D0348082

Susan R. Sloan Omnibus

Guilt by Association
An Isolated Incident

Also by Susan R. Sloan

ACT OF GOD

Susan R. Sloan Omnibus

Guilt by Association
An Isolated Incident

SUSAN R. SLOAN

A *Time Warner* Paperback

This omnibus edition first published in Great Britain by Time Warner Paperbacks in 2004
Susan R. Sloan Omnibus Copyright © Susan R. Sloan 2004

Previously published separately:
Guilt by Association first published in Great Britain in 1994
by Little, Brown and Company
Published by Warner Books in 1995
Reprinted 1995 (twice), 1999 (twice)
Copyright © Susan Sloan 1994

An isolated Incident first published in the United States in 1998
by Warner Books
First published in Great Britain in 1998
by Little, Brown and Company
Published by Warner Books in 1999
Copyright © Susan Sloan 1998

The moral right of the author has been asserted.

A CIP catalogue record for this book is available from the British Library

ISBN 0 7515 3652 0

Printed and bound in Great Britain by
Mackays of Chatham Ltd, Chatham

Time Warner Paperbacks
An imprint of
Time Warner Books UK
Brettenham House
Lancaster Place
London WC2E 7EN

www.TimeWarnerBooks.co.uk

Guilt by Association

I would be more than remiss if I did not acknowledge some of the people who helped make this book a reality.

I wish to thank Lieutenant Mike Pera and Sergeant Angela Martin of the San Francisco Police Department, Sexual Assault Division, and members of the San Francisco Rape Treatment Center, for their invaluable input.

My sincere appreciation goes to Dr. Susan Pendergrass for her expertise, to Susan E. Klein for her research and observations, and to Janine Asch and the library staff of Half Moon Bay, California, for their assistance.

I am indebted to my agent, Esther Newberg, for being one in seventy-eight, and to my editor, Jamie Raab, for creating more out of less.

I am particularly grateful to Linda Stenn for her many contributions, to Howard Schage for his continuing support, and to my little group of readers who kept me going when I was ready to quit.

And my deepest gratitude goes to Sally Sondheim for her unflagging faith in me – and her eagle eye.

For Pamela,
who was there from the beginning,
and got the body up front.

And for Virginia,
who never stopped believing in me.
I know she's smiling.

DECEMBER 22, 1962

I t was cold – the kind of cold, at once heavy and bitter and penetrating, that was so characteristic of New York City in winter. There hadn't been much snow to speak of, only a brief flurry now and again that powdered the sidewalks and dusted the rooftops and then disappeared, as if by sleight of hand, leaving people to wonder whether they had really seen anything at all.

It was three days before Christmas, and Manhattan could not have been described as anything but bleak. Temperatures lurked in the low twenties and skies were filled with sullen clouds that never managed to do more than glower by day and threaten by night.

Margaret Westfield was not used to being awake at six o'clock on a Saturday morning, much less dressed and out. But she had a week's vacation from her job as an assistant bookkeeper for a Seventh Avenue clothier, and she was taking advantage of the time off to spend the holidays with her family in Rhode Island. She wanted to give Brandy, her frisky golden retriever, a good run in Central Park before relegating him to the cramped back seat of her Volkswagen beetle for the three-hour journey to Providence.

Only rich people and crazy people kept automobiles in Manhattan, Margaret knew, but her father had ignored her protests.

'It's just my way of making sure that you'll always have a way to get back home to us,' he said when he handed her the keys.

He knew she had gone to New York to get away from the family or, more precisely, away from the embarrassment of being thirty-three years old and the only one of his eight children who was still unmarried. But he had no intention of abandoning her.

'If traffic's not too bad, we'll be there in time for lunch,' she told Brandy as they crossed Fifth Avenue and entered the park.

It was too early for most New Yorkers to be up and about, and Margaret found herself alone on the path she and the dog usually took to the pretty little lake in the green oasis that ran down the middle of the concrete city. After several yards, she stopped and, reaching down, unsnapped Brandy's sturdy leather leash. The retriever bounded on ahead of her and was soon out of sight.

Margaret pulled her knit cap down over her short brown hair, buttoned her navy pea jacket over her stocky figure and started after him. She wasn't concerned. They took this same route every day and she knew Brandy wouldn't go any farther than East Drive, where he would sit on his haunches, with his tongue hanging out and his tail wagging, waiting for her to catch up so they could begin their game of fetch with the ratty tennis ball she always carried in her pocket. Even in the middle of winter, he couldn't wait to plunge into the lake's icy water. But when she reached the road, the dog was nowhere in sight.

'Brandy?' she called. 'Come on, boy. We haven't got all day.'

There was no response. Margaret frowned, peering up and down the road in the pre-dawn gloom. The four-year-old retriever was impeccably trained, responding to her voice commands almost before the words were out of her mouth, and next to his breakfast and dinner, there was nothing in the world he liked better than his morning play.

Margaret crossed the road and continued along the walk toward the lake, looking in all directions, calling for the dog every fifteen or twenty steps. She was well beyond the boathouse before she heard a faint whimpering sound.

'Brandy, where are you?' she shouted.

This time she received a short urgent bark in response which came from somewhere off to the right. Margaret spotted a narrow path and turned quickly onto it, hurrying along for several hundred yards while it twisted and turned and the retriever's woofs and whimpers grew louder. Around one last corner, the path abruptly widened into a small clearing. The dog was about forty feet away, barely visible, with his rump exposed and the rest of him buried beneath a clump of bushes.

'Brandy, you come out of there,' Margaret ordered. She hoped he hadn't cornered some small animal in the brambles. She had never known him to go after a park creature before, but she supposed there was always a first time.

The retriever looked over at her, gave another short urgent bark, and turned back to the bushes, making no attempt to obey her command. Margaret was totally bewildered. He had never behaved like this before. Sighing, she reached for the leash she had slung over her shoulder and started toward him.

When she was thirty feet away, she realized that, in between his cries and yelps, he was indeed working at something he had found. The last thing she ever allowed him to do was pick up strange food.

'Brandy, no,' she demanded at twenty feet. 'Whatever it is, you leave it alone.'

When she was ten feet away, Margaret stopped dead in her tracks. In the gray dark, she saw a human foot in a black satin pump. Margaret gasped. The body of a girl lay half-hidden under the bushes. Whatever clothes she might have worn were shredded beyond recognition, she was covered with angry-looking bruises, and her skin had a bluish tinge to it. Brandy was crouched on top of her, licking at her face.

'Oh my God,' Margaret murmured, now frightened, inching closer, one hesitant step at a time.

The girl's face was swollen and caked with frozen blood, and ugly purple marks showed on her throat. There was something unnatural about the way one leg was positioned but Margaret didn't dwell on it. She was sure the girl was dead, yet when she mustered up enough courage to push her fingers against the purple neck, she felt a feeble, thready pulse.

'She's still alive, Brandy,' Margaret cried. 'She's not dead – she's still alive. We have to do something.' She tried to think. 'Keep her warm, that's it. We have to keep her warm.'

She pulled off her pea jacket and laid it over the part of the girl's body that the dog wasn't already covering. She didn't have any idea how long the girl had been lying there, or how close she was to freezing to death, but she knew the temperature was low enough to numb her own body in just the few seconds since she had shed her coat.

'Brandy, *stay*,' Margaret ordered the retriever. 'I'm going to find help.'

With the bitter cold urging her on, Margaret ran as fast as she could back up the twisting path, past the boathouse, across the deserted East Drive, and out to Fifth Avenue. She knew it was still too early for much traffic, but she prayed that there would be someone about at this hour. She ran into the middle of the road and stopped the first vehicle that came along.

'What's the matter with you, lady?' the irate taxi driver yelled, slamming down hard on his brakes and skidding to a stop. 'You wanna get us both killed?'

'Help,' Margaret cried. 'Oh, help me, please. There's a girl back there. I think she's been beaten up and she may be almost frozen to death. Please, get a doctor, get a policeman – get somebody.'

'Okay, lady, okay,' the cabby said in a more reasonable voice. 'Calm down. There's a police station right up the road. Just tell me where to bring 'em.'

'It's back there,' Margaret told him, quickly pointing out the direction.

'Yeah, yeah, okay, they'll be able to figure out where that is.' He reached into the back of his cab and pulled up a car blanket. 'Here,' he said. 'It's not much, but maybe it'll help till I can get someone to you.'

Margaret took the blanket and quickly retraced her steps to the clearing and the clump of bushes where her retriever was right where she had left him.

'We have to keep her warm awhile longer, Brandy,' she said. 'Until help comes.'

She picked up her coat and put it back on, jumping up and down a few times until she grew warm inside of it. The last thing in the world Margaret wanted to do was get near the girl. Even the thought of blood was enough to make her queasy, but she suppressed the surge of nausea and forced herself to crawl into the bushes, lie down on the ground as close beside the broken body as she could get, and drape the blanket carefully over all of them. Brandy stirred a little beneath the unfamiliar cover but stayed where he was.

The stench of waste was awful. Margaret shut her eyes and swallowed hard and, searching her mind for anything that might distract her, began to think about the Christmas tree that her family would be trimming tonight.

Unlike any other in the neighborhood, the Westfield tree would be hung with garlands and ornaments that her mother and sisters spent weeks creating, each one hand-fashioned and unique. It was a tradition that had been passed down through generations of Westfields, but Margaret had never really cared that much about it, until now. Now it seemed like the most important thing in the world, and for the first time since she had moved from Providence to New York, she couldn't wait to get home.

She didn't know if the girl she held in her arms could hear her, but she began to talk aloud, about that tree and about her family, and about all the silly, crazy, happy moments they had shared down through the years, one thought leading to another, in a soft, soothing voice.

They stayed there like that for almost half an hour – the girl, the woman and the dog, until the cabby appeared, bursting into the clearing with a burly policeman and two white-uniformed medics in his wake.

PART ONE
1962

We believe no evil till the
evil's done.

– Jean de La Fontaine

one

Karen Kern left the subway at Columbus Circle, deciding on impulse to walk the rest of the way to the Hartmans' West Side apartment.

Office Christmas parties, held on Friday by companies that would be closed on Monday, were ending. Cabbies, cold and irritable, leaned on their horns as they inched around the clogged intersection. Salvation Army Santas in stuffed red suits clanged their bells from every corner, and the tantalizing odor of roasting chestnuts hung in the air.

Karen didn't mind that there was no snow. She had just come down from Ithaca, where almost three feet of it had fallen in forty-eight hours, disrupting traffic, causing accidents, and canceling classes at Cornell University, where she was a junior. She didn't mind the cold, either, although the black cashmere coat wrapped tightly around her slender figure gave little real protection.

Dodging taxis, donating a quarter to the nearest Santa, and skirting knots of tipsy secretaries with a smile, Karen threaded her way through the intersection and headed north along Central Park West. It was December 21, 1962. She was young and healthy, and she had never been happier.

Even in the murky glow of the streetlights, it was clear that her face was too long for classic beauty, her nose too small, her cheekbones too prominent. But her dark Jackie-Kennedy-styled hair gleamed, her blue-gray eyes sparkled, and a pair of impish dimples framed her full lips. Her slim feet in black satin pumps barely touched the pavement.

Her mother might have been devastated when Karen was rejected by Radcliffe, where she would have mingled freely with Harvard men, and refused even to apply to Smith or Mount Holyoke, which were well within striking distance of Yale, but Karen was delighted with her choice. She loved Cornell, with its picture-postcard setting, grand Gothic campus, and amiable atmosphere. Besides, her father was a graduate of the university's dental school, which didn't exactly leave her mother in much of a position to protest.

'Don't waste time with undergraduates,' Beverly Kern had advised. 'Concentrate on the men in the professional schools.'

For a month or so, Karen made a halfhearted effort to comply, ever conscious of her mother's social set, in which success was measured by the number of doctors or dentists or, at the very least, lawyers brought into the fold. It was the direction in which sons were pushed and the end to which every parent of a marriageable daughter openly aspired. But then Karen met Peter Bauer, and her mother's exhortations flew right out of her head.

The very thought of the senior engineering student was enough to deepen her dimples and warm her heart on this frigid night, and she had thought of little else for weeks. After two years of dating, she and Peter had gotten pinned, in one of those incredibly romantic ceremonies, and were already talking about getting officially engaged come summer.

She could still remember how special she felt, standing on the porch of her sorority house, surrounded by all her sisters, grinning from ear to ear, while the men from Peter's fraternity serenaded her. And at the moment when he actually fastened his fraternity pin to her pink angora sweater, she was profoundly sorry for every other girl in the world.

Karen sighed in the chill Manhattan night, watching her breath frost in front of her, and wishing Peter were here beside her instead of in Bangor, Maine, spending Christmas with his family. Despite her mother's importunings, Peter was everything Karen had ever wanted, ever hoped to find in a man, from his quick mind and generous nature to his short crop of sandy hair, warm brown eyes and soft lips that hardly needed an excuse to curl into a grin.

'At least we'll spend New Year's together,' he'd told her when they hugged good-bye at the Ithaca train station. 'I'll see you on the thirtieth.'

Nine days and counting, Karen thought with anticipation. Still, she couldn't suppress a small stab of disappointment because she would have so enjoyed the chance to show him off at the party Jill and Andy Hartman were throwing tonight.

At Seventy-seventh Street, she turned west.

Although Great Neck, the upper-income suburb jutting out into Long Island Sound where Karen had been born and raised, was no more than half an hour's train ride from Manhattan, the very last thing the

Cornell coed had planned to do on the Friday before Christmas was come into the city. But here she was, dressed in her finest and on her way to her best friend's party. Her best friend who had returned from her sophomore year at Northwestern ten pounds overweight and two months pregnant.

What a mess that had been – Jill disgraced, Andy dragged back from his summer abroad, Jill's parents trying in vain to put a good face on everything. No one bothered to mention the option of a back-alley butcher. Instead, there was a hushed, rushed little civil ceremony that was promptly predated six months. Jill's father, a prominent New York attorney, pulled some strings to get Andy transferred from Northwestern to the law school at Columbia. Of course, Jill had to quit college.

Karen could just imagine what her own parents would do were she to get herself into such a predicament. The very thought of her mother's wails and screeches brought her stomach to the edge of revolt. She said a silent prayer of thanks for Peter, who had made a few attempts to get her to go all the way with him, in the back seat of his green Pontiac after they had drunk too much sour-tasting beer, but had never pressed her past a certain point.

Perhaps it was going out of style nowadays, but Karen still believed in the value of virginity and the importance of saving herself for her wedding night. Besides, her mother had certainly warned her often enough about the perils of promiscuity.

'Men might date tramps, but they marry virgins,' Beverly Kern would state bluntly, hammering her message home at every opportunity. 'Would you go into a store and pay top price for used merchandise?'

Karen had to admit she wouldn't.

'And God forbid you got pregnant,' her mother always continued. 'How could we ever hold up our heads in this town again? The tongues would never stop wagging.'

Just the notion of humiliating her family in such a way was enough to make Karen break into a cold sweat. So each time she found herself getting high on beer in the back seat of the Pontiac, a prudent little voice, which always sounded remarkably like her mother's, would begin to echo very clearly in her ear. It was more than enough to keep her resolve firm and her legs crossed.

Karen felt awful for Jill having to quit college, for having to marry so inopportunely, and for having a baby when she was still practically a baby herself. She knew Jill had dreamed of going to Paris after college, of living in a quaint little garret on the Left Bank, painting surrealistic versions of the Eiffel Tower, and hobnobbing with expatriate artists for a year or so, until her graduation money ran out.

For herself, Karen had no such lofty ambitions. While she intended to earn a degree in English at Cornell, a career did not really figure into her future. In fact, there wasn't any fantasy in her head that didn't ultimately end in getting married and having children – a whole houseful of children. Especially since she had met Peter. And while such a goal might have seemed dull or old-fashioned to some, she could hardly wait for the day when, as she pictured it, she would walk down the aisle and begin her real life.

Karen knew a few girls at Cornell who planned to pursue careers after graduation, but her mother had always dismissed a vocation as something to fall back on only in the case of early widowhood, and dismissed Karen's schoolmates as girls who, lacking enough marketable assets to make good marriages, were simply making the best of unfortunate circumstances.

Moreover, Beverly Kern was convinced that anyone with Andy Hartman's good looks and other attributes, having been forced into marriage, would probably divorce Jill at the earliest possible moment, thus ruining her forever.

By the time Karen reached the corner of West End Avenue and Seventy-seventh Street, it was after eight o'clock. The brick building in front of her, which rose twelve stories and occupied almost half the block, was, like so many that lined the streets of Manhattan, a once-elegant structure that was past its prime. In the dreary December night, it appeared more gray than red.

A doorman in maroon livery ushered her in out of the cold and across a softly lit lobby so ornately appointed that Karen imagined it might have been lifted from a palace like Versailles.

'At last,' Jill Hartman exclaimed when the elevator deposited Karen on the eighth floor and she made her way to Apartment G. 'I was beginning to think you'd changed your mind about coming.'

'And miss a good party?' Karen laughed. 'You know me better than that.'

Jill was now eight months pregnant and she looked absolutely radiant. Her long, honey-colored hair glistened, her hazel eyes danced, and her face glowed. This party was her final fling, as she described it, before the baby burst onto the scene.

'Well, come on in,' she cried. 'There are scads of great-looking guys here that ought to keep you from pining for Peter for at least one evening. I'd take you around and introduce you, but the truth is, they're mostly friends of Andy's. I hardly know any of them.' She took her guest's coat and purse and waddled off down the hallway. 'Don't be shy,' she tossed over her shoulder. 'Just jump right in.'

Karen chuckled. Always bright and bubbly, she was anything but shy. So she fluffed out her hair and smoothed down her skirt and looked around. The apartment was truly fabulous, boasting large, airy, cream-colored rooms with high ceilings and intricately carved moldings. Crystal sconces graced the walls, velvet curtains framed windows that overlooked the Hudson River, and those floors that weren't buried beneath thick carpeting were highly polished parquet.

With insolent indifference, the Hartmans had taken this glorious setting and filled it with Danish modern furniture. A makeshift bar sat at one end of the living room, while an assortment of spindly teak sofas and chairs upholstered in ugly brown tweed occupied the other. Across the foyer, a stick-legged dining table sagged under an extravagant buffet supper. The throaty voice of Nat King Cole drifted out of an elaborate hi-fi system that Andy had installed, completing the incongruity.

The crush of guests who filled the apartment were split pretty evenly between the bar and the buffet. Karen wasn't much of a drinker, so she turned toward the dining room. She was in the process of filling a plate with creamed chicken, shrimp curry, and a variety of salads that must have taken Jill a month to prepare, when someone brushed up against her, jostling her elbow, and she felt warm breath tickle her ear.

'You must've just arrived,' a husky voice whispered, 'or I would certainly have noticed you were missing.'

It was so unexpected that Karen promptly spilled macaroni and mayonnaise down the front of her favorite black party dress.

'You're right, I did just get here,' she managed to say, although at the moment she felt more like grinding her high heel into the stranger's foot. 'But now you'll have to excuse me.'

She set her plate back on the table, and, without so much as a glance in his direction, fled down the hall to the bathroom where she stood in front of the mirror and stared in dismay at the oily stain that had quickly spread across the expensive satin.

'Damn,' she muttered, snatching a towel off the bar and beginning to dab at the mess.

'What's the matter?' Jill asked from the doorway.

With a sigh, Karen turned around.

'Good heavens,' her friend cried. 'What happened?'

'Some would-be Don Juan tried to whisper a sweet nothing in my ear as I was helping myself to the macaroni salad.'

'Cornstarch,' Jill said, vanishing and returning faster than Karen would have believed possible, given her friend's present condition, with a box of powdery white stuff, which she proceeded to sprinkle liberally over the black satin. 'Who whispered in your ear?' she asked as the two of them waited for the cornstarch to soak up the oil.

'I don't know,' Karen replied. 'I didn't stop for the formalities.'

'Well, go find out,' Jill suggested when the home remedy had worked its miracle. 'And spill some cocktail sauce down his shirt.'

'Now that's an idea,' Karen chuckled. But she skipped the buffet this time and went to the bar instead, busying herself with a bottle of root beer.

'I'm sorry about your dress,' the voice said from behind her. 'I'd be happy to buy you a new one.'

'That's all right,' Karen told him, wondering whether root beer would do as much damage as cocktail sauce. 'Most of the stain actually came right out, and I think a good cleaning will take care of the rest. But I appreciate the offer.'

She turned around then and looked up into a pair of aquamarine eyes so arresting that she was left with only a fleeting impression of what the rest of him was like.

'It's a beautiful dress,' he said, and Karen actually felt his blue-green glance travel from the rise of her bosom to the turn of her ankle.

'Why thank you, kind sir,' she responded lightly. In fact, it *was* a beautiful dress, a graceful, scoop-necked concoction with a tight bodice and a flattering tulip skirt.

'I'm Bob,' he said with a seductive smile that lit up his face, a very handsome face she now saw, with straight brows, a thick fringe of eyelashes, a thin nose, sculpted mouth, and a small black mole on his right cheek that may have marred perfection but suited him absolutely. The whole was set off by a lot of dark hair that apparently curled too much for his liking, judging by the amount of Brylcreem he had used.

'I'm Karen,' she replied.

'Well, Karen,' he said as though he were actually caressing the name, 'there's no doubt that you're the most attractive woman here tonight.'

She knew it was a line, but he delivered it so well that she couldn't stop a little shiver from skidding down her spine. Bob was taller than Peter, who was far from short, and, where Peter was lean and trim from hours on the tennis courts, Bob was broad and muscular like a football player. She noted that his slacks were sharply creased, his cuffs, peeking from beneath a navy blazer, were fastened with expensive gold links, his tie was modestly striped, and his loafers were polished to a high gloss.

He was obviously quite stuck on himself, but Karen had handled this type before, and she didn't feel she would be betraying Peter any if she let a handsome stranger pay her a compliment or two.

'I think you have exceptionally good taste,' she said, smiling back.

He touched his Scotch highball to her bottle of root beer. 'Well then, here's to getting to know you better,' he said softly.

The party circled around them. Karen was at her best in crowds, moving in and out of various groups with such grace and ease that a professor once observed that she would be a real asset to an ambitious politician. She was included in a conversation about the truth behind the Cuban missile crisis, took part in a discussion of James Meredith and the future of integration, and joined a circle speculating about the future of a shaggy-haired quartet from Liverpool who went by the name of some insect.

The comfortable cloak of Camelot – that invisible sense of security and innocence and well-being – rested gently over everyone.

Karen would have enjoyed spending more time with several of the people she met, but Bob seemed always at her elbow, distracting her. A͟ charge of the drinks, pouring her ͟ glass and adding a little somethi͟ thought she wasn't looking. Karen ͟ the unpleasant combination of Hire's ͟ didn't object. Bob was so attractive and h͟ ͟ng so considerate and, although she knew it ͟s all just harmless flirtation, it made her feel terrific when, several times, she caught the envious glances of some of the other young women.

It's only for tonight, girls, she thought with a self-satisfied smile. Tomorrow, he's all yours.

Bob, as it turned out, was a friend of a friend of one of Andy's former roommates from Northwestern. He told her he was a born-and-bred California boy and had graduated from Stanford.

'Palm trees, sunshine and tequila,' he summed up for her with a nostalgic sigh. 'It was a glorious four-year-long party.'

'Oh, I'm sure of that,' Karen said, laughing.

'But now that I'm at Harvard Law,' he added with a grimace, 'all I get to do is study, study and study. Have to keep the old nose to the grindstone, you know, fourteen hours a day, seven days a week. Would you believe that this is the first real party I've been to in almost a year and a half?'

'Poor baby,' Karen consoled. Another lawyer, she thought with an inner chuckle. He was going to make some girl's parents very happy one day.

'No joke,' he assured her. 'I came down from Cambridge the day before yesterday and I have no intention of going back until I'm partied out.'

'Good luck,' Karen told him.

'You know, Cornell's not all that far from Harvard,'

mmented at one point during the evening, though Ithaca was in fact hundreds of miles from Cambridge. 'Maybe I'll look you up sometime.'

It was on the tip of her tongue to tell him about Peter, but she reasoned his remark was merely party talk and not to be taken seriously, and anyway, she was enjoying the attention too much to relinquish it so soon.

'Let's see, that should be in another year and a half, right?' she quipped.

'Oh, I just might make an exception in your case,' he countered, flashing a dazzling smile.

It was two o'clock before she realized it, and the party was winding down. About a dozen guests remained, wandering around, looking as though they couldn't remember where they were supposed to go. Andy had gotten drunk and passed out on one of the spindly brown tweed sofas. Jill was clearing away the debris.

'Let me help,' Karen offered.

'I'm not doing any heavy cleaning up now,' her friend replied. 'I'm just stashing the leftovers in the fridge. Everything else can wait until tomorrow. Look, it's really late. Do you want to stay over? I'm sure we can find an extra sofa.'

'Thanks, but I'm all set up with my aunt and uncle.'

Edna and Harry Kern lived on East Seventy-sixth Street, across Central Park. Over the years, Karen had occupied their flowery guest room whenever she stayed late in the city. The arrangement was quite convenient. She kept a change of clothes, a pair of pajamas, and a toothbrush in a dresser drawer, and Uncle Harry would leave an extra key with the night doorman so that Karen could let herself in without disturbing them.

'Then you'd better get going or you won't be able to find a cab,' Jill told her.

'It was very nice meeting you,' Karen said to Bob as he helped her on with her coat. 'I had fun.'

'The evening doesn't have to end, does it?' he asked. 'It's still early. There's bound to be a club or two that's open.'

'Thank you very much,' she replied, 'but it's pretty late by my clock and I have to get crosstown.'

'Are you sure I can't change your mind?'

'I'm afraid not. I'm staying with relatives. They're kind of old-fashioned and if I don't show up pretty soon they're apt to send the police out looking for me.'

She knew that Aunt Edna and Uncle Harry had been sound asleep for hours by now, but he didn't. Had circumstances been different, she might have said yes to his invitation. But the party was over and Peter would be coming down in a few days, and that was the way it was.

'Then let me help you find a cab,' he offered. 'I don't like the idea of you wandering the streets alone at this hour.'

She smiled because he really was very nice. 'Thanks,' she said, 'but the doorman will take care of that.'

'Well then, the least you can do is let me accompany you down in the elevator,' he persisted.

'Why not?' she agreed carelessly.

They said their good-byes and departed. When they reached the lobby, however, the doorman was no-where in sight.

'Maybe he had to go to the john,' Bob suggested.

'Perhaps he's on a coffee break.'

They stood around for ten minutes or so, but the doorman did not reappear.

'Look, let me get you a cab,' Bob said. 'I have to find one for myself, anyway.'

Karen shrugged. 'Okay.'

The temperature had dipped down into the teens by the time they emerged from the apartment building and began their hunt for a taxi, walking east, past the Museum of Natural History complex, on their way to Central Park West. The streets were almost deserted at this hour and the sound of their shoes on the pavement echoed off the rows of dark, frowning buildings.

When they reached the edge of the park, they stood on the sidewalk, Karen stamping her feet and rubbing her hands together to ward off the cold, while Bob searched up and down the street for a cab.

'One's bound to come along sooner or later,' he said reasonably.

Karen chuckled. 'With a little luck, before we die of frostbite.' She was glad now for the warmth of the alcohol he had added to her root beer.

They waited fifteen minutes.

'Maybe we should walk down to Columbus Circle,' Karen suggested. 'We might have a better chance there.'

'I have a better idea,' Bob said. 'Why don't we just walk across the park?'

It was an option she would never have considered, going into the park at night. There were a number of stories about how dangerous it had become.

'Look,' she said, 'you've really been very nice, but I can't ask you to go out of your way like that.'

'Sure you can. Where do your relatives live?'

'On East Seventy-sixth Street,' she told him. 'Between Park and Lexington.'

'It happens that I'm staying with friends on Seventy-fourth and Third,' Bob said. 'So you see, it's hardly out of my way at all.'

'Well, in that case ...' She was still a bit hesitant but then not all that anxious to have him walk off and leave her alone. Besides, she supposed this nice broad-shouldered man could protect her from just about any kind of hobgoblin they might encounter. 'I guess it would be all right.'

They crossed into Central Park, following the pedestrian paths, Bob's hand firmly on her elbow, steering her this way and that – to the right, to the left, over a little bridge, then to the right again, until the sights and sounds of the city were far behind them. It was dark and eerie here, and ominously quiet. No voices broke the silence, no moon shone down through the thick clouds to light their way. Spidery branches reached out for them like gnarled black fingers against the grim gray sky.

'I haven't the faintest idea where we are,' Karen admitted after they had been twisting and turning from one path to another for some time.

'That's okay,' he said. 'I know the way.'

He directed her along as though he really did know where he was going and, because she didn't exactly have much of a choice, Karen followed. She remembered him saying that he was from the West Coast and had been locked up at Harvard for the past year and a half.

'How do you know which way to go?' she asked.

'I came this way earlier,' he replied smoothly. 'The

people I'm staying with gave me directions.'

'Oh,' she murmured.

'Trust me,' he said with a smile in his voice.

They walked on, even as the path got narrower and the underbrush thicker.

'It's so dark,' Karen observed, 'I can't even tell what direction we're going in.'

'It's easy,' he said. 'Hear the water? That's the lake. As long as that sound is to our right, we're heading east.'

Karen listened intently but she couldn't figure out from which side the faint slap-slap was coming, and she had a sudden wish that she had dropped bread crumbs in their wake.

'Are we heading for the Seventy-ninth Street Transverse?'

'No,' he told her. 'I don't know that way. But this way comes out right at Seventy-sixth Street.'

'I hope so,' Karen said. 'My teeth are beginning to chatter.'

'Are you cold?' he asked. 'Well, I can certainly take care of that.' He opened his heavy overcoat and pulled her inside, wrapping it around them both. 'There, is this better?'

His unexpected body warmth did help, but he was holding her too close and too tight and it made her uncomfortable.

'That's all right,' Karen told him. 'We can't have that much farther to go. I can make it.' She tried to move a step away from him but he wouldn't release her. 'I'm okay,' she assured him. 'Honestly.'

'Don't be silly,' he insisted, moving her along beside him. 'What would your relatives say if I brought you home frozen solid?'

'Well ...'

She was just about to concede the point when he added in a husky voice, 'Besides, this feels nice.'

Karen stopped short. 'Please,' she said politely yet firmly, 'I appreciate your good intentions, but I really would feel more comfortable if you let me go now.'

'What if I don't want to?' he teased, tightening his grip even more.

Despite the numbing cold, she felt a little spurt of apprehension sprint down her spine.

'Look, you're a very nice person,' she replied, choosing her words with great care, 'but I wouldn't want you to get the wrong idea. You see, I'm engaged to be married.'

Karen rarely lied to anyone, but she felt that, under the circumstances, this slight exaggeration of the truth was justifiable.

'If you're so engaged,' he snapped, 'why do you go around flaunting yourself in front of other men?'

'I wasn't doing anything of the kind,' she retorted.

'Oh yes, you were. And I didn't waste a whole evening for nothing.'

Before she could stop him, he had turned her to him and was kissing her, his tongue pushing its way into her mouth, his hand beginning to grope beneath her coat.

'Stop it,' she sputtered, trying to twist out of his grasp. But he was much too strong and held her easily.

'You can cut the act now,' he said, laughing.

'This isn't any act,' she protested, struggling against him, 'and you're not very funny. Now let go of me this instant.'

Perhaps it was the amount of liquor he had consumed or maybe it was the stress of his law studies, she didn't know, but something inside of him seemed to snap.

'Shut up,' he snarled and slapped her across the face with such force that she fell backward against a clump of brambly bushes.

'What do you think you're doing?' she cried, realizing, too late, that something had gone very, very wrong.

'I'm going to give you exactly what you've been asking for,' he said, tossing aside his heavy coat.

'I wasn't asking for anything,' she insisted, scrambling to her feet. 'I was having a good time at a party – just like everyone else.'

He laughed harshly. 'Don't you think I can recognize a come-on when I see it? That dress alone was all it took.'

'You're crazy,' she shouted, before considering the effect her words might have, and turned for the path.

He reached out and grabbed her by the hair, yanking her back so hard that she lost her footing and fell against him. Then he pulled her right arm behind her back, twisting until, with excruciating pain, she felt it snap.

'Crazy? You think I'm crazy?' he snarled in her ear. 'Well, you're going to be crazy about me by the time I finish with you.'

Whirling her around, he knocked her to the ground with one swift punch in the stomach. Karen lay where she was, gasping for breath, unable to get up, as disbelief turned to fear. Even as she wondered what would come next, she felt the toe of his shoe slam into her rib cage. When she tried to roll aside, he caught her in the small of the back, and when she tried to wriggle in another direction, he kicked her in the abdomen. Wherever she turned, the polished loafer was waiting for her, smashing into her, over and over and over again.

'Please,' she whimpered.

'That's right, beg,' he hissed. 'Tell me how sorry you are you made me angry. Tell me how much you want me to do it to you.'

He straddled her then, threw open her coat and started to claw at her dress, the expensive satin shredding as though it were made of tissue paper. He reached for her bra, yanking it off with a skin-cutting snap. He ripped her garter belt in half, and the delicate silk panties her mother always insisted she wear came apart in his fingers.

She felt his hands sliding down her body, over her breasts, along her thighs, between her legs – places not even Peter had yet been allowed to explore. And following his hands were his teeth, marking her skin in a gruesome trail of his own design.

When she thought she could take no more, he suddenly stopped. But it was only to fumble at the front of his trousers. Then, without further preparation, he shoved himself deep inside that most private part of her.

Karen screamed. She had never known pain like that before. It was as though she had been split in two by a red-hot knife, starting at her thighs and shooting up into her chest. Immediately, one hand closed over her mouth and the other clamped around her throat – cutting off her shriek, and her air.

'I didn't say scream,' he snarled. 'I said beg.'

But she couldn't utter a word, she couldn't move, she couldn't even breathe. She couldn't do anything but lie there as he stabbed at her, again and again and again. Tears streamed from her eyes and her lungs began to burn. She didn't want to believe that such a thing could be happening to her, when she had always been so careful, but the agony she felt assured her that it was.

It was then she knew she was going to die, that he could not let her live, and she prayed it would be quick.

Soon enough, the world around her began to blur, her eyes fluttered. Sights and sounds seemed to fade and she felt herself rising, strangely weightless, higher and higher and higher still, until she was floating above the sinister gray clouds in a soothing white light, where everything was beautiful and no harm could reach her. She thought that being dead was not so bad, after all.

When she opened her eyes, the first thing she saw was the sullen sky. He was gone – his hands no longer closing off her mouth and throat – and the cold had almost numbed her to the pain. She sucked in great gulps of icy air and wondered where the peculiar rasping sound she heard was coming from. She couldn't believe she had survived and she was just beginning a silent prayer of thanks when his face loomed above her.

'Did you like that?' he crooned. 'Come on, tell me how much. I bet you never had it so good before.'

Karen turned her head away.

He slammed her across the face with the back of his hand. 'Tell me,' he barked.

She opened her mouth, but nothing came out except a throaty hiss.

He began to caress her roughly. With every ounce of strength she had left, she moaned and tried to move away, but he was there to stop her.

'Where do you think you're going?' he sneered. 'I'm not through with you yet. On the contrary, I'm just getting warmed up.'

Karen stared at him with revulsion, wondering how she could ever have thought him attractive.

'No more,' she managed to croak.

'The hell you say,' he laughed. 'I have to make up for all those monkish months I spent learning the law, and right now you're the only game around.'

With that, he shoved her over onto her stomach, pushed her legs apart, and forced himself into that place where such an invasion had heretofore been unthinkable.

The shriek that began in Karen's throat died in a mouthful of dirt. As agonizing as the other had been, this was infinitely worse – a battering ram, tearing, plundering, punishing, destroying everything in its path.

For an unspeakable length of time, he rode her like a bull, stripping her of every last shred of dignity, working himself into a mindless frenzy until, with a final grunt, he exploded from the inside. So dazed was she that she hardly felt him withdraw, and could not have said whether it was seconds or minutes or even hours later.

Bodily fluids oozed out of every part of her, visible evidence of a life that was slipping away. She scarcely noticed when he rolled her onto her back.

'Now that was even better,' he said with obvious relish. 'With a little practice, you could be quite good at this.'

Her only response was a raspy breath.

He reached down and pulled her head up by a

handful of hair, causing her to wince in pain from a dozen different places.

'I bet I know how you want it next,' he purred in her ear. 'Sure I do. In fact, I bet you love it that way just as much as I do. I bet you're going to be real good at it, too, aren't you?'

Her eyes were glazed, she could barely see him. She had no idea what he had in mind, but it didn't matter – she knew she couldn't stop him. He would do what he wanted and then he would be done and she would be dead, and that was all right. She couldn't imagine living after this, anyway.

He still had her by the hair and now she felt him tighten his grip. Before she quite understood what he meant to do, he had risen up on his knees and thrust himself deep into her mouth.

'Show me how good you are at this, bitch,' he cried hoarsely. 'Show me how much you appreciate what I'm doing for you.'

Karen couldn't help herself – she gagged and, as she did, her teeth reflexively snapped shut.

Bob squealed in rage and yanked himself free of her. 'I'll teach you to play games like that with me,' he howled and his right fist crashed into her face, shattering her jaw.

After that, Karen knew nothing.

two

Dr. Stanley Waschkowski was in the last year of his residency at Manhattan Hospital. A tall, gaunt man, with thinning brown hair, inquisitive dark eyes and a persistent five-o'clock shadow, he had the pallor of one who spends too much time indoors among the sick and dying. In four years, he had been exposed to almost every possible kind of illness and injury – one advantage of big-city training he would have missed in the small New Hampshire town he called home – and he prided himself on having achieved the emotional separation that a physician needed in order to survive.

'If you give up a piece of yourself to every patient you can't help,' a doctor he greatly admired had once told him, 'pretty soon you'll have nothing left to give to those you can.'

Waschkowski had learned the value of that advice even before he completed his internship. So well, in fact, that he was now frequently referred to, behind his back, as the 'Old Stone Man' by some of the younger residents. He didn't mind. In fact, he was rather proud of the sobriquet, knowing what it had cost him to earn it.

But as he watched an emergency room nurse cut away what clothing remained on the brutalized young woman before him, anger filled his dark eyes, and the iron clamp that held his emotions in check slipped a notch.

'God, she's hardly more than a child,' he murmured.

Waschkowski had two young daughters of his own. The thought of anything like this ever happening to one of them was enough to make him forget his Hippocratic oath.

'Okay, we have respiratory distress,' he told the intern who had summoned him. 'Prep her for a tracheotomy.'

He looked down at the girl as she lay there, bruised and bloody, barely able to breathe, depending on him to help her. He set his jaw and began his grim work.

'Tell me what you can, as soon as you can, Doc,' the corpulent policeman who had accompanied the ambulance said. Despite his age and obvious experience, the officer looked a little green.

'Take a seat, Sergeant,' the doctor said. 'Have a cup of coffee. This might take a while.'

An hour later, a weary Waschkowski emerged from the tiny cubicle with blood splattered on his white coat. 'Do you have any ID on her?' he asked the policeman.

'Yeah,' the officer replied.

'Call,' the doctor said. 'Get someone down here. We need a consent.'

Henry 'Tug' McCluskey was less than six months from retirement. He had put in thirty tough years on the New York City police force, playing it straight and clean right down the line, which hadn't always been easy. His living room wall was lined with commendations, his dress uniform was covered with medals, and his gold watch was waiting for him. In spite of that, he hadn't been able to protect that poor girl.

From one end of Manhattan Island to the other, he had seen more than his share of gunshot wounds, stabbings, mutilations, strangulations and beatings, but in thirty years he had never gotten used to it. Every one of those brutal crimes had taken its toll on him, but none had been as bad as the sight of Karen Kern's broken, bleeding body lying there under a bush.

Sitting in the hospital emergency room on a cold Saturday morning three days before Christmas, he knew he would have traded his commendations, his medals, his gold watch and even his pension, come to that, for five minutes alone in a room with the bastard who had done that to her.

Tug had been raised to respect women, and in turn had taught his four sons to do the same. He was known around town as 'the Gentleman Cop,' even by the hookers he used to roust over on Eighth Avenue. There was no doubt in his mind that, whatever this girl might have done to provoke such violence, she didn't deserve what she had received.

The sergeant hefted his bulk out of his chair and shuffled to the bank of telephones along the far wall of the emergency room to do the part of his job that he disliked the most. Keeping his voice as calm and unemotional as he could, he suggested to the woman at the other end of the line that she get to the hospital as quickly as possible.

'No, ma'am,' he sighed. 'I'm afraid I don't have any of the details yet. But I'm sure the doctors will be able to tell you everything when you get here.'

Although he had to have the results of the medical examination for his report, Tug McCluskey didn't need any know-it-all resident to tell him that Karen Kern had been raped and beaten half to death. But there was no point in telling the parents such a thing over the telephone. There would be time enough for them to hear that when they reached the hospital.

three

Leo and Beverly Kern paced the length of Manhattan Hospital's third floor corridor – a spare little man with rimless spectacles and trousers pulled over his pajamas, and a buxom woman in bright-blue eye shadow and a full-length mink coat – passing each other wordlessly at the midpoint on their way to opposite ends.

Beverly's high heels click-clacked against the stained gray linoleum, sounding sharply out of place in the subdued and sterile atmosphere. Not in all her forty-five years had there been a circumstance so dire that she could not first take the time to attend to her appearance. It was an edict that had been unchallenged in her family for generations – never to leave home without the appropriate outfit and clean underwear.

Leo fussed and fumed as Beverly took the time to shed her nightgown for a stylish woolen dress and camouflage her sags and wrinkles with a varied assortment of cosmetics, but in fact barely fifteen minutes passed before they were in the garage, revving up the engine of the big black Buick and speeding out of Great Neck.

Now, as they paced and waited, it seemed a lifetime ago that they were awakened by the telephone call, but it was actually little more than six hours.

'What could be taking so long?' Beverly grumbled when she had tapped her way up and down the corridor for perhaps the hundredth time.

'There are some things you can't hurry,' Leo responded mildly, 'and surgery is one of them. You wouldn't want them to rush, and risk making a mistake, now would you?'

'No, of course not,' Beverly conceded. 'It's just the waiting – it's so hard.'

Orderlies had wheeled Karen off to the operating room at nine-thirty. It was now two forty-five.

'Your daughter has been badly hurt,' Dr. Waschkowski told them when they hurried into the emergency room, having abandoned the Buick in the hospital parking lot. They had encountered very little traffic and no highway patrol cars on the Long Island Expressway at that early Saturday hour, and had reached midtown Manhattan in a record twenty-seven minutes.

'What happened?' Beverly demanded.

'Apparently, she was the victim of an assault.'

'An assault?' Beverly cried in dismay. 'What are you talking about? There must be some mistake. She was at a party last night. At the home of her best friend.'

'She was found in Central Park at approximately six-thirty this morning,' Tug McCluskey told them. 'I got to the scene a little before seven o'clock.'

He didn't want to tell these frightened parents what he found when he and the two medics followed the cab driver into the clearing.

'I brought your daughter here,' he said instead.

'What was she doing in Central Park?'

'We don't know that, ma'am,' McCluskey said.

'What about her injuries?' Leo asked.

'My preliminary examination indicates that she sustained multiple contusions and fractures and there are signs of abdominal bleeding,' Waschkowski replied. 'We've done a tracheotomy to give her a clear breathing passage.'

'Is she in a lot of pain?'

'No,' he assured them. 'She's unconscious.'

'Dear God,' Beverly gasped.

'That's not unusual in these cases,' the doctor was quick to explain. 'She's had a considerable shock to her system. Aside from the trauma due to injury, we estimate that she was exposed to temperatures well below freezing for several hours.'

'Why would anyone do such a thing?' Leo pondered aloud. 'It couldn't have been a robbery. She wasn't wearing any expensive jewelry. She wasn't carrying much money.'

Waschkowski cleared his throat and shifted from one foot to the other. Next to losing a patient, this was the part he most hated about being a doctor.

'We – uh – don't think the beating was necessarily her assailant's primary intent,' he said as gently as he could, having found evidence of semen in her vagina, her mouth and her rectum. 'She's been raped.'

Beverly cried out and sagged against Leo. Of all the things that could happen to one's child, this was a mother's worst nightmare.

'My baby,' she wailed, 'my baby.' Then she straightened up. 'I want her to have the best possible care,' she said firmly. 'And I want her in the best possible facility.'

'Manhattan Hospital *is* the best possible facility,' Leo told her.

'Then I want top doctors in charge of her treatment,' she retorted. 'No offense, Dr. Waschkowski, but I won't entrust my little girl to a resident. I want the best.'

'I've already taken the liberty of calling in a number of specialists,' Waschkowski assured her. 'There's an oral surgeon, an orthopedist, a urologist, a neurologist and a gynecologist standing by, all highly respected in their fields, and all in agreement that surgery should begin as soon as possible.'

'Of course,' Leo said.

'Well, if they say so …' Beverly muttered.

'One of you will have to sign the necessary papers.'

Leo had gone to do that and Beverly had stayed, waiting for the occasional glimpse she could get into the small white cubicle where nurses and technicians were preparing Karen for the operation to come.

'Your daughter's going to be fine, ma'am,' Tug McCluskey tried to soothe her. 'I've seen a lot worse pull through.'

'Thank you,' Beverly murmured.

Tug cleared his throat, much the same as Waschkowski had earlier. 'I just wanted to say, ma'am,' he added, 'how sorry I am.'

'That's very kind of you.'

'What I mean is, I've got granddaughters of my own, you see, and well, if I ever find the guy who did this to your little girl, I might just kill him.'

'Ohhh,' Beverly groaned, turning away. The thought of all these people knowing what had happened to her baby was almost more than she could bear.

Medical personnel bustled in and out of Karen's cubicle in a constant stream, while Beverly waited helplessly outside. Then, in twos and threes, they emerged, discussing what they had seen in brief sentences peppered with technical terms that were difficult for Beverly to understand.

But, she thought now, pausing outside the doors to the surgical suite, she didn't understand much of anything at all, except that Karen had left home at six-thirty yesterday evening to go to her best friend's party, and twelve hours later had been found unconscious in Central Park. Her bright, pretty, well-behaved daughter – after all the times Beverly had warned her not to have anything to do with strangers, how could this awful thing have happened?

'Maybe we should telephone Jill,' Leo interrupted her.

'What for?' Beverly replied. 'Surely you don't think the Hartmans had anything to do with this, do you?'

'No, of course not,' he murmured. 'I just thought Jill might know something that would help us figure this whole thing out.'

'What's there to figure out?' Beverly moaned, looking down on her husband's shiny bald head. 'It's all painfully clear, wouldn't you say?'

'But shouldn't we at least …?'

'Why don't we wait a bit,' Beverly said. 'There'll be time to talk to Jill. It's bad enough that the police are already involved. Until Karen herself can tell us exactly what happened, the last thing we need is more publicity.'

Leo nodded slowly. 'I guess I didn't think of that.'

He was a myopic little man who, at the age of twenty-six, had traded one mother for another without ever knowing the difference.

They brought Karen out of surgery at twenty minutes to four. An exhausted Stanley Waschkowski met the Kerns in the recovery room.

'She came through just fine,' he told them. 'There was more internal damage than anticipated, but we're confident we were able to take care of everything.'

Later, he thought, when they were stronger, he would give them the details, but they were in no emotional condition to listen now.

'She's going to be pretty uncomfortable for a while,' he said. 'But in time she'll be up and about again, and all this will be nothing more than a bad dream.'

'Is she awake?' Beverly asked.

'No, not yet.'

'Can I see her?'

'Why don't you wait an hour or so, until we move her into the special care unit. She may be awake by then.'

'She needs special care?' Leo asked.

'In cases like this, where there's been severe trauma, we don't take chances,' Waschkowski replied. Your daughter was unconscious when she was admitted. That might be the result of shock, or it might be an indication of some kind of intercranial pressure buildup. We want to watch her closely for a possible kidney involvement as well. With constant monitoring, we'll be on hand to detect any problem and act immediately.'

By ten o'clock in the evening, Karen was running a fever of 105 degrees.

'What is it?' Beverly cried.

'Pneumonia,' Dr. Waschkowski said. 'We had hoped to avoid it but it wasn't unexpected, given her condition.'

'Is it critical?' Leo wanted to know.

'At this point, unfortunately, everything is critical.' The senior resident sighed. 'But we've started her on a program of penicillin, aspirin suppositories, and alcohol baths, and that should help fight the infection. The good news is, so far, there's been no indication of any abnormal cranial pressure or kidney failure.'

Around midnight, the exhausted Kerns were persuaded to leave the hospital.

'There's really nothing you can do, even if she does regain consciousness,' Waschkowski assured them. 'And it may be as much as seventy-two hours before we know if we've beaten the pneumonia. I'm going to be here all night, and I'll call you immediately if there's any change.'

'No matter what the time?' Beverly asked.

'No matter what the time,' he promised.

They went to Edna and Harry Kern's spacious apartment on Seventy-sixth Street. Despite the hour, Leo's brother and his wife were still wide awake.

'We didn't even realize that Karen wasn't here until we got your call,' Edna sobbed. 'We left the key and went to sleep, just like we always do.'

'Don't blame yourself,' Leo said. 'You had no way of knowing this would happen.'

'Of course you didn't,' Beverly added, and making the only possible decision, as far as she could see, she planted her foot firmly on the first rung of the ladder of lies that she would climb in the weeks and months and lifetime to follow. 'How could anyone possibly have known there would be such a terrible ... accident?'

four

At first there were no days or hours or minutes, no way of measuring time or distance. There were no thoughts, no feelings, no recognition, just the murky black of nothingness that cradled her body and wrapped itself protectively around her mind.

Then the darkness began to give way to a thick gray fog, layer on top of layer, roiling around her, tangible, almost touchable, relentlessly propelling her toward unwanted sight, lurking just beyond her mind's grasp.

In the end, despite every ounce of resistance she could muster, awareness overtook her. It began with the voices. She could hear them through the fog – soft, urgent, too low for her to catch the words, annoying. Next came the smells, unfamiliar and unpleasant, that stung her nose with each laborious breath. And finally, there was the realization of pain, and with it, the last agonizing thrust into the harsh light of reality and horror.

Karen opened her eyes.

She was lying in a bed that was not her own, in a place she had never seen before. Shards of bright sunlight slanted through a large window in the opposite wall. Unknown people in white hovered around her. Everywhere she looked, there was white – the gown that clothed her, the sheets that covered her, the pockmarked ceiling tiles above her. She wanted to ask where she was, she wanted to tell someone about the pain, but she couldn't seem to move her mouth or produce anything but a curious gurgling sound.

'Julie, go get Dr. Waschkowski,' a lady with gray hair pulled back into a bun instructed the aide beside her. 'I think she's awake.'

'Yes, ma'am.' A petite strawberry blonde with enormous china-blue eyes dashed from the room and the gray-haired lady leaned over the bed and smiled. Wisps of hair had come free of her bun and drifted around her kindly face.

'You're quite safe,' she said in a reassuring voice that floated gently over Karen. 'You're in the special care unit at Manhattan Hospital. You were brought here after your, uh, after your accident. Now, you're not to worry about a thing. The doctor will be right along and he'll answer all the questions I know you must have.'

Karen tried again to say something and again failed. She tried to raise her right arm to see if she could feel what was holding her throbbing head immobile, but the arm was encased in something white and heavy. She looked out of the corner of her eye at her other arm. It was anchored to a white board, palm up, with a needle protruding from a vein in her wrist. Tubes and wires seemed to be coming out of every part of her. Karen's eyes widened fearfully. She wanted to scream, but as before, only a gurgle escaped.

'Now, now,' the lady in white soothed. 'You just relax, dear. Don't try to talk. You're going to be just fine. Trust me, all this paraphernalia looks much scarier than it really is.'

Rose Thackery had been a nurse for forty-one years. She wasn't sure she could think of anything much scarier than what had happened to this poor girl.

Karen shut her eyes as tears began to ooze out the sides and drip onto her pillow. The pain came from everywhere, her head, her eye, her nose, her mouth, her chest, her arms, her abdomen, her leg. It hurt to move, it hurt to lie still, it hurt to breathe. She dimly remembered being in Central Park with Bob, but that had been at night, and now it was day, and she didn't know what had happened in between. She hoped the nice gray-haired lady had called her aunt and uncle. She didn't want them to worry that she wasn't there for breakfast.

'Karen?' a voice asked. 'Karen, can you hear me?'

She opened her eyes again. The sunlight was gone. It was dark outside the window. A tall man stood beside the bed. In the shadows, he looked like Bob. Karen gasped and began to thrash about. This time, she knew she had to get away from him, and that gave her the strength to ignore the sharp pains that attacked her from every corner.

The Bob-man said something over his shoulder and a woman in white hurried over and handed him something. He leaned down and, flinging aside the bedclothes, plunged a long needle into Karen's hip.

A peaceful warmth flooded through her. She was dancing in a lush meadow and the scent of wildflowers filled her nostrils. The sun was hot on her face.

'Karen?' the voice said again. 'Can you hear me?'

She didn't want to answer. She wanted to stay and play in the meadow.

'Karen, I want you to wake up now.'

The meadow began to slip away, the vibrant greens and the sky-blues fading into colorlessness, the sweet fragrance of flowers and grass turning sour, like disinfectant. She awoke reluctantly. The white world of agony greeted her.

A man stood at the foot of the bed. He had kind brown eyes, a large hooked nose and a warm smile, and the sun picked bronze highlights out of his thinning hair. His hands were long and slender and his fingernails were neatly trimmed. He looked as if he might play the piano.

'Hello,' the man said. 'I'm Dr. Waschkowski.'

Of course, a doctor, not a piano player, Karen thought. She gurgled painfully.

'No, don't try to talk,' he told her. 'Your upper lip is stitched, your jaw is wired and you have a tube in your throat that's helping you to breathe.'

Karen stared at him.

'I know that sounds pretty frightening, but the truth is, things usually sound worse than they are.' His smile broadened reassuringly.

Karen tried to smile back, but couldn't.

'No, you can't smile with your mouth just yet,' the doctor told her, 'but I can see it in your eyes. So I'd like you to do something, sort of play a little game with me, okay? I'll ask you some questions, and you answer me by blinking your eyes. Once for yes and twice for no. Do you understand?'

Karen blinked once.

'Good,' he said. 'Okay, here we go. Is your name Karen Kern?'

Blink.

'Are you twenty years old?'

Blink.

'Do you live in Port Washington?'

Blink. Blink.

'Good girl.' Waschkowski smiled and moved around to the side of the bed. 'Do you remember being in Central Park?' he asked gently.

Karen's eyes filled with tears. Blink.

'All right,' he said with an encouraging nod, 'you've told me everything I need to know for now. As your doctor, I prescribe more rest. We can talk again tomorrow.'

He made a move to go but Karen, using all her strength, raised her right arm in its heavy cast to stop him.

'Don't be afraid,' he said kindly. 'You're going to be just fine. I'm an excellent doctor and I would never let a slip of a girl like you make a liar out of me.'

Blink. Blink.

'Is the pain very bad?'

Blink.

'Up until now, we couldn't give you anything for it, because we didn't want to mask any symptoms. But now that you're fully awake, I'll have one of the nurses give you a shot.' He made another move to go, but again she stopped him. 'Is there something else?'

Blink.

Waschkowski sighed. 'Let me guess. You want to know what all this stuff connected to you is about?'

Blink.

'Why don't you rest for a while and then we can have

a long talk about that later?'

Blink. Blink.

'Okay,' he said with resignation, pulling a chair up to the bed and sitting down on it straddle-style. 'I can tell you're not going to let me get away with anything. Well, let's see. Do you want to start at the bottom and work up, or start at the top and work down?'

Karen blinked once, then twice, then once again.

'Serves me right,' Waschkowski laughed. 'Okay, we'll start at the top.'

One by one, he cataloged her injuries, mentioning the black eye that would be tender for a time and the broken nose they had set and the split lip they had sutured, and then pointing out each of the tubes and wires, telling her in simple terms what it was and why it was there. The enormity of it might have over-whelmed her had he not been careful to maintain a calm, almost matter-of-fact, attitude.

'You have a fractured jaw,' he began. 'We've wired it shut and immobilized your head with a splint. It should be as good as new in a month or so, but until then, your ability to talk and eat will be restricted.'

She could remember Bob's fist crashing into her face.

'Along with that, you have a crushed larynx, which means you *really* can't talk for a while. Think of it as having a very sore throat. We did a procedure we call a tracheotomy, which is a big word that means we put a little hole in your windpipe to help you breathe more easily.'

She remembered Bob's hand closing around her throat.

'Moving on,' Waschkowski said, as though he were a docent describing masterpieces in a museum, 'we have several cracked ribs, which we simply taped up because modern science hasn't yet provided us with a better way of mending them.'

She could feel the toe of Bob's shoe smashing into her over and over again.

He pointed to a tube emerging from the side of her rib cage. 'Now this little beauty is what we call a chest tube. We put that in because one of your ribs went and poked a hole in your right lung. Think of your lung as something like a balloon, and then picture what happens when you stick a pin in that balloon.'

Waschkowski saw her eyes widen. 'Fortunately, a hole in a lung isn't something to worry about these days,' he went on smoothly. 'The tube will drain the fluid out of your chest cavity and then your lung will reinflate, just like that balloon again, and most likely heal all by itself.'

He was so casual about it that Karen supposed having a hole in a lung wasn't such a big deal, after all.

'I bet you can pretty much figure out what the cast on your arm is for.'

Blink.

'I thought so. It was a clean fracture, easy to set. You'll probably have signatures from the entire staff on that cast by the time it comes off.'

She remembered falling out of a big maple tree and breaking her arm when she was eight. She had worn a cast for six weeks. 'I told you so,' her mother's voice echoed.

'Next,' Waschkowski continued, 'we have some discomfort in the abdomen, right?'

Blink.

'That's because we had to open you up inside and fix a few things. Do you know what a spleen is?'

There was a pause before Karen blinked once, then twice.

'Yes and no,' Waschkowski interpreted. 'Well, that's okay. It doesn't really matter, because you don't have one anymore. It was ruptured, so we took it out. Luckily, you can live to a very ripe old age without it.'

He opened his mouth to tell her about the uterus, about how torn it was, about how they had tried to repair it, but failed.

'You also lost a fair share of blood along the way,' he said instead. There would be time enough later, when she was stronger, physically and emotionally, to tell her she would never have children. 'So we gave you a couple of pints of healthy new A positive to fill up those veins again. And last, but not least, we have a smashed kneecap. Now I happen to like the symmetry of it,' he joked, 'seeing as it's your right arm that's busted and your left kneecap that's smashed. But you might prefer to be lopsided.'

Blink. Blink.

'Ah, good,' he said with a grin. 'You obviously share my sense of artistic proportion. We put a splint on the leg, which will immobilize it until we can operate. There's an orthopedic specialist waiting in the wings who'll tackle the job when you're a bit stronger.'

He told her about the pneumonia next, again as though it were an everyday occurrence rather than a potential killer, and about the IV dripping nourishment and antibiotics into her system, and about the sinister-looking machine that monitored her heartbeat and the cuff on her arm that allowed the nurses to take her blood pressure.

Finally, he told her about Margaret Westfield and her dog Brandy.

'Animals have excellent instincts,' he said.

When she was four years old, Karen was bitten by a neighbor's Rottweiler and had since been somewhat wary of dogs. How ironic, she thought, that she might now owe her life to one.

'Your parents are here,' Waschkowski said at the conclusion of his monologue. 'They've been here right from the start, of course, and they've really been keeping us on our toes for the past eight days.'

Karen had listened to the recitation of her injuries with relative calm, but now her eyes opened so wide they threatened to engulf her entire face. Eight days? She had lost eight days? How was that possible? And much worse, in that time, how many strangers had looked at her, examined her, and discovered the awful things that Bob had done to her? It was humiliating to realize what they had seen.

She began to agonize over what they must have thought of her as she lay unconscious and unable to explain. They must have thought her stupid, at best, to get herself in such a situation. At worst, cheap and common. Tears welled up in her eyes again. Even her mother and father knew, before she had a chance to prepare them. Above all, Karen prayed she wasn't pregnant. *Anything but that*, she silently begged a God she didn't know if she still believed in.

At that moment, all she wanted was to rip the tubes and wires from her body and crawl, if she had to, into a hot shower bath, to burn off the layers of skin that the monster in the night had touched, to scrub away all evidence of his existence. Even as she struggled to get her mind around the enormity of her ordeal, she knew that she would never be completely clean again. The tears rolled down her cheeks.

Waschkowski's heart turned over. 'Look,' he said, 'I'm not going to tell you that you haven't had a rough deal here. You have. Rougher than anyone deserves. But you're a strong young woman. The fact that you've made it this far proves that, and you're going to make it the rest of the way. It may take a little time, but you're going to be just fine. In all the weeks and months ahead, you remember that I told you so – and that I'm never wrong.'

He had a sincere face and kind eyes and Karen wanted so much to believe him.

As a doctor, Stanley Waschkowski knew, perhaps better than most, how badly a body could be ravaged by an unexpected injury or a debilitating disease. He had learned how to set bones and treat infections with a reasonable expectation of success. But he had never, in all his years of schooling and practice, been called upon to treat a damaged soul.

five

Karen slept a great deal after that. Deep, dark, pain-free slumber that blotted out reality and hastened the healing. It was so much easier not to have to think and not to have to feel and not to have to remember. She wished it might go on forever.

She would lie in oblivion until the nightmares came to jolt her back into consciousness, and then she would stare up at the reassuring pocked ceiling and around at her cocoon of white night curtains and listen to the soft noises of the special care nurses at work until the panic ebbed and her heart stopped its erratic pounding and she could close her eyes and float back into forgetfulness. She had no concept of hours or days. Her only indicator was that sometimes it was light outside the window when she awakened and sometimes it was dark.

Once, when she opened her eyes, her parents were there. She wanted to smile and tell them not to worry about her, but her wired jaw wouldn't cooperate, and nothing more than the now familiar gurgle made its way past her throat.

'Hello, darling,' Beverly cooed. 'Daddy and I are right here and we're making sure you get the best possible care.'

Gurgle.

'Don't try to talk, sweetheart. You just rest. That nice Dr. Waschkowski says the more you rest, the quicker you'll be all well again.'

Karen needed no encouragement. She drifted off, almost immediately, eager to return to nonexistence. Another time she awakened, Peter was sitting in a chair beside the bed.

'Hi, honey,' he said gently. 'Happy 1963.'

Dimly, she remembered that he was coming down from Maine to spend New Year's with her and that they were going to live happily ever after. But she had slept through New Year's and there was no happily ever after in her nightmares.

By the end of a month, she had been moved out of the special care unit and into a private room at the other end of the third floor.

Here, the walls were painted a surprising pastel-peach color with a broad band, the exact shade of ripe raspberries, circling the room just above eye level. Curtains striped in peach, raspberry, forest green and gray framed the window. Two upholstered chairs, which stood like bedside sentinels, matched the curtains. Except for one swath from the door to the bed, the institutional linoleum that covered most of the hospital's floors had been replaced by a dove-gray carpet. A framed Monet print hung over the bed, a Renoir accented the opposite wall.

'This whole wing was redecorated last year,' Julie van der Meer, the aide, told her. 'The designer convinced the administrator that recovering patients would recover faster if they were surrounded by cheerful colors and a touch of class.'

The special care unit was located in the relatively quiet rear of the building, but this room looked right out onto busy First Avenue. Now, Karen was treated to the drone of traffic, night and day, and the indiscriminate intrusions of squealing brakes and honking horns and angry voices.

Sometimes in the late hours of the night, as she waited for sleep, she would think about the people in those cars and buses and taxis and trucks and wonder where their lives were taking them. It was her first reconnection with the outside world.

The day Karen was able to take her first real food – a chocolate milk shake, from a flexible straw inserted in the corner of her mouth – everyone celebrated. It tasted delicious and she drank almost all of it. She had lost fifteen pounds since entering the hospital, and the doctors were anxious to get some of that weight back on her slender frame.

Now that she was no longer attached to all the tubes and wires, the staff began to fuss over her, bringing nourishing drinks at all hours, sponge-bathing her sometimes twice a day, combing her hair before her parents arrived, giving her muscle-stimulating massages. Karen could see how proud they were of their handiwork, having put the bits and pieces of her back together again. But she was so totally unfamiliar to herself that it was as though they had worked without a pattern and gotten it all wrong. She wished they would stop fussing and go away.

Her parents came to see her almost every day, her father unutterably sad, her mother artificially cheerful. They encouraged her to finish all her liquids and to exercise her arms and legs as though they actually believed that was all that was necessary to make her whole again. Occasionally her younger sister Laura came with them and tried her best not to stare.

And, of course, there was Peter, who sat beside her for hours on end, holding her hand and telling her funny little stories and smiling at her with his warm brown eyes, until the winter recess was over and he had to return to Cornell.

'I'll call you,' he said. 'You get someone to hold the phone for you and then tell me that you're hearing what I'm saying. Of course, you'd better not let anyone else hear what I say,' he added with an impish grin. 'That might be very embarrassing.'

Karen wondered what could possibly be embarrassing to a staff of professionals who had seen and heard every single thing there was to see and hear about her since the moment she had been brought in out of the Central Park bushes.

On her thirty-fourth day in the hospital, she said her first word.

It was early afternoon and her mother sat in one of the striped chairs beside the bed, knitting. She was wearing a black suit over her matronly figure, and had on too much rouge.

'To cover my hospital pallor,' she said with a chuckle.

Her hair was swept stylishly up on top of her head and her eyelashes were coated with an extra layer of black mascara. It occurred to Karen that her mother had been wearing a lot of black lately and it was not a particularly becoming color.

On the day Karen was moved to the private room, flowers had begun to arrive. They came from friends and relatives all over the country, from neighbors, and even from her father's patients, until the combined fragrances of roses, chrysanthemums, tulips, gladiolas and delphinium almost succeeded in disguising the acrid smell of disinfectant. As soon as one bouquet began to wilt, another appeared to take its place. When there was no space left, Beverly would pluck the sender's card from the arrangement and direct an aide to take it down to the charity wards.

In addition to the flowers, dozens of cards came in the mail. Beverly would perch her eyeglasses on the end of her nose and read some of the clever ones aloud. Later, she would reply to all of them, thanking each one, in Karen's name, for the good wishes. She had also sent a heartfelt note of thanks to Margaret Westfield.

On this day, Beverly had just finished with the mail when Julie van der Meer brought in a huge vase of roses.

'I believe this is the third bouquet from Jill and Andy,' Beverly said after a quick glance at the card. 'I beg your pardon,' she amended, scanning the whole message. 'This one is from Jill and Andy – and *Rebecca Karen*, born January twenty-third, seven pounds, two ounces, twenty-one inches, ten fingers, ten toes, all perfect.' Beverly put the card on top of the pile and resumed her knitting. 'A girl. How nice. How sweet to name her after you.'

Jill wanted to come to the hospital to see Karen, but Beverly put her off, as she put off everyone else except Peter, and that was only out of necessity. She explained that just the immediate family was allowed to visit, which was true – Beverly had issued those instructions herself. So the cards and flowers had come instead.

'Shall I take these down to the ward?' Julie asked, the roses still in her hands.

'No, not these, dear,' Beverly replied. 'I think we'll find a place for them here.'

Beverly knit two and purled one. Julie looked for a place to set the vase. Karen looked from one to the other.

'Ba-by,' she said.

It was a half whisper, half groan, hoarse and wheezy, but it was most definitely a word, not a gurgle.

Beverly dropped a whole row of stitches. 'Did you hear that?' she asked, turning to Julie. 'She spoke. I think she said *baby*. Did you hear?'

'I heard,' Julie replied with a broad grin and hurried off to spread the news.

Beverly jumped out of her chair and leaned over the bed. 'That's right, darling,' she encouraged, speaking slowly and distinctly as though her daughter might be hard of hearing or mentally retarded. 'Ba-by. Jill's had her ba-by. Can you say it a-gain?'

'No,' Karen wheezed with an inward smile, wondering whether her mother actually thought she had lost her mind along with her voice.

But Beverly missed the sarcasm. She was much too busy laughing and crying and jumping up and down all at the same time. Her little girl had spoken. In all the weeks of having to sit by and watch the mending process inch its way along, this was what she had been waiting for, praying for – proof that the damage to Karen's body had not affected her brain. Broken bones could be explained, but what could be said about a broken mind?

She had spent countless sleepless nights listening to Leo's staccato snoring and contemplating the possibility of her daughter's emerging from this disaster little more than a vegetable, unable to think or do for herself. Injury aside, minds had been known to crack under a lot less stress than Karen had endured.

It didn't matter that both Dr. Waschkowski and the neurologist had told her, over and over again, that there were no indications of any brain damage. What did doctors know anyway? As long as there was even the slightest chance that they could be wrong, Beverly would wait, hoping for the best, but preparing for the worst.

There would be no question of keeping Karen at home, if it came to that, she was quick to realize. The town gossips would have a never-ending field day with it, and there was Leo's dental practice to consider, not to mention Laura. And now, with one little word, Karen had erased all her mother's fears.

'Sweetheart, it's so good to hear your voice again,' she cried, the tears of joy running down her over-rouged cheeks, tracking her mascara with them. 'I was beginning to think I never would.'

'No-such-luck,' Karen rasped.

'Now, don't overdo it,' Beverly instructed. 'We can't have you wearing out your vocal cords the very first time.'

'I-want-to-tell-you …' Karen croaked, letting the sentence dangle.

'I know, dear, but not now,' her mother said hastily.

The last thing Beverly wanted to hear from her sweet, innocent daughter, she realized, were the gory details of what a madman had done to her. It would be so much easier to believe there really had been an accident.

'You need your rest,' she said. 'We've waited this long, we can wait a little longer. Right now, I'm going to go call your father and tell him the wonderful news.' She gathered up her knitting and prepared to flee. 'When you're a little stronger, the three of us will sit down and have a nice chat.'

A nice chat, Karen thought. How like her mother to put a Hans Christian Andersen face on an Edgar Allan Poe tale. She didn't know anyone who could do it better.

'What do you say, darling? Isn't that the best plan?'

It was difficult enough to challenge Beverly when Karen was well. Now it was impossible. She blinked once, out of habit.

SIX

The word spread like a brushfire, whipping down the hospital corridors.

'She spoke,' one joyfully told another.

'That's wonderful,' came the response.

Doctors, nurses, technicians and aides whom Karen hardly knew were suddenly stopping by to exchange greetings. People she didn't know at all were pausing at her door to give her a friendly smile and a thumbs-up sign. Everyone, it seemed, wanted to be a part of her success.

'I understand you had something to say today,' Dr. Waschkowski said that evening, a big grin covering his dear homely face.

Karen looked up, her throat sore from responding to the steady stream of well-wishers.

'Too-much,' she wheezed.

'I guess what they say is true – you can't keep a woman quiet for long.'

'Fuh-ny,' Karen said.

'Here,' he said, bending over her. 'Let me teach you how to talk through that tube in your throat.' When he had shown her how to place her fingers over the little air hole, he sat down in one of the striped chairs. 'So,' he asked, 'what do you have to say to me, after all this time?'

There had been a measure of protection in her silence, an excuse for not having to participate, not having to communicate. Karen had gotten used to the idea of listening and observing, used to hiding behind the simplicity of one blink or two. She thought about all the questions everyone would now want to ask and the explanations she would be expected to give.

'I want to go back to blinking,' she said.

Sergeant Tug McCluskey arrived the next day accompanied by a thin man with a pinched face, horn-rimmed glasses and a dark-blue suit.

'I don't expect you'd have any way of remembering me,' Tug said kindly, 'but I was there. I mean, I was one of the ones who ... who found you.'

Karen nodded as best she could. The burly policeman had small blue eyes, a prominent nose, and a weathered face, and the jacket of his uniform pulled a little too tightly across his girth.

The other man cleared his throat. 'I'm Michael Haller,' he said. 'Investigator for the district attorney's office.'

Karen shifted her attention. Almost skeletally thin, the investigator's dark suit hung poorly on him, reminding her of a hastily assembled scarecrow. His starched white collar was at least two sizes too big and he had the smallest hands Karen had ever seen on a man. His thick horn-rimmed glasses kept sliding down his nose, and every few seconds he would reach up with his right pinky finger and push them back.

'Now that you're able to talk,' he was saying in a brisk impersonal voice, 'I'd like you to tell us what happened.'

Karen looked at him in dismay. She had spent a lot of time thinking about what she would say to her family and her friends, framing the words carefully, but she never realized she would have to talk to the police.

'Is this really necessary?' she replied, pressing her fingers over the tracheotomy tube as Waschkowski had taught her to do.

'I'm afraid so,' Haller replied, fishing a pad and pen from his jacket pocket. 'You see, the way it works is, Sergeant McCluskey here files a report, and then my office investigates.'

'I see,' Karen conceded. 'What is it you need to know?'

'Do you remember the events of the night in question?'

'Yes,' she replied, thinking how pompous he sounded.

'Why don't you tell us about it?'

She looked from one to the other, wondering whether she could suddenly develop amnesia, but she didn't suppose they would go away until they'd gotten what they'd come for, so she took a deep breath.

'His name was Bob.'

'He told you his name?'

'Yes. At the party.'

The two men exchanged glances.

'Maybe you should start at the beginning,' the policeman suggested.

Karen shut her eyes as images she didn't want to see flooded her mind, images she didn't want to share with these strangers. It took almost an hour for the whole story to come out, in bits and pieces and tears. By the time Haller ran out of questions, Karen's mind was numb, her throat ached, her sheets were damp with perspiration, and her pillow was soaked with tears.

'Why did he do such an awful thing?' she rasped. 'Why?'

Tug sighed. 'There doesn't always have to be a reason,' he admitted. 'There are a lot of psychos wandering around.'

'He didn't seem like a psycho.'

'Some of them don't, until something sets them off.'

'I can't promise that we'll get this guy,' Haller said, returning his pad and pen to his pocket. 'These kinds of cases are difficult at best, and we don't have very much to work with.'

'But don't you worry about that right now,' Tug told her. 'You just concentrate on getting well, and leave the rest to us.'

The scarecrow was already halfway out the door.

Karen blinked, but the significance was lost on the two officers. She watched silently as they left. Maybe it was the way they probed for every tiny detail, almost like voyeurs, going over and over the same ground, but it was as though they had raped her all over again – coldly and callously violating the fragile sense of self she needed so desperately to protect.

She took a small measure of comfort in knowing

that, after this, telling her parents and her friends and Peter would be easy.

'Don't you think you were a little hard on her?' Tug asked as he walked with Haller down the front steps of the hospital.

'It's how you get at the truth,' the investigator said with a shrug.

'So, what do you think?'

The investigator shook his head in disgust and sighed. 'It'll never get to court,' he said.

'You don't think you can find him?'

'Oh, I'll probably find him, if I look hard enough, if his name really is Bob, if he really does go to Harvard. But what's the point?'

'Jesus, Haller,' Tug protested. 'He shouldn't get away with what he did to that girl.'

'Come on, Sergeant, don't go getting soft this late in the game. She knew him, for God's sake. They were partying, they were drinking. She went for a walk with him. At two o'clock in the morning. For all I know, she could have been a willing partner and things just got a little out of hand.'

'You didn't see her the way I did, dumped under those bushes,' the veteran policeman replied. 'I don't think you can call that a little out of hand.'

'So maybe she teased him, led him on a bit and then, when it was too late, changed her mind and went virginal on him, and he lost his temper. That kind of thing happens all the time, you know. Women say no when they mean yes, and yes when they mean no, and who knows what they really want?'

'I don't think so.' Tug shook his head. 'I think it happened exactly the way she said it did.'

'You may be right, Sergeant,' Haller said with another shrug, 'and I'll follow through on the investigation because that's what I get paid to do, and because maybe I feel a little sorry for her, too, all beat up like that. But take my word for it, the DA won't prosecute. You know as well as I do these cases are tough enough to prove even when there are half a dozen eyewitnesses, a ton of physical evidence, and we're dealing with a known offender. But a guy from Harvard Law School? Jesus, he could represent himself and still make mincemeat out of that girl.'

'He shouldn't walk,' Tug insisted.

'Maybe not,' Haller agreed, pushing his glasses up his nose and reaching for his car keys. 'But in the end, it'll be her word against his.'

'If it was one of my granddaughters lying there, looking like that, I'd rip the balls off the bastard.'

Haller sighed again. 'If she were my granddaughter,' he said, 'I'd tell her to go home and forget it – and be more careful the next time.'

seven

By Saturday afternoon, Karen had forgiven the policemen. She reasoned they probably didn't realize they were being offensive. More likely, it was their way of being polite, deliberately trying not to show any emotion as she plodded through her grim recitation.

Still, there was the feeling that they hadn't believed her that kept nagging at her, that they thought her in some way responsible for what Bob had done. But of course that was absurd – she had tried everything she could to stop him. Karen decided that it was only because the policemen were strangers and knew nothing about her values or her upbringing that they had cross-examined her in such a harsh way.

She sipped the last of her afternoon shake as she waited for her parents to arrive, knowing that, even though she would have to tell her grim story again, this time she would be talking to the people who knew her best and loved her and would, above all, understand.

'Hi, sweetheart,' Beverly cooed shortly before four o'clock.

The black was gone. Her mother was wearing a bright-red suit with a cropped jacket and a flattering A-line skirt that Karen had never seen before, and she had been to the beauty parlor. Her hair was perfectly coiffed and her nails gleamed with red polish.

'How's my girl?' Leo asked, looking rather drab beside his flamboyant wife as he took the seat farthest from his daughter.

'Better,' Karen told him. It wouldn't matter if it were true or not; she knew it was what he needed to hear.

'That's good.' He nodded, satisfied.

Leo Kern was the kind of man who found it easier not to see ugliness in the world around him. He spent his days in a sterile stainless-steel cocoon, where defects could be fixed, as if by magic, decay could be drilled out of existence, and discoloration could be polished to gleaming purity. He left his wife to deal with the harsh realities of raising a family, and Karen sometimes felt he was more involved with the lives of his patients than with the lives of his daughters.

'What is that you're doing with your fingers?' her mother asked.

'Closing the hole,' Karen told her. 'So I can talk.'

'And is that what you've been doing since Thursday – talking up a storm?'

'I guess,' Karen answered. 'The police came to see me.'

'The police?' Beverly echoed sharply. 'What for?'

'They're investigating what happened.'

Her parents exchanged a glance that was too quick for Karen to catch.

'What did you tell them?' Beverly asked.

'I told them everything I could remember.'

Beverly settled herself in her chair. 'Well then, I guess maybe you'd better tell us, too.'

Karen took a moment to search for the right words, the right phrases that would convey the facts of that night to her parents without the horror. The last thing she wanted was to upset them unnecessarily.

'You went to Jill's party,' Beverly prompted.

'Yes,' Karen said. 'I went to Jill's party. And right after I got there, I met a friend of a friend of Andy's former roommate, named Bob, from Harvard Law School. I don't know what his last name is – he never told me, but he seemed very nice and he was attentive, and we sort of spent the evening together.'

'Well, that doesn't sound so bad,' Beverly commented.

'That part wasn't,' Karen agreed with an uncustomary hint of bitterness in her voice. 'When the party was over, Bob offered to help me get a cab to Aunt Edna's. It was pretty late, after two o'clock, and I thought that would be all right. We waited and waited but we couldn't find a cab, so then he suggested that we walk across the park.'

'A nice young man from Harvard Law School offered to escort you across Central Park at two o'clock in the morning?' Beverly summarized.

'That's right.'

'Well, I guess that explains how you got there, although God knows why you would go into such a dangerous place in the middle of the night, even if you were with a friend of a friend of Andy's former roommate.'

'It was cold,' Karen told her. 'Walking seemed like a better idea than standing around.'

'So, you were in the park. Then what happened?'

Karen took a deep breath. 'He attacked me.'

'Who attacked you?' Beverly asked, looking blank.

'Bob did. He made a pass. I tried to stop him, but he wouldn't let me go.'

Beverly stared at her daughter with a combination of dismay and disbelief. 'You were, you were … damaged' – she couldn't even bring herself to say the right word – 'by a Harvard Law student?'

'Yes.'

'It was someone you knew?'

'Yes.'

'Why?' Beverly cried.

'Why what?'

'Why would the young man behave like that? What did you do?'

'What do you mean, what did I do?' Karen replied. 'I didn't do anything.'

'Well, there must be something you're not telling us,' Beverly said flatly. 'Nice young men from Harvard don't go around taking advantage of innocent girls for no reason.'

'Well, this one did,' Karen retorted.

'Oh my God,' her mother muttered, springing up, almost knocking over her chair.

'What's the matter?' Karen asked.

Beverly looked to Leo for support, but Leo was looking at the crease in his trousers with a very pained expression on his face.

'I thought we were talking about some maniac. I thought some very sick stranger grabbed you off the street, and you couldn't defend yourself.'

'I couldn't defend myself,' Karen insisted. 'He was too strong.'

'I just don't understand you at all,' Beverly snapped. 'You keep telling us you're madly in love with Peter Bauer. So why on earth would you take up with someone else like that?'

'I didn't take up with him,' Karen protested, tears filling her eyes, forgetting for the moment that Peter Bauer had never fit into her mother's narrow category of acceptable suitors. 'He said he was taking me to Aunt Edna's. That's all. I believed him.'

'And you're sure you didn't lead him on in some way, or give him any reason to expect that you might be receptive to his advances?'

'No.'

'You didn't lean up against him, say, in a manner that he might have misconstrued?'

Karen remembered Bob pulling her inside his coat when she complained of the cold, but that had been his idea, not hers.

'It wasn't like that,' she cried, the tears now flowing freely down her cheeks. 'I didn't do anything wrong.'

'Oh, darling,' Beverly said hastily, grabbing a tissue and dabbing at her daughter's eyes. 'Now don't get yourself into a tizzy. Nobody said you meant to do anything wrong. It's just that sometimes we don't realize how our actions might appear to another person. The way we smile, perhaps, or the way we stand or the way we say things. It's so easy to be misinterpreted.'

'I was just having a good time,' Karen sobbed.

'Of course you were.' Her mother relented. 'Just like anyone else at a party would. You had no way of knowing that this Bob person would take it so seriously.'

'No,' Karen mumbled. This wasn't going at all the way she had thought it would. First the police, and now her parents. She was suddenly very confused.

'I don't mean to distress you,' her mother added, 'but your father and I just can't understand how you could have gotten yourself into such a situation, how you could have been so, so … careless.'

Leo had yet to say a word.

'Neither do I,' Karen sobbed, letting go of the tube to cover her face with her hands.

After a moment, Beverly sat back down in her chair, crossed her legs at the ankles and clasped her hands together in her lap.

'Yes, well, I think we have a pretty clear idea of what took place and we're not going to dwell on it any longer,' she said firmly. 'You'll soon be well again, and I think it's time that we consider this … unfortunate incident over and done, and get on with the rest of our lives.'

Over and done, Karen thought wistfully. Could it really be over and done with a snap of her mother's fingers?

'Do you think so?' she asked.

'Yes, I do,' her mother affirmed. 'I can tell how terribly upset talking about the whole thing is making you, and I don't see any reason to put you through the painful ordeal of repeating this story again. After all, it's none of anyone's business.'

'The police know,' Karen reminded her. 'I told them everything. They're going to find Bob and arrest him and make him pay for what he did.'

'Your father will take care of that,' Beverly said

smoothly. 'The last thing we're going to do is let anyone drag you into some sordid courtroom and smear your name all over the newspapers.'

'But I'll have to testify,' said Karen. 'I want to. I want to see him convicted and put in jail.'

'You'll do nothing of the kind,' her mother declared. 'You're not going to have anything more to do with this whole unpleasant mess. From now on, we'll simply tell anyone who asks that you were taken to the hospital because ... because of an accident.'

'An accident?'

'Yes.' Beverly declared. She studied a speck of lint on her red jacket. 'Actually, that's pretty much what we've been telling people anyway.'

Karen looked from her mother to her father and back to her mother again. 'You told people I had an accident?'

'We weren't very specific about anything, of course. After all, we didn't really know anything. We just sort of intimated that it was an accident. There wasn't any reason to go into the gruesome details.'

'What kind of accident did I have?'

Beverly hesitated a moment. 'I think we'll make it an automobile accident,' she decided. 'That's the most logical choice, isn't it? I mean, considering how damaged you were, we can't very well say you fell out of a tree, now can we?'

Karen's head suddenly began to hurt. 'But that's a lie,' she said.

'Well, if it is, it's only to save you, save us, from a lot of humiliating gossip.' Beverly's full lower lip began to quiver. 'Isn't it enough that we have to know what went on, does the rest of Great Neck have to know, too? We're respected members of the community. There's never been a hint of scandal in our family. Think what it would do to your father's practice if this ever came out.'

'Now, Mother.' Leo spoke up for the first time.

'And think of your sister,' Beverly went on, as thought he hadn't. 'If you go around broadcasting all the ugly facts, people might start asking what you had in mind when you went strolling in Central Park in the middle of the night with a young man you hardly knew.'

'But the people here know there wasn't any automobile accident,' Karen argued, wondering dimly what this had to do with sixteen-year-old Laura.

'Maybe they do and maybe they don't,' Beverly declared. 'Besides, hospital records can be sealed or something, and then we can do whatever's necessary to prevent anyone else from finding out.'

'What about Peter?'

'The time for worrying about Peter was before you went walking in Central Park, I should think,' her mother replied tartly. 'But of course we'll have to tell him the same thing as everyone else.'

'I can't lie to him,' Karen objected.

'Of course you can,' Beverly snapped. 'What chance do you think you'll have to make a decent marriage, to him or to anyone else, if you repeat this dreadful story? Do you really want to ruin the rest of your life? Because that's exactly what will happen if you ever tell anybody what you told us.'

Karen's head was throbbing and she began to pray for the oblivion that had always come to ease her pain to come now and swallow her up forever.

'It's not fair,' she said.

'Fair?' her mother pounced. 'You think it would be

fair to stand up and tell the whole world what you did?'

'What *I* did?' Karen echoed. 'You mean, what *he* did, don't you?'

'Whatever,' Beverly replied, picking the piece of lint off her jacket.

'You're my parents,' Karen whispered. 'You're supposed to love me. I thought you'd be on *my* side.'

'Of course we love you,' said Beverly. 'Of course we're on your side. That's why we're willing to go to such lengths to protect you.'

'No,' Karen accused. 'You think this was all my fault. You don't think he ought to be punished – you think I should. You think I flirted with him and teased him and then enticed him into the park. You think I asked him to do this to me, don't you?'

'I don't think anything of the kind,' Beverly retorted. 'I think there was probably a terrible misunderstanding somewhere along the way and he took advantage of you. Maybe he should be punished for that, but not at the expense of this family's reputation.'

Suddenly Karen couldn't seem to catch her breath. Her right leg was in spasm, her face turned beet-red, her whole body began to heave, and she was clawing at the wires that fastened her jaw.

'Oh my God, what's wrong?' Beverly shrieked.

Leo sprang up and grabbed for his daughter's hand before she could do any serious damage to herself. 'Get a nurse in here,' he told his wife.

Beverly rushed for the door. 'She can't breathe,' she shouted into the corridor. 'Do something.'

Rose Thackery came running. After one look she turned on her heel, returning seconds later with a hypodermic. She hurried to the bed, almost knocking Leo aside.

'Karen,' she said firmly, 'calm down now. You're having a little anxiety attack, that's all. It's nothing to worry about.'

She stuck the needle deep into Karen's hip. Then she took hold of her patient's hand. 'Listen to me,' she said soothingly. 'You're all right. You're safe. Nothing bad is going to happen to you.'

Karen stared at the kind face through the flood of gasps and tears – a face that had always meant comfort and acceptance and good humor, and heard the soft words that had never been anything but supportive.

The panic began to subside.

'Just take a nice deep breath,' the nurse encouraged. 'Come on, just one.'

Slowly, Karen began to draw air into her lungs, and when she could hold no more, she let it all out.

'Now another.'

Karen obeyed. By the third breath, the spasm in her leg had eased and her face was returning to its natural color.

'She's all right now,' Rose Thackery assured the Kerns. 'Do you know what caused this? Did one of you say something to upset her?'

'Certainly not,' Beverly retorted. 'Why on earth would either of us say anything to upset her?'

eight

It was dark outside the window. The draperies had not been drawn and night shadows moved in all directions. A cloud scudded across the moon, a newspaper was swept up in a sudden gust, a taxi slid along a slippery street.

The weary swing shift had departed, the grumpy graveyard shift had arrived. Most of the patients on the third floor of Manhattan Hospital had been asleep for hours.

Karen lay in her bed, wide awake despite her evening sedative, her head pounding even after two doses of aspirin. Try as she would, she couldn't get her mother's words out of her mind. The thing she had feared the most had happened. She had disgraced herself and her family. So much so that her mother was willing to tell a terrible lie rather than have anyone know the truth.

But what *was* the truth? That was the question Karen

struggled to answer in the dark hours before dawn. Had she in some way prompted her own misfortune, as the police had more or less intimated, and her mother seemed so ready to believe?

For the thousandth time, she began to replay that long, harrowing night in her mind, from the moment she spilled mayonnaise down the front of her dress to the instant Bob's fist smashed into her jaw and the world had gone black. She went over every action, every gesture, every smile, every giggle, every word she could remember, but it had all been harmless party flirting to her.

Was it possible that Bob had seen an invitation in her behavior she hadn't meant to be there? Read some signal she hadn't realized she had given? Yes, she had been flattered by his attentions, but had that made her appear easy? Did casual flirting mean she had agreed to have sex? Had she really brought all this on herself?

Two men she didn't know and two people she had known her whole life apparently thought so. Karen groaned aloud in the darkness and wished she could ask for more aspirin. But it was barely half an hour since she had had the last ones.

If only she hadn't thought Bob so attractive. If only she hadn't enjoyed the envious looks of the other girls at Jill's party. If only she had insisted that they wait for the doorman to hail a cab. If only she hadn't worn her favorite black dress. If only she had stayed at home in the first place. Her head throbbed with all the if-onlys that might have kept her from ending up, with her clothes and her life in tatters, under a clump of bushes in Central Park.

Was it only two months ago that Karen had believed there was nothing worse than getting pregnant and having to marry a man you didn't love? It seemed a lifetime ago. How could she have been so naive? Why, compared to the Kerns, Jill's family would be considered fortunate. Next to Karen, Jill had everything.

A small light began to flicker in the darkness of her soul because there was one thing Jill didn't have, and that made all the difference – she didn't have Peter Bauer.

Strong, devoted Peter, who called on the telephone twice a week and sent funny little cards and big bouquets of her favorite yellow roses. No matter how bad things got, Karen could still take courage from the knowledge that Peter was there for her, and that alone was enough to ease the pounding in her head and let the gray curtain of sleep steal over her.

Michael Haller came back two weeks later, wearing the same baggy suit. Tug McCluskey was not with him.

'I found Bob,' he said without social preamble. It was on the tip of his tongue to fill in the last name for her, but he decided there was really no point unless, of course, she asked. 'He was exactly where you said he would be.'

'Did you arrest him?'

'We couldn't really do that.'

'Why not?'

Haller pushed his eyeglasses back up his nose. 'Because we have no proof that he committed any crime.'

'Look at me,' Karen cried. 'You can see for yourself what he did. Isn't that proof enough?'

'Yes, well, the thing is,' Haller replied, studying his scuffed shoes, 'the young man doesn't exactly corroborate your story. Actually, he says it was your idea to walk across the park and that it was *you* who came on to *him*.'

The fact that this Bob had been so easy to find, in plain sight at Harvard Law School, had more or less clinched things in Haller's mind. A man bent on rape didn't normally go around telling his victim where to find him.

Karen stared at the investigator. Part of her was outraged, but part of her, she realized, had almost expected it. The conspiracy, as she now thought of it, was complete.

'He said I asked for it? He said I wanted him to do this to me?'

'He said he didn't do anything – other than accommodate you, that is,' Haller told her. 'He said he simply had sex with you and afterward, when he wanted to leave, you refused to go with him.'

'Did you believe him?' she asked dully.

'He seemed sincere.'

'Did you believe him?'

'It doesn't matter what I believe,' Haller declared in his own defense. 'It's what a jury would believe, if this were to go to trial. We have no real evidence here, no eyewitness, just your word against his and, from everything my investigation has turned up so far, he's a straight-A student from a prominent San Francisco family who's never been in any trouble.'

'Neither have I,' Karen reminded him.

Haller shifted uneasily. 'I know that,' he replied. 'But in cases like these, the burden of proof is on the state. And the reality is that juries just don't convict fine upstanding young men from prominent families of rape without a great deal more evidence than we have here.'

'You mean they'd say I made it all up? That *I* seduced *him* and then went off into Central Park by myself, looking for more, and lured some stranger into the bushes, and begged him to rape me and beat me half to death, and then tried to blame some nice innocent guy who didn't do anything but try to take me home?'

'It could go down like that,' Haller said.

'Even if that's not what happened?'

'Look, if it were up to me, I'd lock the bastard up and throw away the key,' he told her, because he didn't need her anger and he had a perfect out. 'But it's up to the DA, and the DA doesn't go to trial unless he thinks he can win. He just doesn't think he can win this one.'

In fact, the wily politician had all but laughed Haller out of his office.

'You mean, winning is all that matters – not what's true or what's right?'

'Okay, I'll give you that.' The scarecrow sighed. 'But I never said anything about justice. I'm only saying it's the system.'

A justice system that didn't have anything to do with justice? Karen pondered his statement in genuine confusion. It had never occurred to her that truth could be meaningless if no one chose to believe it. Or that lies could be accepted because of expediency, because they were more comfortable to live with.

'Did my father come to see you?' she asked.

'Yes, he did,' Haller said. 'As a matter of fact, both your parents did.'

'Did they tell you that they wanted you to stop this investigation?'

'If they did,' Haller replied, 'it's because they don't

want you going through any more pain, and I happen to think they're right. You're a nice kid. You have no idea what a clever defense attorney would do to you in open court. Trust me, by the time he was finished, he'd have the jury believing you weren't much better than a two-dollar hooker off Eighth Avenue. If you want my advice, forget all about it. You won't get any satisfaction in a courtroom.'

'Thank you for coming,' Karen said.

If the police thought her a liar, if her parents thought her a tease, if a jury would think her a whore, what was the point of protesting any further?

'I'm sorry,' Michael Haller said, annoyed because his words sounded so hollow and inadequate.

'So am I,' she replied.

'No one deserves to be hurt as badly as you were hurt,' he added, to make up for some of it. 'I hope you get well soon.'

The conversation was over. He turned to leave, noting that she hadn't asked for Bob's last name. It was just as well.

Karen shut her eyes so that she wouldn't have to watch him go. Oddly enough, it seemed to be the broken bones and bloody bruises that disturbed people more than anything else. It was almost as though, if they could focus on them, they wouldn't have to deal with what had really happened to her.

nine

Karen was discharged from Manhattan Hospital on the eighth of May. Her jaw had healed, as had her arm. Two more sessions in surgery had reconstructed her smashed left kneecap. Physical therapy two times a day was helping her to regain muscle tone and she had learned how to walk again with the aid of crutches.

The hole in her throat, where the tracheotomy tube had been, was now a small red bump. The hole in her side, where the chest tube had been, was now a little wrinkle of skin between two ribs that she could reach around and feel with her fingers.

Driving home in her father's roomy Buick was almost like seeing the world for the first time. Winter had come and gone during her months in the hospital and spring had burst across Long Island. Karen drank it in.

The mighty maple trees and graceful elms that she

last remembered being naked and gnarled were now dressed in bright new greenery. Tired lawns had been transformed into lush carpets, and everywhere, it seemed, azaleas and rhododendron were in bloom. Little gray sparrows and red-breasted robins hopped from branch to branch, singing of sunshine.

When Leo turned onto Knightsbridge Road, Karen craned her neck for a first glimpse of the circular driveway that fronted the stately brick colonial where she had lived her entire life.

'The cherry blossoms waited for you,' her mother said, as the Buick slid beneath a row of delicate pink petals that were usually gone with April.

Karen sighed happily. It looked exactly as she had hoped it would: the burgeoning trees, the curving beds of begonias and impatiens and peonies that her mother so carefully cultivated, the thick blanket of grass, the neat hedges that separated them from their neighbors. It was good to know that some things never changed.

From the outside, the house looked just the same as it always had. Although Karen had gotten used to the quiet hustle of the hospital's third floor, the constant stream of white uniforms that passed by her door, the ministering routine that never varied, and her wonderful mechanical bed with its infinite positions, it hadn't been home.

Home was like a pair of old slippers that you could snuggle into and be totally comfortable, and it didn't matter how you looked or what you said or even what you did, because you were loved and accepted. But coming home this time was different, because she was different, and the spacious colonial on Knightsbridge Road felt both familiar and strange as she crept back to it and pulled the walls in around her.

At first she hobbled from room to room, learning to negotiate on her crutches, needing to reacquaint herself with everything that had always signified stability and security – the polished mahogany banister she had slid down as a child, the Persian rugs and Duncan Phyfe furniture that seemed lost in the huge living room, the flowered wallpapers and heavy brocade draperies, the Meissen lamps, the Dresden porcelain, the Revere silver, her father's books overflowing the shelves in the library, her sister's Elvis Presley albums and, last but not least, her own room that hadn't been changed since high school, with the moiré curtains, the profusion of yellow ribbons and rosebuds that climbed up and down the walls, the white oak furniture, the cluttered desk, and the cork bulletin board that told the story of her girlhood.

The first night, once she got Beverly to stop fussing over her, Karen locked her door and wept, wishing she had never left her room, never grown up. Long after she felt the rest of the house go to sleep, she snapped on her bedside lamp and rummaged in the nightstand drawer for her box.

It was a wooden keepsake box of her grandmother's, old and scarred, but the intricate inlay was still visible. In it, Karen kept scraps of paper on which she wrote down whatever came into her head. She called them her thought pages.

She pulled out a clean sheet and began to write:

> They say a dog found me,
> torn and bleeding,
> more dead than alive,
> left there like discarded garbage.
> Perhaps I am.

They threw words around me,
like exposure,
massive trauma,
pneumonia.
But I wasn't there to hear them.

They say surgery lasted
six hours.
They removed
more than they left.
But I was already empty inside.

It was days before I opened my eyes.
Weeks before I spoke.
What could I say
after all their fine work –
they should have let me die … ?

Karen put the page into the box and put the box back in her drawer. Then she turned her head into the pillow and cried herself to sleep, her lamp still lit.

She spent many hours in her mother's treasured garden, sitting quietly in a lounge chair with her leg propped on a pillow, alternately reading, sipping iced tea, and staring into space, smelling the gentle fragrances of spring warming into summer. Before long, the hospital pallor began to fade and her cheeks grew pink in the sunshine.

Now that Karen was eating real food again, her mother had instructed Winola, the maid who had been with the family for as long as any of them could remember, to follow the girl around with tempting plates of goodies.

'If you keep this up, I'm going to be as fat as a pig,'

Karen complained, but not too loudly.

She had nothing to think about but getting well as she waited for Peter to come and rescue her – like the princess in the tower that her mother had read to her about as a child.

Twice each week, Beverly drove Karen back to Manhattan Hospital to continue her physical therapy. It would have been much easier to go to the local hospital for treatment but Beverly had waved the idea aside.

'I think it's best that we stay with the people we started with,' she said. 'They're most familiar with Karen's case and I don't mind the drive.'

Actually, Beverly hated driving into the city, fighting traffic in every direction. But this way, she reasoned, none of the personnel at the local hospital, including their long-time family physician, would need to know the truth.

Aside from those Tuesday and Thursday afternoons, Karen stayed at home, making one excuse after another not to leave the house.

'Come to town with me,' Beverly would suggest. 'We'll do a little shopping. It'll do you good to get out.'

'My knee hurts,' Karen would reply, even though her physical therapist repeatedly told her to use the leg as much as possible. But she was sure that all anyone would have to do was look at her to know immediately what had happened to her, despite her mother's fiction, and she wasn't prepared to cope with that just yet.

She tried, on a number of occasions, to talk about Bob and that night, but she was always cut off.

'You had a terrible accident,' Beverly would say.

'And we're not going to dwell on it anymore.'

'But I really need to talk about it,' Karen would press, wanting only the chance to explain her side of things so that her parents could forgive her for being so careless.

'What you need is to put it all behind you and forget it ever happened,' Beverly would declare firmly. 'Believe me, I know what's best.'

'Yes, Mother.'

Just before she left the hospital, Dr. Waschkowski had suggested she talk to a psychiatrist.

'We here are dealing with your physical healing,' he said, giving her a slip of paper with a name and telephone number on it. 'But that's only part of the problem.'

The idea of being able to ask a doctor why things in the park had gone so wrong seemed rather tempting to Karen, but when she mentioned it to her mother, the woman exploded.

'Only crazy people need psychiatrists,' Beverly fumed. 'You may have been careless, but that doesn't mean you're crazy. My God, that's all we need, on top of everything else – a psychiatrist messing around in this.' And she tore the piece of paper to shreds.

Two weeks after Karen's return home, Jill and the baby came to see her.

'Don't worry about the details of the accident, in case she's rude enough to ask,' Beverly counseled in advance. 'It's very normal to be fuzzy after such an ordeal.'

'Yes, Mother.'

It was eerie the way the woman actually seemed able to blot out reality and convince herself that her daughter was indeed the victim of some reckless automobile driver. Part of Karen wished she could do that, too.

Motherhood had transformed Jill. In addition to a healthy, happy glow, her figure, which had always been a bit too thin, had filled out in all the right places.

'It took having a baby to get boobs,' she said, laughing.

But it was the little pink bundle in the crib that most fascinated Karen – a perfect miniature person, with innocent blue eyes, the softest skin, and a fuzzy halo of honey-blond hair.

'She's so tiny. I never expected her to be so tiny.'

Jill grimaced. 'You wouldn't think that if you'd had to deliver her.'

'Do you think I could hold her?'

'Sure.' Jill swung the four-month-old baby out of her carrier and into Karen's waiting arms without hesitation.

Rebecca turned trusting eyes on the stranger who now cuddled her, and smiled.

'I think she likes me,' Karen cried.

'She likes anyone who'll hold her.'

Karen ran her fingers along a round pink cheek. 'If she were mine, I'd hold her all the time.'

'Tell me that after you have one of your own,' Jill retorted. 'When the house has to be cleaned and the diapers have to be washed and dinner hasn't even been started and your back is killing you.'

Karen bit down on her lower lip. Before she left the hospital, right before he gave her the name of the psychiatrist, Dr. Waschkowski had told her there would be no children. Of all the bad moments she had endured up to then, that was the worst – to hear her dreams and her future shatter against his words and know that she would pay for her carelessness for the rest of her life.

It was almost agony to hold Rebecca, to feel the warm little bundle snuggle up against her so trustingly, to smell the sweet scent of baby powder, to hear the contented little gurgles, to feel the tiny hand close itself around her finger and know that she would never experience this joy with a baby of her own.

Karen heaved a sigh of infinite sadness, and, despite her best efforts, a hot tear slipped out of the corner of her eye, rolled down her face, and dripped onto the baby's pink-and-white romper suit.

'Well, I think that's enough spoiling for a while,' Jill said, missing the tear and interpreting the sigh as a sign of weariness. She plucked Rebecca out of Karen's arms and turned to settle her back into her crib. Karen started to protest, but Beverly chose that moment to announce lunch.

'All right now,' Jill said later, after they had eaten Winola's tomato soup and tuna-fish salad and the baby had been nursed and changed and put down for a nap, when the two of them were in the garden with a tray of iced tea and cookies between them, 'enough about me and the baby. I want to know about you.'

'What about me?' Karen countered.

'Oh, come on, I've been waiting for months to find out what happened,' Jill exclaimed. 'The last time I looked, you're leaving my apartment with the hunk of the evening, and the next thing I know, you're in the hospital.'

'What did my mother say?'

'Your mother told us you were hit by a car, of course. But how on earth did it happen?'

Karen began to fix pleats in her cotton skirt. In

fifteen years of friendship, she had never deliberately lied to Jill. They had shared each other's triumphs as well as tragedies, had been each other's counsel as well as critic, and had never broken a promise or betrayed a confidence. She felt certain she could trust Jill with the truth, despite her mother's warning, and she so desperately needed someone to talk to, so desperately needed someone to understand. She opened her mouth but, just as it was all about to come pouring out, Jill began to giggle.

'When we first heard, you know, about you being hurt,' her friend confided, 'before we knew what had really happened and all, you understand, Andy said that maybe the hunk of the evening had been too hot for you to handle.'

Karen's mouth snapped shut and she stared at her friend. 'What would have made him think that?' she made herself ask.

'Oh, you know Andy,' Jill shrugged. 'His mind is always up somebody's skirt.'

'What did you say when he said that?'

'I told him it was ridiculous, naturally,' Jill replied. 'Anyone who knows you, knows that your heart is pure and your body belongs to Peter.'

'Now that you mention it, I think the hunk *was* pretty strong,' Karen said cautiously, testing the waters. 'I suppose it's not implausible for someone to think that he might have ... overpowered me.'

'Don't be ridiculous,' Jill retorted. 'With those looks, why on earth would he need to overpower anyone? He must have women falling all over him at every turn.'

'Do you really think so?'

'Sure,' her friend asserted. 'And I set Andy straight

about it, too. Anyway, we all know that I'm the weak-willed one. I was destined to jump the gun. But you – you're the original iron maiden. You'll never be seriously swayed by anything short of a ring on your finger. So, come on, let's have all the details.'

Weak-willed or iron-tough, Karen digested silently. Were those the only acceptable options? She wondered how Jill could so arbitrarily reject any other possibilities, completely forgetting that, less than six months ago, she herself would have rejected them, too. It was the police and her parents all over again.

'It was a drunk driver,' she recited woodenly. 'A drunk driver hit me with his car. He came out of nowhere.'

'How awful,' Jill exclaimed, having already heard this from Beverly. 'But where were you when it happened? I mean, what were you doing?'

Karen's heart began to pound in her chest and a line of perspiration popped out across her forehead. She couldn't remember what her mother had told her to say.

'I don't really know that much about it.' She shrugged. 'It's mostly just a blur.'

'Oh, come on, you must remember something,' Jill urged. 'Like what street were you on? I mean, let's start with the hunk. You left the apartment with him. Was he involved in the accident?'

'Yes,' Karen began. 'I mean, no,' she hastily corrected herself. 'I mean, yes, I left the apartment with him, but no, he wasn't hit by a car.'

'Wasn't he going to get you a cab?'

'Yes, he was, but he didn't. I mean, we waited but – that is, yes, he did.'

Jill smiled encouragingly. 'Which is it – yes or no?'

'Well, you see, it was very late, and I – ' Karen was now so flustered she made the only excuse she could think of, rubbing at her eyes with feigned weariness. 'I'm exhausted,' she mumbled. 'I'd really like to talk some more, but I think I have to lie down for a while.'

'Absolutely,' Jill agreed with alacrity, noting her friend's sudden pallor. 'Your mother made me promise not to wear you out.'

'It was great seeing you,' Karen added. 'And thanks for bringing Rebecca. She's just adorable.'

'Of course I'd have brought her anyway,' Jill declared as she gathered up the baby's things, 'but I didn't have much choice. She and I are joined at the hip until solid food.'

Beverly met them in the foyer. 'You're not leaving, are you?' she asked.

'I promised Andy I'd be home early,' Jill replied, maneuvering the crib over the threshold, 'and if I don't hit the road pretty soon, I'm bound to get stuck on the Long Island Expressway until all hours. Besides, I don't think Karen's really up to lengthy visiting yet.'

'Well, you must come back when she's stronger. It's very important for her to have her friends around.'

'I will,' Jill promised.

'What happened?' Beverly asked the moment the front door closed. 'Why did she go running off like that?'

'She wanted details,' Karen replied, turning away.

ten

Peter Bauer steered the Pontiac off the Long Island Expressway onto Lakeville Road, heading north toward Great Neck. His back was stiff and his eyes burned in their sockets. He had planned on doing the journey from Bangor in something under twelve hours, but the closer he got, the heavier the traffic grew, and the slower he was able to travel. He had been driving now for almost fourteen hours.

A week ago, Peter had left Cornell with his degree in electrical engineering. It was his family's proudest moment, the first Bauer to graduate from college. He went home to Maine with his mother and father, his four brothers and his two sisters, to bask briefly in the glory of his achievement, and to attend the lavish party his parents had insisted on giving in his honor.

His whole exciting future was before him, and, as he lay in his lower bunk that first night, listening to the sound of his brother's breathing, he knew that everything was going just as he had envisioned on other nights in this same bed. He had gotten his education, his father was about to take him into the family business – a small company that designed and manufactured electrical components – and he had found the girl of his dreams.

Although he and Karen had not discussed it lately, he was confident that, despite her accident, they would get engaged as planned, and then go on to marry. Maybe not as originally scheduled, but as soon as Karen had recuperated enough to finish her degree at Cornell. He knew she would insist on that. Then they would settle down in Bangor and live happily ever after.

Peter pushed his sunglasses up onto his head and rubbed at his tired eyes as he waited for a traffic light. In the five months since the accident, he and Karen had spoken regularly on the telephone, lopsided conversations – at least until she got the hang of that tube in her throat – but he hadn't seen her since January. He had wanted to drive down from Ithaca on several occasions, but Beverly kept putting him off, suggesting that Karen wasn't up to company and it would be better if he waited until she was stronger.

'Her visitors are restricted to the immediate family,' she told him. 'But I can of course keep you posted on her condition.'

Peter didn't exactly feel like company anymore, but then, he supposed, he wasn't family yet, either, and Beverly was as good as her word, calling him weekly with comprehensive progress reports, more often if there were some sort of breakthrough, as when Karen drank her first liquid, said her first word, took her first steps.

It was Beverly, not the doctors, who had told him about Karen's injuries, when he arrived at the Kerns's doorstep at the end of December.

'We won't know what really happened,' she said, 'until Karen herself can tell us. But it appears to have been some sort of accident.'

She told him as much as she knew about the physical damages, except for the hysterectomy, of course. It would have been much too awkward trying to explain exactly why that had been necessary, and she decided there really wasn't any point in telling him something before he needed to know it. Again, it was Beverly who informed him, the day after she and Leo had had to hear the appalling account, that Karen's injuries were the result of an automobile accident.

'She doesn't remember much about it,' Beverly said. 'Which is just as well, all things considered. From what we've been able to piece together, she was crossing the street when a car went out of control and hit her. As simple as that. A hit-and-run. We assume the driver was drunk.'

'Was she thrown by the force of the impact, or did the car actually run over her?' Peter asked.

There was an abrupt pause on the other end of the phone. In the dozen or so times that Beverly had told this story, no one had thought to ask that question, and she found herself unprepared to answer it.

'I don't know,' she said lamely.

'The doctors should be able to tell,' Peter persisted, 'from the nature of the injuries.'

'I never asked them,' came the stiff reply. 'I mean, after all, what difference does it make?' What was this upstart from Maine trying to do? she wondered. Could he tell from her voice that she had fabricated the whole tale? 'The important thing is that she's going to get better, and that's what we should concentrate on.'

At his end of the line, Peter wondered why she sounded so defensive.

'Are the police investigating?' he asked.

'What is there to investigate?' Beverly retorted. 'No witnesses have come forward, and Karen certainly didn't get much of a look at whoever hit her.'

'Sometimes, people don't come forward because they don't realize they saw anything,' Peter suggested. 'But they might, if the circumstances were publicized widely enough.'

That was all they needed, Beverly thought in annoyance. She wanted to slam the receiver down in his impudent ear, but she resisted the urge. Although he intended to be some kind of engineer – an occupation that ranked barely above a garage mechanic by her standards – it was quite possible that this was the best match her daughter would be able to make, under the circumstances, and it would be foolish of her to do or say anything to jeopardize that.

'I think we would all just as soon forget about the past and focus our energies on the future,' she oozed. 'I'm afraid you'll only succeed in upsetting Karen enormously if you insist on pursuing such really unimportant issues.'

As he turned left into the residential village of Russell Gardens, Peter realized that it still rankled him to think that the person who had injured Karen so seriously, and then simply abandoned her there in the street, should be allowed to get away with it.

It was close to eight o'clock when he pulled into the Kerns's circular drive on Knightsbridge Road, and the sun was preparing to set. It danced off the colonial's brick walls, which now seemed more pink than red, set the white trim to shimmering, and glinted off the windows, turning them into solid gold. So it was that he didn't see Karen standing in the upstairs hall window, looking down at him with a mixture of anticipation and apprehension in her eyes.

She had been standing there, waiting, for more than an hour. She had been preparing herself for his visit for more than a week, ever since he had called to say when he would arrive.

'I'll be there the day after the party,' he told her. 'I'll leave early and drive straight through.'

'We'll have dinner waiting,' she promised.

For over two years now, whenever Karen had contemplated her future, it was at Peter's side – as his wife, as his helpmate, as the mother of the children they both wanted to have.

She had stolen many hours from her studies to scribble 'Karen Bauer' in the margins of her notebooks, and fashion elegant monograms out of two *K*s and a *B*. Peter was her biggest supporter, her best friend, her hero – the only man in the world who could make her heart turn over just by smiling. He was so much a part of her life that had she tried to picture it without him she would have come up blank.

Yet, at this moment, as she looked down on his sandy hair and lanky frame, he seemed a stranger to her, standing on the far side of a canyon of catastrophe, without a bridge.

It had been easy to maintain the link from opposite ends of a long-distance telephone line. There was safety in that. He had called twice a week, always with a joke or a story to make her laugh. Between the calls were the cards and the flowers. But now he was here, and Karen was suddenly sweating and shivering at the same time, wondering what he would think when he saw her. Would he be repulsed by the ugly scars, frightened by her frailty, shocked by her crutches? Would his love turn out to be trivial? She shut her mind against the thought, because he was the reason she was struggling so hard to become whole again, when so much of her had been lost. Turning awkwardly from the window, she maneuvered her crutches down the hall in the direction of the stairway.

She looked like a cadaver, Peter thought, as he stood in the foyer with Beverly and watched Karen, closely followed by Winola, negotiate the broad curving steps with infinite care, planting one crude wooden support firmly into the thick carpet, while holding on to the banister with the other hand, hopping off her good right leg, and then swinging the bad left one down under her. She was barely more than skin and bones beneath her cotton dress, her skin had a strange translucent quality to it, and there was something about her eyes, an expression in the blue-gray depths that he couldn't define and didn't remember ever having seen before.

'It takes me forever to get anywhere, but I have to be careful not to fall on this knee,' she said as she finally reached bottom, took her other crutch from Winola, and started toward him across the polished hardwood floor.

A fleeting frown puckered his narrow face and was gone. The Karen he knew would have said something like: 'I didn't want to fall at your feet and risk you getting all swelled in the head.'

'I thought you handled that rather masterfully,' he said with a smile, stepping forward to take her in his arms for the first time in so many months.

Karen stiffened. She had prepared herself for this moment, had even looked forward to the comfort of having him hold her. But, when he drew close, all of a sudden, it wasn't Peter reaching out to grasp her but Bob, and with a little cry she jerked backward, almost losing her balance.

'I'm sorry,' he exclaimed. 'I didn't realize a little hug would hurt.'

'She's still pretty sore,' Beverly said to cover the awkwardness.

'Well, would a kiss on the cheek be okay?'

'Sure,' Karen replied. But she had to steel herself against a shudder when she felt his warm breath on her cheek and his lips graze the corner of her mouth. One of the crutches slipped out from under her.

'Are you all right?' he cried, steadying her.

'These things have a mind of their own,' she said with a brittle smile as she slipped out of his grasp and planted the perverse pole more firmly on the slick floor. 'I figure by the time I get the hang of them, I won't need them anymore.'

'And that won't be much longer now, will it?' Beverly chimed in. 'Since you're making such excellent progress.'

Peter glanced from mother to daughter. 'I'm glad to hear it,' he said.

'Don't you agree our precious girl looks a whole lot better than the last time you saw her?' the mother coaxed.

'She certainly does,' he replied politely, thinking he had never seen her look worse.

'Never mind about me,' Karen said brightly. 'Tell us about graduation, Peter. Was it everything you hoped it would be? And the drive down – was it terribly long? Are you famished? You must be absolutely exhausted. Do you want a nap first? Or would you rather have dinner?'

'Dinner would be fine,' Peter replied. He had stopped outside Portsmouth for a quick lunch, but that was more than eight hours ago, with only a candy bar in between, and his stomach had begun to rumble. He could rest later.

'Wonderful,' Beverly said quickly, thinking if they waited much longer the roast would be ruined. 'Why don't you go wash up and then we'll eat.'

'Do you want me to see you to your room?' Karen offered, although the thought of having to navigate the stairs again, under his watchful eye, made her wince.

Peter grinned. 'That's all right. I know the way.'

This was his third visit to the Kern home, and on each occasion Beverly had put him in the big corner guest room with the damask curtains and antique-rose wallpaper. Peter took his suitcase and climbed the stairs. He had identified the strange expression in Karen's eyes. It was fear.

He took his time in the bathroom, letting the cool water run over his head and neck. Then he changed out of his jeans into slacks and a crisp sport shirt. By the time he entered the dining room, everyone was seated. He shook hands with Leo, who had come to the table in his suit and tie, winked at Laura, a teenager in ponytail and shorts who reminded him of his own sisters, and slipped into the chair beside Karen.

Dinner began. Salad followed the soup, a rib roast followed the salad, and peach pie followed the roast.

Coffee cups were filled, emptied and filled again. Second helpings made their way onto Peter's plate without his asking for them, and, all the while, the Kern family talked around one another, in a strange kind of play in which he was expected to take a part, except that he didn't know any of the lines.

'Spring is such a lovely time of year,' Beverly began.

'You can feel the energy in the air,' agreed Leo, blinking his myopic eyes.

'There's still two more weeks of school,' Laura fretted.

'It's the season when life begins anew,' Beverly continued. 'A fresh start, a clean slate. Isn't nature grand?'

'If you like spiders, mosquitoes and yellow jackets,' Laura parried. 'There's a hornet's nest behind the garage.'

'The garden has never looked so beautiful,' Beverly said proudly. 'Everything is in bloom. It's absolute perfection.'

'Perfection is in the eye of the beholder,' sniffed Laura.

'I thought that was beauty,' Karen put in.

Beverly pouted. 'They said it was going to rain today.'

'I took my umbrella,' Leo replied, 'but I didn't go out.'

'That's why it didn't rain.'

'Probably.'

'My arthritis flared up for nothing.' Beverly massaged her left thumb.

'Do you like the rain, Peter?' inquired Laura.

'Sometimes,' Peter answered, trying to keep up.

Four pairs of eyes turned to him.

'What does *that* mean?' the girl demanded.

'Why does it have to mean something?' her father asked.

'Because,' Laura told him, 'everything means something.'

'No,' Karen said, with an unfamiliar edge to her voice, 'not everything. There are some things that have no meaning at all.'

'We're not going to talk about that, are we?' Beverly exclaimed.

'We're not talking about anything,' Karen replied.

'There you are,' Beverly cried, flinging down her fork. 'A perfectly good pie, ruined.'

'A perfectly ruined pie,' chirped Laura.

'Don't be silly,' Leo argued. 'The pie is perfect.'

Laura giggled. 'There's that word again.'

'Very funny,' Karen said.

'Did someone make a joke?' Leo wanted to know.

'Go ahead,' said Beverly. 'Laugh all you want to.'

But no one was laughing.

'Is there more coffee?' Peter asked, feeling as though he had somehow stumbled into the Mad Hatter's tea party.

'Of course there is,' Beverly crowed, replenishing his cup with a flourish. 'There, you see, Peter understands.'

But Peter didn't understand at all.

'I like the rain when it's fine and misty and you can't hear it and you can barely see it,' he told Laura. 'Then it's fun to go out walking and feel the wet on your face.' It was called Ithaca rain, and he and Karen had often walked in it.

'Oooh, how romantic,' cooed the teenager.

Peter grinned, remembering. 'It can be.'

'We don't have rain like that,' Laura grumbled. 'Here it just pours down and drowns you.'

'It doesn't matter,' Karen replied.

'Romance doesn't matter?' Laura asked.

'I think romance matters,' Peter said.

'The rain doesn't matter,' Karen amended.

'Nothing matters to you anymore,' Laura said moodily.

Beverly dropped her coffee cup, the fine bone china shattering in the saucer. Leo almost choked on a piece of the perfect peach pie.

'Are you satisfied?' Karen glared at her sister.

'Don't take it out on me,' Laura retorted with a toss of her ponytail, her eyes flashing. 'It wasn't *my* fault.'

'Nobody said it was,' Karen hissed.

'No, indeed,' Beverly added.

'Of course not,' Leo soothed.

'*I* wasn't careless.'

There was a sharp intake of breath around the table.

'That's enough of that,' Beverly barked.

Leo sighed wistfully. 'It's been such a nice dinner.'

'I hate living like this,' Laura cried. 'Nobody can ever say anything.' She jumped from her seat and ran from the room. 'I hate it.'

'Teenagers,' Beverly sighed with a dismissive shrug. 'They can be so emotional.' She smiled benignly at Peter and then nodded at Karen. 'It's such a lovely night. Why don't you take Peter into the garden?'

'Yes, Mother,' Karen said obediently.

They went out onto the patio, seating themselves in separate lounge chairs, Karen's crutches drawn up on either side of her. The night air was warm and fragrant, and the lights from the house cast long shadows across their faces.

'What's going on around here?' Peter asked, as soon as they were settled.

'What do you mean?' Karen responded.

'I mean the tension at dinner,' Peter declared. 'It was like everyone was afraid to breathe.'

'Nothing's going on,' Karen told him.

'Is it something about me?' he pressed.

'Of course not,' she assured him. 'Everyone's been looking forward to your visit. I guess they must just have had a bad day, that's all.'

'And what about you?' he asked softly. 'Have you been looking forward to my visit?'

'Of course I have,' Karen replied in genuine surprise. 'How could you even ask that? Why, I was standing in the window for over an hour tonight, just waiting for the first glimpse of your car.'

'I'm sorry,' Peter said quickly.

'But I suppose I do owe you an apology,' she added because it was easier to talk in the dark. 'You know … for my knee being bad, and for you not being able to hug me.'

'You don't have to apologize,' he declared. 'I was just feeling a little sorry for myself. Look, maybe you shouldn't even be sitting out here like this. Maybe you should be in bed with a heating pad or something.'

Karen sighed into the shadows. He was such a good person, always so considerate, so caring, so willing to accept blame that wasn't his.

'We can sit a little longer,' she said.

He smiled broadly, although she could barely see it, and then leaned over to pick up her hand. 'It won't hurt to hold hands, will it?'

'No,' Karen assured him. 'It won't hurt a bit.'

'Is the arm all healed?'

'Pretty much.'

'Do you think you'll be ready for the fall semester?'

Karen looked off somewhere past his shoulder. 'I don't know,' she said. 'I haven't really thought about it.'

'You haven't?'

'No,' she said flatly.

A college degree, which had once been a primary goal, now seemed irrelevant to her, and the cloistered atmosphere of the Ithaca campus incredibly impractical. Nothing she had learned at Cornell had prepared her for, or protected her from, the nightmare of the real world.

'You've only lost one term,' he continued. 'That shouldn't be very hard for you to make up.'

'I don't want to think about it now,' she insisted, a bit more sharply than she had intended. 'I have a lot of other stuff to figure out first.'

'I wasn't trying to rush you,' he assured her. 'It's just that I know how important it is to you.'

Was, she thought sadly. It was strange how she had come to see many of the things that had mattered before December 22 as part of the past, not the future.

'I just need some time,' she said more reasonably.

'Of course you do,' he agreed, letting go of her hand.

'Time to get my priorities back in order.'

There was an awkward silence then, with each of them tense and unsure, trying to figure out what was really going on in the mind of the other.

'Does that mean maybe we should put our plans

on hold for the time being?' he asked tentatively, deciding to give her the option, but hoping she would reject it.

Karen's heart lurched painfully at his words. Her worst fear was about to be realized. Now that he was here, now that he had seen how awful she looked, he had decided he didn't really love her after all, and was trying to find a kind way out.

'If you think that would be best,' she said.

Peter sighed. 'I just want you to be sure.'

'I understand.'

There was another pause as the two of them sat there surrounded by the fragrant darkness, together but apart.

'You almost died in that accident,' he said after a while. 'I suppose an experience like that can have a profound effect. So I think you should take all the time you need to decide what it is you really want.'

'Thank you,' she murmured, wishing he wouldn't worry so much about letting her down easy and just say what he needed to say and get it over with.

That was it then, he thought. But he couldn't let her slip away from him without one last effort. He got out of his chair and stood beside hers, looking down at her through the shadows.

'Just do me a favor, while you're doing all that heavy thinking, okay?' he pleaded. 'Remember how much I love you.'

Karen gasped with relief. He wasn't trying to end their relationship. He still loved her, despite what she looked like, despite how she behaved. What had she been so worried about? She was so caught up in the moment that she didn't notice him bending down to brush his lips against hers.

It was so unexpected, his coming down at her out of the dark, that Karen couldn't help herself, she shuddered and cried out.

'What's the matter?' he asked, startled. 'Are you in pain?' He leaned toward her. 'Are you cold?'

The words came out of her nightmare.

Are you cold? he had asked. *Well, I can certainly take care of that.*

Without warning, she was fighting for air and pushing against him with all her might.

'What's the matter?' he cried.

'Get away!' she wheezed, trying to cover her face. 'Get away from me!'

He tried to grab at her flailing hands. 'Tell me what's wrong,' he shouted. 'Tell me what to do.'

At this angle, the lights from the house slanted across his face. Somehow, through her panic, she could see genuine concern in the brown eyes – *brown* eyes – and realized that it wasn't the demon from Central Park, it was Peter.

'I don't know what happened,' she gulped as her body, soaked with perspiration, went limp. 'I couldn't breathe there for a bit.'

'You scared me half to death,' he admitted, his own heart racing. 'I mean, you were staring at me like I was some kind of monster.'

'Was I?'

'Do you need some medicine or something?' he asked, peering at her, not only with concern in his eyes but with bewilderment.

She shook her head. 'No, no medicine. I'm fine now.'

'Are you sure?'

'Yes, I'm sure. It was nothing, really.'

'I wouldn't exactly call what just happened nothing.'

'I'm fine,' she insisted, feeling like a fool. 'I promise.'

'Well, even so,' he said, still a little unsteady, 'maybe we'd better call it a night.'

Karen let him lead her inside without resistance. She was more than ready to escape his scrutiny. They said their whispered good-nights in the upstairs hallway, just outside her room. Peter ran his index finger lightly down her cheek.

'I do love you,' he murmured.

'I love you, too,' she echoed.

He smiled, a happy smile that spread across his whole face. 'Then, as far as I'm concerned,' he breathed, 'that's all that really matters.'

Karen shut her door with a soft click and leaned against it, wondering if he were right.

Peter Bauer had never been her mother's choice of a suitable husband. Beverly had made no bones about that. He wasn't going to be a doctor or a dentist or a lawyer, he wasn't going to graduate from Harvard or Yale, and his family was not prominent in any way. That was three strikes against him, in her mother's book, which flatly eliminated him from any serious consideration.

He had, however, one thing in his favor, and if truth be told, it was the only reason Beverly had not insisted that Karen put a speedy end to the relationship the moment it became serious. Peter's father ran a very successful small business which, according to all indications, Peter would eventually own. So, although the boy might never set the world on fire, he would at least be able to provide well for his family, even as an engineer, and even if it meant that her daughter would have to live in the middle of absolutely nowhere.

Peter had told them that his father's manufacturing company would soon convert into producing parts for computers. Beverly knew nothing about computers, but Leo did and told her that they were going to be very important one day.

Although Beverly continued to encourage Karen to seek out what she called better options, she had resigned herself to Peter's presence in her daughter's life.

'After all,' she would say with a shrug, 'until you catch a bigger fish to fry, you don't want to let go of the one in the pan, or you may end up with no supper at all.'

Until the 'accident.'

Without bothering to wash her face or brush her teeth, Karen undressed and hoisted herself into bed, snuggling deep under the covers, despite the muggy night.

In the past five months, Beverly had not been able to say enough about Peter – about how thoughtful he was, how sincere, how loyal, and how much he obviously cared for Karen. Suddenly, all the doctors and dentists and lawyers that had been out there for the seeking were forgotten, there was no longer anything so terribly wrong with being an engineer, and she took every opportunity to tell Karen how fortunate she was to have found such an exceptional suitor.

The message was clear: a mere engineer should be grateful to have Beverly's daughter, even though she did come to him a little damaged. After all, he would be marrying up, as they said, and couldn't very well expect perfection. Karen didn't bother to protest the

assumption. Peter was everything she had ever fantasized about in the dreamy nights of her girlhood, and
she wanted nothing more than to marry him and live
the fairy-tale life they had so often talked about.

Abso-u-lutely-topia, he had called it.

'We're going to have it all,' he would say. 'The
beautiful wife, the hardworking husband, the cozy
cottage, the white picket fence – and at least half a
dozen cherubic children. Abso-u-lutely-topia!'

Karen frowned, remembering with a painful tight-
ness in her chest that there weren't going to be any
cherubic children, and that, in the detailed recounting of her injuries, it was the one thing her mother had
somehow neglected to tell Peter.

'You can tell him yourself, when the time is right,'
Beverly had said with a shrug. 'That, but nothing else.'

Karen squirmed at the directive. In her mind, she
referred to it as selective honesty, which, as far as she
was concerned, was the same as dishonesty. Not for the
first time she wondered how she and Peter were going
to share a life without truth.

But what was truth? she asked herself. Her mother,
who had once preached the importance of total
honesty between a husband and wife, now insisted that
it wasn't necessary to disclose every sordid little secret.
She was quick to point out that Peter had never
considered it necessary to share the details of his
previous exploits. Had he done so, Karen might have
found cause not to marry him – just as he might find
cause, were he ever to discover the truth about her
'accident.' It was infinitely better, Beverly concluded,
that they both bury their pasts in the interests of
building a wonderful future together.

Karen reached into her nightstand drawer for her

thought box and pulled out a blank piece of paper and a pen. In the gentle pool of lamplight, she wrote:

> Love is truth,
> the careful truth of time
> and constancy.
> Between eyes,
> between sighs.
> From girl to woman,
> from woman to wife.
> To life.

Without bothering to reread the words, she closed the box and tucked it safely away in the drawer, snapped off the light, and settled back against her pillows. Visions of white lace and rose petals began to dance before her eyes as she saw herself floating down the aisle, Peter standing there, waiting for her. He would smile and take her hand in his, and then he would take her away from all the pain and pity and reproach.

She closed her eyes with a contented yawn and pulled the covers up over her head, as though she were already nestling into that cozy little cottage with the white picket fence. She would find a way to tell Peter they would not be able to have children. He would be devastated, of course, but, as always, he would be loving and understanding, and perhaps, sometime in the future, they would think about adopting. There were bound to be some adorable little ones out there, with shiny faces and bright eyes, just waiting for a picture-perfect home.

At the other end of the hall, Peter lay in the guest bed

with his lamp still lit, listening to the subtle sounds of the Kern household as it settled itself down for the night, thinking how different it was from the rambling home in which he had grown up. The walls and floors back in Bangor creaked and groaned freely to accommodate the noisy brood who lived there. These walls and floors didn't seem to yield at all. Rather, it was the people who did the accommodating.

He laced his fingers under his head and stared up at the ceiling. His body was weary and sore from the long drive and yearned for sleep, but his mind would not cooperate. Not when there was so much to think about.

The change in Karen had almost overwhelmed him. The happy-go-lucky girl he remembered had become a frightened animal. While he could understand her reluctance to think about a future when her present was still somewhat in turmoil, her reaction to him had not been exactly normal.

He was now forced to concede that being run over and left for dead like a dog in the middle of the road had probably been much more traumatic than he had imagined and he could feel his anger rising, almost out of control, toward that nameless person who had stolen not only her health but her self-confidence as well. The quality that had always most charmed him about her was the funny little way she had of combining self-assurance with naïveté which always managed to make him feel just a bit more sophisticated than he actually was, and he loved her dearly for it.

Of course, it went without saying that sexually he was the more experienced. In fact, her innocence was one of the first things that had attracted him. Although he'd made a few half-drunken attempts at tempting her, in the back seat of his Pontiac, he was secretly pleased that she wanted to wait until marriage. He enjoyed the idea of being able to teach her, when the time came, and it meant a great deal to him to know that he would be her first.

Her accident was a setback, but he hoped it was only a temporary one. He wanted to believe that, as soon as she recovered physically, her confidence would return and her emotional distress would dissipate and she would be her old self again.

All she needed was enough love and encouragement to see her through, and that, he realized, was precisely where *he* came in. He could give her as much love and encouragement as she could handle. It was there, bubbling up inside him, in that part of his heart that had her name engraved on it. He would show her, in every way he could, that he was with her to the end. He would find a way to let her know that she could lean on him, depend on him, and share the bad as well as the good with him. A little smile began to play across his face, because he knew exactly how to accomplish that.

He reached over and picked up the small box he had placed on the nightstand beside the bed. Karen had said she needed time, but it was now perfectly clear to him that what she really needed was reassurance – reassurance that his feelings for her hadn't changed and weren't going to change, and that their life together was going to be exactly as they had planned it.

He flipped the box open. Inside, nestled against dark velvet, a diamond engagement ring sparkled in the lamplight.

eleven

The smell of coffee awakened him. For a moment, Peter thought he was at home in Maine, but it was much too quiet for the rambunctious bunch in Bangor. No floors complained, no walls grumbled. He opened his eyes. Sunlight flooded through the window between Beverly's damask draperies.

Peter glanced at his wristwatch, astounded to see that it was almost ten-thirty. He shook his head to clear away the cobwebs. It was practically the middle of the day, and he couldn't remember the last time he had slept so long.

Allowing himself one huge stretch, he jumped out of bed and padded into the bathroom, wondering if Karen was up yet. He had an idea that the two of them could go out for a while this afternoon, maybe even have a picnic somewhere. With the sun shining down on them, and the food between them, and her peculiar family nowhere in sight, they would be able to talk.

He dressed quickly after his shower, in clean khakis and a T-shirt, slipped the little velvet box into his pocket, and made his way downstairs.

'There you are,' Beverly accosted him before he had even crossed the foyer. 'My word, you must have been exhausted. We tried to be quiet. I hope we didn't disturb you.'

'I didn't hear a thing,' Peter said truthfully. "I guess the drive down took more out of me than I realized.'

'Well, you look bright as a new penny now.'

'Where's Karen?' he asked.

'Oh, she'll be along soon, I'm sure,' Beverly told him airily. 'It takes her a while to get going in the morning, you know, ever since the accident. But there's coffee in the kitchen, and Winola will fix whatever you want for breakfast.'

'Hello there, Mr. Peter,' Winola cried when she saw him, displaying a big grin and a deep Mississippi drawl. 'My lands, how good you look. Miss Karen sure is a lucky girl.'

Peter chuckled. 'From your mouth to her ears, Winola.'

The maid began to laugh. 'Yessir, Mr. Peter, I'll tell her. You can be sure of that.'

'Do you think I could have a gulp of that coffee?' he asked, sniffing the aromatic air.

'Why, you surely can.' The maid snatched up a cup and filled it in a flash.

The coffee tasted as good as it smelled and Peter drank it down with relish.

'That's not enough,' Winola told him. 'You's a growing boy, you got to put something substantial under them ribs.'

'What do you suggest?' he asked with a grin.

The maid grinned back. 'How about some of my sour-cream eggs and a plateful of bacon?' she suggested.

'You remembered.'

It was what he had asked for every morning during his last visit, in January, when Karen was in the hospital and he was so worried, and Winola wouldn't let him out of the house without eating.

'Now you just set yourself down, Mr. Peter,' she instructed. 'Breakfast'll be ready in no time.'

'Winola,' he said as he watched her scramble up the eggs and sour cream and blend in her own combination of herbs and spices, 'I need your help.'

'Yes, Mr. Peter?'

'I want to take Karen out today, on a picnic, and I was thinking, if it was all prepared, she couldn't say no, could she?'

They had shared a number of picnics in the past – lazy spring afternoons on the banks of Cayuga Lake, and crisp colorful autumn days down at Cascadilla Park. All fun times, filled with laughter and warmth and closeness. He wanted to recapture that with her, if he could.

'Say no more, Mr. Peter,' Winola cried, her black eyes shining. 'The basket's in the closet, and I'll have it filled before you can finish your eggs. It'll do Miss Karen a world of good to get out of this house for a change.'

The eggs had been devoured and the picnic basket packed by the time Karen appeared, pushing open the kitchen door with the tip of her crutch.

'Good morning,' she said. 'Did you sleep well?'

'Like a log,' he told her.

She was wearing white slacks and a lemon-yellow blouse and her dark hair was tied up with a yellow ribbon. She had that fresh-scrubbed look he remembered so well, and he felt his heart do a cartwheel as she smiled at him.

'It looks like Winola's been taking good care of you.'

'You bet,' he confirmed.

'How about something for you, Miss Karen?' Winola asked.

'Just some juice, Winola, please,' Karen replied.

'That's not enough,' Winola complained.

Karen grimaced. 'If Winola had her way, I'd weigh four hundred pounds and be a circus freak,' she told Peter.

'You don't eat enough to keep a sparrow singing,' Winola muttered, wagging her head.

'Why eat if I'm not hungry?' Karen asked, earning only a scowl in response. 'Okay, I'll clean my plate at lunch.'

Winola grinned suddenly at Peter. 'Well now, I expect that'd be all right,' she conceded.

'What's going on?' Karen asked, looking suspiciously from one to the other. Winola never gave in so easily.

'A surprise,' Peter said.

'What surprise?'

'Winola has been kind enough to pack us a fantastic lunch, and I'd like to invite you on a picnic.'

'A picnic?' Karen echoed. 'What do you mean? You want to have lunch in the garden?'

'No,' Peter told her. 'I was thinking more of going out somewhere, maybe to a park.'

'Oh, I don't go out,' Karen declared.

Peter looked bewildered. 'What do you mean?'

'I mean, I don't go out,' Karen repeated.

'Why not?'

It wasn't an unreasonable question and perhaps she even should have expected it, under the circumstances. But it took her by surprise and left her momentarily flushed and flustered.

'I just don't,' she said lamely.

'Well, maybe you could make an exception,' he pressed. 'We used to have a lot of fun on picnics.'

'A picnic? What a wonderful idea,' Beverly cried, pushing through the door with an armful of fresh-cut roses and catching the end of the exchange. 'It's a gorgeous day outside and I can't think of a better thing for the two of you to do.'

'Mother,' Karen warned.

'Nonsense,' Beverly retorted. 'You've been cooped up in this house for weeks now. If you don't get out soon, you'll forget what the rest of the world looks like.'

'What a ridiculous thing to say,' Karen objected. 'I go to the city twice a week for my physical therapy, don't I?'

'And that's all you do, isn't it?' her mother countered. 'Go to the hospital and come right back home again. A change of scene would do you good.'

'I'll be right beside you,' Peter tried to reassure her. 'I won't let anything happen. If you're still nervous about cars, we won't walk in the street.'

Karen began to breathe hard and her hands, gripping her crutches, grew clammy. She was furious with her mother for interfering.

'I can't,' she whispered.

'Of course you can,' Peter urged.

'But I look so dreadful,' she cried. 'What if we run into someone I know?'

'What if you do?' Beverly countered. 'You smile very politely and tell whoever it is that you're recovering from an accident. What's so hard about that?'

Karen stared at her mother stubbornly. 'It's too soon,' she muttered.

'You'll be with me,' Peter said soothingly. 'You don't have to talk to anyone else if you don't want to. I can talk for you.'

'You can't spend the rest of your life hiding away in this house, you know,' her mother added.

'I'm not hiding,' Karen snapped irritably, because that was exactly what she was doing. It was humiliating to have to have this discussion in front of Peter, who couldn't possibly understand what was wrong, and watch him trying so hard to make it right. 'I'll go out when I'm ready,' she declared with as much dignity as she could muster.

'And when will that be?' her mother, as tenacious as any bulldog, inquired.

'When I'm ready,' came the reply.

Beverly threw up her hands in frustration. 'Take her on that picnic, Peter,' she instructed. 'Even if you have to carry her, kicking and screaming.'

Peter didn't have to carry her. He simply promised to bring her back home the moment she asked. They drove out to Steppingstone Park, a pretty little stretch of green lawn that rolled right down to the edge of Long Island Sound. Only a handful of people idled there on a Monday, mostly nannies with small children who paid no attention to the girl on crutches, and Karen recognized none of them.

There were several rough wood picnic tables scattered about, but Peter spread a blanket on the grass and he and Karen sat down on either side of Winola's basket.

'I'm starved,' Karen announced. 'Shall we see what Winola's packed for us?'

Without waiting for a reply, she dug into the big wicker hamper with all the fervor of a shipwreck survivor who hadn't eaten for a week.

'And to think,' Peter observed dryly, 'it was scarcely an hour ago that you weren't the least bit hungry.'

'It must be all this fresh air,' Karen retorted, a piece of cold chicken in one hand, a forkful of potato salad in the other. In fact, it *was* a beautiful day and she *was* hungry, and who could be serious over a drumstick and a dill pickle?

Peter couldn't help smiling. He had been right to bring her here. Already there was new color in her cheeks and a sparkle in her eye, and she seemed almost her old self again. He ached to be closer to her, the urge to reach out and take her in his arms was almost overwhelming, but something stopped him, a little voice that told him to tread slowly.

Between bites, Karen busied herself with the other goodies Winola had provided. She had laid out plates and napkins and forks and poured two cups of lemonade, like a little girl at a tea party, before she realized that Peter was just sitting there, watching her.

'What are you staring at?' she demanded.

'The most beautiful girl in the world,' he replied.

'Stuffing her face,' Karen added, knowing with a twinge of sadness that he wasn't really seeing her as she was now, but remembering her as she used to be. 'So, how come you're not eating?'

'Half a dozen sour-cream eggs,' he explained.

Karen chuckled. 'You know, one of the first things I wanted when they finally unwired my jaw was a plateful of Winola's eggs.'

'You'd better get her recipe,' Peter advised, 'before she takes it to the grave.'

Karen stopped with a blueberry muffin halfway to her mouth. 'It wouldn't do any good,' she said. 'I can't cook.'

'Surely, you jest,' he cried, clutching his chest. 'I thought acid indigestion was part of every bride's dowry.'

She chuckled. 'I can sew, I can knit, I can play the piano. But put me in the kitchen and I have two left hands.'

'But man cannot live by peanut butter and jelly alone,' he cried.

'Certainly not,' she agreed.

'Have you considered taking a culinary course?'

'Actually, I expect the man I marry to hire a chef,' she teased, as she so often had in other, happier moments.

'Not only the wench can't cook,' he huffed, 'she thinks I'm a Rockefeller. Well, my pride is clearly at stake here, not to mention my stomach. You leave me no choice but to call off the engagement.'

'Call it off?' Karen cried. 'How can it be off before it was even on?' She had almost forgotten how much fun it was to be with him.

'A mere oversight,' he said blithely.

He reached into his pocket and pulled out the velvet box, placing it gently on the blanket in front of her.

Karen stared at the small square shape. 'Is that what I think it is?' she asked, suddenly sober.

'Open it and see.'

One hand slid cautiously toward the box, then stopped. 'I thought you wanted to put things on hold for a while,' she whispered.

'Only because I thought *you* wanted to,' he replied.

She sat there, not moving, barely even breathing. It was about to come true, that one desperate dream she had clung to during all the bleak months of disillusion and despair. All she had to do was reach out and open the box.

'Before I look at this,' she said, 'we have to talk.'

'I'm not pressuring you,' he hastened to assure her. 'I know you need time. This is for when you're ready. It's just so you know that, as far as I'm concerned, nothing's changed.'

She looked at him with anxious eyes. 'Wait,' she warned. 'There's something I have to tell you first.'

'I love you, I want to marry you, and I'm all ears,' he said with a grin.

He wasn't making this very easy, Karen thought with a sigh.

'My mother should have told you months ago,' she began, 'but I guess she thought this was something best left between the two of us. The doctor didn't even tell *me* until just before I left the hospital. But it's something you have to know now because ... well ... it could make a difference.'

'Nothing's going to change my mind,' he asserted with a confident smile.

Karen remembered the way Dr. Waschkowski had explained about her lung, likening it to a balloon that deflated when it was punctured. She felt as though she were about to do some puncturing of her own.

'Peter, I won't be able to have children.'

It took him a moment to absorb her words, and he kept his face blank because he didn't want her to see how shocked he was, how disappointed.

'You mean, because of the accident?' he asked.

Karen nodded, her eyes sliding off his. 'I'm sorry.'

'Sweetheart, don't blame yourself,' he exclaimed. 'It's not your fault.'

'Maybe not,' she whispered, 'but I feel like it is.'

He didn't hold her responsible. How could he? It wasn't Karen who had so cruelly robbed him of the sons and daughters he had hoped to have, but some drunken driver who, in all likelihood, would never know and never care. Peter realized bitterly that the accident wasn't going to go away quite as simply as he had anticipated. Already, the shape of their lives was irrevocably altered.

'Did you really think that would make any difference between us?' he asked.

'Well, I wasn't sure,' she said honestly. 'I know how much you want children.'

'And you were afraid to tell me.'

'A little, I guess.'

'Sure I want children,' he told her honestly. 'But not having them isn't the worst thing I can think of. The worst thing is you being afraid to tell me about it. It makes me think you don't trust me.'

'Of course I do,' she cried. 'And I wanted to tell you, as soon as I found out.' I wanted to tell you everything, she thought, but my mother wouldn't let me. 'I just didn't think it was the kind of thing to discuss over the telephone.'

'I suppose I can understand that,' he conceded. 'But let's make a promise – one we'll never, ever break, okay?'

'What kind of promise?' she heard herself ask.

'Let's promise that we'll always be open and honest with each other. Completely honest. Let's not have any secrets between us. What do you say?'

But Karen couldn't say a word – there was something squeezing her throat.

'I want to know everything about you,' he went on. 'The bad as well as the good. Just as I want you to know everything about me. I mean, what kind of marriage would we have if we were afraid to talk to each other? Besides,' he added with a chuckle, 'secrets always have a nasty way of popping out when you least expect them to, so it's much better not to have any in the first place.'

She wanted to run then, but she could barely walk, and even were she able, there was no place for her to hide.

'What if – well, what if there was something that would maybe hurt the other person?' she asked in a small voice.

'Then you try to find a kind way of saying it,' he replied with a gentle smile.

Karen frowned, wondering if there were a kind way of telling him that she had let another man steal her most precious gift.

'Sweetheart,' he said earnestly, leaning forward, seeing her uncertainty. 'Surely you must know, after all this time, that there isn't anything you can't tell me.'

Her mother's voice went off in her head like an alarm bell. *Do you want to ruin your life?* it screeched. But Karen didn't know how she was going to be able to make the promise Peter was asking of her, when the very promise itself would be the biggest lie of all.

'Sometimes,' she suggested, gazing out across the

water, 'there are things that may be better left unsaid.'

'Between others, maybe,' he allowed, 'but not between us.'

Her blue-gray eyes turned toward him just long enough for Peter to see the anguish in them. 'There's so much you don't know.' She sighed. 'I wouldn't know where to begin.'

Her words were so unexpected, they left him speechless. He sat there staring at her, and despite the warm afternoon sun, he felt cold. This delightful, sincere young woman, who had always hung on his every word – this innocent, guileless girl he had thought he knew almost as well as he knew himself – was now someone he wasn't sure he knew at all.

He didn't know how to respond, or whether he should take her in his arms or turn away. What he did know was that something had suddenly gone very wrong with his master plan.

'So what is it I don't know about you?' he asked at last, when the silence had become excruciating.

She shook her head. 'It doesn't matter,' she replied, toying with a chocolate-chip cookie.

'Are you trying to say you don't want to marry me?' he asked, holding his breath.

Karen dropped the cookie. 'Of course I want to marry you,' she cried. Enough to think I could cheat you and lie to you and steal your life from you, her heart cried.

He let out an enormous sigh of relief. 'Then, whatever it is, whatever's troubling you, we can work it out, I know we can. You just have to trust me.'

She wondered if her mother could possibly be wrong about Peter. She wondered if he loved her and believed in her enough to understand. Karen wanted so desperately to tell him the truth. She couldn't bear the thought of living with this horrible lie for the rest of her life.

Would you go into a store and pay top price for used merchandise? her mother's voice sounded in her ear.

Karen groaned inwardly, knowing she wouldn't, and knowing she had no right to expect that Peter would, either. But, by accident or design, she had already gone too far – as good as admitting she had secrets – and it was too late to retract her words and go on with the lie. She had no choice now but to trust him, and pray. She took a deep breath.

'I know what you want is for us to be the way we were,' she began cautiously. 'But that Karen is gone, Peter. She isn't coming back. Not ever. Whatever our future together might be, it's going to be different than we thought.'

'It doesn't have to be,' he argued, unable even to contemplate life without the sweet, innocent girl he loved so much.

'You don't understand.'

'I understand,' he said. 'I just don't accept it. I realize that not being able to have children of our own is a setback – maybe you could even consider it a serious one. But, what the hell, we'll have each other, and that's what counts. Besides, we can still be parents. There's always adoption, you know.'

Karen frowned, remembering that it was those very same thoughts that had carried her off to sleep last night. But she wasn't tucked up safely in her bed now.

'This isn't just about children,' she told him.

'I know – it's about the accident, too,' he conceded. 'You've had a ghastly experience and I can see that you've lost some of your confidence. But other people have been hit by cars and they get over it and go on with their lives. In time, so will you. I really believe that, and you just have to believe it, too.'

'I want you to look at me, Peter,' she said. 'Just for a moment, I want you to see me, not as you remember me from two years ago, or even six months ago, but as I am right now – as I was last night. Think about it. I cringe whenever anyone reaches for me. I hyperventilate at harmless shadows. I break into a cold sweat at the thought of leaving the house. Do you see me?'

'Yes,' he answered reluctantly.

'All right then, deep down inside, where all your good instincts live, do you honestly believe any of this is about an automobile accident?'

'I guess I don't understand,' he admitted.

'There was no car, Peter,' she said bitterly, 'no hit-and-run, no drunk driver. There was no accident at all.'

'But your mother said –'

'My mother lied. To you, to everyone.'

His eyebrows met over a puzzled frown. 'But then, what happened to you?'

Karen opened her mouth to speak, closed it, then opened it again. The end of the past and the shape of the future lay in her next words.

'I was … assaulted in Central Park,' she said.

'Assaulted?' Peter echoed.

'Yes,' she confirmed. 'The injuries my mother described to you … they weren't caused by a car. They were the result of a beating, a very vicious beating.'

It took him a moment to digest this. 'I don't get it,' he said. 'If you were assaulted by someone, then you were assaulted. Why lie about it?'

'Because that isn't all.' She took a tremulous breath. 'I wasn't just beaten up, you see. He, uh – well, he – he also … raped me.'

Peter stared at her in disbelief. 'Raped?' he finally managed to croak. 'What do you – ? Are you saying that someone – someone actually – ?'

'Yes,' she said.

He sat there, struggling to get his mind around her words. The whole thing was preposterous, way beyond the scope of his comprehension, and yet, with a sharp thrust of pain in his heart, he knew it made perfect sense. It explained Beverly's peculiar evasiveness and her efforts to keep him away from the hospital. It explained that craziness at the dinner table, too. And, of course, now he understood Karen's behavior since his arrival.

'I don't know what to say,' he said.

'I'm sorry,' she replied. 'I wanted to be … to be perfect for you.'

Perfect, he thought. There was that word again, and he almost groaned aloud. He wanted to put his arms around her and assure her it didn't matter, hold her close and promise to protect her for the rest of his life, beg her to believe that not all men treated women as she had been treated. He reached out and patted her hand.

'I never expected perfection,' he forced himself to say, because, of course, he had never expected anything else.

'I did,' she murmured.

'But why hush it up?' he exclaimed. 'It's a crime, for God's sake, and the person who committed it should be put in jail. What's the matter with the police down here? Didn't they investigate?'

Karen shrugged. 'They were looking into it, but my parents didn't want any publicity.'

Despite his turmoil of emotions, he could understand the practicality of that. After all, the world was not entitled to know everything – the right to privacy still existed. But the thought of someone else putting his hands all over her, putting his – and getting away with it! Peter felt as though he were about to throw up.

'Do they know who he is?' he gulped.

The easy part was over, Karen thought. Now came the hard part.

'They know,' she said.

'You mean, they showed you mug shots? You were able to identify him?'

'No … I told them who he was.'

'You *knew* him?'

'I met him at Jill's party. Remember, that's where I was that night. He was polite and attentive. When he offered to take me home, it never occurred to me that he had something else in mind.'

On a bright, sunny afternoon in Steppingstone Park, overlooking Long Island Sound, the bottom fell out of Peter Bauer's world. Of all the things he imagined happening to him in his life, he had never once considered that the woman he would choose to marry would go off with some other man and get herself violated.

He knew she was waiting for him to say something to her, something sympathetic and reassuring, as he always had, but no loving words formed behind his tongue. He felt betrayed.

'I don't understand,' he cried. 'I thought you loved me?'

'I do,' she assured him.

'We were practically engaged.'

'Yes.'

'Then how could you do such a thing to us? To me?'

Karen groaned. 'And you wanted me to trust you.'

'I didn't realize,' he began. 'I never expected – '

'The truth?' she asked softly. 'Peter, I made a mistake, and what happened, happened.'

'Why did you have to tell me?' he exclaimed.

'Would you have preferred to live with the lie?'

'Yes,' he agonized. 'No. I don't know. I just don't understand any of it. Why would you, how could you, let someone – ?'

'I didn't *let* him,' she whispered, tears flowing down her cheeks. 'I tried to stop him. I tried as hard as I could. That's why he beat me up. I never wanted anybody but you to be the first – the only – you have to believe that.'

Peter shut his eyes against her words. 'We don't have to discuss this anymore now,' he decided because his heart was hurting too much. 'We have lots of time. We can talk again tomorrow, or the next day, after we've both had a chance to, well, sort things out.'

Some things, he thought, were better left unsaid.

'If that's what you want,' she said dully.

'Yes,' he replied with a forced smile. 'I think that would be best.' He peered into Winola's basket. 'We came here for a picnic, didn't we? Well then, let's have one.'

Peter heaped his plate with chicken and potato salad and blueberry muffins, although he didn't know how he was going to get a single bite past the lump in his throat.

Karen stared into her lemonade as though it held some kind of answer.

The little velvet box lay forgotten on the blanket between them.

PART TWO
1964

It is said to begin with the father.

– Maxine Kumin

One

Amanda Willmont took the decanter from the table beside her chaise longue and poured another glass of sherry, carelessly spilling several drops on the polished mahogany surface.

The late-afternoon sunlight filtered through the windows of the elegant Jackson Street Victorian that crowned San Francisco's exclusive Pacific Heights, spreading a soft haze over the subtle grays and mauves of the large corner bedroom, just the way Amanda liked it. Life was easier when the edges were a bit blurred.

It was her favorite time of day, just before dusk, when her correspondence was finished, her charity work completed, and her household duties attended to, and she could slip into her favorite silk dressing gown and retire to the privacy of her room, knowing she would not be bothered until Robert came home for dinner – if he came home for dinner.

For the past two weeks, her husband had been noticeably absent three nights out of five, which usually signaled the onset of a new liaison. As was typical in such situations, this was Thursday, and Amanda hadn't seen him since Tuesday.

Not that she cared very much anymore. She had given up whatever romantic notions she might have had about her marriage shortly after the honeymoon, right after she had become pregnant with Bobby, as soon as her trust funds had legally been put into Robert's care.

'You are no longer to be pitied,' he had told her two months after the wedding. 'You now have a husband to parade around in public, a posh home in one of the best parts of town, and a secure place in San Francisco society. In exchange, you're going to let me do exactly as I please.'

What pleased him was to be successful in his own right, to live well, and to sample half the female population of the state of California. Before the Willmonts had reached their fifth wedding anniversary, he had achieved the first two and made a significant dent in the third. What he didn't have much interest in was a house filled with bothersome children. He moved out of his wife's bedroom on the day she announced her pregnancy, and never returned.

Amanda Willmont, who had been Amanda Drayton of the San Francisco Draytons before her marriage at the age of twenty-nine, was the only child of Horace Lowell Drayton, the financier and magnate, whose ancestors had been among the most influential in the city's development since the gold rush days. Her mother, a homely but refined woman, came from one of the oldest families on Philadelphia's Main Line.

Robert Willmont came from nowhere, but he had taken a modest law degree and, with the help of his wife's name and her father's backing, turned it into a partnership in one of the most prestigious law firms in San Francisco. Even Horace, who would never have considered the brash nobody as son-in-law material had his daughter not been descending rapidly into spinsterhood, was forced to concede that the man had made the most of his opportunities.

As public as his professional success was, Robert was careful to keep his personal successes private. It mattered little to him that his wife knew of his various escapades, but he didn't want to run the risk of his father-in-law's finding out and perhaps withdrawing his patronage. It didn't take any great insight to understand that, with her close-set eyes, thin mouth, beak nose and mousy hair, Robert hadn't chosen his wife for her looks.

Over the years, Amanda learned to shut her eyes to the realities of her marriage, and although it was painful, she eventually came to accept the arrangement. The sherry helped, and of course there was Bobby. The complaisant baby she held too briefly in her arms, the dutiful child who suffered her embraces with acute embarrassment, the fine young man who now smothered her with bear hugs whenever he was home – he had become her only reason for being.

Her heart would all but burst when she thought of him, so bright, so handsome, so well-behaved. And such a good boy, so kind and considerate, that he had never caused her a moment's anguish. He was consistently at the head of his class in school, appreciated by his teachers, admired by his opponents, and envied by his peers. In his entire life, whatever he had asked for, she never came upon a good-enough reason to deny him.

Amanda knew she had done herself proud in raising the boy. Going far beyond teaching him his letters and his manners, she had worked hard to instill in him a sense of responsibility for who he was and what was expected of him. He was no ordinary young man, after all, and she felt it was essential that he understand, at the earliest possible age, the tradition into which he had been born.

'Having wealth and influence means nothing in and of itself,' both her father and her grandfather had liked to say. 'True character is the ability to take whatever you are fortunate enough to be given and use it for the good of mankind.'

It was clear to everyone that, although his name was Willmont, Bobby was every inch a Drayton, and no one who had any contact with him doubted that he had an exceptional future awaiting him.

Indeed, Robert had had very little to do with his son's upbringing. On the rare occasion when he was home at all, he would closet himself in the richly paneled library with strict orders not to be disturbed. At the dinner table, he was usually too preoccupied with his own concerns to have much interest in a growing boy.

In just a few short weeks, that growing boy would be graduating, with honors, from Harvard Law School, as he had graduated from Stanford University three years earlier, and he had already been offered positions at no less than three of San Francisco's best firms, one of them being his father's.

'I didn't even know he interviewed with us,' Robert

said with an indifferent shrug when his wife attempted to express her appreciation.

The one and only time that Amanda could ever recall him involving himself in his son's affairs was in the middle of Bobby's third year at Stanford. It had something to do with a girl, and Amanda recalled that Robert had been furious. He ordered the boy home from school late one night. They met in the library, behind closed doors. But they spoke so loudly that Amanda, standing in the hallway, had no difficulty hearing at least part of the conversation.

'How dare you put me in this position?' Robert barked. 'I've worked my ass off for too many years to get myself accepted in this goddamn town to have you destroy it all with one of your stupid blunders.'

Bobby murmured something Amanda didn't catch.

'What did you think would happen, you fool? Did you think she'd say thank you and just walk away?'

Again, Amanda missed Bobby's response.

'He threatened me, that's what he did,' Robert shouted. 'Walked right into my office and threatened me – someone I wouldn't let shine my boots. "I don't really want to go to the police on your boy," he whines, "but my Polly's only seventeen, and someone has to look out for her." Of course he meant *me*. A hundred thousand dollars – that's what it's costing me to clean up your little mess. I ought to take it out of your hide.'

'Look, I'm sorry,' Bobby pleaded, his voice rising loud enough for his mother to hear. 'I didn't think he'd have the balls to go to you. Anyway, I never forced her to do anything. Believe me, she wanted exactly what she got.'

'It doesn't matter what she wanted or didn't want. Get it through your thick skull – she's only seventeen.

That's statutory rape in this state.'

Bobby laughed harshly. 'Let them prosecute. It's my word against hers, and I'll say I never even heard of her. Who do you think they'll believe? This town isn't going to convict me of anything. I'm a Drayton.'

There was the sharp sound of an open hand coming in direct contact with a soft cheek.

'You're a Willmont,' Robert roared. 'And don't you ever forget it. The Draytons are nothing but a bunch of lily-livered snobs, and there isn't a one of them who wouldn't disappear into the woodwork at the first hint of a scandal, including your dear sherry-nipping mother.'

'So what am I supposed to do?' Bobby asked with a mixture of petulance and belligerence in his voice.

'You're supposed to keep your mouth shut, that's what you do,' his father snapped. 'No bragging to your buddies, no boasting about your great conquest, and you make damn sure that you never come within a hundred yards of her again, understand?'

'How can I do that?' Bobby whined. 'She's all over the campus.'

'You see her, you walk in the other direction. Not a word, not a gesture, not so much as a look. Do you hear me?'

'I hear you.'

'I'll pay her medical bills. I'll pay the rest of her way through Stanford. Hell, with a hundred thousand bucks in the bank, she'll be set for life. But that's where it ends. Don't ever expect me to bail you out again.'

'No, sir,' Bobby murmured.

'You get in a mess, you get out of it. If you need to play that rough and tumble, figure out how to do it without having to pay the piper. It's time you learned. Because if you ever put me in a position like this again, I'll cut you off without so much as a cent. And make no mistake – I control all your mother's trust funds and I can do it. And I will.'

'You're not going to tell her about this, are you?' she heard Bobby ask anxiously.

'You mean, malign her sainted son?' Robert sighed. 'No, I'll let her keep her illusions. What else does she have? She probably wouldn't believe any of it anyway.'

The conversation continued, but Amanda had heard enough. Clearly, Robert had had a bad day at the office and was taking it out on the boy, misunderstanding some youthful prank or another. She was undressed and in bed, half an hour later, when Bobby came up to say good night.

He was still smarting from the humiliating encounter with his father. No one had ever spoken to him that way, and at that moment, he knew he would shed few tears if the man were to fall under a cable car. He sat beside his mother and held her hand. At least there was one parent he could always count on to see things his way.

The boy and his mother talked about his classes at Stanford and his position on the football team and his plans to go down to Mexico with friends during the Christmas holiday. Then he stood up and tucked the covers in around her and kissed her on the forehead.

'You're my best girl, you know,' he told her. 'You'll always be my best girl.'

A few minutes later, Amanda heard his sports car roaring out of the drive. Nobody ever referred to the incident again, and over the years, the conversation faded in her memory, until it were as though it had never taken place.

Amanda pulled the ruffles of her dressing gown around her and poured herself another glass of sherry. The amber aperitif had long since lost its taste, but she sipped at it anyway, slowly, hardly more than a drop at a time, as she had been taught to savor fine wines. It wasn't how it tasted that mattered, after all – it was how it made her feel.

Nothing had ever been said to any of the staff, but the large crystal decanter on the table beside the chaise longue was always kept filled. Most of the household help had come to Jackson Street from the Drayton mansion atop Nob Hill on the occasion of Amanda's marriage, and had known her since she was a girl. It didn't matter that they also knew her secret.

It didn't matter that her marriage was a sham, either. All that mattered was Bobby, and the important things he had been born to do. That would be her reward for all the lonely years, all the unfulfilled dreams.

There was a soft tap at her bedroom door. Amanda looked up in surprise. It was still way too early for dinner, and she couldn't think who might be rude enough to disturb her.

'Come in,' she snapped irritably.

The heavy door opened, and as the intruder entered, a big smile spread over Amanda's face.

'Bobby,' she cried in pure delight. 'What a wonderful surprise.' She frowned in sudden confusion. 'But aren't you supposed to be at school? Aren't we coming to Harvard next week to see you get your degree?' She started to whimper. 'Don't tell me I got the dates wrong. Don't tell me I missed your graduation.'

Robert Drayton Willmont bent over the chaise longue and wrapped his arms around his mother's frail frame.

'No, dear, you didn't get the dates wrong,' he soothed. 'I just wanted to see you.'

'Oh, Bobby, how nice,' she cooed. 'I'm so glad.' She smiled at him through blurry eyes. 'I do believe you've grown an inch or two just since Easter. Why, you must be taller than your father by now. Wait till he sees you. I do hope he doesn't have to work too late at the office tonight. He'll be so pleased.'

It was important to her that the boy think well of Robert, and she had played the game for so long that the lies rolled off her tongue like truth.

'How long can you stay?' she asked.

'Just a day or two.'

'You've made a very long trip for such a short visit. It isn't like you to be so frivolous.'

He knelt down in front of her and took both her hands in his, a thing Amanda could not remember him ever doing before, and she began to blink nervously.

'I have something to tell you, dear,' he said softly.

'Is it important?'

'Yes, it is.'

'Then why don't you wait until your father gets home?' she suggested. 'And then you can tell us both at the same time.'

'No, I can't wait for that,' he said with infinite patience. 'You see, there's been … an accident, and Father … well, he won't be coming home.'

'An accident? Did you say an accident?'

'Yes, dear.'

Harold Sutton, senior partner of Sutton, Wells, Willmont and Spaulding, had telephoned Cambridge at three o'clock in the morning.

'It's your father, Bob,' he said with no apology for the hour. 'He died of a heart attack an hour ago. I think you should get back here as fast as you can. It really would be best all around if you were the one to tell your mother.'

'She doesn't know yet?'

The older man cleared his throat. 'No,' he replied with obvious discomfort. 'Your father wasn't home at the time.'

The Harvard law student laughed aloud. He didn't need a road map to tell him where Robert Willmont had been found.

'Well, at least the old man went out with a bang,' he said. 'Good for him – he wouldn't have wanted it any other way.'

'Look,' Sutton entreated, 'your father's private life was just that, and we can't have any embarrassing publicity attaching itself to the firm.'

'Certainly not, sir,' the young man said, instantly somber.

'Yes, well, I'm glad you understand. I've talked it over with the other partners and we've decided to say that he was working late at the office when the, ah, unfortunate incident occurred.'

'Can you square that with the authorities?'

'I believe so. The police commissioner is a personal friend.'

'I'll catch the first plane out.'

'That'll be fine, Bob,' Sutton said. 'Just fine. And, by the way, don't think for a moment that this has any effect on our offer. We're still hoping you'll come with us after graduation.'

'One thing has nothing to do with the other, sir, I know that,' came the correct reply. 'As a matter of fact, after careful deliberation, I've decided to accept your offer.'

In truth, he had not made his decision until that very instant.

There was just the slightest hesitation at the San Francisco end of the line. 'Well, that's good news, indeed,' the senior partner said heartily. 'We'll be looking forward to it.'

'Thank you, sir.'

In Cambridge, a big grin spread across the young man's handsome features. Like father, like son, he could almost hear Sutton thinking.

'Now, you be just as gentle as you can with your mother. She's a bit fragile, you know.'

Amanda Willmont was indeed fragile, never more so than when she had consumed half a decanter of sherry.

'What kind of accident, Bobby?' she whimpered.

'It was a heart attack.'

'A heart attack?'

'Yes, dear.'

'Is he – was it – you mean, he's – ?' Somehow, she couldn't get the word out of her mouth.

'I'm afraid so.'

'When?'

'Last night. He was working late at the office.'

Amanda closed her eyes. Her husband had been dead for almost an entire day, and she hadn't even known it. A heart attack – an attack of the heart. The irony was obvious to her because she knew exactly where Robert had died, and it had nothing to do with the office. How kind it was of Bobby to want to protect her.

In spite of herself, she felt hot tears pressing against her eyelids. Robert had been an absentee husband for twenty-five years and she had learned to live with it. Now that he was dead, she missed him. She had played the part of a happy wife for more than a quarter of a century, and that had been a sham. Now she would play the part of a grieving widow, and that would be real.

'You're all I have now, Bobby,' she sobbed.

'Don't worry, dear,' he said. 'I'll take care of you.'

She smiled at him through her tears. 'You're such a good boy. You've always been such a good boy.'

'And you've always been my best girl,' he replied.

How like his father he was, Amanda thought, so tall and broad, with the same dark hair and beautiful face. In the dim light, it could almost have been Robert kneeling before her, looking up at her with such concern. Except, of course, for the one feature that Bobby had inherited from her side of the family, and which marked him as a Drayton above everything else – the extraordinary aquamarine eyes.

PART THREE
1969

Learn from the past, live for the
present, look to the future.

— *Anonymous*

one

Karen Kern hurried up Fifth Avenue, as quickly as the slight stiffness in her reconstructed left knee would allow, and turned left on Twelfth Street. Both the temperature and the humidity registered in the upper nineties, and Karen was perspiring freely beneath her bulky black coat.

She had regained her health and most of her weight. Her skin glowed a rich bronze from weekends in the sun, setting her blue-gray eyes off dramatically. Her dark hair, which grew well below her shoulders, was pulled back at the nape of her neck. A pale touch of lipstick was her only makeup.

Shifting the sack of groceries she carried, she began to fumble for her door keys when she was still half a block from the solid concrete building where she shared an apartment with Arlene Minniken, her former roommate from Cornell.

'Good evening, Miss Kern,' Martin, the door-man, said as she approached.

Her parents had insisted on her living in a building that provided round-the-clock doormen for extra security.

'Hello, Martin,' she replied with the plastic smile she had perfected for almost every man with whom she came in contact, regardless of the circumstances.

The lobby of the ten-story apartment house was dim and functional, in contrast to the splendid opulence of Jill Hartman's building on West End Avenue, but Karen hardly noticed. She pulled an assortment of bills and advertising circulars from her mailbox and rode the tired, creaking elevator to the sixth floor.

Letting herself into her apartment, she dropped her coat on the floor, deposited the bag of groceries on the kitchen counter, and hurried over to flip the switch on the air conditioner. The unit was old and rattled so much that she and Arlene almost had to shout to hear each other above the racket, but it provided a mod-icum of relief that was better than nothing. Then she kicked off her shoes, fixed herself a vodka collins and collapsed on the living room sofa.

For the past six months, Karen had been working as the assistant manager of the Washington Square Book-ery, which wasn't exactly on Washington Square, but close enough for the owner to get away with the namesake.

Housed in the dim, quiet, faintly musty basement of an old brownstone, the Bookery specialized in pre-viously owned, rare, and hard-to-find books and peri-odicals. Peace posters hung everywhere, along with a sign that read, 'Make Love Not War,' and a cartoon of Lyndon Johnson riding the top of a bomb about to plunge into a crying baby, which said, 'Bombs Hurt.' Burning incense spread a pungent odor over everything.

A number of regulars, mainly friends and neighbors from Greenwich Village, came in to browse and pass the time of day with Demelza, the rather eccentric proprietor, but the shop was not generally frequented by uptown customers. Karen kept track of inventory, placed orders, organized the woefully disorganized owner, and made sure there was always a pot of herbal tea brewing. The job was interesting and just a short walk from the apartment, and the money didn't matter because her parents footed the bill for her major expenses.

When she wasn't at home or at the Bookery, Karen could be found on a bench in Washington Square with her nose deep in one of Demelza's treasures, or wandering around the narrow streets of Greenwich Village peering into secondhand shop windows, or sitting by herself in one of the coffee houses that were an integral part of the area's offbeat charm.

Nobody bothered her. Like marbles bouncing off one another, people of the Village met, touched briefly and then veered away, strumming their guitars, selling their wares, keeping their distance and protecting their own painful secrets behind hard, glossy shells.

Had she had her own way, Karen would have chosen one of the run-down walk-ups that passed for quaint right in the heart of the unique little community, but her parents had been adamant.

'It's bad enough you want to live in the city at all,' her mother had said. 'But as long as you do, we're going to make sure that it's someplace safe and respectable, and not some bohemian enclave overrun by weirdos and freaks.'

There was no way Karen could explain to her parents what it was like when she crossed Washington Square South. More than merely entering another part of the city, it was like entering another life, a life she felt she belonged in – among the weirdos and the freaks.

They settled on the formerly deluxe apartment house on West Twelfth Street, a block off Fifth Avenue. It was quiet and well-maintained and offered enough security to satisfy the elder Kerns, and it suited Arlene, who split her time between Bellevue Hospital and NYU, where she was earning her master's degree in psychology.

Karen never went back to Cornell. Nor did she marry Peter Bauer. The two of them had spoken on the telephone several times after his return to Maine that dreadful spring, but their conversations were short and superficial. Peter spoke of the weather and told her about his job and his family, but he carefully avoided any mention of the future. Karen listened politely and didn't press him. There wasn't really any point. After a while, the phone calls stopped.

'What could you possibly have been thinking of, to tell him that ugly story?' her mother demanded once she had pried the circumstances of the picnic at Steppingstone Park out of her daughter.

'I couldn't marry him under false pretenses,' Karen replied defensively. 'I had to tell him the truth.'

'Truth, my dear girl, is what we want it to be,' Beverly retorted. 'Were you *trying* to push him away?'

'I was trying to find out if he really loved me – or just some fantasy he had of me.'

'Why? What's so wrong with fantasies?'

'Nothing,' Karen conceded. 'I just didn't want to build my marriage on one.'

'I daresay many a marriage has been,' Beverly declared. 'You have to understand – it isn't men who lead women down the garden path, but the other way around. It's all part of the game we play to get what we want. And there's no harm in it, because the men are getting what they want, too.'

'It just wouldn't have been fair to him,' Karen insisted stubbornly.

'Fair?' Beverly exploded. 'Has this whole awful thing been fair to any of us?'

'I don't want to talk about it anymore,' Karen snapped, her head beginning to throb.

Beverly threw up her hands in exasperation. 'Have it your way, then. Just remember that righteousness is a poor excuse for loneliness.'

Karen had hobbled away defiantly, but her mother's words stayed with her. She learned to accept the sympathy she received as the innocent victim of a terrible automobile accident. She never again spoke of what had really happened to her, but pushed it all down into a dark place within her, where no light could shine.

She discarded the crutches. The stiffness in her left knee grew less and less noticeable. The doctors assured her that, in time, it would disappear altogether. She took to wearing long skirts and high collars to hide the scars on her body, and perfected an attitude of polite disinterest to hide the scars on her soul. It was two years before she could bring herself to leave Knightsbridge Road for something other than a brief appointment. But when she did, in the summer of 1965, she left for good.

'Arlene Minniken wants me to share an apartment in the city with her,' Karen announced one evening at dinner. 'She thinks it would be fun for us to room together again.'

'You want to live in Manhattan?' Beverly asked, unsure she had heard correctly. It was her opinion that nice young ladies stayed at home until they married.

'Yes,' Karen replied. 'Lots of girls are doing it these days. Take Arlene, for example.'

'Arlene's home is in Tallahassee,' her mother declared. 'She couldn't very well commute to New York City. But you have a perfectly good home right here. If you want to get away so badly, you can always go back to college.'

'I don't want to go back to college,' Karen responded. 'I just want to live on my own for a while.'

'How will you support yourself?' her father asked.

'I'll get a job.'

'A job?' Beverly questioned. 'What kind of job?'

Karen shrugged. 'I don't know yet.'

'You know that isn't necessary,' her mother exclaimed. 'There *are* other options.'

'Mother, please, let's not start that again. I'm not going back to college, and I have no plans to marry.'

'I suppose we can help out with expenses' – Leo thought aloud – 'at least until you get on your feet.'

Karen beamed at him. With one sentence, he had not only resolved her financial qualms, he had silenced her mother in mid-argument, and that was not a frequent occurrence.

'Thanks, Daddy,' she said. 'That would be fantastic.'

'What with Laura starting at Mount Holyoke in the fall, and now you wanting to live in Manhattan,'

Beverly pouted, 'the house is going to be awfully empty.'

'I'll come back to visit as often as you like,' Karen assured her.

It was the end of summer before she found work. There were not many jobs available to someone without a college degree, certainly not ones her mother considered appropriate, which meant in the right part of town, in an acceptable industry, among respectable people. She took a position as a receptionist at Marilyn's Beauty Salon, where she was allowed to wear full skirts and high-collared blouses and oversized sweaters, and the patrons, mostly older women, patted her hand a lot. In addition to greeting customers and scheduling appointments, it was Karen's job to close the shop at night, making sure that curling irons and blow dryers were turned off. Hardly demanding work, but the pay was steady.

After that, she became a salesgirl at Lord & Taylor's. The department store stood solidly on Fifth Avenue, at what her father called the edge of the high-rent district. Everything about it was elegant – the architecture, the dramatic display windows, the merchandise, the personnel. After her training period, Karen was assigned to the lingerie department, where the senior saleswoman showed her how to recognize the buyers from the browsers and taught her how to clinch a sale to a wavering customer.

She soon discovered that it wasn't only women who bought lingerie. Men, sometimes awkward and embarrassed, came looking for finery for their wives or their mothers or their sweethearts or their mistresses. It didn't take Karen long to learn the difference.

One October afternoon, when she had been at Lord

& Taylor's for almost a year, a customer approached her, gray-haired, distinguished, and obviously wealthy, carrying a black satin negligee in his hands. It was the most expensive that the store offered and one of Karen's personal favorites.

'Excuse me, miss,' he said. 'I wonder if you can help me. I want to buy a birthday gift for my daughter, and I'm not at all sure what would be appropriate.'

Karen concealed a smile. She knew that men did not buy slinky black satin negligees for their daughters, but she had learned how to play the game.

'How old is she?' she asked politely.

'Well, I'd say she's about your age.' He held up his selection. 'Tell me, do you like this?'

'I like it very much,' Karen conceded. 'What size does she wear?'

He frowned at that. 'I don't know,' he admitted. 'But I think she's about your size. Maybe if you'd hold it up, I could get an idea of how it would look on her.'

Karen took the negligee from him and held it awkwardly against her body, fussing with the folds to get them just right. 'How's that?' she inquired.

He shook his head. 'I can't really tell for sure. I don't suppose you'd be willing to try it on for me?'

The hair began to rise on the back of Karen's neck. She had been trained to deal with difficult customers, but no one had told her what to do in this situation.

'I'm afraid not,' she murmured, thinking fast. 'As you can see, I'm alone in the department, and I'm not allowed to leave the floor.'

'Well, that's all right,' he said with an easy smile. 'Why don't I just take it anyway, and if my daughter doesn't like it, she can bring it back and pick out something else.'

Karen wrote up the sale as quickly as she could, the plastic smile fastened to her face, and breathed an enormous sigh of relief when he took his package and left.

The store closed at six. It was six-thirty when Karen slipped out the side door and hurried across Fifth Avenue to catch the downtown bus, joining a small knot of people who were already waiting.

'I think this was meant for you,' a voice directly behind her said. 'Even though you wouldn't try it on.'

Karen was so startled that she fell against an elderly woman standing in front of her.

'I beg your pardon,' she mumbled, as she bent down to retrieve the woman's fallen handbag. Straightening up, she glanced over her shoulder at the gray-haired man.

'I wanted to give it to you right there at the store, but I realized that might not be very appropriate, under the circumstances,' he said. 'So I waited for you. I thought we'd go somewhere for a drink, perhaps have dinner. Get to know each other.'

'I think you've made a mistake,' Karen said, her heart pounding.

'Really?' he asked with a smile. 'I thought you got my message very clearly. I certainly got yours.'

'What message?' she demanded. 'I gave you no message.'

'You knew perfectly well I wasn't buying a present for my daughter.' He chuckled. 'I don't even have a daughter.'

'I didn't know *who* you were buying it for,' she replied truthfully, praying the bus would come.

'I was buying it for you, of course.'

'Thank you very much, but no, thank you,' she said

as politely as she could because he might have been a good customer at Lord & Taylor's and she couldn't afford to offend him. 'That particular item isn't one I have any use for.'

'If you play your cards right,' he told her with a deep chuckle, 'an opportunity might present itself.'

Up the street, Karen could see the bus inching its way toward them, and in anticipation the knot of people began to surge forward. The gray-haired man pressed against her.

'I've been watching you,' he breathed into her ear, his hands, shielded by the press of people, beginning to roam over her. 'On the surface you're cool and proper, but I can tell that underneath the high collars and baggy sweaters you're hot.'

She pushed frantically against the people in front of her, trying to get away from him.

'Wait your turn,' someone snarled at her. 'We all want to get home, you know.'

'You'd better leave me alone,' she cried to her pursuer.

'You don't really mean that,' he cajoled.

'Yes, I do.'

'Your lips may be saying no,' he whispered, 'but your body is saying yes.'

'If you don't stop bothering me,' she shouted at the top of her voice, 'I'll call the police.'

The elderly woman whose purse she had retrieved turned around. 'Is that man annoying you, dearie?' she asked.

'Yes,' Karen half-sobbed.

'You leave this girl alone,' the woman advised tartly. 'She's obviously not buying whatever you're selling.' She shook her head. 'A man your age – you ought to be ashamed of yourself.'

The bus chose that moment to rumble up to the curb and open its doors. The elderly woman put her arm around Karen and guided her up the steps. The gray-haired man melted into the crowd.

After that, Karen stopped wearing makeup and added bulky coats to her shapeless clothing, regardless of the weather. The more unattractive she could make herself look, the safer she felt.

She quit her job at Lord & Taylor's. She answered phones for a Madison Avenue advertising agency, typed bills for a Park Avenue dermatologist, stuffed envelopes for a mail-order house, and stacked books at the public library. But nothing seemed to suit her for long. If the work didn't bore her, some man pursued her, pressing unwanted invitations on her until she sought other employment.

So it was that, in the winter of 1969, she came to the Washington Square Bookery, in answer to an ad for a clerk. The shop, housed in what the owner called a bunker, was long and narrow and crammed with shelves that boasted volumes on every obscure subject from the aalii shrub to zymurgy. In the back, tucked safely into barrister cases, was a treasure trove of first editions and out-of-print copies of works by such authors as Somerset Maugham, Emily Dickinson, Edith Wharton, Sinclair Lewis, Upton Sinclair, and Willa Cather.

The owner was a free-spirited woman in her forties with an ample figure, frizzy black hair that she wore in a thick braid down her back, and soft brown eyes that seemed to reflect the suffering of the whole word. The plight of Biafra was foremost in her mind when Karen first met her.

Her name was Doris Ulasewicz, from the Bronx, but there were very few who knew that. Everyone called her Demelza, after some obscure literary heroine she had unearthed.

'She was a woman with the soul of a saint and the heart of a prostitute,' Demelza explained. 'Something about that always appealed to me.'

'I guess it wouldn't have worked too well if it were the other way around,' Karen observed.

Demelza grinned appreciatively at the young woman. 'I think I'm going to like you,' she said.

'Thank you,' Karen murmured, unaccountably pleased.

'Now to business,' Demelza declared. 'I'm totally disorganized and brilliantly creative. I'm fine with anything under fifty dollars but absolutely frivolous with anything over that. I tend to fly off in too many directions at once, but I'm great at conceptualization. I'm insatiably curious but I never pry. I need someone to bring sanity to my life and work. Think you could put up with me?'

Karen looked around. The few customers that browsed in the aisles seemed harmless enough, the books seemed friendly and inviting, and the pungent smell of incense that tried valiantly to camouflage the basement's mustiness was not unpleasant.

'I could try,' she replied.

'That's all I can ask of anyone,' said Demelza. 'But before you get excited, I'd better tell you that I can't pay more than eighty dollars a week.'

That was ten dollars less than Karen had earned at the library, and she hesitated. With each job she had held, her salary had increased, if only slightly. Her goal was to be financially free of her parents as soon as possible. Yet here she was, actually contemplating taking a step in the opposite direction.

'Maybe I can give you a fancy title to make up for it,' Demelza offered, because she had already decided she liked this girl and had long ago learned to trust her instincts.

'What kind of title?' Karen asked, because she had a funny feeling about this no-nonsense woman with the bizarre name and the out-of-the-way little shop.

'Well, let's see,' Demelza thought aloud. 'Suppose we dub you – assistant manager?'

Karen laughed. 'My mother will love it,' she said.

'Is it a deal?'

'It's a deal.'

Karen practically skipped all the way back to West Twelfth Street, wondering why on earth she should be feeling so good about making less money.

'It wasn't just that I liked Demelza so much,' she explained to Arlene. 'It was something about the Bookery, too. I felt really comfortable there. This is going to sound crazy, I know, but it was almost as if the shop spoke to me and told me I'd be happy there.'

Arlene wasn't a psychology student for nothing. 'Then you made the right decision,' she agreed. 'As for the salary, well, as long as your parents don't mind, why should you?'

In fact, the Kerns were delighted.

'Assistant manager?' her mother exclaimed. 'That's just wonderful, darling. I can't tell you how proud we are.'

Which translated, Karen knew, into how impressed the neighbors were going to be once Beverly got through massaging the facts, and the two-woman operation had become a twenty-person staff on the scale of Barnes and Noble.

'And don't you worry about the money,' her father added from the extension phone. 'You'll get a check from us every month for as long as you need it.'

No one mentioned that this was her seventh job in three and a half years. No one suggested that it would be nice if she would stay in one place for a while. But the words hung in the air as though they had been said.

The focus of Karen's life had been on marriage and children. It never occurred to her that she would have to work for a living. The death of her dream left her aimless. The Bookery gave her purpose. She was not stepping into someone else's shoes that were either too big to fill or pinched her toes – she was creating a totally new position and she found, to her surprise, that she liked it. By the end of a year, Demelza had increased her salary twice.

'I didn't have any choice,' she freely admitted to her friends and customers. 'The girl's got me so well organized, I couldn't exist without her.'

Karen had indeed straightened out the accounts and put Demelza on a budget, and never complained about working long hours. She even developed a plan for increasing business that would draw uptown customers to the out-of-the-way shop.

But, more than that, the two women became friends. The refugee from Great Neck found a lot in common with the expatriate from the Bronx.

'When you're one of six kids and there's not enough food to go around,' Demelza said once, after snatching the last doughnut of the coffee break, 'you learn to be quick. Then, of course, you learn to get out.'

'When you're the older of two and getting so much attention you can't breathe' – Karen sighed – 'sooner or later, you have to get out, too.'

'My parents were delighted.'

'Mine were appalled.'

Karen was an avid reader of popular fiction, but now her employer opened her mind to the beauty of the classics that she had heretofore relegated to the category of required reading.

'You have to sample everything to evaluate anything,' Demelza instructed.

So, for a few precious hours each day, she would crawl into someone else's world and make it her own. Heathcliff haunted her, Becky delighted her, Inspector Jarret infuriated her, Madame Bovary made her blush, and Anna Karenina made her cry.

In addition to her new fictional friends, Karen got to know the scruffy lot who frequented the Bookery. The women wore long skirts and beaded headbands and attended an assortment of classes. The men wore beaded necklaces and hair below their shoulders. Many of the younger men were just hanging out, working temporary jobs until their draft numbers came up and it was time to head for Canada. Some of the others were career dropouts, searching for a reason to get up in the mornings. Several, with a foot in each camp, ran soup kitchens down on the Bowery or taught at places like NYU and Cooper Union. A few composed music or wrote poetry or tried to paint the shapes of their dreams.

Each had a story, and as Karen listened, the ragged clothes, unkempt hair, and shaggy beards disappeared, and she saw instead a group of lost souls, not unlike herself, struggling to find their way in a frequently hostile world.

In the backlash of Camelot, America had splintered into a dozen different subcultures, from the flower children of Haight-Ashbury to the civil-rights marchers of Selma to the drug addicts of Needle Park. Sentiment against the country's involvement in Vietnam was surging and Demelza defiantly displayed every antiwar poster and cartoon she could find.

The Kerns came to visit the Bookery one afternoon when Karen had been there for two months. It was a rainy Saturday in early April and Beverly, dressed in a bright splash of purple and fuchsia, gushed through the door with her umbrella dripping all over a 1923 issue of *Time*.

'My, what a day,' she exclaimed with a shiver. 'It's practically a gale out there.'

'Well, you blew into the right place,' Demelza said cordially, quickly whisking the vintage magazine out of harm's way. 'We have fresh tea waiting to warm you up.'

With cup in hand, Beverly looked around. 'Well, isn't this nice,' she said brightly. 'And so ... cozy.'

'Cramped, actually,' Demelza corrected her.

'Atmospheric,' Beverly suggested.

'Dark,' Demelza said.

'Don't your customers find it a little difficult reading in such light?' Beverly could no longer see her hand before her nose without her glasses.

'Heavens, we don't encourage our customers to read,' Demelza replied, a wicked little smile playing around the corners of her mouth.

'What about Karen? I don't want her to get eyestrain.'

'Demelza's teasing you, Mother,' Karen sighed.

'There are plenty of lights when we need them, but we think the shop has more ambience this way.'

'And it saves so much on electricity,' the newly budget-conscious proprietor put in.

'Ambience?' Beverly echoed with just the slightest hint of disdain.

'Well, we're trying for the archival look,' Demelza confided. 'You know – dusty, musty, hidden away. Isn't that where treasures are usually found?'

'Treasures?' Beverly openly sniffed at Demelza's array of peace and protest posters.

'Let me show you,' Karen beamed, leading her mother off to the special glass cases.

'I don't know about that woman,' Beverly remarked at dinner several hours later. 'She seems very peculiar to me. Don't you agree, Leo?'

'I didn't notice anything very peculiar,' Leo replied, attacking his Peking Duck as though it were a root canal.

'She's not peculiar,' Karen defended her friend and employer. 'She's just a little different, that's all.'

In the bright light of the Chinese restaurant, Karen wondered where the gray in her mother's hair had gone.

'Is she *on* something?' Beverly asked.

'What do you mean, *on* something?'

'You know – does she take drugs?'

Karen chuckled. 'What do you know about drugs?'

'Oh, I'm not as cloistered as you might think,' her mother retorted. 'I know what goes on in the world.'

'Well then, you know more than I do,' Karen replied.

'I smelled a very suspicious odor at that bookshop.'

'That was incense, Mother.'

'Are you sure? It was awfully sharp.'

'I lit it myself, just before you got there.'

'Well, nevertheless, I don't want you mixed up with anyone who takes drugs.'

'If Demelza takes drugs – and I certainly have no knowledge that she does,' Karen asserted, 'she's never done it at the Bookery. As long as she signs my paycheck each week, whatever she might or might not do someplace else is none of my business.'

Which was a neat way of sidestepping the issue, Karen thought to herself now, as the clanking air conditioner began to have some small effect on the stifling apartment. In the four months since that conversation with her mother, she had discovered that many of Demelza's friends did indeed smoke marijuana and she was pretty sure that her employer did, too.

Karen had to confess that the idea of being around people who used marijuana, or pot or grass or weed, as they called it, made her a little uneasy. She knew very little about drugs other than that they were addictive and illegal. Once in a while, someone wandered into the shop behaving a bit off-center, but Demelza usually laughed it off.

The first time, Karen was shocked. 'That guy over there looks weird,' she whispered with wide eyes.

'The word is *stoned*,' Demelza told her with a dry chuckle. 'Sorry, Peter Pan,' she called to the customer in question, 'but this isn't never-never land.'

Once, Karen watched as two young men at the back end of one of the aisles exchanged money for a small plastic packet containing something that looked like baby powder.

'There's someone over there selling talcum, I think,' she told Demelza.

This time, the Bookery owner didn't laugh. 'Where?' she demanded and, following Karen's finger, descended on the two men like a giant bat.

'You're history,' she cried, grabbing each by an arm and thrusting them in the direction of the door. 'We sell books and magazines in here – and that's all we sell.'

'What was that about?' Karen asked.

'There's dope and then there's dope,' Demelza replied. 'Some of it's easy and some of it's hard. No one deals hard stuff in my place.'

'Why do people use drugs in the first place?'

Demelza shrugged. 'Different people – different reasons,' she said. 'Some do it because it's fashionable, some because it's illegal, some because they've become dependent. Most of the people I know do it because, for a little while, at least, it makes the pain go away.'

The doctors had given Karen medicine in the hospital after her 'accident' and she could still remember how it made the pain of her broken body subside. She wondered if the drugs that Demelza was talking about worked the same way.

'What kind of pain do they have?' she asked.

'Not the kind I think you're thinking about,' the older woman replied. 'Street drugs aren't for tooth-aches and back strain. I was referring to the pain of living.'

'The pain of living.' Karen had never heard that before. She tucked the phrase into the back of her mind. Demelza never spoke of it again, but Karen never forgot.

* * *

Dinner was ready by the time Arlene arrived home from the university. Although no one would ever be likely to call Karen a gourmet cook, she had at least mastered the basics.

'Chef salad, iced tea, and French bread from the bakery,' she announced as her roommate passed the kitchen doorway. 'I couldn't bear the thought of turning on the oven.'

Arlene grunted her approval, dropped her books on the dining table, and was shedding her clothes before she even reached the bedroom.

'Look at me,' she cried fifteen minutes later, dripping from the shower, her long blond hair bound up in a towel. 'Soaking wet and sticky all over.'

'I'll call maintenance again,' Karen promised.

'If they can put a man on the moon,' Arlene fretted, referring to the incredible event they had recently watched on television, 'why can't they make an air conditioner work?'

Karen pushed her roommate's books to one side and set two places at the huge oak table with claw feet they had found at a secondhand store. In fact, the whole apartment was done in what Arlene dubbed Early Salvation Army. The overstuffed sofa and wing chairs were comfortable, if faded; the end tables were solid, if chipped; the bureaus were roomy, if warped; and the dining chairs were sturdy, if plain. But the two girls had had a lot of fun picking out each piece.

They were halfway through their salads when Karen said, as casually as she could, 'Have you ever taken drugs?'

Arlene bit into a crusty piece of bread. 'What kind of drugs?' she asked. 'Aspirin? Sleeping pills? Or the mind-control stuff we give the patients at Bellevue?'

'No, I mean street drugs. Like marijuana.'

'I tried pot once,' Arlene nodded. 'Years ago.'

'What was it like?'

Arlene shrugged. 'I guess it wasn't very special. I barely remember, and I've had no great urge to do it again.'

'The effect you got … was it like drinking alcohol?' Lately, and in private, Karen had been learning a great deal about the numbing effects of alcohol.

'No, it was nothing at all like that. Actually, it was nothing much of anything, as I recall. When you drink booze, you usually get fuzzy and your senses get dulled. When you do pot, you're supposed to get a real high. You don't lose awareness, so I'm told, you gain it. Why?'

'I've been invited to a party tomorrow night,' Karen informed her. 'And I think there'll be drugs there.'

'A party?' Arlene couldn't keep the surprise out of her voice because Karen rarely accepted invitations.

'Demelza's having a few people to her place for dinner and she invited me. We're even closing the Bookery early.'

'And she smokes pot?'

'I'm not really sure about that,' Karen replied, 'but I know her friends do and some of them are bound to be there.'

'Well, if you're asking for advice,' Arlene said, 'I'd say, don't do anything you don't want to do.'

'I *am* a little curious,' Karen admitted. 'You know, to find out what it's like.' *The pain of living*, she thought to herself.

Arlene picked up her glass of iced tea. 'Well then,' she said with a careless shrug, 'go for it.'

two

Long after Arlene had fallen asleep, Karen lay awake in the humid darkness, listening to the arrhythmic clanking of the air conditioner and thinking about dinner at Demelza's.

If she chose, she could count the number of parties she had attended in New York City over the past four years on one hand and have fingers left over. Her social life consisted mostly of a dinner out now and then, several movies, one or two Broadway shows, and an occasional concert at Lincoln Center, usually in the company of Jill or Arlene or Demelza.

She had a ready excuse for every man who tried to date her, and after a while even the most persistent stopped asking. If she occasionally caught herself yearning for male companionship, she had only to reflect that few men were interested in friendship at arm's length. With the advent of the contraceptive pill, 'free love' was the catchword on everyone's lips. Even casual dating meant obligatory sex – with all communication carried on between the sheets.

What a different world it was, she thought with a

sigh, and drifted off to sleep thinking about Peter Bauer.

A brief, apologetic note had arrived at the house on Knightsbridge Road a little over a year after the picnic at Steppingstone Park, wishing Karen well and telling her of his impending marriage.

'I wonder what took him so long,' Beverly sniffed.

The nightmare woke her just before dawn and she lay in her bed, sweat-soaked and shivering, until the familiar panic began to subside. It was always the same – something evil chasing her through a thick fog until she couldn't make her feet run anymore, and then the heavy hand reaching out to grasp her by the throat and cut off her life.

She took several deep breaths to settle her heart and thought about trying for another hour of sleep, but fantasies of Demelza's Greenwich Village loft kept her awake. Karen had never been inside a real Village apartment, and she couldn't wait to see what one was like.

Demelza had described her place as a cross between a church and a brothel. It was a fair assessment. The dirty brick building on Bleecker Street had once been a ribbon factory. Visitors reached the loft by means of a rickety self-service elevator with a heavy wooden gate that had to be raised and lowered manually. Karen arrived to find some two dozen of the Bookery regulars already there. She stepped out of the elevator and stood openmouthed at the edge of the single enormous room.

Exposed brick walls alternated with giant arched windows, and the vaulted ceiling was at least twenty feet high. One section of the loft was furnished with

Victorian velvet sofas and ornate side tables, another had two massive pews squaring off over a refectory table, and a third was strewn with half a dozen mattresses, heaped with colorful pillows. Each section was separated by a curtain of beads suspended by wires from the ceiling. Candles burned everywhere, and in the mixture of odors Karen detected the familiar scent of incense. It was different, bohemian, more than a little bizarre, and it suited Demelza perfectly.

'You made it,' the hefty hostess cried, descending on Karen with a highball in one hand and a plate of crudités in the other. 'Welcome to my heaven on earth.'

'This is fantastic,' Karen said, searching for the right adjective. 'It's so, well, it's so ... eclectic.'

'Actually, I think you could call it MGM Extravagant,' Demelza replied. 'And it took years of careful planning.'

'It's definitely you.'

'Well, don't just stand there and gawk,' the Bookery owner urged, taking her guest's bulky coat. 'Take a deep breath and jump on in. You know everybody.'

Obediently, Karen took a few steps forward.

'Hey, Karen,' someone said immediately.

'Hey, Ethan.' She smiled at the slightly off-balanced skeleton beside her.

'You look different,' Ethan observed shyly. 'Not like you do at the shop.'

Karen glanced down at the simple blue cotton skirt and loose-fitting, high-collared blouse she had worn to work.

'It must be the clothes,' she teased.

'Exactly,' Ethan agreed. 'You know, your skirt

matches your eyes. And your eyes are the color of a cloudless sky.'

Her eyes were more the color of a stormy sky, but she smiled at him anyway. Ethan came from Nebraska, she knew, and was on his way to Canada. He was a regular at the Bookery and rather bashful, hovering as he did on the fringe of the group. But he managed to screw up enough courage to test her knowledge of the shop's inventory on a daily basis. Not more than eighteen, with straight straw-colored hair that he kept pushing out of green eyes, something about him always reminded her of a lost puppy.

'My momma's cornflowers are the same bright blue,' he told her, 'and they grow clean up to the sky.'

'Sounds lovely.'

He sighed wistfully. 'I sure hope I get to see them again someday.'

'I hope you do, too.'

'But it probably won't be till after my daddy dies.'

'Why not?' she asked.

'He threw me out – called me a coward and threw me out. He said he didn't have a son no more.'

'Because you didn't want to go to Vietnam?'

'Yeah.' Ethan shook his head sadly. 'He lost a leg on Guadalcanal. I just don't know how he's running the factory without me.'

She could see his pain and wondered how many families across the country were being destroyed by this war of somebody else's that so many young men didn't want to fight.

Ethan pulled out a ragged kind of cigarette and lit it. 'Wanna hit?' he offered after several deep puffs.

Karen knew what it was. She took a half step back.

'No,' she said firmly. 'No, thank you.'

Ethan grinned. 'Demelza said you were a virgin. I didn't believe her.'

'I beg your pardon?'

'She said you'd never used grass.'

'Why didn't you believe her?' Karen asked.

'I don't know,' he said thoughtfully. 'There's just something about you – a look in your eyes, maybe, that says you've been there and back.'

'You know, *you're* different here than at the Bookery, too,' she told him, neatly changing the subject. 'Much more open.' She nodded at the joint. 'Is it because of that?'

'I guess so,' he replied, taking another hit. 'It sort of smooths out the edges and makes everything mellow.'

Karen wondered how it would feel to be mellow. She tried to recall an occasion in the past, but more and more, her memory of that other life was fading into nothingness.

'What's it like,' she asked, 'to be mellow?'

'It's like wearing rose-colored glasses to a horror flick,' he replied.

'Marijuana makes you feel like that?'

He offered the joint. 'Don't take my word for it.'

This time she was tempted. 'Maybe later,' she said. 'Right now, I'm hungry.'

'The food's behind that screen,' Ethan directed. 'On the other side of the pew.'

Karen found the kitchen and soon had a plate heaped with salade niçoise and moussaka. A bottle of ouzo went with the meal. She filled a glass and wandered into the living room, sitting on one of the Victorian sofas. The party drifted around her – long gauzy skirts, flowing shirts, safari shorts, beads, sandals. People stopped to chat about the food or the heat wave or Demelza's outrageous home. Karen began to feel as relaxed here as she did at the Bookery.

A few of the guests were drinking ouzo, as she was, but most were passing pot around the way Karen and Jill used to pass photographs. Two of them were already sprawled on a mattress at the other end of the loft. It wasn't until she saw them shedding their clothes that Karen realized what they were doing and she blushed and turned away.

'Isn't this just the most fantastic party?' Ethan cried, plopping down beside her.

'You bet,' Karen agreed.

'For a small-town boy like me,' he said, taking a hit, 'New York is right out of Oz. I'm going to miss it when I go. I don't think they have anything like this in Canada.'

'Maybe you'll come back someday,' she suggested.

'Maybe I will, if you're still here,' he said, the weed making him bold. 'I guess you know I have this crush on you.'

'No, I didn't,' she replied with genuine surprise.

'Gosh, everybody else knows,' he asserted. 'I thought for sure you did, too. I mean, the way I'm always hanging around you at the shop and everything.'

'I thought you were interested in books.'

'I wouldn't know Henry James from James Michener,' he confessed sheepishly. 'I just like talking to you.'

'I'm very flattered,' she said sincerely. Ethan had always behaved perfectly properly and she didn't feel the least bit threatened by his admission. He was still the lost puppy who waited hopefully for someone to toss him a bone.

'Don't you feel a little funny?' he asked her.

'About what?'

'Well, for one thing,' he said with a grin, 'you're the only one here tonight who's sober.'

Surprised, Karen looked at the other guests – except, of course, for the two on the mattress at the other end of the loft. She had consumed almost a whole glass of ouzo and hardly considered herself sober.

'I am?' she whispered. 'How can you tell?'

'Easy,' he giggled. 'We're all bent one way or another. If you were any straighter, you'd break.'

'Is "bent" another word for mellow?' she asked.

'Not exactly, but close,' he conceded.

More than once, Karen had taken a bottle to bed with her but she would not have described the experience as mellowing.

He held out his joint. 'See for yourself.'

Curiosity got the better of her. She took the butt and put it between her index and middle fingers as smokers did.

'What do I do?' she whispered.

'First of all, you gotta hold it right,' he instructed, repositioning the joint between her thumb and forefinger. 'Okay, now go ahead and pull on it, just like a Marlboro.'

'I've never smoked a regular cigarette,' she admitted.

'Oh,' he said, momentarily confounded. 'Well then, you close your mouth around one end and suck on it real hard and take a deep breath all at the same time.'

Karen did as she was told. Even before the smoke hit her lungs, her insides rebelled, her face turned beet-red, her eyes watered, and she barely avoided losing her dinner.

'I don't feel very mellow,' she gasped.

'It takes more than one hit.'

'What if I'd just as soon not do it again?'

He shrugged. 'How bad do you want to be mellow?'

Karen wrinkled up her nose, put the foul-smelling awful-tasting reefer to her lips and pulled on it. Again she gagged, her insides burned and her eyes watered, but not as much as the first time. By the fourth or fifth hit, she had the hang of it and suddenly began to giggle.

'If my mother could see me, she'd have an apoplectic fit.'

'Does your mother have apoplexy?' Ethan asked.

'No,' Karen replied, wondering why she had never noticed how intelligent he was. 'She has astigmatism.'

Ethan shook his head. 'You're not making any sense.'

'Nonsense,' she retorted. 'I'm making perfect sense.'

For some reason that seemed outrageously funny to her and the giggles began anew.

'I guess I don't have to ask how you feel,' he said.

'Very light,' Karen replied. 'Like I could tiptoe on air. I can't remember ever feeling quite this way before.'

'Maybe that's because you were never mellow before,' suggested Ethan.

Karen stretched up high above her head, wiggling her fingers in the air, and then dropped back against the velvet cushions. It looked as though she might close her eyes and drift right off to sleep, but in the next second she was alert again, every nerve, every muscle at attention.

'Just look at that, will you,' she urged, pointing to the bead curtain that divided the living area from the dining space. 'Look how beautiful those beads are.' She scrambled to her feet and made an unsteady beeline for the partition, motioning him to follow. 'You have to come, too,' she giggled. 'I need a hit.'

Ethan obeyed and passed her a fresh joint. She dragged deeply on it and turned to examine the intricacies of color and design that made up the small wooden balls that hung from high over her head.

'These are absolutely fascinating,' she breathed. As riveted on the beads as she was, something caught her eye and she glanced through the curtains.

'Look,' she cried in surprise. 'Someone's dancing. Oh, how lovely. What kind of dance is that?'

Ethan followed her gaze. Indeed, several couples now occupied the mattresses at the far end of the loft, going about their pleasures with complete abandon.

'I think it's called the mating dance,' he replied with a chuckle.

'I've never seen that before,' Karen said as her body began to undulate in imitation. 'Can we try it?'

Ethan stared at her. 'I guess so,' he gulped.

He seized the joint and took several quick hits, sensing that something far beyond his wildest expectations was about to happen. Trembling, he followed her across the loft. Although he would have sooner died than admit it, the young Nebraskan had never been with a woman.

Karen walked slowly around the mattresses, studying each oblivious couple.

'Aren't they magnificent?' she whispered. 'So graceful, so rhythmic.' She stopped in front of an unoccupied mattress and turned to him. 'What do we do first?' she asked.

'Uh, well, uh, I think we take off our clothes,' he stammered.

She giggled. 'I can't do that.'

'But that's how it goes,' he said. 'We take off our clothes and then we do the dance.'

'Let's do it with our clothes on.'

'Well, I suppose we could,' he ventured, not wanting to seem too anxious.

She stepped onto the mattress and began to twist her body in an awkward version of the mating dance, humming along with a tune only she could hear. Ethan licked his lips and moved toward her, figuring that, when the time came, the undressing part would take care of itself.

He felt her stiffen when he put his arms around her, but she didn't pull away. They swayed together for a few bliss-filled moments, sharing the end of his last joint. Her eyes were closed and her lips were turned up in a small smile. He couldn't resist. He leaned over and kissed her lightly.

Her head snapped back and her eyes flew open. 'That's not part of the dance,' she cried.

'Sure it is,' he said.

Karen squinted at him. 'I don't believe you.'

'Look around,' he invited.

She peered at the couples that surrounded them and, sure enough, she saw that lips were touching lips and hands were touching bodies and bodies were fused tightly together.

'They're so artistic,' she breathed. 'Look how that one's muscles ripple up and down, and how smooth this one's skin is – how it glows in the candlelight.'

Now she was fascinated by the candles, mesmerized by the gentle flickering.

'See how the flames reach for the sky? They look like the tongues of hell.'

One moment she was staring at the candles, the next she was sagging against him and he had to hold her to keep her from falling.

'What's the matter?' he asked.

The whole room had begun to spin out of control and a flurry of bright lights swirled before her eyes.

'Let's sit down,' she suggested.

'Okay.'

He let go of her and she dropped like a sack of flour.

'Plop!' she giggled. 'I need another hit.'

Ethan sat down beside her. 'I think you've had enough,' he told her. 'Besides, we're right in the middle of our dance.'

'So we are,' she agreed with an acquiescent yawn. 'I like the lights, though. Don't turn off the lights.'

He didn't know what lights she was talking about.

'The lights stay,' he said as he pushed her gently back against the mattress. She didn't resist. He slid his hand down her arm, brushing against her breast.

'The colors are so pretty,' she murmured. 'I can see them even with my eyes closed.'

He unbuttoned her blouse.

'They're red and blue and green and pink and purple and silver.'

He unzipped her skirt.

'See how they sparkle.'

He unhooked her bra.

'Look, now they're showering down on top of us.'

He slipped off her panties.

'Why, it's just like the fireworks on the Fourth of July.'

Even in the candlelight, he could see the scars, thin jagged welts from her neck to her knee. He wondered fleetingly what had happened to her as he pulled his T-shirt over his head and unzipped his jeans.

'I feel as though I'm going to break into a thousand pieces of light and float through the air,' she cried.

He had worshiped her from afar for so many months that he could barely contain himself as his hands moved over her body and his mouth found her nipples.

'There's that tune again,' she trilled. 'La-li-la-la, la-li-la-la. Everybody's dancing, the chandeliers are sparkling with a thousand pieces of light. La-li-la-la.'

Without any further ado, he rolled over on top of her and began to fumble between her legs.

Her scream split the loft, a scream not of pain but of terror as, through her daze, she understood what it was he had in mind.

'Stop it!' she shrieked, clawing at him like a cat, pushing against him with all her strength. 'Stop!'

Ethan blanched. 'What'd I do?' he implored. People were staring and he was mortified.

She was crying now. 'It was beautiful,' she sobbed. 'The music, the lights, the dancing, and you ruined it all.'

'I didn't mean to,' he pleaded.

Someone opened a window and Karen felt a sudden draft sweep across her. She shivered and, looking down, realized she had no clothes on. She froze. Images blurred. The music stopped. The lights vanished. The dance was over. Everything went black.

three

A bright shaft of sun was burning through her eyelids. Karen groaned, still half asleep, and pulled the sheet up over her head.

'Rise and shine, Sleeping Beauty,' Demelza chuckled from somewhere above her. 'There's no Prince Charming, but there is fresh coffee.'

Karen blinked several times and forced her eyes open, but everything was fuzzy and white. Then she remembered the sheet and pushed it down under her chin. High arched windows looked down on her. Karen glanced around. She was lying on a mattress in one part of a large room, it was definitely morning – and she didn't know what she was doing there.

'Where am I?' she asked.

Demelza loomed into view. 'In my loft, of course. You came to my party last night. You ate my moussaka, drank my ouzo, and then Ethan must have given you too much of the good stuff, because somewhere around midnight you passed out cold. You looked so comfortable, I decided not to wake you.'

'That's right,' Karen recalled. 'I got mellow, didn't I?'

'Quite,' Demelza chuckled.

'It felt wonderful. I was floating and I could hear this incredible music.' Karen frowned. 'Is that when I passed out?'

'Just about.' Demelza peered down at the girl for a moment and decided that, if she didn't remember anything else, there was nothing to be gained by reminding her.

'I'm so embarrassed,' Karen mumbled. 'Everyone must have thought me terribly rude.'

'I doubt anyone noticed,' Demelza said with a bright smile.

Actually, she had given everyone a terrible fright, screaming and clawing at Ethan like that, as though the devil himself were after her. Demelza didn't grasp the situation immediately, but in the flickering candle-light she saw the scars, and that was enough to make her push Ethan away, grab a sheet to pull over Karen's body, and persuade them all to go on about their business.

As soon as the party broke up, she fixed herself some tea and, bringing the thick mug with her, came back to stare thoughtfully down at Karen. After a while, she pushed the sheet aside and, with some effort, managed to put the girl's clothes back on. Then, tucking the sheet back in place, she sat down on a mattress, her back against the exposed brick wall.

Doris Ulasewicz was the oldest of six children. Her mother was an unstable woman, frequently unable to cope, and her father was a longshoreman who spent more days at the racetracks than he did on the docks. Doris always knew how the ponies had run by how he came home – singing or swinging.

From the time she was eight, she had protected her brothers and sisters from their father's ire and their mother's neglect. She cooked and cleaned, changed diapers, prepared formula and, when the ponies were running badly, she found a way to wheedle the grocer out of one more grapefruit, one more loaf of bread, one more quart of milk.

There was never enough of anything – never enough food, never enough warm clothes, never enough love. When she was thirteen, she slept with the butcher, on a rough wooden floor in a back room, for a pound of hamburger and a scrawny chicken. She stretched the meat into two meals and made soup from the chicken bones and a purloined onion. The following week, she got a pork roast.

At fifteen, she quit school and lied about her age to get a job behind the counter of a luncheonette. The wages were hardly worth her time, but the tips were occasionally good, she was fed a hot meal, and she was allowed to take home whatever scraps she could salvage. She saved every penny, and once a month she would go to the Salvation Army store and dig through piles of used clothing for pieces she could rework into outfits for the children.

Her only refuge was the public library. For a few precious hours each afternoon, she would escape to the musty stacks and lose herself in incredible worlds that were filled with beauty, mystery, and adventure. It was the beginning of a love affair with books that never ended.

On Pearl Harbor Day, she turned eighteen and

forever remembered the occasion, not as the beginning of a war for freedom, but as the beginning of her own freedom. Within a matter of weeks, her father was being called to work on the docks every day.

Doris got a job in a downtown Manhattan bookstore and never looked back. She moved into a cold-water flat on Houston Street, as far away from the Bronx as she could get, changed her name, and found a life. By the time she was thirty, she had gained forty pounds and saved enough money to start her own small business in the basement of a Washington Square tenement.

Her brothers and sisters had long since stopped relying on her, but she never quite got over the urge to nurture. Fortunately, there was always an abundance of needy souls and lost causes for her to champion. And as she sat there in her loft, sipping her tea and watching over Karen, Demelza felt that familiar tug at her heart.

The girl looked like an angel, so innocent and trusting, curled up in sleep, but Demelza had seen the scars and wondered what demons populated her dreams. The Bookery proprietor could not have said how she came to choose her needy souls and lost causes, or whether it was the other way around, but there was a real sense of tragedy about Karen that she had felt from the first day the young woman walked into her shop – and tragedy was definitely Demelza's thing.

Caretaker of the Down and Out, that's what the Village people called her. If there was a person with no place to stay, see Demelza. If there was someone who needed a handout, tap Demelza. If there was an outrage that needed exposing, tell Demelza. Any day of the week, she would gladly give her only warm coat to a freezing vagrant and her last dime to a starving child

Karen wasn't freezing or starving but she was certainly in need of something, if only Demelza could figure out what.

The candles had burned themselves down to nothing and dawn was painting the windows gray before Demelza's eyes closed. When she opened them again, it was past nine o'clock and they were late for work.

'I can't believe I fell asleep and stayed the whole night,' Karen was saying as she came out of the bathroom and helped herself to a cup of coffee.

'You look none the worse for the experience,' Demelza commented.

'I feel fine,' Karen said. 'In fact, I feel terrific. I can't remember the last time I had a better night's rest.'

'Pot has been known to have that effect on people.'

A shadow flickered across Karen's face. 'I didn't do anything to embarrass myself last night, did I?' she asked.

'Not that I saw,' Demelza replied glibly. 'Why?'

'Well, this is going to sound stupid, I know, but I've got this weird picture in my head – a dream, I guess, of me dancing without my clothes.'

Demelza shrugged casually. 'So what?' she said. 'You were among friends.'

Karen blanched. 'I took my clothes off?' she gasped. 'In front of everyone?'

'I don't think anybody was paying much attention,' Demelza reassured her. 'The candles were low, and besides, most of them had other things on their minds.'

Karen looked down at her crumpled blue skirt and

high-collared blouse. 'If I took them off,' she questioned, 'who put them back on again?'

'I did,' Demelza replied calmly.

'Then, you saw …?' Karen whispered.

'If you mean the scars, yes,' her hostess, her employer, her friend said gently. 'Whatever caused them, you must have had a rough time of it.'

Karen felt the prickle of tears behind her eyes, tears of embarrassment and anger that she was never going to live down her past, and tears of frustration that it could still hurt so much.

'It was a long time ago.' She sighed. 'I don't like to talk about it.'

'I didn't mean to pry.'

'You weren't – you never do,' Karen murmured. Demelza listened, Demelza sympathized, Demelza encouraged, but never probed, never criticized and never judged. In the six months that Karen had known her, she had learned to trust the older woman's advice, value her opinions and admire her discretion. In many ways, Demelza behaved the way Karen sometimes wished Beverly would behave.

'I had … an accident,' she said.

'I'm sorry,' Demelza replied with genuine concern.

'I was careless and I ended up in the wrong place at the wrong time. It wasn't exactly the high point of my life.'

Karen felt an unfamiliar flutter in the pit of her stomach. This was the most she had said about the night in Central Park in six years.

'But you're all right now.'

It was a statement, not a question, but it seemed to warrant some kind of answer.

'You probably noticed my left leg is a bit stiff,' Karen

said. 'The kneecap was smashed, but it's getting better.'

'I'm glad to hear it,' Demelza replied, her smile warm and real.

'I guess I'm self-conscious about the scars.'

'I can understand that,' Demelza told her. 'After all, they're a reminder of something you'd rather forget.'

'I can't ever have children,' Karen heard herself say. 'I always wanted to have children.'

'Because of the accident?'

Karen nodded. 'I expected to marry a wonderful man and raise a houseful of children. Now, I don't know what I'm supposed to do with my life.'

Sooner or later, Demelza thought, every riddle had an explanation, and every question had an answer.

'I generally think of life as a great big map,' she said. 'When I reach a dead end on one road, I simply look for another to follow.'

four

Karen crossed Washington Square South and hurried up Sullivan Street. The late-January wind whipped and roared around her, burning her eyes and ears, and pushing its icy way down her throat. She burrowed deep inside her coat, and bent her body into the swirling gale.

The coat was a Christmas gift from her parents. It was made of thick gray wool, and came down to her ankles, and weighed almost as much as Karen did. Her shoulders ached for hours after each wearing, but it kept her warm.

It had arrived in the nick of time. The winter had turned unbearably cold. Piles of dirty snow lined the streets, reducing traffic to single lanes. Sidewalks were salted, but it was too cold for the ice to melt. Vehicles crawled down the middle of roads, honking and skidding. Pedestrians sank into slush over their ankles, cursing.

Reaching the run-down building she sought, Karen scurried up icy steps and pushed through the door. It had once had a lock on it, but that was long before the present tenants.

The structure had four stories. The upper floors were subdivided into studios for artists who sought cheap living in a congenial environment, while the first floor contained four flats of three rooms each. It was toward one of these that Karen headed as she hastened down the narrow brown hall in the light of a single sixty-watt bulb. She stopped at a door on the left and rapped briskly. When her knock was answered, she crossed the threshold and the drab outside world disappeared. She stood in the middle of Paradise. Or, to be more precise, in the middle of the Garden of Eden as it was being painstakingly reproduced, in a Gauguin sort of style, on the walls and ceilings of the once dreary flat.

'Hey, girl, you're late,' cried a bear of a man in a paint-spattered shirt. 'We started without you.'

Mitchell Rankin wrapped her in a hug. He stood over six feet tall and weighed over two hundred pounds. Karen had no clear idea of his face, buried as it was beneath a woolly beard. He never asked to hug her, he just did it, and she had learned to accept it. In the four months she had been coming to Sullivan Street, there had never been anything in his embrace but the simple regard for one person by another.

'Hey, Karen,' a tomboy of a woman called from atop a crudely fashioned scaffold on the far side of the room. 'What do you think of my clouds?'

Karen glanced up at the globs of white pigment that were beginning to scud across one part of the ceiling. 'I think they look very ... cloudlike,' she said.

There was a splash of white freckles across the woman's nose and cheeks. 'I could use an assistant Michelangelo,' she said with a deep stretch.

'Ione, be careful,' scolded Mitch. 'You're doing that balancing act for two, you know.'

'Never mind about us, you big gorilla,' retorted the woman called Ione, as tiny as he was big, as pale as he was dark. 'Just take the girl's coat so I can put her to work.'

Mitch helped Karen out of the gray maxicoat. Beneath it, she wore a long black skirt over black boots and a coarse muslin shirt, loosely bound at the waist with a rope belt. Her dark hair was tied off her face by a beaded headband and she had taken to outlining her eyes in heavy black pencil.

'You can't paint in that outfit,' Ione declared.

Karen shrugged. 'I didn't want to take time to change.'

'Mitch, get the girl my smock,' the tomboy instructed. 'It's hanging on the back of the closet door.'

As Mitch disappeared into the bedroom, a gaunt young man with thick glasses and a wispy reddish beard came out.

'Hey, Karen.' he said with a distracted smile.

'Hey, Kevin.'

'Ione, where's the dictionary?' he asked.

'On the back of the toilet.'

Kevin looked at her quizzically.

'I was doing a crossword puzzle,' she said with a toss of her short blond hair.

With a grunt, he turned back into the bedroom.

'He's got exams,' whispered Ione.

Kevin Munker was in his third or fourth year at NYU, Karen wasn't quite sure. He wasn't a student in the traditional sense, enrolling for four years to earn a degree. Instead, Kevin took the minimum three courses per semester and kept changing his major so that, each term, he would have a whole new list of requirements to complete. As long as he maintained a B average, he could keep his draft exemption.

Mitch reappeared with Ione's smock just as the front door blew open and two women came in. Jenna, barely out of her teens, with carrot-colored hair, deep blue eyes and traces of baby fat still clinging to her, studied fashion design at Cooper Union. Felicity, a stick of a woman at thirty, with high cheekbones and brown hair and eyes, was a dancer who made incredible pieces of jewelry whenever the spirit moved her, and sold them whenever hunger moved her.

'If you're not going to paint,' Mitch ordered, 'stay out until ten.'

Jenna and Felicity weighed the advantages of going back out into the cold. 'We'll paint,' they said together.

Karen couldn't imagine how all five of these people survived in one small apartment together, but they did. They called it communal living, the way of the future, and although unrelated, they considered themselves a family.

Ione Meecham came from the coal mines of Alliance, Ohio, arriving in New York with a fine-arts degree in her hand and stars in her eyes, hoping for a spot at the Metropolitan Museum. Two years later, funds depleted, she took a job teaching art history at NYU, which always amused Karen, since she looked far more like a student than a teacher.

Over the next dozen years, Ione earned a small measure of respect, rose from the rank of instructor to assistant professor, discovered that she really loved teaching, and met Mitchell Rankin, a starving artist with unbridled optimism.

Mitch was a farm boy from Montana who'd spent his young years surrounding himself with paints and canvas instead of comic books and baseball cards, translating the raw splendor of Big Sky country into impressionistic brilliance.

'Something's wrong with the boy,' his father had declared. 'He's not interested in things kids his age are interested in. And he doesn't give a damn about sugar beets.'

'There's nothing wrong with him,' his mother had protested. 'He's just different, sensitive. He sees beauty in the world where everybody else sees brutality.'

Mitch went from high school to Korea, where a mortar burst resulted in a patchwork of scars across his right cheek. He grew a beard to cover them. When he met Ione, he was painting buildings, not pictures, but he still had his dream. She said at least he hadn't been reduced to doing those awful portraits for the tourists who invaded Washington Square. She invited him into her home and her heart.

Next came Felicity Gravois. Mitch found her sitting on a curb, crying, beside a box holding all her worldly goods. She was six months behind in her rent and had been evicted.

'I'm a dancer,' she explained. 'A really good dancer. Only nobody seems to care about that.'

When she was eight years old, a society matron had taken her to see *The Red Shoes*. Felicity decided then and there that she would be a ballerina. She slept, ate, and breathed dancing, took any job to pay for lessons and, when all else failed, made up steps and danced them in her head.

'How long have you been in New York?'

'Three years,' she sniffled.

'Maybe you should think about going home,' he suggested gently. 'This can be a lousy city to be alone in.'

'The Saint Louis Institute for Orphans?' the twenty-three-year-old asked through her tears. 'I don't think so.'

'Come with me,' Mitch said.

'I never knew my parents,' Felicity told Ione. 'The orphanage called me Felicity for happiness and Gravois for the street where I was found. With that name, I figured I couldn't help but become famous.'

Jenna Bell had been sent after high school from Alliance, Ohio, with a letter from Ione's mother.

'This is the daughter of our new minister,' Mrs. Meecham had written. 'She wants to design clothes for a living, and has convinced her parents that she can only do this in New York. Everyone will feel so much better if you keep an eye on her, you being a teacher and all.'

'I'm free,' Jenna had cried her first night on Sullivan Street, whirling around, her carrot-colored curls sticking straight out. 'You have no idea what it's like to be a fourth-generation minister's daughter – with red hair.'

Ione helped the teenager find a job as a seamstress on Seventh Avenue and arranged for her to enroll at Cooper Union.

Kevin was next, and after that, the pattern was set. Sometimes the number taking refuge in the three-room flat swelled from five to as many as ten, depending on who needed a bed at the time. Karen met them in September, through Ethan, who lived there until just before Thanksgiving. When his number came up, they all went down to a street corner near Battery Park to see him off on the first leg of his underground journey to Canada.

There was something very comfortable about these people, and Karen soon found herself spending every possible moment with them. Their secret was that they genuinely cared about one another in a way Karen had never experienced before. There was no rivalry here, no petty jealousies among them. No one had anything another wanted because they shared everything they had – their money, their clothes, their abilities, even their bodies.

Karen knew that Mitch slept with Ione and sometimes with Felicity, and that Kevin slept with Felicity and occasionally with Jenna, and that Jenna spent several evenings a week with John, a sculptor who lived in a studio apartment upstairs. Like Demelza's loft, the bedroom floor was carpeted in wall-to-wall mattresses, and visitors were always welcome to join in.

Once, such an arrangement would have made Karen turn and run, but she had come a long way in a short time. Much of that, she realized, had to do with the matter-of-fact approach these people had to life and living, and the ease with which they accepted one another's boundaries. There was never any pressure. Certainly, no one ever pressured Karen. They took her into the fold and never challenged the limits she set. She was one of the family, on whatever terms she chose, and that was all they cared about. No one ever crossed the line.

Arlene was dating an orthopedist from Bellevue and

often did not come home, so Karen got into the habit of dropping by Sullivan Street several nights a week. The women cooked, the men rolled joints, and then they would meet to share the fruits of their labors. Sometimes, if it got late and Karen was feeling particularly mellow, she would grab a blanket and curl up, undisturbed, on one of the mattresses.

The Garden of Eden had actually been her idea, born while they were toasting in the New Year, having emptied the contribution can and splurged on a rather decent bottle of champagne. The wine bubbled right down to Karen's toes, and with the weed she had already smoked, heaven was a three-room apartment in the run-down heart of Greenwich Village.

'I love you all,' she said when the toast came around to her. 'You took me in and treated me like one of you, right from the start, and you never asked for anything in return. You nurtured me and encouraged me and gave me space, and then you waited to see if I would bloom. I want to thank you for that, and wish all of you as much happiness in 1970 as you gave me in 1969. If this place were a garden, you'd be the most magnificent flowers growing.'

It was the longest speech she had made in seven years.

'What a lovely thing to say,' Ione cried, rushing over to hug her.

'What a lovely idea,' Mitch said. He took a long look around the common room and a big smile slowly lit up his bearded face. 'I bet we could do it.'

'Do what?' asked Felicity.

'Why, turn this dump into a garden, of course ... the Garden of Eden,' he replied. 'I could do the sketches right on the walls to get us started and I can get the paint cheap. All we need is enough manpower to bring it to life.'

'I don't remember the lease on this apartment saying anything about going Michelangelo,' Ione protested.

But the artist was in his element. 'The landlord'll love it once it's done. After all, we're going to provide him with something of inestimable value – an original Mitchell Rankin – free of charge.'

'What the hell,' Kevin said. 'The old place could use a face-lift.'

'I can make new curtains and pillows,' offered Jenna.

'I guess I can handle a brush,' Felicity allowed.

'Then it's settled,' exclaimed Mitch. 'I'll do some preliminary drawings in the morning.' He beamed at them. 'It will be my first masterpiece.'

And, as far as Karen could judge, it was.

Mitch had created a spectacularly lush version of Eden that was perhaps more Tahitian than biblical. A thick green carpet of grass populated by inquisitive little creatures and wildflowers crept up the common-room walls and was bordered by a colorful mass of bushes, out of which poked great stalks of hibiscus and birds-of-paradise.

In the bedroom, fish frolicked in a crystal-clear pool, and the kitchen flaunted a tangle of blooming vines, a preening parrot, and a wide-eyed owl peering through the branches of a jacaranda tree. The whole thing was tied together by fruit trees that dripped with peaches and pears and oranges. A smiling serpent hung down from a bough of apple blossoms. A big yellow sun occupied one whole corner of the ceiling, and in another, Ione's clouds dotted a brilliant blue sky. In addition to basic brushwork, Mitch was using his trademark serrated palette knife to create texture. As a result, the scenes had a three-dimensional look that made them come alive.

They would paint until ten o'clock, stopping only for supper. Then they would sit around, smoke a few joints and contemplate their handiwork. It was finished on the second Sunday in February, the same day Karen turned twenty-eight.

'So we have two things to celebrate,' Ione said, digging deep into the contribution can for enough money to buy a good steak and a bottle of Bordeaux.

Kevin brought some good pot. Felicity even baked a cake. Karen made an excuse not to go home to Great Neck. After the food and wine had been consumed and the best wishes offered, Kevin brought out his pipe and passed it around. Then they turned off the overhead lights and wandered from room to room, surveying their accomplishment by candlelight. Karen had never felt more at home, more at peace, more mellow.

'Would that reality could be like this,' Kevin sighed. He was a philosophy major this term.

'Life sure isn't the way I expected it would be when I started out,' Felicity mused. 'I expected to be dancing on Broadway by the time I was twenty. Then it was twenty-five. Then it was thirty. Now I wonder about thirty-five.'

Jenna giggled. 'I never expected I'd actually come to New York and study fashion design. But in five years, I want to have my own label and be sold in the most exclusive shops in town.'

Ione stretched like a cat. 'I'm going to have a healthy kid, and tenure.'

'In five years, I'm going to be hanging in the Museum of Modern Art,' Mitch proclaimed, 'Or, at the very least, the Guggenheim.'

'I just want to get my degree and get on with my life,' Kevin declared. 'So Nixon better keep his goddamn campaign promise and get us the hell out of Vietnam.'

Everyone turned to Karen, whose only plans were for a life that had nothing to do with her now.

'Where do you want to be in five years?' Ione asked.

Karen closed her eyes and looked into the future. But there was nothing to see because, she realized with dismay, she didn't have the faintest idea where she wanted to be in five *days*, much less five years.

PART FOUR
1971

Evil is easy, and has infinite forms.

– Blaise Pascal

one

May could be the most glorious month in San Francisco, once the winter rains had tapered off and before the summer fog rolled in, when the thermometer reached up into the seventies and the air smelled freshly scrubbed and the sun sparkled off the bay, and people went around with smiles on their faces. It was a month often overlooked by tourists, much to the delight of those who lived there and kept the splendor a closely guarded secret.

On one such perfect Tuesday in early May, Elizabeth Willmont was indulging in her favorite pastime – shopping. It was a rare occasion when a committee meeting was canceled at the last minute and Elizabeth found herself with a free day. She had promptly persuaded her husband to take her to lunch and then she made a beeline for Union Square.

It was no secret to anyone that Elizabeth loved to shop, and with her Modigliani-like figure and substantial bank account, that was understandable. The product of a Colorado millionaire and a French beauty, few things delighted the young socialite more than going from one store to the next, trying on item after item, selecting what pleased her and discarding what didn't.

By mid-afternoon, she had purchased three dresses, two suits, and a whole host of accessories. Ordinarily, this would have put an enormous smile on her face, but as she came out of Maison Mendessolle, the elite salon in the St. Francis Hotel, and turned onto Post Street, it was an uneasy frown that creased her lovely features.

Halfway down the block, Elizabeth stopped as though something in a display window had caught her eye and caught instead a glimpse of the reflection behind her. The girl in the red coat was still there.

Elizabeth sighed. She had first noticed the girl in the fine-china department at Macy's, just a slip of a thing with straggly hair and big brown eyes and blotches on her skin, who showed no interest whatever in Lenox or Minton and surely must have been roasting, all bundled up in that heavy coat.

Next, she turned up in the shoe department at Magnin's, when Elizabeth was buying the silk pumps. And then there she was in Maison Mendessolle, looking terribly out of place but standing her ground, while Elizabeth chose a gown for a charity ball she was helping to organize.

The girl never came close enough for conversation, although it was clear she had something on her mind. But she never let Elizabeth out of sight, either. And in that absurd red coat, she was anything but inconspicuous. Even the saleslady noticed.

'That person over there, Mrs. Willmont,' she whispered, 'do you know her?'

Elizabeth glanced casually over her shoulder. 'No, I'm afraid I don't.'

'Well, she certainly isn't one of our customers, and she's been staring at you for the longest time.'

Elizabeth shrugged it off. It didn't do to tell help any more than they needed to know. Gossip that was started by a careless remark could spread like a brushfire and devastate the select social circle in which the Willmonts traveled. But the girl was making her very uncomfortable. If she had something to say, Elizabeth wished she would say it and get it over with.

Not that she wasn't used to being stared at. As one of San Francisco's most beautiful and stylish young matrons, Elizabeth had been photographed, interviewed, emulated and envied from the moment Robert had brought her to California as his wife three and a half years ago.

Even before that, she had often found herself in the public eye. After all, she was the only daughter of Archer and Denise Avery of Denver, where her father owned Avery Industries, and where her family was every bit as influential as the Draytons were in San Francisco.

Having inherited her elegant French mother's flaming red hair, slanting green eyes, chiseled features and graceful ways, Elizabeth was indisputably the outstanding debutante of 1963, setting a standard for every Denver debutante to follow. By the time it was over, she had received no less than half a dozen marriage proposals. She declined them all, however, choosing instead four years at Vassar and then a handsome young attorney from

California whom she met at Aspen.

It was, as far as Elizabeth was concerned, love at first sight. She had lost one of her ski poles and was having considerable difficulty trying to negotiate the slope without it when he came to her rescue.

'I believe this belongs to you,' he said with a poker face, presenting her with the wayward bamboo stick.

'My goodness,' she exclaimed with a toss of her Raggedy Ann hair, 'I never even noticed it was gone.'

'Well done,' he declared with a hearty laugh and a broad wink of approval.

One look deep into his incredible aquamarine eyes was all it took. After returning to Vassar, she spent several anxious weeks – replaying every moment of their days together, recalling how well his ski outfit fit him, how wind-tanned he had been, what a decidedly sexy mouth he had, and how she had felt when he held her hand – until he finally telephoned.

Theirs was a long-distance romance that consisted of flowery letters and exorbitant telephone bills and three very closely chaperoned visits at the Averys' gingerbread mansion in the heart of old Denver.

'My family's horribly old-fashioned,' she had said, giggling on the occasion of Robert's third stay, during the spring break of her senior year at Vassar, when they were unable to escape from watchful eyes for so much as two minutes. 'I hope you don't mind.'

'Of course I mind,' he grumbled, unused to this cat-and-mouse game he was being forced to play. 'I suppose I'm going to have to marry you, just so I can get you alone.'

It was not exactly the proposal that Elizabeth had spent her girlhood dreaming of, but she hardly noticed. Her feet didn't quite touch the ground for the rest of his stay.

'I think I'd better know something about your prospects, young man,' Archer Avery declared, when his daughter came seeking his blessing.

Elizabeth would never forget it. Robert sat in her father's study, with just the right mixture of self-assurance and deference, and looked the intimidating patriarch directly in the eye, something that few of the boys who courted her had ever been brave enough, or foolish enough, to do.

'I'm a senior associate with Sutton, Wells, Willmont and Spaulding, sir,' he said with confidence. 'I believe that you're acquainted with Jonah Spaulding.'

The older man nodded.

'It was my father's firm, before he died,' Robert continued, 'and I have every reason to believe that I will be asked to join the partnership when the time comes.'

'I assume that means you plan on taking Elizabeth to San Francisco to live?'

'Yes, of course,' Robert replied. 'I'm sure she'll love it there. It's a lot like Denver. But we won't necessarily live there forever. You see, sir, once I've established my reputation at the bar, I'm planning on going into politics.'

Elizabeth's ears perked up. Robert had never said anything to her about having political aspirations.

'Politics?' Archer echoed, stiffening slightly.

'I'm a Drayton,' Robert explained. 'It's a matter of tradition that Draytons give something back. My ancestors have donated parks, established museums, and endowed schools. One set up the Drayton Foundation, which provides scholarships and does other philanthropic work. Several served as judges. Others built bridges and railroads. One even sponsored soup kitchens during the Depression. Each chooses his own way. I've chosen politics.'

Archer grunted and scowled and shifted uncomfortably in his chair. He was a bull of a man and not one who bothered to keep his feelings hidden, but then he had never been able to deny his daughter anything.

'Well, I just don't mind telling you, young man,' he rumbled, 'I don't like the sound of that. I don't like the sound of that at all.'

'I know that politics has always been a dirty word in some circles,' Robert said quickly. 'I can tell you that it certainly has been in mine. But times are changing, and I believe that government thinking has to change, too, if we expect to maintain the proper balance of interests in this country. And that means that some of us, no matter how reluctant we may be, have to do our bit.'

Archer clasped his fingers across his chest and squinted at the lawyer seated in front of him. 'Just how far do you intend to go with your bit, may I ask?'

For a moment, Robert allowed himself to look slightly surprised at the question. Then he grinned.

'Why, all the way to the White House, of course,' he replied.

Their engagement was announced the following week, and three months to the day after Elizabeth's graduation from Vassar, she and Robert were married at St. John's Cathedral, and then feted at a lavish reception for twelve hundred at the Denver Country Club, which the *Post* later described as one of the major social events of the decade.

The new Mr. and Mrs. Willmont honeymooned in

the south of France, at a villa that belonged to one of Elizabeth's French cousins. They spent some of their time swimming in the Mediterranean and browsing around the quaint little towns along the Côte d'Azur, but most of their time was spent between the sheets of the huge wrought-iron bed provided for their pleasure. The staff at the villa was kept busy changing the sheets several times each day.

Elizabeth delighted in every moment of it. Right from the start, Robert was able to generate such a feverish level of desire in her that their mutual climaxes left her laughing and crying and begging for more – far more than even her forthright French mother had led her to expect. She was prepared for an adjustment period, a time during which they would learn each other's bodies and each other's likes and dislikes, but there seemed to be no need for that. Somehow, he knew exactly how to please her.

'Now that you've had a chance to sample the goods, so to speak,' Elizabeth teased her husband one morning, 'I hope I was worth putting up with all that horrid chaperoning.'

But he only grunted and reached for her again. Robert was insatiable when it came to sex, openly fondling her at a restaurant, murmuring seductive suggestions in the middle of a concert, whisking her away from a cocktail party given in their honor by some distant relatives. He thought nothing of cutting short any activity in which they were engaged the moment the urge overcame him.

Elizabeth never objected. On the contrary, she found herself as eager as he. But Robert was a big man who could be somewhat rough in the throes of passion and she was unprepared for the intensity of it all. It wasn't long before she was black and blue on the outside and more than a little tender on the inside.

'Sweetheart, do you think we could maybe not do it for a day or so?' she asked one afternoon when Robert attempted to cut short a shopping expedition to Saint-Tropez.

'What do you mean?' he replied.

'Well, as you have reason to know, I'm not exactly used to all this ... activity' – she giggled timidly – 'and I guess I must be extra-sensitive inside because, well, it's really kind of painful now, everytime we ... well, you know.'

'Shit,' her husband exploded. 'We're on our honeymoon, for Christ's sake. And what the fuck is it that people are supposed to do on their honeymoon?'

'I'm sure it'll be all right again in a day or two,' she protested, wincing at his outburst.

He stamped his foot petulantly. 'And to think I got married just so I could have it whenever I wanted it.'

'Well, I certainly hope that wasn't the only reason,' she replied with a toss of her red hair.

'All those months I waited for you,' he grumbled. 'I never had to wait that long for anyone, but I waited for you. Now we're hardly married a week and already you're pulling the old headache routine.'

'It's not a headache and it's not forever,' she said. 'And the sooner we stop, the sooner we can start again.' She batted her eyelashes at him. 'In the meantime, maybe there's something I can do to make up for it.'

Robert looked at her in surprise. 'Now you're talking,' he said, taking her firmly by the arm. 'Let's go. I can't wait to see what you have in mind.'

What she had in mind – dinner on the terrace, a

bottle of champagne, a long leisurely bath and a back rub – didn't turn out to be exactly what he had in mind.

'That sounds awful,' she protested when he described what he wanted to do.

'I don't see how you can dismiss something until you try it,' he replied, nuzzling her. 'Most of the women I know really get off on it.'

Most of the women in Robert's circle were no doubt chic and sophisticated and older, and despite the fact that he had chosen her over the rest, Elizabeth didn't particularly care to come out on the wrong side of a comparison.

'All right,' she said with a reluctant sigh. After all, he was her husband now and anything between married people was supposed to be acceptable. Besides, she had promised to obey.

Elizabeth had to admit that what he proceeded to do to her was rather thrilling and she achieved three orgasms in rapid succession and was beginning to think she might agree with all those other women of his when he rolled over onto his back and pulled her down on top of him. The ecstasy quickly turned to revulsion.

'I don't know how to do it,' she mumbled, hoping he would suggest an alternative.

Instead, he gave her explicit instructions and held her head firmly so she couldn't pull away.

'I didn't hear you complaining when I brought you off three times,' he reminded her. 'Now let's see what you can do for me.'

Gagging and sputtering, she managed to make the best of it, but the experience was so distasteful to her that the very next morning she slipped down into town and bought some salve.

'That's too bad,' he murmured when she grit her teeth and told him she was no longer sore. 'I rather like it the other way.'

They came home after a month to the house on Jackson Street where Robert had been born. Amanda Willmont insisted that it was much too big a place for her now that she was alone.

'I rattle around in here and there's just no point to it,' she said. 'I want you and Elizabeth to have the house, and I can take a small apartment nearby.'

But Robert wouldn't hear of it.

'This house has been your home for more than thirty years,' he insisted, 'and no one's going to put you out of it. I think we should all live here together.'

'Don't you think you ought to consult with Elizabeth before you make a decision like that?' Amanda asked, trying not to look too pleased.

'Elizabeth will do what I say,' he replied. 'Besides, she's an old-fashioned girl and family means a lot to her. She'll love the idea.'

Elizabeth hated the idea.

'It's not that I'm not fond of your mother,' she said. 'It's just that I'd like us to have a place of our own.'

'But it'll be almost like having that,' he assured her. 'She's an old lady and she rarely comes out of her room. Besides, it really is a terrific house and I wouldn't be able to afford to give you anything nearly so grand.'

'I don't mind starting small,' his new wife replied.

'Well, sure,' he agreed with an irritable sigh. 'I wouldn't either, if we didn't have a choice. But we do, so why don't we take advantage of it?'

'I know I'm being foolish,' Elizabeth said stubbornly. 'But I think couples should be on their own when they get married.'

'Well, I wouldn't want this to be part of our decision,' he said, changing tactics, 'but the truth is, I'm worried about Mother. She's not well and she's getting weaker all the time. I don't think she's going to last much longer and I don't want her to be alone. I just wouldn't feel right if we were off having a grand time on our own and something awful happened to her and I wasn't there. I'm her only child, you know. I'm all she has in the world.'

Elizabeth's green eyes filled with sympathy and she covered his hand with her own.

'Of course you are,' she cried. 'And forgive me for being so selfish. I didn't realize she was that bad off. You certainly can't leave her alone, I understand that now, and I love you for being such a devoted son. Of course we'll move in with her. The most important thing is to help make her last days happy ones.'

Robert beamed. 'You'll see,' he promised. 'Everything is going to work out just fine.'

Within a month of taking up residence at her new home on the crown of Pacific Heights, Elizabeth learned two things. The first was that San Francisco was nothing at all like Denver. The second was that Amanda Drayton Willmont would probably outlive them all.

The city had taken a bit of getting used to. For someone who had grown up with crunchy white winters, rain was a poor substitute. For someone used to towering mountains, the endless stretch of the Pacific Ocean was disconcerting. For someone raised on the flat Denver plateau, the peaks and valleys of San Francisco's streets were a shock.

Once she had married a Drayton, her place in the city's inner social circle was ensured – but not her popularity. That she had to earn on her own. She was asked to join all the right clubs, serve on all the right committees, and sponsor all the right causes. It was an endless round of luncheons and parties and fund-raisers that left her head spinning and her calendar filled.

She said yes to everything, because she didn't realize she could have said no. Very soon, the Jackson Street parlor had been transformed into the principal gathering place for the 'planners of good deeds,' as Robert jokingly referred to them, and San Francisco's social matrons bustled in and out from morning to midnight.

Amanda was furious.

'Turning my house into a meeting hall,' she fussed on more than one occasion. 'That wasn't what I had in mind when I invited you to come and stay.'

'I'm very sorry they disturb you,' her daughter-in-law replied, biting her tongue. 'But the causes are so worthy.'

Perhaps because she was so young and so eager to please, Elizabeth soon became the darling of the elite crowd and, with her wild hair and classic beauty, the darling of the media, as well. Newspaper photographers fell all over themselves to capture her on film. Television cameras seemed to pick her out of a crowd. Although she rarely had anything earthshaking to say, reporters sought her out for comments on everything from haute couture to Haight-Ashbury.

She had inherited her mother's elegant Parisian style which, together with her father's generous allowance and her own boundless energy for shopping, resulted in an exquisite wardrobe that provided her with the perfect outfit for every occasion.

'Does your daddy own the majority stock in Magnin's?' Robert roared when he saw the bills.

'It's my money,' she reminded him. 'And I should think you would want me to look my best.'

'You're a Drayton now,' he snapped, 'and Draytons do not go around flaunting their wealth.'

Elizabeth smiled at him sweetly. 'The only thing I'm trying to flaunt is that I'm the wife of a very successful attorney who will one day be President of the United States. But if you think that's the wrong image, I'll gladly donate all my clothes to the charity of your choice and wear sackcloth to your firm's Christmas party next week.'

'Isn't there a compromise here somewhere?' he grumbled.

Always the politician, she thought with amusement. 'Sure,' she replied, looking pointedly at his six-hundred-dollar suit. '*You* can wear the sackcloth.'

Robert never mentioned her wardrobe again and Elizabeth continued to set fashion standards among her peers in the cosmopolitan city by the bay. Matrons of means tried to emulate her, less affluent ladies envied her, bachelors and husbands alike attempted, without success, to compromise her.

By the end of her first year as Mrs. Robert Drayton Willmont of Pacific Heights, Elizabeth Avery was a social triumph. She was one of the first to don a miniskirt, one of the last to abandon hats, one of the few to forgo the perils of platform shoes, and she stopped conversation dead when she wore a black satin pantsuit to the opening of the opera.

Early in their second year of marriage, Elizabeth

became pregnant, but lost the child in the tenth week. She was devastated, even though her doctors assured her that such occurrences were not uncommon and it in no way meant she couldn't have children in the future.

By the end of the summer, she had conceived for the second time. Fearful of another tragedy, Elizabeth cut her social obligations to a minimum and spent much of her time in bed. Her efforts were in vain. She miscarried again, this time during her fifth month, and along with the fetus she almost lost her life.

The doctors no longer made light of the situation. They suggested that it would be unwise for Elizabeth to risk a third pregnancy for at least a year. They recommended a long rest, perhaps even a change of scene. They advised the young couple to cease all sexual intercourse for at least three months and thereafter to exercise extreme caution.

If she had expected an explosion from her husband, she was surprised. He accepted the warning in stony silence.

'We can do that other thing you like so much,' she offered, because she felt so guilty.

'Sure,' he replied carelessly.

But she noticed that he began to stay up later at night, frequently not coming to bed until she was already asleep. Several times, when she went looking for him, she found him in the library, snoring over a briefcase full of work and a half-empty bottle of Scotch.

A despondent Elizabeth went home to Denver. Her mother and father and three brothers welcomed her back with loving concern and fussed over her as though she were a visiting head of state.

It was marvelous to be back in Denver, but she missed Robert more than she had ever believed possible, and cut her visit short after only three weeks. She returned home to find that he had moved into an adjoining bedroom.

'I just won't be able to sleep next to you and not want to – well, you know,' he said in explanation.

'I understand,' she said, although she didn't, not really.

'So I thought, until the doctors say it's okay again, this would be easier for both of us.'

The weeks slipped into months, the months moved toward a year. Once the doctors gave their permission, the Willmonts began to practice careful sex but Robert continued to sleep in the adjoining room. As time passed, husband and wife settled into a routine. Robert would stay with Elizabeth on Saturday nights, during which they would rekindle some of the hot flames of their honeymoon, and then they would share a long, leisurely breakfast in bed together on Sunday mornings.

But always, in the back of her mind, Elizabeth thought of it as temporary, and she lived for the day when the doctors would tell her it was all right to try again to have a child.

Shortly after Robert had informed Archer Avery of his intention to enter politics, he and Elizabeth had mapped out a strategy. The key, Robert told her, was to start small and build rapidly. He was sure that he could use his Drayton connections to capture a local election, and once he had proved himself a winner, he reasoned, the party bosses would fall all over themselves to promote him – all the way to the White House.

But first, Robert had to become a partner at Sutton, Wells, Willmont and Spaulding. This was essential, he explained, in establishing his credibility. Moreover, to maintain his timetable, he had to do it by the time he was thirty-two.

To keep the odds in his favor, he told Elizabeth upon her return from Denver, it would be necessary for him to maintain a higher visibility in the firm.

'For the past few years,' he said, 'I've been much more interested in my bride than in my business.'

Higher visibility, according to Robert, meant assuming a heavier workload that would involve stretching the limits of his specialization, accepting some of the cases that no one else wanted, and generally calling attention to himself through a clever combination of diligence and excellence.

'And the only way I'm going to be able to do that,' he said, 'is to work longer hours.'

'I hope you're not talking about weekends,' Elizabeth exclaimed. 'We can't possibly renege on any of our social obligations. Why, the telephone's been ringing off the hook ever since I got back, and now there's hardly a weekend right through Labor Day that we're not already committed.'

'Well, if weekends are out,' Robert said with a sigh of resignation, 'then I have no choice but to work late during the week.'

'How late?'

'That's hard to say,' he replied smoothly. 'Why don't we just play it by ear.'

Soon, Robert was staying on at the office one or two nights a week, sometimes not getting home until three o'clock in the morning. Occasionally, when Elizabeth awoke and went looking for him, she would find him sound asleep in his room with all his clothes still on.

'I worry about him,' she admitted to Amanda during one of the increasingly frequent occasions when the two women dined alone together. 'He's going to wear himself out. I'm not sure that becoming a partner one year sooner or later is worth ruining his health.'

But Amanda only shrugged. 'Men must do what men must do,' she said vaguely, leaving Elizabeth more confused than reassured.

'You're not getting enough sleep,' she said to Robert when six months had passed. 'If you keep up this kind of pace, you're going to make yourself sick. I think you ought to ease up a little.'

'I've never felt better,' he assured her. 'Besides, how do you think it would look to the partners if I were to tell them that my wife didn't think I was up to the job?'

'That's not what I said,' she protested.

'What if I did slack off?' he posed. 'You can bet the competition won't, and I can't afford to get left behind.' He winked at her. 'After all, I'm already thirty-one.'

'You know you're going to make partner someday. Does it really matter all that much when?'

'It matters to me,' he said flatly. 'And I thought it mattered to you, too.'

'You matter to me.'

'Then why don't you want me to have what I want?'

'I do want you to have it,' she protested. 'It's just that … I miss you.'

'I miss you, too,' he assured her. 'But we made a plan and we have to stick to it if we want to get where we're going. I intend for you to be the first First Lady of the twenty-first century. And, if accomplishing that means we have to make a few minor sacrifices now, I say it's worth it.'

'When you put it that way,' she conceded reluctantly, not bothering to tell him that being the First Lady was not really one of her greatest ambitions.

But then, for a month, he didn't work late at all.

'Things are a little slow right now,' he explained.

He showed up promptly for dinner at seven o'clock and even sat with her well into the evenings, as he used to, but he was preoccupied much of the time and seemed out of sorts.

Soon enough, the late hours began again. Only, instead of one or two nights a week, it was now three and even four. There was always an excuse, always a promise that it wouldn't be forever, and always a reminder of their ultimate aim.

But Elizabeth was lonely. While her days were filled with one charitable endeavor or another, her evenings were long and empty. Her mother-in-law was little comfort. Amanda retired to her room immediately after dinner and did not encourage company. To relieve the boredom, Elizabeth took to going out for walks after dinner, wandering up and down the steep streets, pausing sometimes to look in the windows of her neighbors, at families who had gathered to share the end of the day together. But then her heart would begin to ache for her two lost babies and she would turn away, searching for something to help her forget the tragedy.

So it was that she came to accept an invitation for dinner and the ballet one Tuesday evening shortly after the Willmonts had celebrated their third wedding anniversary.

It was an innocent-enough occasion, arranged by Marian Pinckton, one of San Francisco's formidable matriarchs, who worked with Elizabeth on a number of committees and who needed a partner for her visiting nephew.

'I apologize for this being such a last-minute thing,' Marian explained. 'But the lady who was supposed to join us came down with influenza this morning and I've been just beside myself trying to think what to do. Then I remembered you saying something about Robert occasionally working late during the week, and I was hoping that tonight might possibly be one of those nights.'

'As it happens, it is, Marian,' Elizabeth replied, barely able to contain her delight. 'And as I have nothing on my calendar for this evening, I'd be happy to fill in for you.'

The nephew turned out to be a fastidious gentleman in his early forties, with sparse hair and an Adolf Hitler mustache, who sat up very straight and didn't have two words to say to anyone around the dinner table, despite Elizabeth's best efforts. From the corner of her eye, she watched him separate his salad into little piles of tomato and cucumber and lettuce and onion, and then proceed to eat each ingredient in its turn. After that, he cut his filet mignon into minuscule pieces and then dabbed his napkin at the corner of his mouth with each tiny bite. Elizabeth half-expected to see him take his fork and spear one green pea at a time, and she had to try very hard not to giggle.

Everyone at the table seemed to talk around him, even his aunt, as though they didn't know how to include him in the topic of conversation and had decided not to bother.

How lucky I am to have Robert, Elizabeth thought to herself, making one of the unfailingly favorable comparisons she had become so fond of making since her marriage. He was so handsome, so winsome, so charming that people couldn't help but warm to him, and he quickly became the center of any group he entered.

Elizabeth felt very sorry for all the women in the world who were still out there looking, especially if her dinner partner were an example of what was available. Mrs. Robert Drayton Willmont smiled a private little smile. She knew she could afford to be just a tiny bit smug, because she already had a lock on the best man in the whole world.

The nephew took Elizabeth's elbow as they crossed the busy intersection at Van Ness and Grove on their way to the Opera House.

'I find that drivers at intersections can be exceedingly unpredictable,' he said. It was the longest sentence he had uttered all evening.

The San Francisco Opera House was an imposing building, with ornately gilded ceilings and crystal chandeliers. Naturally, the Pinckton box was in the center of the dress circle. The nephew sat primly beside her, his legs crossed, his hands folded neatly in his lap, his attention focused on the maroon curtain that would soon rise, making not the slightest attempt at any of the social graces. Elizabeth sighed and began to read her program.

From the second row of chairs, Marian Pinckton leaned forward and laid a hand on Elizabeth's shoulder.

'Don't be offended that he isn't taken with your charms, my dear,' she whispered in her young protégée's ear. 'He's one of *them*, you know.'

Fortunately, the lights dimmed at that moment, sparing Elizabeth the necessity of a reply. If she had understood Marian correctly – and how could she not have – it was the first time she had knowingly been this close to a homosexual person before, and the idea both enthralled and appalled her.

Elizabeth stole a sidelong look at the man next to her, seeing him now in a whole new light. She had a thousand questions, none of which she would ever dare ask. There were some things, she had been taught, that a lady just didn't discuss. Not that his sexual orientation made any difference to her in relation to this evening. She would gladly have partnered King Kong if it meant one less night to spend at home alone.

The curtain went up and the ballet began and Elizabeth didn't think again about her escort until the first act was over and they filed out of the box for the intermission.

'Would you like champagne?' the nephew asked politely.

'Of course she would,' Marian answered for her guest. 'We all would.'

The nephew took Elizabeth's elbow again as the party of eight began to edge its way through the crowd toward the bar.

'I find that theatergoers at intermissions can be exceedingly unpredictable,' he said.

Elizabeth wasn't sure whether he had intended to be witty, but she burst out laughing – a delicious ripple that ran the length of the scale and back again. A nearby group glanced over in curiosity, among them a distinguished gray-haired gentleman.

'Elizabeth?' he inquired. 'Is that you?'

She turned at the mention of her name and looked up into the intelligent eyes of Stanton Wells, the managing partner of Robert's law firm.

'Hello, Stanton,' she said, offering her hand. 'How nice to see you.'

'How nice to see you, too,' Wells said and then glanced around. 'And where's that handsome husband of yours?'

Elizabeth chuckled. 'At the office, of course. You and your partners have him slaving away almost every night these days.'

'Really?' Wells asked in surprise. 'I wasn't aware of that. Well, I can see we'll have to do something to correct the situation.'

'No objection, your honor,' she quipped.

But Wells wasn't looking at her anymore, he was looking to her right. With some embarrassment, Elizabeth realized that the nephew still had hold of her elbow.

'I beg your pardon,' she said, hastily disengaging herself. 'May I introduce Mrs. Pinckton's nephew, who is visiting from Chicago.'

The two men shook hands stiffly.

'Are you enjoying the ballet, Stanton?' Elizabeth asked.

'Very much,' he replied. '*Giselle* has always been one of my favorites.'

'Mine, too,' Elizabeth agreed.

'We were on our way to get champagne,' the nephew said abruptly. 'Before the intermission is over.'

'By all means,' Wells murmured. Then he turned to Elizabeth. 'Enjoy the rest of your evening, my dear,' he said. 'And you can be sure I'll look into that little matter we discussed.'

While it was true that she would have preferred to have Robert at home with her in the evenings, Elizabeth was not the kind of woman to go behind her husband's back. She sat through the rest of the ballet wishing she had not been so flip with Stanton Wells. A complaining wife was not an attractive asset and the last thing she wanted was to damage Robert's chances of becoming a partner at the law firm.

She thought of seeking Stanton out at the end of the performance and asking him to forget their conversation, but she was afraid that would only make matters worse. It had been such a casual exchange, there was a chance he would forget all about it in the light of day. She fervently hoped so, but a nagging feeling told her that he wouldn't and that her flippant words would come back to haunt her.

She was right. The repercussions were almost immediate. Robert stormed into the house the next evening, well before the seven-o'clock dinner hour, the earliest he had been home on a weeknight in months.

'Just what the hell did you think you were doing?' he roared. 'Complaining to Wells about my hours and parading yourself around town on someone else's arm?'

'I wasn't parading myself,' she protested. 'I was doing Marian Pinckton a favor. And Stanton asked me where you were. What should I have said? Would it have been better if I'd told him a lie?'

'If you'd been at home where you belong,' he snapped, 'you wouldn't have had to tell him anything.'

'But it gets so tiresome being alone all week long.'

'Alone? You're not alone. My mother's here, and

you've got a houseful of servants at your beck and call.'

There was no point in telling him that Amanda was less than social, or that a servant turning down her bed or bringing her a glass of warm milk did not constitute company for an evening.

'I don't know why you're making such a fuss,' she said. 'What's wrong with Stanton knowing that you're in the office working? Isn't that what you wanted?'

'Forget about that,' he retorted. 'What's wrong is when one of my partners has to come and tell me that my wife is out cavorting with another man.'

'Stanton Wells didn't say anything of the kind,' she declared. 'And I wasn't cavorting.'

'Then why did this guy have his hands all over you?'

'He had his hand on my elbow, for pity's sake. He was guiding me through the crowd.'

'I don't want any man putting his hands anywhere on you for any reason. I refuse to be humiliated by gossips wagging their tongues behind my back. Besides, you know perfectly well if you give a man a hand, he'll try to take an arm.'

A vision of the nephew behaving as Robert suggested suddenly popped into Elizabeth's head and she began to laugh.

'I don't see anything funny about this,' he growled.

'You would, if you knew,' she gasped.

'Knew what?'

'The other man you're so concerned about – well, he's Marian Pinckton's nephew, on his obligatory annual visit. He separates his salad and he cuts his meat into pieces the size of a crouton – and he's a homosexual.'

'You're kidding,' Robert scoffed.

'Honest Injun,' she assured him.

'How do you know?'

'Marian told me herself.'

'Well, I'll be damned.'

'I tried to wait up for you last night. I wanted to tell you all about it, but I fell asleep. Too much wine, I guess.'

'Nevertheless,' he said, somewhat mollified, 'it doesn't look right for you to go out without me like that. After all, you're my wife, and as such you have your reputation to protect, not to mention the Drayton name. I feel I must insist that you don't do it again.'

Elizabeth sighed heavily. She supposed there might be some truth in what he said. 'I'm sorry if I disappointed you,' she said. 'I won't do it again.'

'Do I have your promise?'

'You have my promise.'

'There's my good girl,' he said, kissing her lightly on the cheek. 'Besides, you're always so busy with all your charity work, I should think a few quiet evenings at home would be good for you.'

'Yes, Robert.'

Elizabeth had been as good as her word, thereafter politely declining all invitations that did not include her husband and even curtailing her nocturnal walks. She had a television set installed in her sitting room and spent the better part of her evenings involved in the triumphs and tragedies of the Partridge Family, who were always able to sing their way out of trouble, or Marcus Welby, who reminded Elizabeth of her family doctor back in Denver, or Ironside, who solved his San Francisco cases from a wheelchair.

* * *

It was eerie, she thought as she left Post Street for the interior of Gump's Department Store, but in some ways the fictional characters that now kept her company had become more compelling than many of the real people she knew.

Except for the girl in the red coat, that is – the one who had been following her all afternoon. She was certainly compelling enough. Elizabeth glanced over her shoulder, and like the proverbial itch she couldn't scratch, the girl was still there.

Gump's of San Francisco was a store unlike any other on earth. A playground for the rich, it boasted an eclectic collection of trinkets from every corner of the world and came within an inch of being a museum – a museum where the entire collection just happened to be for sale. Elizabeth often thought how much fun it would be to work for a while as a Gump's buyer.

She had nothing particular in mind to purchase on this day, but she walked purposefully to the stairs and started up. It was the red coat that finally got to her. Not so much that it was ridiculously out of season as that it was a color she dearly loved but could never wear because of her hair.

The furniture galleries on the third floor were not usually very busy, but there must have been a sale in progress this day. Elizabeth passed quickly through room after room until she finally found one, featuring an elegant dining suite, that was out of the way and empty. Then she stopped and whirled around, catching the girl completely off-guard.

'If there's something you want to say to me, please go ahead and say it,' she suggested kindly enough. 'We're alone here.'

'You're his wife, aren't you?' the girl said, after

taking a moment to recover her composure.

'I beg your pardon?'

'I said, you're Bobby's wife.'

Elizabeth winced. She detested the nickname that Amanda had bestowed upon her son during his infancy, and she had always refused to use it herself. How disconcerting it was now to hear it come rolling off the tongue of this unlikely stranger.

'If you mean Robert Willmont,' she said, 'yes, I'm his wife.'

'I know,' the girl confirmed. 'I've seen your picture in the paper lots of times, and Bobby would kill me if he knew but sometimes I take myself up to Pacific Heights and watch you coming and going.'

Up close, it was clear that the girl was younger than Elizabeth had first thought, probably not even out of her teens, and if it weren't for the blotches and the unkempt hair, she would have been quite pretty.

'You called my husband Bobby,' she said. 'Does that mean you know him well?'

The girl snorted. 'You could say that. Three or four nights a week for almost eight months now.'

Elizabeth felt as though someone had punched her in the stomach.

'Why would you say a thing like that?' she asked with difficulty.

'Because it's true,' the girl declared.

What Elizabeth wanted was to spit in the girl's face, scratch her eyes out, scream obscenities at her. Only, of course, she couldn't do any of those things.

'What do you want?' she asked rigidly.

'I want you to let him go.'

Try as she might, Elizabeth was unable to conceal her dismay. 'Are you talking about divorce?'

The girl nodded eagerly.

'But that's absurd.'

'Why?' the girl demanded. 'What's the point of holding on, now that you know?'

'I'm afraid I don't know anything,' Elizabeth corrected her.

The girl sighed. 'Bobby said you wouldn't understand. He said you'd fight the divorce. He said you don't care anything about his happiness, you just married him because he's a Drayton. I know you don't sleep in the same room together anymore, and you can't even give him children.'

It was like a knife thrust into Elizabeth's heart.

'My husband told you all that?'

'Sure,' the girl replied easily. 'Bobby tells me everything. Sometimes, that's all we do – just talk, for hours and hours. You see, we love each other.'

'He said that?' Elizabeth murmured.

'I know he wanted to tell you himself,' the girl assured her, 'but sometimes men are so slow about things. So I thought if I explained it to you – you know, woman to woman, then you'd see that we were really sincere and that it wasn't just some casual fling. Please, you'll let him go now, won't you – now that you see how it is? We're just meant to be together. I may not be so smart or so beautiful as you, but I guess I know how to make him happy better than you, and I can give him all the children he wants.'

With that, the girl opened her coat to reveal a swollen belly.

The knife twisted agonizingly. 'Are you saying that's my husband's child?'

'Well, of course,' the girl said. 'What'd you think?'

But Elizabeth didn't know what to think. Of all the

demons that had populated her worst nightmares, the demon of duplicity had never been among them. Was it possible that for these three and a half years she had been married to a man she didn't even know?

She looked back on all those evenings she had sat alone, waiting for Robert to come home from work. She remembered how sweet and sympathetic he had been after the miscarriages. She considered how much their Saturday nights and Sunday mornings meant to her. She thought about all their plans for the future. None of it made sense. She wondered if someone were playing a very cruel joke on her, but she couldn't imagine that anyone would hate her that much.

'Did my husband send you to speak to me?'

'Gosh, no!' the girl exclaimed. 'Jeepers, he'd split my lip or worse if he knew I was here.' Seeing Elizabeth's startled look, she shrugged. 'He did that once, when I made him mad. Sometimes, he hits me around when he's had too much to drink. Some men are like that, I guess, but I don't care, because he always comes back. I don't have anyone else.'

Elizabeth stared at the girl, overwhelmed with elation, because she now knew for certain that this was nothing but a horrible mistake.

'Now I know there's been a misunderstanding.' She breathed in relief. 'You see, my husband doesn't drink at all the way you describe. More important than that, he's a gentleman. He would never lay a hand on a woman. So it's obvious you must be talking about someone else.'

The girl reached up and pushed the hair back off her face, revealing a jagged scar down her cheek.

'It took eleven stitches,' she said, 'because he hit me

with the back of his right hand, the one he wears that big Harvard ring on.'

The elation, all too fragile, collapsed like a balloon. Elizabeth felt her knees beginning to buckle and then the room started to spin, and she reached out and grabbed hold of the back of a chair to steady herself.

She tried to think what she could possibly say next, but everything was so jumbled up in her brain that the only thing that came to mind was the hope that this whole confrontation wasn't real, after all, just a horrible scene from one of her television shows, and Marcus Welby was waiting in the wings with a miraculous cure.

Archer Avery had never taken a serious look at anyone other than Elizabeth's vivacious French mother in their entire thirty years together, and it was that kind of loyalty and devotion that Elizabeth had been raised to expect from her own marriage, which now made Robert's betrayal just that much harder to bear.

She wanted to hate the girl as she stood there, blooming with life. She wanted to make her the villain of the piece and blame her for everything. But for some reason, Elizabeth found herself feeling sorry for her instead. Perhaps it was because the girl was so young and vulnerable and because, sooner or later, Elizabeth realized dully, Robert was going to betray her, too.

'I hope you have a healthy baby,' she said in a toneless voice, and then she turned and walked away.

The girl stood stock-still, confusion and uncertainty written all over her face. She knew the interview was over, but she had not gotten what she had come for and time was running short.

Over the past eight months, Bobby had painted a very vivid picture of his wife, describing her as aloof and unemotional and far more interested in embellishing her wardrobe than in pleasing her husband. He claimed that she had lost all interest in sex once the doctors told her she couldn't get pregnant, and that she even went so far as to turn him out of her bedroom without a second thought. He confessed that it was her continuing coldness that forced him, in desperation, to look elsewhere for fulfillment.

But the woman who had faced her here today had been anything but cold. In fact, although the girl had prepared herself for icy indifference and brittle rejection, Elizabeth Willmont, had, under the circumstances, been kind and even compassionate. Still, Bobby insisted that the marriage was a sham, and the only thing the girl cared about was making sure that her baby had a name and a father. After all, however he had been conceived, this child was a Drayton and deserving of his birthright.

She wrapped her coat tightly about her and made her way out of Gump's. If she hurried, she would get home in time to have dinner on the table when Bobby arrived. That and a bottle of wine would put him in a good mood, and one of her special back rubs would make him amorous, and she would do that thing she knew he liked best.

Then they would talk.

two

Elizabeth scrambled out of the taxi that brought her home to Jackson Street and hurried inside. She brushed past Preston, the butler, who was waiting with her mail and her messages, and went directly upstairs to her room, avoiding Amanda, declining dinner, refusing to take telephone calls.

She couldn't bear the thought of having to speak to anyone, and she couldn't wait to get her clothes off. Her fingers clawed at the buttons and yanked at the zippers and ripped at the hooks in her haste. Her teeth were chattering, she was shivering all over and she felt so horribly dirty and defiled. But when her clothes lay in tatters at feet, she realized that simply undressing wasn't enough, so she ran a hot bath and scrubbed at herself with a stiff brush until her skin was as red as her hair.

Then she put on a fresh nightgown and crawled into bed, pulling the crisp clean sheets right up to her chin

– sheets that Robert hadn't yet had a chance to sully. The steaming bath had soothed her only momentarily. As reality slowly crowded in, the shivering resumed, her head began to throb, and it became increasingly painful for her to breathe. She felt like crying but her eyes remained dry.

Outside her windows, daylight was fading. Elizabeth lay in the half-dark and listened to the sounds of the house. A closing door, a creaking floorboard, a muffled voice – proof of life going on around her. She had never really cared much for this house of her husband's, but now she found a peculiar comfort in its endurance.

Sometime around eight o'clock, she rang for a pot of tea and some aspirin and waved aside the concerned inquiries of the maid who brought up the tray. She quickly washed down two of the aspirin with the hot liquid and then, on second thought, another two. But she knew she would need something much stronger than Bayer to get her through this crisis.

Despite her cosseted upbringing, Archer and Denise Avery's daughter was a realist. She understood that there were things to be done and decisions to be made, but not tonight, not when her emotions were so hopelessly muddled. Tomorrow would be time enough to sort it all out. Elizabeth shut her eyes and prayed for the numbing, healing, dreamless sleep that could always make intolerable burdens seem lighter in the morning.

It was not quite ten o'clock when she heard Robert come in. It was the earliest he had arrived home on a Tuesday night in six months. He slammed the front door and barked something at one of the servants, and then he was charging up the stairs and down the hallway.

Elizabeth sighed deeply and reached over to snap on her bedside lamp. She had hoped that he would spend the entire evening out so she would not have to face him so soon. But in a matter of seconds he would be at her door and that meant she had to decide right now how she was going to treat his treachery.

She examined her options. While it would certainly be cathartic to lash out with the full force of her outrage, it might perhaps be more prudent to hide the hurt and preserve what was left of her dignity. She didn't want to give him the satisfaction of knowing how devastated she was, but neither did she wish to leave him with even the slightest impression that she condoned any part of his behavior. Above all, she had to steel herself against any attempt he might make to sweet-talk her into forgiveness. She was still weighing her options when he entered the bedroom.

'Preston said you weren't feeling well,' he said with genuine concern in his voice.

The shivers had subsided beneath the covers and the aspirin had eased the throbbing, but the pain inside was as sharp as ever.

'It's just a headache,' she answered.

He came close and bent down to kiss her, but at the last moment she turned to plump her pillow and his lips brushed her ear. His hair was mussed, his face was flushed, and his clothes were all askew as though they had been put on in a hurry. A spot of red wine marred the front of his shirt. Elizabeth felt her stomach grind.

'Is there something I can do for you?' he asked. 'Rub your head, perhaps?'

Elizabeth could think of a number of succinct

responses to that particular question, but none of them were appropriate for a young lady of her upbringing.

'No, there's nothing you can do,' she replied in a flat voice. 'Nothing at all.'

Robert shifted from one foot to the other. Despite her anguish, Elizabeth had to suppress a smile. She could not recall ever having seen him quite so ill at ease before, and she took a perverse pleasure in that.

'Okay, I think I know what this is about,' he said with a harsh chuckle, realizing this was not a matter that she was going to shrug off. 'But believe me, the whole thing is utter nonsense.'

'There's a spot of wine on your shirt.'

Robert glanced hastily down at his front. 'I didn't notice,' he said. 'It must have happened at lunch.'

'No,' she reminded him. 'We didn't have red wine with lunch.'

'Look, I don't know what she told you,' he blurted, 'but I think you owe it to me to hear the truth.'

Elizabeth's eyes widened slightly. 'The truth?' she echoed. 'Do you mean the girl lied to me?'

'Of course she lied to you,' he asserted. 'All women like that lie.'

'By "like that," do you mean young, vulnerable – or pregnant?'

'Desperate,' he corrected. 'So desperate she'd make up just about any story.'

'Did she make up the pregnancy?'

'So she's pregnant,' he said harshly. 'What does that prove? It doesn't prove I had anything to do with it. All I did was be nice to her a couple of times. She worked in the building and I'd see her in the elevator. So maybe I said she looked good once or twice. Maybe I bought her a drink one night, I don't remember, and now she's in trouble and she sees "meal ticket" written across my forehead.'

'It's late and I'm very tired,' Elizabeth said.

'Look, it's blackmail, I tell you,' he insisted. 'Plain and simple. She probably got knocked up by some nobody or other and grabbed at a chance to make it into the big time.'

'Just picked you out of the elevator, did she?'

'More likely the social register.'

Elizabeth gave her husband a loathsome look. 'She knows about my miscarriages, she knows we don't sleep in the same bedroom, she calls you *Bobby*, for God's sake – and all you did was buy her a drink?'

Robert glared at his wife, wondering why she couldn't be as dim and manageable as his mother. Then, with an exaggerated shrug, he tried a new tack.

'So maybe I saw her a few times. Maybe I told her my troubles. Do you think you're the only one who has troubles? Those were *my* babies you lost, too, you know, but did I ever get any sympathy? No, everyone was always hovering around *you*, consoling *you*, comforting *you*, being strong for *you*. "Poor Elizabeth." "How tragic for Elizabeth." Well, maybe I needed someone to comfort me, and had to find it where I could. But that doesn't mean I slept with her.'

'And the moon is made of green cheese and there really is a tooth fairy,' his wife snapped. 'What if that girl is carrying the only child you'll ever have in this life? Think about that and then ask yourself if you really want to be so cavalier about it.'

Robert sank down on the end of the bed with a groan, because that was the very thought that had been torturing him for months, ever since the girl, grinning with unabashed pride and devotion, had told him the news.

'Okay, so I made a mistake,' he admitted, his head in his hands, his fingers sunk into the thick dark hair that curled fashionably around his ears. 'I'm human. But you know me, you know my … appetites, and I was afraid to touch you, afraid if you got pregnant again too soon, I might lose you, like I almost lost you the last time. So I took up with someone who didn't matter, someone I could use and forget. I never intended it to be anything more than that.'

'Well, it is now,' Elizabeth reminded him.

'Yes, I guess it is,' he sighed.

'All those nights,' she said bitterly. 'All those nights that I sat home alone, while you were supposed to be working harder to advance sooner. I feel like such a fool.'

'You weren't supposed to find out.'

'And that would have made it all right?' Elizabeth shot back. 'What I didn't know couldn't hurt you?' She shook her head sadly. 'And to think I actually felt guilty for going to the ballet with Marian Pinckton's homosexual nephew.'

'That was different,' he protested. 'You were out in public. Whatever I did, I was discreet about it.'

She turned on him sharply. 'You bastard – do you really think you can compare the two?'

'I told you it didn't mean anything.'

Elizabeth glared at him. 'She followed me around all afternoon, in and out of every store on Union Square, to beg me to let you go so you two could live happily ever after.'

'Whatever she may have told you,' he declared, 'I never once said I'd marry her.'

'Whether you did or didn't doesn't seem very important now. In any case, I wouldn't dream of standing in the way.'

Robert looked up sharply. 'What are you talking about?'

'I'm talking about a divorce, of course.'

She had not intended to say that, but the moment the words were out in the open, she felt an enormous burden lift from her shoulders.

'Don't be ridiculous,' he snapped. 'There's never been a divorce in the Drayton family.'

If he had intended to intimidate her by his declaration, he had miscalculated.

'There's never been one in the Avery family, either,' she retorted, 'but that doesn't mean there never will be.'

'You mean you'd really be willing to give up everything we have because of some … some nobody from North Dakota?'

'Is that where she's from?'

He sprang off the bed. 'Who the devil cares where she's from?'

'I guess it's not important.'

'Then tell me you're not going to throw away our lives because of her.'

'If I decide to divorce you, it won't be because of the girl,' Elizabeth declared. 'It will be because I don't want to be married to you anymore.'

'Why not? You wanted to be married to me yesterday, and I'm the same person today that I was then.'

'You really don't understand, do you?' she charged. 'Yesterday I didn't know who you really were. Today I do, and I'm not at all sure I want to stay with someone I can't trust.'

'Well, that's a hell of a thing to say to me.'

Elizabeth shrugged. 'It was a hell of a thing you did to me.'

The starch seemed to melt right out of him.

'Please,' he implored, 'you're my wife. I love you. I picked you over a thousand others I could have married. I've never loved anyone but you and I never will. I need you. God, I never realized how much until this moment. You're my strength, my center. I'm nothing without you. Think of the future, think of all our plans to make this a better country. None of it would mean a damn to me if you weren't there to share it. If you leave me, I'm finished.'

Elizabeth stared at her husband in surprise. Of all the words spoken between them over the years, he had never come close to saying anything like this. There had even been a catch in his voice, and in the dim light of the lamp, she could see tears glistening in his magnificent black-fringed eyes. It was a vulnerable side of him that he had never shown before, and – she couldn't help it – her heart turned over.

'I never realized,' she whispered.

'It's hard for a man to admit he's not as confident as everyone expects him to be,' Robert said. 'It's like admitting he's scared.'

Elizabeth shook her head slowly, more confused than she had ever been in her life. She had been raised with simple values and a very clear understanding of right and wrong. Robert had betrayed her, that was certainly true, but she wondered if perhaps she did bear part of the blame. She had been so consumed with her own grief over the miscarriages that she had failed to consider his feelings. Not only had she accepted all the attention as her due, she had run off to Denver and abandoned him. Had she helped to push him into someone else's arms when he wasn't strong enough to resist?

The threat of divorce had been intended to hurt Robert as he had hurt her. But Elizabeth now realized that, regardless of the anguish he had caused her, she was still hopelessly in love with her husband, and try as she would, she could not conceive of spending the rest of her life without him. Despite her earlier determination, she felt the anger that had been coiled so tightly inside of her beginning to loosen.

'I suppose there might have been fault on both sides,' she conceded. 'Maybe I could have been more sensitive to your needs. But what you did ... I mean, there just isn't anything worse that could happen between a husband and wife.'

'If I could undo it, I would,' he cried, covering his face with his hands. 'I'd make it all go away.'

'It's a little late for that,' she observed.

'Please, give me another chance,' he urged. 'Give *us* another chance. I'll make it up to you, I promise. I'll do penance, I'll toe the line, whatever you want. I swear I'll never let you down again. Just give me one more chance.'

'Even if I would be willing,' Elizabeth sighed, 'there's still the other problem.'

'I'll take care of it,' he said flatly.

'You can't abandon her, Robert, if that's what you're thinking. She's your responsibility. Besides, we aren't just talking about her, we're also talking about a child – *your* child. There has to be some kind of acknowledgment, arrangements made, an understanding.'

'I said I'd take care of it.'

Elizabeth's eyes widened at a sudden thought. 'But it's even worse than that, isn't it? We'll never be able to keep this a secret. Sooner or later, it'll get out – this kind of thing always does. And then your political career will be ruined. I can't imagine this country electing a President with an illegitimate child.'

'Perhaps not,' Robert allowed.

Elizabeth brightened for a moment. 'I don't suppose she would let us adopt, let us give the child a name and a good home, and go back to North Dakota?' she wondered aloud. Then she shook her head. 'No … if it were me, I'd never give up my baby. I'd sooner die.'

'Don't worry,' Robert assured her. 'I'll handle it.' He leaned down and kissed her lightly on the forehead. 'You get some rest now,' he said gently. 'Just put it all out of your head and leave everything to me. There's a solution out there – it's just a matter of finding it.'

He snapped off the lamp and left the room with a self-satisfied smile that his wife missed. Women had been put on this earth to be manipulated, he knew. It was all in knowing the right approach.

Elizabeth snuggled under the covers. It had been a ghastly day, but now it was over. The crisis was past, the healing could begin. Robert would take care of the girl and the child somehow, and even if they never got to the White House, life would go on. In time, the whole episode would be nothing more than an unpleasant aftertaste. Her eyes closed and she slept.

A week later, the body of a young girl washed up on Baker Beach. An autopsy confirmed that she had drowned, and a coroner's inquest, finding no evidence to the contrary, ruled the death a suicide, citing the fact that she was pregnant and unmarried as the probable reason. No one came forth to claim her.

On the sixth of August, Robert was invited to join the partnership of Sutton, Wells, Willmont and Spaulding.

PART FIVE
1979

There is always one moment …
when the door opens and lets
the future in.

– Graham Greene

one

Autumn was a fleeting, frosty breath that swept across Manhattan Island, chasing off the last remnants of summer before vanishing into winter. Snow followed quickly on the heels of Thanksgiving, but didn't stick around for Christmas. Icy air was all that was on hand to welcome in the New Year.

Karen locked the front doors of Demion Five, double-checking to make sure they were secure before she crossed to the curb to hail a taxi.

Burglaries riddled this exclusive section of Madison Avenue, and shop owners had resorted to installing security barriers and sophisticated alarm systems. Pretty soon, she thought with a sigh, New York was going to resemble an armed fortress. In its two years of operation, Demion Five had been burgled three times. The first time, a week after the opening, vandals had destroyed half the inventory. When Karen arrived, she found priceless books soaked with water, canvases slashed, clothing shredded.

'Vindictive bastards,' Demelza exclaimed, surveying the devastation. 'They did this because there wasn't any money.'

'Why would anyone think we'd be stupid enough to leave money lying around?' Karen demanded.

The co-owner of the eclectic uptown establishment threw up her hands in disgust. 'Let's just call it another form of insurance we have to pay. From now on, we make sure that a hundred bucks stays in the register overnight.'

A cab pulled up to the curb to discharge a passenger and Karen grabbed it right out from under the noses of a timid Oriental couple. She pulled the door shut, gave the driver the address of her Sixty-third Street town house, and fell back against the seat. It was one of the less than chivalrous things New Yorkers did to get from one place to another, and doing it always made Karen feel a little mean inside.

The modest girl from the suburbs had been transformed into a cosmopolitan city-dweller. The long hair she had worn through much of the decade had been discarded in favor of a soft curly crop, Elizabeth Arden had taught her the artistry of makeup, and Saks Fifth Avenue had reshaped her style of dress. Slim suits and tailored blouses now occupied her closet. As the Washington Square Bookery once accommodated one kind of clothing, uptown now required quite another.

Demion Five was Ione's brainchild. The art history professor had conceived the idea primarily to help promote her husband's work, but it was also a unique concept in shopping. When her father died, leaving her a bit of money, she decided to act. The first thing she did was approach Demelza.

'I know art, but I don't know anything about running a business,' she confessed. 'I want to open a shop that's not like anything I've ever seen, with rare books and magazines like you have at the Bookery, but also with quality art and fashions and jewelry and things. I don't want a department store – I want this to be like an elegant home where the customers feel comfortable, as though they were calling on old friends. I see a setting with lots of sofas and chairs and carpets and morning coffee and afternoon tea.'

'I always thought the Bookery was like that homey part without the elegant,' Demelza observed.

'Exactly,' Ione agreed. 'I guess what I want to do is add a little something to your act, and take it uptown.'

Karen practically wriggled with excitement. 'I think it's a marvelous idea,' she cried. 'And of course this kind of thing has to be uptown. It would never fly down here.'

Demelza gazed thoughtfully past Ione's shoulder. For the past thirty years, she had intended to live and die in her beloved Greenwich Village, but times had changed. Starving artists were no longer in fashion, and 'bohemian' had become a derogatory term. The war in Vietnam was over and the country was trying to heal itself. Long hair and love beads were out, the Establishment was in. Different was tiresome, causes were boring. It was everyone for himself.

Thanks to Karen, the Washington Square Bookery was doing a brisk business dealing in titles that were unavailable anywhere else, but the customers were now largely citywide and the locals who used to drop by for tea and sympathy had grown fewer and farther between.

The Village was metamorphosing. Most of the innocents who wanted to change the world were gone, replaced by drug addicts and chronic malcontents. The coffeehouses, those bright spots of sawdust and magic where gentle visionaries sang their songs of protest, had become dark corners where sinister shadows dealt their deadly panaceas. Hope had become despair, protesters had become terrorists, love had become sex, music had become noise, 'us' had become 'me,' and the quaint little community was rapidly becoming passé.

So Demelza did the only reasonable thing – she went uptown. She sold the Bookery and added her money to Ione's. The two women knew exactly what they wanted. It took five months before they finally found the right rental on Madison Avenue, and after that, they never looked back.

The result was part gallery, part boutique, part café and part drawing room, concocted of velvet and lace and ribbon, rich woods and lemon oil. It was bright and spacious and cozy and charming and chic all at the same time.

Mitch's paintings adorned the walls as they would in any fine home. Jenna's fashions peeked out of armoires in the upstairs boudoir. Rare books and periodicals filled the shelves in the paneled library. Felicity's one-of-a-kind jewelry creations sparkled from a circular showcase in the foyer. And a selection of superb sculptures done by Jenna's live-in, John Micheloni, were judiciously placed throughout.

Armchairs and sofas that Demelza had procured and Jenna had recovered were scattered everywhere. Small tables and chairs graced the balcony, where coffee and tea and baked goods were served. And wafting into every corner were the gentle strains of Bach or Mozart.

Stepping through the front doors was like stepping into another time, a bit of Victoriana that they had managed to create in the middle of a city that couldn't seem to wait to tear down its past in favor of its future.

It was fresh and fun and trendy, and it caught on. A month after the shop opened, there was a small write-up in the *Times*. After that, people wanted to be seen at Demion Five. Slowly, Mitch's paintings began to sell. Several of Jenna's creations made their way to fashionable Manhattan events. A few of John's sculptures found niches in discriminating homes. And Felicity was accepting commissions that would keep her too busy to pine for Broadway. The partners of Demion Five and their little consortium were becoming successful and embarrassed.

'I've compromised every principle I ever had,' Mitch declared when he agreed to do a painting for Gracie Mansion, the mayor's residence. 'I took a wife, I quit drugs, I pay taxes, I wear suits, I grovel before idiots incapable of understanding my work, and worst of all, I'm getting rich.'

He and Ione had married shortly after the birth of their daughter Tanya. The Rankins still lived on Sullivan Street, because it was so near NYU where, along with tenure, Ione had an associate professorship. But they now owned the run-down tenement and were in the midst of a total renovation.

The rest of the family had moved on. Jenna and John shared a loft in Soho. As soon as the Vietnam war was over, Kevin Munker completed his bachelor's degree. Shortly thereafter, to everyone's amusement, he applied to graduate school and went off to Boston.

Felicity took a flat in Chelsea. Demelza traded Bleecker Street for West End Avenue. Ethan never came back.

'I never had any principles to compromise,' Felicity said with a sigh. 'But it is a little awkward having so much money.'

Jenna giggled. 'I opened a savings account. I think it was maybe the third time I've ever been inside a bank.'

'I made more money in 1978 than my daddy made in any ten years of his life on the docks,' said Demelza. 'I keep thinking there must be something immoral about that.'

The taxi slid up in front of the dun-colored house on Sixty-third Street, between Lexington and Third, which Karen had called home ever since she had become the assistant manager for Demion Five. Her parents had been so thrilled by her decision to move uptown that, although she no longer needed their assistance, they had underwritten the rent for two years.

Karen tipped the cab driver extravagantly, emptied her mailbox, and let herself into the first-floor apartment, turning on the lights and the stereo on her way to hang up her fur-lined coat. WQXR was featuring a Brahms symphony during this hour and the flowing melody suited her mood.

The apartment was a study in browns and whites. White walls, white window treatments, white area rugs, brown velvet sofas and chairs, warm wood accents, polished parquet floors, a few lithographs displayed here and there for a dash of color, and the soft glow of lamplight throughout.

There was a wonderful painting of Mitch's at

Demion Five, done in his inimitable serrated palette knife style, that would have been perfect over the fireplace. On the surface, it was a simple clearing in a wood, yet the longer one looked, the more complex it became, until the outwardly deserted space was seen to be inhabited by hundreds of creatures. It was a riveting canvas, but even with her acceptable salary, beyond her reach.

Karen dropped the mail on the entry table and clacked down the hall into the bedroom, where she kicked off her pumps, shrugged out of her navy gabardine suit and silk blouse, and slipped into fuzzy gray slippers and a shapeless robe. Padding into the kitchen, she tossed some ice cubes into a glass and poured herself a Scotch. Then she headed for the living room, pausing on the way to pick up her mail.

She was completely alone, to do whatever she wished whenever she wished. Even after five years, she hadn't quite gotten used to the idea. Part of her still listened for Arlene's key in the door. More than once she caught herself setting two places at the table. Then she chuckled because all that was behind her.

This place was hers alone. At least, the first floor of the town house was hers. There was a gay man in the basement apartment who taught English literature at Hunter College, and an elderly couple, German refugees who wore long sleeves to cover the tattooed numbers on their forearms, who lived upstairs. But each had their own space, as she had hers. And each had their own secrets, as she had hers.

Once the door was shut, Karen was surrounded by her own choice of furnishings. She knew exactly where things were, she could eat as she pleased, mess around with her thought pages without fear of prying eyes, watch the television programs she preferred, and she didn't have to see or talk to anyone unless she wanted to. There were even times when she would let the telephone ring unanswered.

'I called you last night, but you weren't home,' her mother would say on those occasions. 'Where were you?'

'Out to dinner,' Karen would reply glibly, because she knew her mother would prefer the lie to the truth.

'With anyone special?'

'Just friends.'

Beverly sighed. 'Not those peculiar people you're in business with?'

'Formerly peculiar,' Karen corrected her. 'Now they're all fine upstanding members of the Establishment.'

'I'm glad they're so successful,' her mother said with a sniff.

'But they're still not good enough,' Karen remarked. 'No doctors, no lawyers, not a dentist in the bunch – and none of them even came close to going to Harvard or Yale.'

'Well, really,' Beverly protested, 'you make me sound like such a snob. I thought, once you moved out of that degenerate neighborhood into a decent part of town, you'd be in a position to find more, shall we say ... suitable companionship. You're not getting any younger, you know.'

Karen had stayed on at West Twelfth Street after Arlene got her Ph.D., married her orthopedist and moved to Scarsdale, because it was familiar and convenient and close to her friends. She originally intended to find another roommate, if only to ease the financial burden on her father. But, as the months and then the years passed, she came to understand that she didn't really want anyone moving in on her. By the time she was ready to move uptown, it never occurred to her to seek a roommate.

It was her sister Laura who told her about the apartment on Sixty-third Street. An ex-roommate from Mount Holyoke and her husband were being transferred to Chicago. It was a real find and Karen should rush right over to see it. She did and it took her all of a minute and a half to make up her mind.

Now, as she sat on a brown love seat that faced its mate across a walnut coffee table and sorted through the mail, she wondered about the vagaries of life that could put one in the right place at the right time just as easily as they could put one in the wrong place at the wrong time.

Although she never spoke about that night, now almost half her life ago, the memory dogged her like a relentless shadow. The few men who were persistent enough to get her to agree to a date were soon put off by her aloofness and her insistence that they meet and part in very public places. She didn't mind. Somewhere along the way, she stopped mourning for the life she had lost and learned to live with the life she had, and quite happily spent her time with what she had come to think of as the Sullivan Street set.

Occasionally she saw Jill Hartman. Not unexpectedly, the Hartmans had divorced soon after Andy finished law school. Their daughter was now a delightful teenager.

A lot of things had changed since she and Jill had been girls together. Divorce, for one thing, which had been such an anathema a generation ago, was now an acceptable solution to marital problems. Legalized abortion had removed the necessity for shotgun weddings. And, perhaps most ironic of all, careers were now something that women were looking forward to rather than falling back on. Whereas, twenty years ago, girls had dreamed of marrying doctors and dentists and lawyers, today they dreamed of *being* doctors and dentists and lawyers.

'God,' Jill liked to say, 'were we ever raised in the Dark Ages.'

The Dark Ages, indeed, Karen thought now as she sipped her Scotch. Just the other week, she had read about a man who was actually on trial for raping a woman he had taken on a date. They even called it that – date rape. The prosecution argued that a woman who accepted a date with a man was not automatically agreeing to have sex with him, that she had the right to say no, and he was obliged to believe she meant it. The pendulum had swung. Karen didn't know whether to laugh or cry.

She turned resolutely to the mail, separating the thick stack into four piles: advertising circulars to be tossed away unopened, magazines to be read at a later time, bills to be paid on the tenth of the month, and, finally, the cards – more than two dozen of them, to be opened and read right now.

Today was February 8, 1979, and Karen was thirty-seven years old. Tomorrow, after work, she would make a trip out to Great Neck to be fussed over by her family. Laura had dutifully landed her lawyer and now had two adorable babies, whom Karen took enormous pleasure in spoiling. Winola would make one of her special double-chocolate birthday cakes and her mother would fudge the number of candles on top and no one would dare breathe a word about spinsters or maiden aunts or unmarried women.

But tonight was hers, to scrutinize herself in the bathroom mirror and pluck out the stray gray strands that had mistakenly wandered into her dark hair, open a can of soup instead of taking the time to prepare a proper dinner, contemplate the inexorable passing of time, and wonder how the next year of her life would differ from the last.

The Brahms symphony concluded and she was on her way to the kitchen for another Scotch when the intercom buzzed.

'It's Ione,' the art history teacher replied to Karen's query. 'Can I come in and talk?'

'Sure,' Karen replied.

'Mitch and I had a fight,' Ione groused, following Karen into the living room and dropping into the nearest chair. 'I had to get out of Eden for a while.'

Of all of them, Ione had changed the least. With her short blond hair, big gray eyes and tomboy body, she still looked more like a schoolgirl than a forty-five-year-old wife, mother, professor and business mogul.

'I'm having Scotch,' Karen offered.

'Make it a double,' said Ione.

When Karen returned with the drinks, Ione was gazing balefully at the stack of cards.

'It's your birthday,' she moaned. 'I forgot it was your birthday.'

'No you didn't,' Karen reminded her. 'You sent an adorable card.'

'I mean I forgot right now. You probably have big plans for tonight and I just barged right in.'

Karen shrugged. 'I didn't have anything important

on. Actually, I'm going out to my folks over the weekend and I was just planning to wash my hair tonight.'

'Well, the least I can do to make up for spoiling your evening is to take you out to dinner.'

'Nonsense,' Karen declared. 'I can whip up something right here and you can stay and share it with me.'

'I'm too restless to hang out,' Ione replied. 'I feel like kicking up my heels, going to an extravagant restaurant and raising a little hell. Come on, say you'll go with me.'

'Well, I don't know . . .' Karen began.

'Please,' Ione urged. 'I don't want to go alone.'

'Okay,' Karen gave in.

'Great!' Ione cried, pushing her in the direction of the bedroom. 'I'll give you ten minutes to get dressed. And you can choose the restaurant.'

Karen wore the only one of Jenna's originals she could afford to own, a flowing patchwork dress made of colorful bits of silk and velvet and brocade with a high lace collar, and chose the Sign of the Dove, a nearby French restaurant that featured the most charming garden room. It had been the group's favorite since they had come uptown.

It was eight o' clock when they arrived at the bright yellow building on Third Avenue. The restaurant was packed, there was a long line, and people were being turned away.

'I'm surprised,' Ione admitted. 'I didn't really think the place would be so crowded tonight.'

'I think it's crowded every night,' Karen told her with a disappointed sigh.

'Well, let's just see if they've got some little spot

they're overlooking,' Ione said encouragingly. 'You keep our place in line.'

Before Karen could stop her, Ione pushed her way to the front of the crowd and Karen saw her whisper a few words into the maître d's ear. The man smiled broadly and nodded. Ione turned and motioned Karen forward.

'What on earth did you say to him?' Karen asked, feeling the irate stares of people who had been in line in front of her.

Ione shrugged. 'I told him you were a famous European gourmand.'

Karen was trying to decide how to respond to that when she caught sight of a familiar bulk up ahead.

'Look,' she exclaimed. 'There's Demelza!'

'Really?' Ione grinned. 'Look again.'

Karen looked again and there, too, were Jenna and John and Felicity and even Mitch, along with eight-and-a-half-year-old Tanya, who came bounding over to throw her little arms around her best grown-up friend. Then there were hugs and kisses all around, as if they hadn't seen each other for months.

'Aren't birthdays wonderful?' Tanya cried happily.

'Surprise!' Demelza shouted. At fifty-six, her dark hair was turning white, but she still wore it in a thick braid down her back.

Karen turned to Ione. 'Big fight with Mitch, huh?' she accused with a smile.

It was a wonderful party. They laughed and ate and drank and ate and laughed and drank some more. For a while, it almost seemed that they were just as they used to be. Except, of course, Karen knew with a small pang of sadness, they weren't. Success, and the times, had changed them all. Going uptown had been much more than a geographical move – it had been a psychological one as well. Not so long ago, they had ridiculed people who went to restaurants like this. Now they thought nothing of dropping six or seven hundred dollars for someone else to do the cooking and the dishes.

Karen could remember when having a little money in the contribution can meant they could splurge on a good bottle of wine. Now they were hiring financial advisers and buying real estate and investing in high tech companies. They had traded the *Village Voice* for the *Wall Street Journal* and the mellow edges of marijuana for the numbness of Scotch. They no longer spoke of the future and what they hoped to accomplish, only of the present and what they had already accomplished. Dreams had become responsibilities. They had joined the Establishment.

The little family that had been her anchor for so long was gone. Like a rough diamond that had been cleaved into brilliant but separate gems, they would never be one again.

'I really miss you guys,' Karen heard herself saying.

'Yeah,' Mitch agreed. 'We should do this more often.' He was trimmer than he had been in their lean days, and his woolly beard had been reduced to a neat graying fringe.

'At least once a month,' Felicity said. Now almost forty, her wafer-thin body looked more anorexic than stylish.

'Or even once a week,' John added.

Karen had always thought of the sculptor as an awkward Ichabod Crane, but with the onset of affluence, he had developed a distinct resemblance to Sherlock Holmes. He admitted to being from New

Jersey where, it was rumored, his people had more than a nodding acquaintance with organized crime. To his credit, even in his leanest years – and there had been many – he had never taken a dime from any of them.

'Then it wouldn't be special,' Jenna reminded him. The carrot-topped, rosy-cheeked former teen had matured into a Rubenesque delight.

At that, a busboy wheeled up a cake, the top aflame with exactly the right number of candles. As the waiter popped the cork on a bottle of champagne and began to pour, Karen caught a glimpse of the label. Dom Perignon. She smiled softly to herself. They had indeed come a long way.

When the glasses were filled, Demelza rose to her feet.

'I know it's Karen's birthday,' she said, 'which is lovely and all that, but not really why we're gathered here tonight.'

Tanya held up her glass with the two drops of precious bubbling wine her mother had allowed her to have.

'Do we drink now?' she whispered.

'Not yet,' Demelza told her. 'After my speech.'

'Will you tell me when?'

'Yes.'

'Do you promise?' the little girl insisted. This was going to be her first taste of champagne and she didn't want to miss the moment.

'I promise,' Demelza said. 'As you all know, I've been the manager of Demion Five for the two years of its existence,' she continued. 'Two embarrassingly successful years, I might add. God help me, I have entered the top tax bracket.'

'Who'da thunk it,' Mitch muttered.

'Of course, there's a perfectly good reason for all of this. Demion Five has become a bigger winner than we ever thought it would. Let's face it, it's one thing to fantasize about something and quite another to turn it into reality. It took nothing less than a superhuman effort to put five such distinct specialties into one house and make it work so well, as though they were joined at the hip from birth and always intended to enhance one another. Ione dreamed it, I designed it, but the truth is, ladies and gentlemen, and little lady,' she said with a wink at Tanya, 'Karen made it happen.'

Everyone turned and applauded Karen.

'The only reason I was able to sell the Bookery for enough money to join up with Ione in the first place was because Karen turned it into a decent business. In her quiet way, she sees what needs to be done and does it.'

'Hear, hear,' everyone saluted. Karen blushed.

'Now?' Tanya asked.

'Not yet,' Demelza murmured. 'So, as the manager of Demion Five,' she continued, 'I wanted you all to be the first to hear that I am no longer the manager of Demion Five. Say hello to your new manager. To Karen.'

'To Karen,' everyone echoed, raising their glasses.

Demelza turned to Tanya. 'Now,' she prompted and they all drank.

'Speech!' everyone cried.

Karen looked around the table, stunned. 'I – I don't know what to say,' she stammered. She turned to Demelza. 'If you make me manager, what will *you* do?'

'Same thing I already do. Get in everyone's way, make a general nuisance of myself. Nothing's going to change. You've been doing the work from the beginning, you deserve to have the title. Besides, I miss my books. Now that I'm a woman of means, I want to spend more time poking through them and maybe even travel around in search of new treasures.'

'I still don't know what to say,' Karen admitted.

'Demelza didn't mention it,' Ione put in, 'but there's a significant raise that goes along with the promotion.'

At that, a happy grin spread across Karen's face. 'Now I know what to say,' she said. 'I can buy Mitch's painting.'

two

The woman appeared to be about Karen's age, short and round with asymmetric blue eyes and dark-blond hair worn in a ponytail with straight-cut bangs, and this was the third time in less than two weeks that she had braved the blustery winds of March to come and look at the Micheloni sculpture.

It was one of John's best creations, a representation of Paul Revere on his midnight ride, a rough black mass that vaguely resembled a horse, topped by a sweep of translucent alabaster that suggested a cape. It stood barely a foot high, but it had enormous impact. And a five-figure price tag.

Karen had placed it on a marble pedestal in a lighted niche at the back of the oval foyer, a position she set aside for only the most spectacular pieces. Like Mitch's painting of the clearing in the wood that now hung over the fireplace in her apartment, it was a work of art she truly appreciated. But her admiration was reserved for working hours because not even her significant boost in salary was enough to cover the cost.

The woman circled the pedestal slowly, considering the sculpture from every angle, with an expression of adoration mixed with indecision.

'Excuse me,' she said finally, taking a deep breath and walking over to Karen. 'Would it be possible for me to see the manager?'

'I'm the manager,' Karen replied, smiling politely and introducing herself. 'How may I help you?'

'Well, it's come down to a choice,' the woman announced. 'Either I take that exquisite thing home with me, or I move into your shop.'

Karen chuckled. 'I know exactly how you feel. If I had the money, it would have gone home with me a long time ago.'

'That's just it,' the woman acknowledged. 'I can't afford to buy it, but I can't resist. You see, my husband just got a big promotion at work, and he's a Revolutionary War buff, and I thought this would be a really special way to celebrate.'

'This is certainly special,' agreed Karen.

'But he'd kill me if he knew how much it cost. So I was wondering if maybe we could work something out.'

It wasn't the first time a customer had inquired about the possibility of financing a purchase. Demion Five's usual policy was to refuse courteously and suggest a lower-priced item. But Karen found herself hesitating because there was something engaging about the woman, and a candidness that showed clearly in her delightfully asymmetrical face – one blue eye being noticeably larger than the other.

'Would you care for a cup of tea?' she asked. 'I always deliberate better over a cup of tea.'

'I'd love one,' the woman replied.

'Okay, now, what did you have in mind?' Karen asked when they were settled at a table on the balcony with a pot of Earl Grey and a plate of Ione's fresh apple-berry muffins between them.

'My name is Nancy Yanow and I'm a photographer,' the woman began. 'At least, I used to be before I became a mom. I worked for the *Philadelphia Inquirer* one summer and the *Reading Times* for several years, and I had a pretty good reputation. I won an award for my series on Kent State in 1970. Anyway, I got to cover some pretty exciting stuff. The *New York Times* bought one of my pictures once. My name was still Nancy Doniger back then.'

'That sounds exciting,' Karen offered.

'It was,' Nancy replied wistfully. 'Anyway, my kids are both in school, and that leaves me with lots of free time. Newspaper work wouldn't fit my life now, but I was thinking about maybe going out on my own, you know, into artistic photography. I've kept up with my camera and I know quality work is selling these days and I thought that, if you liked the kind of thing I'm doing, we might arrange a trade where I could pay for, say, half of the sculpture and then give you enough of my stuff to cover the other half.'

It was an intriguing idea, Karen thought. Not that Demion Five wasn't doing just fine as it was, but adding a new dimension could have benefits.

'We've never had an arrangement like that,' she said slowly, although she knew the idea of bartering would appeal to both Demelza and Ione.

'Oh,' Nancy sighed.

'But that doesn't mean we couldn't.'

'Oh?'

'Of course, I'd have to see your photographs – that is, before I could commit to anything, and I'd have to discuss it with the owners, too.'

'Of course,' Nancy concurred, her whole face lighting up. 'I could bring in some samples tomorrow or the next day if you're available, or, better yet, you could come up to my place and see just about everything.'

'Let me check my schedule,' Karen suggested.

The two women went into the back, where Karen had her tiny cluttered office.

'If you're the least bit claustrophobic,' she warned, 'I don't recommend that you come any further.'

'I'm more curious than claustrophobic,' Nancy said, following her inside. 'Besides, this is at least twice as big as my darkroom.'

Karen flipped through the pages of her appointment book. 'The only day I have available this week would be Thursday.'

'Thursday's fine,' Nancy replied.

'It probably makes more sense for me to see everything you have, and I can't really concentrate that well here, so why don't I come to you?'

'Wonderful,' said Nancy. 'Come at noon and I'll make lunch.'

'You don't have to do that,' Karen assured her.

'I know,' Nancy declared. 'Here, let me give you the address.'

The brownstone in which the Yanows lived was on West Seventy-eighth, in a quiet little block tucked behind the Museum of Natural History. Nancy was waiting at the front door, opening it against the gusty wind before Karen even had a chance to push the buzzer.

'Hi,' she said. 'Come on in. I've got a good fire going and some hot cider to warm you up.'

'Sounds great,' Karen replied.

Nancy led the way up a flight of stairs. 'We have the top two floors,' she explained gratuitously. 'My brother's got the bottom two.'

'Did you flip a coin?'

'No,' Nancy chuckled. 'It's my brother's house. We rent from him.'

The upper duplex was spectacular, with heavy beamed ceilings and hardwood floors and window walls overlooking a garden in back. The top floor was divided into thirds, with two bedrooms at one end, a master suite at the other, and a large playroom in between. Downstairs, each room opened naturally into the next – kitchen into dining room into living room into study. The darkroom was a closet off the kitchen that had most likely started out as a pantry.

The furniture was a hodgepodge of styles and periods. Oriental carpets were scattered throughout and Navajo throws were draped over the sofas. Most of the exposed brick walls were lined with shelves that were in turn crammed with books, but several framed photographs were hung here and there for dramatic effect. One was a portrait of an ancient woman with a youthful twinkle in her eye. Another highlighted a solemn little boy with a big tear on his cheek. A third captured a boy and a girl sharing an apple.

'Did you do these?' Karen asked.

'Uh-huh,' came the reply.

'They're great.'

Nancy beamed. 'I did them when I was in my people

phase. Now I'm in my place phase.'

'I can't wait to see more.'

'I thought we'd eat first, if that's all right,' Nancy suggested. She ushered Karen into the kitchen, where wood blended into tile and the tile gave way to wood again.

'I thought my apartment was impressive,' Karen observed. 'But what you've done here is ... well, it's incredible.'

'I wish I could take the credit,' Nancy said.

'Your brother did all this?'

'We knew from the time he was six that he was meant to be an architect. He could do the most fantastic things with Lincoln Logs.'

'From the looks of it, you were right.'

'He lost his wife to cancer three years ago,' Nancy confided. 'He got through it by taking on this place. He gutted the building practically to the foundation and rebuilt from there.'

The lunch, which more closely resembled a banquet, was delicious. The two women chatted throughout the meal like old friends rather than potential business colleagues. Somewhere between the crab bisque and the baked salmon, Karen learned that Nancy's husband Joe was the sales manager for a large industrial products firm and that her son Roger was in the second grade and her daughter Emily in the first.

'It sounds like you have a great family,' Karen said.

'Are *you* married?' Nancy asked.

'No,' came the reply.

'Are you interested?'

'I was once,' Karen replied, and for an instant the mask slipped. 'But it didn't work out, and I don't really think about it much anymore.'

A little smile fluttered around Nancy's mouth. 'Well, you just never know when you might stumble over the right opportunity again, now do you?' she murmured.

She led Karen into the study and sat her down on an overstuffed sofa. Then she hefted a large black portfolio onto an oak coffee table and flipped it open. Faces of every age and emotion stared up at Karen, each with a tale to tell, speaking silent volumes, even in black and white. Karen picked one up. In it, an old man sat on a bench staring into space with an expression of such emptiness that Karen felt her eyes moisten.

'He looks like he's waiting to die,' she whispered.

'He was,' Nancy said. 'His wife had just died. They'd been married for sixty-three years. They used to go to the park every afternoon so she could feed the pigeons. Hundreds of pigeons would wait for them at that bench. He told me that the day after she died he went to the park because he knew the pigeons would be waiting, but when he got there, they were gone. It was as if they knew.'

Karen looked into the old man's face, into his eyes. Even if Nancy hadn't told her the story, she felt she would have known it.

In the next picture, a little boy had slipped on a jungle gym at a playground and was dangling precariously. Above him, a teenage boy reached out a helping hand. The teenager was black. Karen saw both fear and relief in the little boy's eyes as he grasped for the helping hand. She needed no explanation for that story.

'Hollywood may think it invented talking pictures,' she murmured, 'but these are the real thing.'

'Now for talking places,' Nancy said, lifting another portfolio onto the table. Inside, Karen saw New York

City as she had never seen it before – a block of empty shops on the Upper West Side with boarded-up windows that even the rats had abandoned, an elite block of Park Avenue on garbage day, the Queensboro Bridge coming out of the dawn, Broadway during a blackout, the Empire State Building in a snowstorm, a Lower East Side tenement house burning out of control, a foggy shadow of the Staten Island Ferry.

'Look,' Karen said when she had seen everything, 'I don't claim to be an art critic, or know anything at all about design or composition, but if these are half as good as my instincts tell me they are, you and your husband are going to own a John Micheloni sculpture that I would give my eyeteeth for.'

'You really like them?' Nancy breathed.

'Not only do I like them, I think they're going to raise the level of Demion Five at least one notch.'

'You know, you're the first outside person I've actually shown any of these to. Joe kept telling me they were good, but of course he's not exactly what you'd call objective.'

'Nancy, they are good,' Karen asserted. 'Really good – and not even your delicious lunch would make me say that if I didn't mean it.'

The photographer grinned. 'I was so nervous the other day when I approached you. At first, I was just going to ask if you would do some sort of payment schedule for me. But once we started talking, well, you were so nice, and I just had this feeling that you'd understand what I was trying to do here.'

'I want you to bring both portfolios into the shop first thing Monday morning,' Karen instructed. 'Can you do that?'

'Of course I can.'

'I'll have the owners there and maybe a couple of other people and we'll see what the reaction is.'

'I'll be there,' promised Nancy. 'And if this deal works out, if I get Paul Revere, I promise you can have all the visiting rights you want.'

three

By the time the bitter winds of March had given way to the gentle rains of April, limited-edition photographs were a fixture at Demion Five. By the time spring flowers had begun to blossom beneath the May sun, Paul Revere had become the focal point of the Yanow living room, and Nancy was as good as her word – Karen had become a regular visitor at Seventy-eighth Street.

The two women spoke daily on the telephone, met for lunch, and spent Saturday afternoons together. Karen had to go all the way back to her girlhood, to the lazy weekends she had spent with Jill, to find a time when she had enjoyed as close a friend.

On the first Saturday in August, Nancy arrived at the town house on Sixty-third Street at ten o'clock in the morning.

'You're two hours early,' Karen protested when she opened the door wrapped in her terry-cloth bathrobe, her hair soaking wet. 'I just got out of the shower.'

'Joe's taking the kids to the beach,' said Nancy by way of apology. 'He dropped me off on the way.'

'Well, have a seat,' Karen told her. 'There's fresh coffee. I'll be ready in half an hour.'

Nancy poured herself a cup and took it into the living room. She loved the serenity of Karen's apartment, the muted browns and stark whites, the brief flashes of color, the simplicity of the furniture, the quiet. It was easy to relax here, where there was never a need to worry about tripping over toys or sitting on something sticky. Fastidious Karen, Nancy thought with a smile. You could eat off her floor, you could see your reflection in the polished surfaces of her wood, and there was never a thing out of place.

Except, this morning, there was a scarred wooden box that had been left open on top of the desk. Nancy was not by nature a snoopy person. It was the incongruity of the box that drew her attention. She peeked inside. On top was a page covered with Karen's neat, precise handwriting. Nancy couldn't resist – she picked it up and started to read.

> The death of a dream
> is surrounded by pain,
> emptiness,
> regret,
> guilt.

> The tragedy of life
> is filled with opportunity,
> unrecognized,
> ignored,
> lost.

* * *

Fascinated, Nancy picked up the next page.

Half an hour later, Karen appeared in navy-blue slacks and a flowing white blouse, her hair smartly fluffed.

'As long as we have some extra time,' she was saying, 'I thought we could – '

The words died in her throat as she saw Nancy with the wooden box on her lap and the thought pages beside her.

'Stop!' she cried instinctively. 'Those are private.'

'I'm dreadfully sorry!' Nancy was both startled and embarrassed. 'I didn't realize … I saw the box sitting there, and my curiosity just got the best of me. I didn't think.'

Karen gathered up the papers and stuffed them back in the box and then shoved the box into one of the desk drawers.

'They're nothing important,' she said woodenly. 'Just a bunch of silly doodlings.'

'They *are* important,' Nancy contradicted her. 'And I had no right to read them without your permission.'

There was a long and distinctly awkward pause.

'I suppose you're wondering what that stuff was all about,' Karen said finally.

Nancy's uneven blue eyes reflected nothing but genuine caring. 'Not if you don't want to tell me,' she said.

'It was a long time ago,' Karen murmured, looking down the tunnel of years. 'I was very naive and I made a terrible mistake, and I had to pay the price.' She let out a shaky breath. 'Some mistakes you can simply shrug off because you know you won't ever make them again, but there are others that … well, I've had to learn to live with what happened. I don't talk about it very much. The notes and things – nobody was ever supposed to see them – they help.'

Nancy heard the sigh and felt the pain. 'I'm so sorry,' she apologized. 'I never meant to intrude.'

Karen shrugged. 'Well, it's over and done.'

'But since I did,' Nancy continued, 'I want to tell you something. The things I read – they were very good.'

'Don't be silly.' Karen shrugged. 'They're nothing.'

'You're wrong – and you ought to do something with them.'

'Perhaps I should wallpaper my bathroom.'

'Perhaps you should publish them.'

Karen laughed outright. 'Who'd publish my non-sense?'

'Literary publications take poetry all the time, and most of it is written by people who are working through problems, just like you. I've read stuff in periodicals that isn't half as good as yours. You had one poem in there about winter that actually gave me chills on an eighty-degree day in August.'

'Look, I appreciate the compliment, but my stuff is just for me,' Karen said with finality, now mortified that she had made such an issue of it. 'So let's pretend you never saw any of it and we can forget it and be on our way, okay? As long as we have time, I want to stop at the cleaner's.'

Only Nancy did not forget. In fact, an idea that had been lurking around the edges of her mind for some time began to come into full focus.

'I want to say something,' she said two weeks later, when they were enjoying a late lunch, 'and I don't want you to say a word until you've heard me out.'

'Okay,' came the casual reply.

'I'm doing well, right? I mean, my photographs are selling, right?'

'Right,' Karen said.

'Well, I was thinking, if my prints are popular – how about a book?'

'A book of photographs?'

'Exactly. You see, I've had this idea for a while now, and it's something I can't really do with a single print. I want to do a whole year in Manhattan, all four seasons, and how the city changes with each one. Different perspectives, all tied into the calendar. The man who sits on a bench three hundred and sixty-five afternoons a year – how do the seasons affect him? The mother who pushes a baby carriage around every morning – what difference do the seasons make to her? How is a river affected, or a park, or a schoolyard? What do you think?'

'I think it's good,' Karen replied, the wheels beginning to turn. 'A book, if it's priced right, could be a real hit. We could sell it right out of the shop.'

'There's just one hitch,' Nancy said.

'What?'

'Well, the book I'm imagining needs to have more than just photographs in it. It needs to have words. Words that will tie everything together, you know, the way illustrations enhance stories. I want to "illustrate" my photographs with words. But I don't want to use any stuff that's already been written. I want ideas that are just as fresh and original as my pictures. Only I wouldn't know how to do that myself.'

'Then find someone,' Karen responded without hesitation. 'It's such a good idea, I don't know how anyone could turn you down.'

'That's what I hoped,' Nancy said with a Cheshire cat grin that spread all over her face.

Karen choked. 'Don't be silly. You can't mean me. I'm not a writer.'

'As it happens,' contradicted Nancy, 'I'm in a position to know better.'

'Well, I'm certainly not a professional writer,' Karen pointed out.

'So what? You're as good as many professionals I know. I want you to illustrate my book with poetry.'

Karen frowned. 'My things aren't the kind of things you could use for something like this,' she argued.

'I'm not talking about what you've got in your box at home,' Nancy assured her. 'That's private and it should stay that way. I'm talking about you and me going out and creating something brand new and exciting together.'

There was a long pause.

'You really think I could do it?' Karen asked finally.

'Absolutely,' Nancy confirmed. 'Look, five months ago, you took a chance on a nobody photographer just because your instincts told you that you were right. Well, don't insult me by assuming that my instincts aren't every bit as good as yours. I say you can do it. I *know* you can do it.'

Karen didn't believe it for a moment. She had done enough reading in her lifetime to know that the pages in her box were little more than sophomoric jottings. That anyone might want to buy them was ludicrous. And yet, the idea was tempting. To create a work that would live and breathe all on its own would, in some ways, be like creating a new life, something she was so often reminded she could not do.

She took a deep breath. 'When do we start?'

four

Karen added a final coat of lip gloss, fluffed out her hair, and stood back to consider herself in the mirror.

Labor Day had come and gone, taking with it the pastel clothes and white shoes of summer. Although the midday temperature had climbed well above seventy, it was October, officially autumn, and time for more sober attire.

It had taken two hours of trying first one thing and then another before Karen settled on a simple taupe dress that had hung in her closet since being purchased, patiently waiting for an occasion to be taken out and worn. Matching pumps and a thick gold bracelet created by Felicity completed the outfit.

She turned, checking from every angle, looking for anything that might be amiss. But everything was just as it should be. With a satisfied sigh, she picked up her purse, let herself out of the apartment and walked over to Lexington Avenue in search of a taxi that would take her to the West Side.

'It's just a small get-together for my brother's fortieth birthday,' Nancy had explained in early September. 'He's been an absolute recluse since his wife died and I want to do something special for him. Joe's sister and brother will be there with their spouses and offspring.'

'But it's a family gathering,' Karen objected. 'I don't belong there.'

'Of course you do,' Nancy insisted and would hear no argument.

In truth, the Yanows were almost like family. In the past six months, Karen had been in and out of their house as if it were her second home. Although she'd never met the guest of honor, she probably knew Nancy's husband and their children better than she knew her own niece and nephew and brother-in-law, now that Laura had moved to Boston.

'Can I help with anything?' she asked.

'Yes,' Nancy replied. 'I have my eye on that new Rankin, the little one with the clown. I think my brother would love it. If I give you a deposit, do you think you could put it away for me?'

The painting was a whimsical Rankin, with the subject balancing nonchalantly on a unicycle while the rest of the circus whirled all around him with dizzying speed. 'Sanity-in-sanity,' Mitch called it, and it always made Karen smile.

'Done,' she said. 'But I won't put it away. I'll just mark it 'sold' and leave it hanging. Better for business.'

Now the painting was wrapped and waiting in

Nancy's study and all there was for Karen to do was get herself crosstown.

Joe Yanow answered her ring. A jovial man, even rounder than his wife and almost as short, with crinkly laugh lines and thinning hair, he gave her a broad smile and a big hug. It was a Mitch Rankin kind of hug and Karen had become used to it.

'Nancy's in the kitchen, the kids are up in the playroom, and everyone else is in the study watching the Orioles cream the Pirates.'

'I'll try the kitchen,' Karen decided as a huge groan escaped from the study, 'in case the hostess needs a hand.' She had never been able to muster much enthusiasm for baseball, not even the World Series.

The kitchen was in turmoil, which meant that Nancy had everything under control. After the barest of greetings, the hostess shoved a platter of canapés into Karen's hands.

'With all the complaining going on in there, a diversion is surely in order,' she suggested.

Karen carried the assortment of ham rolls, stuffed celery and deviled eggs into the study.

Up close, there was a good deal of resemblance between Ted Doniger and his sister except that Nancy was short while Ted stood at almost six feet. They shared the same sharp nose, easy smile, square jaw and blond hair, but Nancy's eyes were a cool blue, while Ted's were a rich hazel with warm gold flecks in them.

He was wearing gray slacks and a pale-yellow turtle-neck sweater that looked like cashmere, and he was smoking a pipe that smelled delicious. He might not have been what some considered handsome, but Karen thought he had a nice face, a comfortable face.

'I'm not sure what all the excitement is about,' he

whispered as he helped himself to a ham roll and a deviled egg from the plate of canapés. 'We hated the Pirates when we were kids growing up in Reading.'

'That's okay,' Karen whispered back. 'To me, a strike is when workers want more wages, a batter is what I whip up to make pancakes, and a run is something I'm always getting in my stockings.'

The gold flecks began to dance in his eyes. 'That's pretty good,' he said appreciatively. 'Of course, some of the others might consider it heresy.'

'Then I won't repeat it,' Karen told him as she moved on with her platter.

As if by design, the children clambered downstairs the moment the final pitch was thrown. Roger and Emily rushed to give Karen a hug, but the others hung back.

'The snot-nosed monsters are mine,' Joe's sister announced, nodding to two scruffy little boys.

The three Doniger girls peered out from behind their father.

'I don't think she bites,' Karen heard Ted whisper.

The oldest, blond like her father, round and blue-eyed like her aunt, took half a step forward.

'I'm Gwen,' she said. 'I'm twelve.'

'Hello, Gwen,' Karen answered with a smile. 'I'm Karen. I'm thirty-seven.'

Gwen gasped and the others giggled.

'That's pretty old, isn't it?'

'It depends on the day,' she was told.

'I'm Jessica,' the middle girl ventured. She had straight brown hair and her solemn brown eyes were fixed warily on the strange woman. 'I'm almost nine.'

'When I was nine,' Karen responded, 'I was in the fourth grade.'

'I'm in the fourth grade,' Jessica said.

'I'm Amy,' the youngest piped up. 'I'm five and my mommy's in heaven.'

Karen smiled at the towhead with her father's golden eyes. 'You're very grown up for five,' she said, 'and I'll bet your mommy is looking down at you right this minute and feeling very proud of you.'

'Do you think she can see me right through the roof?' the little girl asked, searching the heavy beamed ceiling.

'I think she can see you anywhere,' Karen declared. 'That's what's special about being in heaven.'

'Do you think Herman can see me, too?'

'Oh, Amy,' Gwen exclaimed.

'Who's Herman?' Karen asked.

'He's our hamster,' Jessica explained. 'He died last week and we buried him in the yard.'

'I think all those we love find a way to stay with us,' Karen said, 'even after they're gone.'

The five-year-old tucked her hand inside Karen's and leaned close. 'I kept his little red ball,' she whispered. 'It was his favorite toy. I sleep with it under my pillow.'

'When I was your age, I had a kitty,' Karen whispered back. 'When he died, I did the same thing.'

Nancy had stretched her classic Sheraton dining room table to its limit to accommodate the eight adults and seven children who crowded around it. She had planned to seat Karen between Joe and Ted, but Amy insisted on sitting beside her new friend and Gwen slipped quickly into the seat on Karen's other side.

'Well,' Nancy said and smiled, 'so much for my place cards.'

The dinner was sumptuous. Mrs. Peagram, the stout

matron who kept house for Ted and the girls, did the serving and clearing, which allowed Nancy to stay with her guests.

The company made its way through lemon consommé and butter-lettuce salad to individual Rock Cornish hens stuffed with wild-rice pilaf and served with tiny glazed carrots and onions and tender tips of asparagus. Karen wondered where Nancy had found fresh asparagus this time of year.

'Shouldn't they have let this poor chicken grow up first?' Gwen murmured.

'It's not a chicken – it's a special kind of hen that doesn't get any bigger,' Karen just had time to reply before she felt a tug at her sleeve.

'Would you cut my meat for me, please?' Amy asked. 'I'm too little to do it by myself.'

Karen smiled. 'One meat-cutter coming right up.' She started to slide the child's plate over and then changed her mind. 'If I put my hands on top of yours,' she suggested, 'we can do it together. Then, when you're old enough, you'll know how.'

'Oh, let's do it that way!'

Karen placed Amy's small hands in the correct position on the knife and fork, then covered them with her own hands and carefully guided the utensils until they had reduced the hen to bite-sized pieces.

'Oooh, that was fun,' the little girl exclaimed. 'Can we do it again next time?'

'Only if you promise to eat every morsel.'

Amy's eyes widened in dismay. 'But I'm a picky eater,' she exclaimed.

'Who told you that?'

'Mrs. Peagram,' came the solemn reply. 'She says it all the time.'

'Well, I used to be a picky eater, too,' Karen confided. 'Then one day, I ate everything on my plate. That plate was so clean it didn't even have to be washed, and everyone was so surprised that their mouths hung open. After that, they called me a piggy eater.'

Amy giggled and then frowned. 'But I don't like to eat what's good for me.'

'Oh, but that's not how it works,' Karen told her. 'You don't eat because you have to – you eat because it's so much fun. Corner that onion, crunch that carrot, down that rice, chomp that hen. The carrot says, "If she thinks I'm good for her, she won't eat me and I'll escape." The onion says, "If I make myself slippery, she won't like me and I'll escape." It's all a big game, you see – you against the food. Now, the question is, who's going to win, you or the food?'

Amy turned immediately to her plate and speared a piece of carrot with her fork. At the foot of the table, Nancy grinned. Across the table, Ted Doniger watched.

five

'I don't know,' Mitch said, cocking his head to one side. 'It still looks crooked to me.'

Karen leaned as far back off the ladder as she dared and squinted up at the painting.

'We've almost got it,' she insisted.

'A little more on the left,' Mitch directed.

'My eye tells me more on the right,' she replied.

'Look, I'm the artist,' Mitch insisted. 'I tell the manager. I say, on the left.'

'I'm the manager,' Karen declared. 'I *sell* the artist. I say on the right.'

'Get the spirit level,' Mitch demanded.

'What spirit level?' Karen retorted. 'I've never needed a spirit level. I've got a perfect eye.'

'Then get another opinion.'

'A little more on the right,' a voice behind them said.

Karen turned so abruptly that she almost fell off the

ladder and Mitch had to grab hold of her to make sure she didn't. Ted Doniger was standing there with his feet apart and his hands in his pockets.

'That's what I said,' she affirmed.

'How can you say that?' Mitch argued.

Ted shrugged. 'I've got a perfect eye,' he replied with a smile.

'You'd better believe him,' Karen told Mitch. 'He's an architect. He also owns one of your paintings.'

'And if you stop fussing over this one long enough for me to get a good look at it,' Ted said, 'I may own two.'

Mitch looked at Karen. 'A little more on the right,' he grumbled.

Karen pushed the right corner up a fraction of an inch and climbed down off the ladder.

'There,' she said to Ted. 'Now you can look all you want.'

Mitch had taken to the sea this time to create a violent storm that threatened to topple a solitary sailboat into the teeming, roiling depths.

'The movement is great,' Ted observed. 'The urgency, the recklessness, the precariousness – all balance so well. It's got very much the same feeling as my clown, and yet it's totally different.'

Karen smiled. 'I wasn't sure at first, but Nancy really did choose the right gift.'

'Nancy spent too much money,' he replied.

'So, what brings you here?' Karen asked.

In the month since the birthday party, she had seen him several times – at a Sunday brunch, once or twice in passing on the weeknight evenings when she and Nancy worked on their book, on the Saturday afternoon when they had all gone to the Hayden

Planetarium – and a friendship had begun to grow
between them in the nice slow way that lasting
friendships always grew, like her friendship with Mitch
and John and Joe Yanow had grown.

They found they had a lot in common and that it was
easy for them to talk to each other. They made each
other laugh.

'I come bearing an invitation,' Ted announced.

'Sounds promising so far,' Karen said with a warm
smile. 'Speak more.'

'Mrs. Peagram is making the turkey, Nancy is making everything else, and the girls and I would very
much like you to come to our place for Thanksgiving.'

The smile dimmed. Thanksgiving was the one traditional holiday that Beverly Kern took very seriously.
Friends and relatives were culled from as far away as
Palm Beach and Grosse Pointe. Laura and family were
coming down from Boston, of course, and Karen's
appearance at Knightsbridge Road was mandatory.

'I wish I could,' she sighed, 'but that's the one day
of the year, above all others, that I'm obligated to
spend with my parents.'

The disappointment showed clearly in his eyes.
'That's too bad,' he said. 'We'll miss you. You've sort of
become part of the family.'

It was true. As the Sullivan Street set had once
accepted her into the fold, so now did the Doniger/
Yanow clan, going out of their way to include her in
many of their activities.

'That's because you've made me feel so welcome,'
Karen responded. 'It's been a little like discovering a
whole new brother and sister I never knew about.'

'I'm very glad you feel that way,' he said. 'I mean,
you know, comfortable with us.'

Karen grinned. 'So comfortable I don't even mind you seeing me in my sweats.'

He had caught her one Sunday morning, dropping off a book Joe had ordered from Demelza, when she was in a hurry and hadn't bothered to dress.

'But I like your sweats,' Ted protested. 'They look very ... comfortable.'

The two of them laughed.

'Someday,' she said, 'you wait and see, sweats are going to become haute couture.'

'Are you going to be spending the whole Thanksgiving weekend with your family?' he asked.

'Not a chance. I have to work on Friday. It's always one of our busiest days.'

'Well then,' he declared, 'all is not lost. You can come for leftovers.'

'I thought you'd never ask.'

'One condition, though – you have to promise to wear your sweats.'

Karen poked him in the ribs. 'Very funny.'

Ted turned back to Mitch's oil. 'How much?' he asked.

'Forty-five hundred,' Karen told him.

'Why not bring it with you when you come and we'll see how it looks.'

It was the first time Karen had been invited into the downstairs half of the house on West Seventy-eighth Street, and it was every bit as dramatic as the upstairs, with the same high beamed ceilings, exposed brick walls, and polished floors. But the resemblance ended there.

While Nancy's taste ran to the eclectic, Ted's was strictly modern. Leather, chrome, and glass dominated the furnishings, with only a few touches of warmth. A bentwood rocker had found its way into the study, Breuer chairs surrounded the thick glass slab that served as the dining table, and the sleek desk in the study was made of black walnut. Neutral-colored rugs had been used sparingly. The whole effect came amazingly close to Karen's own concept of interior decoration, and she was enchanted.

'This is exactly the effect I tried to achieve in my apartment,' she exclaimed. 'Clean, airy, elegant.'

'Then you should feel right at home,' he said with a smile.

The Doniger girls declared the leftover party to be even better than the holiday, and to be honest, Karen thought so, too. After dinner, they tried Mitch's painting everywhere, except in the study, where Ted had already hung the clown. They would even have considered the kitchen, but Mrs. Peagram shooed them out. They settled finally on the living room, over the mantel.

'That's it,' Ted declared, as Karen and Nancy held it in place. 'Perfect.'

'Quick! Get the hammer and hooks,' Nancy directed her husband, 'before he changes his mind.'

The Rankin really did look wonderful there, against the dark-red brick, above the rough stone fireplace. Ted had it fixed in place in no time.

'What do you think?' he asked with a mischievous wink. 'A little more on the right?'

Karen hooted.

'What's so funny?' Nancy inquired, looking from one to the other.

Ted winked at Karen. 'You had to be there,' he said.

* * *

The week before Christmas, Karen mailed her presents home to Great Neck – a brocade-covered photograph album for Beverly, a cashmere scarf for Leo.

'I'm going to stay in town on Tuesday,' she told her mother.

'Why?' Beverly wanted to know.

'Because we're open until nine on Monday, and we open again at nine on Wednesday, and to try to do Great Neck in between would be too much of a hassle. But I won't be alone. I've been invited over to Nancy's.'

'It seems to me you're spending a great deal of time with that family,' Beverly observed. 'Just like you used to with those Village people.'

Even after the enormous success of Demion Five, there was still a note of disdain in her mother's voice when she spoke of the Sullivan Street set.

'They're nice people,' Karen said mildly, 'and I like them.'

'Who are they, exactly?'

Karen sighed. 'You know perfectly well who they are. Nancy is a friend I met at the gallery.' She had not yet told her parents about the book. 'And Nancy's husband, Joe, and their two children, and also her brother and his three children, who share the same house.'

'What about the brother's wife?'

'She died a few years ago.'

'Oh?' There was a note of sudden interest in Beverly's voice. 'What does he do?'

Karen sighed in exasperation. She wanted desperately to tell her mother that Ted was a garbage collector, just for the effect she knew it would have.

'He's an architect,' she said flatly. 'And a friend.'

'An architect?' Beverly echoed. 'Is he starving, that

he has to live with his sister?'

'Hardly.'

'What has he built?'

'I haven't the faintest idea.'

Her mother sighed. 'Well, I suppose it could be worse. Anyway, we'll miss you. Everyone will be here. I'll tell them that an indigent architect was more important.'

Architects, Karen was well aware, ranked even lower than engineers in that outmoded pecking order Beverly Kern still clung to, despite the fact that her daughter was in her late thirties and still unmarried.

'We're friends, Mother,' Karen repeated.

'Yes, dear.'

It was the best Christmas Karen could remember, from the moment she arrived, barely past dawn, to participate in the official present-opening, to the moment she departed, near midnight, with Ted insisting on seeing her safely to her front door.

Gwen had asked her aunt to take a photograph of herself and her two sisters, and her father had helped her frame it. 'So you won't forget what we look like when you're not here,' she said when she gave it to Karen.

'I'm going to put it on my desk at work,' Karen told her. 'Since that's where I spend most of my time.'

Jessica had made a small ceramic box in school. 'For your most precious things,' she whispered.

'I'll keep it right next to my bed,' Karen promised, 'so it'll be the last thing I see at night, and the first thing I see in the morning.'

Amy had drawn a picture of a little blond girl with a big shaggy dog.

'Who's that?' Karen asked her.

'Me, of course,' she said.

'No – that person next to you?' Karen said, pointing to the dog.

Amy giggled. 'That's not a person. That's Duster.'

'Who's Duster?'

'He's the dog I'm going to have one day.'

'I think I'll put this on the door of my refrigerator,' Karen decided. 'That way, every time I go into the kitchen I can wave to the two of you.'

Ted laid a package gently in her lap.

'Let's see,' she said, weighing it. 'This feels heavier than a feather, but lighter than a bread box.'

The girls giggled. 'Open it! Open it!' they cried.

It was a book on modern interior design, with hundreds of color photographs of the most exquisite rooms, done by some of the foremost decorators in the world.

Karen's mouth hung open as she turned the pages. 'It's fantastic,' she said. 'One room's more magnificent than the next. I intend to spend months going through this.' Her eyes shone up at Ted. 'You couldn't have picked anything better.'

He smiled. 'I'm glad you like it.'

'I love it,' she assured him. 'I really do.' Then she jumped up. 'Now it's my turn.'

Karen had worked with Jenna for weeks. Together, they had created a sweat suit for each of the girls, as well as one for Ted. Gwen's was red with patchwork appliqués of plaids and prints, Jessica's was pale blue with diagonal paisley insets, and Amy's was bright pink and decorated with pastel circles, squares and triangles. Their father's was done in navy and featured bold stripes in red and green and yellow.

Ted laughed until there were real tears in his eyes,

and the four of them had to go and try on their new outfits before they would touch another present.

'You look fabulous,' Nancy said, searching for the camera when they paraded back in.

'They did turn out rather well, didn't they?' Karen was immensely pleased with herself.

'You couldn't have picked anything better,' Ted said, the gold flecks twinkling in his eyes.

After the presents, it was time for a hearty breakfast.

'Opening all those presents really works up the appetite,' Joe insisted as he helped himself to a third stack of pancakes.

When the last biscuit, the last egg, the last drop of maple syrup had disappeared, the two men bundled the children into their snowsuits and took off for a romp in the park. Karen and Nancy tackled the kitchen, but no sooner had they gotten the breakfast things cleared away than it was time to start on dinner.

'Now I know what they mean when they say a woman's work is never done,' Karen groaned with a grin.

Nancy chuckled. 'I can't tell you how much it's meant to have you with us,' she said as they began to soak bread crumbs and chop up the celery and onions. 'I don't just mean today, I mean the whole past ten months.'

'Well, you make me feel like one of the family,' Karen told her.

'You make it easy,' Nancy said. 'You might not see it, of course, because you didn't know them before, but your being around has really made a big difference in Ted and the girls. It's put the light back in their eyes.'

'You give me too much credit,' Karen murmured. 'I think it's probably more a case of grief just running its course.'

Nancy gave her a sidelong look. 'Well, whatever,' she murmured.

It was much later, after the trip to the park, after dinner, when everyone was stuffed to the limit and sprawled in front of a crackling fire, listening to the last of the Christmas music on the stereo, that Gwen and Jessica crept up on either side of Karen.

'Will you come spend New Year's Eve with us?' Jessica asked, her solemn brown eyes now full of trust. 'Daddy says if you come we can have real champagne at midnight instead of apple cider.'

'Daddy says the sad times are over,' Gwen added. 'And he says if you come it means that 1980 will be an extra special happy year.'

Karen looked over at Ted. He was sitting on the floor, with his back up against Nancy's chair, cradling a sleeping Amy in his arms. Karen couldn't remember ever seeing Laura's husband do anything like that with her niece and nephew, and she couldn't help but envy Nancy enormously.

If God had told her to go out into the world and pick herself a brother, she knew she wouldn't be able to find a better choice than Ted Doniger.

'I guess we've been monopolizing quite a lot of your time,' Ted said afterward as he left the car motor running and walked Karen up the steps of her town house. 'We really would love to have you join us on New Year's, but of course we'll understand if you have other plans.'

'Well, as a matter of fact, I *am* expected somewhere else,' Karen admitted, handing him her cache of gifts as she fished for her keys.

The Sullivan Street set's New Year's party had long since gained the status of an annual event, and this year's celebration was doubly special. The Rankins had finished their renovation, having divided the old tenement building into four truly elegant duplex suites, each five times the size of the flat they once rented.

'I see,' Ted said.

'It's an annual thing, with a group of friends. It all started when we were very young and very poor and needed one good meal a year to keep us going.'

He smiled. 'It goes that far back, does it?'

'Little did we realize what success would do to us,' Karen said, only half in jest. 'But I'm pleased to say that I'm not totally spoiled. I would be willing to share the evening.'

'You would?' he said, brightening.

'What if I went off to my party for a while and then came around to your place?' she offered. 'In time for the champagne, of course.'

'That would work,' he replied with a nod. 'Is the party nearby?'

'It's in the Village.'

Ted frowned. 'You're not going down there by yourself, are you?'

Karen chuckled. 'If you're asking whether I have a date, the answer is no. But I always take a taxi, so it's quite safe.'

'Still, it's no night for you to be chasing all over the city on your own.' He scraped his toe against the top step. 'Look, maybe this is out of line, and you can tell me if it is, but I'd feel a whole lot better if you'd let me take you down there and then bring you back.'

Karen couldn't help staring at him. It had been a very long time since anyone had been that concerned about her welfare. She decided he really was the big brother she had never had.

'I love it that you're so concerned about me,' she said, 'but I wouldn't dream of letting you do that. However, I am willing to negotiate.'

'Oh?'

'How about you coming along to my party with me? I'm sure the Rankins would be delighted to have you, at the very least because you're the proud owner of two of Mitch's best paintings. Besides, they've just finished renovating their building and they kept a very special room in it that you might get a kick out of seeing.'

A broad grin spread quickly across Ted's face. 'You've got a deal,' he declared.

With that, he handed her back her packages, brushed his lips against her cheek and was gone, bounding down the steps two at a time.

To anyone observing from a distance, he looked far more like a carefree teenager than the middle-aged, widowed father of three.

SIX

Ted Doniger married his high school sweetheart two weeks after he received his license to practice architecture, and expected to spend the rest of his life with her.

They met when Ted was a junior and Barbara a freshman. What began as an intense adolescent infatuation eventually evolved into committed adult love.

'You're too young to tie yourself down to one girl,' his mother argued when Ted was saving up for a ring. 'You haven't experienced anything of life yet.'

'Your mother's right, son,' his father felt compelled to agree. 'What happens when you go off to college and meet somebody else?'

'I'll probably meet hundreds of girls,' Ted replied, thinking only of the young woman with the straight brown hair and solemn brown eyes. 'But none of them will be Barbara.'

With his dream and her determination, his good humor and her good sense, his energy and her serenity, they were two sides of the same coin – opposite and inseparable. There was never anyone else for either of them. From the very beginning, they knew that one day they would be husband and wife. But that day would not come until Ted could properly afford to support her and the family they would have. He was adamant about that.

'You're not going to scrub, you're not going to scrimp, you're not going to do without,' he said the afternoon she saw him off to Yale. 'We're going to have a decent place to live and a car and enough extra money for movies and ice cream and vacations every summer.'

It took eight years.

His first job was with a small firm on the outskirts of Philadelphia, which was barely close enough to Reading for him to commute every day from the little cottage behind her parents' house, but not close enough to allow him very much time with his new bride.

'We can afford to live closer, if you like,' he told her. 'But if your parents are really willing to let us have this place, just for the cost of fixing it up, maybe we should grab it.'

Barbara Doniger was not only in love, she was very wise. If she could wait patiently for him to finish four years of college, two years in the army and two years of graduate school, she could wait for him to come home for dinner.

'We'll start a savings account,' she said. 'And every month we'll make a deposit, just as if we were paying rent, and before you know it, we'll have enough to build our own dream house.'

'A dream house, eh?' He smiled. 'Is that the plan, Mrs. Doniger?'

'That's the plan,' she told him firmly. 'And it isn't going to cost so very much, either, because I happen to know an exceptional young architect who'll design exactly what we want for free.'

Five mornings a week, Ted got up before dawn, leaving the house at six to drive to Philadelphia, some sixty miles away. Barbara got up with him so they could share breakfast together, packed him a lunch so they could save money, and got into the habit of fixing a peanut-butter-and-jelly sandwich for herself around three in the afternoon so she could wait to have supper with him when he came home at night, which could be anywhere between eight and ten o'clock, depending on his workload.

One day in April of 1967, he made the usual two-hour trip home in eighty-six minutes, reaching the hospital in Reading just seconds after his first daughter was born.

'I guess I didn't plan very well,' Barbara yawned as she drifted off to sleep. 'I thought it would take much longer.'

Jessica was born in Hartford, Connecticut, a year after Ted took a job with a medium-sized firm that specialized in the kind of steel-and-glass office buildings that had begun to pop up all over the northeast. Amy was born in New York, six months after Ted accepted a junior partnership in a large and prestigious firm known for its distinctive hotels and unique office complexes.

Each time, in each place, he and Barbara resolved to build their dream house, and each time they were thwarted by a better offer in another city. But this time Barbara would not be denied. They rented an apartment on the west side of Manhattan for convenience, and spent their weekends driving from one suburb to another, from New Jersey to Long Island to Westchester County, hunting for just the right place. One crisp September afternoon they drove into Hastings-on-Hudson and knew their search was over.

'Here,' Barbara said.

'Here,' Ted agreed.

The very next week, they placed a deposit on a beautiful two-acre site that sloped down toward the river and began to design their house.

'I want large rooms, high ceilings, and lots of windows,' Barbara declared. 'And a big pantry in the kitchen. And closets – endless closets.'

'Every room will have a river view,' Ted decided. 'The house will have two arms that extend out, sort of like a V with a flat bottom, and the girls will have one wing and we'll have another.'

'Can we have a garden?' she asked.

'Of course,' he told her. 'And we'll have a play area for the girls, and a patio with a barbecue, and a front porch where we can sit in the evenings and watch the sun go down.'

'I can't wait,' she breathed.

But Barbara was already sick. Every specialist Ted consulted told him the same thing – a year, perhaps two, no more than that.

They kept the seriousness of it from the children and from each other and even from themselves as long as they could. Every night, Ted would snuggle close beside her, willing his strength into her body and praying for a miracle even as he watched her slowly fading away.

'She's always been there,' he told his sister wretchedly one drab day in May when the ambulance had been summoned to rush Barbara to the hospital for the last time. 'She's not just my wife, you know, not just my friend – she's the best part of me. She's my strength, my purpose. Whatever dreams have come true, whatever plans have worked out, whatever I've accomplished – all of it – it's only because she was there, backing me up. What will I ever do without her?'

'What you have to do,' Nancy told him, holding tight to his hand. 'You'll go on.'

The doctor, a well-meaning but taciturn man, came out of Barbara's room just then and tapped Ted on the shoulder.

'She wants to see you,' he said.

Ted started to stand up but his knees buckled under him.

'Get hold of yourself,' Nancy hissed. 'You have to be strong now, for her.'

He nodded numbly and struggled to his feet. It was only a few steps across the corridor, but it took an eternity for him to reach her door and all his effort to push it open. She looked so small lying in the hospital bed, so helpless, her brown eyes too big in her pale face. What was left of her glossy brown hair barely grazed the pillow. The tubes were gone, the masks, the wires, the machines – symbols of modern medicine that had not been able to heal. Had they been there, he might have smashed them with his fists.

She tried to smile at him as he came toward her and

that pitiful attempt alone was enough to fill his eyes and pinch his throat.

'Hi,' she whispered.

He sat down on the bed beside her and held her shoulders and kissed her lightly.

'I love you,' he said in an unsteady voice. 'I've always loved you. I guess I haven't said it anywhere near as often as I should, but that doesn't mean I don't feel it.'

'I know,' she murmured.

'I've never loved anyone but you – not anyone. Not from the moment I first saw you in that ridiculous pom-pom skirt.'

'No sillier,' she breathed, 'than you in your Bermuda shorts.'

'We made quite a pair, didn't we?' he said with a painful chuckle.

Her eyes flickered closed for a moment and he thought she might be slipping away, but then they opened again.

'The children . . .' she sighed, her voice weaker, her effort stronger.

'What?' he asked. 'What about them?'

'Love them . . .'

'Always,' he told her.

'Find someone . . .' she managed, and he had to bend close now to hear her. 'Make a family ... build ... build that house . . .'

'No!' he cried.

'Promise . . .'

'No,' he sobbed, burying his head against her. 'You can't ask me to do that. I could never love anyone but you. Never! I'll take good care of the girls. I'll be the best father to them that I know how to be, but I don't want anyone else. Please, don't make me promise.'

But Barbara could no longer hear him.

Ted took her home to Reading to be buried. Nancy stayed behind with the girls. For two days he allowed himself to be surrounded by people who knew and loved him and who had known and loved Barbara.

'I'm sorry,' he kept saying to her parents. 'I'm so sorry.'

'It wasn't your fault, son,' they told him. 'It was nobody's fault. Don't blame yourself.'

But he did. He blamed himself for all those years he had made her wait, all those lost years they could have had together.

When he returned to New York, he and Nancy and the girls had a quiet ceremony of their own. It was a godsend having Nancy there to take care of everything, but eventually she had to go back to Reading. Joe needed her and she did have two little ones of her own.

'Why don't you take a couple of weeks off?' she urged her brother. 'Go away somewhere, get some rest.'

'It's better if I work,' he told her.

'Well then, why don't I take the girls home with me? Mom's already said that she and Dad would love to have them for a while.'

'Gwen and Jessica have school,' Ted said. 'I don't want to disrupt their routine any more than necessary.'

'Will you be all right?'

'Sure.'

'How will you manage, I mean, with everything?'

'I don't know,' he said. 'I suppose I'll have to hire a housekeeper. Someone to cook and be here with the girls when I'm not home. I think that would be the best solution.'

Nancy hired Mrs. Peagram before she left. The plump little widow, with the knot of gray hair on top of her head, had lost her husband in the Korean War, before there were any children, and had never re-married. She was fair, if strict, and believed in reward-ing success more than punishing failure. The girls never entirely warmed up to her, but she had the household running smoothly in no time.

Ted went ahead and purchased the property in Hastings-on-Hudson but he never built the house. The idea of living there without Barbara was much too painful. Occasionally, he would drive up on a Sunday and walk the boundaries of the site or sit on the slope and look out over the steady river while the children played catch or tag or munched on a lunch that Mrs. Peagram had prepared.

He bought the house on West Seventy-eighth Street instead, and not only did he design the new interior, he did much of the actual renovation work himself. It was hard, mindless labor and exactly what he needed. While he and Barbara had dreamed of getting out of the city as soon as possible, his decision to stay was based on practicality. The fifteen-minute commute to and from his office, even at the height of the rush hour, gave him more time to spend with the girls.

When the Yanows moved to New York a year later, Ted offered them the upstairs apartment. The ar-rangement suited everyone. Nancy slipped into the role of surrogate mother that Mrs. Peagram had never quite filled and Ted soon settled into a comfortable routine – with his work to sustain him, his children to fulfill him, and his sister to support him.

He had no interest in meeting women. The very idea of dating seemed a betrayal. For the most part, he was quite content with his neat, safe life. If he sometimes missed the kind of intimacy that could be found only with a woman, it was a momentary distraction. For him, the act of love was as emotional as it was physical. On the few occasions when he even bothered to look at the women who continually circled around him, there wasn't one among them with whom he felt the slightest desire to share anything intimate.

Until now.

Now, as he puttered in his little patch of garden under a thin April sun and watched Gwen pulling weeds and Jessica teaching Amy to do a cartwheel, it occurred to him that, as usual, Barbara had been much wiser than he. She had tried to tell him not to bury himself beside her and shut his heart to the idea of being whole again. He had never dreamed that someone would come along to fill even a portion of that aching void inside him. But someone had – when he wasn't looking, when his guard was down, when he least expected it.

It was Nancy's fault, of course, for bringing her into the house, first as a business associate, then as a friend, and finally blending her into the very fabric of the family.

'She's nothing to do with you,' his sister had insisted the day before his fortieth birthday party. 'She's my friend. We're working on a book together, Joe and the kids adore her, and I thought it would be nice to include her. But if the idea really bothers you that much, I'll just tell her not to come.'

'You can't very well do that once you've invited her,' Ted grumbled.

'Then grin and bear it.'

From Nancy's careless account of her career-oriented friend, he expected something of a barracuda to show up – insecure, power-hungry, and typically overdressed, overconfident, and overanxious. He was totally unprepared for the gentle, amiable, utterly delightful woman who had captivated his daughters in less than thirty seconds.

'You've very good with children,' he told her on that first evening. 'The girls are usually quite shy with strangers.'

'I love kids,' she said simply.

He couldn't understand why she wasn't married, with a houseful of her own to nurture, but as winter slipped and skidded its way into spring, he realized how very glad he was that she wasn't.

It began on his birthday with just a vague recognition of someone new entering his space. By Christmas, he had become comfortable with her. By Easter, he thought of her as a good friend. By Labor Day, he found himself inventing opportunities to see her. And by the time 1981 rolled around, he was ready to put aside his guilt and acknowledge that he wanted her to be a lot more than a friend.

She was bright and amusing and self-reliant, and still there was something terribly vulnerable about her – a way she had of holding back sometimes, to observe rather than to participate, or an expression in her eyes when she didn't know he was watching.

On New Year's Day, he invited her up to Hastings-on-Hudson. A foot of snow lay on the ground and chunks of ice floated slowly down the river. The girls immediately set to building a snowman and Ted and Karen began to walk.

'It's magnificent up here,' she breathed when they had tramped the length of the property. 'I'm so sorry you and Barbara didn't get to build your dream house.'

'I think you would have liked her,' he heard himself say. 'I know she would have liked you.'

'Knowing you, knowing the girls,' Karen replied, 'it's obvious she must have been very special.'

He was well aware that she saw him as a sort of surrogate brother, and was quite comfortable with him on that basis. He had no inkling of how she would view a change in that status. In the eighteen months they had known each other, she had not once indicated, by a single word or deed, that she desired anything else. All by itself, that set her apart from almost every other woman he had met in the five years since Barbara's death.

It occurred to him that he really knew very little about her. She rarely spoke of herself, except to provide brief answers to direct questions. Their conversations were mostly about him or the girls or the Yanows or Demion Five. She had walked into the middle of his life, but as of yet, he had not been invited into hers.

'I suppose you're one of those feminists,' he suggested once when she teased him about his tendency to cling to traditional gender roles. 'An emancipated woman who chose career over family.'

'Sometimes,' she replied enigmatically, 'life has very little to do with choice.'

'What does it have to do with, then?' he probed.

For a moment, Karen's face clouded over and a haunted expression filled her eyes.

'Survival,' she said. Then her face cleared and she was smiling and teasing him once again.

It was the first time he had seen beneath her sunny, serene surface, the first glimpse he had of a darker side. He wondered what misfortune shrouded her past, but he didn't press her. He didn't want to appear to be prying and run the risk of pushing her away. Besides, it didn't really matter. In the silence of the night, and the emptiness of his bed, he couldn't stop thinking about her.

Two or three evenings a week, when he knew she was upstairs working on the book with Nancy, Ted would invent a reason to come knocking on the door. After a while, the frequency of his visits prompted Nancy to observe, privately, that she had seen more of him in the past several months than in the past several years.

'Is that a complaint?' he asked.

'Nope,' she said with an impish grin. 'In fact, let me know when you run out of excuses. I'm sure there are a few I can suggest.'

At Ted's instigation, Sunday evenings became family occasions. Either upstairs or downstairs, the Yanows and the Donigers would gather together for dinner, a few games, a little conversation and a lot of fun. Karen was always included.

Late one summer Sunday, when the children were asleep and the adults were lingering in the garden, Amy woke up screaming from a nightmare and neither Ted nor Mrs. Peagram could manage to calm her.

'Let me try,' Karen offered.

She sat down on Amy's pink-and-white canopy bed in the little girl's candy-cane room, and calmly took the child into her arms. Her voice was too low for Ted to catch the words, but it didn't matter. In less than ten minutes, his youngest daughter was sound asleep again.

'What did you say to her?' he whispered.

'I told her that her mother had sent me to chase away the hobgoblins and keep her safe while she slept.' He caught a sudden mischievous glint in her blue-gray eyes. 'Then I bribed her.'

'With what?'

'I promised that, whenever I'm here, I'll come and tell her a story before she goes to sleep so that her dreams will be filled with beautiful things – and there won't be any room left for scary monsters.'

It became a ritual. Three, sometimes four nights a week, Karen would sit on the edge of Amy's bed and spin magical tales of little girls and little boys in a faraway world where the sun always shone and birds always sang and flowers always bloomed, and there was no such thing as sadness.

'Is there such a place?' Amy asked her.

'Oh yes,' Karen told her. 'If you believe.'

Before long, Jessica and Gwen, too, were sidling into Amy's room, climbing up on the end of the bed to listen, and from the doorway, Ted watched and realized how much his daughters needed a mother. Mrs. Peagram kept the house spotlessly clean and the girls properly fed and clothed and supervised their homework, but she wasn't very good at nurturing. She just didn't have the knack.

Karen had the knack. She wasn't Barbara, of course – no one would ever be Barbara. Yet, in some ways, she was a lot like Barbara. She seemed to know many of the same things Barbara had known and she did many of the same things Barbara had done, and more and more, he couldn't seem to keep himself from smiling whenever she was around.

She was interested in his work, genuinely fond of the children, and perfectly at ease in his environment. Without even being aware of it, he began to picture her running the house, raising the girls, and growing old beside him.

'Is Karen coming tonight?' Jessica asked, interrupting his thoughts, and yet not really interrupting them at all.

'Is today Sunday?'

'Sure.'

'Then Karen's coming.'

'I want to show her my science project before I turn it in.'

'Good,' Ted replied. 'As I recall, she was the one who gave you the idea.'

'Yeah.' Jessica grinned. 'She did, didn't she?'

'Watch me, Daddy!' Amy cried suddenly. 'I'm going to do a cartwheel!'

'I'm watching, sweetheart,' he called.

The effort was a bit lopsided but the chubby youngster managed to pull it around.

'Did you see?' she chortled, jumping up and down. 'Did you see?'

'I saw, and it was wonderful.'

'Will Karen be here before it gets dark? I want to show her, too.'

'I think so.'

'Make sure, Daddy, will you? I want her to see me.'

'You know, Dad,' Gwen observed idly, 'if you

married Karen, we wouldn't have to keep asking when she's coming all the time. She'd already be here.'

'You mean every night?' Amy asked, overhearing.

'Sure,' Gwen told her, 'and mornings and afternoons, too.'

'Would she be here to tie my shoes for school?' the first-grader pressed.

'Of course,' Jessica put in. 'She'd be here just like Mommy used to be.'

Amy's eyes widened. 'Just like Mommy?' she gasped, although she was too young to have a very clear image of Barbara.

'Well, not exactly like her,' modified Gwen, the only one of the three of them who could really remember. 'But almost.'

The little girl turned to her father. 'Are we going to marry Karen, Daddy? Is she going to be almost like Mommy?'

'Would you like that?' he asked, amazed at how simple the most complex things could become when seen through the eyes of a child.

'Oh yes,' Amy breathed.

'Sure,' Jessica said.

'Why not?' Gwen shrugged and then lowered her voice to a whisper. 'She's a lot nicer than Mrs. Pea, anyway.'

As if on cue, Mrs. Peagram came to the back door. 'It's time for lunch,' she announced in her high-pitched Boston twang. 'Come on in now, girls, and let's get those little hands washed.'

Ted thrust his trowel into the soft dirt of the flower bed and stood up with purpose.

'You go on in with Mrs. Peagram and have your lunch,' he directed his daughters.

'What about you, Daddy?' Jessica wanted to know. 'What are you going to do?'

'I'm going to go clean myself up a little,' he told her, looking down at his soiled jeans, 'and then I have an errand to run, across town.'

seven

Karen sat cross-legged in the middle of her living room floor, in a baggy red sweat suit, surrounded by black-and-white photographs. A yellow pad lay beside her, a ballpoint pen was clamped between her teeth. There was a smudge of ink on her chin.

The book that she and Nancy had envisioned nearly two years ago was almost finished. They had made the final photo selections, from among the thousand images captured on film, just last week. All that was wanting now were the words.

'No pressure,' Nancy had assured her, handing over a thick stack of prints. 'Just take these home with you, live with them for a while, and see what comes.'

At first, nothing had come. Karen spent hours staring at a blank pad, chewing on the end of her pen, trying to think like a poet. Finally, she tossed the pad and pen aside, stopped thinking, and began to stare instead at the images themselves, spreading the prints out around her, concentrating on their stories.

Eventually, she found words to describe the children of Harlem as they stood in the path of a gushing fire hydrant on a suffocating summer day, and the cold breath of death that reached into a Bowery doorway in the middle of winter to claim a man beneath a blanket of newspapers, and the rebirth of the earth as the first spring crocus pushed its head through the hard crust of clay along Riverside Drive.

But autumn had totally frustrated her. With a sigh, and time running out, Karen reached for the twelve visions of that enigmatic season for perhaps the hundredth time. This time, one of them caught her attention and she reached out and pulled it toward her. It was a bleak illustration, in which Nancy had caught the last leaf falling from the only tree in an otherwise treeless section of Morningside Park. She yanked the pen out of her mouth, grabbed her pad, and began to write.

> The last tear of autumn
> falls unnoticed.
> A silent cry,
> frozen on the cheek of winter.

Now, at least, she had a beginning, a direction.

An hour later, she had covered half a dozen pages. So engrossed was she that the unexpected sound of her door buzzer severed her concentration like a chain saw.

'Hi,' Ted said when she opened the door.

'Hi,' she replied, wondering why he was standing on her doorstep, looking so freshly scrubbed, in the middle of the day. 'Don't tell me I forgot something,' she gasped. 'Did we have plans?'

'No, no,' he assured her hastily. 'I just happened to be in the neighborhood, so I thought I'd stop by. But if you're busy, I can be on my way.'

'Don't be silly,' she told him, because the mood was broken now and the words were gone. 'Come on in.'

'I thought maybe you'd be out on a day like this.'

Karen was quickly gathering up her papers, stacking them neatly on the desk. 'I've been trying to work.'

'And I interrupted you, didn't I?'

He sounded so genuinely distressed that she felt her irritation at the intrusion melt away.

'It's all right, really,' she assured him. 'I wasn't having much success, anyway.'

Ted had been to her apartment on a number of occasions over the past year and a half, and each time he entered he was surprised by how familiar it felt. When he sat down on one of the love seats, it was just like slipping into a comfortable old sweater.

'I think this book is a wonderful idea,' he said, glancing down at the photographs on the floor. 'I know it's going to be a success.'

'Providing I hold up my end of the bargain.' Karen sighed. 'I don't know why I let Nancy talk me into this.'

'Someday you'll be glad she did,' he said with such genuine conviction that Karen smiled.

From the very beginning, he had put her at ease, teasing her like a kid sister, treating her like a valued friend, until it was hard to remember that they hadn't known each other all their lives. In large part, she supposed, the instant comfort came from his being Nancy's brother. But Karen knew it was also because he had never attempted anything more than a quick peck on the cheek or a hand on an elbow to guide her across a street that she felt as close to him as if there were actually a flesh-and-blood connection between them.

Like his sister, Ted was bright and clever, and Karen looked forward to the now frequent occasions when she saw him. But even more important to her than the time spent with him was the time she spent with Gwen and Jessica and Amy.

In many ways, the three girls had come to symbolize the innocence Karen had lost, the daughters she would never raise, the children she would never bear. She answered their questions, cheered their successes, and basked in every smile and every giggle they chose to share with her. And always behind them stood their father, steady, sober and safe.

Still, she hadn't realized how deeply entwined she had become in the lives of the Donigers until this very moment – because this was the first time Ted had ever appeared on her doorstep unannounced.

'Can I get you something to drink?' she asked, suddenly remembering her manners.

'A glass of water would be fine,' he replied.

'How about some iced tea?'

'Only if you'll have some, too.'

She returned from the kitchen with two frosty glasses and a plate of cookies.

'Looks good,' he said.

They sipped in silence until Ted set his glass down on the coffee table and stood up, walking to the fireplace and pretending to study the Rankin oil that hung above the mantel.

'Amy would like you to come before dark tonight,'

he said. 'Jessica's taught her how to do a cartwheel, and she wants you to see.'

'Of course I will,' Karen replied warmly.

'And Jessica wants to show you her science project.'

Karen nodded. 'Oh, good. I've been anxious to see how it turned out.'

Their words sounded strangely formal and stilted to them both. Karen shifted uncomfortably in her seat, wondering what had happened to their usual light banter. Ted ran a finger along the edge of the mantel.

'Uh, Gwen thinks we ought to get married,' he said, trying to make his tone light, 'so we wouldn't always have to schedule appointments to see you.'

'Oh, she does, does she?' Karen replied with a smile, relieved to have the conversation back on track.

'Actually, all three girls would like that,' he added.

'Those little devils.' She chuckled. 'You never know what they'll come up with next.'

Ted turned around to face her then. 'As a matter of fact,' he said softly, 'all four of us would like that ... very much.'

Karen opened her mouth to say something clever and then closed it again when she realized he was serious. But it didn't make any sense, because they didn't have that kind of relationship. They were just – friends.

'I don't understand,' she stammered finally. 'I mean, you never – that is, I didn't – I mean, you and I aren't – well, you know – like that.'

'Just because we haven't been doesn't mean we couldn't be,' he observed.

'But we're friends,' she protested. 'Good friends. I count on your friendship. I don't want that to change.'

He shrugged. 'I happen to think that friendship is a pretty solid foundation to build on.'

Just like an architect, Karen thought wryly, beginning to squirm anew in her seat. She valued the relationship they had forged more than she could ever say, and she wondered whether it would survive her turning him down.

'I'm really very flattered,' she began gently, 'but the idea of marrying you – well, it just never entered my head.'

'I know I'm not exactly the knight in shining armor you probably expected to come riding over the hill,' he conceded. 'I've had some of the stuffing knocked out of me, I admit it. I'm too much of a workaholic and not enough of a romantic. I like theater and the symphony, but I don't go very often. I'm not much of a party animal. I guess you could say I'm a real stick-in-the-mud. I'm not well-traveled or well-read. On top of that, I'm middle-aged, I've buried a wife, and I've got three kids to raise – altogether, nobody's idea of a prize package. But I'm faithful and honest and a good provider, I think, and the thing is, I care for you in a very special way, and I think we could make a good life together.'

He stopped talking suddenly, surprised that he had actually managed to make that whole speech without stumbling.

'How can you say all those awful things about yourself?' Karen demanded. 'You're certainly no more middle-aged than I am, and you're terrific at parties. You may not say much, but you're a great listener. I don't go to the symphony all that often myself, and the bookshelves always seem to be filled at your place. I'm not so well-traveled, either, I'll have you know. I've never even been to Europe. And there are a whole lot more important things for a person to be in life than romantic – like sensible and stable and sincere, and your children are absolutely terrific. How can you say you're not a knight in shining armor? I can't imagine any woman who wouldn't be proud to ride off with you.'

'Is that a yes?' he asked.

Karen stopped short. She had been so eager to come to his defense that she hadn't really given much thought to the effect her words might have on him.

He was so terribly nice and the last thing in the world she wanted to do was hurt him. But she had long ago resigned herself to the idea of being unmarried, choosing instead to devote herself to a career, whatever it turned out to be, and she was not uncomfortable with that decision. Now all she had to do was find a way to let him down gently.

'I think maybe you should give me a little time,' she heard herself say. 'You know, to kind of sort things out.'

'Of course,' he exclaimed. 'Take all the time you need. I know this is a pretty big decision for you to make.'

The biggest, she thought. 'Thank you,' she murmured.

Ted reached for his iced tea and politely drained the glass. 'Why don't I let you get back to work,' he said. 'I mean, it's not as though I''m not going to see you again in a few hours, right?'

'Right,' she agreed.

The moment the door closed behind him, Karen made for the kitchen, filling her tea glass with Scotch and drinking it down in one long swallow.

The plastic composure she had cultivated for the past eighteen years, that singular ability to draw a curtain across her emotions, crumbled as she giggled and cried and shivered all together. She refilled her glass and went back to the living room, where she collapsed in a heap. Halfway through the second Scotch, she began to feel very foolish.

'Why didn't you just come right out and say no?' she reproached herself aloud. 'Why did you have to leave him dangling as though there were some hope?'

The day Peter Bauer walked out of her life, Karen had been devastated. Although, clearly, she had been the one to betray him, she had been unable to shake the feeling that, in some indefinable way, he had betrayed her as well. She determined that she would never again put herself in that position. The yardstick of the 1960s still hung over her in the 1980s. In her heart, she knew that no man would ever be able to forgive her for what she had let happen on that cold December night, as Peter had not, and would shrink from her at the first mention of it – at the first sight of the result. Of course, she had to admit, she had never been willing to let anyone close enough to test her theory.

Instead, she had come to terms with being single. In many ways, she found she was well-suited to the solitude, and the consequent peace and privacy it afforded. Then, too, the state of spinsterhood no longer carried the stigma it once had. Karen knew women who were enjoying a whole new kind of life-style. They were out in the business world, being successful and single. Some lived intimately and openly with men to whom they were not married. A few were even choosing to have babies without having husbands.

Downing the last of her Scotch, Karen sighed a sigh of defeat, knowing in her heart of hearts that, even though she had truly made peace with the way her life had turned out, she would gladly have given up Demion Five and her posh East Side apartment and her Rankin oil for just one day of being elbow-deep in diapers and dirty dishes and Tinker Toys. That was the irony of what Ted had come across town to suggest. Had he offered her Mrs. Peagram's position instead of a marriage proposal, she might have been tempted to accept.

Karen laughed outright. Nothing less than two stiff drinks could have brought her to admit anything like that. But it was true. In just a few short months, she had become so involved in the lives of Gwen and Jessica and Amy that she couldn't imagine a more rewarding assignment than to spend every single day with them, helping them to learn and grow and blossom into beautiful young women. It would go a long way toward making up for the children she could never have.

Sometimes she liked to imagine, when she sat on Amy's bed in the evenings and spun out her stories, that these three little girls were indeed her very own. She couldn't have loved them more. But to marry a man just so she could stay close to his children? There seemed something not quite honest about that.

It wasn't that she didn't like Ted. On the contrary, she liked him enormously and probably even loved him, as a sister would love a brother. But the thought of having to share a bed with him, or let him see the ugly scars that screamed the truth of her youthful indiscretion, made her shiver all over again.

No, she would have to tell him again how flattered she was by his proposal, and then decline – even knowing it would mean she would lose the girls, because things would be too awkward after that. How many men who had been rejected would still want the woman who rejected them underfoot all the time?

Karen bit her lower lip and felt tears stinging her eyes. She was going to miss the children terribly, she knew. Not only that, she was truthful enough to admit that she was going to miss Ted terribly, too.

eight

The photographic essay was finished and scheduled for production the second week in May.

'Jesus,' Demelza breathed when she saw it. 'I knew Nancy could take pictures, but I never dreamed Karen could write this kind of poetry. This is dynamite. We'll order five thousand copies.'

'Do you think you can sell that many?' Nancy gasped.

'At least,' the co-owner of Demion Five told her. 'What are you going to call it?'

After considerable debate, the two women had named the book *Four Seasons* because, after all, that was exactly what it was.

'Not to be confused with Vivaldi,' Nancy said.

'Or the restaurant,' Karen added.

Demelza priced the book at $49.95.

'My goodness,' the photographer exclaimed. 'Isn't that a bit steep?' Actually, she considered it outrageous.

'It's a bargain,' Demelza told her. 'Fifty Yanows for a dollar apiece? Fabulous presentation? Even without the poetry – which could be a lovely little book in its own right – it's an absolute bargain.'

'I had no idea,' Nancy conceded, even though her single prints, which were limited to a run of fifty, sold for as much as two hundred and fifty dollars each. But then, they were individually signed and numbered.

'You have to remember,' Demelza continued as though she had read the photographer's mind, 'it's not so very different from marketing your prints. We're still talking limited edition.'

'Five thousand doesn't sound so limited to me,' Nancy observed.

'If we start promoting by the middle of July,' Demelza said, 'we should be sold out by Christmas.'

'Sold out?' Nancy exclaimed. 'Are you serious?'

Demelza smiled. 'I suggest you start planning your next book.'

Nancy's head was spinning and Karen was feeling as giddy as a newborn colt as the two women made their way over to Ninth Avenue and a new, highly touted Italian restaurant. They had promised themselves a night on the town when *Four Seasons* was finished.

'Why do I feel as though I'm in a leaky rowboat about to plunge over Niagara Falls?' the photographer wondered as they were shown to their table.

The poet chuckled. 'Well, look at it this way,' she suggested. 'It's not your life you're in danger of losing, just your credibility.'

'Thanks,' Nancy replied dryly. 'That makes me feel lots better.'

It was a prix-fixe restaurant without a menu. The fare was whatever the chef felt like preparing that particular evening. Reservations were required, and the place, which could accommodate only forty diners at a time, was booked at least two months in advance.

They discussed different ways of promoting the book through the minestrone, the in-store fanfare that Demion Five would be likely to launch over the hot and cold antipasto, and the incredible idea that their work could become a coffee-table necessity between bites of cheese ravioli.

It wasn't until they had begun to dig into their veal scallopini that Karen casually dropped her bombshell.

'Ted asked me to marry him.'

The fork fell from Nancy's hand and her uneven blue eyes almost popped from her head.

'And you waited through three courses to tell me?' she cried indignantly.

'Well, actually, it's been a bit longer than that.'

'How long?'

Karen shrugged. 'About a month.'

'A month?' Nancy squealed. 'A whole month and you never breathed a word of it?'

'Well, I wasn't sure how you'd take it.'

'How I'd take it? I've been hoping and praying for this for a year and a half now.'

Karen picked at her three-star food.

'The thing is, you see, I've never really thought of Ted in that way,' she mused.

'Oh?' Nancy said, and the word hung there between them.

'Don't misunderstand. It's not that I don't care about him,' Karen insisted. 'I do, a great deal, and you know how much I adore the girls. But, well, I wasn't planning on getting married.'

'Why not?' was all Nancy could think of to ask.

'It's just a choice I made, a long time ago,' Karen replied, gulping her Chianti.

Nancy had decided that Karen was ideal for her brother the first day the two women met at Demion Five, over tea and muffins and Paul Revere. She wasn't sure what it was about the stylish boutique manager, among all the other women she had considered and rejected, that made her so positive so immediately, but the idea had caught on something inside her head and refused to be dislodged.

'Why would you make such a ridiculous choice as that?' she asked, as Karen toyed with her veal.

'I've been alone so long,' came the reply. 'I'm set in my ways. I need my space.'

'It's about a long time ago, isn't it?' Nancy asked softly, shrewdly. 'About what happened to you – what you wrote about?'

Karen looked away. 'It's about a lot of things,' she murmured.

'But things can change,' Nancy insisted. 'If we want them to.'

There was a pause then, neither of them knowing quite where to go next.

'I believe that everyone has two selves,' Karen said finally. 'The public self that they show to the world and the private one that sustains them. For some people, the public self is merely an extension of the private self. For others, though, the public self is a mask for the private self, and without it they wouldn't survive.'

Karen stopped there, and Nancy considered her words. This woman had been her closest friend for two years, in great part because they shared so many common interests, common values and common instincts, and Nancy had long ago seen beneath the self-assured facade.

'Sometimes sharing can be a means of survival,' she suggested.

'Not in this case,' Karen asserted. 'You'll just have to take my word for that.'

'I think you're selling yourself short,' Nancy declared. 'And Ted, too.'

'Perhaps I just have a different perspective.'

'Then why say anything at all?'

'Because you and Ted are so close and I don't want this to come between you. And because you and I are close and I don't want it to come between us, either.'

'He might not come to me.'

Karen thought about that for a moment. 'Then go to him. There are so many good women out there. Don't let him shut the door because one failed him.'

'He really cares about you, you know.'

A shadow flickered across Karen's face. 'He deserves better.'

The next evening, she dropped by for a bedtime story unannounced, choosing the tale of the princess and the pea. As soon as she finished, she tucked the covers around Amy, kissed Jessica and Gwen good night, and went in search of Ted, finding him in the study, of course, hunched over his drafting table, the light from the lamp glinting off his golden hair.

'Are you busy?' she asked hesitantly.

His face lit up when he saw her.

'Never too busy for you,' he replied, snapping off the lamp and standing up to stretch his back muscles.

Then he moved over to sit on the sofa. 'Are the girls in bed?'

'One is, another is on her way and the third is probably on the telephone.'

'Come sit down,' he invited, patting the sofa.

Karen chose the chair across from him.

'You must have thought I was ignoring you,' she began.

'Nonsense,' he told her. 'I know how hard you and Nancy have been working to finish the book.'

It would have been so much easier, she thought, if he weren't always so nice and so understanding about everything.

'Well, I didn't want you to think that I'd forgotten your ... your kind offer.'

He grinned at her, the gold flecks in his eyes dancing. 'You make it sound like we're talking about a job.'

'Oh, I didn't mean to,' she apologized. 'It's just that I ...'

Karen faltered. She had simply meant to thank him, decline his proposal, and then leave, as quickly as possible.

'It's been such a short time,' she heard herself saying instead. 'We barely know each other. I mean, we're friends, and I really do like you, but ...'

'... you don't love me,' he finished for her.

She looked down at her hands twisted in her lap. 'It's not that so much,' she whispered, wishing she didn't have to do this. 'But there are things about me, things you couldn't possibly understand that – well, it isn't you, you see, it's that – well, I can't marry anybody.'

He looked at her thoughtfully for a moment, while

she struggled with her hands.

'For a long time after my wife died,' he said finally, 'I was convinced that I never wanted to get close to anyone again. Losing her had hurt too much, and I knew I couldn't risk going through anything like that a second time. So I built an invisible wall around myself, a bomb shelter, if you will, and I locked myself into it so I could be safe. I had my work, I had the girls, and I figured that was enough. But I was wrong, because all of life is a risk – and safe is as good as already dead.'

Karen pried her eyes away from her hands to glance up at him. He was sensitive and he was caring and he was trying so hard, but he just didn't understand.

'And for me, it's the other way around,' she told him. 'Safe is the only way I can live.'

'Does that leave any room for negotiation?'

Her glance slid past his shoulder. 'I do like you, in a very special way,' she said. 'I trust you more than any man I know. I feel good when I'm with you. I look forward to the time I spend with you and the girls, and all that means more to me than I can say.'

'That's a start.'

'But it's not enough.'

'Why not?'

Her eyes fastened on her hands once again. 'Because I can't ... I can't be a wife to you.' She sighed. She had come to think of other women as being lush and green inside, where she saw herself to be brown and shriveled.

A pensive frown creased his forehead. 'I'm not going to pry,' he said. 'I don't need to know any more than you want to tell me.'

'I had ... an accident,' she heard herself say, when

she hadn't intended to say anything at all. 'It was a long time ago, but because of it, there are – things that don't work like they should.'

'I'm not looking for grand passion at my stage of life,' he replied sincerely. 'I don't really expect to have again what I had with Barbara. But the feelings I have for you are warm and comfortable and constant, and that's enough for me. I'd just like you to be a part of my life, to share all the laughter that's ahead, and the tears, too.'

'You make it sound so simple,' she responded. 'Only it isn't that simple.'

Ted took a deep breath. 'It can be,' he assured her. 'It can be as simple as taking on three little girls who adore you, and their father who thinks the world is an okay place again because you're in it. And it wouldn't ever have to be anything more than that, unless, of course, you wanted it to be.'

'I do believe you *are* offering me a job,' she said with a sudden grin. 'Mrs. Peagram's job.'

'Well, that may not be exactly what I had in mind,' he returned with a grin of his own. 'But I'll take what I can get.'

Karen sighed again. He made it sound almost idyllic, as in the fairy tales she told the girls, where the prince and the princess, no matter what problems stood in their way, always rode off into the sunset together to live happily ever after. But fantasy was one thing and reality was quite another.

'I wish – ' she began.

'Look,' he interrupted. 'I have to run up to New Haven tomorrow. I'll be gone two, maybe three days. Why don't you think about it some more, until I get back. Then we can sit down and talk again.'

'Well, if you insist,' she conceded, although the last thing she wanted was to have another conversation like this.

'Let's put it this way,' he said. 'I know you came here tonight to turn me down. That's pretty obvious. So I have very little to lose by postponing the moment – and maybe a great deal to gain.'

Karen couldn't help chuckling. 'This would be a whole lot easier if I didn't like you so much.'

'I'm counting on that,' he replied.

'What's happening in New Haven?' she asked.

'Something of an honor, actually,' he told her. 'My alma mater has invited me to participate in a symposium on changing trends in architecture and then I've been asked to submit a proposal for a new computer complex.'

'Yale is in New Haven,' she said.

'Indeed it is,' he agreed.

Karen began to laugh as she hadn't laughed in years because there were some things that had no rhyme or reason, they just happened, at a time and a place of their own choosing, and there was no point in trying to figure out how or why.

'You went to Yale?' she sputtered.

'Twice,' he confirmed. 'Both undergraduate and graduate school. Why? Does that make a difference?'

'Not to me,' she giggled. 'But my mother is going to love you.'

nine

Four Seasons, by Yanow and Kern, was presented to the public on the thirteenth of August. Its appearance at Demion Five was preceded by a solid month of promotion, designed to whet the appetite of every status-conscious patron of the arts within a hundred-mile radius of Manhattan.

'By the time this little item hits the shelves,' Demelza predicted, 'there won't be a self-proclaimed connoisseur anywhere within hailing distance of this city who'd let himself be caught dead without a copy on his coffee table.'

Karen and Nancy were on the scene that Thursday from two until six, seated behind a table, as the stack of books in front of them slowly dwindled, autographing every first-day purchase with a flourish. Trays of canapés were passed about, champagne bubbled, and the shop was jammed.

'I told you they'd come,' Demelza murmured,

breezing by with a platter of rumaki.

Finally, it was closing time. The last canapé had been eaten, the last drop of champagne drunk, and the last paying customer politely ushered out the door.

'My right hand will never be the same,' Nancy complained as she flexed her fingers in agony.

'Oh, the price of fame and fortune,' Demelza declared.

'That remains to be seen,' Karen remarked. 'Two hundred copies sold does not five thousand make.'

'After twelve years in my employ,' Demelza chided, 'I can't believe you haven't learned how to recognize a winner. Hasn't any of my clairvoyance rubbed off?'

Karen shrugged. 'I guess in this case, I'm not exactly what you'd call objective.'

By the end of October, two-thirds of the limited edition of *Four Seasons* had been spoken for.

'Trust me, the rest will be gone before Christmas,' Demelza proclaimed.

'I don't believe it,' Nancy gasped when Karen handed her a five-figure check for her share of the profits.

'I know,' Karen agreed, having banked a similar check earlier in the afternoon. 'Too bad we didn't print ten thousand copies.'

'That's okay,' Nancy told her. 'I've got a great idea for our second effort.'

Karen laughed. 'I was afraid you'd say that.'

Nancy shrugged. 'Well, at least you didn't say no.'

They began work on *Mirror Images*, a contrasting study of the people of New York, two days later, finishing the layout at three o'clock on the afternoon of November 14.

Four hours later, Karen and Ted were married in a simple ceremony in a judge's chamber, after which they celebrated with close friends and family at the elegant Four Seasons Restaurant.

'How appropriate,' gushed Beverly Kern. She smiled benignly at her new son-in-law. 'Was this your idea?'

'Actually, it was Karen's,' he told her.

'How very clever of you, darling,' she trilled at her daughter.

'Thank you, Mother,' Karen responded graciously.

'He's one of the most successful architects in the country,' Beverly had informed her sister-in-law Edna shortly after the engagement was announced.

'I'm so happy for Karen,' Edna replied. 'For a while, there, it didn't seem that she was ever going to settle down.'

'Well, I suppose it did take her longer than it might have,' Beverly sniffed. 'But then, she wasn't about to marry just anybody. He had to be suitable. Ted's a Yale man, you know.'

'No, I didn't know.'

'I suppose an architect is better than no one,' she said to her husband with a heavy sigh. 'But a widower with three small children? What can Karen be thinking of?'

'What's wrong with that?' Leo inquired. 'Seems like a pretty good fit to me, all things considered.'

'To have someone else's children foisted on her? How can that turn out to be anything but disastrous?'

'You worry too much,' Leo told his wife.

* * *

'We're so happy for Karen,' Beverly told Ted's mother during the reception. 'Your son is such a lovely man and so successful, too. And those adorable little girls of his – why, they're just an extra added bonus, aren't they?'

'We think so,' Ted's mother replied.

Karen never discussed what finally tipped the scales in Ted's favor. Not with Nancy or Jill and especially not with her mother. She told everyone it was because he had made it very easy for her to say yes and impossible for her to say no. But of course there was more to it than that.

There was knowing that a career, while not a totally unsatisfactory substitute for marriage and mother-hood, was still just that – a substitute. There was, in the final analysis, the desire to be connected to another human being, not to be alone any longer. And there was curiosity. Or perhaps it was that, in the secret place where her best instincts dwelled, Karen believed she had come upon a man who might care more about who she was than about what she had done.

It had always been her fantasy that a knight in shining armor would simply appear one day, like a sunburst, to claim her. He would ignore her imperfec-tions, look deep into her eyes and take her breath away.

Ted Doniger had sneaked up on her. There was no sunburst, no breathless moment of awareness. In the guise of a friend, he gained her confidence. In the guise of a surrogate brother, he gained her affection. Before she quite realized how it happened, she began to trust him with her laughter, her hopes, and her fears. From that grew the fervent faith that he would not turn away from her defiled body, and the belief that he would protect her from the harsh glare of an indifferent world. Further, she knew this was likely her last chance to have the life she had been raised to want – the children, the home, the status, the security, and he had offered it to her on whatever terms she chose to name.

'A good marriage is your only chance for happiness,' she could still hear Beverly saying. Although her values were no longer her mother's, she knew she would be a fool to turn Ted down.

'I know what a private person you are,' he had said, 'and how much you value your own space. I wish the apartment was big enough for separate rooms, but we can at least have separate beds, if that would make you more comfortable.'

Ted Doniger was a man of infinite patience. He intended to spend the rest of his life with this woman, and he was prepared to wait as long as necessary for the intimacy that so obviously troubled her. Just having her in the house all the time, where he could look at her and talk to her and watch her with the girls, would be enough.

'Do you want to go on a honeymoon?' he asked.

'I hadn't thought,' Karen murmured, uncomfortable with the implication of the question. 'Is it … obligatory?'

'I think it's up to the two people involved,' he replied casually. 'But since I'm still in the middle of the Yale project and you and Nancy are just starting a new book, it might work out better if we didn't plan anything right away.'

'That sounds reasonable,' she agreed with relief.

A honeymoon, with all that the word implied, would have been too much for her to handle, and she silently thanked him for his understanding. It was going to be difficult enough to change her whole life, not to mention her home, and she was counting on having the children around to help smooth the transition between dropping by and moving in.

They asked Felicity to create their wedding rings and she produced complementing free-form chunks of gold, Ted's plain, Karen's set off by a thin row of diamonds. Karen asked Jenna to design her wedding dress, requesting something simple, without a veil or a train, and not white – she would not have been able to deal with the deceit of wearing white. Jenna created a short swirl of pale-peach satin that suited Karen's coloring and figure perfectly and complemented Ted's dark-blue suit and tie.

The ceremony was brief but dignified and the reception was later described as elegant. Afterward, however, Karen could remember very little of either, except that she had been surrounded by all the important people in her life. What she did remember vividly was going home to West Seventy-eighth Street.

With the best of intentions, Nancy had whisked the girls upstairs following the festivities, bundling them into bed beside her own Roger and Emily. Mrs. Peagram had been given the weekend off.

The downstairs apartment was dark when Ted unlocked the door, and ominously quiet. For a moment, Karen had the foolish thought that they had come to the wrong address. She walked behind him into the kitchen, her high heels tapping smartly against the hardwood floor, echoing her heartbeat.

'It's so different here without the girls,' she murmured.

Ted snapped on the kitchen light. There was a bottle of champagne in a bucket of ice on the counter, with two long-stemmed glasses standing beside it. A card was propped against the bucket. It read: 'To a long and happy life together' in Nancy's distinct, slanted handwriting.

'My sister the romantic,' Ted chuckled. 'She must have sneaked down here just ahead of us.'

He reached for the bottle and extracted the cork with a resounding pop.

'Leave it to Nancy.' Karen smiled, wishing fervently that she was back in her own town house, standing in her own kitchen, about to down a shot of brandy before going to sleep in her own bed.

Ted poured just enough champagne into each goblet so it would not overflow. Then he handed one to her.

'I may not have much control over how long a life we'll have,' he said, smiling at her and touching his glass to hers, 'but I promise that I'll do everything I know how to make it a happy one.'

He was unfailingly nice and he was trying so hard to put her at ease. Karen was glad they still had on their coats so he couldn't see how hard her knees were knocking. Except she could see that her hand, holding the champagne, was trembling.

'Shall we light a fire?' he asked, noticing. 'We can sit and enjoy our champagne while we warm up.'

It sounded exactly like the kind of thing her knight in shining armor would have suggested.

'It's really late,' Karen heard herself reply. 'And I'm exhausted. Would it be all right if I just went on to bed?'

'Sure,' Ted said easily. 'You go ahead.' He leaned over and kissed her lightly on the cheek, the way he always did. 'I think I'll stay up for a while and unwind. Just holler if you need anything.'

Karen went quickly down the stairs, intending to be fast asleep by the time he finished unwinding. During the past week, she had moved her clothes and personal items over from East Sixty-third Street. She knew which bed was hers, which bureau, which closet, which shelves in the medicine cabinet, where the towels were kept, and how the light switches worked. She would not need any help.

It took her less than five minutes to undress, wash off her makeup and brush her teeth, pull a nightgown over her head and slip between the sheets, leaving only the lamp on Ted's side of the room lit. In addition to trading the double bed he had shared with Barbara for twins, Ted had fashioned a kind of partition out of draperies which had the effect of splitting the space in half.

Karen lay stiffly in the unfamiliar bed, staring at the unfamiliar half-room, and wondered what on earth she was doing there. This house, which had always echoed with light and laughter, now seemed like a silent tomb, with menace lurking in every corner.

'Please, let me go to sleep,' she whispered into the shadows. 'Let the morning come quickly. Let the girls come back early.'

The mist became fog, collecting at her feet, stealing up her legs, swirling about her body, engulfing her. Soon, she could see less than a yard ahead through the thick gray soup. She looked frantically around, searching for the path that had been there just seconds before –

but it was gone, gone in the fog, and she was lost and alone. With him.

She knew she couldn't stand still, she had to keep going. She plunged ahead blindly, running as fast as she could, knowing that outrunning him was the only thing that would save her. Her breath was coming in short, hard gasps now, and a sharp pain began to knife its way through her chest, but there was no stopping. Above the pounding of her heart, she could hear him behind her, getting ever closer.

She summoned one final burst of speed to push herself forward and fell head over heels into a thicket of bushes. Familiar bushes, with brambles that scratched her skin and snared her hair. She knew she had been there before. With every last ounce of energy she possessed, she tried to scramble free, but it was too late. He was already there.

The flames licked around the logs in the fireplace, radiating a comforting warmth. Ted sipped at his champagne and thought about what he had done. He had married a woman who didn't love him because he didn't want to be alone any longer. Yet he felt more alone now than he had before.

He couldn't fault Karen, he knew. She had been totally honest with him. He was the one who had insisted it didn't matter, that he could live with it. But had he been honest with her, or with himself?

It was their wedding night, the only one they would ever share, and all he had wanted was to sit quietly with her for a while and perhaps talk a bit, not about anything terribly important, just to know that she was warm and alive and really there with him. Only she had fled instead, and he didn't know how he was supposed to interpret that.

They had always been so easy with one another, so companionable, that her abrupt departure had thrown him off-balance. He thought back over the past several weeks, in search of any clue that might help him understand, but he could find none. She had been her warm, beguiling self right through all the wedding preparations, arranging the details of the reception, moving her things into place, putting most of her furniture into storage, subletting her apartment. They had seen each other almost every day, discussing at length every decision that needed to be made. And through it all she had been so positive, seemed so happy.

During the ceremony, she looked beautiful in the dress that Jenna had designed, and her eyes sparkled. Her hand even quivered engagingly when he slipped the ring onto her finger. And then, at the Four Seasons, she was absolutely radiant, smiling and laughing a lot, standing beside him with her arm tucked in his.

No, it was only after they left the restaurant that her mood changed, once they were alone with each other. He wondered if the one thing neither of them had wanted to happen had happened, after all – that, in getting married, they had indeed spoiled their friendship.

The fire so lulled him and his thoughts so absorbed him that he didn't know how long the sound had been pushing against the edges of his awareness before it forced its way in. It was an eerie sound, part moan, part sob, part shriek, more like a wounded animal than anything human, and it took him several seconds to realize that it was coming from inside the house. He was on his feet in an instant, crossing the living room in three strides and charging down the stairs.

Karen appeared to be in the throes of a nightmare. She had obviously been thrashing around the bed because she was all tangled up in the sheets. The harder she struggled, the more ensnared she became, and the more ensnared she was, the more desperate her cries became.

Ted touched her shoulder, shaking it gently to awaken her. 'Karen,' he whispered. 'Karen, wake up.'

But she only gasped and shuddered and pulled away.

He shook her a bit harder. 'Karen, it's all right,' he told her. 'I'm here, you're safe. It's only a bad dream.'

The bedding was soaked with perspiration, and her nightgown was slippery as she resisted him, so that he had difficulty getting a firm grip on her. He sat down on the side of the bed and, reaching over, tried to pull her into his arms, to hold her to him and rock her back and forth as he had done so often with one or another of his daughters during the first years without Barbara. But she wouldn't let him. While his daughters would wake up and calm down as soon as they realized where they were, Karen flailed at him, her sobs and screams growing louder and more urgent.

With one hand, Ted snapped on her bedside lamp, hoping that the sudden light might awaken her and she would see that he was with her and there was nothing to fear. But when he looked, he saw that she was already wide awake.

'It was just a bad dream, that's all,' he soothed, still trying to catch hold of her and remembering how she had been the one to get Amy past her bout with nightmares. 'Just a bad dream. It's all over now, see?

You're in your new home and I'm right here and you're perfectly safe.'

But his words didn't seem to make any difference. Her fists continued to lash out against his chest as though her life depended on fighting him off, and she was staring at him as though he were a monster from hell.

PART SIX
1981

Who shall fill up his cup, for he
has drink enough to spare.

– Theocritus

one

The Boeing 727 slid smoothly up to the gate at San Francisco Airport, the door opened, and the United States congressman from California, followed by his wife and their two-year-old son Adam, stepped out and started the long walk toward the terminal.

At forty-three, his handsome face was beginning to show the wear that was often called 'aging' in a woman and 'character' in a man. A light frosting of gray dusted his dark hair.

'Congressman Willmont,' called a pretty young reporter, detaching herself from a loose knot of newspeople on the other side of the security barricade and brandishing a microphone in his face. 'Rumor has it that you've come home early to announce for the Senate. Do you have any comment on that?'

The congressman flashed a dazzling smile and allowed his aquamarine eyes to twinkle ever so briefly.

'Miss Evans, isn't it?' he asked the attractive blonde.

'Yes, sir. Janice Evans, Channel Seven.'

'Well, Miss Evans,' he said, scooping a half-asleep Adam up into his arms as the cameras began to click, 'you know I never comment on rumors.'

'Make an exception,' the brown-eyed blonde urged.

'Come on, Congressman, give us a break,' another of the journalists complained. 'It's been a slow news day.'

Robert Willmont chuckled. 'I wondered what you were all doing out here in the middle of the afternoon.'

'Help us out.'

'I'd like to, but the simple truth is, my family and I have come home for the holidays, just as we do every year.'

'But why two weeks early?' someone asked.

'If you must know,' the congressman replied pleasantly, 'my mother hasn't been very well, and it's important to me to spend as much time with her as I can.'

This was not news. Amanda Drayton Willmont's health had been precarious for as long as any of them could remember.

'Perhaps your wife would tell us,' the persistent Janice Evans pursued. 'Mrs. Willmont, how would you like to be the wife of a United States senator?'

Elizabeth Willmont smiled, the way she had been taught from early childhood to smile at prying strangers.

'I'm very proud of my husband in whatever capacity he chooses to serve,' she replied.

'Come on, Bob,' a veteran from the *Chronicle* urged. 'You *do* want a shot at that Senate seat, don't you?'

'Someday, perhaps,' Robert agreed. 'But right now, I'm perfectly comfortable in the seat I have.'

'Someday's awfully indefinite,' someone objected.

'I'll make you all a promise,' Robert said. 'When I decide to run for higher office, you'll be among the first to know.'

'Thanks for nothing,' someone else muttered.

'Would you rather be among the last?'

Most of the group shrugged good-naturedly.

'Whenever you're ready,' a KRON mainstay drawled, 'all you have to do is whistle, and we'll come running. You do know how to whistle, don't you, Bob?'

Everyone hooted, including the congressman, but his smile was turning brittle around the edges by the time Randy Neuburg pushed his way through the crowd.

'Where the shit have you been?' Robert snarled as his aide quickly ushered the Willmonts toward the exit.

'Caught in a traffic jam,' came the reply.

'This wasn't supposed to be a media event, god-damn it. No one was even supposed to know we were coming in today. Now I'm standing here with egg all over my face – will I run, won't I run?'

'Sorry, boss,' Randy apologized. 'There must have been a leak.'

'Well, see how fast you can get us out of here.'

'The limo's right out front. I'll send it back for the luggage.'

Randy Neuburg had served as Robert's aide since the charismatic partner of Sutton, Wells, Willmont and Spaulding had been elected to Congress three years earlier. He was unusually bright and intuitive for one so young, and totally committed to the causes Robert espoused, and Robert had very wisely plucked him from the associate ranks of the law firm and taken him to Washington.

Like the man he worked for, Randy was a product of Harvard Law School, but unlike Robert, he was West Virginia born and bred and had completed his undergraduate work on scholarship at Princeton. It was a sense of adventure that prompted him to accept the offer that the San Francisco firm tendered him in the spring of 1977. He had never been to the sand-and-surf nirvana called California. It was a sense of destiny that persuaded him to sign on with Robert. Two summers clerking for a West Virginia state senator had left him with a lingering taste for politics.

Randy was a skinny youth who developed into a slight man, with large ears, an unruly shock of red hair almost as bright as Elizabeth Willmont's, a face full of freckles, and clear blue eyes behind horn-rimmed glasses that never lost sight of an objective. Some of his less charitable schoolmates at Princeton used to liken him to Alfred E. Newman, the character from *MAD* comics, but Randy shrugged the epithet off. Let them say what they would, he knew he was smarter than the whole lot of them put together.

To underscore that, he went back to Princeton for his fifth reunion, counselor to a United States congressman – and a congressman who was enjoying a growing reputation as a real up-and-comer at that.

It was the Ridenbaugh case that first catapulted Robert's name onto the front pages and evening newscasts around the state. Joseph Ridenbaugh was accused of swindling some three hundred people out of almost $15 million dollars by selling home sites for the Happy Sands Retirement Community in a part of the California desert that had no water and no hope of getting any for less than $250,000 per house. When the whole scheme began to unravel, Joseph liquidated what he could, transferred the balance of his assets into his mother's name, and took off for Trinidad.

Robert accepted the case on behalf of one Samuel Pappas and the 302 other persons who had been defrauded. He launched an intensive investigation that some felt more closely resembled a witch hunt. Together, he and a new associate assigned to him – one Randy Neuburg, fresh out of Harvard – spent three months digging into every corner of Joseph Riden-baugh's life, hunting for any legal lapse that would give them what they needed. Just when they were gray with exhaustion and about to concede defeat, Randy unearthed an ancient partnership agreement between Joseph and his mother, Alice, with no recorded dis-solution, that had somehow slipped through the cracks.

Applying a liberal interpretation to the agreement, Robert argued that its existence made the mother as liable as the son. He attached every piece of real property he could find in Alice Ridenbaugh's name and sued the partnership. The defense attorney hoped the jury would feel sorry for the gray-haired lady who claimed to have no head for business and no idea about her son's activities.

They didn't.

When the dust finally settled, the duped investors got at least some of their money back and Alice Ridenbaugh was facing criminal prosecution as an accomplice to fraud. Joseph, having set up house with a native girl on Trinidad, showed no inclination for returning to the United States, at least not as long as his Cayman Islands bank account held out.

Robert was heralded as a crusader, a champion of the little man, a benefactor of senior citizens. Two months after the verdict, he was approached by a certain group of people who suggested he might consider running for the United States Congress.

Robert was nothing if not quick to take advantage of an opportunity. With a prayer of thanks to *Pappas* v. *Ridenbaugh,* and with the full weight of the old Drayton name and his law firm's connections behind him, he jumped feet first into the political whirlpool. Even in the affluent district where he campaigned, he was able to defeat the conservative incumbent by a comfortable margin.

'It played almost like the war-hero scenario,' Randy, a student of history, observed on the day after the election.

'Stick with me, kid,' said the congressman-elect, who had been a child during World War II, an adolescent during Korea, and too well-connected to get within a continent of Vietnam. 'There's no telling how far we can go.'

But James Randall Neuburg knew exactly how far they were going to go, and he had already reserved his ticket for the full ride.

Capitol Hill was a prestigious plateau, and over the years many had carved out a piece for themselves and settled into it with considerable complaisance and limited vision. But in Randy's clear blue eyes, the House of Representatives was nothing more than a brief resting place on the journey up Pennsylvania Avenue.

The West Virginia lawyer had no great desire to

reign over the Oval Office himself, understanding
clearly that the qualities one needed to be elected
President of the United States had nothing to do with
the qualities one needed to run the government. But
he knew at first glance that Robert Willmont, with his
looks and charm and his utopian philosophy of
making America strong again, would make an excellent leader. And Randy Neuburg, standing in the
shadow of power and quietly wielding a substantial
share of it, would be the one to transform his mentor's
ideals into a practical road map for steering the nation
into the twenty-first century.

It was pretty heady stuff for the twenty-six-year-old
son of a West Virginia steelworker and a seamstress.

'You got brains, Randy, and determination, and they
got you a scholarship to Princeton,' his father told
him. 'Make the most of it.'

Randy intended to.

'There's only one thing that really means a damn,'
he once overheard the state senator say, 'An' it ain't
money, and it ain't sex, and it ain't no sheepskin from
some snot-nosed Ivy League college, either. It's power.
That's what it is – power, pure and simple. Gettin' it,
holdin' on to it, knowin' how to use it.'

It was a message the young law student never forgot.
Now, halfway through Robert Willmont's second congressional term, Randy was seeing it in action.

'So, what's the word from upstairs?' Robert asked
once they were safely settled in the limousine. 'Go or
no-go?'

'Upstairs' was a euphemism for the particular machine that controlled party politics in California. They
were no longer the cigar-smoking back-room boys of
old, they were now chief executive officers, bankers,

financiers and image makers who met in fortieth-floor penthouse suites and were a hundredfold more powerful than their predecessors had been.

No candidate was elected to public office in the state without their endorsement, and few who had it were defeated. They saw something in Robert Willmont that greatly appealed to them – an attractive, intelligent man who successfully straddled the fence between conservative and liberal interests, who carried the weighty Drayton mantle with polished assurance, and who was a proven vote-getter.

They saw him as a man who believed in a strong America but an America that was generous, a man who believed that the balance of trade meant exactly that, and that free enterprise was not in conflict with a worker's right to earn a fair wage. They noted that he was not above deploring the quality of education in California – once in frustration he had even suggested that the best solution might be to bus every school child into Oregon.

He campaigned in one of the wealthiest sections of San Francisco, where he himself had been born and raised, on a platform that said: 'If we can't get past the philosophy of *me first* in this country, we're going to wake up one day and find *us last.*'

His sincerity couldn't be questioned – the Draytons were too well known for their generations of philanthropy. And it soon became clear that he could stir a crowd in the same youthful, energetic way that John F. Kennedy could in the days of Camelot. In the rarefied air where the power brokers met and considered and orchestrated, he got the nod.

'It's a go,' Randy said.

A broad grin spread across the congressman's face

and he reached across and slapped his aide on the knee.

'Well, all right!' he exclaimed.

Randy had been sent back to San Francisco a week earlier to open a dialogue with the nameless, faceless upstairs people. He had prepared his speech carefully, with exactly the right mixture of confidence and humility.

The House of Representatives was an excellent training ground, but the congressman was a quick learner and easily bored. He was eager to take the next step up, into the Senate. Everyone knew the doddering incumbent standing for reelection was vulnerable.

Randy's mission was to feel the upstairs people out and, if possible, get the green light. The time was right. Robert knew it, Randy could feel it. Upstairs agreed. The young congressman's record in the House, while perhaps not dramatically distinguished, was certainly consistent. In his one-and-a-half terms, he had accomplished exactly what he had set out to accomplish. He had learned the ropes, played the game, and earned the respect of his colleagues. He had made his deals and kept his promises, and had won the devotion of his constituents as a sincere representative of his district who, although born to wealth, possessed genuine compassion for those less fortunate.

Furthermore, *Pappas* v. *Ridenbaugh* still lingered in the minds of a substantial number of Californians. It was a significant issue that they felt went right to the heart of Robert's character. Randy knew they would be able to capitalize on that during their campaign against the grandfatherly incumbent. He also knew that, if they were forced to wait until the next Senate seat was contested, *Pappas* v. *Ridenbaugh* would be past history, and useless to them.

'Get Mary Catherine out here – tomorrow, if possible,' Robert was saying, 'and let's start the wheels in motion.'

'Yes, sir,' Randy replied, jotting the congressman's trusted administrative assistant's name down in his notebook.

Robert turned to the woman sitting beside him, holding the sleeping child. 'So tell us, Mrs. Willmont,' he mimicked the pretty young reporter, 'how would you like to be the wife of a United States senator?'

Elizabeth had been paying only marginal attention to the conversation, yet she forced a weary smile.

'Step two,' she murmured obediently, but her words lacked enthusiasm.

As far as she was concerned, the birth of her son was the crowning achievement of her life, and it had taken a great deal out of her. It was her fourth pregnancy, the other three having ended in miscarriages. The doctors had warned her that not only were the chances of her being able to carry a baby to term slim to none, but the risk to her health was considerable, and they had embellished their dire predictions with a lot of multi-syllabic words she couldn't pronounce and didn't understand. Elizabeth thanked them politely, paid their exorbitant fees, and proceeded to ignore their advice.

Robert was then in his first term in the United States House of Representatives. He was busy and excited and each moment brought him new challenges. Elizabeth was able to share in his glory, but not in his day-to-day involvement. Once the fervor of the campaign and the election were over, her life seemed to lose its focus.

'I know something you can do,' Robert told her when he came home one night a week after the election. 'You can find us the right place to live.'

'To rent or to buy?' she asked.

'To buy,' he replied with a confident grin. 'I think you can count on us being in Washington for a while.'

Elizabeth spent a month searching for the perfect house, finding it finally on a graceful wooded acre in Rock Creek Park, and she spent another three months having it redone. At last, this was the home that would truly be just hers and Robert's. She put all her energy into the redecorating, supervising the entire project herself, thinking and then rethinking even the smallest detail, personally selecting each fabric, approving every paint sample, shopping endlessly for exactly the right pieces of furniture.

The result was gracious and comfortable and spoke softly of good taste and breeding. Those who were fortunate enough to be invited into it were charmed.

It took no time at all for the nation's capital to be as enchanted with the lovely Mrs. Willmont as San Fransicso had been a decade earlier. Soon her style was being imitated by other Washington wives, and her advice on fashion, always a step ahead of vogue, was being sought by women from Capitol Hill to Embassy Row.

'They know class when they see it,' Robert observed to Randy when, only a few months into his first term of office, Elizabeth was asked to join the planning committee of one of the capital's most prestigious annual balls.

But once the Rock Creek Park house was completed, Elizabeth again found herself without focus. Her charity work, while certainly worthy, no longer gave her the satisfaction it once had, and the various luncheons and teas she chose to attend each week filled time but not the growing emptiness inside. She knew only one solution to that particular problem. So, at the ripe old age of thirty-four, she made one last stab at motherhood.

'Why would you want to go and do that?' Robert asked in dismay when she told him she was pregnant.

'Because I heard my biological clock ticking,' she replied. 'Very loudly.'

'Do you think it was wise, under the circumstances?'

'I guess I wasn't thinking wise, I was thinking baby.'

'Sweetheart, you don't have to do this, you know,' he assured her. 'Not for me.'

'I'm not doing it for you,' she replied.

'But children aren't essential for us anymore. I mean, we're doing fine just the way we are.'

'No, you're doing fine, Robert,' she told him. 'I'm doing carpeting and fund-raising.'

'What about the doctors – did they say it was all right to try again? I mean, the risk?'

'I don't care about the doctors,' she declared. 'I want to have a baby.'

'Don't you think maybe we're a little old to be starting a family now?' he persisted.

Elizabeth shrugged. 'Apparently not.'

'But won't it look, well, a little strange to people? I mean, at our age?'

'If you mean people here in Washington, who cares?' she retorted. 'If you mean people back home, I rather think that voters like having a family man in office – young or old.'

'Really?'

'Really,' she confirmed. '*I* certainly do, at any rate. I

automatically assume that politicians with children are ... well ... more stable than ones without.'

'I'd have to see some polls on that,' he retorted.

But by the time Adam Drayton Willmont was born, ten days before 1980, Robert no longer cared about polls. His wife had made it through the delivery, and he had an heir.

Almost from the start, Elizabeth had problems with the pregnancy, but she was determined not to lose this baby. She curtailed her charitable activities, accepted very few social invitations, and managed to keep up a brave front for her husband, which wasn't too difficult because he was so preoccupied with his work that he often left for Capitol Hill well before she awoke in the morning and came home long after she was asleep.

But she couldn't hide from her doctors. They saw her weekly, changed her diet, pumped her full of vitamins, and performed endless tests to monitor fetal progress. Her first miscarriage had occurred early in the pregnancy, her second in the fifth month, her third in the fourth. The day she entered her sixth month and felt the baby kick for the first time, Elizabeth cried with relief.

'Don't get your hopes up yet,' the doctors cautioned, knowing that a sixth-month abort or even a still birth, with her history, was a very real possibility. 'You have a long way to go.'

'I'm going to make it,' she told them fiercely. 'We're both going to make it.'

She began to bleed two days later.

'What do I do?' she begged the doctors. 'Tell me what to do.'

'Nothing,' they replied. 'Absolutely nothing.'

They meant exactly that. Elizabeth spent the last

four months of her pregnancy in bed, and she almost didn't survive the eighteen-hour labor, but Adam was perfect.

The doctors called it a miracle.

Even after two years, Elizabeth was still struggling to regain her strength, and the long flight from Washington had taken its toll. She yearned for her bed, although it was barely the middle of the afternoon. It wasn't that she was no longer interested in her husband's political ambitions, it was more that she had just so much energy to expend, and she chose to expend it on her son.

Adam was her life now. Her charitable activities, her social commitments and her congressional obligations became peripheral. When Robert was at home, he was included in what she thought of as her heart circle. When he was not, she rarely thought about him at all. Her days were full of Adam – his first words, first steps, first lessons. Her nights were filled with planning – for his education, his future, his happiness.

Robert wanted to employ a nanny. Elizabeth refused.

'I have no intention of letting a stranger raise my son,' she declared.

'You're the wife of a congressman,' he retorted, 'and a Drayton. You have obligations.'

'I'll maintain an association with one or two worthy charities and I'll attend every social and political function that you feel is necessary to your advancement,' she said firmly. 'But my only obligation is to Adam.'

Although it was often beyond her endurance, she forced herself to accompany Robert to as many as three social events a week without complaint, charming even the crustiest of statesmen with her sweet smile and well-bred manners.

It was the little pink pills that got her through. Her doctors prescribed them when she complained of lethargy. One per day, they said, would fix her right up. By the end of six months, she was taking as many as three a day, sometimes four if she were facing an especially late evening.

Elizabeth had been looking forward to the Christmas break, and was delighted when Robert told her they would have an extra two weeks away from Washington. Even the thought of Amanda's grousing hadn't dimmed her anticipation of the quiet month ahead. But what she had just half-heard had.

If Robert intended to announce his candidacy for the Senate during the holiday, there would be no rest. Instead, there would be a nonstop round of press conferences, photo sessions, and interviews, with people underfoot every moment, and she would be expected to participate. She sighed deeply and made a mental note to have her prescription refilled.

Robert settled back against the leather cushions. It was going to happen just as he had dreamed it, and one day very soon he would have it all. The endless schooling, the long apprenticeship at Sutton Wells, the confining proper marriage, the petty congressional duties he performed, the tiresome committees on which he was obliged to serve – each was merely a rung up his ladder to the White House. When he looked at it like that, he knew it was worth it.

The limousine pulled up in front of the house on Jackson Street. Robert took Adam, Randy helped Elizabeth, and the four of them went up the steps.

'I want to spend a few minutes with Mother,' Robert

told his wife, handing the boy over. 'And then Randy and I have some people to see.'

Elizabeth hardly heard him.

'Where are we headed?' Randy asked half an hour later as the two men climbed back into the limousine.

'I don't know where *you're* headed, old man,' replied the congressman with a sly wink. 'But I'm on my way to give an interview.'

Randy grinned on the outside but cringed on the inside. It wasn't that he was a prude. In fact, he wasn't in the least. But, after three years, he knew that Robert's sexual appetites sometimes got the better of his good sense – and boffing a news reporter on the eve of announcing for the United States Senate was certainly not what Randy considered using good sense.

two

The jumbo jet sped steadily toward the sunset. Mary Catherine O'Malley sipped her champagne, nibbled at her smoked-salmon appetizer, and contemplated the strategy session that would begin almost the moment the plane touched down – the announcement that would result from that session, and the impact it would have on the rest of her life.

She had been working for Robert Willmont for a scant three years now and he was considered damn lucky to have her, because Mary Catherine was regarded by many to be the best administrative assistant on Capitol Hill. She had earned that reputation over almost thirty years of shepherding congressmen through the political quagmire.

For a girl from the wrong side of the Winston-Salem railroad tracks, with only a high school education to her name, who had started her career as a temporary filing clerk, that wasn't half bad.

She did her share of stumbling in the beginning, but she was a quick learner and it took her hardly any time at all to realize that she was smarter than most of the duly elected world-beaters with their multiple degrees who moved in and out for a few years at a time.

By the time Mary Catherine attended her sixth congressional swearing-in ceremony and her third Presidential inaugural, she was on a first-name basis with just about everyone in Washington who counted. She was invited to most of the parties that mattered, the press courted her, insiders sought her advice, and politicians trusted her. Over the years she discovered where all the bodies were buried, where all the skeletons lurked, and which pairs of shoes hid Achilles' heels, and she accomplished it all without ever having to take off her clothes.

Mary Catherine was barely five feet tall, but people rarely realized that. They noticed instead that, at the age of forty-eight, she still displayed a classic hourglass figure, an abundance of glossy brown hair, and brown eyes that were faintly reminiscent of Bambi.

She managed her staff with the patience of Penelope and the determination of a drill sergeant, she managed the public with humor and impartiality, and she managed her congressmen with the utmost tact and discretion.

Robert had inherited her from his predecessor, and two months into his first term, he had actually written that conservative gentleman a note of appreciation.

'If you don't know what to do or how to do it,' he was soon telling everyone, 'ask Mary Catherine.'

Born seventh in a family of nine to a schoolteacher mother and an alcoholic father, Mary Catherine had learned the wisdom of knowing the right answers and keeping a low profile by the age of six. Her gentle North Carolina drawl camouflaged an exceptional mind and her soft Southern ways managed to convince many a man that he was really the one in charge.

When she was twenty-nine years old, a White House aide asked her to marry him. He was reasonably handsome and fun and even quite bright, and by that time, they had been enjoying each other's close company for some months.

'What will you do after your Administration is out of office?' she asked him.

'Oh, we have five years before we have to worry about that,' he said and laughed.

'But then what?' she persisted.

'Go back to Boston, I guess,' he replied. 'It's too hard to tell your friends from your enemies in this town.'

But after all it had taken to get herself established, Mary Catherine had no intention of leaving Washington, in five years or ever. She refused his proposal with sincere regret. While the two of them vowed to remain intimate friends, less than a year later, when the Administration he worked for ended so abruptly, so tragically, the aide said good-bye and faded into memory.

Robert Willmont was Mary Catherine's third congressman from California. With her ability and experience, she could easily have had her pick of the biennial crop, but she liked Californians. They had a style that other members of the House often lacked. Women seemed to sit up straighter in their presence, men tended to order wine instead of bourbon.

This one, however, had a lot more than style. He had looks and he had brains and he had an ambition that wasn't going to quit with a third-floor office on the House side of the Capitol Building. This one was on his way up, as they said, and he was the one Mary Catherine had been waiting for.

Like almost everyone else who came with purpose to the nation's capital, the soft-spoken North Carolinian dreamed of ending her career in the White House. For decades, she had studied the mostly indistinguishable features of those who took up residence in the Senate and the House, looking for just the right combination of qualities that she could help hone into a presidential great. In the part of her gut where her most trusted instincts lay, Mary Catherine knew that Robert Drayton Willmont was the one.

The prestigious law firm of Sutton, Wells, Willmont and Spaulding, while officially neutral when it came to politics, was nonetheless pleased to provide the congressman, and former partner, with a suite of offices on the twelfth floor of its Front Street building.

Five days after Mary Catherine hit San Francisco, she had leased an apartment on Telegraph Hill for herself and anyone else from out of town who might need it, outfitted the Front Street headquarters, hired two secretaries and a clerk from a local temporary agency, and called in two assistants from Washington to help set up operations.

At two o'clock in the afternoon of Thursday, December 17, perfectly timed to take advantage of the evening newscasts, she stood beside Randy Neuburg, just outside the glare of the television lights, as Robert Willmont announced to the press and the people of California his intention to be a candidate for the United States Senate.

Mary Catherine approved of Randy. He was smart and realistic, and under her tutelage was developing into one of the most savvy aides in Washington. To the congressman's right was his lovely wife, holding their cherubic little boy Adam in her arms. A nice touch, the shrewd administrative assistant conceded. Mary Catherine approved of Elizabeth Willmont, too. Not only was she beautiful and fashionable, she had the kind of grace and charm that was considered an enormous asset in Washington and which would play very well in the media.

From the corner of her eye, the assistant scanned the local newspeople she would get to know again in the eleven months to come. In the front row sat a pretty young blonde with brown eyes, a short tight skirt, one leg thrown ever so casually over the other, and an insolent little smile on her face. She was the only member of the group who wasn't taking notes. Mary Catherine frowned. She had seen that same smile on a number of other pretty young faces over the past three years and it always triggered an alarm bell in her head. A slight sigh beside her told her that Randy was noticing, too.

'I think it went well,' Robert observed once the lights had been turned off and the reporters had rushed away with their stories.

'It'll play in Pasadena,' Randy agreed.

'So long as the conservative voters of our good state continue to focus on my sound fiscal policies and the liberal voters concentrate on my progressive social programs,' the candidate summed up, 'I think we've got it made.'

He stretched broadly and made a point of glancing at his wristwatch. 'See that Elizabeth and the boy get back to Jackson Street, will you?' he directed his aide. 'I'm late for an appointment.'

Randy and Mary Catherine exchanged glances.

'I don't have anything down in the book for you this evening, Congressman,' the administrative assistant noted.

Robert grinned. 'It's just a quick stop.'

Quick, as in before she has to do the six-o'clock news, Mary Catherine interpreted.

Quick, as in quickie, thought Randy.

'Do you think that's really such a good idea?' the aide wondered aloud. 'I mean, the media is bound to be all over you every minute from now on.'

The congressman chuckled. 'Oh, I've become an expert at dodging those snoops.'

'Still, you know, all it takes is one slip,' Randy persisted.

'Well, if I do slip,' came the reckless reply, 'I know you'll be there to pick me up.'

'It's the blonde in the first row,' Randy said as soon as Robert had departed.

Mary Catherine nodded. 'Janice Evans, from Channel Seven. Another reporter! You'd think he'd learn, wouldn't you?'

'All I can say is that he'd better make damn sure there are no hidden cameras around this time.' Randy sighed. 'I've done my last second-story work.'

Shortly before the congressman's reelection to the House, Randy had actually been induced to commit burglary to clean up a particularly messy liaison. The wide-eyed young woman in question had claimed to be a graduate student in political science from some Midwestern university, spending the summer soaking up the Washington scene. But she was actually a scandal-sheet stringer hoping to make it big on a major-city newspaper.

Only after Randy had broken into her apartment and retrieved some incriminating photographs and negatives was the congressman able to dump her. Then, in case she might have had in mind to spread any unfortunate publicity, he arranged, with the help of a small-time lowlife who owed him a favor, to have the stringer implicated in a prostitution and drug deal, thereby destroying her credibility. He never even blinked when she was arrested, convicted, and sentenced to nine months in prison.

Mary Catherine sighed. If Robert Drayton Willmont had one fault, one weakness that could cost them all everything were he not very careful – were she and Randy not constantly vigilant – it was that he didn't know how to keep his zipper zipped.

PART SEVEN
1991

It is circumstances and timing
that give an action its character,
and make it either good or bad.

– *Agesilaus*

one

Karen emptied the last of the wardrobe containers and heaved a sigh of relief. It was the thing she hated most about moving, trying to find places in a new home for all the things they had so easily accumulated in the old, and this was the fourth occasion in ten years she had had to do it.

It was especially difficult this time because the house here in San Francisco was smaller than the one in Tucson had been. When they had made the first move, from New York to Atlanta, they had gone from the compact brownstone apartment on West Seventy-eighth Street into a stately six-bedroom colonial. Again, when they went from Atlanta to Houston, it was into a sprawling hacienda that had taken Karen almost an hour to walk from end to end. And when they had to make the hop from Houston to Tucson, they had found an equally spacious adobe. But now, with Gwen grown and Jessica almost finished with college, they had no need for all that acreage.

Karen secretly thought Atlanta and the colonial too pretentious, Houston and the hacienda too hot, and Tucson and the adobe too dry. But she liked this house, set on a hill overlooking the Pacific Ocean, at the southern edge of San Francisco, in a section of the city known as St. Francis Wood.

It was quasi-Mediterranean in style, with stucco walls and a red tile roof, inlaid wood floors, high arched windows, and a stunning art deco skylight. There was a delightful solarium off the kitchen that they turned into a breakfast room, and a sunporch off the master bedroom that they glassed in.

'Quintessential 1920s,' Ted said when he saw it.

'We don't really need more than three bedrooms,' Karen told Gwen over the telephone, 'now that Amy is the only one at home full-time.'

'But what if Larry and the twins and I want to come out when Jessica's there?' her oldest stepdaughter had protested from her home outside Philadelphia. Brightest of the three girls, she was the image of her father except for her blue eyes.

'Your dad has already thought of that,' Karen assured her, thinking of the sunporch.

'How come you picked San Francisco?' Jessica asked from her dormitory at the University of Colorado. The middle girl was the tallest of the three and the only one with her mother's brown hair and eyes and quiet determination.

'As usual, it picked us,' Karen replied. 'Your father's been commissioned to design a megacomplex in China Basin.'

'Why do we have to move again?' Amy complained. She had grown into a lively teenager, combining her father's coloring with her mother's serenity. 'I only have one more year of high school. It'll be absolutely awful to have to go to a new school for just one year. I won't know anyone, I won't have any friends, I'll be miserable.'

'I know the timing isn't very good,' Karen conceded with a sigh. 'But we didn't have much choice. It's an important project and your father couldn't turn it down.'

'It's not fair!' the teenager exclaimed.

Karen had to agree it wasn't.

There were more than enough hotels and shopping malls and office complexes being built on the East Coast to have kept Ted busy for two lifetimes. But his eyes had always been fixed on some distant horizon.

If Karen had thought that, by wrapping herself up in Ted's ready-made family, she would automatically have the idyllic life she had dreamed of having, she soon learned otherwise. Trying to meet her personal needs for privacy and orderliness and fulfillment in the midst of four other people who had long since resolved those issues among themselves required constant compromise and difficult periods of adjustment. With every assignment Ted was unable to resist in yet another new city, she was forced to abandon whatever nest she had painstakingly constructed and begin building again, compounding the problems.

She felt isolated by the southern hypocrisy of Georgia, awed by the sheer size of Texas, and haunted by the eerie desert winds of Arizona, but she eventually grew accustomed to each – just in time to leave. She made very few friends along the way, and those she did make were superficial.

Karen missed Demion Five more than she had ever

expected she would, not to mention the Yanows, Demelza, and the Sullivan Street set. She saw her life now as quite dull compared to the excitement she had left behind. She turned inward to her family, only to find her family striking outward. Ted was absorbed in his work and the girls were involved with their schools and activities. The more they blossomed, the less they seemed to need her. That left only her partnership with Nancy.

In ten years, the two women had collaborated on seven books. Their second effort, *Mirror Images*, completed just after the Donigers moved to Atlanta, sold well enough at Demion Five for a major New York publisher to approach them with a proposal for future endeavors.

'We'll get a lot more exposure working with a publisher than we do printing our own books and selling them through Demion Five,' Nancy had told her. 'Besides, we've just about exhausted the New York market anyway.'

What Spectrum Publishing had in mind was to take the same format they had used in their first two books and go national with it.

'You mean, take a good cow and milk it until it's dry?' Karen had observed. But she had to admit the idea appealed to her and would go a long way toward easing her loneliness. Within a few weeks, Nancy was on a plane to Atlanta.

'As long as you were already here,' she said, 'Spectrum figured this was as good a market as any.'

The team of photographer and poet spent three weeks exploring the city as Karen never would have on her own. They titled the book *Phoenix Risen*, choosing to concentrate on the triumph over devastation that truly set the Georgia city apart from much of the Civil War South.

They did Washington, D.C., next, focusing on the two separate cities that shared the same space, and produced a black-and-white indictment they called *Dichotomy*. It soon became mandatory for anyone who aspired to be someone in the political sphere to claim it in his library.

Then came Houston. The two women called that effort *Southern Comfort*. They took a detour through the antebellum elegance of New Orleans to do *Amazing Grace*. And then, in Arizona, they broke tradition and did their first book in color.

'This can't be done in black and white,' Nancy declared emphatically at the end of her first visit to the Southwest. 'Look at all the colors – they're just bursting to be told.'

They decided not to focus on any one city, either, as they had before. Instead, they wove the peoples and places of the whole state together, and named the result *Tapestry*.

The endeavor brought Nancy out west six times and took almost two years to put together, a luxury they hadn't enjoyed since their first book, but it was worth it. They were rewarded with a product that reviewers declared embodied a great deal more than a photographic journey through the Southwest, and an extraordinary initial printing of twenty thousand copies.

The cover featured a Hopi youth, standing on the boundary of his reservation, staring out toward the mountains. About him, Karen had written:

> The color of pain
> is purple

for distant peaks
never to be reached,
and green
for the land
never to be roamed.

The color of pain
is brown
for the blood
of countless ancestors,
and red
for the pride
that still burns within.

The color of pain
is gold
for the hope
that rises with the sun
and sets with the moon.

The color of pain
is gray
for the apathy
of yesterday
and the indifference
of tomorrow.

As far as Karen was concerned, the best part of
Tapestry was the four months that she and Nancy spent
together, crisscrossing the state in a four-wheel drive,
from the Grand Canyon to Chiricahua and from Yuma
to Mexican Water. Each time they set out on one of
their forays, she had the strange sensation that she was
escaping.

The girls were growing up so fast. First it was Gwen, graduating from high school with honors, going back east to the University of Pennsylvania, and then on to business school and a nice young man from Wharton. Then Jessica, surviving her sister's limelight and departing for the University of Colorado, with ideas about medical school after that. And before long, it would be Amy's turn to find her niche in the world – such a different world than it was when Karen was her age. The concept of home, which used to be a noisy, crowded place, in whatever city they happened to be, was too rapidly becoming a silent, empty place.

Over the years, Karen's relationship with Ted had settled into one of uneasy intimacy. The nightmares grew less frequent, until their occurence was rare, and the strangeness of blending two adult lives into one slowly dissipated; but the carefree camaraderie they had shared before their wedding night never fully returned.

The energy that Ted hoped to put into his marriage and family he put into his profession instead, working long hours, six and sometimes seven days a week. The drapery wall he had erected between them back in New York came down, but not the invisible one that neither seemed able to penetrate. The twin beds were pushed together to look like a king-sized one, but it was illusion rather than reality.

What passed for lovemaking between them began a few weeks after the wedding, with Ted admitting to himself that being able to look at Karen and talk to her was not going to be enough, after all. It started with casual gestures of affection – a kiss, a hug, a touch, and slowly progressed to acts of consummation that mostly occurred when, for whatever reason, Karen had consumed more alcohol than usual.

The first time they attempted actual intercourse, she bit down so hard on her lip that it bled, and clutched the sheets so tightly that they tore. Neither of them ever mentioned it. Eventually, she learned how to separate Ted from her nightmare and was able to meet his needs with a modicum of liquor and a minimum of panic. There was no thought of her own satisfaction. Too many layers of guilt and shame and humiliation were in the way.

To the rest of the world, however, theirs looked like the perfect marriage, the embodiment of the American Dream. The girls were bright and attractive. The parents were well-dressed and soft-spoken. They had a sheepdog named Duster and a tabby named Cat, and an unnamed station wagon. And there was enough money. But the things they once believed they had in common were not strong enough to bind them together, so they grew apart.

They never discussed what was happening – or not happening – between them. They discussed the children, the house, their work, but never the serious issues that, board by invisible board, were pushing the wall between them higher and higher. It was almost as though they were fearful of saying or doing anything that might spoil the illusion, so they surrounded themselves with the girls for as long as they could and, when they were obliged to be alone with each other, they were considerate but not close.

'I sometimes think we should never have married,' Karen said on one of those occasions.

'Probably not,' Ted agreed.

'I would understand if you wanted a divorce.'

'I don't … Do you?'

'No.'

So they went on the way they were, because something was better than nothing and the illusion seemed more important than the reality. Until one hot Thursday in the spring of 1990, when Amy's tenth-grade class took a field trip out into the Arizona desert and her horse, spooked by a rattlesnake, set off at a dead run.

Amy was a good rider but the bolt was so unexpected that she lost her balance and was thrown from the saddle almost immediately, which would not have been so bad except that her right foot caught in the stirrup and she was dragged a hundred yards or more before two of her classmates were able to head her off and stop her horse.

At the hospital, the doctors found multiple contusions and abrasions, two broken legs, a dislocated right hip, and a skull fractured in three places.

Karen and Ted paced the hospital corridors until well after midnight, the scene in different ways all too familiar to both of them, but the doctors couldn't say anything except that surgery had gone as well as expected and that the next forty-eight hours would tell.

They dragged themselves home in a daze, Karen helping an exhausted Ted to undress and get into bed. Then she went into the kitchen and downed two stiff shots of brandy before returning with one for him.

'This will help you sleep,' she said, sitting down on the side of the bed and holding out the glass.

'I don't want to sleep,' he cried, although he was shivering with fatigue. 'I want to be awake in case she needs me. I should have stayed there with her.'

'The doctor said he would call if there was any change,' she reminded him. 'The hospital is only ten minutes away.'

'It's all my fault,' he sobbed suddenly.

'What is?' she asked.

'I've been so wrapped up in my work I haven't had time for her. I know so little about what she's doing, what she likes, what she thinks. We hardly see each other anymore. I can't even remember the last weekend we spent together.'

'All the weekends in a lifetime wouldn't have prevented this accident,' Karen said. 'You're a wonderful father, and if you could ask her, she'd tell you she couldn't have wished for a better one.'

'It all goes so fast,' he mumbled. 'One day, they're babies, the next, they're teenagers, and the day after that, they're grown up and gone, having babies of their own.'

'That's what it's all about,' Karen observed.

'But are they ready?' he asked. 'Are they strong enough? Are they wise enough? Did we do a good enough job? That's what I don't know.'

'We did the best we could.'

The platitude seemed to work for a moment. He swallowed some of his brandy and looked as though he would calm down, but then his tears broke out afresh.

'I'm so lonely,' he cried from the very center of his soul. 'I don't want to be lonely anymore.'

Before she quite realized what was happening, he had his arms around her and she was holding him, as she had so often held the girls when they were frightened or unhappy.

'I'm here,' she murmured. 'Don't worry. I'm here.'

The first night they spent in the house in Atlanta,

Amy had awakened screaming. When Karen reached her room, she found the eight-year-old cringing on the floor.

'This is a scary place,' the child sobbed over and over. 'This isn't my room – it's a scary place. I'm all alone here. I want to go home.'

'It's not your *old* room,' Karen told her, sitting down on the bed. 'It's your *new* room.'

'I want my old room,' Amy cried.

'Tell you what,' Karen said. 'Why don't you come up here with me so the two of us can take a good look at this room, and then maybe it won't be so scary.'

Uncertain, Amy crawled up next to her stepmother.

'You know, a room just doesn't get to be your very own room until you've looked at it from your very own bed,' Karen told her. 'Wait a minute now – this *is* your very own bed, isn't it?'

Amy nodded. It was her familiar pink-and-white canopy bed from home.

'Well, then, are these your very own sheets?'

The bedding was white with pink ribbons and brown teddy bears frolicking across it.

Amy nodded again.

'So far, so good,' Karen declared. She glanced around the generous L-shaped space that they had hung with pink-and-white festooned wallpaper. 'Now let's see – is that your very own toy chest against the wall?'

A third nod came in reply as the child eyed the gaily decorated trunk that housed her favorite things.

'Is Snoopy sound asleep inside?'

'Yes,' Amy admitted. 'Unless I woke him up.'

Karen listened. 'I don't hear a single peep, do you?'

The little girl shook her head.

'Well, I guess that means he's just as snug as that old bug in a rug,' Karen declared. 'But I think we should whisper anyway, just in case.' She lowered her voice. 'Is that your very own dresser and desk and chair over there?'

Amy looked at the pink-painted furniture that had been brought from her room in New York. 'Uh-huh.'

'Now peek inside that closet – are those your very own clothes hanging up?'

'And that's my bathrobe on the bedpost, and my slippers on the floor, and my Raggedy Ann and my panda and my picture of all of us at the wedding.'

By this time, Karen was leaning against the head-board and Amy was nestled in her arms.

'Well then, you'd better tell me: What are all these things doing here if this isn't your very own new room?'

The little girl shrugged. 'It's bigger than my old room, and it's shaped funny, but I guess it isn't so scary after all.'

'In that case,' her stepmother suggested, 'suppose you snuggle down under the covers and close your eyes and think about how special this room is going to be, just because it's yours, and about all the new friends you're going to make who'll want to come here to play.'

'Are there any little girls my age nearby?'

'I have it on good authority that there's one right next door.'

'Maybe I can meet her tomorrow,' Amy ventured, stifling a yawn. 'I can't wait till tomorrow.'

'In that case, the sooner you go to sleep, the sooner tomorrow will come.'

'Don't go yet.'

'Don't worry. I'm right here.'

'Are you going to turn off the light right away?'

Karen smiled. 'Not until you're in dreamland.'

'Promise?'

'Promise.'

Ted found them both there the next morning.

As she had once held her daughter, so now Karen held her husband on the night of Amy's accident and the unexpected honesty held them both. He thought he had married a woman, but she knew he had married a shell. She thought she had married a shell, only to discover that she had married a man. With a silent splinter, the first crack appeared in the invisible wall.

'It's going to be all right,' she murmured. 'You'll see, everything's going to be all right. Amy will be fine. We'll all be fine.'

Somehow, she thought.

Amy recovered. She missed the last month of school but had no trouble making up the work. She spent the summer in a wheelchair, but by the fall she was back in class, first on crutches, then with a cane, and finally on her own two feet again. The skull fractures healed, having done no serious damage. Her hair grew a little funny around the scars, and she fretted until it was long enough to cover them, but that was the worst of it.

The best of it was that Karen and Ted began to talk to each other, first during the long nights of Amy's stay in the hospital, then during the months of her convalescence.

'I married you for the wrong reasons,' he acknowledged. 'I didn't realize it then, but I do now. You see, you were like Barbara in so many ways, and I missed her so much, and I thought I could make her come alive again through you. But of course I couldn't, and I blamed you when I shouldn't have.'

'I married you for the wrong reasons, too,' she conceded. 'I thought I could get back some of the things I felt I'd been cheated out of, without having to pay the price. But I ended up cheating you instead.'

'What sort of things?' he asked.

'The chance to know what being married was like,' she replied. 'The chance to have children to raise. The chance to have the kind of life I was brought up to believe I was supposed to have.'

'The accident you had – it prevented all that?'

'Yes,' she said truthfully. But she didn't elaborate.

Of course, he had seen the scars and wondered about them. But he would never ask.

'I didn't realize it was that bad,' he mused.

'The doctors had to remove my uterus,' she explained. 'My college sweetheart couldn't handle it. I guess he wanted children more than he wanted me. After that, I guess I just withdrew. I was afraid of being hurt again.'

'I can understand that,' he said. 'I suppose men can be very selfish and insensitive sometimes.'

'Well, it might not have been all his fault,' she heard herself say.

'Marrying me wasn't what you expected, was it?' he observed. 'I turned out to be selfish and insensitive, too.'

'No,' she said quickly. 'Don't blame yourself.'

'Well, where do we go from here?' he asked, holding his breath. 'Do you want a divorce?'

'Do you?' she countered, not daring to breathe.

His response was rapid and sincere. 'No, I don't.'

Karen sighed with relief. 'Neither do I.'

'All right then,' he declared, 'as far as I'm concerned, we start our marriage over again – from right this minute – and not only do I promise to love and honor you and keep you in sickness and in health, but I promise to keep you safe from harm for as long as we both shall live.'

Less than a year later, they moved to San Francisco.

Karen took her mid-morning cup of tea into the living room. The three Rankin oils she and Ted owned between them were stacked against one wall, waiting to be uncrated. The clown would go in the office, they had already decided on that, but it was up to Karen to choose where to hang the other two. She was about to begin ripping the first crate apart when the front doorbell rang.

A large woman in her late fifties, with full lips, a broad nose, narrow brown eyes, and frizzy salt-and-pepper hair pulled back into an unfashionable bun, stood across the threshold with a casserole in her hands. There was something about her that reminded Karen of Demelza.

'Hi,' she said, when the door was opened. 'I wanted to bring this to you yesterday, because I know how horrific moving-in day can be, but I had an emergency at the office and just didn't get home in time to get it done. So I took this morning off, and here it is. I hope you can use it.'

'Thank you,' Karen replied. 'That's very kind.'

'I'm Natalie Shaffer and I live across the street,' the woman continued, nodding in the direction of a stately Tudor two houses down. 'Welcome to The Wood and to San Francisco and even to California, come to that.'

Karen introduced herself. 'I guess I have to admit to

all three,' she said with a chuckle. 'We came from Tucson.'

'Never been there,' Natalie announced. 'But if you have time to come over for a cup of coffee, you can tell me all about it.'

'I've just made a pot of tea,' Karen ventured. 'Why don't you come in and join me?'

'Tea?' Natalie echoed, stepping into the foyer. 'My goodness, you're civilized. I thought Arizona was still one of those wild and woolly places.'

Karen laughed. 'In many ways it is, but I'm originally from New York.'

'Are you?' pounced Natalie. 'How delightful – we're twice neighbors. I'm from Pennsylvania.'

'My husband comes from Pennsylvania,' Karen exclaimed. 'From Reading.'

'Well then, we're practically family,' Natalie assured her. 'I'm from Scranton.'

Karen poured another cup of tea and found a box of cookies in the cupboard, and the two women sat down at the breakfast-room table.

'I'm amazed you can find anything, a day after moving in,' Natalie marveled, biting into a cookie.

Karen shrugged. 'I used to be the manager of a shop that depended on my being able to unpack and organize in record time. My employer used to call me the Unbearable Neatnik. I guess some habits are hard to break.'

'I wanted to be a flower child,' Natalie said with a chuckle. 'My husband used to call me the Unbearable Beatnik.'

Karen sipped her tea with a soft smile. After ten years and four moves, she knew she was about to make a real friend.

'What do you do that you have emergencies and you get to take mornings off?' she asked.

'I'm a psychiatrist,' replied Natalie and immediately burst out laughing. 'I'll wager no one's ever accused you of having a poker face,' she cried. 'It froze like a sphinx the minute that word came out of my mouth.'

'Did it?' Karen managed to say. 'I can't imagine why.'

The neighbor grinned. 'It gets worse, I'm afraid – my husband's one also.'

'Really? Both of you?' Karen blurted in her discomfort. 'I guess psychiatry must be … profitable.'

Natalie chuckled. 'Shrinks are in, shame is out. With ninety-eight percent of the population among the walking dsyfunctional these days, there's no longer anything wrong with an otherwise perfectly sane person seeking help.'

'I didn't mean to offend you,' Karen said hastily.

'I'm not offended,' Natalie replied. 'On the contrary, I think this is the beginning of a great friendship.'

By the end of three weeks, Karen no longer thought about Natalie in terms of her profession. They were having too much fun together. Soon, the Shaffers were coming to dinner every other Friday night, and the Donigers were going across the street for brunch on alternate Sundays.

The Shaffer home was a collector's bad dream, crammed with antiques representing every period from Elizabethan to Bauhaus. Threadbare Orientals that rightfully belonged in a museum covered the floors, original Tiffany lamps lit the rooms, a real

Fabergé egg kept the papers on a side table from scattering, and Karen found a cabinet of first editions tucked into a corner that would have had Demelza drooling. Mostly, however, there was clutter – papers, books, magazines and dust.

'Neither of us is particularly good at housekeeping.' Natalie shrugged without guilt.

Herbert Shaffer was a jolly man of sixty, with bushy eyebrows and a funny little mustache. It seemed to be a race whether he would go bald before he went gray. He had a surprising interest in architecture, and he and Ted hit it off immediately.

The first Friday the Shaffers came to dinner, they sat in the green-and-cream living room afterward, drinking brandy from crystal snifters and carrying on an animated discussion about everything from movies to music to food to California wines, and eventually to the five-year-old drought.

'Isn't that the most beautiful book?' Natalie exclaimed during a break in the conversation, nodding toward a copy of *Tapestry* that Ted insisted be kept on the coffee table. 'I saw it down at B. Dalton's and – I don't know – there was just something about it. I had to have it. I guess that's where I got my wild and woolly notions about Arizona.'

'Yes,' Karen murmured noncommittally.

'I understand the authors travel around the country in a jeep. A couple of free spirits, I guess.'

Amy giggled.

'What's so funny?' Natalie inquired.

'That you call my mother and my aunt free spirits,' she replied.

'Your ... what?'

'Nancy Yanow is my aunt,' Amy explained. 'She

takes the pictures. And Mom writes the words. But she uses her maiden name so no one will know it's her.'

'That's not why at all,' Karen objected. 'It's just the way we started.'

Natalie gaped at Karen with a mixture of astonishment and admiration.

'You never said,' she complained.

Karen shrugged. 'It never came up.'

'I asked you what you did,' the psychiatrist insisted. 'You said you were a housewife.'

'I am.'

'And a mom,' Amy put in.

'That's right,' Karen said, giving her stepdaughter a hug. 'The other is just a hobby.'

'You've done a first-rate job with your Amy,' Natalie remarked one day during a shopping excursion. 'I'm looking forward to meeting Gwen and Jessica.'

'I'm afraid I can't take much of the credit.' Karen sighed. 'The girls aren't mine. I only wish they were. Their real mother died when they were young.'

'You look pretty real to me,' Natalie observed.

'That's not what I meant.'

'I know what you meant, but you don't know what you're talking about,' the psychiatrist said bluntly. 'Amy is the way she is as much because of you as anyone else.'

'Well, perhaps.'

'How come you never had any of your own?'

'I had ... an accident some years ago,' Karen confided reluctantly. 'I wasn't able, after that.'

'Not something you care to discuss,' the psychiatrist suggested. 'Me and my big mouth.'

'It doesn't matter anymore,' Karen replied with a shrug.

'One of the by-products of being a shrink,' Natalie said casually, appraising her friend through the professional corner of her eye, 'is that you get in the habit of asking too many questions. Of course you also get to be one hell of a listener. So, if you ever feel like talking, you know, about anything at all, I'm just across the street.'

Karen smiled politely, a bit of the old plastic smile, but said nothing. Years ago, she had told Nancy all she intended to tell anyone about the assault in Central Park. Since then, she had managed to put the past behind her and now she wanted only to leave it there. Despite their new understanding, she had not even told Ted. Several times, she thought she might, but the fear stopped her – the same fear that the truth would disgust him and he would turn away from her as Peter had.

She sometimes wished there had been someone to tell who might have listened without condemning, who might have understood, who might have been able to help her deal with the anger and frustration. But there hadn't been anyone there for her.

Now it was a different world. Rape was a topic that was being discussed openly, and rape-counseling centers were springing up all across the country. Along with date rape, acquaintance rape was beginning to gain acceptance. More and more, women were coming forward to say: 'Yes, I went with him, but I did not want to have sex with him. I said *no*.'

How desperately Karen had longed to say those very words to the New York police, to her mother, to Peter, to the whole world, and have someone stand up beside her and agree. But no one had, and after almost thirty years, she had pretty much convinced herself that she had been the villain of the piece instead of the victim.

* * *

The balmy days of September stretched into October and the Bay Area held its collective breath, hoping for rain. The drought had brought severe water rationing.

'We had enough water when we were in the middle of the desert,' Karen observed wryly. 'Now here we are, surrounded by water, and the reservoirs are dry.'

'It's not the weather, it's the politicians,' Natalie told her. 'Down in southern California, they're swimming in their pools and watering their lawns just like they always did, while up here we're recycling every possible drop and taking communal showers.'

Karen had never had much interest in the workings of government, at any level. Although she dutifully voted in every election, she paid scant attention to the players. She had the general impression that politics had degenerated to a fairly dismal level, that corruption was everywhere, and behavior once considered abhorrent was now being condoned.

Over the last decade, a growing distrust and disgust with the business of politics had culminated in total disinterest. Karen stopped reading newsmagazines altogether, began to skip the front sections of the paper, and paid no attention to the evening news. She made an effort to watch some of the Thomas-Hill hearings, but the entire spectacle appalled her.

'It's progress,' the psychiatrist told her. 'A generation ago, a woman would never have been allowed to confront such a man about his behavior. Anita Hill may not have stopped the Thomas confirmation, but she accomplished something just as important. She opened a door that won't be easily shut again.'

Karen pondered that for a while. 'I suppose you have a point,' she conceded, 'but I'm suffering from an incurable case of apathy. I don't even know – or care – who's going to run for President next year.'

Natalie nodded. 'I understand how you feel. But it happens that we have someone right here in California that I wish would take a stab at it.'

'Why?'

'Because I think he's a good man. It's clear he really cares about the state and I think he cares just as much about the country, too. I heard him speak at an AMA luncheon last month, and he was honest enough to tell us what a mess we're in, and smart enough to show us exactly how he'd fix it.'

'What's his name?' Karen asked. 'If he runs, maybe I'll vote for him.'

'Willmont,' Natalie replied. 'Robert Drayton Willmont.'

two

On Thursday, October 24, Randy Neuburg squeezed his way past a throng of media representatives into Robert Willmont's private office in the Old Senate Office Building, shutting it firmly behind him.

'It's a zoo out there,' he exclaimed. 'I've never seen so many reporters stuffed into one place before. How do you think they all knew it was today?'

Robert leaned back in his chair and grinned. 'Mary Catherine told them.'

It was still the same boyish grin, but now it spread across a face that showed the erosion of middle age and the pressures of responsibility. 'Handsome' had described him in his youth. At fifty-three, the more appropriate word was 'distinguished.'

'Well, every single paper in the country must have sent someone hightailing it over here, not to mention all three networks and CNN,' Randy informed him.

'They've just about finished with the lights. Are you ready?'

'As ready as I'll ever be, I guess.'

They were brave words and bravely spoken, but Randy hadn't served this man for thirteen years and learned nothing about him. He knew that, behind the cool facade, the senator had to be as nervous as he had ever been. Only halfway into his second six-year term, he was about to take the biggest gamble of his life.

As though he had read his aide's mind, Robert sighed. Like a runaway horse on a slippery hill, he felt out of control. The slow, careful journey to the White House that he had plotted so many years ago had turned into a reckless dash. Somebody else was holding the reins – a group of somebody elses, actually, and he was helpless to do anything but hurtle and leap in whichever direction they chose.

'It's too soon,' he had argued when the upstairs people approached him in the middle of summer. 'My game plan was to finish up this term and then be in position for 1996.'

'Fuck your game plan,' they replied. 'Now's the time.'

'What if we can't take him? I'm finished.'

'You can take him,' they said with easy assurance.

'But I promised my wife she'd be the first First Lady of the twenty-first century.'

'She'll get over it.'

In fact, Elizabeth Willmont didn't even seem to remember the promise. But then, with the little pink pills never far from reach, she sometimes didn't seem to remember very much of anything. She regarded her husband's consuming desire for the White House as the fulfillment of his dream, and focused all her attention on the fulfillment of her own.

Adam was eleven years old now, smart as a whip and as striking as his parents, with the flaming Avery hair and the extraordinary Drayton eyes.

'He has your cunning and my curiosity,' Elizabeth told her husband once, because she knew he was too busy to notice.

Mother and son went everywhere together – the zoo, the ballet, the Smithsonian. They hiked in Rock Creek Park and in Muir Woods, graced the Drayton box at the San Francisco Opera, sailed Chesapeake Bay, and watched hang gliders swoop across the cliffs at Fort Funston.

'Would you like to try that?' she asked him once.

Adam, nine at the time, considered the kitelike figures and then shook his head. 'It looks like fun,' he said, 'but a kid could get killed doing that sort of thing.'

'What are you going to be when you grow up, young man?' his paternal grandmother asked him. The dowager socialite was past eighty and still hanging on.

'Useful,' the boy answered.

Elizabeth delighted in him. He entranced her as Robert once had and more than made up for his father's frequent absences – absences she had long since ceased to care about.

'What would you say to closing out this century in the White House instead of starting the new one?' Robert asked her one late-August evening over dinner in Rock Creek Park.

'Whatever you think best,' she replied absently.

'God,' he exclaimed in disgust. 'You'd think I was talking about buying a new car.'

Elizabeth glanced up. 'Do we need one?'

Robert looked at the still beautiful but now indifferent woman across the table from him and wondered where the naive, adoring girl he had married had gone.

'Tell them it's a go,' he instructed Randy the next day. 'And let's start testing the waters.'

Randy cleared his throat. 'Uh, there's something maybe we should talk about first.'

'Sure,' the senator replied. 'Shoot.'

'Gary Hart,' the aide said.

'What about him? He was a damn fool who had a shot at the White House and shot himself in the foot instead.'

Randy leveled a look at his boss that said it all and the expression on Robert's face suddenly darkened.

'You're way out of line,' he snapped. 'What I do on my own time is my own goddamn business.'

'In California, where you can do no wrong, maybe. But once you become a national candidate, what you do becomes everyone's business,' Randy insisted. 'And since you pay me a lot of money to give you advice, maybe you ought to listen to some of it.'

The senator sighed. 'All right, say it.'

The aide knew he would have to phrase his next words very carefully. 'There are people out there who don't know a thing about your extracurricular activities, and wouldn't care if they did,' he said. 'And there are people who do know but believe the things you stand for are more important than a minor transgression here and there.'

'I should hope so,' Robert interjected.

'But also out there are the Moral Righteous, who believe they were appointed by God to tell everyone else how to live. And sharing the ears of these paragons of virtue is the media, who don't give a damn what you stand for or what you could do for the country or for the world. The polite days are gone, Senator. All that counts now is the story – the front-page, three-inch-head, above-the-fold story.'

Unexpectedly, the senator chuckled. 'And you want me to promise that I won't give them the one they're looking for?'

'A sizable group of folks have worked long and hard to get you to this point,' Randy replied bluntly. 'You owe it to them – to us – and, yes, to the country – not to blow it.'

'Hart should have had you in his corner.'

The aide shrugged. 'He misjudged both the press and the people. It was a blunder that no one, with the exception of the incumbent, of course, wants to see you make.'

'None of that nonsense made any difference back in JFK's time,' the senator said with a sigh. 'Back then, people were able to separate what was important from what wasn't.'

'That was thirty years ago,' Randy observed. 'Things have changed since then, and you have to accept that.'

Robert was not stupid. He knew his dalliances were potentially dangerous for a politician, but he was still a man – a man with substantial needs and a wife who had lost all interest in satisfying them. It was a pity that the media were no longer as well-bred or as tolerant of the human condition as they had once been. It was going to make the next year very tedious.

'Okay, I hear you,' he said. 'But there's one thing I'm going to insist on, and I won't compromise.'

'What's that?' Randy asked, not sure he wanted to hear the answer.

'No Secret Service. I won't have any official watch-dogs monitoring my life – knowing what I eat for breakfast every morning, where I keep my socks, when I take a crap.'

'What about protection?' his aide protested in panic. 'You know what kind of nuts there are out there.'

'If you feel it's necessary, we'll hire a private firm, a discreet firm. One that will answer only to me, not to Washington. I promise you I'll be as good a boy as I can, but I'll do it on my own terms.'

Randy sighed, knowing it was pointless to argue and reasoning that half a bargain was better than none. 'All right. When it comes to it, we'll decline the Secret Service. And I'll have Mary Catherine start scouting around for the right private group.'

The senator smiled benignly. 'Anything else?'

In answer, Randy placed a folder on the desk. 'These are some of the areas the upstairs people have targeted,' he said. 'I recommend we start testing the ones on the top page.'

Robert scanned the sheet. Locations in a dozen major political markets across the country jumped up at him.

'Looks good,' he remarked. As always, his aide was two steps ahead of him.

'I also recommend we hire a public relations firm to handle you.'

'Handle me?' Robert inquired, raising an eyebrow.

'You know, image builders,' explained Randy. 'They do media strategies for politicians, all based on numbers and high-tech prestidigitation. They analyze a candidate and they figure out the best way to present him to the public.'

'I haven't had any trouble with my image up to now,' Robert objected.

'Not in California, no,' Randy agreed. 'But you've kept a low profile in Congress – making allies instead of enemies – building your political base. That's left you basically unknown across the country. So now we're going to push your national awareness up as high as we can, make you a household name.'

'I see your drift,' murmured the senator.

'I've done some research,' Randy continued, 'and I think that Smoeller and Dobbs is our best bet. It's a small firm, but dedicated, with impeccable credentials.'

'They're not the ones remaking Willie Smith, are they?'

'No,' Randy said emphatically. 'We certainly don't want any connection whatsoever with that debacle.'

'And I don't want to be associated with those people who went around promoting the Kuwaiti incubator scam, either.'

'Absolutely not. Smoeller and Dobbs is a firm with a spotless reputation.'

The senator appraised his aide. 'One of the smartest things I ever did was to take you on, wasn't it?'

'The true test of any leader' – Randy grinned – 'is whether he's wise enough to surround himself with his equals. Speaking of which, Ms. Dobbs will be here at three o'clock.'

Mariah Dobbs was a no-nonsense lady who looked more like a *Playboy* centerfold than the successful businesswoman she was. She displayed a short skirt over long legs, a generous curve beneath her suit jacket, intelligent gray eyes behind oversize designer glasses, and a radiant mane of gold hair.

'Given enough access, enough money, and the right buttons to push,' she said at the start of their first meeting, 'I can sell anything – or anyone – to anybody.'

'That sounds encouraging,' Robert replied, flashing his dazzling smile and feeling a familiar rise in his groin.

'If I agree to take you on, Senator, we'll naturally be spending a considerable amount of time together,' Mariah said pleasantly. 'So I think we should have a clear understanding of our relationship right from the start.'

'Certainly,' Robert murmured, shifting ever so slightly in his seat.

'I keep my professional life totally separate and apart from my personal life,' the public relations expert declared. 'Which means that the only portion of our anatomies that will interact will be our minds.'

'I wouldn't have it any other way,' Robert demurred.

'On that basis,' she went on as though he hadn't spoken, 'I plan to study your persona, in depth, over the next few weeks, familiarize myself with your political philosophy as well as your particular strengths and weaknesses, so that we'll be better able to promote you. Off the top of my head, however, I'd say that since a significant part of your message appears to be quite liberal, it might be prudent if the rest of you came across as being fairly conservative. I recommend white shirts, dark suits, traditional ties, keep your hair cut short, and skip the beach this summer.'

'I can handle that,' he said. I can handle you, too, he thought. There wasn't a woman in the world he couldn't have, if he wanted her. Some took a bit more persuasion than others, perhaps, but it was all part of the game. It would be no different with this one.

'People are going to know that you're a rich boy,' the public relations executive continued, 'but I want them to see that you're *using* your wealth, not just enjoying it.'

'I hear you, Mariah.' He caressed the name.

'Dobbs,' she corrected. 'Professionally, I prefer to be known as Dobbs.'

'All right, Dobbs,' Robert corrected himself.

'Also,' she added, refusing to be sidetracked, 'trade the Lamborghini in for something more conservative. A Mercedes is okay, if you're fixated on European cars, but make it black. Red is fine for a playboy, but I don't think that's the image you really want to promote in Peoria.'

'Okay, the Countach goes,' Robert agreed, thinking she had certainly done her homework. The Italian sports car was kept at home, in the garage at Jackson Street, where he drove it infrequently but flamboyantly, at a hundred and ten miles an hour down the treacherous Coast Highway.

'And whenever you go out socially, I recommend that you go with your wife, or with your wife and son. We want people to see you as a dedicated family man.'

The senator shot a look at his aide. 'I *am* a dedicated family man,' he asserted.

'Yes, well, that's all I'm prepared to say for now,' Mariah concluded. 'I'll go through the background material your staff has put together and touch base with you in a week or so with a more complete proposal.'

She slipped the thick folder Randy had provided

into her briefcase, coolly shook Robert's hand, and turned to leave. But at the last moment she turned around and, removing her glasses, produced the definitive *Playboy* smile.

'Well, gentlemen, will I do?'

The senator laughed outright. 'You'll do,' he said, adding to himself – you'll do just fine.

'Good,' she replied with a toss of her gold mane. 'Because I plan to retire on what you're going to pay me.'

Randy produced a broad grin the moment the door had closed behind her. 'With that little ace up our sleeve, how can we lose?'

'Let's not get too cocky,' Robert suggested. 'By Labor Day, we should have a clear picture of where we stand.'

By Labor Day, the picture was indeed clear. According to every major newspaper, poll, and political pundit in the target areas who could squeeze himself onto the Willmont bandwagon, the senator from California was someone with a legitimate chance of unseating the incumbent.

No one close to the senator was very surprised by his swift climb up the political ladder. He was that rarity of rarities – a man of both image and substance. He had the dashing looks, the persuasive charm, the keen intelligence – and the right message at the right time.

'I believe in a balance of trade with Japan or no trade with Japan,' he assured the auto industry in Detroit.

'Hear, hear,' his audience applauded.

'But I won't force Japan to buy American automobiles. Hell, *I* won't even buy American automobiles.'

'So what are you telling us?' bristled a CEO into sudden silence.

'Learn how to make a Toyota.'

'Half of every federal tax dollar is used just to keep up with interest payments on the national debt,' he told a caucus of housewives in Cleveland. 'Isn't it time Washington learned what all of you have known for years – that you can't spend what you don't have?'

'I'm four-square behind foreign aid,' he assured a contingent of Third World diplomats in New York, 'as long as it comes after American aid.'

'It's time to take responsibility for your own actions,' he suggested to the NRA. 'Either you find a way to get guns out of the hands of children, or I promise you – I will.'

'Contrary to popular doctrine, the meek are not going to inherit the earth,' he assured a group of industrialists in Dallas. 'By the time we get through with this planet, not even the cockroaches will survive.'

He became the king of the sound bite, but even the media sensed there was more to him than one-liners. He made some of the people angry and he made some of the people laugh, but he made enough of the people go home and take a good long look in the mirror. By the end of October, all that was left was the announcement.

Mary Catherine poked her head in the door. She was wearing a new red wool dress, she had a fresh perm in her gray hair and her Bambi eyes sparkled.

'We're all set,' she said.

'Is Elizabeth here?' Randy asked.

'She and Adam just came in.'

Robert pulled himself out of his chair, reached up to straighten his tie, and stepped out from behind the desk.

'How do I look?' he asked.

'Like a man about to step off a cliff,' replied Randy with a grin.

'Like the next President of the United States,' Mary Catherine told him.

'Okay,' he said. 'Then let's go do it.'

three

'I don't think we should do a book on San Francisco,' Karen told Nancy on October 24.

'Why not?' Nancy queried. 'It's one of the most popular cities in the country.'

'That's why,' Karen explained. 'As far as I can tell, it's been photographed, lithographed, silk-screened, etched, sketched and painted to death. It's already so overexposed that I'm not sure we could find anything new to say.'

'Spectrum's not going to want to hear that.'

'Well, I have an alternative.'

'I'm all ears,' declared Nancy.

'I'd like to do a book on water.'

'Water?' came the blank response.

'Water. When we lived in Tucson, there was always plenty of it. We were in the middle of the desert and we took it for granted. But here in San Francisco we're surrounded by water and we literally have to count drops. There's the ocean and the bay and the delta and rivers and streams and lakes and ponds and, if someone's been careless, even a puddle. And, all the while, people are taking family showers and trying not to flush their toilets.'

'I didn't realize it was that bad,' Nancy murmured.

'It's just the irony of it,' Karen told her. 'Besides, it may be the only story left to tell about this place.'

'Water, huh?'

'Well, why don't you think about it,' Karen suggested, 'and run it past Spectrum.'

'Don't have to,' Nancy said. 'I think it's a terrific idea. Let's do it.'

'Really?' asked Karen.

'Really.'

'My sister-in-law is coming out in the beginning of December,' Karen told Natalie. 'We're starting another book.'

'About San Francisco?' the psychiatrist asked.

'About water.'

Natalie threw back her head and roared.

'I'll want an autographed copy of that one,' she said.

'I'd like you to meet Nancy, if you have time.'

'I'll make time,' Natalie asserted with more than a hint of sarcasm. 'That is, if I can tear myself away from the Willie Smith rape trial.'

'Oh … that.' Karen stiffened imperceptibly, but good psychiatrists were trained to see imperceptibles, and Natalie Shaffer was very good.

'Not planning to watch, eh?' she said.

'No,' came the short reply. Then a shrug. 'He'll be acquitted.'

'Why do you say that? Do you think he's innocent?'

'I think he's guilty,' Karen replied. 'But he'll be acquitted anyway. The jury will say it was her fault because it was three o'clock in the morning and she went with him.'

'Come on,' Natalie argued. 'This is the 1990s and rapists are getting convicted every day.'

'Acquaintance-rapists?'

'All kinds, although admittedly acquaintance rape is a lot harder to prove.'

'He'll be acquitted,' repeated Karen.

'Nancy's coming out in December,' Karen told Ted when he came home that evening.

Her husband grinned. 'The new book?'

'She liked my idea about water.'

'So do I.'

'Would you like a glass of wine?' she asked.

'Sure,' he replied, heading toward the study.

Since coming to California, the Donigers had been making a conscientious effort to switch from Scotch to wine. On evenings when Amy was in her room doing her homework, Ted would drink a glass with the national news, and Karen would sip at hers as she fixed dinner.

It was just past seven and the newscast was in full swing. As usual, Karen was not paying attention. She inserted a corkscrew into a chilled bottle of chardonnay.

'. . . *surprise move, an unexpected hat has been thrown into the Presidential race,*' the anchor was saying.

With a practiced jerk, Karen pulled the cork free.

'*Robert Drayton Willmont, the charismatic senator from California, made his announcement at a press conference held in Washington late this afternoon.'*

She half-filled two glasses.

'Ladies and gentlemen,' another voice said. *'My wife Elizabeth and my son Adam have set their hearts on being the next residents of sixteen hundred Pennsylvania Avenue.'*

The voice paused for a titter of appreciative laughter. Karen took Ted's glass and started down the hallway that ran from the kitchen to the study.

'Since I have always made every effort to give these two very special people in my life everything they ask for, I am today declaring my candidacy for President of the United States.'

She reached the door of the study and, for some reason, an icy shiver slid down her spine.

'It should come as no surprise to anyone that this country is in very serious trouble,' the candidate continued. *'To be more specific, we are standing on the brink of moral, intellectual, and economic bankruptcy. I believe that America deserves a leader who will first recognize that, second, admit to it, and third, do something about it.'*

It was something about the voice, something familiar. She was sure she had heard it before, and the memory pushing its way into her consciousness was not a pleasant one.

'I saw a bumper sticker the other day,' the voice went on. *'It read: 'New World Order – Same Old Lies.' Now if that's what you want for four more years, then turn off your television sets and put aside your newspapers for the next twelve months, because I'm not interested in anyone's megalomaniacal new world order at the cost of those who are suffering in America now.'*

She took three steps into the study and stopped. The television set was behind her, so that the voice seemed to come through her rather than toward her.

'I say you've been lied to enough. I say you've been deceived

*enough. I say you have the right to know what's going on.
After all, it's your country. And it's in trouble. But I think we
can keep it viable. Yes, even after twelve long years of trickle-
down leadership, even after decades of neglect, I'm not ready
to give up on America yet. But I can't do it without you. So
I'm going to take advantage of every opportunity the media
will give me to tell you the very unpleasant but necessary truth
about what has been done to you and what is still being done
to you, and exactly what we have to do to fix it.'*

'That would be different,' drawled Ted.

As though the whole world were now running in
slow motion, Karen turned to face the face on the
television screen. The once-dark hair was almost
buried in silver, and the crevices of middle age etched
his face. After twenty-nine years, she might not have
remembered the set of the jaw or the shape of the
mouth or the angle of the nose or even the little black
mole on his right cheek – but she would never ever
forget those eyes.

The wineglass shattered against the hardwood floor.

It was ten o'clock the following evening when Karen
crossed the street and pressed the Shaffers' doorbell. It was the dream that drove her there – the
dream about being chased through the fog that she
hadn't had in years, but which had come back last
night.

She had stayed indoors all day, drinking cup after
cup of tea laced with brandy, not even bothering to
dress until just before Amy came home from school.
Dinner was a scramble of leftovers.

It was the unbelievability of it that she couldn't seem
to grasp, that after all these years she should have to
come across him again – and the unfairness that he

had not only escaped retribution of any kind but had become so successful.

'I'm sorry to bother you so late,' she apologized when Natalie answered the door in her bathrobe, 'but you said – if I ever needed to talk . . .'

'Come on inside,' the psychiatrist replied instantly, leading Karen to the back of the house and the room they had turned into a cozy office.

'I don't know what to do,' Karen whispered. 'I thought it was all over and done with long ago, part of the past – and now it's all back, just like before, and I don't know what to do.'

Natalie closed the door behind them. 'Sit down,' she invited and watched Karen squirrel into a deep leather chair. 'Now, what don't you know what to do about?'

Shadowed eyes peered out of the chair. 'I want to kill him,' Karen said.

'Kill who?'

'I didn't want to tell Ted. I thought *he* might kill him and I couldn't let him do that. I couldn't let him ruin his life. But my life is already ruined – he ruined it, so what difference would it make if *I* did it ... if I killed him?'

'Ruined what?' Natalie asked. 'Kill who?'

Karen suddenly giggled, a high, shrill, scary sound.

'Here he is, after all this time, and he's running for President, can you believe that? He's running for President! I could have gone the rest of my life never having to see him again, and what happens? I end up in California, and he's running for President.' The giggle turned to a groan and she began to shiver. When she spoke again, her words stumbled over chattering teeth. 'He doesn't deserve to be President.

He doesn't even deserve to be alive.'

Natalie hustled over to a tray on a sideboard and poured a glass of brandy.

'Here,' the psychiatrist ordered. 'Drink this down.' She had to hold the glass herself to keep it from spilling.

'I never thought I'd see him again,' Karen went on. 'I thought I was done with it all. The nightmares had gone away. Ted and I were starting to put our marriage together. Sometimes, days went by and I didn't even think about it. And then there he was, big as life, coming right through the television screen, talking about truth, for God's sake – truth!'

With a gasp, Natalie sank into the opposite chair. 'Are you talking about Robert Willmont?' she asked in disbelief. 'You want to kill Robert Wilmont?'

'Why not?' Karen flared. 'He almost killed *me*.'

The words hung in the air for a moment, until Natalie was able to absorb them.

'Why don't you tell me about it,' she suggested calmly, although she felt anything but calm.

'I never knew who he was – that is, his whole name,' Karen began. 'No one had a last name back then. So he was just Bob when I met him. Bob from Harvard Law School.'

Natalie knew the California senator had gone to Harvard Law School.

'Do you remember,' Karen asked, 'when I told you I'd had an accident and because of it I could never have any children of my own?'

'I remember.'

'Well, *he* was the accident.'

The psychiatrist listened in silence to the story that Karen had to tell, and Karen told it all, beginning with the party at Jill Hartman's, describing the assault in Central Park, detailing her months in the hospital and the biased police investigation, moving on to her parents and their incredible reaction, and ending with Peter Bauer.

She told it as she had never been allowed to tell it, not just chronicling the bare facts, but clothing them in her deepest-buried feelings, exposing her fears, revealing her humiliation and degradation. Even though she was recounting something that had taken place more than half her life ago, she could recall every detail as vividly as though it had happened yesterday.

From a quarter of a century of professional practice, Natalie Shaffer had learned the art of detached listening, a method of filtering information without betraying anything other than objective interest. But the technique failed her now. Robert Drayton Willmont, the man she had voted for in two senatorial contests, the man she intended to support vigorously in the upcoming presidential campaign, the man she looked upon as the one real hope for the country, was turning into a monster before her very eyes.

'He told the police that you initiated the sex and then refused to leave the park with him?' she asked when the story was finished.

'That's what the investigator said.'

'And you're positive this is the same man? You couldn't be mistaken? After all, it was such a long time ago.'

'There are some things you never forget,' Karen said stonily. 'Maybe I could have mistaken the face, or even the voice, but as long as I live, I'll never forget those eyes.'

Natalie got up from her chair and went to pour a brandy for herself. 'I think *I* need one of these now.'

'I didn't mean to burden you,' Karen apologized, 'but I just needed to talk to someone. You know, someone who would maybe understand my side of it.'

'What's not to understand?' Natalie shrugged. 'It's the old guilt-by-association ploy. You were there – ergo, what happened must have been your fault.'

'In all this time,' Karen confessed, 'you're the first person I've ever told.'

'Besides Ted, of course.'

Karen shook her head. 'I couldn't tell him. I was too afraid he wouldn't want me if he knew, that he'd run away, like Peter.'

Natalie sighed. She desperately wanted Karen to be mistaken, to find some loophole in her story that would show that the man responsible for the terrible things she had described was someone other than the charismatic senator from California who had come forward to lead the nation back from the brink of disaster. But the psychiatrist had been trained to detect even the hint of duplicity, and Karen's years-old recollections were far too clear, far too detailed to leave much room for doubt.

'In December,' she mused aloud, 'voters in Louisiana will go to the polls to choose between a crook and a racist. If what you say is true, next year this country may be asked to choose between an incompetent and a rapist. I'm not sure I know what's to become of us.'

Karen's eyes widened. 'You called him a rapist,' she whispered.

'Of course I did,' Natalie replied. 'What else would I call him?'

Karen began to laugh and cry at the same time. 'Are you saying you don't think it was my fault?'

'Not from what you've told me,' Natalie declared, and then turned a thoughtful glance on her visitor. 'Why? Do *you* think it was your fault?'

'Everyone seemed to think it was,' sobbed Karen. 'They said I went with him and so I must have been looking for trouble. I must have teased him and led him on. They said he was a fine upstanding citizen, so why would he have done such an awful thing unless I had provoked him. The police, my parents – they told me what was past was past and to forget about it and get on with my life. But I guess I never did.'

'Of course not,' said Natalie. 'You're still struggling with what happened to you because no one ever let you deal with it.'

'What do you mean?'

'I mean, when a person is assaulted, as you were, it isn't just the body that needs to heal. The mind also has to heal. The doctors mended your body, but no one understood how important it was for you to mend your soul as well.'

'I never thought of it that way,' Karen marveled.

'You were never allowed to talk about it, you were never allowed to confront your attacker, you were never allowed to work through your fear and anger. Instead, you were made to feel guilt and shame, because that's what the people around you were feeling.'

Tears ran down Karen's cheeks. 'I always felt exactly that way,' she whispered, 'even though I never really thought I did anything wrong.'

'What was that?' Natalie asked.

'I said I felt that way even though I didn't think I did anything wrong.'

'I'm sorry, I didn't catch that last part.'

'I said I didn't think I did anything wrong.'

'Once more,' the psychiatrist urged.

Karen took a deep breath. '*I didn't do anything wrong*,' she almost shouted.

Natalie sat back in her chair. 'You've just taken the first step toward healing.'

'But how can I heal when he's still out there, walking around as free as the wind? When there are still people – my own family – who think that what he did was my fault?'

'As long as *you* know it wasn't,' the psychiatrist said, 'does it really matter what anyone else thinks?'

'It matters,' Karen said bitterly. 'Because it isn't fair. My whole life, ever since that night, I've felt so unworthy, so dirty. All my parents wanted to do was sweep it under the rug – sweep *me* under the rug. They couldn't even call it what it was, you know – they always referred to it as my "accident."'

'You can blame them, if you need to,' the psychiatrist replied. 'But the truth is, they probably didn't know how to deal with it any more than you did.'

'Maybe not,' Karen conceded. 'But that's no excuse for them not believing me, is it – my own parents? All these years, I doubted myself because of them. I had no confidence in my own judgment. I could hardly bear to look at myself in the mirror. I was never able to have a decent relationship with a man. I believed the most important thing was that no one ever find out, that as long as no one knew, everything would be all right. But all the time I thought I was coping, I wasn't coping at all. Everything is still churning around inside of me, like a volcano waiting to erupt.'

'Let it,' Natalie advised.

'You don't mean I really should go out and kill him, do you?'

'Is that your only solution?'

'I can't deny the idea has real appeal,' Karen declared.

'I don't doubt that,' Natalie replied reasonably. 'But, on the other hand, what will killing him accomplish? Will it give you back what he took from you? Will it justify all your years of torment? Will it restore your self-respect?'

'Well, I won't really know until after I do it, will I?'

Natalie stared at her visitor for a minute before she began to chuckle. 'Well, at least you still have your sense of humor.'

Karen shrugged. 'I feel like I have to do something.'

'I agree,' Natalie assured her. 'But now that capital punishment is back on the books, killing Robert Willmont will only succeed in ending what's left of *your* life, too, and where's the justice in that?'

'Maybe I don't care,' Karen said. 'Can you honestly tell me he deserves to live?'

'Perhaps not, but *you* do,' the psychiatrist observed. 'Despite the years of pain and anguish and betrayal you've suffered, look what you managed to create. You have a marriage with real potential, you've raised three beautiful girls, you're producing a series of wonderful books. Now, I'm certainly not saying that you wouldn't have had a happy life if you'd never met up with Robert Willmont. I'm only saying that, on balance, you've done very well for yourself, and I'd think long and hard before I decided to throw all that away on a momentary act of revenge.'

'Tell me the truth,' Karen urged. 'Do you think the man who did those things to me deserves to be in the White House?'

There was a long pause.

'I'd like to think that people can change,' Natalie said slowly. 'That a man who raped you and beat you half to death at twenty-three could have learned how to build rather than destroy at fifty-three. But to be honest with you, even though I sometimes think the White House has become little better than a whore-house, no, I guess I have to say I don't think Robert Willmont belongs in it.'

Karen smiled an almost luminous smile. 'I can't believe how good it feels to finally tell someone, to say all the words right out loud, for God and the whole world to hear.'

'Don't stop there,' Natalie suggested.

'What do you mean?'

'I mean, go home. Talk to Ted. It's time, and if I'm any judge of character, you may be in for a very pleasant surprise.'

The idea of telling her husband dredged up all the painful memories of Peter in Karen's mind. But she knew Natalie was right. Ted was a good man – understanding, compassionate, supportive, and they had lived with the lie between them long enough.

'In spite of myself, I guess I'm a lot stronger now than I was then,' she said, knowing it was true. 'If Ted turns away from me – like Peter did – it'll hurt, but I can handle it.'

'I do believe you can,' declared the psychiatrist.

With a little nod, Karen stood up. 'Thank you for

listening,' she said sincerely. 'I can't tell you how much it's helped.'

And it had. By sharing her pain, she had lightened its load. By letting the ugliness out of the dark, she knew she could begin to put the excruciating episode into some sort of perspective.

'What will you do?' Natalie asked.

'I'm going to take your advice,' Karen replied. 'I'm going to tell Ted.'

'And then what?'

Karen shrugged. 'We'll see,' she said.

It was after midnight when Karen let herself back into the house, but Ted was still awake, sitting patiently at the breakfast-room table with a fresh pot of tea ready.

'I waited up,' he said simply, 'in case you wanted to talk.'

'I do,' Karen responded, sitting down across from him.

He poured tea for both of them, adding the dollop of honey he knew she liked in hers. Then he wrapped his hands around his cup and waited for whatever was to come.

Half an hour later, they were both drained.

'I should have told you long ago,' she said, 'and I've felt guilty all these years for deceiving you. But I knew you'd never have married me if you'd known. So I let myself behave very selfishly and kept it from you.' She stared at the bottom of her teacup. 'If you want that divorce now, I won't blame you.'

Instead, he came around to sit beside her.

'I guess I can't honestly say how I would have felt back then,' he said slowly. 'But I don't think it would have been much different than I feel right now, which is appalled and devastated and outraged – but not at you. Never at you.'

'Really?' she breathed.

'Despite what the police or your parents or Peter might have thought, I know you well enough to know that you could never have been to blame for what that man did to you.'

She blinked as though she hadn't heard properly. 'You honestly mean that?'

He put his arm around her and drew her against him. 'Of course I do. I guess, on some level, I always knew there was more to it than an automobile accident, because the scars on the inside always seemed so much deeper than the ones on the outside.'

'You could see that?'

He nodded. 'You shouldn't have had to live with this all alone for so long,' he said. 'But at least you won't have to anymore. You've got Natalie to help you now, and I trust her. And you've got me to support you in any way I can. If you want, I'll even go out and kill the bastard for you.'

'No,' she murmured with a little smile. 'I don't want that.'

'Whatever it takes for you to work through all this, just know that I'm right here with a shoulder to lean on or cry on, or anything else you need or want.'

They made their way upstairs, into the peach-and-aqua master suite, where they undressed in the dark and got into Karen's bed and held each other as tight as they could.

'You're safe now,' he murmured into her sweet-smelling hair. 'I'll never let anyone hurt you again.'

four

Janice Evans hurried down Front Street in the November sunshine, on her way to the Willmont campaign headquarters.

The newly announced presidential candidate and his entourage had been in town for little more than a week and already they had everything organized. Mary Catherine had telephoned her at eight-thirty.

'The senator has agreed to an interview,' she said. 'But he wants to make it very clear that he intends to choose the topics.'

'Agreed,' Janice replied. 'I can be there in an hour.'

'The senator can see you at eleven,' Mary Catherine informed her.

The pretty blond reporter had come a long way since the day when, as a fledgling staff member of a local television station, she had stuck her microphone in the face of a congressman at San Francisco Airport, and much of her success was directly attributable to the exposure she had received from covering his subsequent campaign.

During his numerous forays up and down the state, Robert had used her as his official press-pool representative – and his unofficial bed companion. He would feed her information that she would then dutifully share with the rest of the media.

The networks got to see a lot of the attractive, well-spoken, well-informed journalist, and liked what they saw. When the campaign ended, Janice was brought to New York as a background reporter for one of the major television news-talk programs. Today, she was one of a quartet of rotating hosts on the show and had earned the respect of her colleagues.

She had kept her figure, but her blond hair now received a lemon rinse every month to hold its highlights. The laugh lines around her mouth and eyes, which used to come and go, now came and stayed, and she found herself using heavier makeup to keep her complexion looking fresh and clean. She was thirty-six years old.

'When I'm elected President,' the newly elected senator promised, 'the job of press secretary is yours, if you want it.'

'I want it,' she said.

Janice Evans had developed into more than just a pretty, if somewhat hardened, face. She was also articulate and single-mindedly dedicated. She would eventually have risen to the top of her profession even had she not gone to bed with Robert Willmont, but the shortcut certainly hadn't hurt. They were two of a kind, the journalist and the politician, and they used each other, with total understanding, at every opportunity.

'Janice Evans to see the senator,' she said when she reached the twelfth floor.

'Is he expecting you, Miss Evans?' a striking African-American receptionist asked with a polite smile.

'I believe he is.'

'Just a moment, please,' the woman said, reaching for the telephone.

The one thing they had each insisted on was discretion. Public knowledge of their relationship would have ruined them both. Janice suspected that Randy Neuburg and Mary Catherine O'Malley knew what was going on, but if they did, it went no further than that. As far as the rest of the world was concerned, she was just another newswoman covering a story.

'I have an idea I'd like to pursue,' she said to her producer on the fifteenth of October. 'I think Robert Willmont is going to be our next President, and I'd like to do an in-depth segment on him. You know, give the public an advance peek inside the man.'

'What makes you think he's even going to run?'

'Come on,' she admonished. 'I've been on his trail for ten years. I know his organization. They're gearing up.'

'Well,' the producer said, unconvinced, 'we'll see.'

On October 25, he stopped by her office. 'That idea you had about Robert Willmont,' he said. 'It's a go.'

Janice hid a smug grin. 'Do I get a free hand?'

'If it's quality.'

'Have I ever given you anything but?'

'No,' the producer had to admit. 'You haven't.'

It was true. Janice had an uncanny nose for news and a discriminating eye. Her results were frequently fascinating, occasionally explosive, but always in good taste.

'The senator will see you now, Miss Evans,' the receptionist said cordially, turning from the telephone.

'Hi there, beautiful,' Robert beamed as soon as they were alone. 'How's New York?'

'Getting chilly.'

'Well, if you lock that door, I'll do what I can to warm you up. God, I've missed you. Randy's had me living like a monk for months.'

Janice chuckled. 'If the press could hear you now.'

Robert sighed. 'I liked it better when the press knew its place. Or at least when reporters recognized that a man's sex life has nothing to do with his ability to run the country.'

Sex for Robert, while admittedly more pleasurable, was as fundamental as feeding or relieving himself. When he was hungry, he ate, and he wasn't particular what food was put before him. When his bladder was full, he emptied it, and it didn't matter whose bathroom he used. And when his libido swelled, he thought nothing of turning to whatever acolyte was at hand. And there were always many. Even the reality of AIDS failed to curtail Robert's appetite. The past few months under Randy's watchful eye had been pure hell.

'Well, if you're in real need,' Janice said, 'I'll be home later on tonight.'

She had kept her Cow Hollow flat, well aware that, in the media business, nothing was permanent.

'Unfortunately,' the senator replied with a grimace, 'so will I.'

'In that case . . .' Janice reached back and snapped the lock on the office door.

* * *

Randy perched on the corner of Mary Catherine's desk and glanced at his wristwatch. 'What time did she come in?'

'About eleven,' the administrative assistant replied. 'They skipped lunch.'

'Jeez, it's two-thirty,' Randy groaned. 'You'd think he'd have more sense. Going at it in his office, for God's sake, where anyone can breeze right in.'

'They locked the door.'

'Doesn't he have an appointment or something this afternoon?'

Mary Catherine shook her head. '*Time* was supposed to be here at three, but the photographer got stuck in Chicago, so they rescheduled for tomorrow.'

'How much longer, do you think? The *Chronicle* wants a comment on the Yugoslavia sanctions, and ABC wants a statement on the bombing in Beirut.'

'Considering how long you've had him on the straight and narrow' – Mary Catherine shrugged – 'another hour or two.'

'And it's only November,' sighed Randy.

five

Karen stepped out of the Jacuzzi that Ted had installed in the master bath as part of remodeling the St. Francis Wood house and began to towel herself dry. She normally used the tub in the evenings, to relax before going to bed, but had chosen to take advantage of it this morning.

On Natalie's advice, she had thought long and hard about the unique opportunity that fate had given her. Once she calmed down, she could see that the psychiatrist was right – murdering Robert Willmont might provide a momentary pleasure, even a genuine sense of satisfaction, but not much else, and she had no intention of settling for that.

'What will you do?' Ted asked.

'I don't know,' she replied honestly. 'I don't know what I *can* do.'

But she knew she would do something. The feelings she had buried for so long could no longer be denied.

It was ironic to think she might have heard or read his name many times, might even have seen a newspaper photograph of him, and it would have meant nothing to her. It wasn't so unreasonable – she hadn't been looking for him. Rather, she had stuffed the image of him down inside of her where, over time, he became less and less of a man and more and more of a monster. It was one of the techniques she had developed to cope with the guilt and the shame and the loss.

As much as she had hoped, during the long years of recuperating, reevaluating and refocusing, that he would come to some agonizing end, as all monsters should, she now came to realize that what she really wanted, even more than his destruction, was vindication for herself. She wanted the whole world to know exactly what he was – underneath the slick facade, behind the dazzling aquamarine eyes – and she knew that nothing less than exposing him in some horribly humiliating way would satisfy her.

Her plan was ridiculously simple. She would seek him out, in a public forum, where there were bound to be members of the media interested in a juicy story. They would be able to tell, the moment they saw the shock on his face when she confronted him, that she was speaking the truth. He might live, but he would be politically ruined. And he would never be President of the United States.

The forum she picked was an early-December ceremony in Golden Gate Park where the senator was scheduled to preside at the groundbreaking for the Natural History Museum's new Drayton Pavilion. In addition to social and political VIPs, the press would be there in full force, hoping to persuade the candidate to make a few off-the-cuff comments that would play well on the evening news. It was a perfect setting.

Karen tucked her towel around her and leaned over the sink to brush her teeth, but the terry cloth slipped and dropped to the floor. She stared at herself in the mirror. In two months, she would be fifty years old, half a century, and she was pleased to note that she had not yet succumbed to middle-age sag. Her figure had retained its slenderness and regular exercise kept her muscles toned. Once clothed, the disfiguring scars could not be seen. Her skin was still good and a trip to the beauty salon every six weeks removed the gray in her dark hair. With just a modicum of makeup, she knew she could pass for thirty-five.

She slipped into a winter-white turtleneck, matching stirrup pants, and a red-white-and-black tweed raw silk jacket. Winter-white pumps and a pair of Felicity's chunky gold earrings and matching bracelet finished the outfit. She brushed her hair off her face, catching the shoulder-length curls with a black velvet bow at the nape of her neck.

The ceremony was scheduled for two o'clock. Just after noon, Karen drove her Volvo wagon into Golden Gate Park and down John F. Kennedy Drive, stopping a block and a half from the museum. Traffic-control barricades had already been put in place, personnel in mobile television vans were setting up their equipment, and the area was beginning to fill with curious onlookers who sensed the makings of a media event.

It was one of those magnificent winter days for which San Francisco had long been famous – sunny, windless, and sixty-five degrees. Karen melted into the crowd that milled around the area and waited.

At five minutes before two, a pair of motorcycles

with lights flashing led a convoy of limousines into the parking lot that flanked the main concourse and fronted the five museums that shared this section of the park.

The crowd, which had swelled to over a thousand, pushed forward, taking Karen along with it. She was perhaps twenty feet away when he stepped out of the second limousine, and in the first instant of actually seeing him, she thought she might faint. It was only the people pressing against her for a glimpse of the candidate that kept her upright.

The other limousines were emptying now and the party of some thirty dignitaries, surrounded by reporters, television cameramen and still photographers, was making its way to the bandstand at the far end of the concourse.

The new mayor was there, along with several members of the board of supervisors and a fair selection of the city's most prominent personalities, but Karen didn't recognize anyone. She barely even looked at them, so focused was she on the self-assured man with the memorable eyes.

She paid no attention to the overblown speeches that honored the Drayton dynasty. She simply waited for the right moment, the brief lull that was bound to come, when she would step forward and face him. She had it all very carefully rehearsed – every word, every move.

'Hello, Bob,' she would say, planting herself in his path. 'You remember me, don't you – and what you did to me? Of course you do. I can see it in your eyes, and now so will the rest of the world. They're known as the Drayton eyes, aren't they? Well, the Draytons should have gouged them out the day you were born.

You raped me, you beat me, and you left me for dead all those years ago, without so much as a second thought. And now you think the people of this country should elect you President of the United States?'

The moment came and almost went before she recognized it. The speeches were over, the group of dignitaries was moving away from the bandstand toward the museum for the symbolic shovel of dirt. As expected, reporters were shouting out their questions.

'What do you think about the Sununu resignation?' one called.

'Come now, Dave,' the senator admonished the newsman. 'We're here today for something that has nothing to do with politics.'

'Everything you do between now and next November has to do with politics, Senator,' the newsman replied.

The candidate grinned. 'In that case, Mr. Sununu was merely the first of the rats to desert a sinking ship.'

'How about the Keating verdict?' another asked.

'If they put him in jail and destroyed the key, it wouldn't make up for what he's done,' Robert replied.

'And the Kennedy Smith trial?'

'No comment.'

'Thank you, ladies and gentlemen,' a redheaded man who looked like a dwarf beside the candidate said smoothly. 'The senator would now like to get back to the purpose at hand, the groundbreaking for the Drayton Pavilion.'

He put his hand on Robert Willmont's arm to guide him through the crowd. But Karen Doniger stood in the way. She stared up at the monster who had invaded her dreams for so many years and opened her mouth to say the words that would damn him to eternity. But he looked right at her, from less than two feet away, with a polite smile that held not so much as a flicker of recognition.

She had taken him by surprise, leaving him no time to prepare. He could not possibly have been that good an actor – he didn't know who she was.

In the seconds it took for that to register on her, he moved on past, the crowd surging after him. Stunned, she dug her heels into the grass and stayed where she was. The moment was gone, she would have to find another.

Karen turned and hurried away, not looking back and not pausing until she reached her car. With shaking hands, she unlocked the door and scrambled behind the wheel, started up the engine and sped off, coming out of the park onto the Great Highway, which ran along the Pacific Ocean.

She parked the car and, kicking off her shoes, walked along the beach. It was low tide and the soggy sand curled beneath her weight. She went down to the water's edge and stood there, staring out into the depths, as the frigid foam lapped around her feet and sucked the coarse brown granules from beneath her stockinged toes.

Finally, she went back up the beach and dropped down on the dry sand. Her head was spinning. It was inconceivable to her that the horror which had etched itself like acid into her very core meant so little to him that he wouldn't even remember her – that the most catastrophic episode of her life was nothing more than a minor encounter he had long since forgotten. Of all the scenarios she had conceived, this had not been among them.

She didn't know how long she sat there, watching the gentle waves flow and ebb, letting the sea spray drizzle over her, before she began to laugh. Hugging her knees to her chest, she threw back her head and laughed, peal after peal swallowed up by the pounding surf.

A whole new perspective engulfed her, and with it came the realization that, to a large extent, she had created her own hell. She had allowed the monster to torment and terrify her for almost thirty years. But today, she had stood two feet away from that monster – and seen that he was in fact nothing more and nothing less than a man. She had looked into the aquamarine eyes of a *man*, a man she knew she would never again have cause to fear.

Slipping her shoes back on, Karen got up and walked slowly back to the Volvo. There would be another opportunity for her to expose Robert Willmont for what he was, of that she was sure. She would just have to think of a different approach, now that it was clear he did not remember her.

There was no hurry. There was still plenty of time.

SIX

'No one's going to stop us now,' Randy exclaimed the morning after Super Tuesday. The Willmont candidacy had taken half of the dozen primaries with at least fifty-three percent of the vote.

Robert grinned. 'We're looking good, my boy. We're definitely looking good.'

'Jeez, we even took forty-two percent of Texas.'

'It's all in the message,' the candidate said smoothly.

'I know you weren't keen on hiring her, but you've got to admit that Dobbs is worth twice what we're paying her.'

The public relations expert had deftly created an image of the California senator that was all but irresistible. Men responded intellectually to Robert's no-nonsense manifesto. Women reacted emotionally to his carefully groomed good looks and boyish charm. Senior citizens viewed his conservative appearance as sincere and approved of his obvious devotion to his mother as well as his wife and son. People everywhere found themselves listening to what he was saying.

The issue was clear – if America was going to be saved, everyone had to do his share. No one would be exempt and no one would profit at the expense of others. 'Save America!' the banners read, and in a few brief months those two words had become synonymous with Robert Drayton Willmont.

Mariah Dobbs had indeed done her job, and the only negative ever expressed by the senator was that ice water ran in her veins. In the four months that she had been on his team, traveling with him, sitting beside him on airplanes, in limousines and at endless strategy meetings, sharing early-morning breakfasts and late-night dinners, sometimes even sharing hotel suites, she had never thawed. The end of an evening was always followed by a polite good-night and the firm snap of a lock on a bedroom door.

For a sexually active man being kept in rigid check, it was agonizing. He began to dream about her, waking before dawn with thoughts about the things he wanted to do to her and the things he wanted her to do to him. More and more, as time went by, hotel maids found his sheets wet and sticky.

'Are you a lesbian?' he asked her once in frustration.

Cool green eyes appraised him. 'No, Senator,' she replied.

'Then why the deep-freeze act all the time?'

'I believe I made it clear at the beginning that I don't mix pleasure with business.'

'We could put it on a business basis, if you prefer.'

'I can leave, if you prefer,' she retorted.

It was exasperating. He rarely had a problem getting a woman into bed. On the contrary, he was usually fighting them off. But this one didn't seem the least bit inclined. Several times he had come very close to forcing the issue, but then backed off, knowing he could not risk alienating her. But he wasn't used to a woman being in control of him, and the more unattainable she was, the more he wanted her.

'I'm sorry if my presence bothers you,' Mariah remarked with a frosty edge in her voice. 'I'm sorry if your marriage isn't everything you need it to be. But, as it happens, mine is.'

'I didn't know,' he muttered, taken by surprise. No one had told him the bitch was married. Not that it made any difference to him, but it did help to explain her lack of interest.

'It wasn't necessary for you to know,' she told him. 'All that's necessary is for you to convince the voters that you are first and last a devoted family man.'

She was the only woman he had ever met, he confessed to Mary Catherine, who flat out intimidated him.

'Dobbs is okay,' he said now, with a shrug. 'But she didn't go out and win those primaries. I did.'

Randy smothered a grin. There weren't many women who failed to fall under Robert's spell. In fact, he could remember only one, a staff secretary during their first term in the Senate. She was right out of Brigham Young University – fresh, eager, lovely, and clearly not buying what Robert was selling. She was also smart, and solved the problem of unwanted attention by not staying around very long.

But this time, the senator had met his match.

Whenever Mariah was around, Randy would catch his eyes following her. He would stand a little straighter and laugh a little louder, but in vain. Mariah maintained her professional demeanor and gave him nothing else. Whatever frustrations were building up inside of him, he had no choice but to keep his distance.

What Robert didn't know was that Mariah more often than not warmed herself in Randy's bed.

'He thought I was a lesbian,' she giggled one night as they lay apart, waiting for the sweat of passion to dry on their bodies.

'You're kidding!'

'What an egotist! I guess it was the only explanation he could come up with for my lack of interest.'

'He's not used to women turning him down,' Randy felt obliged to explain. 'Very few do.'

'Maybe that's his problem,' she observed. 'He's always had everything too easy.'

'I guess you could say that,' Randy had to admit. 'As a matter of fact, I can think of only one other woman in the last thirteen years who refused to give him a tumble.'

'Who was that?'

'She was a secretary. Her name was Maggie Holden, and damned if she didn't look just like Julia Roberts. She distracted the hell out of him.' Randy chuckled. 'It was really funny sometimes, watching him around her, preening like a peacock. But he was old enough to be her father and I honestly think that was the way she saw him.'

'What became of her?'

'Who knows? She was there one day and gone the next. That happens more than you might think in D.C. A lot of people just can't handle the pressure. It was a little weird, though, because when she went, she really went. She never called, never even came back to clean out her desk. When Mary Catherine finally packed up her stuff and took it around to her apartment, her roommate said she'd gone home to Utah.'

'It sounds like maybe it was the senator she couldn't handle,' Mariah said. 'There were some women, you know, who refused to put up with sexual harassment even then.'

'I don't believe it went as far as sexual harassment,' Randy protested. 'I think all he did was flirt with her.'

'Perhaps she didn't see it that way.'

'Well, whatever, it was too bad. I think she could have had a career in Washington, if she'd wanted it. She wasn't only a knockout, she was damn smart.'

'Well, based on my own personal experience,' declared Mariah, 'I'd say that the senator can be very persistent when he wants to be and he doesn't handle rejection very well.'

'I'm sorry about that. Do you want me to talk to him?'

'No, of course not.' She laughed. 'I'm a big girl. I can take care of myself. But I suppose you should know – I elected to tell him a small untruth.'

'What sort of small untruth?'

She shrugged. 'I told him I was married.'

'Why did you do that?'

'I thought it would shake him loose for a while.'

Randy sighed. 'As you've probably figured, Robert needs a lot of … exercise,' he explained. 'We've been keeping him on a very short leash.'

'He's not a baby, for heaven's sake,' Mariah snapped. 'He's fifty-four years old. Isn't it time he learned how to control himself?'

'He is what he is.'

'Well, if a little lie keeps him from hitting on me,' she said with a yawn, 'that's all I care about.'

Randy reached out and pulled her into the warm circle of his arms. 'Maybe someday that won't have to be such a lie,' he murmured.

Mariah snuggled against him. 'Maybe, someday,' she said, already half asleep.

By the end of March, Robert was steamrolling toward a first-ballot nomination. With his eye fixed on the June 2 California primary, he returned to San Francisco for a two-week round of politicking. Janice Evans had long since left the campaign and gone back to New York to put together her segment on the man behind the candidate. It was scheduled to air a week before the primary.

'I'm doing my part to win you the nomination,' she told him over the telephone. 'So long as no one catches on why.'

'You're going to make one hell of a press secretary,' he replied, shifting in his chair and wishing she were in town because he'd already gone without for too long.

The Willmont campaign headquarters on Front Street was cranked into full gear. Although still two months away, winning the California primary, and winning it big, was considered essential to put Robert on top going into the convention. The suite of offices was filled to overflowing with teams of tireless volunteer workers, mimeographing dozens of press releases, licking thousands of contribution envelopes, and manning an intimidating bank of telephones.

Mary Catherine had arrived the week before, while the senator was still campaigning in Wisconsin. By the time he appeared at Front Street, on April 2, every last detail of his two-week stint had been arranged.

'Maximum exposure, minimum wear and tear,' she told him. 'It's a work of art, but I can't take the credit.'

'Why not?' he asked.

'Because the volunteer staff did it. One woman in particular, who's a whiz at organization. She put the schedule together, made all the reservations, prepared press releases for the locals at every stop, and now she's working on half a dozen different promotional packets.'

'Point her out,' Robert requested.

Mary Catherine scanned the busy work area. 'There she is, over there by the Xerox machine, the one with the dark hair and the designer dress.'

Across the room, the senator caught a glimpse of a neat, attractive woman who looked to be in her middle thirties. She was nothing at all like Mariah Dobbs – dark where Mariah was light, slender where Mariah curved – but there was something about the way she moved, something about the cool efficiency with which she worked that connected the two women in his groin.

'She could be useful,' he murmured.

'Forget it,' Mary Catherine told him. 'She has a very successful career and no long-lasting interest in politics. And in case you've got something else in mind, she's also very married.'

'What kind of career?'

'Have you seen a book called *Tapestry*?'

Robert shook his head.

'I have,' Randy said. 'Pictures and poems about the Southwest. It was impressive, as I recall.'

'*Tapestry* is one of a whole series of books that she

and another woman have done about America,' Mary Catherine noted.

'They're the same two who did *Dichotomy*,' Randy added. 'You know, the book on D.C. that everyone was raving about a few years ago.'

Robert did remember that one. Elizabeth had had it out on the coffee table for months.

'She's a photographer?'

'No. She's the poet.'

'What's she doing here?'

'I guess poets must be voters, too,' Mary Catherine said with a shrug. 'She wandered in one day and said she had some free afternoons, and you were the first politician to come along who wasn't afraid to tell it like it is.'

'Wait a minute,' Robert said with a sudden frown. 'Do I know her? I think she looks familiar to me, but I can't seem to place her.'

'I can,' Randy told him. 'If I'm not mistaken, she was at the groundbreaking ceremony back in December. In fact, I'm pretty sure she wanted to say something to you that day, but then I guess she changed her mind.'

'I must have made quite an impression,' the candidate replied, flashing one of his famous grins and standing up a little straighter.

Karen had been working for the senator's campaign for three months. She spent Tuesday and Thursday afternoons promoting a man she had every wish to see chewed up into tiny pieces and spit out, and the sheer perversity of it all made her smile while she worked.

'I need to do this,' she told Ted the night before her first day at Front Street. 'Don't ask me why, I just need to do it.'

'I *have* to ask you why,' he protested.

'I'm not sure I can explain it,' she replied. 'But this is a man who almost killed me and certainly changed my entire life – and I don't even know who he is. Natalie said that maybe a man who destroyed at twenty-three could have learned to build at fifty-three. I want to find out if he has.'

'Surely there's another way,' he argued.

'I can't learn the things I need to learn about him from reading articles and watching interviews,' she declared. 'I know it might sound crazy to you, it does a little to me, but I need to know who he really is, from up close. I have a right to know who he really is.'

The Xerox stopped grinding out copies and Karen bent down to pick up the stack. Straightening up, she turned in the direction of the collating machine, only to collide with a navy-blue suit. Pages scattered in all directions.

'I'm terribly sorry,' the suit said. 'Here, let me help you.'

Robert scrambled to gather the errant papers. Up close, he could see she was perhaps a bit older than he had first thought, but certainly no less attractive.

'We haven't met,' he said. 'I'm Senator Willmont.'

'I'm Karen Doniger,' she replied, amazed at how calm her voice sounded.

He put out his free hand and, while it took all the courage she could muster, she took it.

'I understand you're something of an expert on America,' he declared.

'I beg your pardon?'

'Your books.'

'Oh,' she said in some confusion. 'I didn't realize you were familiar with my work.'

'To be perfectly honest, I'm not. My staff is.'

She allowed herself a slight smile at his ingenuousness. 'From a certain, very limited perspective,' she conceded, 'I suppose you might say I'm an expert.'

'Your perspective could be very useful to me,' he said. 'Maybe we can find time to discuss it.' He still had hold of her hand.

'Maybe,' she returned, disengaging her fingers with apparent unconcern.

It was a noncommittal answer to a non-question. The opening gambit had been played. He returned the stack of papers he had collected with a dazzling smile.

'I'll look forward to it,' he promised, caressing her with his eyes exactly as he had on a December night so many years ago.

seven

'You didn't forget that I'm going over to DeeDee's for dinner tonight, did you?' Amy asked at breakfast the following Tuesday. 'I have to help her study for the history exam.'

'No, I didn't forget,' Karen replied, putting a bowl of cereal in front of her stepdaughter, and thinking how easy her transition to San Francisco had been, after all.

'I've got that meeting with the supervisors tonight,' Ted said. 'It's bound to run late.'

'That's okay,' Karen replied with a smile. 'Contrary to popular opinion, I can handle an evening on my own.'

'Are you sure?'

'Of course I'm sure. In fact, if they ask you to join them for dinner after the meeting, go ahead. A little hobnobbing with the politically lofty can't hurt.'

'Okay,' Ted replied with a smile. Ever since she had

gone to work for the Willmont campaign – a decision he wasn't entirely easy about – the ins and outs of politics seemed always on her mind.

Karen spent a long time in the shower, washing her hair, applying a deep conditioner and pampering her body with rich moisturizing lotion. When she came out of the bathroom, snuggled inside a thick terry-cloth robe, she spent a long time in front of the big picture window that offered an ever-changing panorama of the Pacific Ocean right from her own peach-and-aqua bedroom, and gave her a whole new perspective on water.

She did busy work in her office for an hour. Nancy had already made two trips to San Francisco and had planned her last for late July. Once the photographs for their new book, *Reflections*, were selected, Karen would be swamped, but until then, there really wasn't much to do, and she went upstairs with plenty of time to prepare for her afternoon in the Willmont camp.

Left to her own devices, she would have whiled away the rest of the day in front of the picture window, watching the freighters and tankers go by, watching the seabirds swoop down around the fishing boats, watching the undulating water stretching all the way out to the horizon. But, she conceded with some reluctance, she had other things to do.

She hung her robe on the back of the bathroom door, peered into her closet, and pulled out a simple navy silk pleated dress with long sleeves and white trim. She added low-heeled navy pumps and transferred her wallet and keys and makeup case into a navy handbag.

It was one more magnificent Bay Area afternoon as

she backed the Volvo out of the driveway and headed downtown. The sky was radiant blue, the breeze was soft, and the temperature was in the high sixties. She parked in a garage half a block from the campaign headquarters and stopped at a little coffee shop on the corner for a container of fresh orange juice, which she sipped on the way up in the elevator.

'Am I glad you're here,' Mary Catherine greeted her the moment the doors slid open at the twelfth floor. 'The senator wants a press reception set up for tomorrow afternoon, complete with promotional stuff. Randy sent over some notes. Can you work them up?'

'I'll get on it right away,' Karen promised. 'What's the topic?'

'A woman in San Jose asked the senator why we burn crops, leave grain to rot in silos, and pay farmers not to farm when there are millions of people starving in America.'

'That sounds like a reasonable question to me,' Karen observed.

'That's what *he* said – so now he's hell-bent to make a campaign issue out of it.'

It was seven-thirty by the time Karen had selected the appropriate boilerplate and reworked Randy's notes into readable prose with the help of the user-friendly Macintosh on her desk. The rest of the volunteer staff had long since disappeared. If nothing else, she mused, her experience here had banished the dread of computers that had kept her clinging to a pad and pen all her life. She typed the final period, printed out a fresh copy, and headed for the Xerox machine.

'How are you doing?' Mary Catherine asked.

'Almost done,' Karen told her.

The administrative assistant glanced through the copy. 'Say, this is good,' she praised. 'Very good. I think you've just created your first position paper.'

Karen chuckled 'And I thought that political pundits had to ponder those things forever.'

'You'd be surprised,' Mary Catherine retorted. 'Can I help you finish up?'

Karen shook her head. 'There's not that much left to do. Besides, my family has deserted me for the evening, so there's no reason why I can't stay and get it done.'

Mary Catherine smiled. 'I really don't know what we'd do without you,' she said.

By the time Karen finished the Xeroxing and turned to the collating machine, it was almost eight.

'I thought the senator might stop in,' Mary Catherine said, purse in hand. 'But I guess he decided not to. So I'm going to go find myself a Scotch and sandwich. Care to join me?'

'No, thanks,' Karen replied. 'I've a few more things left to do here and then I think I'll just head on home.'

'In that case, I'll see you tomorrow. Just close the door when you leave. It locks automatically.'

The clatter of the collator was too loud, some twenty minutes later, for Karen to hear the outer door open and close, so the senator took her completely by surprise.

'Do I pay you enough to work these hours?' he asked.

'Probably not,' she replied, noting that he was alone, with neither Randy Neuburg nor the private security detail following in his wake.

'Where's everyone?' he inquired, looking around.

'Gone home.'

'Except you.'

'Except me, for about five more minutes. Mary Catherine decided you weren't going to come in this evening.'

'I wasn't,' he said. 'It was a last-minute idea. I thought of it after I gave my shadows the night off.' He grinned. 'But I guess I'm safe enough for one evening. Anyway, all that constant scrutiny tends to get to you after a while.' He peered over her shoulder. 'Is that the stuff for tomorrow?'

'Yes,' she replied, inching a step away.

'Good. I wanted to get a look at it.'

'Help yourself,' she murmured.

He leaned against the collator and flashed his famous smile down at her.

'You know, I've been meaning to find the opportunity to tell you how much we appreciate your dedication to the campaign. How much *I* appreciate it.'

'It's for a worthy cause, isn't it?' she said obliquely.

'Look,' he said, checking his wristwatch, 'why don't you let me buy you a drink or something, to thank you for all your time and effort.'

'That's not necessary.'

'I know, but I'd like to do it anyway,' he pressed. 'Besides, there's your unique perspective on America that we were going to talk about, remember?'

Karen snapped off the collator and began to staple the press packets together.

'Thanks,' she said, 'but I really have to get home.'

She finished the stapling and carried the kits over to the long worktable beside Mary Catherine's desk, knowing he was watching her every move. She was out of the building, into the parking garage and behind the wheel of the Volvo before she could banish the sensation of his eyes on her body.

She shook her head, impatient at her foolishness, and twisted her key in the ignition. Nothing happened. She tried again, and again nothing happened. The engine refused to turn over.

'Just what I need,' she groaned, popping the hood and climbing out of the station wagon, although she knew next to nothing about cars and realized it was highly unlikely that she would recognize any kind of problem.

'What's the matter?' Robert asked.

She couldn't believe he was standing there and wondered if he had followed her.

'My car won't start.'

'Let me see.'

Before she could protest, he had slipped into the Volvo and was turning the key. There was no response. He tried wiggling and thrusting and pumping, but his efforts were in vain.

'It's not the battery,' he said with assurance. 'But it might be the starter.'

'What does that mean?'

'If it's the starter, it means you'll have to leave the car here until morning and then get it towed.'

'Damn,' she muttered.

'Can your husband come get you?'

Karen checked her watch. 'He won't be home yet,' she sighed. 'He's at a dinner meeting.'

'Well, don't worry about it,' he said with a reassuring smile. 'I can drive you home.'

'Oh, that's not necessary,' she declared. 'I can take a taxi.'

'Nonsense,' said Robert firmly. 'I won't hear of it. After all the hours you've put in on my behalf, it's the very least I can do.'

Karen looked at him for a long moment with an expression he couldn't define.

'Well, all right,' she said finally, 'if you're sure it won't be an inconvenience.'

'Not at all,' he replied with a smile. 'Maybe we can even stop on the way and have that drink. I really do have a lot of questions to ask you.'

She couldn't think of a polite way to decline. 'We could go across the street,' she suggested, referring to a popular bar on the corner that she felt certain would still be busy at this hour.

'Done,' he said.

Over three Scotches, a bucket of steamed clams, and the constant interruption of political supporters glad to find him unencumbered by a wall of security, he encouraged her to talk about her books and experiences, inserting a question every now and then. Karen found herself describing the special characteristics of New York, Atlanta, Houston and Tucson without even realizing she had noticed them.

It was ten-thirty by the time they returned to the garage. They tried the Volvo again but it was useless. So they moved on to Robert's black Mercedes, parked just a few spaces away.

He opened the passenger door for her, making sure the pleats of her navy blue dress were safely tucked in before he closed it again with a firm click and went around to the driver's side.

Despite the three Scotches, which usually had a numbing effect on her, Karen's heart began to flutter as he steered the Mercedes out of the garage and she realized she was now more alone with him than she had ever been before. Part of her couldn't believe she was here, even as she knew that in the peculiar twists and turns of fate it was inevitable. It was a testimony to how far she had come that she was able to sit there without dissolving into a cowering, mewling blob.

They spoke little. At that hour, traffic was light and he took advantage of it. He drove with speedy assurance straight up California Street, veering around whatever vehicles they encountered, left and right and left again, before taking the Presidio Transverse into Golden Gate Park, the most direct way to St. Francis Wood ever since the Embarcadero Freeway had been damaged by the earthquake two and a half years ago.

It might have been his driving, or the Scotch, or the realization of what she was doing, but suddenly her stomach began to churn with ominous intent.

'Please,' she gasped. 'I think you'd better pull over. I'm not feeling very well.'

'What's the matter?' he asked.

'I'm sorry,' she said, 'but I think I'm going to be sick.'

eight

It was halfway between dark and dawn when Arthur Gertz trotted down the steps of his house, jogged across Lincoln Way, and entered Golden Gate Park.

Streetlights cast a faint yellow beacon into the mist as the solid night sky began its slow dissolve into the distinguishable gray shades of morning. The phosphorescent digits on his sports watch told him it was not quite five o'clock.

It certainly wasn't Arthur's idea of fun to get up an hour early every morning and go running around the city like some health nut. He had just gotten tired of listening to Essie's nonstop nagging.

'You're fifty-six years old, Arthur,' his wife had harassed him for a year. 'You're overweight and out of shape. Overweight, out-of-shape men drop dead of heart attacks at fifty-six.'

For his fifty-seventh birthday, she gave him a warm-up suit.

'What's this for?' he asked.

'So you should live to be fifty-eight.'

But it was rising before five in the morning that was going to kill him sooner than anything else, he grumbled to himself as he jogged along.

Arthur was a certified public accountant in one of those big firms that merged so often he sometimes didn't know the latest company name. He had spent his adult years organizing his life into neat sections – his job, his family, his stamp collection, his Tuesday-night bridge game, his Robert Ludlum novels. Jogging didn't fit into any of those categories, and Arthur was not a man who took easily to change.

But Essie left him no choice. She stopped serving red meat at home, eliminated dairy products from their diet, and bullied him into beginning a program of sensible exercise. To shut her up, he carved an hour out of the section of his life marked 'sleep' and plotted a daily route through the morning mists of Golden Gate Park that would take him exactly fifty-two minutes to complete, and he never deviated from that course by so much as one yard.

On this particular Wednesday morning, however, he was looking to shorten his route by seven minutes. Last night at the bridge table, he had made a stupid mistake that cost him the rubber. He agitated over it so much afterward that it took him an extra twenty minutes to fall asleep. As a result, he awakened twenty minutes late.

He made up one minute by selecting the jogging shoes that fastened with Velcro. Then he calculated he could make up four minutes by not washing his hair, three minutes if he didn't floss when he brushed his teeth, and five minutes by refusing a second helping of oat bran and skipping the obituary section in the morning newspaper. That left seven minutes, and it explained why, on this particular day, Arthur Gertz took a detour.

Instead of his usual run along Martin Luther King, Jr., Drive, around the Arboretum and down past the old Kezar Stadium, he opted for the shorter route up to Stow Lake and around Strawberry Hill.

Afterward, he couldn't remember what caught his eye, what turned his head in that direction, what made him take a second look, and then a third. He was only glad that he did.

She was lying half-concealed beneath a clump of bushes, bits of her clothing scattered around her. Even in the early light, he could see that her face was cut and battered, her lip split and bleeding, one eye blackened. He noticed an angry trail of bruises down her body.

She was slender but not young. He wondered how she had gotten there, what persuasion had drawn her into the park at such an early hour. Arthur could pretty much guess what had happened to her. He was sure she was dead. She lay so still and her skin was so pale that he actually jumped when she moved. It wasn't a big move, more of a shudder, really, and then he heard a low moan.

'Oh my God,' he muttered. 'Oh my God, she's alive.'

He turned every which way, hoping someone else would be in the park at this hour of the morning. But they were alone with each other. He crept closer and knelt down beside her.

'Take it easy,' he said. 'You're hurt, so just lie still. I've found you, I'll take care of you, you're going to be all right.'

Blue-gray eyes fluttered open to focus on him for a second or two and then closed again.

Arthur thought fast. He didn't know how badly she was hurt but he knew enough not to move her. If he hurried, he calculated it would take him roughly four minutes to get back to Lincoln Way, where he would at least be able to find a telephone. He stood up, stripped off his warm-up jacket and placed it carefully over her. It wasn't much, but it was better than leaving her the way she was.

'I'll be right back,' he told her, although he wasn't at all sure that she heard him. 'I'm going to go get help and then I'll be right back. Don't move. Just lie there nice and quiet until I get back.'

With one last look at her, he took off at a dead run.

'My name is Azi Redfern,' the short, redheaded Native American said to the woman lying motionless on the table in the curtained cubicle. 'I'm from the Rape Treatment Center and I'm here to help you in any way I can.'

It was less than fifteen minutes from the time the call came into the Center that Azi and a nurse-examiner reached the Emergency Room at San Francisco General Hospital.

'Is she conscious?' Azi had asked the resident on duty.

'Dazed, but conscious,' he replied.

'Anything serious?'

The doctor shook his head. 'A number of abrasions and lacerations, but no evidence of internal trauma. Her nose is broken, she's got a split lip and a black eye. The rest appears to be superficial, but she took quite a beating.'

The counselor nodded to the nurse-examiner. 'Let's go,' she said.

The resident pulled aside the curtain and allowed the two women to enter the tiny cubicle ahead of him.

'The doctor is going to treat you first,' Azi told the victim in a gentle, soothing voice. 'He's assured me that your injuries are minor and that you're in no danger. So try to relax as much as possible. Do you understand?'

The woman blinked once and closed her eyes.

When the doctor was finished, Azi touched the woman's shoulder.

'The nurse needs to examine you now,' she said, 'to collect as much physical evidence as possible.' The woman's eyelids fluttered and Azi quickly reached down and took hold of her hand. She smiled reassuringly. 'It's purely routine.'

When she was thirteen years old, Azi Redfern's father sent her from the reservation to an uncle in Santa Fe for a proper education. Three weeks later, her uncle raped her, the first of what became a weekly occurrence that lasted until she was seventeen, when she was awarded a scholarship to the University of New Mexico in Albuquerque.

She was too ashamed to tell her father, too ashamed to tell anyone, until she met a psychologist at the university who was able to help her deal with the pain and the anger. After college, she went on to become a counselor, knowing she could draw on her own experience to help other victims of sexual abuse.

Half an hour later, the nurse-examiner had filled a dozen or more plastic bags with swabs of vaginal secretions, slides of semen residue, pubic hairs, fingernail scrapings, torn underwear, what was left of a navy-blue silk dress, shredded nylon stockings, grass specimens, and blood samples. A female police officer had slipped into the cubicle to observe the examination. A police photographer had snapped twenty or more images of the battered woman from every conceivable angle. Azi still had hold of her hand.

'Why do you do all that?' the woman mumbled through her swollen, sutured lips, as she watched the nurse label each of the plastic bags and then gather them together into one large envelope, which she sealed and handed to the policewoman.

'It's what we call the chain of custody,' explained Kelly Takuda, one of the two uniformed officers who had responded to Arthur Gertz's frantic call. 'First we collect the physical evidence, then we seal it all up to make sure that no one tampers with it, then we have the police lab analyze it. Later, we can use this analysis to identify the person who assaulted you just as positively as if we had actually seen him do it.'

'Oh.'

The police hadn't found her purse or any identification on her person.

'Can you tell us your name?' Officer Takuda asked.

'Karen,' the woman said. 'Karen – Doniger.'

'Is there someone you would like us to call for you?'

'. . . .my husband.'

Karen gave the telephone number, and Kelly Takuda wrote it down and passed it to her partner outside the cubicle.

'Now,' she urged, 'can you tell us what happened?'

Karen took a tremulous breath. 'I felt sick,' she replied. 'I guess maybe I drank too much, or maybe it was the clams, but I felt sick. I asked him to stop the car.' Tears began to roll down her cheeks, stinging smartly when they reached her raw, swollen mouth. 'He pulled off the main road and then onto a side road, and I got out and started to walk around a bit and take some deep breaths, you know, so I'd feel better. And then, all of a sudden, he – he grabbed me and – and – and he was too strong and I couldn't get away from him.'

She was shivering now, choking on her tears and words and Azi pulled a blanket up around her and held her with an arm about her shoulders.

'It's all right,' she murmured. 'You're all right.'

'Do you know your assailant, Mrs. Doniger?' Officer Takuda asked. 'Can you identify him?'

Karen's head was throbbing. She tried to focus on the policewoman but saw only the uniform, and, with a small groan, she turned her head away. Kelly glanced at Azi, but the rape counselor shrugged and shook her head.

'I guess that's enough for now,' Officer Takuda said kindly. 'Perhaps we'll be able to get a more detailed statement from you later, when you're feeling better.'

The call came just before seven o'clock. Ted was so frantic by then that it was actually a relief to hear that Karen was only injured. He had spent much of the night talking to the police and calling every hospital in the city, afraid she might be dead. He reached the Emergency Room just as the two officers were leaving.

'She's had a bit of shock, Mr. Doniger,' Kelly Takuda said. 'And she's a little banged up. But she's all right, and the doctor says she can go home whenever she's ready.'

'What happened?' he asked.

'Why don't we let her tell you about it,' the policewoman replied diplomatically. There were just some things, she had long ago concluded, that belonged between a husband and wife, at least in the beginning.

Ted knew then, of course, like a knife plunging itself into his heart. There was only one kind of injury that the police hesitated to discuss.

Karen was still huddled beneath the blanket when he entered the cubicle. A redheaded woman was holding both of her hands and talking to her, too low for him to catch the words. He came up and put his hand on his wife's hair and smiled down at her. Tears of relief that she really was alive and even well enough to be sitting up filled his eyes.

'I was so worried,' he said.

'I'm sorry,' she whispered.

'No, don't,' he cried. 'It's enough that you're all right.' But he saw her eyes slip away from his and knew that she wasn't all right at all.

The redhead took the change of clothes that Ted had brought along and began helping Karen to dress.

'I'm a crisis counselor,' Azi said, after introducing herself. 'I've been here since the ambulance brought your wife in.'

He saw the angry bruises on Karen's thighs and, without either of them saying a word, he knew what kind of crisis counselor Azi Redfern was. The knife twisted itself deeper, and he wanted to scream and bash his fists into somebody's face, as someone had so obviously done to Karen.

'Thank you,' he murmured.

With some encouragement, Karen managed to stand up, but she couldn't seem to coordinate her legs well enough to walk.

'I'll get a wheelchair,' Azi offered.

'That won't be necessary,' Ted told her. He lifted his wife into his arms as though she were a feather and carried her out of the hospital.

The doorbell rang at two o'clock.

'My name is Lamar Pope,' drawled the giant of a man standing on the threshold. He was dressed in a western shirt and jeans, a leather jacket with fringe, and an exotic pair of tooled leather boots. He handed his card to Ted. It identified him as a sergeant for the Bureau of Investigations, Sexual Assault Division.

'Come in, Sergeant,' Ted invited hesitantly. 'My wife is resting. I don't know if she's up to seeing anyone yet.'

'I won't stay any longer than necessary, Mr. Doniger,' Lamar assured him. 'But we like to get the facts as fresh as possible, you understand.'

Karen was curled up on one of the pale-green sofas in the living room, inside a cocoon of fuzzy blankets. Azi had just brought her a fresh cup of tea.

'I'd sure like to get a statement from you, ma'am, if I could,' Lamar said after the introductions. 'To get the investigation going. Tomorrow or whenever you feel up to it, you can come down to the department and make it official.'

Karen looked up at him apprehensively. Azi, noticing, sat down beside her.

'They have women investigators in the division,' she said softly. 'We can request one, if you prefer. But you won't find anyone better than Lamar. He's not just a great detective, he's one of the most decent men I know.' She glanced up at him and he gave a short nod. 'Twenty years ago, his daughter was raped and murdered by a young man who got off because the prosecution didn't do its job right. Lamar's been involved in sexual-assault investigations ever since.'

The heavyset officer with the shock of white hair and bizarre cowboy clothes looked nothing at all like her memory of Michael Haller.

'I guess it's all right,' Karen consented.

Lamar sat down in the opposite chair and produced a pad, a pen, and a microcassette recorder from various pockets.

'This is so I don't forget anything,' he said, gesturing to the recorder. 'And this,' he said, holding up the pad and pen, 'is so that I have something to do with my hands. I'm trying to quit smoking.'

'Would you like something to drink, Sergeant Pope?' Ted asked.

'Well, sir, if that's tea your wife's having, I wouldn't say no to a cup if it was offered.'

Azi went to the kitchen to get the tea and Ted retreated to the study, leaving Karen and Lamar alone.

'I'm sorry about your daughter,' Karen murmured.

'I appreciate that, ma'am,' he drawled. 'I surely do.' He pressed the little red button on the recorder. 'Well now, suppose you tell me, in your own words and at your own pace, exactly what happened.'

It took Karen almost an hour to recall it all, from the moment Robert had approached her in the downtown parking garage to the moment he left her in Golden Gate Park. Lamar scribbled copious notes, stopping her every now and again to ask for a clarification or a further detail.

And through it all, the soft-spoken giant was kind and gentle and supportive.

'You're doing just fine, ma'am,' Lamar said when Karen began to falter. 'And we're almost through.

Now, you say that, after he forced you to have sex with him, the man got into his car and drove away, and just left you there?'

'I think so,' Karen replied. 'I mean, I guess he must have, because I was still there when the jogger came along. But I really don't remember very much about what happened – you know, afterward.'

'What kind of car was he driving?'

'A Mercedes. Black.'

'What was he wearing?'

Karen thought a moment. 'I think it was a gray suit with a little stripe in it, a white shirt and a gray-and-maroon tie. And black loafers with little tassels.'

'All right,' Lamar coached. 'You say you met him in the garage and he took you for a drink and then offered to drive you home.'

'He offered to drive me home first and then we went to have a drink,' Karen corrected.

'At any point in the evening, did he happen to tell you his name? Where he lived? Where he worked?'

Karen stared long and hard at the police investigator. He seemed so fatherly, with his white hair and careworn face. But behind the sympathetic blue eyes, she knew, was a keen mind. She wondered if it was also a fair one.

'He didn't have to tell me his name,' she said finally. 'I knew who he was. That's why I agreed to let him drive me home. I've been working as a volunteer at his campaign headquarters for three months. His name is … Robert Drayton Willmont.'

Lamar's left hand shot out and hit the stop button on the microcassette recorder. He sat there frozen with shock, wondering what the hell he had stumbled into, and why it had been his accursed misfortune to be the investigator on call this particular day.

There was no point in asking if she was positive of her identification. Obviously, she was. There was no point in asking if there were any political motivations behind her accusation. If there were, she would certainly not admit it. There was no point in asking her anything more at all until he had time to digest what he had already heard.

'I think that about does it,' he said finally. 'I will ask you not to discuss this with anyone until the department completes its investigation and decides how to proceed. Due to the rather special circumstances involved here, I think it would be wise if the press were kept out of this as long as possible.'

'I have no intention of talking to the press,' Karen declared with dignity. 'Or anyone else.'

Lamar dropped the recorder back into one pocket, stuffed his pad and pen into another, and hefted himself to his feet.

'I thank you for your time, ma'am,' he said. 'No need to bother your husband. I can see myself out.'

'Goodbye, Sergeant.'

Karen watched him go. Thirty years ago, it had been a fine, upstanding Harvard law student who had never been in any trouble. Now, it was a United States senator who was seeking the highest office in the land. Her word against his. And another male police investigator. She wondered if there was any justice to be had in the world.

It was evening. Ted had sent Amy off to spend the night with DeeDee because Karen didn't want her stepdaughter to see her the way she looked. Then he called Natalie.

'She won't admit it but I know she's in pain,' he said after a brief explanation. 'I need to go out and pick up a prescription the doctor ordered, but I don't want to leave her alone. Can you sit with her until I get back?'

'Of course I can.'

'I won't be long.'

Natalie knew her own remedy for pain. She took a full glass of brandy up to the bedroom.

'Drink,' she instructed.

Karen sipped the fiery liquid but it had little effect.

'Did Ted tell you?' she asked through swollen lips.

Natalie nodded. 'I can't believe it,' she lamented. 'I feel like this is all my fault. I didn't argue when you said you were going to join his campaign. I realize now I should have. I guess, way down deep, I wanted to believe he had changed. It just never occurred to me that this could happen twice.'

'Or me,' Karen said. 'That's why I got into the car with him. I thought, well, he's an important person now, he's certainly older, and he should be wiser, and besides this is 1992 and he's got so much to lose, he'd be crazy to try anything – so why should I be afraid?'

'What are you going to do?'

'I'm not going to do anything. It's up to the police to decide what they're going to do.'

'Talk about a bombshell,' Natalie murmured. 'Nobody's going to want to come within a hundred miles of this.'

'You and Ted and the investigator are the only ones who know who it was. If the police don't prosecute him, I don't want it going any further.'

Natalie groaned. 'I'm so sorry,' she repeated.

'Please don't blame yourself,' Karen said. 'It's not your fault. I'm an adult. Whatever I did, I did all on my own.'

Ted held her all night long, rocking her, caressing her. With Natalie's help, he had gotten some hot soup into her on top of the brandy, but she couldn't seem to get warm.

'I didn't tell them,' she said.

'You didn't tell them what?'

'About ... about the other time. They would have thought me so stupid to let it happen again.'

'But shouldn't they know?'

Karen shrugged. 'It was so long ago, and it was my word against his. Besides, that was then and this is now, and it would only confuse things.'

He remembered the night, barely six months ago, when she had told him about her first encounter with Robert Willmont. He remembered holding her tight and promising her that he would never let anyone hurt her again.

He was sick inside because he hadn't been able to keep his promise. He couldn't understand what kind of man would brutalize a woman, then not even remember it and turn around and do it again. He had not been thrilled when Karen said she wanted to work for the Willmont campaign, but he hadn't argued all that strenuously against it, either. Not when she was sure it would be a positive step toward putting the past behind her. But now he wished, with the impassioned accuracy of hindsight, that he had objected.

'Save America!' was rapidly becoming a powerful slogan throughout the country, a heady concept that was rallying thousands to the cause every day – and the man behind it all had turned out to be nothing but a brutal rapist.

Ted Doniger was a gentle, caring man, a true Libra, who believed that sufficient good existed in everyone to balance out almost any bad. It was just that, as his father used to say, you had to look a little harder to find it in some. As hard as he now looked, Ted was unable to find sufficient good in Robert Willmont.

He stared into the darkness, choking on an unfamiliar anger that burned so hot inside him that, had he owned a gun, he knew he would have gotten up in the night and used it.

nine

It was a point with Lamar Pope that he never used elevators if he could help it. More a matter of innate impatience than any specific effort at exercise, he habitually walked up to the fourth floor of the Hall of Justice, the solid gray building that occupied a whole block of Bryant Street and looked so oddly out of place in the dismal neighborhood of warehouses, factories, and body shops.

This morning was no exception. Lamar climbed the steps, taking two at a time, and lumbered down the corridor to Room 436, where the Sexual Assault Division was located. Going directly to the rear of the shoulder-high partitioned space, he spent some minutes rummaging through the bottom drawer of his desk before making his way into the lieutenant's cramped office and dropping heavily into a chair.

It was eight-thirty on Friday and he had been sitting on his bombshell for almost forty-eight hours.

'You're not going to believe this,' he said.

Lieutenant Mike Perrone had been a policeman for twenty-three years and in charge of investigations for five. There wasn't a whole lot he wouldn't believe. Every day, as he got ready to leave for work, he told his wife he didn't know how much longer he could stand to stay in the Sexual Assault Division. Too many of the victims had begun to haunt his dreams.

'Lay it on me,' he invited.

'Okay,' Lamar nodded. 'I've got a woman who claims she was raped by Robert Willmont.'

'*Senator* Robert Willmont?'

'That's the one.'

Perrone, a medium-sized man with a barrel chest and a thin mustache, threw back his head and guffawed.

'You're right,' he cackled. 'I don't believe it.'

Lamar shrugged. 'The trouble is,' he responded, chewing the end of an unlit cigarette, 'it may just be true.'

The smile on the lieutenant's face slowly faded. 'The Prince of Pure? The squeaky-clean people's advocate? The trumpeter of "Save America!"?'

'Yep.'

'Well, I'll be damned. When? Where?'

'Tuesday night, Golden Gate Park.'

'Where's the report? I haven't seen anything about it come through. All hell hasn't broken loose.'

'I buried it,' Lamar declared. 'All things considered, I thought that was the smartest li'l ole thing to do until we knew where this was going.'

Perrone nodded. 'Okay, what have you got?'

'I've got her statement,' Lamar told him. 'I've got her physical condition. I've got all the stuff that the

Rape Treatment Center collected, including finger-nail scrapings – she says she scratched him pretty good. I've got a footprint at the scene. And I've got her positive identification.'

'Hell, this smells like a setup to me,' the lieutenant muttered. 'What is it – two months before the primary? Shit! That's a pretty timely coincidence.'

'The thought did cross my mind,' Lamar agreed. 'That's why I've been playing it so close to the vest. But I have to lay it on the line. I've spent the last forty-two hours checking her out. If she's got any political axes to grind, I can't find them. On the contrary, every-thing I've learned about her so far leads me to believe that she was honestly committed to Willmont's philos-ophy.'

'Christ,' Perrone breathed. 'You don't really think it's possible, do you?'

'Gut feeling?' Lamar asked.

'Yeah.'

'Anything's possible.'

'What do you want to do with it?'

'I think we've got enough for a friendly chat.'

'Well, make sure you cover our asses first, but good,' Perrone said. 'What have you done with the stuff?'

'I relabeled the RTC evidence. Now no one but me can find it. I listed the cast we made of a footprint at the scene under a John Doe. I took the report filed by the uniforms that answered the call and the medical report and the photographs that were taken at the hospital and lumped them all under an alias. I erased the mention of his name from my tape record. I guaran-damn-tee you this isn't going to leak until we're ready to make a move.'

'All right,' the lieutenant sighed. 'Let me look at the

report. If I agree with you, we'll call him in.'

If there was one thing Mike Perrone had learned in the last five years, it was that Lamar Pope was never wrong.

'He won't come in,' the investigator replied.

'Hell, I know he won't,' Perrone snapped. 'But we damn well gotta follow procedure.'

'I tell you, Hal, it's absurd,' Robert Willmont raged at his attorney over the telephone. 'The woman's a goddamn liar. This whole thing is a frame, can't you see that?'

'Then you have nothing to worry about,' Hal Sutton replied calmly. 'Besides, they just want to talk to you.'

'The hell you say. They're not going to haul me down there for one of their interrogations like I was some common criminal.'

'I'm sure we can arrange a compromise,' the son of the former senior partner of Sutton, Wells, Willmont and Spaulding said. 'I'll handle it. But first, you'd better tell me exactly where this is coming from.'

'She's a volunteer who works at headquarters,' the senator explained. 'Her car wouldn't start, so I offered her a lift home. We went across the street to a bar and had a few drinks and talked for a while. Then, on the way to her place, she got sick or something, asked me to pull over. She got out of the car and disappeared, so I got out, just to make sure she was okay, and the next thing I know, she's jumping me. I mean, she was worse than those crazy groupies who follow after rock stars. She was all over me, scratching and biting. Hell, I couldn't get away from her.'

'She was that strong, eh?' Sutton asked.

'Well, all right,' Robert admitted, 'maybe I didn't try

very hard. You know how it is, a little alcohol, the stress of the campaign, a woman throwing herself at you. So maybe my resistance was low – okay, she was a cold and I caught it. After all, I'm only human, and Randy's had me living in solitary confinement since December. But if she thinks she can get away with crying rape, she's got another think coming!'

'Don't worry,' Sutton assured him. 'Acquaintance rape is a very muddy charge and the hardest kind to prove. If it's not true, believe me, she won't get away with it.'

'But if it goes to trial, that alone will be enough to ruin me,' Robert argued, considering the big picture. 'I haven't come this far to be done in by some crazy person.'

'Well, you might consider pleading to a lesser charge.'

'Like what?'

'Maybe simple assault.'

'That's still a felony, and a felon isn't going to get elected President of the United States.'

'It's better than rape.'

'What if I just denied everything?' Robert suggested. 'Said I was never there and had an alibi to prove it?'

'I would never knowingly let you perjure yourself – or anyone else you may be thinking of involving in this,' the respected partner of Sutton, Wells, Willmont and Spaulding replied tartly. He and Robert were not exactly friends, but they had known each other for over twenty-five years. 'Besides, they're bound to have DNA evidence, at the very least, that can place you at the scene just as surely as an eyewitness from a foot away.'

'I've been in the inner circles long enough to know

that evidence can ... disappear,' Robert said casually. 'All it takes is enough money and the right connections, and I've got both.'

'You've built your reputation on honesty,' his attorney reminded him. 'My advice would be to stick to that.'

'It was just a thought.' Robert sighed, wondering what good an honest reputation was going to do him in the middle of a maelstrom. 'So now what?'

'Let me sort things out,' Sutton said, 'and I'll get back to you.'

Lamar trudged up the steps of the Jackson Street house just after three-thirty that afternoon and pressed the bell. A faint melody of chimes sounded from somewhere inside, and a moment later an elderly man in black livery opened the door and, without so much as a word, ushered him into a room off to the left of the entrance foyer.

Three men awaited him in a richly appointed library of the type that Lamar had heard about but had never been invited to enter. He recognized Robert Willmont, of course. The second man was perhaps ten years older than the senator, not as tall but equally distinguished-looking, with a full head of silver hair. The third man was shorter, younger, thinner, with receding red hair and glasses.

'I'm Hal Sutton, Sergeant Pope, Senator Willmont's attorney.' The silver-haired man stepped forward but did not offer his hand. 'This is the senator's aide, James Randall Neuburg. And, of course, you know the senator.'

'Gentlemen,' Lamar acknowledged.

'I appreciate your cooperation in allowing this

meeting to be held here, instead of at Justice,' the lawyer continued smoothly. 'Discretion is vitally important in this instance for reasons you can readily understand.'

'I assure you that I would have preferred to meet the senator under very different circumstances,' Lamar responded in kind, but he wasn't one for social chitchat. 'So, with your permission, I suggest we get right to the matter at hand and get it over with as quickly and painlessly as possible.'

'Certainly, Sergeant.'

They sat down on facing sofas. Lamar pulled out his tape recorder. 'Do you mind, sir?' he asked with just the right note of deference. 'It helps me to remember.'

'Not at all,' came the senator's reply after a quick glance at his attorney.

'Thank you.'

'You know that I would be well within my rights not to make a statement at this time,' Robert declared.

'Oh, I know that, sir.'

'The only reason I'm doing so is because I want this whole thing to go away before it does some real damage.'

'I appreciate that.'

'All right, then, where do you want me to begin?'

It took less than twenty minutes for Lamar to obtain the senator's account of the events of Tuesday evening.

'I'm sure you understand,' the senator concluded, 'there could be any number of people out to get me. Someone in my position is always vulnerable. Was I foolish, under the circumstances, to succumb to a woman I hardly knew? Of course I was. But I assure you, foolishness is the only thing I'm guilty of. Now I hope this will be the end of it.'

'Well, sir, I can't exactly promise you that,' Lamar replied. 'Needless to say, your version conflicts some-what with the lady's, and that means we'll have to do a little more investigating.'

'You certainly aren't going to take her word over mine, are you?' Robert asked with a sharp edge in his voice.

'It's not up to me, Senator,' Lamar told him. 'I just gather the information.'

'Well, who then?'

'Once my investigation is completed, it'll be up to the district attorney's office.'

The senator glared at Lamar. 'I don't believe this,' he snapped. 'Some deranged woman comes out of nowhere and tells a big fat lie, and because it involves someone respectable and important and very much in the public eye, you people jump all over it.'

In the background, Hal Sutton cleared his throat.

'Yes, well, what more can I say or do, Sergeant?' Robert went on in a more reasonable tone. 'What will it take to convince you that I didn't rape anyone?'

'Perhaps you'd be good enough to show me the clothes you were wearing on Tuesday.'

'My clothes? What the devil do you want with – ?' Robert began. 'Of course – you're looking for evidence that may support one story or the other. Well, I certainly don't know what my clothes can tell you that I haven't already told you, but you're welcome to them.'

He jumped to his feet and crossed to the door, yanking it open. 'Preston,' he barked at the aged man who waited in the hallway. 'Bring down whatever clothes I was wearing on Tuesday. Suit, shirt, tie, everything.'

'Shoes,' Lamar prompted.

'Yes, and my black loafers.'

The four men stood around looking uncomfortably at one another until the butler returned with the clothing.

'I'm sorry, sir, but the shirt has already been sent to the laundry,' he said, apologizing for his efficiency.

Robert shrugged. 'Then this will have to do.'

'In that case, sir,' Lamar requested, 'I hope you won't object to unbuttoning your shirt.'

'I damn well do object!' the Senator snapped. 'Who the hell do you think – ?'

This time it was the redhead who cleared his throat.

'Certainly, Sergeant,' Robert said stonily.

He ripped off this tie and undid his shirt. Four angry-looking red lines slanted down his chest.

'Yes, she scratched me, if that's what you're looking for,' he conceded. 'But I assure you it came out of her … exuberance, and not from any effort to fight me off.'

'Thank you,' Lamar said, gathering up the senator's clothing. 'I believe that's all I need for now.'

'What do you think?' Robert asked the moment the door closed on the police investigator.

'I think they'll probably charge you,' Sutton replied.

'Shit!'

'When they start asking for clothing and looking for scratches, it's a pretty good indication,' Randy agreed.

'But I didn't do it,' Robert protested.

'I think we could still plead it out,' Sutton advised.

'If he pleads to anything,' Randy declared, 'it ends his political career right there.'

'Maybe so, but it might keep him out of jail.'

'No,' Robert sighed. 'The only chance I've got is to be cleared in open court.' He turned to his aide. 'Get Dobbs on this. Let's turn it into a cause célèbre. A real civics lesson that will prove to the whole country that the system does work.'

'What if it doesn't?' Randy asked softly.

'Of course it will,' the senator assured him. 'Don't forget – this is my state, my town, my people. No jury here is going to convict me of something I didn't do.'

At nine forty-five on Monday morning, Jay Agar, the Deputy District Attorney for the City of San Francisco, walked resolutely down the third-floor corridor of the Hall of Justice and stopped at an office barely larger than a moderate-sized closet. A window with a broken blind overlooked the freeway and took up most of one cracked beige wall. The scarred desk took up most of the floor space.

Agar rapped on the open door to catch the attention of the woman inside.

Teresa Maria Yacinta Escalante, hands down the best ADA he had ever had the good fortune to work with, glanced up from the stack of files in front of her. She was a black-haired, black-eyed beauty with very white teeth that flashed when she smiled. She was smiling now.

'I heard you coming,' she admitted. 'But I was hoping you would pass right by. Just look at this desk. I can't possibly handle a single other thing for the next two months.'

'I'm sorry, Tess,' Agar sighed, dropping a folder on

her desk. 'You don't know how sorry I am.'

Tess flipped the folder open, knowing it had to contain something big because he hadn't even bothered to pose his usual questions about her weekend. She scanned the pages quickly and her already large eyes grew even larger.

'This is a joke, right?' she charged. 'Like in April Fool's?'

'No joke.'

Tess frowned. 'You mean, someone is really accusing Robert Willmont of rape?'

'So I'm told.'

'*Senator* Robert Willmont?'

Agar sighed. 'He's the only one I know.'

'Why me?' she protested. 'You usually grab on to all the biggies. Why aren't you grabbing on to this one?'

'The Stepaner case,' Agar reminded her. 'I can't tell the judge in the middle of a triple murder trial that I'm sorry but something else has come up.'

He didn't bother to mention that the Stepaner case was a notorious one, bound to enhance his reputation, while this one was clearly destined to be a no-win situation, whichever way it went.

Tess leaned back in her chair, her brow furrowed, and tapped her pen against her left palm.

'It doesn't make sense. Willmont's got to know there's a goddamn microscope trained on him,' she observed shrewdly. 'He's just about got the nomination sewed up. Why would he risk it? Does it strike you that the timing here may be just a little too perfect – that this might be a setup?'

'Sure.' Agar shrugged. 'But it doesn't matter what I think,' he said. 'The DA is afraid it's too solid to ignore. What you think is up to you.'

'Why me?' she repeated.

'Because you're honest, non-partisan, and the best – and everyone knows it. If I put anyone else on this, both sides would cry foul.'

'But I'm already over my head.' She gestured to the mountain of paperwork on her desk.

'I know, and I'm willing to let you lay off as many of your other cases as necessary. Needless to say, this one gets top priority.'

'No kidding,' she grumbled.

'Look, will it help if I tell you that you've got Lamar on this one?' he coaxed.

'Don't try to butter me up,' retorted Tess. 'I wouldn't touch this case without him and you know it.'

Tess Escalante and Lamar Pope were a team, the best ADA in San Francisco and the best sexual-assault investigator in the country.

The beefy ex-Texan brought a degree of dedication, intuition, and sensitivity to his work that surprised everyone but Tess, and kept him digging after most others would have given up. On more cases during the last five years than Tess cared to remember, she knew she would have been dead in the water without him. But even with Lamar Pope in her corner, the last thing Teresa Maria Yacinta Escalante wanted to do was go after a United States senator – especially this one.

She wasn't any more or less political than any other assistant district attorney whose career hung on the reelection of the administration that employed her, but neither was she blind to what was happening in America. She liked the things Robert Willmont was saying, although the majority of her colleagues considered him too radical.

The daughter of migrant workers who had escaped the border patrols to live and die stooped over the crops they were lucky enough to pick, Tess could see the writing on the crumbling wall of America. What both surprised and pleased her was that she was apparently not alone, judging from the impressive number of primary victories that the senator from California was piling up.

There had never been so much as a hint of a shadow over Robert Willmont's private life, which meant that either the public relations pabulum being fed to the people about him was accurate, or he was very discreet. Tess considered Edmund Muskie and the forged letter that was his downfall, Geraldine Ferraro and her husband's business affairs, Michael Dukakis and Willie Horton, and the more recent flap over Bill Clinton and Gennifer Flowers, and she couldn't stop the specter of dirty tricks from looming large in her mind.

'All right, go on and get out of here and let me do my job,' she said, waving Agar off. 'But you're going to owe me for this one. Boy, are you going to owe me.'

She read through the folder again, this time studying the preliminary police report, Azi Redfern's account, and the two statements made by Karen Doniger. Then she looked at the police photographs. Finally, she read Robert Willmont's account of the event. By the time she finished, Lamar Pope stood in the doorway to her office, filling it up.

'So who are you voting for in the primary?' she asked.

'I don't vote in primaries,' he drawled. 'I've been a registered nonpartisan my whole life.'

Tess chuckled. He was the only one in the office who could get away with wearing jeans and fringe to work.

The cowboy with the college education, she thought, as she shoved the folder away from her and looked squarely at him.

'How did you ever get Willmont to make that statement?'

Lamar lowered his bulk into the chair across the desk from her. 'He offered. He said he wanted the truth to be known right up front.'

'Well, what do you think?'

'I'm not sure yet,' the investigator admitted. 'With the primary just around the corner, I can't figure out why the man would be so stupid.'

'More or less the same thing I told Agar,' Tess agreed.

'Are you thinking it could be a frame?'

Tess sighed. 'I don't know what I'm thinking – except that right now I wish I'd never left Salinas.'

ten

Mary Catherine sat at her desk in the gathering dark, the outer door of campaign headquarters safely locked. She had sent the staff home the moment the story broke, the moment Robert Willmont had been arrested on charges of sexual assault and battery, the moment he had been escorted downtown to be fingerprinted, photographed, and booked, the moment the office had begun to be bombarded by the media.

'I'm sure it's all just some horrible mistake,' she assured the wide-eyed workers who stood in a daze as they watched the first telecasts from outside the Hall of Justice and saw a behemoth in cowboy clothes conducting their beloved senator inside. 'You know, one of those cases of mistaken identity. By tomorrow, I'm sure it will all be cleared up, and everyone will be right back on the job.'

But in her heart, her bones, or whatever it was that

had deftly guided her through forty years of politics, she knew better.

She told the flood of reporters she had no official comment, but as a woman who had known the senator for over a decade, she personally could not believe there was any merit to the charges.

'What can you tell us about the alleged victim?' they cried.

'Nothing,' she said. She had been warned not to talk about Karen Doniger, not to the media, not to anyone.

'But you do know her, don't you?'

'I'm sure the senator will have a statement for you in the next day or two,' she replied.

Then she politely ushered them all out, locked the door and turned off the telephones.

Mary Catherine had no idea why her most valued volunteer had cried foul, but she could not bring herself to believe that this was a question of assault and battery. She knew Robert Drayton Willmont was far too desirable a man to have to resort to forcing a woman to accommodate him.

Still ... Karen Doniger didn't seem either unbalanced or the type to let herself be used as a political pawn. On the contrary, she was bright, competent, and to all appearances perfectly normal – in fact, just the kind of woman who was likely to appeal to the prurient side of Robert Willmont. Not that it really mattered, Mary Catherine reasoned. Whether he was found guilty or innocent, he was going to be politically dead in the water. The Moral Righteous would turn away from him like so many stampeding cattle, and even the thinking segment of the population would, in the backs of their minds, remember the old saw about where there's smoke – there's likely to be fire. The administrative assistant, who had to all intents and purposes grown up in Washington, D.C., knew that the stain of accusation would never wash off.

They had met at Jackson Street on Saturday – Robert, Randy, and Mary Catherine – to work out a contingency plan should worse actually come to worst.

'I can't believe this,' Robert had fumed. 'The woman practically rapes me, and *I* may end up being arrested. Maybe *I* should charge *her.*'

'We don't have time to waste on anger,' Randy suggested mildly. 'We have to decide how to handle the situation. You have three scheduled appearances this weekend. Do you want to go public now with your side of the story? Do you want to claim political motivations on her part?'

Robert turned on Mary Catherine. 'What do we know about her?' he growled.

'We know she's attractive, accomplished and efficient,' the administrative assistant replied. 'She's married, she has three stepdaughters and two step-grandchildren, and she writes popular poetry.'

'What does her husband do?'

'He's an architect,' Mary Catherine told him. 'In fact, he's *the* architect on the China Basin project.'

Robert's eyes narrowed thoughtfully. 'Can we bring any pressure to bear there?'

'I think it's too late for that,' Randy said.

'Why didn't I just deny the whole damn thing and tell everyone to go to hell?'

'As your attorney already advised you,' his aide told him, 'that kind of bluster wouldn't have worked very well.'

'Why not?' the senator shot back. 'It sure worked for Clarence Thomas.'

'Clarence Thomas was judged by his peers, in every sense of the word,' Mary Catherine declared with more than a touch of cynicism. 'You won't be that lucky. You're going to be judged by the voters.'

Robert sagged against his seat. 'Needless to say, I've been in touch with all of my top campaign advisers, every one of whom has counseled me to brazen it out. But the two of you are still my best political weather vanes. What do you think?'

'First,' replied Randy, 'you keep your mouth shut for the time being, and carry on as scheduled. You don't want to open any can of worms unless you have to.' He had spent over two hours on the telephone with Mariah, discussing strategies and probabilities.

'I agree,' Robert said.

'Second, we hire the best damn private detective agency in the country to find out every last thing there is to know about Karen Doniger.'

'Mary Catherine, get on that,' Robert directed.

'Done,' she said. She already knew the right firm to contact.

'Third, if and when it becomes necessary, you admit to a very foolish mistake – cry stress, cry exhaustion, you can even cry temporary insanity, if you like. Voters love to forgive repentant sinners when they sound sincere, so you'd better sound sincere.'

'I *am* sincere.'

'Fourth, you suggest that this is nothing more than a political frame; since you are clearly about to capture not only the nomination but the election as well, someone needed to find a way to stop you. But be careful you don't make the issue a partisan one. In this case, it would be wiser to hint that it could have come from either side, not to mention the auto industry, the NRA, and a few foreign countries who are heavily dependent on American aid.'

'I like that,' Robert said. 'I like it a lot.'

'Fifth, if it comes to trial, you call in every marker you can to push for an early date. Who knows, if we can expedite matters and win a fast acquittal, we might still be able to salvage something.'

'What do you mean *if?*' Robert barked. 'Of course I'll be acquitted. I'm innocent, damn it.'

'Sixth, for however long it takes, you and Elizabeth are joined at the hip.'

The senator shifted uneasily. 'To be honest, I don't know how that's going to go over with her. We haven't been especially ... close lately.'

'Well then, we'd better have her in and find out,' Randy declared. 'Because without her we don't have a prayer.'

Elizabeth Willmont had spent the afternoon at the beach with Adam, where she delighted in her son's agility with his new surfboard. She returned with glowing cheeks to find Robert and his two associates anxiously awaiting her.

'I understand you wanted to have a word with me,' she said, floating into the library.

'We need your help,' Randy said simply, before Robert could respond.

Elizabeth smiled. She had always liked Randy Neuburg. Even at forty, he retained a boyish charm that was direct, unaffected, and appealing.

'Has this anything to do with all the closed-door meetings that have been going on around here the past couple of days?' she inquired.

Genuinely startled, Randy turned to Robert. 'Doesn't she know?' he demanded. 'Haven't you told her?'

'Know what?' Elizabeth asked.

'I didn't really see the point,' the senator replied uncomfortably. 'I mean, you know, unless it turned out to be necessary.'

'It's necessary,' Randy retorted. He strode across the room and took Mary Catherine by the arm. 'We're going to take a walk around the block,' he said meaningfully. 'We've been cooped up in here all day and it's time to stretch our legs. We'll be back in half an hour.'

When they returned, the glow was gone from Elizabeth's cheeks. Her eyes were narrowed and her chin was set. On the table beside her were a glass of water and her pillbox.

'If you thought this would come as a surprise to me,' she said coolly, 'you were wrong. In fact, I knew it was only a matter of time before his promiscuous ways caught up with him. Of course, I always thought it would be something like gonorrhea or AIDS, which is why I've refused to sleep with him for years. But don't worry. I'm his wife, and for better or worse, I'll stand by him. I'll even lie through my teeth in court, come to that.'

Then, with as much dignity as she could muster, she stood up and left the room.

What a woman, Randy marveled to himself. She had known about the senator all along and kept her silence. In a time when wives were divorcing their husbands for a good deal less, Elizabeth had been able to focus on the big picture. She was stronger than he had suspected, despite the vagaries caused by the pills, and he was now confident that, however messy things might get, she would stick.

She must want to be the First Lady a whole lot more than anyone realized, Mary Catherine mused with increased respect, knowing that, if she herself had been married to the good senator, she would have long since kicked him out of more than her bedroom – White House or no White House.

Robert cleared his throat. 'Naturally, I won't hear of her saying one word publicly,' he said. 'Unless, of course, worse comes to worst.'

Worse came to worst on Monday, April 13, at two o'clock in the afternoon, when Lamar Pope met the senator at his home, presented him with a warrant for his arrest, and escorted him down to the Hall of Justice.

Mary Catherine sighed deeply. She knew she ought to be doing something other than sitting there in the office in the dark. Pack some of her things, perhaps, or make arrangements for a flight back to D.C. But she didn't move. She went on sitting there because she was sixty years old and it was too late to pick up and start over again.

There would be no more bright-eyed idealists to teach, to guide through the political quagmire, to cultivate and mold. No, it was time to take her prudently managed savings and retire somewhere.

A little after eight o'clock, the elevator doors slid open and closed and she heard the sound of a key fitting into the lock on the outer door. It was the sound she had been waiting for.

Randy came in and snapped on the lights. 'I thought

you'd be here,' he said wearily. 'But why in the dark?'

'It seemed suitable,' Mary Catherine replied. 'Where is he?'

'At home. Hal had everything arranged. The booking, even the arraignment. I left them at Jackson Street. The preliminary hearing is set for the twenty-third.'

'That's pretty fast, isn't it?'

'We would have opted for tomorrow, given the chance.'

Mary Catherine nodded. 'How is he?'

'Incredulous … confused … outraged,' Randy reported. 'About the same as I would be, if my whole life suddenly exploded in my face.'

'Does he know?'

Randy shrugged. 'On some level, I think he knows. But he'll never admit it. He's sure he'll beat this thing and that the people will rally behind him.'

'Voters have done crazier things, I suppose.'

'I suppose.'

'The media's having a field day,' Mary Catherine said wearily. 'He has to make some kind of statement.'

'He's going to call a press conference for tomorrow,' Randy told her. 'He wants to get his side of the story to the people while the woman is still hiding behind anonymity.'

'What does Hal say?'

'He says it can't hurt.'

'I'll set it up.'

'Make it before three,' Randy directed, 'so we can catch the national newscasts.'

Even in the midst of disaster, her last protégé was in charge – the dedicated aide, the political engineer who had almost made a dream come true. Mary

Catherine peered at the man she had nurtured and taught so well for so many years.

'How are *you*?' she asked gently.

'Numb … angry … frustrated.' He sighed. 'We were so close.'

'What will you do?'

He thought for a moment. 'Go back to practicing law, I guess. Get married. Have a life.'

'That sounds pretty good to me.'

'Damn it, though, it just isn't fair,' he raged. 'That somebody can come along and ruin someone else's whole life, just like that.' He snapped his fingers for emphasis.

Mary Catherine hauled herself to her feet and picked up her purse. 'Come on,' she said. 'Let's go get drunk.'

eleven

The lights in Tess Escalante's third-floor office had burned well into the night for a week, until less than twelve hours remained before she would present her evidence at the preliminary hearing, and ask that Robert Drayton Willmont be bound over for trial on charges of sexual assault and battery. Even though she normally had weeks instead of days to put a case together, she felt she was prepared.

At the start, she had resented Jay Agar for dumping this hot potato in her lap, but now she was forced to admit that her interest had been piqued. Regardless of her position as prosecutor, the ADA had been fully prepared to dislike the alleged victim and to disbelieve her story, if only because the man Karen Doniger had accused of rape was the man whom many, Tess among them, truly believed to be the last hope of a desperate country.

The whole staff watched the senator's press conference, the day after his arrest, and it served only to strengthen Tess's convictions.

'As some of you still may not know,' he had said, looking straight into the camera and holding tight to his wife's hand, 'I was charged yesterday with rape.'

His face openly showed both fatigue and stress.

'Did I have sex with the woman in question?' he went on, carefully avoiding the use of her name, as he had been instructed. 'Yes, I did. I'm not going to lie to you. I knowingly broke my marriage vows, and I have no excuse for that, at least none worth offering you. But did I rape her? *No, I did not.* Our encounter was mutual and brief and we parted on what I believed were amicable terms.'

As a silent affirmation, Elizabeth Willmont moved half a step closer to her husband.

'How do you defend yourself when a woman cries rape?' he asked. 'How do you call her a damn liar without sounding like a cad? How do you convince anyone that, while you may have behaved stupidly, you did not behave criminally? How do you suggest that the timing was too perfect – that, because of who you are and what you stand for, someone would plot to discredit and disgrace you?'

Despite themselves, a ripple ran through the collected attorneys who sat watching with Tess.

'There are those who are saying that my candidacy is dead,' he declared. 'Certainly, if a jury of my peers convicts me of this heinous crime, they're right. But I believe in the system. I believe that America is still a country where truth matters and the innocent are acquitted. And if it is, then I will be acquitted.'

Behind the senator, members of his staff lifted their heads a little higher and stood a little taller.

'Now, I could request that my attorney employ the type of tactics that would delay this matter for years,' the candidate continued, his voice rising oratorically. 'But instead, I have instructed him to expedite it, to pull every string and call in every favor to get my case before the court as soon as possible, so that I may be freed of this stigma and allowed to return to my life's work.'

He paused unblinkingly for five full seconds.

'There are those who think that candidates for high office should be heros, saints, even gods,' he concluded in a more normal voice. 'But the truth is, most of us are just men – vulnerable, fallible, very human men, doing the best we can with the tools we're given. And that's exactly who I am and have always been – just a man who believes that he can help his country get through a terrible time. I know of no way to convince you to give me the benefit of the doubt until this awful business is behind me and my innocence is established. I can only hope that you will.'

Tess sat staring at the screen long after it had gone blank.

'He should have been an actor,' one of the ADAs said with a chuckle.

'Nah,' replied another. 'The last thing we need is another actor in the White House.'

'But you've got to give him points for style,' said a third.

'How about you, Tess?' someone asked. 'What do you think?'

'I think he's a very smart man,' she replied.

Guilty or innocent, he had done absolutely the right thing. He had put his case before the public himself, with dignity and alacrity, and more than anything, Tess

Escalante wanted to believe him.

But after only one meeting with Karen Doniger, it was clear that the alleged victim was no one's political ploy, no mental case who manufactured events, no eccentric in search of notoriety. In fact, just the opposite seemed to be true.

'I don't really want to be here,' the woman declared after the formalities, her words slurring softly through her stitched lip.

'Then why are you?' Tess asked bluntly.

'Because Azi convinced me I had to at least come and talk to you,' she replied, nodding to the RTC counselor beside her.

'Yes, I did,' the Native American confirmed. 'I told her it shouldn't matter that the man who raped her is somebody big and important, because, as big and important as he might be, in the eyes of the law he's no bigger and no more important than she is.'

'I agree with that,' the ADA said.

'Is it true,' the woman asked, 'that I can refuse to testify?'

'Yes,' Tess told her, 'that's your right. And if you exercise it, the charges against the senator will be dropped and the case will be closed. Of course, if he actually committed the acts you claim he did, he will then be free to go out and commit them again.'

'I know,' the woman whispered, and Tess saw a haunted look come into her eyes.

'I don't want to deceive you,' the ADA said. 'A rape trial is very often every bit as vicious and as humiliating for the victim as the original assault. Is that what you're afraid of, that you might not be able to stand up under the pressure?'

'I don't know,' came the reply. 'Maybe, if I thought

he would be convicted, I could convince myself that anything was worth it. But to tell you the truth, Miss Escalante, I don't think he'll be convicted, and I don't want to go through an ordeal that will surely devastate and maybe even destroy my family and my life for nothing.'

'I happen to think we have a very strong case against him, Mrs. Doniger,' Tess assured the woman. 'Why don't you think he'll be convicted?'

Blue-gray eyes looked straight into black ones.

'Because men like that are never held accountable for what they do,' the woman declared. 'What they want, they take. What they can't buy their way out of, they lie their way out of. There are still a lot of people in this world who don't really believe that a woman can be raped, that she can be held down and kicked and punched and forced to have sex. Even with all the evidence in the world against him, it will still come down to my word against his, and he's an elected politician who can do a lot of good for this country. Who am I?'

Tess eyed the woman thoughtfully. One of the things that made the ADA so very good at her job was her talent for objective evaluation. Despite her strongest-held beliefs, she was able to interpret every piece of evidence, every scrap of testimony, every glance, every nuance with unbiased clarity.

'He did it, didn't he?' she breathed, feeling her heart sink to the bottom of her stomach.

'Yes, Miss Escalante,' the woman said clearly. 'He did it.'

'Then Azi is right. It doesn't matter how important he is. No one is above the law and he *can* be held accountable.'

'Perhaps you believe that,' the alleged victim agreed. 'But I watched enough of the Willie Smith trial to know better.'

'I see.' Tess nodded with understanding. 'And you're afraid I might turn out to be as inept as you apparently feel Moira Lasch was?'

'It was clear, even to the experts, that the defense didn't win that case,' the woman said. 'For whatever reason, the prosecution gave it away. Now, I have nothing against you, Miss Escalante. I don't even know you. But I have children I care a great deal about and a husband whose work depends on public acceptance, and I've even enjoyed a bit of success in my own right. I can't afford to have happen to me what happened to Patricia Bowman. I don't think I'm as strong as she is. And even if you believe in me one hundred percent, you aren't going to be representing *me* in the court-room, you'll be representing the people. If you lose, what does it really matter to the people? But I'm branded a liar, an adulteress, or worse, for the rest of my life.'

The ADA sighed. 'All right,' she said, 'I'll grant you the system isn't perfect, but it does work.'

'I don't doubt the system works,' countered the alleged victim. 'I doubt that justice is always served.'

'For most people it is.'

'Perhaps. But Robert Willmont isn't most people.'

'Mike Tyson was convicted.'

'Yes,' the woman conceded. 'But I think he may have been convicted more because he was black than because he was guilty.'

'I'm good at my job, Mrs. Doniger,' Tess said. 'Very good. I do my homework. I don't make many mistakes. I don't go into court unless I'm convinced I can win.

It's true that you can never totally predict which way a jury will jump, but my conviction rate happens to be a pretty decent seventy-three percent.'

The alleged victim looked over at the RTC counselor.

'I've known Tess for five years,' Azi said. 'And even though, technically, she won't be representing you, I don't think you could be in better hands.'

'More importantly, Mrs. Doniger,' the ADA added, 'if you don't agree to testify, if we have to drop the charges and let him walk, it's as good as saying that what he did to you is okay. Do you really believe that what he did to you is okay?'

There were tears in the blue-gray eyes as the alleged victim studied her hands, considering the truth of those words and agonizing over her decision. It seemed like a lifetime before she looked up at Tess.

'My name is Karen,' she said.

The accelerated pace dictated by the defense resulted in Tess's having to lay off every other case in order to prepare for this one. Now, on the eve of the preliminary hearing, she was going through everything one more time, looking for flaws, loopholes, contradictions, anything that might cause a failure to secure an indictment.

'I thought I'd find you here,' Lamar drawled from the doorway. 'Piling on the overtime.'

'Just a formality,' she assured him. 'We've got more than enough for probable cause. What about your end?'

Lamar flopped into the chair across from her. 'You know, every time I take on one of these investigations, I see it as a giant jigsaw puzzle. And I know that, as soon as I put all the pieces together, the picture will come clear. It's what keeps me interested in the process. Only, in this puzzle, there's a piece missing.'

'What do you mean?'

The big man scratched his right ear. 'I don't rightly know, it's just this feeling in my gut that I'm missing something somewhere.'

Tess had learned to trust her investigator's gut. 'Like what?' she pressed.

'Like this whole thing doesn't make any sense to me,' he sighed. 'Because I believe Karen Doniger. I would stake my reputation on the fact that she's telling the truth, that what happened to her happened exactly the way she says it did.'

'So?'

'So my gut says that Willmont just may be telling the truth, too.'

'Well, they can't both be telling the truth.'

'That's the point,' Lamar agreed, 'isn't it?'

'You know,' Tess mused, 'there are some men who really don't understand the word '*no*,' or, more precisely, they don't believe it can apply to them. For whatever reasons, they think of themselves as above rejection, which frequently makes them incapable of accepting it. It's possible that Robert Willmont is one of those men.'

'Maybe,' Lamar said, but he wasn't convinced.

'Look, the way Hal Sutton is rushing us, you haven't had enough time to do your usual thorough investigation. We'll get our indictment tomorrow, and then I'll make sure you have enough time to pursue your elusive missing piece.'

'You like Karen Doniger, don't you?' he asked.

Tess nodded. 'Yes,' she answered. 'I do like her. A

lot. There's something terribly vulnerable about her, and yet very brave. There's a lot of pain there and you can almost see inside her as she struggles to deal with it.'

'Yes, I sensed that about her,' Lamar agreed.

'She's such a private person, too, and I know this public invasion is going to be as dreadful an experience for her as the assault was, whatever the outcome.'

'That's the part I hate the most.'

Tess smiled. 'I do believe you like her a bit yourself.'

'She's a real lady,' Lamar declared. 'And the truth is, you don't get to meet too many ladies in my line of work. It's just that …'

'I know,' Tess finished for him. 'There's a piece missing.'

PART EIGHT
1992

There is no such thing as justice –
in or out of court.

– Clarence Darrow

one

The Honorable Oliver Wendell Washington was suffering from an acute case of gastritis. In fact, he had been suffering from just such attacks every single day since he learned that he would preside over the trial of *The People* v. *Robert Drayton Willmont*.

'Why me?' he groaned to his wife as he made his second dash of the morning to the bathroom.

'Because you're a judge, I expect,' Thelma Washington reminded him through the bathroom door. 'And someone obviously thought you were the right judge for the job.'

'I wish I was a janitor,' moaned the former Stanford University law professor.

'You do not,' she chuckled. 'You're just as pleasured as pie to be a judge.'

'No, my *mama* is pleasured as pie,' he corrected her. 'It was her dream. She had it in her head from the day I was born that I was going to be a judge. That's why she named me Oliver Wendell – so I'd never forget.'

'And you've done your mama proud.'

'You don't understand,' he grumbled. 'I'm up for reelection in November. If I make one mistake in this trial, lean too far in either direction, I can kiss Mama's dream good-bye forever and probably send her to an early grave.'

'Early?' Thelma scoffed. 'She's eighty-eight, if she's a day.'

'Maybe if I just lie down for a minute or two.'

'If you do,' Thelma declared, 'you're going to be late to court – and *that'd* be a mistake.'

'If I called in sick right now, before jury selection starts, they'd find someone to replace me.'

Thelma wagged her head. 'I declare, I think I'd see a yellow streak running down your back – if your skin wasn't so black.'

'But it's the truth,' he insisted. 'Look at me. I can't get more than ten feet from the john.'

'Oliver Wendell,' his wife admonished in a voice that brooked no nonsense, 'now you stop all that whining and be about your business. You're a fair and impartial judge and everyone in this town knows it. That's why you were given this case. And you're going to do fine. But, just in case, I'll pack the Kaopectate in with your lunch.'

Department 21 of the Superior Court, Criminal Division, was referred to by those who worked at Justice as the Glass Courtroom. Positioned at the end of the inner third-floor corridor, it resembled the other courtrooms in modest size and unimpressive style, with its center aisle, its gallery of uncomfortable flip-down spectator seats, its yellow wood paneling and

Naugahyde chairs right out of the 1950s, and its California bear anchored beside the Stars and Stripes. And like all the courtrooms in the row, it was windowless. The one significant difference, and hence its sobriquet, was the ominous bulletproof partition – two thick panes of tempered glass bonded to fine wire mesh – that separated the spectators from the proceedings.

'Isn't that a bit overdramatic?' Lamar observed when Tess told him where to meet her.

'I guess no one wants to take any chances on some weirdo with a water gun slipping through,' she said with a shrug.

But now, as the ADA threaded her way through the milling throng in front of Department 21, Lamar was nowhere to be seen. It was Thursday, June 4, two days after Robert Willmont had won the California primary with a resounding eighty-two percent of the vote. All things being equal, the race for the nomination was over.

'Hey, Tess,' a reporter yelled. 'What do you think your chances are of convicting the next President of the United States?'

'About the same as any other citizen,' she replied with a professional smile.

'How can you do this awful thing to such a fine man?' a woman in a faded housedress cried.

The ADA didn't bother to respond to that. She showed her badge to the armed guards at the door and slipped inside the Glass Courtroom.

It was twenty minutes to nine. The left side of the gallery was already filled with members of the media and other interested parties. In less than half an hour, the seats on the right side would be taken by prospective jurors and the process of selecting the twelve, plus two alternates, who would decide this case, would begin.

Tess was wearing what she described as her jury suit – a classic gray gabardine with a gently fitted jacket and a slim skirt that was just short enough to attract the men but not short enough to distract the women, and expensive enough to establish the credentials, but not the extravagance, of a confident professional.

She laid her briefcase on top of the table to the right of the center aisle, closest to the jury box – which wasn't really a box but two rows of chairs, the second row raised one step above the first – and began to pull out the various files and folders she would need, arranging them neatly in front of her.

The past month had been busy, to say the least. Not counting the preliminary hearing, the ADA had been in and out of court half a dozen times on motions, during which the judge had denied a motion to dismiss, upheld a motion to expedite, denied a motion to exclude, upheld a motion to disclose, and denied the application of Court TV to produce what would surely have become a summer spectacular.

All in all, Tess felt she had come out even. She settled down in her chair and opened one of the files. In it were the names of two hundred registered voters who had been summoned for jury duty during this calendar quarter and would be available for this trial, and it was this list of names that had occupied her overworked staff for the better part of two weeks. Finding out who they were and what they did and how they lived and what they thought was as crucial to a verdict as building the case.

As the jury-selection process began, the ADA would

be searching for the right combination of men and women who would best be able to judge the testimony and weigh the evidence, and every scrap she could learn about each of them would help her in making that determination. While one or two staunch conservatives wouldn't hurt her cause, and a Bible-thumper, a couple of radical feminists, and a senior citizen might help, the best she could hope to get were twelve open minds.

There were three specific things Tess looked for when she questioned a prospective juror – eye contact, straight answers, and the ability to listen. Karen was right about there being people who would refuse to believe that a woman could be raped, no matter what, and Tess was always on the alert to spot them.

Next to her own judgment, the ADA most trusted Lamar's. The beefy cowboy would slouch in the chair next to hers, with his arms crossed over his belly and his leather-tooled boots sticking out from under the table, and pretend to doze. But each time she returned to her seat, a piece of paper would be waiting with either an 'aye' or a 'nay' scrawled on it.

Tess glanced at her watch and then over her shoulder. Lamar usually beat her into court – it was not like him to be late. In the five years they had worked together, she had come to rely on him, much like a security net, to catch her should she fall. An anxious frown crossed her face.

Hal Sutton chose that moment to enter the courtroom, flanked by a striking brunette in a Chanel suit, a good-looking African-American who reminded Tess of the guy on *L.A. Law,* and a stocky man with a shiny head and brand-new wing tips that creaked with every step. Covering all the bases, she thought, the frown becoming a wry smile.

In addition to being a formidable trial attorney, Hal Sutton was a smooth, attractive, impeccably dressed man who belied approaching retirement by keeping himself in excellent physical condition. He was referred to, around Justice, as the Silver Fox. Male jurors envied him, female jurors fantasized about him. Robert Willmont couldn't have made a better choice.

Sutton gave Tess a cordial nod as he and the others arranged themselves around the defense table to the left. Sitting by herself, Tess felt a little like David going up against Goliath, and she looked around again for the giant who was supposed to be on *her* side.

A few minutes later, the first group of some forty potential jurors filed into the courtroom. Tess heard them shuffling into their seats but she didn't turn around. It was a superstition of hers – not to speculate about them as a whole, but one at a time.

At exactly nine o'clock, Robert Willmont appeared, dressed in a neat dark suit, a crisp white shirt, and a conservative tie. Accompanying him were his wife in tailored taupe, his mother in lavender lace, a slight man with thinning red hair, freckles, and glasses, and a middle-aged woman with gray hair wearing a black dress that was far too warm for the season.

The senator took great care to seat his aged mother in the first row of chairs behind the bulletproof window and give his wife a kiss on the cheek before he joined Hal Sutton at the defense table. The block of jurors took it all in. Tess smiled to herself. The show was on.

At ten minutes past nine, the bailiff stepped to the front of the courtroom and began his speech.

'All rise,' he intoned.

There was a general scraping of chairs and rustling of clothing as everyone stood.

'Department 21 of the Superior Court of the City of San Francisco is now in session. Case number 458-026, *the People of the State of California* versus *Robert Drayton Willmont*. The Honorable Oliver Wendell Washington presiding.'

With that, the door to the left of the bench opened and the former Los Angeles prosecutor, former San Francisco attorney, former Stanford law professor emerged. Swathed in his robes, the judge looked half again his already considerable size. His intelligent brown eyes revealed a mixture of resignation and discomfort, and his usually shiny black face had a definite gray tinge to it.

'I apologize for my tardiness,' Washington mumbled after clearing his throat. 'Are the People ready, Miss Escalante?'

'The People are ready, Your Honor,' Tess said.

'Is the Defense ready, Mr. Sutton?'

'Yes, Your Honor.'

Washington nodded to the bailiff. 'You may call the first name.'

The bailiff rotated a small black cylinder several times before reaching in and pulling out a slip of paper.

'Agnes McFaddan.'

A tiny woman in her seventies scrambled out of her seat and made her way to the jury box. Tess found the name on the list – unmarried, librarian, registered Democrat.

The ADA stood up, took a deep breath to quell the butterflies that always took flight inside her stomach during the first stages of a trial, and approached the woman.

'Good morning, Miss McFaddan,' she said with a pleasant smile. 'How do you feel about being here today?'

The woman considered for a moment. 'About the same as I felt all the other times.'

'How was that?'

'Proud to do my duty, sad to have to sit in judgment on a fellow human being.'

'And how many juries have you served on?'

'Four in my lifetime.'

'Do you remember what those cases were about?'

'Of course I do. It's not something you can forget so easily.'

'Tell us about them,' Tess invited.

'Let's see, one had to do with a young man accused of robbing a liquor store. There were three eyewitnesses – we had to convict him. Another was about a drunk driver who killed a little boy. I'm afraid we had to convict him, too. The third was about a man who was supposed to have plotted to kill his wife, but the prosecution didn't convince us he had done any such thing. And the fourth was about a woman who shot her ex-husband when he broke into her house. We acquitted her.'

'What do you think this trial is about?'

'I *know* what it's about,' Agnes McFaddan declared. 'It's been in all the newspapers and on every television channel for weeks now, hasn't it? Why, CNN devotes half an hour to it every single evening, it's that important. This trial is about rape.'

'And how do you feel about rape, Miss McFaddan?'

'I think it's a crime,' the prospective juror replied.

'And I rank it right up there next to murder and kidnapping.'

'And how do you feel about the defendant?'

A big smile broke out across Agnes McFaddan's face. 'I think he's a fine man, and a fine senator. I'm sure he'll make a fine President.'

'I don't think there are many here today who would disagree with you on that,' Tess conceded. 'But the question is, would you be able to put aside your high regard for him as a politician and vote to convict him of the crime of rape if the evidence presented was overwhelming?'

There was another pause as the elderly woman pondered her response. Then she looked straight into the ADA's eyes. 'It would make me sad,' she said, and sighed, 'but I guess I'd have to, now wouldn't I?'

'Thank you, Miss McFaddan,' Tess said with a flash of white teeth. 'I have nothing more.'

She turned to sit down and was delighted to find Lamar sprawled in the chair next to hers. On the table in front of her was a folded piece of paper with the word 'aye' scrawled across it.

The bald, stocky man in the creaky wing-tip shoes was named Andrew Cardigan. He was one of an emerging breed of analysts whose advice on jury selection was being taken very seriously by defendants able to afford the high price tag.

He sat to the left of Robert Willmont, with his own stack of profiles in front of him, and continually passed notes across the senator to Hal Sutton and his assistants. In addition, two of Cardigan's associates were stationed in the spectator section of the small courtroom, monitoring the responses of the jury pool and keeping constant, muffled radio contact with Cardigan by means of transmitters on their lapels and tiny receivers in their ears.

'How long have you lived in San Francisco, Mrs. DeMaio?' Hal Sutton asked a twenty-three-year-old newlywed.

'All my life,' the young woman replied. 'The only move I ever made was when I got married. Then I went from my father's house in the Sunset District to me and my husband's place on Potrero Hill.'

'Do you know much about this case?'

She shrugged. 'Only what's been on the news.'

'Have you formed an opinion, as a result of what you've seen on the news, about the guilt or innocence of my client?'

'No.'

Andrew Cardigan slipped an urgent note down the table to Sutton's black assistant, who glanced at it and then audibly cleared his throat. Sutton turned around and took the note, read it, stared for a moment at Cardigan, then turned back to the young woman.

'Let me rephrase. Have you formed an opinion, based on anything at all, about the guilt or innocence of my client?'

'Look,' she replied. 'Two years ago, my baby sister was raped on her way home from school. He came up to her as nice as you please, telling her she reminded him of his own little girl, and then he dragged her into Sigmund Stern Grove and raped her. She was eleven years old, for God's sake. So, as far as I'm concerned, if a woman says a man raped her, he raped her.'

'Did you vote in the primary on Tuesday, Mr. Hiltz?' Tess asked a gangly garage mechanic in his thirties.

'Sure did,' the man replied.

'Mind telling us who you voted for?'

'Sure don't. Voted for the senator over there and proud of it.'

'Why?'

'Because he's not like them other shysters that make big promises just so's they can get themselves elected and then conveniently forget them the very next day. He may be rich, but he knows how to speak for the workin' slobs like me.'

'And what do you think of the crime the defendant is charged with having committed?'

'Crime? What crime?' Hiltz asked. 'I don't see as it's a crime to give a dame what she's askin' for.'

'Are you a feminist, Miss Chu?' Sutton inquired of a pretty young dental hygienist.

'If you're asking me whether I believe that men and women are equal, yes, I do. Even though my family comes from a country that doesn't yet comprehend that, my father always treated my mother with great respect.'

'Do you think adultery is a crime?'

Elaine Chu though for a moment. 'A moral crime, yes, but I wouldn't know about it being a legal one.'

'Would you be more likely to convict a man of rape if you knew he had committed adultery?'

'I wouldn't convict a man of rape,' the dental hygienist replied, 'unless I was convinced he had raped.'

'Do you believe that a woman has the right to say no to a man, Mr. Barstow?' Tess asked a forty-two-year-old computer software salesman wearing a polka-dot tie.

'Yes and no,' he replied. 'If she says it right up front, yes, absolutely, and a man ought to respect that. But if she leads him on, teasing him and getting him all excited and everything, and then up and thumbs her nose at him, well, I'm not so sure that's right, either.'

'Would you be able to listen to the evidence presented with an open mind?'

'I think so.'

'And do you think, after hearing all the evidence, you would be able to render an impartial verdict in this case?'

'Yes, I would,' Brian Barstow said.

'For a while there, I didn't think you were going to make it,' Tess said to her investigator over hamburgers in the Flower Market Café shortly after noon.

'I may be on to something,' Lamar told her.

She stopped in mid-bite.

'Something usable?'

'Don't know yet,' he said. 'Got some more digging to do.'

'I can go it alone if you need the time,' she offered.

He shrugged. 'I have a meet set up but it's not until later. I'll stick.'

'How are we doing?' Robert asked his team at the end of the day.

'I think we're doing great,' Cardigan said. 'Those people love you. For the life of me, I can't understand why the DA didn't ask for a change of venue.'

'Tess Escalante is smart,' Sutton replied. 'She wants everyone to believe that her case is so strong she can beat us right here in the senator's backyard.'

'Is it?' Robert asked.

'Let's not kid ourselves,' Sutton said. 'If we can't find some kind of motive in this, her case is going to come across as pretty damn convincing.'

Robert turned to Mary Catherine.

The administrative assistant sighed. 'I'm sorry. The detective agency I hired is top drawer all the way, strictly ex-FBI. They've got over a hundred people out there digging, but so far they haven't turned up a thing.'

'Why don't you tell them they don't get paid if they don't get results?' Robert snapped in frustration.

'What *do* we know about her?' Randy asked.

Mary Catherine opened a pitifully thin folder. 'She's fifty years old. She was born and raised in Great Neck, Long Island, New York. Her father's a retired dentist, her mother's a housewife. The parents moved to Florida seven years ago. There's one sister who lives in Boston, the husband is an attorney, they have two children.'

'Anything there?' Robert asked.

'No. He's an estate planner, no particular political affiliation.'

'Go on.'

'She went to college, didn't graduate. On the fringe of the counterculture back in the late 1960s, early 1970s. Hung with a group of anti-war, popular-cause types. Held a series of nondescript jobs. Managed a posh Manhattan art gallery for a while. Married an architect in 1981, a widower with three children. Received some national recognition for a series of photographic essays on America.'

'What about her partner?'

Mary Catherine shook her head. 'The photographer is her sister-in-law. Nothing there.'

'Why didn't she graduate from college?' Randy asked.

The administrative assistant flipped through the pages. 'Let's see. I remember there was something about an accident. Yes, here it is. During her junior year, she was involved in some kind of accident and pretty badly injured. The hospital records are no longer available, lost or something, they said, but people who were there around that time seemed to remember it was an automobile accident. She spent several months in the hospital and then, apparently, she had a couple of years recuperating at home. Just decided not to go back to school after that, I guess.'

'No political ties?'

'None.'

'No mob connections?'

'None.'

'What about her history with men?'

'Other than an old college boyfriend in Maine who told our detective to go to hell – and her husband, of course – the agency hasn't been able to find a single solitary man who can so much as lay claim to having kissed her.'

'Where does that leave us?' Robert asked.

'With Snow White incarnate,' Randy said. 'But only if you believe in fairy tales.'

'Keep digging,' Robert instructed.

Jury selection took the better part of two weeks. In the end, the prosecution and the defense were able to agree on five men and seven women, Agnes McFaddan, Elaine Chu, and Brian Barstow among them, and two female alternates, who would decide the fate of Robert Drayton Willmont. Both sides congratulated themselves. Both sides predicted success.

two

'How are you holding up?' Tess asked, a matter of hours after the jury was sworn in, the day before the trial was to begin. The ADA had arrived at the Doniger home in St. Francis Wood to find a swarm of reporters had taken up residence on the front lawn.

'I've been working on the new book as much as I can,' Karen replied, shutting the door quickly against the barrage of rude questions that followed Tess inside. 'It keeps my mind off things. I don't go out very much and I try not to watch television.'

It was barely a month before the convention, and Mariah Dobbs was making the most of every opportunity to portray Robert Willmont as a pilloried savior – although, granted, a savior with a slightly tarnished halo.

Each day, after court, the senator would stop on the steps of the Hall of Justice to tell the media how deeply sorry he was to have broken his marriage vows and, in so doing, allowed some vague and nameless villain to take advantage of his momentary weakness. Always by his side were his wife and his son and his mother.

'My boy is innocent of this vicious allegation,' Amanda Drayton Willmont would declare whenever anyone inquired. She was eighty-four now and palsied, but her voice was still strong and clear. 'If you ask me, this is all the work of people who are afraid of their fat pocketbooks if my Bobby is elected President.'

'I know the enormous stress my husband has been under,' Elizabeth Willmont said on a national morning talk show, looking lovely in pink. 'I know how difficult it can be for someone to resist temptation when he's pushed himself past the point of exhaustion. I've forgiven his transgression, and I hope the country can, too.'

In addition, much of the media – not an institution known for maintaining its neutrality one minute longer than was deemed absolutely necessary – had flocked to the side of the senator, screaming outrage and crying 'dirty tricks' in chorus with the majority of the public. Every night, it seemed, another prominent commentator was coming forth to proclaim the candidate and denounce the alleged victim.

'It's probably best that you don't watch,' Tess agreed.

Karen picked up the morning newspaper. 'Unfortunately,' she said with a sigh, 'I haven't stopped reading.'

The three-inch headline read: 'Volunteer Accuses Senator of Rape – Trial Begins Tomorrow.' The accompanying article contained just about everything but her weight and bra size.

'I'm sorry about that,' Tess apologized, 'and about

the mob scene out front. But I assure you, the leak didn't come from our office.'

'I know that,' Karen replied, recalling the personnel files that were kept at the Willmont campaign headquarters. 'It was bound to get out, sooner or later. Actually, I'm surprised they waited as long as they did.'

The stunned, skeptical, supportive telephone calls had begun well before seven o'clock California time.

Laura called from Boston. 'It was all over the news this morning,' she confirmed. 'Your name and everything. I couldn't believe it. It's so weird, having them talk that way about my own sister. Is there anything I can do?'

'We've been following the story for weeks, of course,' Jill Hartman proclaimed from her summer home on Shelter Island, 'and we were all positive it was a political setup. We never dreamed it was you.'

'It's incomprehensible,' Arlene Minniken Slarsky, the Scarsdale psychologist, ex-Floridian, ex-roommate drawled. 'Let's face it – on the surface, Robert Willmont is an absolute dreamboat who could probably have any woman in the world he wants just by snapping his fingers. It makes you wonder why someone like that had to resort to rape.'

'A private detective came snooping around here, looking for dirt,' Peter Bauer told her. He had taken his father's company beyond every expectation and now sat at the forefront of computer electronics. He and his wife had five children and four grandchildren. 'I sent him packing.'

'Thank you for calling,' Karen said. 'It means a lot.'

'Look,' he added awkwardly, 'I have three daughters. Each in her own special way has helped me realize how badly I behaved back then. I know I can't ever make it up to you, but if there's anything I can do, please, let me know.'

'Why did they have to say it was you?' Gwen exclaimed indignantly the moment the twins had gone down for their naps. 'They had no right to say it was you right out in the open like that.'

'I guess they thought they did,' her stepmother sighed.

'I'll be there tonight,' Jessica declared during a coffee break from her summer job as a hematology intern at a Denver hospital. 'I've got everything all arranged, so don't argue.'

'Are you sure you don't want me to come out?' Nancy pressed. 'I can at least answer the telephone and the door and keep the press off your back.'

'We're with you, dear,' Ione assured her.

'Hang in there, girl,' Demelza instructed.

Then the call came from Palm Beach.

'Are you satisfied now?' Beverly Kern demanded. 'Your father's had a heart attack.'

Leo had had two small coronaries in the past five years. The doctors recommended bypass surgery, but the seventy-eight-year-old retired dentist didn't trust their judgment. He was trying, instead, to get his wife to cut cholesterol out of their diet.

'How is he?' Karen asked.

'Well, I suppose he'll live,' her mother conceded, 'no thanks to you.'

'Tell him I'm pulling for him.'

'Why are you doing this?' Beverly moaned. 'At your age, for heaven's sake, you should know better. You were always a good girl. How could you even think of doing such a dreadful thing to us?'

'I'm not doing anything to you, Mother,' Karen replied. 'I'm doing what I have to do for me.'

'But what will people say?'

'Is that really what's most important – what the neighbors will think?'

'You may not realize it, but we live in a very small community down here,' Beverly said. 'I can't go anywhere without meeting someone I know. The phone's been ringing off the hook all morning.'

'About me?'

'Well, they ask about your father, of course, but I know that's not why they're *really* calling.'

'Give Daddy my love.'

'You're ruining this family and that's all you have to say?'

'Tell him I'll call him soon.'

The line went dead.

'She was just upset,' Ted said reassuringly. 'She was probably worried about your father.'

'Don't make excuses for her,' Karen replied as she hung up the phone. 'She's been that way her whole life.'

'Everyone's been really terrific,' she murmured now as she poured a cup of tea for Tess. 'Well, almost everyone.'

The two women were seated at the table in the

breakfast room, at the back of the house, away from prying eyes.

'Don't let it get you down,' the seasoned ADA told her. 'We've still got a long way to go.'

'What about the jury?'

'About average, I'd say. One Asian, two blacks, two Hispanics, two Jews, one born-again Christian, one Irish Catholic, two WASPs and an atheist. Four Republicans, eight Democrats, and they're split right down the middle as far as blue collar/white collar. I think it's a good enough mix not to make for bias on either side.'

'So then,' Karen said with a big sigh, 'tomorrow's the day.'

'Not to worry,' the ADA replied. 'We have a strong case.'

'I just hope I don't let you down,' Karen murmured.

Tess smiled in spite of herself. Oddly matched though they were, the two had become close. It amused the ADA that Karen had begun their relationship by fearing the system would let her down, and now she worried that she might fail the system.

'If you tell it like you told it to Lamar and to me,' Tess reassured her, 'you'll do just fine.'

Karen sighed and her gaze slid out the window. Ted had taken the afternoon off and he and Amy were out working in the garden, a small walled space at the back of the house, protected by a locked gate from the prying eyes and insensitivity of the press.

'Have you ever been married, Tess?' she asked.

'Once,' the ADA replied, 'for about forty-eight hours.'

'*Two days?*'

Tess half-shrugged. 'It was a long time ago.'

'How long?'

The attorney sighed. 'We met in college. It was one of those cases of instant magic. You know, bells ringing, feet never touching the ground. His name was Eddie – Edward Parker Hilliard. I was there on full scholarship. He was there on full parentship. For three years, neither of us dated anybody else, and the day after graduation, we eloped. It was foolish, I suppose, but so romantic. We dreamed of having a little apartment and going to law school together. Then we came back and told our parents the glorious news.'

Karen listened intently. Other than an occasional story about her family's stoop-labor life, Tess never talked about her past.

'My parents were thrilled,' she went on. 'They really liked Eddie. But the Hilliards – well, that was a different story. They were furious. You see, they had no intention of allowing their son to contaminate the bloodline. They tried to buy me off, but I wouldn't hear of it. Next they tried to buy my father off, with more money than he would earn in his entire lifetime. To his credit, he told them to go to hell. Then they threatened to pull strings and have my scholarship to law school revoked, and finally, they swore they would disinherit Eddie and see to it that he never went to law school, either.'

Here, she paused for a chuckle, but it held no humor. 'I was feisty even back then. I said we didn't need their dirty money, that we loved each other and we could make it on our own. But I guess Eddie wanted to be a rich lawyer more than he wanted to be a poor husband. Anyway, the next day, his parents began the annulment process and I never saw him again. End of story.'

'And since?'

Tess tossed her head. 'Too busy to look, I guess.'

'I was almost forty when I married,' Karen reflected. 'I liked my husband but I wasn't in love with him. He just happened to be the one who was there when I realized it would probably be my last chance. We had a pretty bad time of it, you know, a lot of conflicting expectations, but now – now I don't know what I'd do without him.'

Tess leaned forward and pressed Karen's hand.

'It's going to be okay,' she promised.

The doorbell at St. Francis Wood rang at eight o'clock that evening. Karen was in the kitchen with Amy and Jessica, finishing up the dinner dishes. She heard Ted open the door and then there was a flurry of muffled conversation before the door slammed shut. Drying her hands, Karen started out of the kitchen and bumped into Ted coming to get her.

'There are some people who'd like to say a few words to you,' he said, unable to conceal the big grin on his face. 'I didn't think you'd mind.'

Ever since the press had descended on them, Ted had been her shield, letting no one but Tess, Lamar, and the Shaffers through the door. Curious, Karen took several steps past him and looked down the hall.

'Hi, kiddo,' Mitch Rankin greeted her. He was still a bear of a man at fifty-nine. 'If we'd known how popular this address was, we'd have come a lot sooner.'

'Now don't be upset with us, dear,' Ione urged, a gray Peter Pan at fifty-eight. 'We just had to come.'

'We figured you could use some friendly faces out

here in West Hostile,' Demelza added. At sixty-nine, her once thick black hair was now thin and white and she kidded about how it had taken the ravages of colon cancer to trim her figure down to gaunt.

'The truth is,' Jenna said, her arm linked in John's, 'we needed a vacation.' Jenna had kept her carrot-colored hair and her baby fat, even into her forties, and John looked even more like Sherlock Holmes now that his face was creased from half a century of living.

'I think it's nothing short of amazing that it never occurred to me to come to California before this,' Felicity declared, still straight as a stick at fifty-two, still the dancer.

'We're already camped out at Campton Place and we're staying for the duration,' Mitch concluded, referring to one of San Francisco's finest hotels. 'And we won't hear another word about it.'

Ted came up behind Karen and squeezed her shoulders. 'I think they mean it,' he whispered.

The pillars of her shaky past, she thought, the stalwart Sullivan Street set, who had always been there to defend her, protect her and support her, were still lining up behind her without question, without judgment. Tears crowded her eyes.

'I'm so glad you're here,' she cried.

'We have it all planned,' Ione told her as they settled themselves on the pale-green sofas that faced each other across the living room. 'We're going to court every day and do our best to remember everything that happens. That way, when you put together what each of us saw and heard, we're bound to come up with a pretty complete picture.'

'Not necessarily objective, mind you,' Demelza conceded, 'but complete.'

'Then, after court, you'll all come here for dinner,' Karen announced, glancing at Ted for confirmation. 'It won't be too much work and it'll give me something to do.'

'Amy and I will make sure it's not too much for her,' Jessica put in. 'She won't let us go to court.'

'Certainly not,' Karen retorted. 'I won't have you being hounded by the media any more than you already are.'

The doorbell rang again at nine-fifteen.

'Now, don't say a word,' Nancy Yanow ordered, pushing her way past the tactless mob of reporters and shutting the door firmly in their faces. 'So I'm a month early – you won't even know I'm here. I can bunk in the sunporch or on the sofa or anywhere there's a horizontal space, and I'm not leaving. If you think for a moment I'd go back out there, you're crazy.'

Karen hugged her sister-in-law and closest friend, who had grown even rounder with the passing of time.

'As long as you brought your camera,' she said, 'it won't be a total loss.'

'Of course I did.' Nancy grinned, her asymmetrical eyes twinkling. 'You didn't think I'd come all this way just for you, did you?'

Ted disappeared into the kitchen, returning with a tray of glasses and two bottles of champagne.

'I was saving this for after the verdict,' he said. 'But I think we should drink it now.' He popped the corks and poured. When everyone had a glass, he raised his own. 'To justice,' he said.

'To justice,' everyone else echoed. 'To convicting the bastard.'

'Yes, indeed,' Karen murmured, taking a small sip. 'To justice.'

* * *

The clock ticked past midnight. There was little more the defense could do. They had spent a thousand hours and hundreds of thousands of dollars trying to find the answer, but no answer had been found, and they had run out of time.

The senator sat at his desk in a pool of lamplight, spinning a paper clip on the end of a pencil. Randy was slouched in a chair across from him. The campaign offices were dark and silent.

'Feels like a funeral in here,' Robert observed wryly.

'Oh, I wouldn't dig the grave just yet,' Randy said buoyantly.

'I'm not.' The senator chuckled. 'I just figured everyone else was.'

'Not quite,' Mary Catherine said from the doorway. She was holding three glasses and a bottle of champagne.

'What's that for?' Robert asked.

'Two months ago, if you'd asked me,' she replied, 'I'd have said that not only the campaign but your whole political career was over. But I must have been reading from the wrong script because, despite this whole mess, here you are, with practically the whole country rallying behind you, one step away from the nomination. All that's standing between you and the White House is an acquittal.'

What a fickle world it was, Robert mused. Not that long ago, a politician had been crucified for a harmless little peccadillo in Bimini, and now here *he* was – being forgiven. He wanted to believe it was because he was a more important person, but he knew it had more to do with the sorry state of the nation.

'And if the voters believe you're telling the truth,'

the administrative assistant added, 'why shouldn't the jury?'

'She's got a point,' observed Randy. 'Even though we couldn't find a plausible reason for the woman to cry rape, it's still all going to come down to her word against yours.'

'That's right,' Mary Catherine confirmed. 'And you can bet the prosecution will have a pretty hard time trying to convince anyone that a man like you would have to use force.'

'Then let's drink to an acquittal,' Robert suggested.

Mary Catherine poured the champagne and the three of them raised their glasses, the click of touching rims echoing through the silent suite of offices.

'To the acquittal,' they toasted.

Lamar Pope did some of his best thinking just before dawn. He rarely slept more than four hours a night anyway, and even then his restless dreams were filled with images of Darcy, his bright, beautiful little girl.

He had never stopped blaming himself for her death. Because back then, being a cop was his life, all he thought about, all he needed. Being a father had come a distant second. Even after his wife died, leaving him alone with a twelve-year-old he hardly knew, it didn't change anything. He always meant to spend more time with her, get to know her better, but somehow the weeks, months, years slipped by and he kept putting it off. Until it was too late.

Then he learned about her after she was gone, from other people who had taken the time to know her and make a place for her in their lives.

'She was an angel,' they said. 'We were blessed to have known her.'

'She loved you so much and was so proud of you,' they told him. 'And she always knew you were there, looking out for her.'

But he hadn't been. Instead, he had been out looking for some sleazy stool pigeon the night she was raped and beaten to death.

He spent the weeks after the funeral stumbling around in a drunken stupor, knowing that, if she had meant little to him when she was alive, she meant everything to him now that she was dead. Around the time he sobered up, the punk who had brutalized her walked.

'The motherfucker has an airtight alibi,' the homicide detective who handled the case told him. 'Of course we know it's bogus, but we can't break it.'

Lamar nodded calmly. 'Mind if I take a look at some of the files?'

'Shit, no,' the detective said. 'If it was my kid that had been offed like that, I'd sure want a peek.'

The files told Lamar that the punk was a rich college kid, a football jock, and that his team had lost a crucial game the evening Darcy was murdered. The alibi had come from several of the punk's teammates, who swore he had been with them the whole night.

Lamar put the files away. Then he began to probe. It didn't take him long to learn that the punk had been involved in three other incidents – one in El Paso, one in Lubbock, and one in Abilene – over the past two years. None of them had resulted in anything as compelling as a death, but each time the punk had been arrested and then released, either because the charges were mysteriously dropped or because he was provided with an airtight alibi by his friends.

Darcy's father began to watch and wait. He was in no

hurry, he knew his opportunity would come. It took seven months, but sure enough, the punk made his last mistake.

On a spring night, in the middle of final exams, the football jock took another high school girl for a ride into the desert west of Amarillo – another high school girl who was too drunk or too naive to know what he had in mind.

Lamar heard her screaming as he braked to a stop behind the red Corvette. He was out of his car in less than three seconds, his gun already in his hand and aimed at the punk's head. He never thought twice, he just pulled the trigger.

The girl was too frightened and too grateful to wonder how Lamar happened to be there. She just clung to him and sobbed. He wrapped her in a blanket and drove her home. Then he went down to the station to report the killing.

Once the girl told her story, he was exonerated of any wrongdoing. No one seemed to care why he was in the middle of the desert in the middle of the night. They were only grateful that he was. He even became a bit of a local hero.

Amarillo had been good to Lamar for more than forty years. He could have stayed, but he left. Too many memories of too big a failure made him pack and go. He never remarried. He knew he had nothing to give a woman. And although it was clear to him that he could never be anything but a cop, he intended to be a different kind of cop.

For the twenty years since Darcy's death, Lamar had concentrated on putting puzzles together, special kinds of puzzles having to do with only one kind of crime, until there was no one better at it.

Now, as the hands on his wristwatch inched toward six, he stared one last time at the scribbled notes in front of him. Page after page, hiding a hint here, offering him a clue there. He had crisscrossed the country three times in the past six weeks, digging, probing – doing what he did best. Finally, it had come down to two sheets of paper, one culled from a report filed by a deceased New York police investigator named Michael Haller, the other scribbled during a reluctant conversation with a Dr. Stanley Waschkowski from New Hampshire. Lamar placed the two sheets side by side on his kitchen table and sat there looking from one to the other.

'I'll be damned,' he muttered slowly.

He knew the defense would never figure it out. After all, they were investigating Karen Doniger, not Robert Willmont. He was the only one who was investigating them both. He also knew there was nothing he could do about what he had discovered. And he was honest enough to admit that there was probably nothing he *would* do, even if he could. It was enough just to know he *was* right. And he *was* right. He knew it inside – by the little click he always felt when the missing piece of a puzzle finally fell into place.

three

The inner third-floor corridor at the Hall of Justice was packed. Media representatives from every corner of the country milled around with literally hundreds of curiosity seekers who had been disappointed by the space limitations in the Glass Courtroom.

Under pressure, Judge Washington had agreed to a closed-circuit TV setup wired to an adjoining courtroom where the media overflow could follow the proceedings. The curiosity seekers were out of luck.

Tess Escalante and her staff assistant, a plain, spare woman with a photographic memory named Anne Jenks, made their way through the crowd.

'I knew this was going to be a circus,' the ADA yelled above the din. 'But I never expected anything like this.'

Lamar was waiting for them inside.

'I've got something interesting for you,' he announced. 'Unfortunately, it's FYI only. You can't use any of it.'

'Show me,' Tess said.

He pulled out a sheet of paper he had drafted less than an hour ago and handed it to her.

'It seems our senator may not be the human saint that he and his PR people would like the world to believe.'

'Where on earth did you get this?' she marveled as she scanned the page.

'Don't ask.'

Tess smiled briefly. It was his standard response. She stared at his scrawled notes. She was the only ADA in the department who could decipher his handwriting.

'His father paid off the one in college?'

'Yes,' Lamar confirmed. 'She agreed to talk to me, but only in private. She's married now, with a family, and she won't come forward.'

'And this one?'

'I had a hunch.' Actually, he had researched every sex or seemingly sex-related crime in the city of San Francisco for the past thirty years. 'I was able to track down two of her old neighbors. They said he was a regular visitor, three or four nights a week. She used to tell everyone she and her Bobby were going to get married. The neighbors said they would have gone to the police when she died, but they were told it was a suicide. Besides, they didn't believe for a moment that such a nice young man could have had anything to do with her death.'

'What about this reporter who went to jail?'

'She claims she was framed because she had secretly taken some pictures of them together. Of course, I've only got her word for it, but part of her story checks out – her apartment *was* broken into the week before she was arrested and nothing of any value was taken. I talked to the D.C. police, and they confirmed that it was an anonymous tip that led to her arrest on drug and prostitution charges.'

'The old anonymous tipster.'

'Yeah. She maintained that someone called and set up an interview for her in that particular hotel room, but she didn't know who the caller was. That, plus a known dealer who had also gotten a mysterious phone call and two kilos of crack the police found under the sofa pillows, put her away.'

The ADA chuckled. 'I bet she'd just love to testify.'

'Hell, yes, but it wouldn't help us. She says he certainly liked sex but she never said he raped her, so there's no relevance. The relationship she says she had with him is hearsay, and she's a convicted felon. He could deny everything and come out smelling like a rose. Not to mention that Sutton would cry foul before she ever opened her mouth.'

Tess knew her investigator very well. 'What have you got,' she asked, 'that isn't on here?'

'Well, there was something about an assault when he was in law school,' Lamar replied casually, reflecting on those last two pieces of paper he had studied so late into the night. 'But our boy flatly denied culpability and no charges were ever filed.'

'Another payoff?'

'Who knows?'

'So, what do you think we're dealing with here, an innocent bystander or a slimy bastard?'

Lamar looked around the almost full courtroom. 'Rumor has it he's been doing a certain TV journalist on and off for the past ten years. Left side, second row, aisle seat.'

Tess glanced at the attractive brown-eyed blonde with the highly recognizable face and sighed. 'We won't get any help there, for sure.'

'You'll just have to rely on the strength of your case,' Lamar said, 'and trust in the jury's better instincts.'

'I always do,' Tess agreed, slipping the sheet of paper into her briefcase. 'Still, I wouldn't have minded a slight edge. After all, it's his town, his people, his whole damn country, and that doesn't exactly put the odds in our favor.'

'I'm sorry I couldn't get you more,' Lamar said.

'That's okay,' she told him with a toss of her shiny black hair and a twinkle in her dark eye. 'I'm at my best when I'm the underdog. It's just that I'm even better when I have an ace up my sleeve.'

Like some macabre wedding party, the family and friends of Robert Willmont gravitated to the left of the spectators' gallery, unofficially designated as the defense side, while Karen Doniger's supporters arranged themselves on the right.

Janice Evans sat in the second row, directly behind Elizabeth Willmont and Amanda Drayton Willmont. In front of them, through the bulletproof glass partition, she could see Robert sitting quietly among his impressive entourage of attorneys and advisers.

Her piece on his campaign, which was first yanked by the network and then hastily revised to reflect recent events, had aired a month ago.

'Get on out there and do a follow-up,' her producer told her. 'Your segment pulled a bigger share than the fucking Super Bowl. So, whichever way the trial goes, we're bound to top our time slot.'

'I'm sure he'll appreciate all your care and concern,' Janice observed wryly.

The producer shrugged carelessly. 'To the extent that he's salable, I care a whole lot.'

'You know this is clearly a case of political sabotage,' the reporter insisted. 'Forged letters are passé – sex is the weapon of the 1990s.'

'If you're right,' the producer said, 'you'll be able to name your price in this industry.'

Janice was on a plane to San Francisco two days later.

Now, as she studied the faces of the twelve jurors and two alternates that filed into the courtroom and took their seats, she wondered if it were possible that they might find him guilty, might actually believe the ridiculous lies of some frustrated, rejected, middle-aged woman? They looked so pompous sitting there, puffed up like peacocks with their own importance. Janice wondered what they were thinking, indeed whether they were thinking at all. She wished she could have five minutes with them to set them straight.

'Can't you see what's happening here?' she would shout. 'Can't you see there are evil forces at work, determined to keep him out of the White House at any cost? Look at him! Isn't it obvious that he doesn't need to assault used-up old women when he's got vibrant young ones lined up for the privilege of being fucked?'

She smiled to herself. Perhaps the last part wasn't exactly appropriate. Especially after all the efforts of Smoeller and Dobbs to promote Robert as a devoted family man. It was ironic, mused Janice, when those in the know knew that he probably made it with every halfway decent-looking woman under the age of forty who crossed his path.

Take the prosecutor, for example. That was one he wouldn't miss were circumstances otherwise. She was a knockout in an Hispanic sort of way, and she knew how to dress. Her slim burgundy suit with matching pumps breathed competence and confidence, and the thin gold chain around her neck added exactly the right touch of femininity.

Power dressing, as it had come to be called, was something the New York newswoman knew a great deal about, and with a sinking heart she realized that an attorney who was sharp enough to wear an outfit like that into court was probably sharp enough to destroy Robert Willmont.

Across the aisle, Felicity Gravois was studying the twelve faces just as intently as Janice Evans.

'They look pretty ordinary,' she remarked to Demelza.

'Most people do,' the Demion Five co-owner commented.

'But are they bright enough to know the truth when they hear it, and not be taken in by the rich and famous?'

'I certainly hope so.'

'Do you really think there's a jury in this city that would convict him?' Mitch Rankin asked his wife.

'Look at the prosecutor,' Ione replied. 'The one in the smashing burgundy suit. I'd say she knows what she's doing.'

'Maybe,' Mitch cautioned. 'But the defense attorney doesn't look like any slouch either.'

Ione's response went unspoken because the bailiff stepped forward at that moment to make his speech, those present scraped to their feet, and the Honorable Oliver Wendell Washington, in his flowing black robes, swept into court and took his seat on the bench.

It was one minute past nine o'clock on Thursday, June 18. The trial of *The People of the State of California* v. *Robert Drayton Willmont* had begun.

'I will remind the gallery that there are to be no outbursts or demonstrations of any kind,' Judge Washington intoned from his side of the bulletproof wall. 'You are guests of the court and as such can be removed at the whim of the court. I will also remind everyone – members of the media, in particular – that guests of the court are prohibited from taking photographs during these proceedings or using any kind of recording devices.'

There was a general shifting in the gallery as everyone glanced around at everyone else and then settled down. Judge Washington clasped his hands in front of him and nodded to the prosecutor.

Tess pushed back her chair and stood up.

'Good morning, ladies and gentlemen,' she addressed the jury. 'My name is Teresa Maria Yacinta Escalante, and I represent the People of the state of California.'

Her voice was melodious and clear and carried easily to every corner of the room.

'That's why this case is called *The People versus Robert Drayton Willmont*. When a crime has been committed, it is up to those who represent the People to collect every possible scrap of evidence, examine even the most minute detail, and analyze every available piece of information to determine who may have perpetrated that crime. Only after we have done all that to the best of our ability do we come here, to a court of law, to ask a select group such as you to tell us how well we've done our job.'

She stepped out from behind the table.

'There was a time, not all that long ago, when the courts of our country refused to recognize such a thing as rape. When people actually believed that if a man took advantage of a woman it was because he either had some preordained right, or because she had asked for it. Thank God that time is past. Thank God our courts are now willing to prosecute those who rape, and thank God there are juries brave enough to convict them. Because there are few crimes in this world as heinous as rape, and fewer still as heinous as acquaintance rape.'

The ADA walked slowly toward the jury box.

'It's one thing, ladies and gentlemen, for a woman to be pulled into a dark alley and assaulted by a total stranger. We can get our minds around that. We can say he was a maniac and she was an innocent – and that makes the crime clearly definable and the circumstances acceptable to most of us. But it's something quite different to be assaulted by someone you know, perhaps even admire, but certainly trust – to put yourself innocently into the hands of such a person and then to be betrayed in such a vicious and violating manner.'

Tess glanced casually toward the defense table.

'That's the distinction that the courts don't always make. That there is more than one kind of rape, and that each must be viewed and evaluated separately. That's the distinction that you are going to be asked to make here. It is the People's position that just because a woman goes to a bar with a man she knows – sits and drinks with him and even agrees to let him drive her home – does not mean she has agreed to have sexual intercourse with him.'

She looked directly into the eyes of each of the jurors.

'There have been some celebrated trials concerning this very issue recently, with juries who, comfortable or not, dutifully considered the facts and delivered their verdicts. Now, it's your turn. There are no eyewitnesses here, as there rarely are in such circumstances, and so the People's case will come down to two things: credibility and evidence. Whose story will you believe, and what proof will sway you?'

The ADA nodded slowly.

'I think the credibility of the victim will be obvious. And the evidence will show, beyond a reasonable doubt – no, beyond a shadow of a doubt – that Robert Drayton Willmont raped and beat Karen Doniger on the night of April seventh and then left her, like so much garbage, in the middle of Golden Gate Park. It doesn't matter who his family might be or what high office he seeks. All that matters is that he did it. *He did it.* And if those of us who represent the People weren't absolutely sure of that, we wouldn't be here today.'

With a small nod, Tess walked back to the prosecution table and sat down.

'Way to go,' murmured Mitch on the right side of the gallery.

'Shit,' Janice Evans mumbled on the left.

Judge Washington gestured to the defense and Hal Sutton rose to his feet.

'My name is Hal Sutton,' the Silver Fox began. 'But that's not very important. What's important is that I am the attorney who represents Senator Robert Drayton Willmont. In fact, that's all that's important here.'

He glanced over at Tess.

'The assistant district attorney says it doesn't matter who my client is, or what high office he seeks,' he went on. 'I say that's exactly what matters. In fact, that's what this case is all about. And it's one of the oldest stories in history. Let a man be brave enough to stand up and say: "Come with me, I know the way," and immediately there are those, too frightened or greedy to follow, who must plot to destroy him. Two thousand years ago, such a man died on the cross.'

'Wonderful,' Demelza muttered under her breath. 'So now we've got Jesus Christ Willmont on trial here.'

'Ladies and gentlemen,' Sutton continued smoothly, 'if you understand anything at all about this proceeding, you must understand that, were Robert Drayton Willmont not exactly who he is, were he not running for the highest office in the land, there would be no cry of rape here, there would be no trial, there would be no slander to this honest and decent and hard-working man who has spent the last fourteen years of his life in the service of his country.'

He put his hand on Robert's shoulder.

'Yes, my client admits to having sex with Karen Doniger. He is, alas, not God, merely one of His imperfect sons. But the fact is, it was *she* who encouraged *him*, *she* who seduced *him*, *she* who took advantage of *him* – morally weakened as he was by stress, fatigue, and Scotch – not the other way around. And then, surprise of surprises, she cries rape. What does that say to you, members of the jury? What does that suggest about the frightened and the greedy?'

He paused for a moment to let his words sink in.

'Senator Robert Drayton Willmont is a devoted son, a devoted husband and a devoted father,' he went on. 'His family sits in this courtroom today as testimony to that. And he has been a devoted public servant, too. His election and reelection to both the Congress and the Senate, and his overwhelming victories in this year's presidential primaries are testimony to that. Does it seem plausible that such a man, on the brink of his greatest achievement, would risk it all on a momentary exercise?'

He pressed Robert's shoulder lightly and the defendant got to his feet.

'Take a good look at him, ladies and gentlemen. A son of one of San Francisco's founding families, a true beacon of hope in our country's time of crisis, a man of wealth and stature and intelligence and charisma, who has chosen to dedicate his life to his country. Is this a man who would have to resort to rape?'

He held his client motionless for a full fifteen seconds before allowing him to retake his seat.

'The evidence to which the assistant district attorney refers,' Sutton concluded, 'will indeed show that Senator Willmont and Karen Doniger were intimate. That they had a few drinks together at a downtown bar and then drove to Golden Gate Park, where they got out of the senator's car and engaged in sexual intercourse. My client does not and has never denied that. But it's a far cry from consensual copulation to rape. And that, despite what the prosecution will attempt to make you believe, my client did not do.'

'Right on,' murmured Janice Evans on the left side of the gallery.

Across the aisle, John Micheloni shifted uneasily in his seat. 'He's damn good,' he muttered to Jenna.

four

Tess took a sip of cold coffee and stretched her aching back muscles, swearing for the umpteenth time that the city had better get her that posture-perfect chair she had been requesting for over a year now before her spine became permanently bent.

All in all, however, she had to admit that there was little to complain about. The first two days of the Willmont trial had gone well.

Arthur Gertz began the case for the prosecution and his testimony was every bit as effective as she had anticipated it would be. The precise, yet emotional recounting of his pre-dawn jog and his grim discovery at Stow Lake set a chilling scene that had enormous impact on the jury, an impact that Hal Sutton's brief cross-examination was unable to dissipate.

Next, Officer Kelly Takuda's dispassionate testimony had fixed two things in the jury's mind: that Karen Doniger had been found semi-conscious in

Golden Gate Park and that all indications were that she had been the victim of a brutal assault.

'Officer Takuda,' Sutton had inquired when Tess finished her direct examination, 'was it possible to tell from anything at the scene, or even from the condition of the woman herself, who initiated the sexual activity?'

'No, sir,' the witness responded. 'There was nothing to indicate how it began. All that was discernible was the result.'

'So it's entirely possible then,' Sutton pressed, 'that what you found at Stow Lake on the morning of April eighth was not the result of an assault, as you previously described, but the result of a consensual sexual act that might have been performed more, shall we say, exuberantly than most?'

The policewoman considered for a moment. 'Anything's possible, I guess – but it's not probable.'

'But is it possible?' Sutton drilled.

'I suppose so.'

'Thank you, Officer Takuda,' Sutton said resuming his seat. 'That's all.'

'Officer Takuda,' Tess said on redirect. 'How many incidents relating to sexual violence have you personally investigated in the past six months?'

'About forty,' Kelly replied.

'And last year?'

'Maybe a hundred, a hundred and ten.'

'Then based on your experience, having dealt with perhaps as many as a hundred and fifty such investigations in just the past eighteen months, when you reached Stow Lake on the morning of April eighth, was it your conclusion that the semiconscious woman you found there, bruised and bleeding, had participated in a consensual sexual encounter?'

'No, it was not,' the policewoman confirmed. 'My conclusion was then, and is now, that she was the victim of sexual assault and battery.'

'Just one more thing, Officer Takuda,' Tess concluded. 'Do you think it's possible – not probable, mind you, but possible – that the sky will fall tomorrow?'

'Objection!' shouted Hal Sutton.

'Miss Escalante,' Judge Washington admonished, 'you know better than that.'

'Withdrawn, Your Honor,' Tess conceded with a contrite smile. 'I have nothing more.'

The Rape Treatment Center nurse-examiner's testimony, detailing the procedures she used to collect the evidence and the precautions she took to keep the chain of custody intact, closed out the second day of the trial. She was a solid witness in the prosecution's case, confirming that everything she had observed during the course of her examination was totally consistent with forced sex. Sutton had been unable to dislodge her.

Now it was Friday night and tomorrow would begin the third day of the trial. While the court was not usually in session over the weekend, pressure by the defense for a speedy resolution had caused Judge Washington to adjust the schedule. Officially, he explained the Saturday session as an effort on the part of the court to have the proceedings concluded and the jury dismissed by the July 4th holiday.

Actually, Tess was pleased. She planned to put the police lab technician on the stand in the morning, and his testimony and cross-examination would probably last the entire day. Tess would have him go over each item, each piece of Karen's clothing, each grass stain and dirt smudge and blood smear and trace of semen. Next, she would have him detail his examination of Robert Willmont's clothing, the tear in his jacket, the split seam in the trousers, and whatever stains, smudges, smears and traces had been found on them. Finally, she would have him produce the highly technical, dreadfully boring but absolutely essential DNA evidence.

If all went well, the jury would retire to the Sheraton Hotel with two vital facts to mull over until Monday morning: first, the DNA unequivocally placed Robert Willmont's semen inside Karen Doniger's vagina and mouth; and, second, the condition of her clothing as well as the traces of blood in the vaginal smear clearly indicated that force had been used.

The ADA stretched again and stood up. Through her window, she could see a steady stream of headlights along the freeway, weekend traffic heading out of town. All those people with somewhere to go, she mused, unmindful that the biggest theatrical of the decade was being played out right here at home on the stage of the Glass Courtroom.

What had begun for her as a dubious duty had become a crusade. From a distance, Robert Willmont seemed a bright promise, but up close, he had lost much of his shine. There was something about the combination of humble contrition and angry indignation he portrayed to the outside world at every opportunity that rubbed Tess the wrong way and made her even more positive of his guilt.

'We're going into court with the strongest case I've seen in years,' she continued to assure Karen. 'And let me tell you that I've won verdicts with a great deal less.'

'I trust your judgment,' Karen said.

'What?' She chuckled. 'You've found new faith in the system?'

'I never doubted that the system works,' Karen corrected her. 'What I said was that there can be a big gap between the system working and justice being served.'

It was true more often than Tess liked to admit.

She remembered that now as she finished the last of her preparations for tomorrow's session, snapped off her desk lamp, closed the door of her office, and made her way down the third floor corridor toward the elevator. She had meant what she said about the case being strong, but she also understood the vagaries of a jury. No, understood wasn't the right word. She had never been able to understand juries, she had just learned how to work with them.

'You sound tired,' Mariah Dobbs said from the New York end of the telephone line on Sunday night.

'I guess I am,' Randy admitted from his studio apartment in the Marina district. 'And lonely.'

'You do understand why I can't be there with you, don't you?' she asked.

'Sure,' he sighed. 'You've got other clients who need you.'

'Exactly,' she agreed, although the real reason had more to do with distancing herself and her firm from Senator Willmont's unfortunate circumstance. 'There's really nothing more I can do for him at this point, anyway. It's in the hands of the jury now, and I have no way of influencing them. But if he's acquitted, you can count on my being around to launch a media bombardment that, come November, will dump him right at the door of 1600 Pennsylvania Avenue.'

'Two months ago, I wouldn't have given him an ice cube's chance in hell,' Randy admitted.

'Neither would I,' Mariah agreed, thinking that, despite the primary victories, she still wouldn't.

'It was your honesty gambit that saved him,' the aide told her. 'If he hadn't done the mea culpa bit right up front, and thrown himself on the mercy of the people, he'd be dead in his political grave by now.'

'The voters love him and they want to believe in him,' she conceded. 'So they're willing to give him the benefit of the doubt – until the jury comes in.'

'I sit in court and watch them,' Randy told her, 'and try to figure out what's going through their minds. I used to think it would take millions of people to decide whether we went to the White House or not, but now it's all come down to twelve – five men and seven women – who are going to make us or break us.'

Mariah chuckled. 'Interesting choice – the White House or the Big House. That's the fat and the lean of it, the up and the down, the yin and the yang.'

'Don't,' Randy groaned.

'How are things really going?' Mariah asked.

'Not great,' he admitted. 'The lab expert was on the stand yesterday. All the DNA stuff was very technical and dreadfully boring. I saw several of the jurors yawning, and it almost put me to sleep. But I've got to admit, the physical evidence is pretty damning.'

'What does the senator say about that?'

'He says he has no idea how any of it happened.'

'He'd better have more to say than that when he gets on the stand,' the public relations expert suggested. 'What does the lawyer think?'

'Hal keeps things pretty much close to the vest,'

Randy told her. 'If you press him, he says to wait until we have our shot, but between you and me, I think he's worried.'

'And the candidate?'

The aide paused. 'To be honest, I don't think he worries about anything,' he said. 'He just assumes that things will work out the way he wants them to.'

five

The surgical resident who treated Karen's injuries in the Emergency Room of San Francisco General Hospital was first to take the stand on Monday morning. He painstakingly detailed and categorized each of her bruises and abrasions, the number of stitches taken in her lip, the setting of her broken nose.

'Your Honor,' Tess said, 'I would like, at this time, to introduce People's exhibits sixty-six through seventy-two, and ask that they be presented to the jury.'

'I must renew my objection, Your Honor,' Hal Sutton exclaimed. 'The prosecutor has already elicited volumes about the physical condition of the alleged victim. The photographs add nothing new.'

'On the contrary, Your Honor,' Tess argued. 'Hearing about a broken nose or a split lip or a bruised thigh is not the same as actually seeing it.'

'The prosecutor knows full well, Your Honor, that

those photographs are deliberately inflammatory.'

'Mr. Sutton is correct, Your Honor,' Tess agreed, 'if you look at them from his client's perspective. But I want the jury to look at them from an objective point of view.'

'Objection!' Sutton stormed.

'That will do, Miss Escalante,' Judge Washington said. 'The photographs are admissible. Objections overruled.'

Tess handed the jury one picture at a time, presenting the entire group with an opportunity to take a good look. It pleased her to see most of the jurors wince.

'Now, Doctor,' she continued, when the last grisly image had been passed around, 'are the bruises you've described, the injuries shown in these photographs, the kind that you would expect to find from consensual intercourse?'

'No, Miss Escalante, they are not.'

'How would you describe them, then?' she pressed.

'I would describe them as being completely consistent with the use of force.'

'Thank you, Doctor.'

'Tell me, Doctor,' Hal Sutton asked. 'Is there any way to tell whether or not all of these bruises were inflicted by the defendant?'

'No, not specifically.'

'For example, isn't it entirely possible that the split lip or the broken nose might have been caused by bumping into a tree in the dark, or tripping and falling face down onto the pavement?'

'There was certainly no indication of that.'

'Could the injuries have been so caused, Doctor?'

'I suppose they could.'

'Thank you,' Sutton said. 'That's all.'

'Where is he going with that?' Anne Jenks whispered in Tess's ear.

'Wherever his limited options will take him,' Tess replied.

After the lunch break, Lamar Pope took the stand. He spent the balance of Monday and much of Tuesday detailing his interviews with both the alleged victim and the defendant, referring frequently to his notes.

From him, Tess elicited testimony relating to, among other things, the footprint found at the scene that matched the senator's loafer and the scratches on the senator's chest that matched the skin scrapings taken from under Karen Doniger's fingernails. Then the topic turned to Karen's missing handbag.

'As part of your investigation, Sergeant,' the ADA inquired, 'did you have reason to search the defendant's car on the afternoon of April tenth?'

'I did.'

'What, if anything, did you find?'

'I found a navy-blue handbag with identification and other items in it belonging to Karen Doniger.'

'Did the defendant offer any explanation for why the handbag was in his car and not with Karen Doniger?'

'No, he did not. He seemed surprised to see it there. Apparently, it had slipped between the seats and he hadn't noticed it.'

'Thank you,' Tess said. 'Nothing more.'

'Was Senator Willmont cooperative in your investigation, Sergeant Pope?' Sutton asked.

'Yes, he was.'

'Did he answer the questions you put to him to the best of his ability?'

'Yes, he did.'

'Did he decline to answer any of your questions?'

'No, he did not.'

'Did he deny having been with Karen Doniger on the night in question?'

'No, he did not.'

'Did he deny having sex with her?'

'No.'

'Now let's go back to those scratches for just a moment, Sergeant,' Sutton invited. 'Did Senator Willmont give you any explanation as to how he had gotten them other than you have already testified?'

'Yes,' Lamar replied, consulting his notes. 'He said they were the result of passion, not resistance.'

'Now, about the handbag.'

'Mr. Sutton,' Judge Washington interrupted, feeling a gastric attack coming on. 'It's already well into the afternoon. I know I'm tired of sitting and I can only assume that the jury is, too. If you are planning a lengthy cross-examination, and all indications seem to be that you are, may I give you every opportunity to complete it in the morning?'

'Certainly, Your Honor.'

'We're getting nowhere, aren't we?' Robert asked on the way back to Jackson Street.

'Evidence is just evidence.' Sutton shrugged. 'It's all in how it's interpreted. And you know as well as I do that it's never really interpreted until the very end.'

'But those photographs,' Robert groaned. 'I saw the shudder when the jury looked at them. They make me come off like I'm some kind of monster. Do you think they retouched them to make her look worse?'

'No, I don't think so.'

'Well, I don't remember her being that banged up. I may have gotten a little rough with her – hell, she asked for it. But I don't remember her looking anything like that.'

'The pictures certainly didn't help our cause,' Sutton agreed.

'At first, you know, I just assumed that no one with any common sense would buy her story,' Robert confided. 'I mean, who would believe that a United States senator running for President would deliberately go out and rape someone? But I was watching the faces of that jury today. Some of them looked like they wanted to lynch me.'

'Well, don't despair just yet,' Sutton said calmly. 'We haven't had our turn yet, you know.'

It was the same thing he always said. In the past, his words had been able to soothe Robert, but now they began to grate on him. Sutton was a longtime associate, but after all, what real difference would it make to him if he won or lost this case – he would still get his million-dollar fee, he would still be free to practice law, and he would even find a way to remove whatever tarnish might rub off on his spotless reputation.

The candidate sighed, knowing it was too late now to wonder whether he had been wise in his choice of attorney.

'Dr. Linderman,' Tess inquired on Wednesday afternoon, following the completion of Lamar's cross-examination and Azi Redfern's virtually unchallenged testimony, 'what is your primary work?'

'For the past three years,' Philip Linderman, the

respected Berkeley psychiatrist, replied, 'I've been involved in a research program dealing exclusively with the psychology of rape.'

'Will you please describe this program for the jury.'

'In the first part of it, we selected a random sample of four hundred and fifty convicted sex abusers and, through interviews, therapy sessions, and testing techniques that were formulated specifically for the program, we tried to develop a psychological profile that would help in the identification of potential rapists.'

'Would it be fair to say then that, as a result of your work in this program, you've become a recognized expert in this area?'

'Yes, I think it would be fair to say that. I have presented no less than half a dozen papers on the subject, both nationally and internationally, and I am a frequent contributor to the *American Journal of Psychiatry.*'

'Your Honor,' Sutton broke in. 'Defense is willing to stipulate to Dr. Linderman's credentials.'

'In that case, Doctor, tell us,' continued Tess, 'have you indeed developed the definitive psychological profile of a rapist?'

'Yes, and no,' he answered.

'Please explain,' the ADA invited.

'Well, we found we were unable to develop one basic profile because, as it turns out, there are several.'

'Several, Dr. Linderman?'

'Yes, Miss Escalante. One profile concerns what people generally think of when they hear the word 'rapist' – the total stranger who pulls a woman into a dark alley. There is another profile that deals with the domestic violator – the husband, the boyfriend, the father, the step-parent, the older brother. And a third profile concerns what we have in recent years come to call the acquaintance-rapist – the man who knows, and is known by, his victim – who already has a relationship of some sort with her, be they friends or neighbors or co-workers.'

'So what you're saying, Doctor, is that your research has determined that there are several distinct types of rapists who commit distinctly different types of rape.'

'That's correct,' Linderman confirmed. 'Even though the crimes have a violent orientation and lead to more or less the same conclusion, defining one in terms of another would be like trying to make apple-sauce out of oranges.'

'Will you please describe for the jury how the profiles you developed for the stranger-rapist and the acquaintance-rapist differ?'

'Certainly,' the psychiatrist replied. 'We determined that the stranger-rapist requires anonymity and his actions stem from deep-rooted anger, low self-esteem, and emotional impotence. He hates women, he some-times hates the whole world, he certainly hates him-self, although he frequently believes just the opposite. His purpose is to control his victim, to dominate and degrade her, as he feels dominated and degraded, and in the only way he can – sexually. For him, rape is not about sex, it's about violence and intimidation. It's about the release of his anger on someone who isn't strong enough to repel him, which represents a reenactment of some ongoing relationship of his own, where he is the weaker party. In other words, it's about the acting out of his unexpressed rage toward some-one he *does* know on someone he *doesn't* know and, therefore, someone who is safe for him to attack. It makes him feel temporarily potent. But the feeling is short-lived and, like a narcotic, once it wears off, he must rape again to get it back.'

'Are there any patterns to this type of rapist?'

'Frequently. His victims, for example, may all look alike if he is deliberately choosing women who resemble the real object of his anger – his mother, a female employer, a girlfriend who rejected him. Even if they don't look alike however, there will usually be something that connects them – blond hair, a style of dress, a profession. Often, he may use the same ploy to find each of them, riding a specific bus, or shopping in a certain market. He will tend to use them the same way, make them do the same things, threaten them with the same weapon, or tie them up in the same fashion. He may say the same things, using the same or similar words. He may have one particular outfit that he wears every time he goes out to rape. He sees it as his protection; in a way, his suit of armor.'

'Nice guy,' Mitch murmured on the right side of the gallery.

'But not our guy,' Ione replied.

On her side of the aisle, Janice Evans turned to Randy, who was now sitting beside her. 'Where is the prosecutor going with this?' she whispered. 'None of it applies here.'

'I'm sure she has her reasons,' Randy replied dully.

'Now, Dr. Linderman,' Tess pursued, 'tell us about the acquaintance-rapist.'

Hal Sutton rose to his feet. 'Your Honor, while this is surely most enlightening, I fail to see the relevance.'

'Miss Escalante?' Washington queried.

'We believe it's essential to our case, Your Honor,' the ADA replied, 'that the jury be able to distinguish between one type of rape and another, and between one kind of rapist and another. One of the defense's primary thrusts has been to ask, "Why would someone like Senator Willmont need to resort to rape?" As though all women should just naturally fall at his feet simply because he's rich and attractive and politically powerful. I think I have every right to try to blow that theory out of the water.'

'Although that argument might better have been made during rebuttal, I'm inclined to allow it,' Washington said. 'Objection overruled.'

'Once again, Dr. Linderman,' Tess went on smoothly, bridging the interruption, 'will you describe for the jury the last profile you developed?'

'The acquaintance-rapist is a different breed,' the psychiatrist said. 'Unlike the stranger-rapist, he's not necessarily motivated by low self-esteem. He generally likes women, although he rarely respects them, and he may even go out of his way to be charming and attentive. He flirts and woos and convinces himself that any woman he singles out should be honored to accommodate him simply because of who he is. He wants the woman he rapes to know him, because he wants her to be impressed with his facade – his name, his looks, his background, his job, his home, his income and, by extension, his sexual prowess. He has two delusions: one is that all women find him irresistible; the other is that he's entitled to take whatever he wants. It's strictly a power play for him. We call it the "Me-Tarzan-You-Jane" syndrome. He pursues until she succumbs. But when he comes across a woman who doesn't succumb, he views his violation of her as just part of the game. He was raised on the concept that all women want to be taken – by force, if necessary.'

'Now *he* sounds familiar,' Demelza murmured under her breath.

'That's where she was going,' Randy muttered under his breath.

'Dr. Linderman,' Tess asked, 'are there any general parameters for this profile?'

'Some,' the psychiatrist replied. 'In our program, we found that the acquaintance-rapist tends to be more highly goal-oriented and professionally successful than the stranger-rapist. Like the stranger-rapist, he is usually the product of a dysfunctional family environment, but where the stranger-rapist is himself frequently the victim of incest or physical abuse, the acquaintance-rapist tends to be the victim of either parental overpampering or neglect. In a number of cases we studied, we found that the acquaintance-rapist had learned how to manipulate women at a very early age.'

'Is there any kind of discernible pattern to this type of rapist?'

'I call it more of an anti-pattern,' the psychiatrist replied. 'Where the stranger-rapist will plan ahead, and generally very carefully, the acquaintance-rapist rarely plans ahead. He is much more likely to be motivated by the moment and act on impulse. He might go to a party or a bar with the idea of finding someone to have sex with, but he doesn't set out to rape the woman. In macho terminology, he's going to hunt, pursue, and conquer.'

'Conquer?' Tess interjected. 'As in war?'

'Sexual dominance was once considered an acceptable form of victory in battle. There's a famous painting that depicts that attitude. It's called *The Rape of the Sabine Women*.'

'Victory in battle,' Tess echoed.

'Your Honor,' the Silver Fox protested. 'Is my client now being accused of ravaging an entire nation?'

'Point taken, Mr. Sutton,' Washington said. 'Miss Escalante, may we confine ourselves to the matter at hand?'

'Certainly, Your Honor,' the ADA conceded. 'So, Dr. Linderman,' she continued, turning her back to her witness, 'our typical acquaintance-rapist is super-macho, spoiled, fancies himself irresistible, and goes out looking to conquer?'

'That pretty much covers it. Of course, he doesn't necessarily go out on the prowl. He might be interested in someone who lives in his neighborhood or works in his office, and then he might simply wait for the right opportunity. Again, however, he would never consider what he intends as rape, because he assumes any woman would happily submit to his advances. It's only when she resists his attentions, when his manipulations fail, that the deep-rooted anger which motivates him flares up and he resorts to violence.'

'Gotcha!' Jenna breathed.

'Shit,' Randy sighed.

'The key to the acquaintance-rapist,' the psychiatrist summarized, 'is that he is generally attracted to the woman he ends up violating. What he can't accept is that *she* might not be attracted to *him*. Starting usually with his mother, women have always done his bidding, so he has every reason to expect this one will, too. If she resists, he tells himself she must be playing hard to get. In the end, it isn't that he intends to rape – it's that he's psychologically unable to accept rejection.'

'In your opinion, Dr. Linderman,' Tess concluded,

'and as an acknowledged expert, does anything in the profile you've described excuse the acquaintance-rapist's behavior?'

'Absolutely not. Once the woman says no, even if the man doesn't believe her, if he then forces her into compliance, he is guilty of sexual assault, Miss Escalante, no matter what he tries to tell himself, or anyone else.'

'Thank you, Doctor,' said Tess. 'I have no more questions.'

'Did I hear you correctly, sir?' Hal Sutton inquired. 'Did you say that, even though a man may sincerely believe he is participating in consensual sex, you believe he is guilty of rape?'

'If the woman resists, yes.'

'I assume that's a medical opinion, not a legal one, or are you also an attorney?'

'No, Mr. Sutton. I'm just a psychiatrist.'

'Well then, as just a psychiatrist, Dr. Linderman, how do you account for all the women we hear about who resist a man because they think they're supposed to, not because they really want to? Women who need to have men dominate them sexually in order to overcome what used to be considered a gross lapse in morality?'

'Thirty or forty years ago, perhaps, there might still have been women who reacted like that,' the psychiatrist conceded. 'Today, I doubt there are more than a handful.'

'But suppose we're talking about a woman who was raised back then, Doctor – say, a woman raised in the 1950s who still remembers the tenets of her upbringing?'

'Objection,' Tess called. 'Calls for speculation. How

can Dr. Linderman be expected to speak for women raised in the 1950s?'

'He's been accepted here as an expert on the psychology of rape, hasn't he?' Sutton argued. 'Did the prosecution mean to stipulate that his knowledge was restricted to one specific decade?'

'You're still asking him to be a mind reader,' Tess persisted.

'Hardly,' the Silver Fox responded silkily. 'I'm simply asking him to speak from the depths of his considerable experience.'

'Objection overruled,' Washington said. 'You may answer the question, Doctor.'

'I suppose such behavior patterns could continue up to the present,' the psychiatrist replied reluctantly.

'Thank you, Doctor. Now tell us, as part of your extensive research, have you worked at all with alleged victims of rape?'

'As a matter of fact, the second part of our study is devoted to victims, and we are currently working with a group of women whose attackers were both convicted and acquitted.'

'Let's talk specifically about those women in your study who exhibited significant injuries as a result of what they claimed were acquaintance-rape encounters, injuries not unlike those being represented in the case now before this court.'

'What about them?'

'Was one of those women named Marion Healy?'

'Objection, Your Honor,' Tess interrupted. 'Relevance. What does one particular research subject of Dr. Linderman's have to do with the matter at hand?'

'I assure the court that I will make the connection,' Sutton said smoothly.

'I'll allow it,' the judge declared.

Tess murmured something quickly to Anne Jenks in the seat beside her, but the staff assistant already had her eyes narrowed in concentration.

The Silver Fox turned his back to his quarry. 'Now, Doctor, I repeat, was one of your research subjects a woman by the name of Marion Healy?'

'Yes, I believe so.'

'And during the course of your interviews with her, what did you learn about the circumstances of her alleged rape?'

'How did you get access to my files?' snapped Linderman.

'I don't know that I had,' Sutton replied blandly. 'The case is a matter of public record. My staff may well have learned about Miss Healy from some other source. Again, Doctor, what did you learn?'

'She admitted that she had encouraged the man to have rough sex with her because that was the way she needed it, and that it was only when she saw how badly bruised she was, and after the man refused to pay for her medical bills, that she changed her mind and reported the incident as a rape.'

'Nevertheless, an innocent man was convicted and sent to jail, wasn't he, Doctor?' Sutton demanded.

'Your Honor!' Tess protested.

'Mr. Sutton!' Washington barked.

'May it please the court,' Sutton argued. 'This expert witness has been called to the stand to give us his learned opinions about rape. I think I have every right to ask him to present both sides of the story to the jury. Prosecution opened the door by referring to the research program, and by basing her witness's expertise in the field on it.'

The judge sighed. 'I think he may have you there, Miss Escalante.'

Tess shook her head in disgust.

Anne Jenks picked up a pen and began to scribble on a piece of paper.

'Again, Dr. Linderman,' Sutton pressed, 'Marion Healy, whose bruises described in court appear to be somewhat similar to those of the alleged victim in this case, later admitted that she had participated in, and even solicited rough consensual sex, did she not?'

'Yes, Mr. Sutton.'

'Thank you, Doctor. That's all.'

'Thank God he was able to get that part of it in,' Mary Catherine murmured from the seat on the other side of Randy.

'I don't think the judge should have allowed any of that,' Felicity grumbled.

Anne Jenks slid a scribbled sheet of paper over to Tess, who looked at it and jumped up.

'Dr. Linderman,' she said on redirect. 'You mentioned earlier that there were four hundred and fifty men in your research program. How many women were there?'

The psychiatrist pulled a notebook from his jacket pocket and flipped through the pages.

'Seven hundred and ten,' he replied when he found the right page.

'And how many of those seven hundred and ten women were the alleged victims of acquaintance rape?'

Linderman peered again at his notes. 'Three hundred and forty-two.'

'And how many of those three hundred and forty-two had been injured in some way by their attackers?'

'Forty-eight.'

'All right, in how many of those forty-eight cases did the victim later admit to falsifying the charges?'

'One.'

'Was that one Marion Healy?'

'Yes, it was,' Linderman confirmed. 'And I'd like to say something about that, if it's all right.'

'Certainly,' Tess invited.

'Marion Healy is a disturbed woman who may or may not have been raped. But the man who was first convicted of the crime and then later released when she changed her story is currently serving a twenty-five-year sentence in a Nevada prison for sexual assault and battery.'

'Thank you, Doctor,' Tess said. 'That's all.'

'That's enough,' Janice groaned.

'Way to go,' Mitch exulted.

'What hat did you pull that rabbit out of?' Tess whispered to Anne Jenks.

'I remembered seeing something about it in the Nevada newspapers a while ago,' whispered the staff assistant, who seldom forgot anything she had seen or read or heard.

SIX

At ten minutes past nine the following morning, Tess got to her feet.

'Your Honor,' she said clearly, 'there are a number of character witnesses I had originally intended to call before the court, but in compliance with the defense's expressed wish for a speedy resolution to this matter, we will present just one more witness. The People call … Karen Doniger.'

With a collective gasp, everyone was suddenly alert. People were sitting up, twisting in their seats, eyes trained on the double doors at the entrance to the courtroom. It was what they had all been waiting for. They had been hearing her name for weeks now, but for many of those present, including the jury, this was the first time they would actually see the alleged victim in person.

A photograph of her, taken from the dust jacket of *Tapestry*, had been splashed across the front pages of some of the seamier newspapers, and had even managed to creep onto a few respected television channels, but Robert Willmont's accuser had held no press conferences, made no public statements, and allowed no interviews. *Hard Copy, Inside Story* and *A Current Affair* had all been turned away with their hundred-thousand-dollar checks still in their pockets.

The doors opened and, with a watchful deputy on either side of her, Karen entered the courtroom. She paused for perhaps five seconds on the threshold before she squared her shoulders, walked straight down the aisle, looking neither to the right nor the left, and marched resolutely through the bulletproof opening toward the witness box, wedged, as it was, between the judge and the jury.

She was wearing a silk suit in a deep mauve color and an ivory Victorian-style blouse with the traditional high lace collar. At her throat was an opal cameo that Natalie had given her to wear for courage, and on her wrist was a new gold bracelet created by Felicity that Ted had given her.

Jessica had styled her stepmother's hair back off her face, while Amy kept bringing up fresh pots of tea. Nancy had pressed her suit. And Natalie had fussed for over an hour, choosing just the right shade of stockings and appropriate pair of pumps.

'Nothing too spiky,' Nancy warned. 'She should look conservative.'

'And nothing too bright,' Natalie agreed. 'We wouldn't want her to appear flashy.'

Everyone took a hand in her makeup, giving her a little more rouge and a little less mascara and then deciding on a soft-pink lipstick and pale eye-shadowing.

And all the while, Karen stood in front of the full-length mirror and wondered who the woman was who looked back at her. The swelling had gone down around the nose and lip, and the ugly bruises had all but faded, but the cheekbones seemed too prominent, there was something disconcerting about her eyes, and the set of the jaw was new and unfamiliar.

Yesterday, when she had ventured out into the garden for a breath of fresh air, she discovered that a rude reporter had scaled the wall.

'So how does it feel to take down the greatest man in America?' he yelled at her.

Fortunately, Nancy was there to take a broom to him, sweeping him away like a speck of dirt, but Karen was left wondering, for perhaps the thousandth time, if she were doing the right thing.

'. . . your right hand,' the bailiff had already begun. 'Do you solemnly swear that the testimony you are about to give before this court is the truth, the whole truth, and nothing but the truth, so help you God?'

'I do,' Karen said, her voice clear and firm.

'State your name.'

'Karen Doniger.'

'State your address.'

She gave the number of the house and the name of the street in St. Francis Wood.

'Be seated.'

The chair took her by surprise. It was deep and almost too comfortable for such a formal occasion. She was still settling herself into it when Tess stood up and walked toward her.

'Good morning, Mrs. Doniger,' the veteran ADA said with courtroom cordiality, tempered by an encouraging smile.

'Good morning,' Karen murmured, sitting up straight and folding her hands in her lap.

'To begin at the beginning, tell the court how you came to be working for the defendant's political campaign.'

'One of the things I've done a lot of over the last ten years is move around the country,' Karen replied, remembering to look at the jury as often as possible, as Tess had coached her to do. 'I've never been very political. I mean, I vote, but not for any particular party, only for a candidate if I like what he or she seems to stand for.'

'As many of us do,' Tess murmured.

'I was raised to believe that the United States was the greatest country on earth, but in some of the places I've lived, it would have been impossible not to see that something was going very wrong with the American Dream.'

'An opinion shared by many,' the ADA suggested. 'Please continue.'

'It bothered me a lot, but I didn't really know what I could do about it. After we moved to San Francisco, I became aware that Senator Willmont not only saw what was happening to the country, but believed he knew exactly what to do about it. When he announced his candidacy, I thought – this is something I can do. I can work for someone who understands the problems and might even be able to solve them.'

'So you volunteered at the Willmont campaign headquarters?'

'Yes, two afternoons a week.'

'What did you do there?'

'In the beginning, I stuffed envelopes and ran the Xerox machine and made telephone calls, all the usual volunteer things. But one day, they were rushed for a press release and no one seemed to know what to do, so I just took the material and sat down and wrote something. After that, they started asking me to write more releases and promotional kits, and I even wrote a position paper on hunger. In fact, that's what I was doing when … when … well, that night.'

'Suppose you tell us, for the record, what it is that you do, and why the campaign staff would trust you to write so much of their material.'

'Well, I don't really know if it was a big factor, but I'm the co-author of a number of pictorial books on America. My partner takes the photographs and I write the accompanying poetry. Some of the staff members had seen my books, so I guess they assumed I knew how to write.'

'Your last book, *Tapestry*, was highly acclaimed, wasn't it?'

'Yes, it was,' Karen confirmed. 'It was by far our most ambitious project.'

In the third row on the right side of the spectator section, Nancy smiled, and Ted, sitting beside her, squeezed her hand. Demelza looked over her shoulder and winked.

Meanwhile, Tess had taken several steps back toward the prosecution table before she stopped and turned.

'Mrs. Doniger, how many times have you been married?'

'Once,' Karen replied.

'And how long have you been married to your husband?'

'It will be eleven years this November.'

'Have you ever, during that time, had an affair with another man?'

Even though Tess had prepared her for the question, Karen felt herself color. 'I was thirty-nine years old when I got married, Miss Escalante,' she said with dignity. 'And, unbelievable as it may seem, I never had an affair with another man before my marriage and I have not had one since.'

'A thirty-nine-year-old virgin?' Janice Evans murmured. 'I bet there's one hell of a story in that.'

Beside her, Randy shifted uncomfortably.

'Now, let's turn our attention to the night of April seventh,' Tess suggested. 'Why were you at campaign headquarters so late on that particular evening?'

'I was working on a position paper, the one I mentioned before. The senator had decided to make hunger in America a campaign issue, and he wanted some material ready for a press reception the next day. My daughter was spending the evening with a school friend and my husband was going to be out for dinner, so I was able to stay until I was finished. The senator came in a few minutes before I was ready to leave.'

'Was anyone else there?'

'No. His administrative assistant was there earlier, but she had already gone. I was alone in the office when he arrived.'

'Tell us what happened.'

Karen carefully recounted the details that had led up to her accompanying the senator to the bar across the street.

'How long did you stay at the bar?'

'About two hours, I think. Long enough for each of us to have three Scotches and share a bucket of steamed clams.'

'What did you talk about?'

'We talked about my books, mostly. When we could.'

'What do you mean?'

'Well, the bar was pretty crowded and people wouldn't leave him alone. They kept coming over to the table. But he seemed to take it all in stride, so I guessed it was like that wherever he went.'

'When you could talk, what besides your books did you talk about?'

'He talked about the campaign for a while, about how well it was going, and about how hard it was to have to be on the road so much, and how lonely it was, and how glad he'd be when it was all over.'

'Anything else?'

'I don't remember anything else, specifically.'

'All right, what happened after you left the bar?'

'We went back to the parking garage and got into his car and he started to drive me home. The most direct way to get to my house is to go through the park. That's exactly what we were doing when I got sick.'

'You got sick?'

'Yes. I don't know whether it was the Scotch or the clams or what, but all of a sudden I got sick to my stomach and I asked him to stop the car for a moment.'

'Did he?'

'Well, he said he couldn't do anything on the crossover, but he'd stop the first chance he had. I thought he meant after we left the park, but, when we got to the traffic light, which is less than a block before you come out of the park, he suddenly turned left onto Martin Luther King Drive. I said I had to get out and walk a bit, but he said that if I was going to be sick I should have privacy, so he turned up the little road to

Stow Lake and stopped there.'

Here, Karen paused. Her heart had begun to race and her breath was starting to come in little gasps.

'Would you like to take a brief break before we get to this next part?' Tess invited.

'No, that's all right,' Karen replied, sucking air deep into her lungs. 'I'm okay.'

'Are you sure?'

'Yes,' Karen said more firmly. 'I'd rather keep going. I'd like to get through this before I lose my courage.'

'All right,' Tess agreed. 'Tell us what happened after he stopped the car.'

'I got out and started walking around a bit, taking some deep breaths to settle my stomach, and then there he was, right behind me. I must have jumped a mile. I didn't even realize he'd gotten out of the car.'

'Did he say anything?'

'He asked me if I was going to be sick. I told him if I could just walk around in the fresh air for a minute or two I'd be okay, at least until I got home.'

'Did you?'

'Yes. Then I started back toward the car. He was leaning against the hood. I told him I felt better and I thought it would be okay to go. I opened the car door but he said he was in no hurry and I should give it a little longer, just to make sure. He said his car was still new and I guess he didn't want to take any chances. So I walked around the car a couple of times and then he came up very close behind me. He asked me if I was cold and he took off his jacket and started to put it around me, but I told him I wasn't cold and I sort of moved away a little. But he said I was shivering and he wanted to be sure I stayed warm in case I was coming down with something, and he was right next to me, and when I tried to get away, he ... he grabbed me.'

Nancy felt Ted stiffen in the seat beside her. She slipped her arm through his and held on tight.

Across the aisle, Elizabeth Willmont took a deep breath and thought about taking Adam to the beach.

'Tell us what happened then,' Tess urged softly.

Karen blinked back hot tears. 'I tried to push him away, but he was too strong, and then he kissed me. He said he'd been wanting to do that all evening, and he could tell that I wanted him to. I told him he was wrong, that I was happily married, and that ... I wasn't interested in him in that way, and all I wanted to do was go home. I tried to pull away, but he just laughed and held me tighter. He said he knew a come-on when he saw it, that I'd been flirting with him all night, and just begging for it.'

'Begging for it?'

Karen nodded. 'I told him he was crazy, but I guess that was the wrong thing to say because he sort of went wild. He slapped me so hard that I fell against the car. When I tried to get up, he started yelling that I'd be crazy about him by the time he finished with me, and then he ... he dragged me off the road and threw me down on the ground.'

Tess waited calmly while her witness fumbled around in her purse for a handkerchief and dabbed her eyes.

'We can stop for a bit, if you need to,' she offered, but Karen shook her head. 'All right, then, tell us what happened next.'

In fits and starts, Karen described in agonizing detail how the defendant had torn aside her dress and stripped off her panties, and how he had then forced himself into her. As almost everyone in the courtroom squirmed uncomfortably, she told how he had laughed at her protests, and how she had managed to reach out and scratch him, and how he had reacted by hitting her again and pinning both her hands beneath her.

In his seat two rows behind the defendant, Randy squirmed with the rest of the gallery and tried not to listen to the words that damned the California senator with every syllable. This woman, whom he had first admired through her work, and then liked for her dedication, and now wanted to despise because of her betrayal, was clearly having a devastating effect on the jury, on the entire court. Even the judge looked queasy, and the typically acerbic Janice Evans was silent beside him.

Randy was a closet romantic who had waited until he was forty to fall in love. Raised to respect women, he knew in his soul there was no place for the kind of violence that Karen Doniger was describing. He had no illusions about the world being a perfect place, but he still had some illusions about the people he knew and had chosen to follow.

Robert Willmont could be inconsiderate, Randy knew, and even downright nasty when the situation called for it, but that was a far cry from the vicious animal this woman was making him out to be. He wondered what silent forces had gotten to her with their evil message.

He had offered to testify himself.

'I've known the senator for fifteen years,' he told Hal Sutton. 'No one has been closer to him. Let me tell the jury that he just couldn't do the things they're claiming.'

'Have you spent every minute of every day of those

fifteen years with him?' Sutton asked.

'Well, certainly not *every* minute,' Randy had to admit.

'Then you can't help,' Sutton said kindly but firmly. 'If we need character witnesses, we'll go to one or two of his colleagues in the Senate, or a couple of his supporters on the Supreme Court, or the mayor or the governor or several of his more influential backers here in California. No offense, but I'm sure you understand.'

Randy understood. But it didn't help his anxiety as he squirmed in his seat and steeled his heart against the respectable middle-aged woman who seemed determined to cut his friend and mentor up into a messy pile of pieces.

'I tried to fight him,' Karen was continuing, tears dripping slowly down her cheeks, 'but he was just too strong. I was crying and choking and gasping for breath, and he kept telling me how much he knew I'd enjoy it, and how long he'd been waiting for this opportunity. But I'd only met him a few days before. And then, just as, well, just as he was, you know … concluding, he gave this strange kind of laugh and he said, "It was only a matter of time, Mariah, until you gave me what I wanted."'

Randy Neuburg's head snapped up.

'He called you Mariah?' Tess queried. 'Not Susie or Sally, or even Elizabeth, but Mariah?'

'Yes.' Karen nodded. 'I'm certain. It was Mariah.'

Janice Evans turned to the senator's aide and chuckled. 'Has Bobby been fantasizing about the human iceberg?'

But Randy wasn't amused. He gripped the arms of his chair until his knuckles whitened and a hard knot formed in his stomach. Two rows in front of him, separated from him by a bulletproof wall, Robert Willmont didn't move a muscle.

'Do you know anyone named Mariah, Mrs. Doniger?'

'I believe the senator has an adviser by that name, but I've never met her.'

'An adviser ... I see.' Tess nodded. 'All right. Let's pick up right after he called you Mariah.'

'Well, he kept saying how I'd probably never had it so good before,' Karen said in a choked voice. 'And then he – he said he knew exactly what I wanted next.'

'Did you know what he meant?' Tess asked.

'I didn't at first,' the witness gulped. 'But then I did.'

Under the ADA's guidance, Karen tremulously recounted how the senator had pushed himself into her mouth.

'He said that was the way he liked it best. And he said ... he said he was sure I'd like it just as much as he did.'

On the right side of the gallery, Ted Doniger groaned.

On the left side of the gallery, Elizabeth Willmont barely concealed a gasp.

'What happened then?' Tess asked.

'I gagged,' Karen replied. 'And I guess I must have bitten him or something, because he yelled and pulled away. Then he said he'd teach me to play games like that, and he punched me in the face with his fist. The next thing I remember clearly, a man in a jogging suit was putting his jacket over me.'

'Thank you,' Tess said. 'Well done,' she whispered.

The ADA walked over to the prosecution table and

leaned on it for a moment with her back to Karen. Then suddenly she straightened up and whirled around.

'Mrs. Doniger, did you at any time during that evening, in the garage, at the bar, or in the car, give the defendant any indication that you wanted to have sex with him?'

'No, I did not,' Karen declared. 'You see, I *didn't* want to have sex with him, so why would I have given him any reason to think that I did?'

'You did not consent?'

'No, Miss Escalante, I did not consent.' The response was quick and emphatic.

'You did nothing at all that could possibly have been construed that way?'

'Nothing. Unless having a drink with him and agreeing to let him drive me home means I gave him some kind of implicit permission to do what he did to me.' Karen looked up at the judge and then over at the jury and finally turned her eyes on Tess. 'Did it?'

The seasoned ADA considered her witness for a moment. The question had come as a surprise, but it was perfect.

'No,' she replied. 'I don't believe it did.' Then she, too, took a deliberate moment to look around, at the jury, at the gallery, at the defendant. 'And I would hope that there is no one in this courtroom who does.'

'You did just fine,' Ione said during lunch at Campton Place. 'You answered every question as well as you could, and it was obvious, at least to everyone in the gallery, that you were telling the truth.'

The moment Judge Washington called the noon

break, two deputies had escorted Karen and her entourage out a rear door where Ted had a limousine waiting. They chose the dining room at Campton Place because it was quiet and exclusive and there was no better food to be found in the city. But Karen just picked at her plate.

'Truth is a very elastic thing,' she murmured, 'that can be stretched to mean whatever people need it to mean.'

'I was watching the jury,' Demelza said. 'They were just as appalled as the rest of us.'

'I was watching the defendant,' Jenna said. 'He sat there through the whole thing like he was made of stone.'

'What did you think of Karen Doniger's testimony, Senator?' a reporter called as Robert and his party made their way down the front steps of the Hall of Justice.

'It was quite emotional,' the senator replied calmly, holding his wife's hand, 'quite theatrical, quite calculated, quite inaccurate.'

'Do you have any idea why she's trying to smear you?' someone sympathetic to the candidate inquired.

'She certainly hasn't confided in *me*, if that's what you're asking,' Robert said. 'But I think it's very sad when a woman is as unhappy, as frustrated, and as desperate as she must obviously be to have involved herself in such an outrageous and malicious lie.'

'She sounded awfully convincing.'

'Not to me.'

'What about the jury – do you think they believed her?'

Robert flashed one of his brilliant smiles. 'I think

the jury is smarter than that, don't you?'

'Will your attorney be able to discredit her?'

'For what I'm paying him,' the senator said, chuckling, 'I sincerely hope so.'

But it was a different story, fifteen minutes later, in the Sutton Wells conference room on Front Street.

'She buried me, damn it,' Robert cried, 'and I had to sit there and listen to her do it.'

It was a last-minute strategy session with Sutton and his associates to make sure they were prepared for the afternoon's cross-examination. The candidate insisted on being present at all such meetings.

'I won't lie to you,' Sutton conceded. 'She was a very compelling witness for the prosecution.'

'Compelling? It was an Oscar-winning performance. Can you trip her up?'

Sutton shrugged. 'I'll certainly try. There are a few soft spots in her story that I think we can expose.'

'Why do you think the prosecution quit so soon?'

'I think it was just a clever maneuver to turn our haste back on us,' Sutton replied. 'Escalante was trying to send a message to the jury that her case was so strong, she didn't need to waste time with character witnesses.'

'Is it?' Robert inquired bluntly.

'Let's just say it's not time to worry yet,' Sutton assured him. 'Don't forget that we have a few compelling things on our side. We have your reputation, which, until this little … lapse, has been spotless. We have the Drayton name, which carries enormous weight in this city. And we have the total lack of motive for you to risk your whole career in such a frivolous way. In the final analysis, it won't be evidence or expert witnesses, but credibility, that will decide this case, and

I think it's fairly accurate to say that your credibility in this community is rock solid.'

'Mrs. Doniger,' the Silver Fox inquired as the afternoon session began, 'you said that, on the night in question, you worked late at campaign headquarters to finish a project that the senator needed for the following day; is that correct?'

'Yes,' Karen replied after a three-second pause. Tess had coached her to wait that long before answering, in case the ADA wished to object.

'Were you expecting the senator to return that evening?'

'No, not necessarily.'

'Were you perhaps taking longer on the project than you might have because you were hoping he would return?'

'No.'

'Whose idea was it that your daughter spend the evening with a friend?'

'Hers.'

'Whose idea was it that your husband have dinner out after his meeting?'

'I guess it was mine, but that was only because – '

'So, would it be fair to say,' Sutton interrupted her smoothly, 'that you were prepared, as early as that morning, and before you knew anything at all about the position paper, to stay late at campaign headquarters?'

'No.'

'He's twisting it all around,' Jenna complained. 'He's trying to make it look like she was planning to get raped.'

'That's his job,' Mitch told her.

'The man is just about to earn his fee,' Mary Catherine murmured.

'Returning to your earlier testimony,' Sutton went on, 'you said you were motivated to join the senator's campaign because you believed he might be the only man who could help solve America's problems; is that correct?'

'More or less.'

'Was there any other reason?'

'I don't understand.'

'Well, let me rephrase my question. Did you consider the senator handsome?'

'I suppose he's handsome.'

'Did you find him charming?'

'Yes, he appeared to be charming.'

'Were you curious about the senator personally, what the man behind the politics was really all about?'

'On some level.'

'You were attracted to him, then?'

'Professionally, perhaps. Not personally.'

'Didn't you ever fantasize about what he might be like when he, say, took off his clothes?'

'No.'

'Or what it might be like to have sex with him?'

'No.'

'So, according to your testimony, the senator was handsome, he was charming, you were curious about him, you thought enough of him to spend two days a week working for his election – but you weren't the least attracted to him?'

'No.'

'The man's a genius,' Janice Evans observed.

'Why doesn't the prosecutor object?' Felicity cried.

'To what?' Demelza sighed. 'He has every right to try to discredit her.'

'Let's move on now to the parking garage,' the Silver Fox proposed. 'You claim you couldn't get your car started; is that correct?'

'Yes.'

'You said you were about to look under the hood when the senator came along?'

'Yes.'

'You said you thought he might have followed you?'

'Yes.'

'Were you hoping he would follow you?'

'No.'

'Where was his car parked?'

'Several spaces away from mine.'

'Then is it possible that he was simply going to his own car when he saw you in trouble and offered to help?'

'It's possible.'

'When you couldn't get your car started and the senator graciously offered to take you home, why did you agree?'

'Because he was insistent and I didn't want to appear discourteous.'

'But if you hadn't wanted to go with him, you could have refused and taken a taxi, couldn't you?'

'As I said, I didn't want to appear discourteous.'

'Whose idea was it to go to the bar across the street?'

'To go to a bar was his idea. To go to the one across the street was mine.'

'Do you frequently go to bars with men and drink three Scotches in the course of a two-hour conversation?'

'No.'

'But you did on this particular occasion?'

'Yes.'

'And the next day, after you accused my client of raping you, when your husband had a towing company come to collect your car – what did they find wrong with it?'

'There was a loose wire.'

'Not a dead battery?'

'No.'

'Not a faulty starter?'

'No.'

'Just a loose wire that anyone could have reached under the hood and pulled free – anyone, that is, who might have wanted an excuse to be in the garage when the senator came for his car?'

'I know absolutely nothing about cars, Mr. Sutton,' Karen declared. 'I have no idea how the wire came loose.'

'All right, let's go back to your quite extraordinary statement that you had never had an affair with a man before your marriage. That was your testimony, wasn't it?'

'Yes.'

'A remarkable thing in the 1970s, Mrs. Doniger. You're to be commended. You were practicing safe sex before anyone knew there was a deadly reason to do so, weren't you?'

The gallery tittered.

'Objection, Your Honor,' Tess said in disgust. 'Mr. Sutton's attempt at humor demeans this proceeding.'

'I agree,' the judge snapped, smacking his gavel sharply at the gallery and scowling at the defense attorney.

'Withdrawn,' the Silver Fox demurred. 'During the years of 1969 through 1977, Mrs. Doniger,' he asked instead, 'where were you living?'

'On West Twelfth Street in New York City,' the witness replied.

'Were you at that time familiar with a section of New York known as Greenwich Village?'

'Very familiar. I worked there and I had very good friends who lived there.'

'These friends, did they live on Sullivan Street, by any chance?'

'Yes.'

'Will you please tell the court something about the living arrangements of these friends?'

Karen considered the attorney for a moment. 'Like a great many people at the time,' she said finally, 'and for economic reasons as much as anything else, they had what you would probably call a commune.'

'A commune – where several unmarried people of mixed sexes shared the same apartment?'

'Objection,' Tess called. 'Where's the relevance?'

'Your Honor,' Sutton argued, 'this morning, Mrs. Doniger testified to having had no sexual relationships before her marriage. I'm simply pursuing that line of inquiry.'

'Objection overruled,' Washington said.

'Again, Mrs. Doniger, this particular commune – was it shared by both men and women?'

'Yes.'

'How many men and how many women?'

'Different numbers at different times,' Karen replied. 'The lease was held by a woman who allowed friends with no place else to go to come and stay as long as they liked.'

'Would you describe these friends who came and stayed as having been part of a counterculture? What were commonly referred to as "hippies"?'

'Yes.'

'Did these hippies who came and stayed engage in sexual intercourse with one another?'

'Sometimes.'

'In fact, didn't the bedroom of that apartment contain wall-to-wall mattresses?'

'It was a small apartment. There wasn't enough space for all the separate beds they would have needed.'

On the right side of the gallery, Ione shifted in her seat. 'Where did he get all this?' she hissed.

'From the ex-roommate, I'll bet,' Demelza muttered.

'Or the ex-landlord,' Mitch growled.

Across the aisle, Janice Evans sat forward. 'Maybe not so lily-white, after all,' she murmured.

'But it was quite common for two or three or even four different couples to – er – make intimate use of those mattresses at night?' Sutton pursued like a bloodhound.

'Yes.'

'And, from 1969 to 1977, you visited at the Sullivan Street apartment quite frequently, did you not?'

'I did,' Karen confirmed. 'As I said, they were my friends.'

'And how often would you spend the entire night there?'

'Sometimes once, perhaps twice a week.'

'Once or twice a week – you stayed the night at an apartment where unmarried couples were openly engaging in sexual activities?'

'Yes.'

'And yet you want this court to believe that you never had an affair before your marriage?'

Karen glanced at Tess. A small smile tugged at the corner of the ADA's mouth, but the Silver Fox missed it.

'What made those people so very special to me, Mr. Sutton,' the witness responded serenely, 'and the reason why I spent so much of my time with them, was that they never pressured me into doing anything I didn't want to do.'

'And you want the jury to believe that you spent night after night in a room full of mattresses and never once participated in any of the activities that were going on all around you?'

'The jury doesn't have to believe me,' Karen said. 'Most of the people from Sullivan Street are sitting right there in the gallery. Why don't you ask *them*?'

As though it had been rehearsed, five spectators on the right side of the aisle rose silently to their feet. The jury craned their necks to get a good look at the prosperous-looking middle-aged group.

'I'm sure that won't be necessary,' Sutton murmured as smooth as satin. 'I think the jury already has the picture. Now, suppose we turn to the night in question, the night of April seventh.'

For the rest of the afternoon session, the Silver Fox probed and prodded, searching for ways to exploit a weakness, highlight a contradiction, uncover an inconsistency.

'So,' he concluded at the end of the long day, 'after admitting you considered the senator handsome and charming, after arranging to work late at campaign headquarters that night, after making sure you were in the parking garage when the senator arrived, after suggesting that you go to the bar across the street, after consuming three Scotches, after thinking up an excuse to get the senator to stop his car in a remote part of Golden Gate Park, you still expect this jury to believe that the defendant raped you?'

'Yes, Mr. Sutton,' Karen retorted. 'Because he did.'

'I have nothing more for this witness,' the defense attorney said with a dismissing wave of his hand.

Tess Escalante stood up and addressed the bench. 'The People rest, Your Honor,' she declared.

'Did we make a dent?' the defendant asked after court.

'Hard to say,' Sutton replied in his taciturn way.

Robert sighed. 'Maybe trying to make her out to be some middle-aged, sex-starved groupie wasn't the right approach.'

'Without a clue as to her motive, what other choice did we have?' the attorney argued.

'I know,' the senator conceded. 'I'm just wondering how effective it was.'

'Juries can be hard to read,' Sutton reminded him. 'But don't sell them short. We've planted the right seeds, and as long as there aren't any last-minute surprises, I'm sure some of them will take root.'

'What kind of last-minute surprises?'

'Someone who can corroborate her story in some way.'

Robert gave a short laugh. 'I don't think you need to worry about that. Besides, if the prosecution had unearthed an eyewitness, we would already know about it.'

'Then it's just her word against yours,' Sutton said

agreeably, 'and the jury will hear your word last.'

'You were sensational,' Ted told her that evening. 'So calm and collected. It was almost as though you knew the defense attorney was going to ask about Sullivan Street.'

'I didn't,' Karen admitted, 'but Tess did.'

'He was sure barking up the wrong tree. Trying to make the jury think you set it all up. But I guess if I were the defense, that's exactly what I'd do – see if I could put the jury off-track by giving them other possibilities to think about.'

In Tess's dream, a perfect spring day was marred by the incessant whiz of a bumblebee that hovered around her head. In reality, someone was leaning on the door buzzer of her Russian Hill flat.

Tess opened her eyes and glanced at the clock radio on her nightstand. The ghostly green digits told her it was almost three o'clock. She climbed out of her canopy bed and stumbled toward the door, wrapping her fluffy chenille robe around her as she went.

'Who is it?' she yawned as she pressed the intercom.

'Lamar,' said the box.

Tess pushed the button that would spring the outer release and unlocked her door. 'This had better be good,' she cried when his bulk appeared in the hallway. 'Do you know what time it is?'

'Make some coffee,' the investigator suggested.

He was always amused at the way she lived, in a world of lace and ruffles and 'froufrous,' as his mother used to call them, when her professional facade was so tailored. Neat Victorian sofas and small Edwardian tables and a froth of chiffon at the windows. A company of stuffed animals, fresh flowers, a Persian carpet. She was the complete opposite of the police investigator, who flaunted his outrageous western attire and lived like a Spartan.

'Coffee?' she echoed.

He nodded. 'I want you wide awake for this one.'

It wasn't often that Lamar Pope appeared at her door in the middle of the night. Tess padded into the kitchen. Five minutes later, they were seated in her living room with their hands wrapped around steaming mugs of instant coffee.

'What? You expected percolated on such short notice?' she grumbled when Lamar grimaced over the first gulp. 'Now, tell me why I'm sitting here with you at this ungodly hour when I should be sound asleep so that I can be bright-eyed and bushy-tailed in court at nine o'clock?'

'I'm on to something,' he said, setting his mug down and fumbling in his jacket pocket for his notepad. 'I've been talking to a woman named Margaret Smith of Provo, Utah.'

'So?'

'It seems Mrs. Smith once worked as a secretary for Robert Willmont.' Indeed, he had painstakingly tracked down every female employee of the defendant, from his days at Sutton Wells to the present. 'In 1984, a year and a half into the senator's first term, she claims he raped her and then told her if she ever said a word about it to anyone he'd not only deny it – and who would take her word over his? – but he'd see to it that she never worked in Washington again.'

'Tell me I'm not dreaming,' Tess implored, any idea of returning to sleep forgotten.

'Wait – it gets better,' Lamar declared. 'She says he

then sat down and wrote out a check for two hundred and fifty thousand dollars, right on the spot, and told her it would be good only if she got permanently lost.'

'Two hundred and fifty thousand?' the ADA gasped.

'Yep.'

'So she got permanently lost.'

'You guessed it. But first she went to a hospital. The doctor had to make a report, so of course the police came around. She told them she'd been raped but that she didn't get a good look at her assailant. Hell, between a quarter of a million dollars and little assurance of a successful prosecution, she figured she'd take the money and run.'

Tess shrugged. 'It's beautiful, but it's nothing more than her word against his.'

'Not exactly,' Lamar corrected with a slow smile. 'It seems she took a copy of the hospital record – made up some excuse about needing it for her own doctor, and then, before she cashed the check the senator gave her, she ran it through a li'l ole Xerox machine.'

'She still has it?'

'Yep. Tucked away nice and safe for a rainy day.'

Tess's eyes widened. 'Will she testify?'

Lamar nodded, neglecting to mention the hours it had taken him to persuade her. 'She's been following the trial and she's ready to help you nail the bastard. She's been married the last five years and only just got around to telling her husband what happened. But he's obviously a good guy because he's behind her one hundred percent.'

'Did you check everything out?' Tess asked, hoping she already knew the answer.

'Sure,' Lamar nodded. 'I got onto the hospital in D.C. she said she went to. Don't ask how, but I tracked down the police officer she said she talked to. I called a couple of people I know who were on Capitol Hill around the time. And I just woke up a former congresswoman from Connecticut. I didn't want to come to you until I was sure that everything checked out. As far as I can tell, it does.'

'How soon can she get here?'

'She can be on a plane in the morning.'

There was a shrewd glint in the ADA's black eyes as she considered her options. Lamar could almost see the wheels whirling inside the razor-keen mind.

'No,' she said slowly. 'Call her and tell her to pack her bags but not to come out until Tuesday night. Then tell her to call my office on Wednesday – make sure it's after nine o'clock but before noon – and leave a message for me. Tell her to say something about having information that may pertain to this case.'

'I know that glint,' Lamar observed. 'It means that what you've got in mind may be slightly left of ethical.'

'Just slightly,' Tess conceded. 'Sutton's got a lineup of witnesses that will probably take us through Wednesday, and if he's as smart as I think he is, he'll play his ace last. He's going to count on the senator's charisma to win over the jury, and I'm going to play along. I'm not going to reopen the People's case – I'm going to keep Mrs. Smith for rebuttal.'

Lamar nodded. 'I like it.'

A satisfied smile spread across Tess's face. 'In fact, I'm going to do everything I possibly can to help the good senator put the noose around his own neck.'

seven

Just as Tess had predicted, the defense paraded a staggering array of technical, psychological, and character witnesses past the jury which lasted through the following Tuesday, and included a Harvard pathologist, an Oxford psychiatrist, the mayor of San Francisco, two female members of the House of Representatives, two notable United States senators, a justice of the Supreme Court, and even a famous entertainment personality who had been flown in from Hollywood for the occasion.

The two congresswomen, who testified to having worked closely with the defendant in a number of capacities, described the senator as a dedicated public servant who had never treated them, or any other woman, to their knowledge, with anything but the utmost respect. The Harvard pathologist assured the jury that the mountain of physical evidence presented by the People was not nearly as conclusive as the prosecution believed and was clearly open to other interpretation. On the basis of a twenty-minute interview, the Oxford psychiatrist pronounced the senator emotionally stable, mentally alert, well-focused, and not the least bit inclined to violence.

Tess's cross-examinations were perfunctory.

Finally, on Wednesday morning, Robert Drayton Willmont was called to the stand.

'There is no one in this court, or in this state, or probably even in this country, who doesn't know who you are, Senator Willmont,' Hal Sutton began. 'But I think it would be appropriate for you to tell the jury something about the man behind the public face.'

'I'd be happy to,' Robert replied.

And so the first hours of the defendant's long-awaited testimony were spent in congenial commentary about his background, his family, his work, his personal values. He wasted little time in telling the jury that he was a devoted son, a proud father, and a loving husband.

'I've been my mother's strength and support ever since my father died,' he said. 'I still tuck her up in bed at night every chance I get.'

In the gallery, Amanda Drayton Willmont wagged her head in agreement.

'My boy Adam is going into eighth grade in September,' Robert boasted. 'He's already almost as tall as I am – and at least twice as smart.'

Sitting beside her mother-in-law, Elizabeth Willmont wondered where he had found the time to notice.

'My wife and I are going to celebrate our silver wedding anniversary in October,' he said brightly. 'She's given me twenty-five wonderful years and the best home a man could ask for – and I'm afraid I was ingenuous enough to promise her the White House in return.'

A faint ripple of amusement ran through parts of the gallery. A faint smile was all Elizabeth could muster.

'My family has always meant everything to me,' Robert expanded. 'Elizabeth, especially. It's true what they say, you know, about there being a smart women behind every successful man. I've been exceedingly fortunate. Elizabeth and I are very close. We understand and respect each other. We discuss every important decision before I make it, we examine every action before I take it. She's my motivation, my inspiration. Without her behind me, believing in me, supporting me, I would probably still be an associate in my father's law firm.'

With a palsied hand, Amanda reached over to pet the daughter-in-law she had always resented.

Next, Robert praised his elementary and high school teachers, proclaimed his good luck to have attended the two finest universities in the country, waxed eloquent about his decade and a half in public service, and then spoke at length about his decision to run for President.

'I believe in America,' he declared. 'I believe in an America where people will work together to ensure that the greed of today doesn't impoverish the children of tomorrow. An America where the middle class can have a fair shake instead of always being made to bear the burden of the rich and the profligate. Even though I was born into money – no, *because* I was born into money – I was not only able to see where many of the problems were coming from, I could see practical ways to fix them. And it was clear to me that only as President of the United States would I have a real opportunity to implement my solutions.'

'He's making a goddamn campaign speech,' Mitch grumbled. '"Forget that I raped a woman, folks. I'll put money back in your pockets."'

By the time the Silver Fox elicited the desired response to a final preliminary question, Judge Washington was ready to call for the noon break.

'Clever,' Tess observed to Anne Jenks. 'Sutton is going to make very sure that his direct examination doesn't end until we adjourn for the day. That way, the jury will get to take the defendant's uncontested words to bed with them.'

'Why didn't you object to all that irrelevant patting himself on the back he was doing?' her assistant asked.

But Tess just smiled. 'Because I want the senator to have every possible opportunity to hang himself.'

'Will he?'

'He already has,' the ADA replied serenely. 'Oh, by the way,' she added, almost as an afterthought, 'notify Judge Washington's clerk at the end of court today that we might be presenting a rebuttal witness.'

'I can take care of that right now, if you like,' the efficient staff assistant offered.

'No,' Tess said firmly. 'At the end of court today.'

The afternoon session began promptly at one-thirty.

'Will you tell the court, in your own words, Senator,' Sutton requested without further preamble, 'what really took place on the night of April seventh?'

Robert turned toward the jury with a look of sincere regret etched into his handsome face, and throughout his recital the aquamarine eyes fastened on first one and then another of the five men and seven women who would be deciding his fate.

'I came home to San Francisco at the beginning of April to make some speeches, to raise some money, and to get out among you, and listen to what you had to say,' he began. 'After three very strenuous months of campaigning, I found myself physically, mentally, and emotionally drained. This city is where I was born and raised, it has always been the fountain of my strength, and it will always be the place I'll come home to.'

Here, he took a deep breath and slowly let it out.

'On April seventh, a woman from San Jose asked me why this country destroys so much of the food it produces when there are Americans who go to bed hungry every night. I'm ashamed to say I didn't have a very good answer. But I decided, then and there, that our agribusiness policy had to change. We talk a lot about the sad state of the economy and health care and education, but we are all suddenly silent when the conversation turns to a child crying in the night because his stomach is empty, or an old man sleeping on a park bench because he has no place else to go.'

The jury shifted a bit under the direct aquamarine gaze.

'I realized that these issues could no longer be shoved under a rug and I directed my staff to prepare a start-up document that I could use as the basis for serious change.'

'Someone should tell him he's already won the California primary,' Mitch muttered.

'Look at that,' Janice Evans murmured to Randy. 'He's got the jury by the tits and balls.'

'I returned from San Jose at about eight o'clock that

evening and made the unfortunate mistake, as it turned out, of letting my security people go. They'd been working very hard and I thought they deserved a break. It was afterward that I decided to go down to the office to get a look at the press material my staff had prepared.'

He reasoned it wasn't necessary to mention that his mother had already retired for the evening and the big house on Jackson Street was empty and depressing.

'Mrs. Doniger was at the office and she had obviously spent a great deal of time putting the information together. On the spur of the moment, I invited her out for a drink as a simple expression of appreciation. When she refused, I didn't argue. I took a copy of the packet she had prepared, read through it to make sure it was accurate and complete, put it in my briefcase, and left.'

'Were you aware that Mrs. Doniger had already left the office?' Sutton inquired.

'Yes,' Robert replied. 'She had said good night, and asked me to lock the door on my way out.'

'Did you go directly to the parking garage?'

'Yes, I did.'

'For what purpose?'

'For the purpose of getting into my car and going home.'

'What did you find when you reached the garage?'

'I found Mrs. Doniger having trouble with her car.'

Robert's account of the following few moments did not differ substantially from the testimony Karen had given.

'What happened then?'

'We went to a bar across the street for a drink.'

'She seemed in no hurry to get home?'

'No.'

'And how did she seem at the bar?'

'She was very animated and she seemed quite impressed by all the people who stopped by the table to wish me well. She laughed a lot and I remember she brushed her leg against mine several times.'

'Did this continue once you left the bar?'

'No. As I recall, she didn't have very much to say at all, once we were in the car. She sat very close to the door. Then, as we were crossing the park, she suddenly said she was sick and asked me to stop the car. I was driving in the left-hand lane and I couldn't very well stop in the middle of the road, so I said I'd pull over as soon as we were out of the park. But she said she couldn't wait that long.'

'She said she couldn't wait until you left the park?'

Robert nodded. 'I thought she was going to be sick any second, so I did the only thing I could. I turned left onto King Drive. I was about to stop the car when she said that, if she was going to be sick, she wanted more privacy, so would I please drive on a little further. When I came to the road that goes up to Stow Lake, she told me to turn there. I must have driven several hundred yards before she said it was all right to stop.'

'*She* asked *you* to drive up to Stow Lake?'

'Yes, she did,' Robert asserted with a sincere glance at the jury. 'Then she got out of the car and dis-appeared. I waited for perhaps five minutes, and then, when she didn't come back, I naturally got a little worried, so I got out and went to look for her. She was over by some bushes and she looked like she was shivering, so I took off my jacket and put it around her. But then she laughed and said she wasn't cold, the fresh air had fixed her up just fine, and it was such a great night, she thought it would be fun to go for a walk around the lake.'

'A walk around the lake?'

'That's what she said. I said that sounded nice but I really had to get home and I started back to the car. But just as I got there she comes flying out of the dark and she's all over me – she actually had me pinned against the hood. And she starts telling me how she's been dreaming of this moment ever since she first saw me, and that she just couldn't stand it any longer, to see me and not be able to have me, and no one ever had to know, it would stay between the two of us because she wouldn't want her husband to find out any more than I would want my wife to.'

'Are you telling this court that Mrs. Doniger approached *you*?' Sutton asked slowly, deliberately. 'Suggested intimacy to *you*?'

'Approached me? She attacked me,' Robert declared. 'I swear to God – and this court – it was all her idea.'

'But you didn't resist?'

The senator sighed deeply. 'I wish I could say I did. How I wish I had. But no, after my initial surprise, I didn't resist. I'm not normally much of a drinker and I'd had three highballs, I was exhausted and I hadn't slept in days. No, I'm ashamed to say, I didn't resist. She dragged me off into the bushes – she was like a tiger, ripping at her clothes, tugging at mine. And she kept crying things like "Hurt me, hurt me," and "The rougher you do it, the better I like it." Then she scratched me down the chest to prove the point. And all the time she was moaning and groaning and saying things like "You're irresistible. You're incredible. You're fantastic. I've never had it so good."'

'Can you believe this garbage?' Ione hissed.

'Anyone who knows Karen knows how ridiculous it is,' Jenna retorted.

'Sure,' Demelza observed. 'But the jury doesn't know Karen.'

Janice Evans leaned toward Randy. 'I can certainly testify to the senator's irresistibility.'

'What happened then, Senator?' Sutton pressed.

'I ... well ... I wasn't able to respond very well at first, because of the fatigue and the Scotch and all, but she said she knew how to get me going, and then she started performing oral sex on me.'

Here, Sutton urged his client to provide explicit details, while the jury shifted in their seats, the women trying not to look too embarrassed, the men trying not to look too interested.

'After a while,' Robert concluded with a properly chagrined expression, 'what she was doing began to work and I achieved an erection. As soon as that happened, she said something like "Great, let's go!" But she wasn't exactly as ready as she led me to believe.'

'What do you mean?' the Silver Fox inquired.

The witness replied in even more graphic detail. The jury continued to look uncomfortable. So did the senator.

'I tried to tell her it wasn't working, but she wrapped her legs around me and wouldn't let me stop. Finally, I managed to penetrate her and then, before I knew it, well, it was over.'

'You climaxed?'

'Yes.'

'Did she?'

'She may have – I don't know. I don't think so.'

'Was she upset by your ... quickness?'

'She didn't seem to be. I apologized, rather profusely, as I recall, but she just smiled and said it was exactly how she expected it to be.'

'Then what?'

'I got up and put on my clothes and said it was time to go, but she didn't move. She said she thought she'd stay for a while and maybe take that walk around the lake. I told her it was getting late, but she said she didn't want to see her husband just yet, or maybe she didn't want him to see her, I don't know. I explained that I couldn't wait around, I had to get home. But she waved me away and said it was all right, she would find a taxi when she was ready. I tried to argue with her, I really did. I even tried to grab her to force her into the car, but she pulled away from me. I mean, I didn't want to leave her there all by herself in the park in the middle of the night, but she wouldn't listen. She just ran off. I tried to find her, but she was either gone or hiding. So, finally, I got into my car and left.'

'A real gentleman,' Felicity drawled.

'He never apologized to *me* for coming too fast,' Janice muttered under her breath.

'Senator Willmont,' Sutton continued, 'you saw People's exhibits sixty-six through seventy-two, the photographs taken of Mrs. Doniger when she was admitted to the hospital on the morning of April eighth. I ask you now, under oath, are you responsible for the injuries depicted in those photographs?'

'No, I am not,' Robert stated emphatically. 'She encouraged me to be rough with her, she said that was the way she liked it, but I never did any of those other things.'

'She looked perfectly all right when you got into your car and drove away?'

'Well, her clothing was torn a bit, mostly by her own doing, I might add, and there may have been a few bruises on her arms and legs, but that was all.'

'Then how do you account for what we saw in those seven photographs?'

'I can't. It was horrible, how she looked, all beat up that way. But I swear she didn't look anything like that when I left her.' Here, Robert turned and faced the jury. 'I made a mistake, I admit it. Unfortunately, it was a big mistake, and I'll spend the rest of my life regretting it. But I'm not a sadist, I'm not a maniac, I'm not a pervert – why would I do such a thing to anyone?'

'Senator Willmont, did you rape Karen Doniger?'

'No, I did not,' Robert replied, again looking straight at the jury. 'I engaged in consensual sex with her – at her suggestion – no, at her insistence.'

'Did you, in the course of that intimacy, beat her, slap her, punch her, and leave her, barely conscious, in Golden Gate Park?'

'No, I did not beat her, slap her, or punch her, and she was fully conscious when she insisted that I leave her in Golden Gate Park.'

'Do you know of any reason why Karen Doniger would claim that you did these things to her?'

'No,' Robert admitted. 'She seemed like a very nice person. Maybe she was afraid to tell her husband the truth. Maybe she was being manipulated by some political group. I don't know. But I do know that she lied to this court. I'm a candidate for President of the United States, for God's sake. Why would I deliberately risk destroying my chances of being elected by raping and beating a volunteer worker on my own staff? It just doesn't make any sense.'

'Thank you, Senator,' Hal Sutton said. 'I have nothing more.'

'Ready?' Janice Evans called.

She stood on the steps in front of the Hall of Justice, straightening her skirt and buttoning her jacket, and then running a quick hand over her hair to smooth it down in the gusting wind.

'Ready,' the Minicam operator replied.

'Ready,' the engineer echoed.

'Okay, roll.'

The cameraman hit the button.

'I'm standing in front of the Hall of Justice here in San Francisco,' Janice said in her best on-air voice, 'where not just the fate of Robert Drayton Willmont is going to be decided, but perhaps the fate of America, as well. A few short months ago, the remarkable senator was a rising political star, streaking toward a first-ballot nomination. Now, rather than the voters, his political career will depend on just five men and seven women who, very soon now, must choose a side in what is perhaps the most celebrated he-said/she-said controversy of our time.'

She began to walk slowly down the steps, into the camera.

'But whose side will they take? That's the question that has the entire country glued to the evening newscasts and embroiled in endless arguments. No cameras have been allowed inside Judge Oliver Wendell Washington's courtroom, and the outside world has heard only filtered accounts of the proceedings from those who are witnessing this high drama. I've been sitting in the gallery, peering through the ominous bulletproof shield that separates the spectators from the participants, trying to separate fact from fiction. It's a monumental task, and as each day unfolds, I wonder, more and more, how the jury will be able to do it.'

Janice stopped at the bottom of the steps.

'Okay, that's a wrap for here,' she told her crew. 'Let's pack up and get over to Jackson Street.'

'I've never heard such a load of crap,' Mitch declared in the cab they had squeezed themselves into to get over to Campton Place. 'Not even back when the politicians were still trying to defend being in Vietnam.'

'And the jury was just eating it all up,' Felicity said.

'Because, deep down in their hearts, they want to believe him,' Demelza observed. 'They want any excuse to acquit him.'

'The sad truth is,' Ione commented with a sigh, 'you don't have to know how to govern to get elected in this country – you just have to know how to lie.'

The senator sat next to his wife on a rich leather sofa in the dignified Willmont library that had been his father's favorite room, the unblinking television lights illuminating every wrinkle, every blemish.

'One might be able to fool a live audience,' he said wryly, 'but it's impossible to lie to a camera, isn't it?'

'Were you thinking of lying?' Janice asked from the sofa facing him.

'No,' he replied simply. 'I was just wondering why so many people think they can get away with it.'

The newswoman crossed her ankles, licked her lips,

and nodded to the half dozen technicians.

'The last time we spoke, Senator Willmont,' she began in her on-air voice, 'you were planning for your future to be decided by the majority of voters in this country. How do you feel now – about it being decided by a handful?'

'Sad,' Robert said thoughtfully. 'Sad for my family and sad for America, that such an outrageous charge was allowed to be brought into court in the first place. But I also feel confident – confident that this jury is not going to let itself be taken in by so blatant an attempt to smear me.'

'Then you think you'll be acquitted of all charges?'

'I believe in the system,' the senator replied. 'I believe that the innocent are protected under the law. I believe the jury will exonerate me.'

'Even though your story of being attacked like a tiger by a middle-aged woman half your size sounds awfully far-fetched?'

'But that's the whole point, isn't it?' Robert exclaimed earnestly. 'The truth is too bizarre for me to have made it up. If I were going to lie my way out of this, I assure you I would have come up with something a lot more plausible.'

'If you are acquitted,' Janice observed, 'you will in all likelihood receive the nomination for President. Do you think you'll be elected in November?'

Robert considered for a moment. 'I think so, yes,' he said with the confidence of a man who has never learned to accept rejection.

'Even though you're a confessed adulterer?'

'I believe I may be elected in part *because* I confessed, because I didn't deny it or try to lie to the people. I came right out and admitted my mistake, whopper though it was. There are precious few perfect people in this world, Miss Evans, and I'm obviously not one of them. There'll be some pure souls who will feel they have to turn away from me, but I hope that most of the people will respect me for being honest about my imperfections.'

'If you are acquitted, will you sue Karen Doniger for character defamation?'

'Why?' Robert sighed. 'The verdict is all that matters to me. I have no interest in humiliating the woman or her family any further. My only hope is that they use whatever money I would have won from them in a lawsuit to get her the psychiatric help she so desperately needs.'

eight

'Senator Willmont,' Tess began on Thursday morning, the thirteenth day of the trial, 'I would like to go back over certain portions of your testimony from yesterday, if you don't mind.'

'I don't mind, Miss Escalante,' the senator responded with a pleasant, confident smile.

'Beginning with your glowing tribute to your marriage.'

Robert produced a boyish grin. 'I could probably talk forever on that subject.'

'I don't think forever will be necessary,' Tess replied. 'I'm interested only in the basics of your relationship with your wife. You testified yesterday that you and she discuss every decision before you make it and examine every action before you take it; is that correct?'

'Yes, I said that. Yes, it's correct.'

'Did you and your wife discuss your having sex with Karen Doniger before you had it?'

'Well, no, of course not,' Robert replied. 'As I said, it was a spur-of-the-moment thing.'

'Does that mean you would have discussed it with her had it not been a spur-of-the-moment thing?'

The senator sighed. 'Had I stopped to think about what I was doing that night, Miss Escalante, I wouldn't have done it. So there would have been nothing to discuss.'

'Does that mean you and your wife have discussed your intent to commit adultery on less impulsive occasions?'

'Objection,' Sutton called. 'What does it matter what he does or doesn't discuss with his wife?'

'Your Honor,' Tess argued, 'the defendant testified that he discusses everything with his wife before the fact. I'm simply trying to determine if he was telling the truth when he made that statement.'

'Your client opened the door himself, Counselor.' Judge Washington sighed. 'Objection overruled. But you're skating on thin ice, Miss Escalante. Be careful.'

'Yes, sir,' Tess agreed, returning to the witness. 'One more time, sir: Have you ever discussed with your wife your intent to commit adultery?'

'I was referring, of course, to political issues when I made that statement.'

'Then the decision of whether to commit adultery is not one you discuss with your wife, but one you make on your own?'

'I don't think that's what I said.'

'I beg your pardon,' Tess said politely. 'What did you say?'

'I said this was an isolated incident,' Robert retorted.

'By "isolated," do you mean that it was the only time

you had committed adultery, or the only time you didn't have the opportunity to discuss it beforehand with your wife?'

'You're twisting my words,' the witness objected.

'I certainly wouldn't want to do that, Senator,' Tess murmured. 'So, let me rephrase my question. Have you ever discussed infidelity with your wife?'

'There has never been cause,' Robert Willmont declared.

'What does that mean, Senator? Are you testifying that, aside from your untimely encounter with Karen Doniger, you have never been unfaithful to your wife?'

'I'm saying that I made a mistake, Miss Escalante. One I will regret for the rest of my life. I hurt my wife, I embarrassed my family, and I disappointed a lot of good people who believe in me. I can't begin to say how sorry I am.'

'For what, Senator?' the ADA inquired. 'Are you sorry you raped Karen Doniger – or just sorry you got caught?'

'Objection!'

'Miss Escalante,' the judge admonished.

'I withdraw the question, Your Honor,' the ADA conceded. 'Prior to the night of April seventh, Senator Willmont, had you ever been unfaithful to your wife?'

'Objection!' Sutton complained. 'Prosecution is badgering the witness.'

'Your Honor,' Tess argued, 'this man has painted himself into a Norman Rockwell example of marital devotion and we seek only to confirm or deny its validity. The defense tried its best to portray Karen Doniger as a counterculture nutcase who hunted down the defendant like a predatory animal for no apparent reason. Shouldn't I be allowed the same opportunity to suggest that Robert Willmont is a man of insatiable appetite who wants what he wants, and is not above taking what he wants, by force, if necessary?'

'She has a point, Counselor,' Washington suggested. 'Besides, you could have made a pre-trial motion to exclude prior behavior. You didn't.'

'Because it wasn't necessary, Your Honor,' the Silver Fox explained. 'Everyone knows that the senator is above reproach.'

'Then your client has nothing to worry about, does he?' the judge declared. 'Objection overruled.'

'Prior to April seventh, Senator,' Tess repeated, 'had you ever been unfaithful to your wife?'

Randy Neuburg and Mary Catherine O'Malley exchanged worried glances, Janice Evans slid an inch or two lower in her seat, and Elizabeth Willmont sat frozen, afraid that her carefully composed mask might crack.

Across the aisle, the Sullivan Street set held their collective breaths, and those on both sides of the gallery leaned forward just a little so as not to miss a syllable.

'I have a beautiful and loving wife,' Robert replied. 'Prior to April seventh, I had no cause to be unfaithful to her.'

A sibilant sigh floated across the courtroom.

'That was slick,' Randy murmured.

'The man's a born politician,' Mary Catherine agreed.

'He didn't answer the question,' Felicity protested.

'You noticed,' Demelza observed.

'Hardly a direct response, Senator,' Tess suggested. 'But then, I suppose we'll have to chalk it up to your having been in Washington for so long.'

'Your Honor!' Sutton complained.

The ADA shrugged. 'Sorry.'

'Don't abuse the court's tolerance, Miss Escalante,' the judge suggested.

'I'll try not to, Your Honor,' Tess acquiesced, pausing a beat. 'Who is Mariah?' she asked the defendant suddenly.

Randy held his breath.

Robert stiffened slightly. 'If you mean Mariah Dobbs,' he replied carefully, 'she's a media consultant.'

'Someone you've had, or hoped to have, an affair with?'

'Certainly not.'

'I see – she's just someone whose name you happened to cry out at the height of passion, for no particular reason?'

'Your Honor!' the Silver Fox complained.

'Yes, Mr. Sutton,' Washington agreed. 'Move on, Miss Escalante.'

'Yes, sir,' Tess conceded. She took two casual steps away from the defendant. 'Not including April seventh, Senator Willmont,' she asked in a clear voice, 'how many other women have you raped?'

'Objection!' the defense attorney exclaimed.

'It's all right,' Robert declared, forestalling the judge. 'I don't mind answering the question. *Including* April seventh, Miss Escalante – none.'

'None, Senator?' Tess parried. 'You mean that you never in your life had to force a woman to have sex with you? They all came to you willingly?'

'I believe they did,' the witness replied. 'I wasn't exactly a monk before my marriage. Like most young men, I sowed my share of wild oats, and I assure you that the lovely young ladies in question, who shall naturally forever remain nameless, were all quite willing.'

'They all freely participated in consensual sex, just as you claim Karen Doniger did?'

'Yes,' Robert assured her. 'They did – just as Mrs. Doniger did.'

'To sum up then, Senator: Prior to April seventh, you had never been unfaithful to your wife and, to the best of your knowledge, you have never raped a woman. Is that your testimony?'

'It is.'

Tess smiled, the slow smile of a cat who has cornered a mouse.

In the gallery, Randy frowned uneasily.

The ADA spent the rest of her cross-examination going over the details of the night of April seventh, but her questions were now mostly routine. She already had everything she needed. The rest was just for window dressing.

'How long did you stay at campaign headquarters after Karen Doniger left?'

'I'd say about fifteen minutes.'

'And you said that, while you were there, you read the promotional packet she had prepared?'

'Yes.'

'How large was that packet?'

'Perhaps twenty pages.'

'Would it surprise you to know that the packet in fact contained almost forty pages?'

'I guess it could have.'

'Are you a speed reader, Senator?'

'No, but I can scan pretty quickly when I know what I'm looking for.'

'So it is your testimony that you spent about fifteen minutes in the office, reading, after Karen Doniger left?'

'Yes.'

'Were you in any particular hurry to leave?'

'I was tired, but not in any particular hurry.'

'Not too tired to invite Mrs. Doniger out for a drink?'

'That was a spur-of-the-moment gesture.'

'Yes, so you said. So, even though you weren't rushing to get anywhere, you scanned almost forty pages of what you yourself considered to be a vital document and still managed to be at the parking garage in time to help Karen Doniger with her car?'

'I had no way of knowing she would still be there.'

'What would you say if I told you that the log in the lobby of your office building lists Karen Doniger as having signed out at eight-twenty-five that evening, and lists you as having signed out at eight-twenty-nine?'

'I would say that I don't recall what time it was. In fact, I don't normally sign the log at all.'

Tess picked up a thick ledger and approached the bench.

'Your Honor, at this time, I would like to introduce into evidence People's exhibit seventy-five, the log book from the building where the Willmont campaign offices are located.'

Sutton jumped up and came over to authenticate.

'No objection,' he sighed. The log was genuine. His own signature was featured prominently on many of the pages.

'So entered,' Washington said.

'You're correct about not signing the log that night,

Senator,' Tess said. 'The doorman has become accustomed to doing it for you, and I'm prepared to call him as a rebuttal witness, if necessary.'

The defendant and his attorney exchanged glances.

'In the interests of time, Your Honor, defense will stipulate,' the Silver Fox said.

'In that case,' Tess continued, 'kindly read to the jury the first entry pertaining to you on the night of April seventh.'

'It says that I arrived at eighteen minutes past eight.'

'And the second entry?'

'It says I left the building at eight twenty-nine.'

'So, according to this log, and even assuming you took the express elevator to the twelfth floor, you could not have remained in the office, reading, for fifteen minutes after Karen Doniger left, could you?'

'I guess not,' Robert conceded.

'In fact, you left immediately after her, didn't you? Probably by the very next elevator.'

'I wasn't really paying attention. I certainly wasn't following her, if that's what you're getting at.'

'No, of course not,' Tess murmured, taking the log from him and placing it on the evidence table.

'How tall are you, Senator?'

'Six feet two.'

'How much do you weigh?'

'About two hundred and fifteen pounds.'

'Would you say you were in good physical shape?'

'Fairly good. As good as a candidate on the road six days out of seven can be, anyway.'

'And yet you say that a five-foot-six-inch, one-hundred-and-ten-pound woman pinned you against the hood of your car?'

'Yes.'

'You then say that this unbelievably strong, although small, woman dragged you into the bushes and demanded that you perform sexual acts on her and abuse her in the process?'

'Yes.'

'And you obliged her?'

'I'm not proud of it, but yes, I had sex with her.'

'And you bruised her?'

'She begged me to be rough with her. I may have bruised her slightly.'

'Slightly? You consider a black eye, a broken nose, and a split lip that took seven stitches slight?'

'I don't recall doing any of those things.'

'And you also claim she scratched you, and that it was from passion and not an attempt to fight you off?'

'Yes.'

'And these scratches, were they hard enough to dig into the skin on your chest and cause actual bleeding?'

'Yes.'

'Did it hurt?'

'I suppose it did.'

'Yet you did nothing about it? You didn't cry out, you didn't protest, you didn't slap her, you didn't pin her hands beneath her to keep her from doing it again?'

'No.'

'You just went right on doing whatever it was you were doing?'

'Yes.'

'And after you had this consensual sex, you simply got into your car and left her there, in the middle of Golden Gate Park, in the middle of the night, with her clothes in shreds, her nose and lip bleeding and no visible means of getting home?'

'I never saw any blood,' Robert protested. 'And I would have taken her home. I didn't want to leave her there. She insisted.'

'She needed medical attention, she was practically naked, her purse was in your car so she had no money for a taxi, or even a telephone call, and yet you want this jury to believe that she insisted on staying where she was?'

'I know it sounds crazy now, but yes, she did.'

At ten minutes after two in the afternoon, Tess finished her cross-examination of the defendant and returned to her seat with a nod to Lamar Pope, who stood at the rear of the courtroom.

'Senator Willmont,' Hal Sutton redirected, 'did you rape Karen Doniger on the night of April seventh?'

'No,' Robert declared. 'I did not.'

'The defense rests,' the Silver Fox said.

'Miss Escalante?' Judge Washington inquired.

Tess stood up. 'The People have one rebuttal witness, Your Honor. We call Margaret Smith to the stand . . .'

Sutton looked at his client. The senator shrugged and shook his head.

'. . . Margaret Holden Smith.'

In the second row of the gallery, Randy and Mary Catherine looked at each other in surprise. At the defense table, Robert Willmont blanched.

'Stop her,' he hissed at his attorney. 'Whatever you have to do, stop her.'

'Uh – may we approach, Your Honor?' Sutton cried, jumping quickly to his feet.

Washington nodded and covered his microphone with one hand as he gestured the two attorneys forward with the other.

'What is it, Mr. Sutton?'

'Defense has had no prior notification of this witness. The name does not appear on any of the lists we received. We object to her testimony being presented.'

Tess swallowed a smile. 'I apologize for the short notice, Your Honor, but I wasn't even contacted by Mrs. Smith until yesterday, after court had begun. As soon as possible, after receiving her message, I had my associate notify your clerk about the existence of a potential rebuttal witness. But, until I had the opportunity to interview her in person, which wasn't until late last night, I couldn't be sure her information was relevant.'

'The assistant district attorney is correct, Counselor,' Washington concurred. 'We did receive notification. She did follow procedure.'

'Then, at the very least, Your Honor, I would want a continuance,' the Silver Fox argued, entirely unsure of his footing, 'until defense has had the opportunity to take the witness's deposition and then has had time to study it and conduct a thorough investigation of its own.'

'And just how long would you anticipate this taking, Counselor?' the judge asked.

'I would think it might take two or three weeks at a minimum,' Sutton estimated.

'Somehow, that's what I thought you'd say.' Washington sighed. 'Miss Escalante?'

'It's July the second, Your Honor. Even two weeks would put us past the convention, and I seem to recall that the reason I had barely two months to prepare for this case was because defense wanted a resolution before July thirteenth.'

'She has a point, Counselor,' the judge acknowledged.

'May I have a moment to confer with my client, Your Honor?' the defense attorney requested.

Washington nodded.

Tess kept her face carefully blank.

'What the hell is going on?' Sutton demanded with his lips to his client's ear. 'I'm operating blind here. Just how far do you really want me to go with this?'

'As far as you have to,' Robert declared.

'We're not going to be able to exclude this witness's testimony. Escalante went by the book. The best we can get is a continuance that will take us past the convention. What can this Margaret Smith do to you?'

Robert looked at his attorney for a moment. 'She can bury me,' he said.

'My client seeks a continuance, Your Honor,' Sutton said, returning to the bench.

'In chambers,' declared Washington, advising the jury and sweeping from the courtroom. 'Now, what's this all about?' he demanded as soon as the door had closed.

'The senator realizes that a continuance will take us past the convention,' explained Sutton, 'but he feels his rights would otherwise be compromised.'

'What have you got, Miss Escalante?' asked the judge.

'The senator said, under oath, that prior to April seventh he had never been unfaithful to his wife and had never in his lifetime raped anyone,' Tess responded. 'Mrs. Smith is prepared to rebut both statements.'

'Hearsay,' snapped Sutton.

'Not exactly,' corrected the ADA. She turned to the judge. 'I believe you know me better than that, Your Honor. I've never had a case come back on me.'

The judge nodded slowly.

'Besides,' Tess continued, 'had I had the proper length of time to prepare my case, defense would have had all the time necessary to prepare its cross.'

Washington sighed. 'Both the district attorney's office and my office did everything in their power to expedite this trial, Counselor,' he told Sutton, 'in order to get you the speedy resolution you not only requested, but demanded. So I'm not particularly inclined to grant you any lengthy delay. But I'll tell you what I *will* do – I'll allow Miss Escalante to present her witness and then, if you wish to take the long weekend to prepare your cross-examination, you may do so. However, I intend to have this case wrapped up and sent to jury by the middle of next week. Do I make myself clear?'

'Yes, Your Honor,' both attorneys replied.

'Then let's get on with it.'

'You can't let her testify,' Robert hissed when Sutton returned to the courtroom and resumed his seat.

'I can't stop her,' the Silver Fox hissed back. 'But we have the weekend to plan a rebuttal.'

Maggie Holden Smith, looking even lovelier than Randy and Mary Catherine remembered, walked to the witness stand and took the oath.

'Mrs. Smith,' Tess began, 'will you tell the court how you came to be acquainted with the defendant?'

'I worked as a secretary in Senator Willmont's office

in Washington, D.C., from January to June of 1984,'
the rebuttal witness said in a naturally husky voice.

'Did you enjoy working there?'

'For the most part. The job was exciting, the pace
was incredible, and there were really important
people coming and going all the time that, before
then, I had only read about in newspapers or seen
on television.'

'This was important to you?'

'I graduated Brigham Young University with a degree in political science and all I wanted to do was
work in Washington. I was twenty-two years old and full
of ideals, and this was my first exposure to the world of
power and politics.'

'You said you liked your job, for the most part. What
part of the job didn't you like?'

'I didn't like it much when the senator was there.'

'Why not?'

'Because he used to hang around my desk a lot,
making comments that embarrassed me.'

'What sort of comments?'

'Oh, things like how distracting I was to have
around, or how he wished he were single when he
looked at me, or how he could be arrested for what he
was thinking when I walked across the room. Things
like that.'

'Did you take these remarks seriously?'

'I thought he was probably kidding, but it made me
very uncomfortable anyway.'

'Did you discuss how you felt with Senator Willmont? Did you ask him to stop?'

'Heavens, no. I was just a kid, all on my own in the
big city, and I really needed my job. I was afraid if I said
anything to him I might get fired. But after a while I

got up enough courage to tell his administrative assistant. She said that was just the way he was and I should try not to let it bother me. But she must have seen how upset I was because she promised she would talk to him. I guess she did because he stopped doing it for a while.'

In the gallery, Mary Catherine nodded slowly. She remembered the lovely young woman almost in tears, and the senator's shrugging off her remonstrations with a laugh.

'Then what happened?'

'About a month or so later, it started again, only it got worse. Even though I wasn't his personal secretary, he would ask me to bring him coffee or files or something, and then when I came into his office he would stare me up and down. He said he'd like it better if I wore low-cut clothes because it would show off my bosom, and he wished miniskirts were still in style so he could see more of my legs.'

'When the senator made these remarks, weren't you able to just laugh them off?'

'I come from a very conservative, very religious family, Miss Escalante, where making remarks about such matters just isn't considered decent. He made me feel like I had no value as a person, and it was humiliating.'

'What did you do?'

'I started looking for another job.'

'Did you find one?'

'I had a final interview with a congresswoman from Connecticut scheduled for the third Wednesday in June. She really liked me and I think I would have gotten the job.'

'Your Honor, I fail to see any relevance in a

discussion of Mrs. Smith's employment history,' Sutton objected.

'If the court will allow me to proceed,' Tess rejoined, 'I'm sure it will find this witness's testimony to be entirely relevant.'

'Objection overruled,' Judge Washington decided. 'But let's get to the point, Miss Escalante.'

'What happened on the day before your final interview with the congresswoman from Connecticut?'

'The senator's secretary was out sick,' Maggie replied, 'and the senator asked me to stay and retype a paper he had written. I didn't really want to, but he promised it would only be for an hour or two and I didn't know how to refuse without sounding like a real idiot, and I needed the overtime anyway, so I agreed. But he kept making changes and I had to keep retyping, and it was almost ten o'clock by the time I was finished. He offered to buy me dinner, in appreciation, but I said it was too late. So then he offered to drive me home. He said it was the least he could do.'

In the second row on the right side of the gallery, the Sullivan Street set began to look at one another with growing anticipation and Ted sat up a little straighter in his seat.

Across the aisle, Randy felt the cold knot that had been occupying the pit of his stomach begin to tighten. Beside him, Mary Catherine sat like a stone.

'Did you accept his offer?' Tess inquired.

'Well, it *was* late,' Maggie replied, 'I was tired and the buses weren't very reliable at that hour. Besides, he hadn't been offensive during the evening, and I didn't want him to think I was rude, so yes, I let him drive me home.'

She shivered and clutched at the arms of her chair.

'Would you like a glass of water?' Tess asked gently.

The witness shook her head. 'I'm okay,' she said in an uneven voice. 'It's just hard to talk about, even after all these years.'

'Take your time.'

Maggie took a deep breath and let it out slowly. 'I lived in Alexandria, which is about forty-five minutes out of the city, and when we got there he asked if he could come in and use the bathroom, being that it was such a long drive back to Rock Creek Park, where he lived. The apartment was a mess. My roommate had just left for vacation and half her wardrobe was left where she'd dropped it and I didn't really want to invite him in. But how do you tell a United States senator that he can't come in and go to the bathroom because your roommate's closet is all over the floor? So I let him in and then I just waited by the front door to let him right out again. But when he came out of the bathroom he was taking off his jacket and untying his tie and he said, "You can close the door – I'm not planning on leaving just yet."' The former secretary took another deep breath. 'And then he raped me.'

A startled gasp rose up from every corner of the packed courtroom and met the echo of Margaret Holden Smith's words.

'Your Honor, I object to this totally uncorroborated testimony!' the Silver Fox cried.

'Sit down, Counselor!' Oliver Wendell Washington barked. 'You'll have your chance to cross-examine.'

'Senator Robert Willmont raped you?' Tess pressed the witness.

'Yes,' Maggie confirmed. 'He told me I had been asking for it for months, teasing him, enticing him with my sexy dresses and phony modesty, and it was time to end the game. He forced himself on me, and when I tried to resist – tried to scream – he beat me, slapping me with his open hand and punching me with his fist. When he finished with me, he got up and straightened his clothes and told me maybe it would be better if I didn't come back to work at his office. I told him I had no intention of coming back. I told him I was going to the police.'

'What did he say to that?'

'He laughed. He said I could do whatever I wanted but he would deny everything, and who did I think the police would believe – a respected United States senator or a nobody sexpot who thought she could sleep her way to the top? Then he started to leave, but right at the door he stopped and came back. He said, on second thought, he didn't want there to be any hard feelings between us, and then he sat down on my sofa and wrote out a check for two hundred and fifty thousand dollars.'

'The defendant wrote you a check for a quarter of a million dollars?'

'Objection!' Sutton called. 'Witness is testifying to material not in evidence.'

'Sustained.'

Tess walked over to the prosecution table and picked up a sheet of paper. 'Your Honor, at this time, I would like to introduce People's exhibit seventy-six, a Xerox copy of a bank draft, number 8038, drawn on account 331-020-665, dated June 20, 1984, in the amount of two hundred and fifty thousand dollars, written to Margaret Holden and signed by the defendant.'

'Objection!' Sutton cried. 'Best evidence, Your

Honor. There's no proof that any such check ever existed. This Xerox could be a forgery, or it could be an altered version of a check relating to an entirely different matter.'

'This is *not* best evidence,' Tess agreed. 'We would much prefer that the senator provide us with the original.'

There was a hurried conversation between defendant and attorney.

The Silver Fox sighed. 'I'm sorry, Your Honor. It seems that, like most honest, hard-working people, the Senator does not keep personal records for longer than the seven years required by the IRS. Whatever checks he may have written in 1984 have been destroyed.'

'Then I ask the court to accept this photocopy in lieu of the original,' Tess countered.

'Approach,' Washington barked, covering his microphone. 'I assume you have precedents, Miss Escalante?' he asked.

'Yes, Your Honor.'

'Okay, into chambers.'

The judge suspended proceedings with a bang of his gavel. A well-armed Anne Jenks followed Tess and the defense contingent out of the courtroom. Ten minutes later, when they reappeared, Tess had a slight smile on her face and Hal Sutton was trying to conceal a scowl.

'I'm going to overrule the objection,' Judge Washington declared for the record, as his bowel complained. 'Subject to controverting testimony or presentation of the original check, the photocopy will be entered into evidence.'

'Exception!' Sutton snapped.

'Noted,' Washington snapped back. 'You may continue, Miss Escalante.'

'Where did this copy come from, Mrs. Smith?' Tess asked as the trial continued.

'I made it,' the witness replied. 'When the senator gave it to me, he said it would be good only if I left Washington immediately and never said a word to anyone about what happened. He said if I didn't, he would see to it that I never worked in Washington again, and that my family would be ruined, too. He said he had the resources and the power to do that.'

'What did you do?'

'I'm ashamed to say I took the check. I was scared to death. After all, he was a big important man, and I figured he was probably right. Who was going to take my word over his after I'd let him drive me home and then let him into my apartment late at night? All he would have to say was that I consented. How could I prove I didn't? But I wanted to have something, just in case he changed his mind and tried to hurt my family anyway. So, right after he left, I went to an all-night store where they had a Xerox machine, and I made the copy. Then I went to the hospital.'

'Your Honor, at this time, I would like to introduce into evidence People's exhibit seventy-seven, a copy of Margaret Holden's hospital record on the night of June 20, 1984.'

Sutton took a perfunctory look at the document and shrugged. 'No objection.'

'What injuries, if any, did you suffer that night, Mrs. Smith?' the ADA asked.

'I had a black eye, a fractured cheekbone, multiple bruises and two crushed ribs.'

In the gallery, Mary Catherine silently began to cry.

'Your Honor, the hospital record just entered into evidence will show that Margaret Holden did indeed suffer, and was treated for, those injuries on the night of June 20, 1984.' Tess turned back to the witness. 'Did you talk to the police?'

'Yes. The hospital said they had to call them. But I was so scared that I told the officer I didn't get a good look at the man who raped me.'

'And then you left Washington?'

'Yes. The very next day. I went home to Utah. I didn't call anyone before I left. I didn't even go back to the office to clean out my desk. I was so embarrassed. I knew how I looked. I didn't know how to explain.'

'You kept your silence for eight years,' Tess observed. 'Why are you breaking it now?'

'Out of guilt, I think,' Margaret Holden Smith replied. 'And because he can't hurt me anymore. When Sergeant Pope found me, I'd been following the story in the news, and all the time I was thinking, if I'd been stronger back then, if I'd stood up to him instead of taking his dirty money and running away with my tail between my legs like a kicked dog, maybe Karen Doniger wouldn't have had to go through what she did.'

'Objection!' Sutton exclaimed.

'Sustained. Confine your answers to only those facts in evidence, Mrs. Smith,' Washington advised.

'I have no more questions, Your Honor,' Tess said.

Tears were running down the witness's cheeks. 'It wasn't fair, Miss Escalante – all I ever wanted, my whole life, was to be a part of the process and work in Washington. I was good at my job. I was learning. I could have gone places. It wasn't fair that he was allowed to take that away from me.'

'No,' Tess agreed. 'It wasn't.'

'Why the hell didn't you tell me?' Sutton snapped later that evening.

'I didn't think it was that important,' Robert said.

'Not that important?'

'It was her word against mine – how was I supposed to know the cunt would make a copy of the check?'

'Is what she said true? Did you rape her?'

'Of course not,' Robert dismissed the idea. 'Why would I have to rape anyone? So maybe I got a little rough with her, but that's all. She'd been coming on to me for months, with her tight clothes and her holier-than-thou attitude. She wanted me to take her home that night. She was clearly giving me the message. So I gave her what she wanted. I only wrote the check because it was my first term in the Senate and I didn't want any problems.'

'You should have been honest with me, Robert,' his attorney declared, massaging his temples. 'Then maybe I could have prevented this. At the very least, I could have moved to exclude past behavior.'

'We couldn't do that,' the senator reminded him. 'We needed to be able to discredit Doniger, remember?'

'Except that it didn't quite work out that way, did it?' Sutton retorted. 'Instead, Escalante set a trap and we walked right into it, like a pair of first-year associates.'

'The bitch,' Robert mumbled. 'So now what do we do?'

'We can argue irrelevance, we can try to discredit, we can attempt to paint this Margaret Smith as the whore of Capitol Hill, we can move to exclude, but I don't know. I'm very much afraid the prosecution has established perjury.'

'Okay, maybe I made a mistake,' Robert admitted. 'Maybe I should have told you about Maggie. Maybe I shouldn't have been so cavalier on the stand when Escalante pressed me about the infidelity issue. But what happened back then has nothing to do with this case. I didn't rape Karen Doniger, Hal. Believe me, she asked for it.'

'That may be,' the Silver Fox said, 'but I'm no longer sure I can convince the jury of that.'

Sutton spent most of Monday trying to undo some of the damage that Maggie Holden Smith had done. He called for a mistrial. Judge Washington denied. He tried to have the witness's entire testimony stricken. Again, Washington denied. He tried to discredit her story. He harped on her refusal to identify her assailant to the police. He suggested that the senator might have had cause to interpret her actions as provocative. He even went so far as to speculate that she had asked the senator to drive her home that night, instead of the other way around, and perhaps even invited him into her apartment in an attempt to further her career. Then he sought to intimate that she had set the whole thing up as a blackmail scheme. Finally, he dredged up a handwriting expert who was willing to testify that it was possible the Xeroxed check was a forgery.

It wasn't clear whether his effort had any significant impact on the jury, but the media, which had since April been overwhelmingly sympathetic to the senator, were suddenly scrambling like cockroaches in a bright light.

nine

Closing arguments were presented on Tuesday.

Sutton argued eloquently and vigorously that his client was simply the innocent victim of political sabotage. It didn't seem to matter that he had been unable to prove this theory with direct evidence and sworn testimony, and he played on the socio-economic climate of San Francisco to hammer his point home.

'The one man who can make a difference,' he declared, 'the one man with the vision to change this country for the better – that man cannot be allowed to survive. Why not? Because he's the only real threat to the superwealthy who, thanks to twelve long years of incompetent government, have gotten America right where they want it – with the poor getting poorer, and the rich getting richer. One man stands in their way. Robert Drayton Willmont. A rich man who refuses to play their self-serving little games. And how better to rid themselves of this very real threat than to have a woman cry rape!'

In the gallery, Amanda Drayton Willmont nodded.

Mitch grinned. 'It's a downright conspiracy.'

'Cry rape today, ladies and gentlemen,' Sutton exhorted, 'and the whole world stops to listen. The images it conjures up are lurid and loathsome. A woman entices a man into a compromising situation and then claims he took advantage of her. How does he defend himself without sounding like even more of a heel than he would had he actually done the deed?'

'He's a heel, all right,' Jenna murmured.

Elizabeth Willmont sat beside her mother-in-law. She had swallowed a handful of pills during the noon recess and now she was twelve years old again, basking in the glory of a Denver summer.

'There are people walking among us who just could not let this man become President of the United State,' Sutton said, looking directly at each juror. 'They are people who will stop at nothing to preserve what they have, at the expense of the rest of us. And they found a way to destroy him, didn't they? They found a middle-aged ex-groupie who would agree to cry rape.'

The attorney paced back and forth for a moment.

'Could it have happened the way Karen Doniger said it did?' he wondered aloud. 'It could have. After all, she had to concoct a believable story, or there would have been no case. But couldn't it just as well have happened exactly the way the defendant said it did? Couldn't he have been drawn innocently into the middle of an insidious plot? Of course he could have.'

Sutton nodded sagely.

'And that's why they didn't stop there. No, they couldn't risk that you might be smart enough to see through their little scheme. Not when, despite their dirty trick, the candidate was still out there piling up victory after victory in the primaries, with the nomination almost in hand. They realized that one woman might not be enough to do the foul deed. So what did they do? They went out and found themselves another woman – a disgruntled ex-employee who harbored a grudge against her former employer, who waved a piece of Xerox paper around that was conveniently eight years old and about as legitimate as the forger who probably wrote it, and they convinced *her* to cry rape, too.'

The Silver Fox wagged his head as though it were all just too overwhelming.

'Can Robert Drayton Willmont survive *two* pawns bent on destroying him? Are they going to win, after all? Is our country destined to have four more years of disastrous leadership? Will we have to stand by and watch while America is bled dry by the greedy until there's nothing left to save? If you convict this man of a crime he did not commit, that's exactly what will happen. They will win and the country will lose.'

Sutton peered intently at each of the jurors in turn. 'Ladies and gentlemen of the jury,' he said solemnly, 'it's up to you.'

'Amen,' the defendant's mother breathed.

Demelza scowled.

With one deep sigh that seemed to bear all the weight of the world, the Silver Fox reclaimed his seat, just as Tess Escalante rose from hers in rebuttal.

'Sinister cliques? Insidious plots? Scare tactics?' she cried scornfully. 'I think the defense attorney should have been a mystery writer. The key to a good mystery is the ability of the author to misdirect the reader. Boy, have we just been misdirected.'

'Amen,' Demelza said.

The defendant's mother scowled.

'To hear the defense tell it,' Tess continued, 'Robert Willmont is a bona fide saint, sent to us to save the world, who just happened to be in the wrong place at the wrong time. Who just happened to invite Karen Doniger out for a drink. Who just happened to show up in the parking garage four minutes after she did. Who just happened to insist on taking her home. Who just happened to drive his car to a remote area of Golden Gate Park. Who just happened to have sex with her, break her nose, split her lip and blacken her eye.'

The ADA shook her head in disgust.

'Never mind that the defense was unable to provide one shred of evidence that Karen Doniger was manipulated by any political motives. They want you to take their word for it anyway, on faith. Well, let's separate the facts from all that fiction, ladies and gentlemen. Let's make sure we have it perfectly clear. Robert Drayton Willmont is a rapist – and the worst kind of rapist, too. The kind who builds trust and then betrays. The kind who not only forces himself sexually upon defenseless women, but who likes to beat up on them, as well.'

Tess allowed a visible shudder to run down her slender body.

'The facts of this case were clear from the moment Karen Doniger spoke them, no matter how hard the defense attorney tried to contort them. But even if there remained a flicker of doubt in the most stubborn of minds, Margaret Holden Smith had to have doused it. Because if the defendant did not rape these two women – who have never met and have never spoken to one another – how then did they manage to come up with almost identical stories? The answer is painfully simple. They couldn't have. Robert Willmont raped both of them, exactly as they said he did, and that's the sad fact of it. He's a rapist, ladies and gentlemen. The great hope of America is a rapist. As brilliant as he may be politically, that's how warped he is personally. And that's the only sinister plot at work here.'

Amanda Drayton Willmont clutched her handbag to hide her anger.

Felicity clutched her handbag to keep from clapping.

The crafty ADA sighed deeply.

'But why would he have to resort to rape, this United States senator and presidential candidate who, on the face of it, has everything? This matinee idol who walks along the path of life with women literally dropping at his feet? That was the one question that I wrestled with, the one thing that I couldn't understand, until I heard the testimony of Dr. Linderman. If ever a man fits his psychological profile of an acquaintance-rapist, one who sets out to seduce and ends up choosing to violate, it's Robert Willmont, a man used to taking what he wants – even when it's not offered.'

Now it was Tess's turn to pace.

'This isn't about political intrigue, ladies and gentlemen of the jury, about secret cliques out to seize America for themselves. This is about one two-hundred-and-fifteen-pound man overpowering one one-hundred-and-ten-pound woman in the middle of Golden Gate Park – and you saw for yourselves the graphic and gruesome results of her resistance.'

Now it was Tess's turn to look each juror in the eye.

'Robert Drayton Willmont raped Karen Doniger, despite his background, despite his position, and despite the extent of his exposure. Why would he be foolish enough to risk it? Perhaps that's the simplest question of all – *because he thought he could get away with it.* Because he thought that his looks, his charm, his power, and his money would protect him from things that ordinary people like you and me are held accountable for every day. Look at him. Payoffs, perjury, denial, coercion – those are the ways of his world. What he can't lie his way out of, he'll try to buy his way out of.'

Tess didn't think Karen would mind her borrowing the line. She raised her left arm and jabbed her finger in the direction of the defendant.

'Sitting over there is a man who thinks he's above the law,' she declared. 'Ladies and gentlemen of the jury, tell him he's not.'

Oliver Wendell Washington took almost an hour to charge the jury, making sure that he walked the fine line of neutrality without a slip. He was known as a by-the-book judge, and by the book he went. By the time the five men and seven women retired to consider their verdict, there was no doubt in their minds about what they could and could not do. It was four-thirty in the afternoon.

Robert Willmont went home and closeted himself in the library. Randy Neuburg did not go with him. Mary Catherine O'Malley went to her apartment on Telegraph Hill and began to pack. Hal Sutton went to his office and sat at his desk, staring into space as he waited for the telephone call he knew would not be long in coming.

Tess left word with Anne Jenks that she could be reached at the Donigers' home in St. Francis Wood.

'I want to be in the courtroom for the verdict,' Karen announced. 'I have the right.'

The ADA nodded. 'I suppose you do,' she said. 'But what if it doesn't go our way?'

'I can handle it,' Karen replied. 'I just want to be there. I need to be there.'

'I'll be with her,' Ted said. 'We'll all be with her.'

Everyone was at the house, preparing for the vigil without knowing how long it would last. Felicity and Ione were cooking. Amy and Jessica were setting the table. Demelza was sitting quietly in the study. In the laundry, Jenna was ironing the simple beige dress Karen had chosen to wear. Mitch was pacing nervously up and down the living room. John was fixing drinks. Nancy was outside, talking with the reporters who still lingered on the front lawn.

'They've certainly changed their tune,' she observed with a chuckle when she came back inside. 'They were actually polite.'

'How long does this sort of thing normally take?' Jenna wondered as they seated themselves at the table.

'I've learned never to try to second-guess a jury,' Tess replied as the salad was passed around. 'They could be out a day, they could be out a week.'

'If he's convicted, will he go to prison?' Amy asked.

'Yes.'

'For how long?'

'Maybe for the rest of his life.'

'What makes it so complicated?' Felicity asked.

'There are two separate charges that the jury must deal with,' the ADA explained. 'The charge of sexual assault, which is the rape, and the charge of battery, which is the beating. All twelve jurors must agree on each count.'

'You mean, they could find him guilty of the battery but not the sexual assault?'

'Yes. They might decide that Karen contributed to the rape but was in no way responsible for the beating.'

'You mean, just because she had a few drinks with him and let him drive her home?'

Tess sighed. 'As hard as you try to read the people you put on a jury, you never really know how they'll react. You also have to consider the dynamics of the group and what kind of peer pressure will be brought to bear.'

'I served on a jury once,' John said. 'Not a big case, like this one, and I remember how two of the jurors squared off against each other and tried to force everyone else to take sides.'

'What happened?' Amy wanted to know.

'They hung the jury.'

'Can that happen here?' Jessica asked Tess.

'Anything can happen,' the ADA had to admit.

'But it's not going to,' Ione said, bringing in a huge pan of lasagna. 'It might take the jury a while, but I watched them and I know, in the end, they'll get it right.'

The telephone rang at ten minutes past seven.

Karen sat beside Ted in the third row on the right side of the gallery, her hand tightly clasped in his. From the corner of her eye, she could see Elizabeth Willmont across the aisle. Whichever way this went, she felt sorry for the woman. Beyond the glass partition, the defendant sat calmly in his chair, waiting.

The courtroom was bursting. Every inch of space that was not taken by friends and relatives was filled with reporters. The closed-circuit television camera next door had been fine for the trial, but everyone wanted to be on the scene for the verdict.

Tess stared at the jury, trying to read something in a stray glance or a shift in position. The five men and seven women sat silent and unmoving, with their eyes on the judge.

'Has the jury reached a verdict?' Washington intoned.

'Yes, we have, Your Honor,' replied Brian Barstow, the computer software salesman and elected foreman.

'How do you find?'

A sudden stillness fell over the entire courtroom as those with and without any vested interest strained to hear.

'On the count of battery,' the foreman read from the slip of paper in his hand, 'we find the defendant ... guilty as charged.'

From every corner of the gallery, there was a sharp intake of breath. Karen's hand tightened in Ted's.

'On the count of sexual assault,' Barstow continued, 'we find the defendant ... guilty as charged.'

'So say you all?'

'So say we all.'

The courtroom exploded. Reporters scrambled to get out, everyone wanting to be the first to file the story, the first to get it on the air. A number of Willmont supporters wailed in protest, even as the small contingent of Doniger allies shouted in glee.

Robert sat as though paralyzed, stone-faced with disbelief and rage, oblivious of his attorneys, who were reassuring him of an appeal; of his wife, who rose and quietly left the courtroom; of his mother, who was unable to grasp what had happened. He was oblivious of everyone, even the two bailiffs who took up positions behind him.

Hal Sutton was on his feet demanding that the verdict be set aside, even though it was clearly nothing more than a formality. Judge Washington was futilely banging his gavel, shouting over the din as he thanked and dismissed the jury and set the sentencing for September 14 at 2:00 p.m.

It was over.

Karen felt so weak she wasn't sure she could stand. In all her dreams, she had not dared to hope that this moment would ever come, and now it was here – after thirty years of anguish, it was here. So she stayed where she was and savored it for a time, closing her eyes and letting it wash over her like a gentle rain. And Ted put his arm around her and sat wordlessly by her side.

She didn't see Robert jump from his chair, knocking it over in the process, or push past the startled bailiffs as he stormed up the aisle. She was aware of him only when he stood in front of her, his aquamarine eyes glaring down at her.

'Why, goddamn you?' he insisted. 'Why?'

A cold winter night came into focus in Karen's mind, a night when she could do nothing – and merged with a mild spring night a lifetime later, a night when she could do anything. She saw the clump of bushes by Stow Lake, as much like Central Park as she could find. She saw her face, as bruised and bloodied as she felt she needed to make it. She saw a soul that was shattered finally made whole again.

There were any number of times during the past few months when she felt her confidence slipping and doubted she would get away with it. But in the end she was strong enough to pull it off and the irony of it did not escape her. Thirty years ago, she had told the truth, and was not believed. This time, *he* had told the truth, and was not believed. She couldn't remember now how the idea had come to her – to frame him for the crime he had already committed – but it didn't matter. All that mattered was that she had succeeded.

An eye for an eye, the Bible said. So be it. As he once took from her the thing she wanted most in the world, now had she done the same to him, and she felt no remorse.

She looked up at him, her blue-gray eyes calm, her conscience clear.

'December 22, 1962,' she said softly.

I am indebted to Howard Schage, Sally Sondheim, Susan Klein, Joyce Valentine, Betta Ferrendelli, and Linda Stenn—my supporters, my contributors, my friends. For only friends are required to tell the truth. And to Fredy-Jo Grafman, Mona Kunen, and Kasey Todd Ingram for their pinpoint research, and their willingness to participate in the creative process.

I must also thank Chief of Police John Sutton and Detectives Loretta Faust and Steve Cain of the Bainbridge Island Police Department for their patience, their wisdom, and their good humor. I hope I got at least most of it right.

I am grateful to Becky Fox Marshall, editor of the *Central Kitsap Reporter*, for sharing with me her experiences and her insight.

Finally, I wish to express my appreciation to the DNA experts at the Washington State Crime Laboratory, and the good people in the Kitsap County Prosecutor's Office for taking the time to answer all my questions, no matter how silly they sounded.

Without such help, this work would never have been accomplished.

PART ONE

The Crime

"Murder, though it have no tongue, will speak."
—*William Shakespeare*

1

Death came without warning. She saw the knife in the moonlight, grasped in his hand, but she thought he meant it only as a threat, and never dreamed he would actually use it. Then it plunged through the fabric of her skirt, somewhere just below the waistband. That was how she thought of it, in the split second she had to think, that he had ripped her skirt—not that he had driven the blade deep into her flesh.

Surprised, she peered down through the darkness, curious about the damage he had done to her skirt. Then her hands, following her eyes to the spot where the knife had been, met a rush of warm stickiness. The surprise turned to disbelief.

Still, she didn't fully realize his purpose until he came at her again, and looking up, she saw his eyes, devoid of all expression, all charity. Then she understood, and the disbelief turned to absolute terror.

Her instinct was to run, of course, to try and get away from him, to survive. But he must have guessed that and was ready for her, reaching out and grasping her by the hair, holding her easily within arm's reach. Then she felt the third thrust of the knife, inches from the first two, and then the fourth and the fifth and the sixth. After that, she lost count.

She felt herself growing weak and then dizzy, and then her vision began to blur. Finally, she no longer stood by her own will, only by his, as he continued to hold her erect with one hand, and carve her up with the other. A roar like the sound of sea surf pounded in her ears, yet she heard him clearly when he spoke.

"I'm sorry," he said, his voice like his eyes, "but I just can't let you do it. I can't let you ruin my life."

She thought of her own barely lived life, of all the things she had planned to do and would now never do. The places she would go, the people she would meet. Far from here, in a land of sunlight and forgiveness. She had wanted to be good, to do good. It seemed so unfair.

The warm stickiness was oozing from too many places now. She knew she could no longer hold it in. It would leak out of her until there was nothing left, and then she would be dead. Yet she didn't struggle. It was almost as though she accepted what was happening to her as God's will.

From her earliest moments, she had sat in church and listened, mesmerized, as Father Paul spoke about the better life that awaited the faithful, about the preservation of the soul, about the rewards of heaven. He had always sounded so reassuring and she wanted so much to believe. But in the last seconds of consciousness, she couldn't help herself—she wondered what death would really be.

When she felt a white hot explosion in her chest, she knew her heart was breaking. Summoning one final spurt of energy, she opened her mouth and screamed. It didn't matter that there was no one to hear her, to save her. It wasn't meant for that, but as her only remaining protest—an excruciating sound, made all the more unbearable because it was born not of pain, but of betrayal.

2

It was usually with great reluctance that the Pacific Northwest let go its gentle grip on summer and made the sharp turn into autumn. The season could be weeks old before the air began to crackle with burning leaves, hum with fresh sea breezes, and catch up with the chatter of schoolchildren. Before the pleasant odor of wood smoke returned to banish the evening chill. Before the endless rains came to soak the spirit as well as the earth.

This year was no exception. It was already the middle of October and morning skies were still blue, night skies still starry, and temperatures still mild, even as the days grew short.

At six-thirty on the second Sunday of the month, Tom Hildress drove his Dodge pickup through the entrance of Madrona Point Park, turned to his right, and followed his headlights through the predawn darkness toward a blue Dumpster that sat against the far edge of the large gravel parking lot.

This was the designated weekend for Seward Island's annual fall cleanup, and Dumpsters had been placed at a number of strategic points for the disposal of bulky items that could not fit into regular household garbage containers. Although Madrona Point, the densely forested area that sprawled across much of the northwest end of the Island, was the most remote of the designated drop-offs, it was the most convenient for the Hildresses, whose home was less than a mile away.

Tom had spent yesterday cleaning out the garage, and he was getting an early start this morning because he had two more loads to dump, and he had promised his wife that he would be finished in time to shower and dress and go to church with the family.

He backed his truck to within six feet of the Dumpster and killed the engine. "You go on top and I'll pass stuff up to you," he suggested to the tow-headed nine-year-old sitting beside him.

"Okay," Billy Hildress agreed, jumping down from the cab and darting up a makeshift set of steps that had been pushed against the front of the big container. "Yuck," he said, wrinkling his nose as he reached the top. "Something in here really stinks."

He squinted over the edge. Dawn would not be breaking for another hour yet, but in the grayness of not quite night, he could see that the Dumpster was already half filled with everything from bald tires to broken-down refrigerators. A dilapidated sofa lay in one corner, a thick roll of rug had been flung against another.

"Jeez, Dad," he called down to his father. "I bet you could just about furnish a whole house with the junk that's in here."

Tom Hildress was well known around the Island for the many patient hours he spent sifting through other people's castoffs in search of unrecognized treasures that he could restore, with loving patience, to their original glory. The Eagle Rock Methodist Church's annual Christmas bazaar was always a huge success thanks to his keen eye and clever hand. Any other morning, he would have bounded up beside Billy, eager to have a look.

"No time," he replied with a sigh, passing an armful of flattened cardboard boxes up to the boy. "Mom gave us strict orders."

Billy heaved the boxes toward the far corner of the Dumpster and reached for more. Turning back to toss the next armful in the same direction, he suddenly froze.

The first load of cardboard had hit against the rolled-up rug, causing it to come open at one end, and revealing what looked, in the dimness, like a head of blond curls and part of a shoulder that were much too big to belong to a discarded doll.

"Say, Dad," Billy said in a strange voice, "I think there's someone up here."

"Who's that?" asked Tom, who had little time to waste and was concentrating on a third stack of cardboard.

"A person," the nine-year-old replied. "A real person. I think maybe there's a body up here."

Tom frowned in the direction of his son. "What are you talking about? Is someone going through the trash?"

Billy shook his head. "Come look," he said, backing slowly down the stairs.

Controlling his impatience, Tom climbed past the boy to peer into the Dumpster. At once, the same fetid odor that Billy had smelled assaulted his nose. His eyes searched the pile of refuse from left to right until, coming to rest on the rug in the far corner, he saw what Billy had seen.

"Oh, my God," he gasped.

He vaulted over the side of the Dumpster and waded into the rubbish. Regardless that Tom was a tall, spare man in excellent physical condition, the going was slow—in places, the trash reached above his knees—and his heart pounded painfully with every step. By the time he reached the spot, he was telling himself that life-sized dolls were not unheard of, even as the stench of waste grew stronger and he knew, just as Billy had known, that he wasn't going to find a doll.

The first thing he saw clearly was the blood. The rug seemed to be soaked with it. Then he saw the girl. She was young, in her teens, and had apparently been wrapped inside the bit of carpet and then tossed onto the garbage heap. Tom couldn't help himself, his stomach heaved, and he turned away and vomited until there was nothing left inside of him.

"What is it, Dad?" Billy called from below.

"Don't come up here, son," Tom told the boy as soon as he could catch his breath. "Go wait for me in the truck. I'll be there in a minute."

Swallowing hard, he reached down and carefully unrolled the rest of the rug, exposing the body. Pieces of denim that might have been a skirt were stuck to parts of her; denim that had probably been blue, but now appeared dark red. A blood-drenched T-shirt fanned around her in shreds. Although Tom was no expert, it didn't take one to realize that she had been stabbed repeatedly. He could almost feel the fury of the attack just by looking at her, and he wondered what kind of maniac, loose on Seward Island, could have done such a thing.

He bent down and made himself touch one of the wounds. The blood was still sticky, telling him it was only a matter of hours since her life had oozed out of those grisly gashes. He was close enough to her so that, despite the lack of daylight, he could see she wore a small gold cross around her neck. Avoiding it, he pressed his fingers against her throat, just to confirm what he already knew. She was quite dead.

The bile began to rise in him again. He didn't want to move her or touch anything else—he was already thinking ahead to finding a telephone and calling the police. But several deep breaths later, he leaned forward and gently pushed the blond curls aside.

An eye stared up at him, wide and glassy and fixed in fear so palpable that Tom stumbled backward onto his heels. Her mouth gaped—grotesque, distorted, and frozen in a silent, agonizing accusation.

3

Ginger Earley had called Seward Island home from the time she was three years old. In fact, it was the day after her birthday that her family had moved from Pomeroy, a small city in the southeast corner of Washington State, so that her father could assume the job of bailiff at the Puget County Courthouse.

In part because it may well have been true, but mostly because of an acute sense of insecurity, Ginger's mother had always harbored the belief that the locals, a great majority of whom had lived on Seward for generations, looked down on her. As a result, it became her life's work, almost to the point of obsession, to see to it that her children were the neatest, the cleanest, the best spoken, and the best behaved on the Island.

Her efforts were reasonably successful as far as the three Earley boys were concerned, but Ginger was another story. The youngest, and by far most stubborn, was more than a match for her mother.

From her earliest days, and perhaps to some extent to frustrate her mother, Ginger declined to go by her given name, Virginia, insisting instead that she be allowed to use the pet name her father had bestowed upon her. She rejected dresses and patent leather shoes in favor of blue jeans and bare feet. She skipped dance classes to participate in touch football games, and practiced tree climbing instead of the piano. She knew nothing about the proper way to pour tea, but she knew everything about gentling a horse. She couldn't stand more than ten minutes in the company of her mother's gossipy friends, but she could spend hours in the woods where deer and chipmunks ate from her hand.

Ginger was taller than average, having achieved her full height of five feet nine inches by the time she was twelve years old. Along with her stature went a head of unruly red hair that her mother always claimed must have come from her father's side of the family, a face full of freckles, and large eyes that were brown and green and gold all at the same time. She wasn't beautiful, although someone once called her looks "arresting," which proved to be a source of private amusement to her later on, and she was far too athletic to arouse much romantic interest in the opposite sex during her growing-up years. But Ginger didn't seem to care. She was the only girl ever invited to play on the boys' varsity soccer and softball teams, and she more than held her own on both. She could fly a kite with the best of them, sit a horse better than anyone on the Island, and she held the Seward High School track record at 500 and 1,000 meters for three consecutive years.

There finally came a point where her mother threw up her hands in disgust. "Go ahead and be a tomboy then, be a total embarrassment to us," she cried one day, when Ginger was sixteen years old and chose a basketball game over a ballet.

"Don't blame *me* for what I am," the fiery redhead shot back. "It's *your* genes that made me this way." It became the last word on the issue.

Despite her mother's discomfort over the people of Seward Island, Ginger loved the place. In the days of her childhood, barely four thousand independent souls laid claim to the twenty-one square miles of rolling hills, lush valleys, thick woods, and sandy beaches. That left plenty of room for a free spirit to kick up her heels.

As much as was possible in the Earley household, Ginger thought her own thoughts and did her own thing. She was loyal to her friends, bright enough to be admired by her peers, and she would not back down from a just fight. Being tall and strong for a girl, she could beat up most of the boys her own age. When she couldn't, she would call on her big brothers to help make her point.

She became notorious for one incident. When the neighborhood bully doused the Earley cat with gasoline and set her on fire, Ginger promptly doused the bully with gasoline and set *him* on fire. Although the boy was more scared than hurt, it caused an uproar.

"Why didn't you just beat him up?" her father, a gentle bear of a man, asked in exasperation when the boy's parents threatened to sue.

"Because I wanted him to know exactly how Mittens felt when he did that to her," replied the eight-year-old. "Now he does, and I bet he'll never do it again."

The police conducted an investigation. The Islanders were divided right down the middle on the issue. After some negotiation, the matter was dropped.

The tomboy image suited Ginger. More than the freedom it gave her to be herself, it allowed her to conceal the fact that she was highly competitive. She discovered early in life that being as good as her brothers was not good enough—she had to be better to be equal. Despite the fact that she was the brightest of the four, and clearly the apple of her father's eye, she saw it was to the boys that he turned for what he called "man talk." It was their perspectives he sought and their opinions he considered, not hers. As much as Ginger resented that, she had to concede that it was to her father that *she* went with her problems and questions and doubts, not to her mother. She decided there had to be a way for her to be accepted by men as an equal, and still be respected as a woman.

When she graduated from high school near the top of her class, her friends and family expected that she would enter college and then go on to become either a veterinarian or an attorney. She surprised them all.

It was not her outward toughness that led her into the police academy and a career as a law enforcement officer. It was more a combination of her loyalty and her intelligence, an overwhelming sense of what was right, and at least the hope of a level playing field. And, too, there was her pride in her father as a dedicated civil servant.

"Tell me what you think, Dad," she said. "Tell me what you really think."

"I think you could do just about anything you set out to do," Jack Earley replied, because he could deny her nothing, and besides, none of his sons had chosen to go into his line of work. "But to join the force—well, I can't think of anything that would make me prouder."

"I thought you were going to be a lawyer," her mother said, thinking how nice it would be to have a professional in the family. Her three boys were all fine young men, but one had chosen the Navy, another worked for Boeing, and the third had a wife and a child by the time he was twenty, and a steady job with the telephone company.

"It was *your* idea for me to be a lawyer," Ginger told her mother, "not mine."

Ironically enough, her first job after the academy was in a small city in eastern Washington, less than thirty miles from Pomeroy where she had been born. She lived with an aunt and uncle while she was there. They introduced her to a tall young man who was in the farm equipment business with his father, and she promptly fell in love. The two of them dated exclusively for almost a year and a half, but when it came right down to it, he apparently couldn't handle the idea of having a policewoman for a wife. She was devastated, six months later, when he married someone else.

Her second job brought her back to western Washington, too far away to live at home, but close enough to visit on her off-duty weekends. For the next five years, she worked hard and learned well, and deserved her promotion to the rank of detective. Occasionally, she would date, but there was no one serious; or perhaps there was no one she was willing to let become serious.

When the opening on Seward Island was posted, she was one of the first to apply. It was no coincidence—she had always intended to come back. There were sixteen other candidates who interviewed for the position, all of them men. Despite the fact that some had more experience and some had handled more responsibility, Ginger never doubted the job would be hers; not necessarily because she was smarter or more intuitive than anyone else, but because she had the one asset the rest of them lacked—she had been raised here, and she understood the Island and its people better than all sixteen of the others put together.

Which explained why she knew, within minutes of arriving at Madrona Point Park, that what Tom and Billy Hildress had discovered in the blue Dumpster was going to destroy her home.

4

Seward Island sat in the middle of Puget Sound like a diamond on a bed of blue velvet—radiant and rare.

It had originally been claimed by a Commodore Nathaniel Seward, who, sailing in the wake of George Vancouver at the end of the eighteenth century, was said to have been so taken by the beauty of his discovery that he promptly came ashore, dispatched his ship back to Portsmouth for his family, and proceeded to live the life of a landed English gentleman well into his eighties.

In its way, Seward Island was as exquisite as any of the tropical paradises the Commodore had encountered in his travels. Towering evergreens graced the hills, clover-rich grass carpeted the valleys, and a breathtaking panorama greeted the eyes from almost any vantage point, sweeping from the jagged Olympic Mountains in the west to the rippling Cascades in the east, and highlighted by craggy Mount Baker to the north and the sky-scraping Mount Rainier to the south.

By the middle of the nineteenth century, however, the Commodore's descendants had grown tired of the isolation of island living, paradise though it may have been, and many began to sell off their holdings and move on.

Anxious for a new beginning, Englishmen from the mills of Manchester and the mines of Newcastle came seeking land of their own. Norwegians emigrated in droves to the Pacific Northwest, bringing with them long traditions of fishing and shipbuilding. Germans fled the farms of Alsace-Lorraine and Schleswig-Holstein in the face of war. And the Irish came, escaping the potato famine, looking to put down new roots.

The warm summer sun, mild winter rains, and rich soil made the tranquil island perfect for growing almost anything. From North Point to South Cove, flowers bloomed and fruits and vegetables flourished. Chickens were brought over from the mainland, and fresh eggs found their way to the local market. Horses grazed the meadows of Cedar Valley, and cows dotted the slopes that led up to Eagle Rock. Salmon filled fishing nets, clams littered the beaches, and crab pots overflowed. Businesses sprang up to service the residents, and a small shipyard began operation.

Eventually, Seward incorporated and became the seat of Puget County—a string of little islands bound together by geography and a lack of imagination as to what else to do with them. The citizens elected a mayor and a city council. Soon thereafter, a tax structure was set up, the roads were paved, electricity was brought across the water, police and fire departments were organized, a medical clinic was established, and a limited amount of light industry was encouraged.

Nonetheless, the Island managed to retain much of its rural charm in the midst of the great Pacific Northwest expansion, due in large part to the fact that it was accessible to the mainland only by boat. A marina on the south side of Gull Harbor provided mooring for one hundred and fifty private yachts, and Washington State operated a daily ferry service.

By the last decade of the twentieth century, the peaceful paradise boasted a population of just under twelve thousand, and the town, perched atop the harbor's central slope, was a little corner of old England that had been carefully constructed by the Commodore and his descendants, and lovingly preserved by those who came after.

Almost a third of the residents took the forty-five-minute water commute to Seattle and back every weekday, and tourists flocked to the Island on weekends. Not as many as crowded onto nearby Bainbridge and Whidbey, perhaps, but enough to browse in the quaint shops along Commodore Street, fill the charming tearooms that accented Seward Way, purchase the homemade jams, jellies, and lemon curd, and even sample the select vintages of the local Corkscrew Winery.

"Welcome to Seward Island," one of the resident artisans had carved into a rustic sign that greeted visitors coming off the ferry. "A good place to visit—a great place to raise a family."

The local newspaper had once observed that the sign said everything that needed to be said. The air was the cleanest in the Puget Sound area, the crime rate was among the lowest in the entire state, and the population was ninety-three percent Anglo-Saxon, Celtic, Teutonic, and Scandinavian, with a sprinkling of other Europeans, a handful of Middle Easterners, and a small community of Asian-Americans making up the remaining seven percent.

In this mostly homogeneous environment, Chief of Police Ruben Martinez was an anomaly. Smuggled over the Mexican border when he was two months old, and shuttled from one stoop-labor farm to another up and down the valleys of California until, at the age of twelve, he was sent to an uncle in East Los Angeles, Ruben was lucky to have survived his teens. He grew up lean and hard and hungry.

It was sheer strength of will that got him out of the barrio, and the belief that his parents had more in mind for him than a repetition of their own miserable lives. He took a keen intellect, a sharp eye, and the cunning of a street fighter to the Los Angeles Police Academy, where he graduated third in his class.

Ruben's intention was to stay in southern California and work with the barrio gangs he knew so well, but an errant bullet lodged too near his spine cut his days on the street short.

"It's a crapshoot, Sergeant," a Los Angeles doctor told him bluntly. "If we leave the bullet where it is, you'll have some level of pain and some reduction in mobility, but you'll still be able to function. If we try to remove it—well, the chances are fifty-fifty that you could end up paralyzed."

The bullet stayed where it was. Ruben was fitted with a back brace to help ease the strain, and a prescription for painkillers that made him fuzzy. He tossed the pills down the toilet after the first week.

For a while, he took a desk job, but it bothered his back to sit around all day, and his feet itched for action. He left Los Angeles for a smaller city in central California where police life was considerably less demanding. Then came a string of other small cities in which he gained valuable experience and honed his skills. Along the way, he married. His wife gave him a daughter before she died. After that, he chose his jobs with a different eye, basing his decisions more on the quality of a town's environment and the caliber of its school system than on the degree of its commitment to law enforcement.

It was a circuitous route that brought Ruben Martinez to Seward Island, but he came with impressive credentials, and a solid reputation for honesty and efficiency. The mayor and the majority of the city council were convinced that they could not have made a better choice for their new chief of police.

"He's certainly the best qualified," said one.

"Probably overqualified," agreed another.

"It'll look good on the record," suggested a third.

"He's an outsider," cautioned a fourth.

"He's exactly what we want," Albert Hoch, the giant pear-shaped mayor, declared.

The terms of Ruben's contract included a tidy, two-bedroom frame house on the outskirts of town, a three-minute drive from the police station and five blocks from Seward High School where his daughter was now a sophomore.

Fifteen-year-old Stacey Martinez was the linchpin in her father's life—a slip of a thing that combined her mother's pale hair and delicate features with his own tawny skin and dark eyes. He had cared for her all by himself from the time she was two until she was ten, when she had begun to take care of him. The arrangement may have gone a long way toward explaining why he had never remarried. As he saw it, he and Stacey were a team; they didn't seem to need anyone else.

Of course, he knew it wouldn't last forever. She was growing up so fast. Soon enough it would be time for her to leave him for a life of her own; time for him to reevaluate his situation. But there was no point in his dwelling on that until it happened, and for now he was quite content with things as they were.

In the three years since Ruben had been chief of the Seward Island police, the department had dealt with numerous outbreaks of petty vandalism, an alarmingly steady increase in teenage drug-related incidents, an occasional drunk and disorderly, a number of traffic violations, frequent minor injuries, some domestic violence, several burglaries, one armed robbery, two rapes, and three accidental deaths. To the best of anyone's recollection, there had never been a homicide.

Although Ruben was technically on call twenty-four hours a day, seven days a week, he generally worked Mondays through Fridays, stayed within hailing distance on Saturdays, in case of an emergency, and took Sundays off to spend with Stacey. Which was why, when the telephone awakened him at seven-thirty-five in the morning on the second Sunday of October, he was surprised to hear Detective Ginger Earley at the other end.

"Sorry to spoil your Sunday, Chief," she said in a voice that was clearly strained. "But I'm at Madrona Point, and I think you'd better get out here right away."

Going more by the urgency of her tone than by her actual words, Ruben didn't take time to shower. He pulled on his clothes, took three gulps of orange juice from a glass Stacey poured for him, and headed for the garage. Fifteen minutes later, he swung his black police-issue Blazer into the Madrona Point parking lot and pulled up next to Ginger's black-and-white.

"What have you got?" he asked, climbing out.

"I've never seen anything like it," the twenty-eight-year-old redhead, who in nine years on the job had seen her share of gruesome bodies, replied with a shudder. "I swear, this is awful."

Her fresh, freckled face had a greenish tinge to it that was more than familiar to Ruben from his days on the streets of East Los Angeles. She motioned him toward the Dumpster, and then led him up the makeshift steps. Dawn had broken and there was now no mistaking what lay mutilated on the bloodstained rug. Ruben got as close as he dared and then hunched over for a better view.

Although it was difficult to tell, due to the excessive amount of blood, there appeared to be somewhere around a dozen sharp-force injuries to the body. He looked at the color of the blood, then dipped the tip of his little finger in it to check the consistency. Next, he noted the bluish color of her skin, which in this warm weather, was more likely to be indicative of blood loss than hypothermia. Finally, he lifted an arm to gauge the extent of rigor mortis. Based on the kind of experience that someone in his line of work rarely forgets, he estimated that she had been dead for at least six hours.

"Did you touch her?" he asked the detective.

"No, I didn't have to—Dirksen was here," she said, referring to the young uniformed officer who had taken Tom Hildress's call and then summoned her. "He said he went in and touched her, but only to confirm she was dead."

"Did anyone else disturb anything around her?"

Ginger shrugged. "I was careful, but the call came in from a local who was dumping trash with his son. I haven't interviewed him yet, so I don't know what he did."

"Well, get on the horn," Ruben instructed almost by rote. "Get the whole park cordoned off. I don't want anyone within a hundred yards of this place until we're finished with it. And get someone down to the ferry to check things out. Hell, get the whole department out of bed, if you have to. I want this whole island crawling with uniforms, looking into every corner, questioning anything that moves. Then, of course, you'd better put in a call to Doc Coop and get hold of Charlie."

Magnus Coop was the town physician who doubled as the county medical examiner, and Charlie Pricker was the police department's other detective, in charge of gathering physical evidence.

"Dirksen is securing the site," Ginger replied. "Two uniforms are already at the ferry and a half dozen more should be out cruising by now. I had to leave a message for Magnus; he was busy delivering twins. And Charlie's on his way."

"Good," Ruben acknowledged, allowing himself a small smile because, as usual, she was way ahead of him.

"You know who this is, don't you?" she asked.

The police chief squinted down at the teenager. "She looks familiar," he murmured, but he was unable to place her.

"Tara Breckenridge," Ginger told him.

The name clicked. He knew who she was now. He looked at the brutalized body. "Jesus," he breathed.

She was the same age as Stacey, even, he thought, in a couple of the same classes at school. He knew that, with just a different toss of the dice, he could as easily have been looking at his own daughter.

"This is going to turn the whole island upside down," Ginger predicted.

Ruben struggled to his feet and climbed out of the Dumpster, feeling a sharp stab across his back because, in his haste, he had neglected to put on his brace. It was years since his last murder case, at least a decade since he'd had to deal with anything like this. He was a month short of his forty-sixth birthday, but at this moment, he felt closer to sixty-six.

He sighed an unhappy sigh. "I guess it was bound to happen someday," he said.

"What?" Ginger asked.

"Seward Island's first homicide."

5

Church services had barely begun before word of the murder had spread to every corner of the little island, leaving residents in a state of total shock. In the entire history of the peaceful community, nothing like this, nothing even remotely approaching this, had ever happened before. Almost everyone had either known the victim or knew her family, but even those few who didn't were outraged by the brutal and senseless death. The entire population felt violated.

"If something like this can happen to Tara," they whispered to one another over the telephone, across picket fences, at street corners, "it can happen to anyone."

To be sure, Tara wasn't just anyone. She was the daughter of the most prominent family on the Island. Her father, Kyle Breckenridge, was president and CEO of the Puget Sound Savings and Loan, and her mother, the former Mary Seward, was a direct descendant of the old Commodore himself.

In addition, Kyle was on the board of the chamber of commerce, a deacon in the Episcopal church, past president of the PTA, and a respected member of Rotary, the Elks, and the Hunt Club. It was generally known that he held the mortgages on at least half the Island's homes, and had never seen fit to foreclose on any of them.

Mary was a member of the Garden Club, worked tirelessly in behalf of Children in Need, a local Christian charity, and just recently had been instrumental in helping to establish the first halfway house in the county to shelter battered women.

Fifteen-year-old Tara was the Breckenridges' firstborn. There was also another daughter, Tori, just turned twelve. Blond and blue-eyed, Tara was the image of her father, and generally considered one of the prettiest girls on the Island. Along with her good looks and her sweet, if somewhat shy, personality went a true concern for those less fortunate than herself, a trait she had inherited from her mother, and that had always made her a community favorite. Just three days ago, she had been elected Harvest Festival Princess by an overwhelming majority of the population.

The housekeeper opened the huge front door at South-wynd, formerly the Seward estate, now known as the Breckenridge estate. The home sat on twenty prime acres in the southeast corner of the Island. It had been built of local cedar and stone by the Commodore's only surviving son in 1830, and added onto by each succeeding generation until the original house was lost in a sprawling architectural amalgam.

Crowning a gentle rise of lush green grass punctuated by blue spruce and maple trees, it afforded a splendid view across Puget Sound to Seattle and Mount Rainier beyond. It was the kind of place that, despite how far he had come in life, still made Ruben feel he ought to look for the service entrance.

"Mr. and Mrs. Breckenridge are not at home," Irma Poole replied to the police chief's question. "They went to Seattle for a christening."

"And the girls?" Ginger asked.

"They're here, of course," she said, and then stopped herself. "No, wait a minute. Just Miss Tori is here. I don't think Miss Tara's come back yet."

"Where did she go?" Ruben inquired obliquely.

"I don't know. Out somewhere, visiting a friend, I think."

"Did she spend the night with this friend?"

"Oh no, she doesn't spend nights out of the house."

"You mean, she went to a friend's house this morning?" Ginger prompted.

"I guess. And early, too. She wasn't at breakfast, and I made apple pancakes."

"Why do you think she's visiting a friend?" Ruben asked.

The housekeeper shrugged.

"Because that's what her father said, when she wasn't here," she told them. "He said that's probably where she went."

Ginger glanced at Ruben. "What time do you expect them back, Mrs. Poole?"

The woman shrugged again. "They didn't say."

"Does Mr. Breckenridge carry a cellular phone with him?" Ruben asked.

"Yes," the housekeeper replied.

"May we have the number, please?"

"I'm not supposed to give that out," the woman said. "Can't it wait until they come home?"

"No," the police chief said gently. "I'm afraid it can't."

Kyle Breckenridge looked much more like a movie star than a bank president. Nearing fifty, he was over six feet tall, with ice blue eyes and blond hair that was turning gray in just the right places. He kept himself in excellent physical condition, and cultivated a year-round tan that was regularly enhanced during the winter months at a local tanning salon. By contrast, his wife, Mary, was a frail, pale thing wearing an unflattering shade of brown.

There was always an air of purpose to Kyle's movements, a

trait that he had cultivated in his youth because he thought it made him look important. It was particularly evident at two o'clock on Sunday afternoon when he strode into the white clapboard building that housed the Puget County Medical Center, his wife almost a shadow in his wake.

The clinic interior was a pleasant surprise. Decorated in soft colors, with flowery wallpapers and comfortable furniture, it resembled the gracious home it had once been far more than the institution it had become. Magnus Coop, the Seward family physician for close to forty years, waited in the foyer with Ruben Martinez.

"All right, what's going on?" Kyle demanded as soon as he was through the front door. "You tell us to get on the next ferry back, but you won't say why."

"I'm afraid we have some bad news, Mr. Breckenridge," replied Ruben. "I didn't think it was something you'd want to discuss on the phone."

Mary Breckenridge gasped. "Is it Tara?" she whispered. "Did something happen to Tara?"

"Why would you think that, Mary?" Coop asked. Barely as tall as she, the doctor closely resembled a gnome. He had a shock of white hair and his small brown eyes, which peered through steel-rimmed spectacles perched halfway down his nose, missed very little.

"Because," she replied, darting a look at her husband, "she wasn't home this morning when we left to go to the christening."

"Do you know where she was, Mrs. Breckenridge?" Ruben asked.

"We thought she might have gone to visit a friend," Kyle answered for his wife.

"A specific friend?"

"I don't know, a girlfriend, a classmate," he said. "But never mind that. Please tell us what this is all about."

Coop cleared his throat. "I'm sorry," he said gently. "There's no easy way to say this . . . Tara is dead."

Mary Breckenridge began to wail, an eerie sort of sound that rose to an unearthly shriek as she stared first at her husband, then at the police chief, and finally at the medical examiner. "Tara . . . dead? Did you say Tara was dead?"

Her husband assisted her into the nearest chair, and Coop deftly administered a hypodermic he had been wise enough to prepare in advance.

"What do you mean Tara is dead?" Kyle then demanded, turning on Ruben, his face ashen. "How do you know she's dead?"

"She was found early this morning," the police chief told him.

"Found?" Kyle repeated, not comprehending. "What are you talking about?"

"An Island resident discovered her body at Madrona Point," Ruben said carefully. "It appears she was stabbed to death."

"Of course, we don't know all the circumstances yet," the medical examiner added. "We just brought her in."

"Stabbed?" Kyle said slowly, as though it were a word with which he was unfamiliar. He stared at the police chief. "You mean, it wasn't some kind of accident? She wasn't hit by a car? She didn't fall or drown? You're saying that someone actually . . . murdered her?"

Ruben nodded. "I'm afraid so," he murmured.

"It appears that way," Coop concurred.

The starch seemed to drain from the bank president's body. He clutched at the high back of Mary's chair to keep himself upright. "How could this have happened?" he managed to cry. "Why?"

"We don't know yet," Ruben said with a leaden sigh.

"But we intend to find out," Magnus declared. He glanced down at Mary. The fast-acting sedative was already taking effect;

the woman was slumped in the chair, the eerie shriek subsiding into a tuneless lament. She was no longer paying any attention to the conversation. "We need you to sign some papers, Kyle."

"What kind of papers?"

"For the autopsy."

Breckenridge gave the medical examiner an agonized look. "Autopsy?" he rasped. "No—no autopsy. I can't let you cut her up." He glanced down at his wife. "What do you want to do—kill Mary, too?"

"I'm afraid it's necessary, sir," Ruben told him. "An autopsy is essential to our investigation. Whether we like it or not, a crime has been committed. In order to find out who did this awful thing, we have to be allowed to collect every possible piece of evidence."

"I can appreciate your position, Chief Martinez," Kyle replied, "but I hardly think that anything essential will be gained from disemboweling my daughter."

Ruben barely knew the banker, but Magnus Coop had known Kyle Breckenridge for twenty years, ever since the man had arrived on Seward Island and won the hand of the town's wealthiest young woman.

"Well, the thing is, you see, we don't really need your permission," the doctor said kindly but firmly. "Signing the papers is just a formality. In homicide cases, an autopsy is mandatory."

Breckenridge's face froze in anguish. "Then go ahead and do whatever it is you have to do," came the abrupt reply.

"I want to see my baby," Mary wailed suddenly. "Take me to see my baby. Maybe it isn't Tara. Maybe you've made a horrible mistake."

Out of her line of vision, Coop shook his head at Kyle, thinking of the mangled body he had brought in from Madrona Point less than an hour ago, and that now lay on a table in the back room that served as the morgue, covered with a sheet.

"If Magnus says it's Tara," Breckenridge told his wife, his expression ragged, "then you can believe it's Tara. Do you really think that he'd put us through this if he weren't sure?"

"I need to examine her first, Mary," Coop said gently. "And find out what happened to her. After that, of course you can see her."

"That's exactly what you always say when she gets sick," Mary murmured.

"Yes, I guess it is."

"Well, that's all right then, Magnus," she conceded with a pathetic smile. "You take all the time you need to make her well again."

Deborah Frankel spent her Sundays doing the laundry. In an overcommitted life, it was the only time she had. During the week, she took the ferry to Seattle and her job as a vice president of a major investment firm. Saturday mornings, she did the marketing, and whatever other shopping was necessary. Saturday afternoons, she allotted to her husband, Jerry, and their eight-year-old son, Matthew.

This Saturday, they had spent their time together bicycling around Madrona Point, and as usual Matthew had tried too hard to keep up with his father, and ended up falling, scraping his knees and getting blood all over his brand-new jeans. Deborah had taken the pants from the boy immediately after they got back home, making far more of a fuss than the incident probably warranted, and deposited them in the sink to soak overnight.

As a result, when she finished folding the clean sheets and towels, and set about sorting the clothes, separating the whites from the colors and the lights from the darks, she was confused to find, buried in the pile, the light gray sweatshirt with the Seward Island emblem on it that Jerry had worn yesterday, also splattered with blood.

She located him in the library—an alcove, really, off the living room in the Northwest-style cedar and glass house, where they had put his books and papers and his antique rolltop desk so that she could have the spare bedroom for her high-tech home office. He was sprawled in a soft leather recliner they had managed to squeeze between the desk and the window, scowling over the *Sunday Times* crossword puzzle. It was almost nine months since they had left Scarsdale, but he still insisted on keeping his subscription to the New York newspaper.

"How did your sweatshirt get all bloody?" she asked, holding it out at him.

Jerry Frankel looked up in surprise. He had a nice face with even features that seemed to light up from within when he smiled. Dark hair fell across his forehead in boyish fashion. His warm brown eyes focused on something just past her shoulder.

"I cut myself," he replied after a blank second or two, and held up a bandaged thumb.

"All that blood from one little cut?"

He shrugged. "It was a deep cut."

"Why didn't you say something about it?" she persisted irritably.

"I did it last night," her husband replied, "working in the shop. It was after you went to bed. I didn't want to wake you."

"Couldn't you have washed the shirt out? Or at the very least put it in the sink with Matthew's jeans?"

He shrugged again. "I didn't think of it," he told her. "What's the big deal? I knew you were doing laundry today."

Deborah sighed and took the shirt to the sink in the utility room. She removed Matthew's jeans, filled the basin with fresh water, and added a good measure of Clorox. If the bloodstains had not yet had time to set, she thought, there was a chance they might come out.

6

Gail Brown was a third-generation Islander who left after high school for a bachelor's degree in English from Wellesley College in Massachusetts, a master's in journalism from Columbia University in New York, and a series of jobs on half a dozen Eastern newspapers before coming home to assume the editorship of the *Seward Sentinel*.

For decades, the publication had enjoyed a comfortable reputation as a commentary on the community's social life. Gail signaled her return by throwing a rather large wrench into the well-greased works.

"It's no longer enough to report that the Garden Club held its annual meeting," the anorexic brunette with a bushy ponytail and thick eyeglasses told her staff, "or that Susie Sweetpea celebrated her sixteenth birthday with a luncheon at Gull House. That kind of stuff just doesn't do it for the majority of our residents anymore—or advertisers, in case you haven't been noticing."

There were some nods and shrugs and a couple of sighs from those who had crammed themselves into the editor's office.

"If we wish to maintain our exorbitant salaries," Gail continued, pausing for the little titter she knew would come, "we quite simply have to increase revenue. To do that, we need to increase circulation. So from now on, the *Seward Sentinel* is going to become Puget County's newspaper of record. We're going to start dealing with the real issues—the serious issues that confront us, on the Island and around the whole county—politics, religion, education, land use, taxes, corruption—all the things people need to know to make informed decisions about the future of the place where they live. No one will be exempt from our legitimate scrutiny, and no topic will be off limits."

"Don't we risk losing the current subscribers who like the paper the way it is?" someone asked.

"If there are some who don't cotton to the new concept, let's invite them to write and tell us about it," the editor suggested with a mischievous grin. "We'll print their comments."

In six months, the newspaper's circulation had tripled. Within a year, advertising was up by forty percent. And before the end of Gail's second year at the helm, "Letters to the Editor" had grown from a lackluster weekly column to two full pages of. often vigorous debate in almost every issue.

"If you really want to know what's happening on Seward Island," it came to be said, "just read the letters."

It was true.

"The character of a community is not defined by what happens there," Gail shrewdly observed. "It's defined by people's reactions to what happens there."

The day after Tara Breckenridge's death, the editor was at her desk by dawn, composing a suitably sympathetic, yet uplifting editorial. Engrossed as she may have been in her task, she was nonetheless aware of the steady stream of locals who were hand-delivering their written statements to the front counter just beyond her office.

The *Sentinel* operated out of a pretty gray building with white gingerbread trim that sat off by itself on Johansen Street, at the southernmost end of town. As the story went, the place, known as Curtis House, had originally been built in 1915 by one Adelaide Curtis, the town's most infamous madam, who had the audacity to erect it right at the juncture of Commodore Street and Seward Way. The city leaders were in an uproar, apparently caused not so much by moral outrage as by their desire not to be seen frequenting the establishment. They literally had it moved, at the taxpayers' expense, of course, to its present, somewhat less conspicuous location. Gail was never able to document the truth of the tale, but just the idea gave the little house a delicious dash of character.

At eight-ten, Iris Tanaka, the *Sentinel's* diminutive editorial assistant, poked her head into Gail's office. "This is unbelievable," she exclaimed. "We've already got over two hundred letters about Tara Breckenridge, and they're still pouring in."

"Everyone wants his fifteen lines of fame," the editor said with a sigh, removing her glasses to rub the bridge of her nose.

"But what are we going to do with them all?"

"Sort through them," Gail told her. "Deep-six the ones that are obviously just about currying favor with the Breckenridge family. Then pick half a dozen of the more eloquent ones that genuinely mourn Tara for all the right reasons, and two or three of those that, despite the tragedy, just can't resist blaming the victim."

Iris wrinkled her nose in distaste. "At a time like this, do you really want to open that can of worms?"

The editor replaced her glasses. "Healthy debate is good for a community," she replied, turning back to her computer. "And it sells."

Jerry Frankel swung his maroon Taurus wagon into the space assigned to him in the teachers' section of the Seward High School parking lot. Climbing out, he buttoned his brown tweed jacket over his tan checked shirt, brushed the hair out of his eyes, grabbed his briefcase, and hurried up the covered walk to the north entrance of the building that had grown from a one-room schoolhouse, constructed in 1865, into a sprawling brick complex that included a gymnasium, an indoor swimming pool, a theater, and a science laboratory that were the envy of the Pacific Northwest and a testament to the generosity of the Island's residents when it came to the well-being of their children.

It was eight-twenty. Deborah had taken the early ferry into Seattle, leaving Jerry with the task of getting Matthew up, dressed and fed, and delivering him to his elementary school. Now the history teacher had barely enough time to get to his classroom.

The early ferry wasn't the only reason he was late. He had overslept because of a toothache that had begun to nag at him on Sunday afternoon, and by evening had progressed to a throbbing pain that kept him tossing and turning most of the night until Deborah had finally gotten up and given him a sleeping pill.

Jerry reached his second-floor classroom a scant two minutes before the bell. Fortunately, he reflected, as he began to pull an assortment of books and papers out of his briefcase and set them on his desk, Matthew had inherited his mother's teeth.

His lower jaw was throbbing unmercifully. Picking up a piece of chalk and beginning to scribble the lesson for this period on the blackboard, Jerry tried to calculate how long he had to wait before he could safely take another dose of aspirin. So absorbed was he by his own discomfort that it was a full five minutes past the bell before he realized that half the seats in the room were still empty.

"What's going on?" he asked. "Where is everybody this morning?"

"In shock," Hank Kriedler, a clean-cut blond sophomore, replied from the back.

"Haven't you heard?" a teary-eyed Jeannie Gemmetta said from her seat in the first row. "Gosh, I thought everybody would've heard by now. Tara's dead."

"Dead?" The teacher turned startled brown eyes on the chubby teen. "What do you mean Tara's dead?"

"She was murdered Saturday night."

"Murdered?" Jerry sagged against the corner of his desk. He had missed the weekly staff coffee, and hadn't had time to stop at the office, or even check the message board. He looked at the empty desk in the middle of the third aisle and felt weak. "I'm sorry," he said to no one in particular. "Does anyone know what happened?"

"She was stabbed," Jack Tannauer said.

"At least two dozen times," Melissa Senn amplified from her seat near the door, a raven-haired beauty who had come in second to Tara in the Harvest Princess election.

"And then dumped in a Dumpster," Jeannie finished, thinking that the history teacher was suddenly looking quite pale.

Jerry swallowed hard. "Do they have any idea who did it?" he managed to ask.

The students craned their necks in the direction of Stacey Martinez, who sat by the window.

The police chief's daughter did not appreciate the scrutiny. "I don't think so," she replied. "But then, I really don't know anything about it."

The Seward Island Police Department was housed in a square cinder block building at the eastern end of Commodore Street. It was affectionately called Graham Hall, after the Island's beloved first police chief.

Designed in 1949, when the population was less than three thousand and the department employed only six people, it was totally inadequate for the present complement of seventeen. The walls were badly in need of paint, the desks were battered gray metal, the floors were scarred gray linoleum, and the uniformed officers worked practically one on top of another in the cramped space. For five years in a row, ballot initiatives that would have allowed for the renovation and enlargement of the building had been voted down by the citizenry.

At exactly nine o'clock, Albert Hoch, the broad-beamed mayor of the city, sometimes referred to behind his back as the Bald Eagle because of his prominent nose and shiny pate, barged unannounced into the police chief's closet-sized office.

"Talk to me, Ruben," he bellowed, his voice carrying easily throughout the building. "We don't have violent crime on this island. Nobody's ever been murdered here."

"Well, somebody certainly has now," the chief responded mildly.

"Kyle Breckenridge is one of my closest friends," Hoch snapped. "And that 'somebody' was my goddaughter, goddammit. Now, I want to know whatever it is you know so far, and I expect to be updated every single day until this case is solved."

Ruben sighed. It wasn't that he disliked the pompous official. It was that Albert Hoch possessed very little acumen for police work.

"So far, all we know is that she was stabbed to death sometime late Saturday night or early Sunday morning, and then tossed into a Dumpster out at Madrona Point," Ruben told him. "Of course, we should know more once the autopsy is completed, and the investigation of the crime scene is finished."

"Do you have any clues?" Hoch persisted. "Do you have any idea who could have done it?"

"Nothing concrete as of this moment," Ruben said. "But then, we're just beginning."

The city official was not known for his discretion any more than his acumen, and Ruben had long ago learned that it was unwise to tell the mayor anything the police didn't want immediately spread all over the Island.

"Who are you going to put in charge of the case?" Hoch asked.

"I'm in charge," the police chief replied. "Ginger Earley will be running the investigation. Charlie Pricker will be responsible for the evidence. Before this is over, I expect everyone will be involved, one way or another."

In a department as small as this, it was always how they worked. It seemed absurd to Ruben to be sitting here, reassuring the mayor of what he already knew. After all, the Seward Island police force employed only two detectives: Ginger, whom he had hired himself a little less than two years ago, and Charlie, whom he had inherited, and just last year promoted out of the uniform ranks.

"Jesus," Hoch breathed, wagging his bald head back and forth. "What was Tara doing out at that hour? How did she get all the way to Madrona Point? How did she end up in a Dumpster, for God's sake? Why the hell would anyone do such a thing?"

All good questions, Ruben thought. None of which had an answer. Yet.

"I think Mr. Frankel was really shook up," Melissa Senn said during lunch period.

"Yeah," Jeannie Gemmetta agreed. "Did you see his face? It went so white, for a moment there it looked like he was going to pass out or something."

"I saw that," Melissa confirmed. "He looked totally tragic— almost like he'd lost his best friend."

"Well, Tara was a real looker," Jack Tannauer said. "Who knows—maybe they were getting it on together."

"Don't be ridiculous," Jeannie scoffed. Jack's father managed the Island's movie theater, and some of his son's ideas seemed to come right out of Hollywood. "I think he's just that kind of person. You know, someone who cares about other people." A smile spread across her round, homely face. "I wouldn't mind too much if he cared about me," she said recklessly. "You have to admit, he's awfully cute."

"You think so?" asked Melissa.

"Sure," Jeannie replied. "Those dreamy eyes of his—when they fix on me, it's like he's seeing right into my soul."

"Come on, he's gotta be old enough to be your father," said Bill Graham, a gangly sixteen-year-old with an unhealthy pallor that his friends decided was the result of spending too many hours in the back room of the mortuary where his father worked.

"So what?" Jeannie retorted. "He doesn't look it. In fact, I think he looks a little like Brad Pitt."

"Well, now that you mention it, I guess he *is* pretty cute," Melissa conceded with a giggle.

"Except for his nose," Hank Kriedler said.

"What's wrong with his nose?"

"It's kinda big, don't you think?" the big blond teen replied with a sneer.

"I never noticed," Jeannie admitted.

"It's because he's a Jew," Hank told her.

"He is?" Jeannie exclaimed. "I didn't know that. How do you know that?"

Hank shrugged. "What world have *you* been living in? I thought everybody knew."

"There isn't very much to go on yet," Albert Hoch reported, having been summoned to Kyle Breckenridge's spacious office on the corner of Commodore Street and Seward Way shortly before the end of the day.

The president and CEO of the Puget Sound Savings and Loan sat behind a sleek rosewood desk that seemed to float on a sea of aquamarine carpeting, and fixed hollow eyes on the portly mayor.

"I want to know whatever there is," he said.

"Well, Ruben's got everyone working on the case, of course. It's got top priority. The autopsy is in progress, and so is the crime scene investigation. Magnus should be giving Ruben his report in a couple of days, and Charlie Pricker will probably be done at the crime scene sometime tomorrow. Of course, you know it could be weeks, if not months, before anything comes back from the labs. Ginger Earley's already out talking to people—you know, people who knew Tara."

"I suppose that means someone will be coming out to Southwynd," Breckenridge said with a heavy sigh. "To be honest with you, Albert, I don't know how much more of this Mary can take right now."

Hoch nodded. Mary Breckenridge was not a strong woman, he knew. "Anything Phoebe and I can do, you know . . ." he murmured.

"Yes, of course, I certainly appreciate that," Kyle acknowledged, aware that the mayor's wife was at least as big a gossip as the mayor himself. "You two have already been more than kind." He blinked several times and then sat up a little straighter in his chair. "Do you know if there are any viable suspects yet?" he asked. "Has Martinez come up with any possible motive? Does he at least have a theory?"

Hoch twisted his big frame in his seat. Actually, the chief of police was not as forthcoming as the mayor would have preferred, apparently determined to keep whatever speculations he might have to himself, and Hoch had not really pressed him.

"I don't think so," he told Breckenridge. "I know there are situations where the evidence is so overwhelming, and the motive so obvious, that the killer can be identified almost immediately. But that doesn't seem to be the case here. Suspects aren't exactly crawling out of the woodwork. Ruben is going to have to go out and find the bastard. But then, that's what we hired him for, isn't it?"

"One of my students died over the weekend," Jerry Frankel told his wife during dinner Monday evening.

"That's too bad," Deborah murmured, her concentration

split pretty evenly between a plate of linguini and a hefty report that had to be read before breakfast the next morning.

"No, I mean, she was murdered."

Deborah looked up. "Somebody was murdered—here on Seward Island?" Her husband nodded. "My goodness, what a shock," she said. "I didn't think folks did anything more exciting around this place than watch the cedars grow."

They were alone in the soft gray dining room. Jerry routinely fed Matthew at six, then got him bathed and into bed. Deborah rarely got home before eight, but she was usually in time to kiss the boy good night. Jerry would have dinner on the table when she came down—he had become a fairly decent cook—and if anything worth discussing had happened that day, they would discuss it while they ate. Unless, of course, she had brought work home with her. It was one of the compromises they made when they agreed that Deborah would ask for the transfer to her company's Seattle office, and the only teaching job Jerry could find in the middle of a school year was on an isolated island with an inflexible ferry schedule.

"The kids were all talking about it," he told her now. "Matthew even mentioned it when he came home from school."

"Did you know her well?"

"I knew her, but not all that well," he said, casually winding his linguini inside a large spoon. "Her name was Tara Breckenridge. She was one of the students I taught in summer school, and she was in one of my sophomore classes this semester."

A shadow flickered across Deborah Frankel's light eyes. "What happened to her?" she asked.

Jerry frowned at the pasta coiled inside his spoon as though he were unsure whether he wanted to put it into his mouth. "According to what the kids say, she was stabbed to death, and then somehow ended up in the Dumpster at Madrona Point."

Deborah didn't know anything about Tara Breckenridge,

but the Frankels had been at Madrona Point just two days ago. A little shiver ran down her spine.

"How dreadful," she murmured as she forked up a mouthful of her linguini and turned to the next page of her report.

"Everyone at school is real upset about Tara," Stacey reported to her father that evening. "It's all they could talk about. Every single period, they kept asking me if I knew anything. I hate it when they do that, like I'm really going to tell them anything you tell me."

"I don't suppose you *do* know anything, do you?" Ruben asked with a sigh.

"Not really," Stacey said thoughtfully. "It's funny, you know. Everybody liked Tara. But when you listen to what they say, not that many kids actually knew her. They kind of just knew *about* her. She wasn't spoiled. In fact, I think her parents were pretty strict with her. She wasn't a snob or anything like that, either. She never lorded her money or her looks or her social position over any of us—she always went out of her way to be real nice to everyone—but she sort of, I don't know, kept to herself most of the time."

"What did you think of her?"

Along with his eyes and complexion, Stacey had inherited Ruben's keen mind, and he had learned that he could trust her instincts about people.

"I really hardly knew her—even though she was in two of my classes in eighth grade, three of my classes last year, and two again this year. You see, that's exactly what I mean—she would never let you get too close. I always thought she was a pretty decent student, but I guess maybe her grades had slipped or something because somebody said her parents made her go to summer school. The longest conversation we ever had was over some algebra notes."

"Who were her friends?"

"Let's see . . . the only girls I ever saw her with on a regular basis were Melissa Senn and Jeannie Gemmetta."

"Any boyfriends?"

Stacey shook her head. "She and Melissa and Jeannie ran with Hank Kriedler and his crowd sometimes, but I'm pretty certain it was just a group thing."

"Are you sure you never saw her alone with any of them? With anyone?"

The teenager considered that for a moment because there was something that seemed to hover around the edge of her memory, just out of reach. But then she shrugged and shook her head.

"If I did, I guess I've forgotten," she said.

7

"Tara Breckenridge wasn't just dumped at Madrona Point," Charlie Pricker declared first thing Tuesday morning. "She was killed there, too."

He was seated in Ruben's tiny office, the spare chair tipped back against the wall. His rimless glasses rested on top of his curly brown hair. The police chief sat at his desk, which left Ginger with a small square of standing space by the door.

"How do you know that?" she asked.

Pricker grinned. "We found the spot where he did her," he said. "It was about twenty yards from the Dumpster. Lots of blood. Looks like he tried to sop it up with something—maybe that rug he rolled her into because it was soaked and I found pieces of gravel in it. When that didn't work, I guess he figured to cover it up by moving the gravel around. I don't think he could really see too well in the dark." The detective wagged his head. "Here's hoping that these people don't learn that you can never get rid of all the blood."

"Why didn't he just leave her where she fell?" Ginger wondered aloud.

Pricker shrugged. "He's a meticulous man, our perp; a regular clean freak. Didn't want to leave a mess, I guess. Or maybe he put her in the Dumpster because he thought no one would find her there. You know, he actually went into the park bathroom after he did her and washed up. We found blood in there, too."

"Hers or his?" Ruben asked.

"Don't know," Pricker said. "All I can tell you is that she was type A and so was some of the blood we found in the bathroom. But we also found some type AB and some O, which may or may not be related. And I'd say at least a hundred fingerprints, which again may or may not be related."

"Public park? After a busy weekend?" Ruben mused. "A long shot at best. Any of them bloody?"

"No, none of them," Charlie replied. "But we got a partial print from the cross Tara was wearing."

At that, both Ruben and Ginger leaned forward.

"Bloody?" the police chief asked.

The detective shook his head. "Sorry."

"Well, it's something anyway," Ginger said. "It doesn't guarantee it got put there at the time of the murder, but we might be able to use it."

Ruben rubbed his back against his chair. "The first fortyeight hours in a homicide case are the most important," he told the two detectives. "That's when you expect to find the bulk of the evidence that will eventually connect the crime to the killer."

"So what do we have?" Ginger queried.

The Breckenridge case was forty-nine hours old. Ruben sighed. "Not enough," he replied.

They had an approximate time of death. They were pretty certain the autopsy would show that Tara Breckenridge had died of multiple stab wounds. They had eliminated both Tom and Billy Hildress from any suspicion. They knew the killer had removed the rug in which Tara had been rolled from the Dumpster, because sixty-six-year-old Island resident Egon Doyle had come forward to identify it as having belonged to his recently deceased mother. He told the police that he had personally deposited the rug in the Dumpster sometime around five o'clock on Saturday afternoon. They had eliminated Egon Doyle from any suspicion. And now they knew for certain that Madrona Point was the scene of the actual crime. Other than that, they had no eyewitnesses, no murder weapon, no apparent motive, no suspects.

"People around here desperately want to believe that this was done by some psychotic transient, you know," Ginger said. "The idea that Tara could have been brutally murdered by one of their own is just too frightening for them to contemplate."

"I can understand how they feel," Ruben conceded. "I don't blame them."

Ginger looked at him shrewdly. "You don't think it's a transient, do you?"

The police chief shook his head. "No," he admitted. "But I could be wrong. It's just a feeling I have, a hunch, about the nature of the crime."

"Well, I think we can rule out anything drug-related," Ginger said. "According to everyone I've spoken to, Tara was so straight she never even took aspirin. And nobody ever saw her anywhere near the junk druggies."

Marijuana, crank, and crystal meth were the current drugs of choice among teenagers, and police records showed that Island usage was more than double the national average.

"Charlie, can we rule out drugs?" Ruben asked.

The detective nodded. "Yup," he replied. "According to Magnus, she tested clean for both drugs and alcohol—and aspirin."

"If this was a random attack by some lunatic, either on or off the Island," observed Ginger, "it could be just the beginning."

"If this was random," Ruben said, "I'm going to lock my daughter in her room forever."

"Unless we come up with a motive," Ginger persisted, "what else can we assume?"

Ruben stood up and stretched his back. "Obviously, it isn't going to do us much good to sit around and assume anything at this point," he declared. "Charlie, go find us a smoking gun—or at the very least, a bloody knife. Ginger, go talk to everyone who knew her." He paused, remembering what Stacey had told him. "Talk to everyone who knew anything about her."

"I'm gone," said Charlie. "If you need me, I'll be at Madrona Point."

"I'm gone, too," Ginger told him. "If you need me, I'll be at the high school."

Ruben nodded. "If you need me, I'll be at Southwynd."

He rang the front doorbell at exactly ten o'clock.

"Come in, Chief Martinez," Mary Breckenridge invited, answering the door herself. "My husband is expecting you."

She was very pale. Her eyes were red, and there were dark circles around them, giving her a rather ghoulish look. Her light brown hair looked uncombed. Her black dress was obviously expensive but not flattering.

"I'm sorry to have to bother you in your time of grief," Ruben murmured.

She led him down a pale green marble corridor, enhanced by ancestral busts on graceful pedestals and huge vases of flowers, to a paneled library with gleaming leather furniture and thick red carpeting. Books of every conceivable size and category were crammed into floor-to-ceiling shelves. Among them, Ruben caught a quick glimpse of what were most likely first editions of works by Stevenson, Kipling, Hardy, and Maugham.

Slivers of morning sun slanted through windows covered with narrow wooden blinds. A small fire burned in a huge stone fireplace. This was clearly not a room that children played in. It was exclusively a man's room, and it was immaculate. As far as

Ruben could tell, there was not a speck of dust on any surface, nor a single item out of place.

"I'm more than happy to tell you whatever you want to know," Kyle Breckenridge said. "But I don't think I know anything that will help."

He was dressed in a dark gray business suit, with a crisp white shirt and charcoal tie. His normally tan skin had a definite gray tinge to it.

"Well, it sometimes happens," Ruben told him, "that a seemingly unimportant piece of information can turn out to be the key to a whole case."

Breckenridge gestured to two wing chairs that faced each other in front of the fire. His wife started to back out the library door.

"Please don't go, Mrs. Breckenridge," Ruben forestalled her. "If it would be all right, I'd like this conversation to be with both of you."

She looked at her husband and he shrugged, so she pulled up a side chair and sat down on the edge of it. This was obviously not a room in which she spent a great deal of time, Ruben guessed. He extracted a pad and a pen from his jacket pocket.

"Suppose we start with last Saturday," he suggested in a gentle, low-key tone. "When was the last time you saw Tara that evening?"

"I think it was about ten o'clock," Kyle replied. "We had dinner at seven-thirty. Then we watched some television. At nine o'clock, our younger daughter went up to bed. Then at ten, my wife retired with a headache, and I came in here to read for a while."

"And Tara?"

"When my wife went upstairs, Tara went to her room to do her homework."

"Was that customary?"

"What?"

"For Tara to spend Saturday evenings in her room doing homework?"

"I don't know if I'd call it customary, but it was something she often did, especially when she had an exam to study for, or a project due."

"Did she have an exam or a project?"

Breckenridge glanced at his wife. "I don't really know," he replied.

"Do you know, Mrs. Breckenridge?" Ruben asked politely.

"No, I don't," Mary Breckenridge almost whispered. "But I guess she must have."

"What did Tara generally do on those weekends when there were no exams or projects?" The question was directed to the mother, but the father replied.

"If my wife and I had plans to go out, she would stay home with her sister."

"And if not?"

"Sometimes we would all go out to dinner or to the movies," Breckenridge said. "Occasionally, we would go into Seattle for a concert or a play."

"Did Tara ever go out with friends on Saturday nights?"

"Once in a while," Breckenridge responded.

"Did she have a boyfriend?"

"No," the father said flatly. "We didn't allow her to date. She was only fourteen years old."

"Fifteen," the mother murmured.

Ruben glanced briefly from one to the other. "Where was Tara on Saturday during the day?" he asked.

"She went into town with her sister," Mary replied. "I dropped them off myself a little before eleven. They had lunch and they went shopping, and then I picked them up. We were home by three." The mother's gaze wandered toward the fire. "They were very close."

"And from three o'clock on, Tara was here?"

"Yes."

"Did she get any phone calls? Or make any that you know of?"

Kyle shook his head. "I wouldn't know. I was in a golf tournament on Saturday. I didn't get home until shortly after six."

"Do you know, Mrs. Breckenridge?" Ruben inquired.

Mary shook her head. "I didn't hear her make any calls. But there's a telephone in her room, so she could have."

"All right now," Ruben said as kindly as he could, "based on our current information, we believe that Tara's death occurred between midnight and two o'clock on Sunday morning. Which means that she had to have left the house sometime after ten, when you last saw her, and probably before midnight. Do you know why she would have gone out that late?"

Kyle shrugged. "No, I don't."

"And she said nothing to either of you before she went out?"

"As I've already told you, I was here in the library, reading. I didn't see her after she went upstairs, and I didn't hear her go out."

Ruben turned to the mother.

"I was in my room," she replied to the unasked question. "My headache."

"But you know it was after ten o'clock?"

"Yes," the father said.

"Did Tara often do that kind of thing?" Ruben asked.

"What kind of thing?"

"Go out late at night?"

"No, of course not," Breckenridge replied. "She was a good girl, very well behaved. She was always in bed by eleven o'clock on Saturday nights. Unless, of course, we were out."

"But that wasn't the case this Saturday night, was it?"

Kyle shifted in his seat. "No, I guess not."

"And she left the house without telling you."

"Apparently."

"And in the morning, when she wasn't here, you assumed she was at a friend's house."

"Yes."

"Why?" Ruben asked.

"It seemed the most reasonable assumption," Breckenridge admitted. "She had said something at dinner about needing to return some chemistry notes."

"But when she wasn't here for breakfast, you weren't concerned?"

Breckenridge frowned. "I was surprised, and I admit even a little annoyed because she hadn't bothered to tell anyone she was going out, but I wasn't concerned," he said. "This has always been such a safe island. Besides, we didn't know she'd been out all night, so we didn't think we had any reason to be concerned."

"Did anyone look to see if Tara had slept in her bed?"

"I did," Mary said. "The sheets seemed wrinkled. It looked as though she'd slept in them."

"It never occurred to us that anything could have happened to her," Breckenridge said. He sighed deeply. "How I wish I'd checked on her before I went to bed."

"You couldn't have known," Ruben told him.

Kyle closed his eyes. "No," he said. "I suppose not."

"By the way, what time *did* you go to bed?"

"About eleven-thirty, I think," Breckenridge replied. "Maybe a little later." He looked at his wife. "What time was it when I came up, do you remember?"

Mary Breckenridge blinked several times. "About eleven-thirty," she said.

"You're sure of that?" Ruben prodded gently.

She nodded wordlessly.

"The housekeeper can tell you," Breckenridge said suddenly. "Now that I think of it, she was in the front hallway, turning out the lights, when I went upstairs."

"Was there any kind of an argument during the evening that you recall?" Ruben asked. "Was Tara upset about anything? Were either of you angry at her for any reason?"

"No," Breckenridge replied. "There was no argument. No one was angry."

"Could there possibly have been something personal that was bothering her?"

"What do you mean?"

"Well, I've got a fifteen-year-old at home," Ruben said with a wry smile, "and I know she occasionally has problems that seem insurmountable to her at the time. Often, at that age, kids find it hard to discuss personal things with their parents."

"Why are you asking all these questions?" Breckenridge asked with a groan.

"I know how terribly painful this must be for you," Ruben said. "But the only way we're going to find out how and why this terrible thing happened to Tara is to learn all we can about her and her habits."

Breckenridge sighed. "Well, Chief Martinez, if she had a personal problem that she didn't feel she could discuss with us, then we wouldn't know about it, would we?"

"How about you, Mrs. Breckenridge?" Ruben asked. "Did you notice if there was anything that seemed to be troubling her?"

"No," the woman whispered, tears filling her eyes.

"How about her sister? You said they were close. Would Tara have talked to *her*?"

"Tori is barely twelve years old," Breckenridge said. "If Tara did talk to her, it couldn't have been about anything more important than dolls and hair ribbons. As I told you before, Tori went to bed at nine o'clock on Saturday night. She knows nothing—we've asked her. She's very upset by the death of her sister, and I would beg you not to make things worse right now by interrogating her about it. Perhaps in a week or two, when it's not so—so painful."

"Of course," Ruben conceded. "I certainly understand. All right then, you said something about chemistry notes. If Tara had decided she needed to return those notes that night, where would she have gone? To a classmate? A friend? Do you know who that might have been?"

"I guess I wouldn't know," Breckenridge admitted after a few seconds. "I didn't really know much about her classmates or her friends."

"Would you know, Mrs. Breckenridge?" Ruben inquired.

"Melissa, perhaps, or Jeannie," she ventured, dabbing at her cheeks with a sodden handkerchief. "I think they had chemistry together."

"Assuming she was on foot, do both of these girls live within walking distance?"

There was a momentary pause.

"Jeannie lives on the other side of the Island," Mary Breckenridge replied. "Melissa lives about half a mile away. There may be other classmates who live nearer. I don't know."

"You know, it's possible that all she did was go out for a walk," Kyle said suddenly. "I mean, not to go anywhere specific, just to get some fresh air. It could be that simple."

"Fresh air?" Ruben repeated politely.

Breckenridge nodded. "The weather was beautiful on Saturday, quite warm for the season. Maybe she just went out walking, and some psycho came cruising by, and for some terrible reason, she let him pick her up. Not anyone from Seward Island, of course," he added hastily. "I mean a stranger, out for his own sick kind of fun."

"You could be right," Ruben conceded and veered onto another subject. "Does your housekeeper live in?"

"Yes, she does," Breckenridge confirmed.

"Anyone else?"

"No."

"Does she have visitors?"

"No. Mrs. Poole is a widow. She has no children, no visitors. We're probably the closest thing she has to any family. She's been with us for more than twenty years."

"Perhaps I might have a word with her," Ruben suggested. "Just to get everything straight in my head."

Breckenridge reached over and pulled on a thick silk cord that hung beside the fireplace. The three of them sat in silence until Irma Poole knocked softly on the door and entered the room.

"Chief Martinez is here about Tara's death," Kyle told her. "He's looking to confirm our whereabouts on Saturday night. I've already told him that I saw you turning off the lights as I was going up to bed. Mrs. Breckenridge and I believe it was around eleven-thirty. What do you remember?"

Irma Poole looked at her employer and nodded. "It was just eleven-thirty," she said.

"You're sure of that?" Ruben asked.

"Quite sure," the housekeeper replied.

"How do you come to remember the time so exactly?"

"Because I always turn off the lights and lock up at eleven-thirty," Irma Poole said.

"Did you see or hear anything out of the ordinary that night? Anything at all that you might not have thought important at the time, but now strikes you as unusual?"

There was a slight pause. "No," she said finally, and this time she looked straight at Ruben, her eyes filled with sorrow. "I didn't see anything and I didn't hear anything."

"Thank you, Mrs. Poole," Kyle said, and the housekeeper withdrew.

"She loved Tara," Mary said with a pathetic attempt at a smile. "Everyone loved Tara."

Ruben glanced at Breckenridge; the man was staring into the fire, his face drawn and gray. He hated putting them through this, but he had to do it.

"If it became necessary, Mr. Breckenridge, would you be willing to take a lie detector test and give us a sample of your blood?"

Mary gasped openly at that, and Kyle fixed the police chief with a glacial stare.

"Are you serious?" he demanded. "Do you really think I could have done such a thing to my own child?"

Ruben shrugged. "I'm sorry," he apologized. "But I wouldn't be doing my job if I didn't investigate even the most unlikely of possibilities."

"Then, at the point when you find sufficient reason to believe that I am implicated in this case in any way," came the stiff retort, "I will present myself at Graham Hall for whatever tests you wish to perform—given my attorney's consent, of course."

"Thank you," Ruben said smoothly and moved on. "Can either of you think of anyone who might have had a reason to harm your daughter?"

At that, Mary, already too close to the edge, dissolved into tears, burying her face in her handkerchief to muffle her sobs.

Kyle Breckenridge shook his head. "As my wife has already said, Chief Martinez, everyone loved Tara. She didn't have an enemy in the world."

"Well then, how about someone who might have wanted to get to *you* through her?"

"Me?" Breckenridge asked in genuine surprise. "But I have no enemies, either. My whole life has been about helping people. There couldn't possibly be anyone who could hate me so much that he would take it out on that beautiful girl."

His voice faltered on the last few words, and the composure he had tried so hard to maintain finally cracked. He turned away from the police chief.

One of the things Ruben had learned over the years was to know when enough was enough.

"Thank you both for your time," he murmured. "I can see myself out." He stuffed his pad and pen back into his jacket and got up to leave. But when he reached the door to the library, he stopped, wanting to say something relevant to these devastated people. "My daughter means more to me than my life," he said. "I know how I would feel if anything like this happened to her. Please accept my condolences."

At that, Kyle Breckenridge gathered himself together and stood up. "I know you have an investigation to conduct, Chief Martinez," he said in a leaden voice, "and I don't want to hamper you in any way. But we need to bury our daughter and do our grieving. I think the whole island needs that. So please, if you could expedite things so we can do what we have to do, that would mean more to us than anything else right now."

Ruben nodded. "I'll see to it that the body is released as soon as possible."

Now there were tears in the father's eyes. "Get the bastard who did this to my little girl," he whispered.

Ruben drove back to Graham Hall with his mind more on his interview with the Breckenridges than on the road he was following.

It was a sad commentary on the world in which he lived, he decided, that his investigation obliged him to establish Kyle Breckenridge's whereabouts at the time of the murder. The man was obviously grief-stricken, and as a father Ruben couldn't help but put himself in Breckenridge's place. The very idea that anyone might think he could harm a hair on Stacey's head made the police chief's blood run cold with anger, and he knew how he would have responded to such a suggestion.

All things considered, Tara Breckenridge's father had remained a gentleman.

"The police are proceeding on the assumption that Tara Breckenridge was accosted by an assailant or assailants while walking near her home sometime after ten o'clock Saturday night," the *Seward Sentinel* began its lead story the following day.

"According to Mayor Albert Hoch, the popular Island teen might have been on her way to visit a friend, or just out to get some fresh air.

"Said Hoch: 'We have reason to believe that Tara was somewhere in the vicinity of Southwynd when she was abducted by this person or persons, and then taken to Madrona Point, where she met her tragic end.' "

"If there is anything good that can be said of such a terrible tragedy," a member of Seward Episcopal Church where the Breckenridge family worshiped wrote to the editor, "it's that the grief we feel over dear Tara's death has made us cherish every single moment with our own precious children that much more."

"Whether we like it or not, violent crime has come to our island," wrote a crusty fisherman whose son was serving a two-year sentence in a California prison for possession of cocaine. "Perhaps, the only way to keep our young people out of trouble is to keep them off the streets."

8

Malcolm Purdy lived on the west side of Seward Island, on a thirty-acre parcel of land that had been left to him by a great-uncle he never knew. The first thing the crusty ex-Marine did upon acquiring title to the property was to erect a high stone wall around it, secured by an iron gate. The second thing he did was to electrify it.

He had come from nowhere one day about ten years ago, driving off the ferry in a new Jeep Cherokee with a one-eyed dog seated beside him. No one on the Island had ever been able to figure out what he did for a living. He had no apparent job, no visible assets, and aside from his military pension and his modest inheritance, no income anyone could readily identify. He lived alone in the cottage his great-uncle had built, and except for one month each year when he was absent from the Island, he rarely left it.

Those few, mostly delivery people, who got past the gate reported that he was doing nothing with the land. His neighbors said he spent much of his time at target practice, the sound of his rifles carrying easily over the wall. The woman who worked for him three days a week, who did his cleaning, his laundry, and his shopping, and stayed on the property for the entire month he was gone, was as taciturn as her employer. Some said she was also his mistress, but if that were so, it didn't seem to bother her husband very much, a grizzled fisherman who lived aboard his boat for months at a time.

For the first couple of years, Malcolm Purdy was the hot topic of conversation on Seward Island, fueled on by the insatiable curiosity of small-town people to know everything there was to know about everyone. They were told when his fancy computer arrived from a mail-order catalogue company. They knew, almost to the penny, how much he spent on ammunition down at Gus Landry's gun shop. They took note of the NRA literature that regularly filled his mailbox. They assumed he had a small arsenal on his land, but since none of them was ever invited inside to see, they could never prove it. Most of all, they speculated about what he did during the month each year that he left the Island. They would have given almost anything to know where he went, but there was no one to tell them.

Eventually, interest died down, and for a while anyway, the recluse was left to live in relative obscurity. Then strange men began to show up on the Island and find their way to his electrified gate, to stay for a month or two and then be gone.

Shortly after the arrival of the first few visitors, a significant quantity of lumber and other materials was delivered to the property, and the neighbors related that the sounds of target practice had been replaced by the sounds of saws and hammers. Sure enough, a mainland man who installed septic tanks reported that Purdy was building a bunkhouse behind his cottage. A local plumber later confirmed the report.

The Seward gossips began their speculations with renewed fervor. What was going on out there? they wondered. Was he training terrorists? Was he plotting insurrection? Was he harboring wanted criminals?

If Purdy knew how preoccupied the Islanders were with his life, he never let on. It was as if they walked and talked on another planet. He was an orphan from Alabama, who had been handed around from one distant relative to another until he was eighteen years old. The Marine Corps had for many years been everything to him. It gave him an identity he had never had, comrades he would never have found, the discipline he had always lacked, the focus he would otherwise not have gained. And it taught him how to kill: swiftly, cleanly, and without remorse. As much as he was able to love anything, Malcolm Purdy loved the Marines.

He had a wife once, and what he thought was a life with her. One day he came home unexpectedly and found her in bed with another man. He killed them both; coldly, calmly, each with one deliberate shot to the head.

His attorney, a sharp major, managed to exonerate him of any wrongdoing, claiming he had acted out of acute pain and uncontrollable rage in the commission of a justifiable crime of passion, even intimating that the woman and her lover had somehow deserved to die for what they had done.

But the Corps had its image to protect. After twenty-three years of dedicated service, Purdy was quietly and speedily discharged, with all accrued benefits. He didn't blame the Corps; he understood.

He was left with two young daughters, one who was five years old, the other almost three. He took them to a second cousin and her husband in Mobile who were in their thirties and childless.

"I want you to legally adopt the girls," he told them. He gave them a duly executed document in which he renounced all present and future parental claim. "They need a regular home and a good woman to raise them. They don't need to know their mother was a whore and their father was a murderer."

"Where will you go?" his cousin asked. "What will you do?"

"I don't know," he said. "Don't let it concern you."

A month later, a lawyer representing the estate of his great-uncle contacted him.

In the ten years since then, Malcolm Purdy had made no effort to communicate with his cousin, or to find out what had become of his children. He sent no birthday cards and no Christmas presents. But the day after Tara Breckenridge's death was reported in the paper, he picked up the telephone and called Mobile.

"I just wanted to know they were all right," he said.

"They're perfect," his cousin told him. "Bright and beautiful and normal and happy."

"Do they—do they remember . . . anything?" he asked.

"I think they remember only good times," she replied. "Would you like to talk to them?"

"No," he said abruptly. "I just wanted to know they were all right."

9

"All efforts to identify the assailant or assailants whom police believe abducted Tara Breckenridge near her home, and then brutally murdered her, have so far been fruitless," the *Sentinel* told its readers.

"Police are asking anyone who might have seen or heard anything unusual in the vicinity of the Southwynd estate or Madrona Point Park, either late Saturday night or early Sunday morning, to please contact the police as soon as possible.

"'We believe we are looking for a transient,' Mayor Hoch told this reporter. 'Someone who does not live on Seward Island, but was just visiting on the day of the murder when he committed this random act of violence. If anyone saw, spoke to, or knows anything about such a person, we need to hear from you.'

"'Sometimes, just the smallest piece of information,' Detective Ginger Earley said, 'no matter how insignificant or unrelated it may seem, can bring about the resolution of a case.'"

"It is our failure to provide our children with good Christian morals that is causing them to go astray," one of the Island's most righteous religious residents wrote to the editor. "They are falling prey to the hedonism that permeates our society, and we must do everything in our power to bring them back to God."

"Tara Breckenridge's death was a sad and horrifying thing," wrote a housewife and mother of four, "but lack of morals didn't kill her—some deranged lunatic did, and we should not lose sight of that. Our kids are basically good kids."

"If Tara Breckenridge had been at home where decent girls should be instead of out walking somewhere in the middle of the night," wondered a divorced carpenter who rarely saw his own daughter, "would she be dead today?"

Magnus Coop sat at one end of a rectangular metal table in the small, windowless room at Graham Hall that the police used for interviews or meetings of more than three people. The morning paper lay open in front of him. "Sometimes, I don't know which is worse," he declared peering at the newsprint through the steel-rimmed spectacles perched on his nose, "the facts or the speculation."

"Lack of the former often leads to a proliferation of the latter," the police chief, seated opposite him, observed. He looked at the folder in front of the medical examiner. "I assume that's the autopsy we've been waiting for."

"It is."

"So what have we got?"

"I should warn you, Magnus," Ginger said, seated along the length of the table, between the two men, "despite what you may read in our esteemed local newspaper, Ruben doesn't think our perp is a transient."

"You don't?" Coop inquired, fastening his beady eyes on the chief of police. "Why not?"

Ruben shrugged. "I'd like to. In many ways, it would make this case a whole lot easier. But it doesn't add up. Besides, I tend to go with the statistics. Well over eighty percent of all homicide victims in this country are killed by someone they know."

"This is true," the medical examiner agreed. "But that does leave a few percent, doesn't it?"

"Okay, just for the sake of argument," Ruben was willing to consider, "let's say our perp *is* a transient, and he just happens to be visiting the Island, and he just happens to be driving by Southwynd in the middle of the night when Tara comes along, and she just happens to let him pick her up and take her out to Madrona Point Park, where he kills her. My first problem with that is—why would Tara go anywhere with a perfect stranger? From all accounts, we're not talking about some wild teenager here, out looking for kicks. She was sweet and shy and well brought up. She didn't do drugs, she hadn't even started to date yet. Would a girl like that really have gotten into a car with some-one she didn't know in the middle of the night?"

Charlie Pricker was slouched across from Ginger. "He could have forced her."

"With a gun, yes, but with a knife? From inside a car? In that neighborhood? She would have screamed. She would have run."

"Maybe he got out of the car," Charlie suggested.

"And maybe there were two of them," Ginger added.

"Well, I don't know about that," Charlie said. "We have no indication there was more than one perp."

"Okay," Ruben continued, "let's say, one way or another, the person we're talking about finds a way to force Tara into his car and get her to Madrona Point where he kills her. My question is—why? Don't forget, we saw the body; that poor girl died a brutal death. This was no whim. It was clearly a crime of uncon-trollable anger. Now remember, we're dealing with a stranger here. What was his motive?"

"Maybe nothing more complicated than that he was mad at the world," Charlie suggested.

"Then let's say he's mad at the world. So he takes a ferry to a remote island—one that rolls up its sidewalks at nine o'clock at night—to find a victim? And long after most of us are tucked up in our beds, he's still out roaming around, and when he happens on Tara walking along in the most exclusive part of town, he knows exactly where to take her?"

"Isn't something like that possible?" Ginger asked. "Maybe he's been here before; maybe he's a regular."

"Okay, let's suppose that for a moment," Ruben conceded. "He's a repeat visitor, and he picked Tara up, took her out to Madrona Point, and for whatever reason, he killed her. How did he get off the Island? Even assuming the earliest possible time of death, the last ferry was already long gone. And he had to have had blood all over him—we know he tried to wash himself up in the park bathroom. What did he do for the rest of the night? Check into the Island Inn? Sleep on the street? Even if he stayed where he was, where did he go in the morning?"

"That's right," Ginger said with a frown. "He couldn't have been at Madrona Point past six-thirty, or Tom Hildress and his boy would have seen him."

"And the first ferry doesn't leave until eight o'clock on Sunday," Ruben added, "so he could hardly have been at the dock without being noticed. Keep in mind, we had the park, the ferry, the whole island covered by seven-forty-five that morning. How many killers, even mad-at-the-world ones, would set up a mark on an isolated island, and then get themselves trapped with no way to get off?"

"I see what you mean," Ginger murmured. "But maybe he didn't mean to kill her. Maybe he just meant to take her someplace and rape her, and it went down wrong."

"No," Coop said.

Ruben looked at him quickly. "Why no?"

The medical examiner sighed. "Because there were no indications that she had been raped or sexually molested in any way.

There were abrasions on her arms consistent with someone trying to restrain her, and a laceration on her face consistent with someone slapping her, and there were also some contusions on her scalp which I'll get to later, but there was no sign of semen and no anal or vaginal bleeding or bruising."

"What else?"

"The cause of death is what I told you it was," Coop said with a heavy heart. "There were thirteen sharp-force injuries—nine in the abdomen and four in the chest. It was one of the last four—a direct penetration of the left ventricle—that finally killed her."

Ginger shuddered. "What a nightmare it must have been for her."

The medical examiner nodded grimly. "This was not a merciful death," he said. "But surprisingly enough, while I found blood on her hands, there were no defensive wounds, and nothing under her fingernails. Brutal as the assault was, she apparently didn't make any effort to protect herself."

Ginger had little experience with this kind of homicide. "Is that unusual?" she asked.

"When you're attacked, especially with a knife," Coop told her, "the typical reaction is to defend yourself. In a situation like this, Tara should have had cuts and abrasions all over her hands and forearms."

"What else, Doc?" Charlie inquired.

"The majority of the wounds were very deep," the medical examiner continued, "in most cases, right up to the hilt, indicating that whoever killed her was reasonably strong. It's my opinion that all the injuries are consistent with having been made by one person, using one instrument—in all likelihood, a single-edged knife with a curved blade, about six inches long and approximately one and one eighth inches at its widest part. In other words, a hunting knife; the kind of hunting knife that can be bought in no fewer than a hundred places within a fifty-mile radius of here, and is probably already present in at least thirty percent of the homes on this island. Hell, I know for a fact that Jim Petrie's got a whole case of them over at the hardware store."

"That really narrows it down," Ginger muttered.

"Well, maybe it does in a way," Coop said. "Because it's also my opinion, based on the angle and position of the wounds, that our killer was left-handed."

"Left-handed?" Charlie echoed, perking up.

"The way I reconstruct it," the doctor said, "he was holding her by her hair. There were several contusions on her scalp resembling knuckle imprints that conform to a right-handed grasp, and confirm my opinion that he held her with his right hand and stabbed her with his left. It's what I state in my report."

"Okay," declared Ginger, "so now we know our killer is strong—at least strong enough to inflict the injuries and then hoist her into that Dumpster—and he's probably left-handed." She turned to Ruben. "Now what?"

But the police chief had been only half listening, his attention caught on one of the doctor's earlier statements.

"Did you say nine out of the thirteen stab wounds were in the abdomen?" he asked.

Coop's eyes blinked behind his steel-rimmed spectacles. "That's what I said—nine in the abdomen."

Charlie Pricker hunched forward in his seat.

Ginger glanced from one to the other. "Did I miss something?"

"Not yet," Ruben said, and fastened his glance on the medical examiner. "What is it you don't want to tell us, Doc?" he asked softly.

Magnus Coop sighed with unutterable sadness. Barely fifteen years ago, he had brought this child into the world, so clean and innocent and perfect, and now he was about to destroy her, as surely as had some madman with a knife. From now on, whatever else people remembered about her, they would first remember this.

"Tara Breckenridge was pregnant."

10

When Ginger thought about her childhood, one of the first things that always came to mind were the hundreds of jigsaw puzzles she had done with her father. The long rainy winter evenings when the two of them would huddle in front of the living room fire over little interlocking bits of landscapes that increased in difficulty as she increased in years. It never ceased to fascinate her, how all those oddly shaped pieces eventually fit together to form one complete picture.

At the time, she had no way of knowing that an evening's entertainment was also an important learning experience. But as she would later say, doing jigsaw puzzles taught her how to concentrate on the forest, one tree at a time. It also taught her patience. And that combination went a long way toward explaining why she took so readily to police work. She saw each case as a similar sort of puzzle; finding the next clue to put in the proper place or context to reach, ultimately, the one incontrovertible truth.

"You were right all along, and I should have seen it," she told Ruben the moment the medical examiner had departed and Charlie had gone off to review the autopsy report in detail. "We aren't dealing with a transient, and this wasn't a random act. Our perp was someone she knew."

"So it would seem," Ruben concurred.

"That's why she got into the car with him. He wasn't a stranger; she had no reason not to. And that's our motive—he got her pregnant, and then he decided maybe that wasn't such a good idea."

"A pretty drastic form of abortion," the police chief said with a sigh.

"Maybe she didn't give him any alternative," Ginger responded.

"Maybe."

"And of course that's what she was doing that night, too," the detective continued. "She wasn't out for some fresh air, or going to visit a friend—she was meeting *him*. They had a date she didn't want her parents to know about. She probably told him about the baby. Maybe she refused to have an abortion, they got into an argument, and he panicked. All those wounds in the abdomen—he wanted to kill the baby."

"Conjecture is fine," Ruben allowed, "so long as you don't let it cloud up the real picture. Yes, he obviously wanted to end her pregnancy, but does what we know so far tell us that this crime was just about dealing with unwanted fatherhood?"

Ginger considered for a moment. "No, it doesn't," she decided. "He could have talked his way around paternity, he didn't have to slash her to pieces. What it tells us is that this is someone who had a lot more to lose than just becoming a daddy."

"Give me a profile," Ruben prompted.

"All right," Ginger began thoughtfully. "He's someone who's strong, very likely athletic, probably left-handed, and known by his victim. Which means he could be a high school student who has big plans for college or career. He could be a relative or a friend of the family with a high profile. He could be a teacher or a minister or a doctor, or anybody else in a position of respect or authority in the community. He may be married. He either is, or believes himself to be, highly vulnerable. He's almost certainly somebody Tara trusted."

"Who have we excluded?"

"So far, Tom and Billy Hildress and Egon Doyle."

"Who can we include?"

"Everyone else—that is, everyone else who happens to be left-handed." She paused for a moment. "Can we rule out Kyle Breckenridge? He's partly left-handed."

"Partly?"

Ginger shrugged. "I happen to know he's ambidextrous. I've seen him write with his left hand, but he plays golf right-handed."

"He's also got a confirmed alibi for the time of the murder," Ruben told her. "And the sympathy of the entire island. Without any direct evidence that leads us right inside his front door, I think we'd best take him off the list for now."

Albert Hoch had been adamant about that. The mayor was on the telephone barely an hour after Ruben's interview at Southwynd had concluded.

"That man's done more for Seward Island than anyone in the last hundred years," Hoch screamed in Ruben's ear. "I happen to know he's devastated by the death of his daughter. So unless you can wrap the actual murder weapon around his neck and no one else's, don't you dare go dragging his good name through the mud."

"Getting back to our profile," Ruben continued. "If we assume everything you've said so far to be so—what was our perp's greatest fear?"

As before, Ginger took a moment to think. "Exposure," she declared. "And not just to the wrath of the Breckenridge family, although that would have been considerable. But Tara was only fifteen—which means, even if she consented, he was still looking at a rape charge. A felony conviction. A prison sentence. Total ruin."

"So what else can we add to the profile?"

"He's at least eighteen years old."

"And you got nothing on a boyfriend?"

Ginger shook her head. "I talked to the kids Tara hung with. They were positive she wasn't seeing anyone."

"So were her parents," Ruben said.

"Do you think they knew she was pregnant?"

"I'd say there's a good chance the mother didn't know, but the father's a hard read. He might have suspected, but I think he wanted to protect his daughter, and he figured, if it didn't come out in the autopsy, it was none of our business."

"None of our business?" Ginger cried. "It just defines the whole case. It just establishes that we're looking for someone right here on Seward. Look out, folks, he could be living in the house next door."

"Or in the bedroom upstairs," Ruben murmured.

The detective sighed. "Nobody's going to like this, you know. But in a way, it could be a good thing. Most of the locals are decent people. They're just used to taking potshots from a comfortable distance instead of getting involved up close and messy. Now they're going to know that we aren't dealing with a transient, that the killer is one of their own, still here, and to all intents and purposes, ready and able to kill again. No mother on this island is ever going to turn in her son, and most wives would have a pretty tough time turning in their husbands, but knowing he's here may motivate someone else to give him up."

Ruben smiled. Whatever her personal opinions might be on an issue, he could always count on her for a clear and accurate analysis of the place and the people she had known for the better part of her life.

"I sure did a smart thing when I hired you, didn't I?" he thought aloud.

Unaccountably, Ginger blushed, even as her hazel eyes twinkled. "For such a hotshot cop, it took you long enough to figure that out," she retorted.

It rained the day of Tara's funeral. A downpour that Father Paul, the aged priest of Seward Episcopal Church, was quick to attribute to the tears of God at having to take one so young into His fold.

There were hundreds of people in attendance, all of them wanting the opportunity to say a final good-bye. The high school had canceled classes for the afternoon so that those students who wished to do so could be present at the service. Local businesses had shut down for two hours so that workers could pay their last respects. Housewives did their shopping early that morning. Commuters flocked home on the midday ferry.

There were also sizable contingents from both Seattle and Olympia in attendance; mainlanders who felt motivated to make an appearance. The Sewards had pioneered this part of the country, and the family's interests spread across Puget Sound.

The grand stone church that crowned the north end of the Village Green was by far the largest and most prestigious on the Island. The original building dated back to the days of Nathaniel Seward and his tribe. On this day, its ancient carved mahogany pews overflowed, the crowd spilling out of the antechamber, an armada of umbrellas bobbing over a soggy sea of grass.

The ceremony was sad and beautiful. The choir sang the hymns that Mary Breckenridge identified as Tara's favorites. At least two dozen people spoke, each recalling funny, happy, touching little stories about the girl who had been part of their lives for such a brief moment in time.

"She may have been beautiful, and she may have been rich, and she may have had all the advantages that the rest of us just dreamed of having," Melissa Senn said. "But she was just too nice for anyone to hate. So we loved her instead."

"She was not just my goddaughter," sobbed an emotional Albert Hoch, "she was one of His favorites here on earth. And there's no doubt in my mind that she'll go right on being His favorite now that she's with Him in heaven."

"I gave Tara her first smack on the bottom and her first vaccination," Magnus Coop recounted. "Every time she came to my office, she earned a lollipop for good behavior. I sat with her when she had the measles and the mumps. I put her arm in a cast when she broke it, and taped up her ankle when she sprained it. I watched her grow from a beautiful child into a lovely teenager. I have the marks on my office wall where we measured her height each year; just like a lot of you, she got to put her name below it. As long as I live, that wall will never be repainted."

Out of respect for Tara, the chairwoman of the Harvest Festival announced that the festivities would be canceled for this year. Nobody objected.

Ruben and Ginger stood at the back of the church.

"Remember the old detective stories," Ginger whispered, "where the inspector goes to the funeral to see who's there who doesn't quite fit?"

The police chief nodded. "You mean the one who can't quite help looking guilty?" he whispered back.

"Yeah," Ginger said. "That's the one."

Ruben smiled. "Do you really think he showed up?"

Ginger studied the crowd: the family, the friends, the entire bank staff, various civic leaders, representatives from Mary's numerous charitable organizations, Kyle's golf buddies, members of the Rotary, the Elks, and the Hunt Club, and the crowd of students and teachers.

"Oh, he's here, all right," she murmured. "He couldn't risk not showing up."

◦   ◦   ◦

Jerry Frankel left the church in the company of half a dozen other teachers from the high school, quite moved by the out-pouring of sympathy for the dead girl.

"It's rather extraordinary that one so young could have touched so many lives," he murmured.

"I know you're relatively new here, but don't be naive," someone replied cynically. "That show wasn't about Tara. It was about being seen."

"Are the Breckenridges really that important?" Jerry asked.

"Let's put it this way," another teacher responded. "I wouldn't want to get on the wrong side of them. Old man Seward, Tara's grandfather, had a teacher summarily dismissed some years back for referring to the Commodore as a pirate."

Jerry laughed. "He *was* a pirate," he said. "One of the best of them, too."

The other teachers looked around hastily.

"You'd be wise to keep your voice down and your opinions to yourself," one of them said. "Kyle Breckenridge isn't exactly a person to mess around with, either."

Mary Breckenridge walked slowly down Southwynd's grand second-floor hallway, hugging the wall as though to diminish her-self. She had been taught to walk that way by nuns. Her mother, being Catholic, had insisted on sending her daughter to a con-vent school in Seattle. Mary was always so quiet and obedient that perhaps the woman hoped the girl would take to religious life.

She didn't. Quiet, she may have been, and obedient, most definitely, but Mary had her own ideas about the kind of life she wanted for herself, and it had nothing to do with a solitary exis-tence shut off from such things as marriage and children.

"She's a good girl," reported the nuns, "but not suited to the sisterhood."

Like a flower, Mary had the kind of looks that were fresh

and delicate as a girl and faded into womanhood. She met Kyle Breckenridge when she was twenty years old and a sophomore in college. He had come to work at her father's bank and was ten years her senior.

"That young man has a damn good head on his shoulders," her father said after a month. "If he sticks with the banking business, he could be a real asset to us, I think."

"And he has such fine manners," her mother added. "He obviously comes from a good family that took the time to raise him properly."

In fact, Kyle Breckenridge was the ninth of twelve children born to a Minnesota strip miner and his common-law wife. The state had been mostly responsible for raising him until the age of eighteen, whereupon he turned an athletic scholarship into an honors degree from the University of Minnesota, followed by a graduate degree in finance from the University of Chicago, and never looked back.

He taught himself how to speak and how to behave by watching Cary Grant movies over and over again, invented a tragic background to explain the absence of family, and proposed to the bank president's daughter a year to the day after they met.

Mary was delirious. She had hoped and dreamed and fantasized, of course, but despite her wealth and position, she had never really expected that anyone as charming, as attractive, or as exciting as Kyle Breckenridge would fall in love with her. As a result, she promptly fell madly, deeply, completely, and irrevocably in love with him.

She abandoned college, they married, she gave him two daughters, he took over the bank after her parents drowned in a tragic boating accident, and they lived in the gracious home that had first been built by her great-great-great-great-grandfather. And slowly, so slowly that Mary didn't even realize it was happening, Kyle's needs became her needs, his dreams became her dreams, and his life became her life, until she almost ceased to exist.

Everyone they knew applauded them for their dedicated community involvement, appreciated them for their charitable support, admired them for their obvious family commitment, and envied them their affluent lifestyle. But Mary knew it was only an extension of their own desires. Like a house with shuttered windows, no one ever really saw what went on inside. They never glimpsed the heartache that Mary lived with every day, once she was forced to accept the fact that Kyle had married her not so much for love as for a bank and an estate and everything that went along with that.

And it was never more obvious than right now, when she needed him the most, when her whole carefully constructed world was about to explode into a million irretrievable pieces, and he was somewhere else.

Almost at the end of the hall, she reached the door to Tara's room—a pink and yellow cocoon that had once nurtured such promise, so briefly occupied by the beautiful little girl who had always made her mother so proud. It was all ruined now. Her daughter had gone to a place where Mary was unable to reach her, to hold her, or to wipe away her tears. And as if that were not bad enough, her precious memory would soon be forever tarnished. Once tomorrow's issue of the *Sentinel* reached the breakfast tables, everyone who had applauded, admired, appreciated, and envied them, everyone who had sobbed as the casket was lowered into the cold, wet ground, would know that the image of sweet innocence that had always defined Tara was nothing more than a facade.

A facade, Mary thought bitterly, much like a marriage could be. Sinking down on the pink and yellow canopy bed and wrapping her arms tightly around her body as though to keep herself from falling apart, she wept.

○　○　○

Despite the combined protests of both Albert Hoch and Kyle Breckenridge, news of Tara's pregnancy did indeed find its way onto the front page of the newspaper the morning after the funeral.

"Revealing this information to the general public could seriously hamper the investigation," the mayor told the editor.

"That's a load of crap and you know it," Gail Brown shot back with an indignant toss of her ponytail. "The fact is, it might just help find the bastard."

"Don't go up against me, Ms. Brown," the bank president warned, "or I'll damn well put you and your newspaper right out of business. I'll call in your loan, and if that doesn't do it, I'll lean on your advertisers until they turn and run."

"Go ahead," Gail retorted fearlessly. "I'll print what you just said, in the presence of a witness, and let not just Seward Island but the whole of Puget County decide the issue of the people's right to know."

"But running this story will make you so unpopular," the mayor pleaded. "All it will do is ruin the good name of an innocent girl."

"I'm not in the popularity business, I'm in the newspaper business," the editor declared. "And I don't make the news—I just report it. Besides, whatever you know about today, Albert, the whole world will know about tomorrow anyway, so what difference does it make if I print it?"

"I hope you'll at least have the sensitivity to wait until after the funeral," Kyle said.

"As a result of startling new evidence that has been confirmed by the county coroner's office," the *Sentinel*'s lead story began as promised, "local authorities now believe that Tara Breckenridge's killer was not a transient, as had been previously assumed, but a resident of Seward Island who almost certainly knew his victim."

• • •

"Well, at least she waited until the poor girl was buried,"
Charlie Pricker observed, tossing the paper into the trash can.

"A lot of comfort that'll be to the family," Ginger said with a
sigh.

The story eclipsed the funeral, even the murder itself, as the
main topic of conversation down at the Gull Harbor Drug Store,
the Commodore Street Bakery, the Seward Island Library, and
the Waterside Cafe, where little knots of people spoke in hushed
whispers that broke off in mid-sentence if either Kyle or Mary or
young Tori Breckenridge happened by.

"It's twice the tragedy," an assistant librarian felt compelled
to tell the editor. "Now the Breckenridges have been devastated
by two murders instead of one."

" 'The wages of sin is death,' " quoted the wife of the Baptist
minister, with her husband's permission. "Tara Breckenridge
sinned and has been punished for her sin. May God have mercy
on her soul."

"If parents can't properly educate their kids about sex, and
if churches won't even admit that teenage sex is here to stay,"
wrote an angry biologist, "maybe it's time we let the schools dis-
pense condoms."

Everyone, it seemed, had an opinion, whether it was about
the murder or about teenage pregnancy or about the recklessness of unbridled youth. But as the days began to slip into weeks,
no one stepped forward with any information that would assist
the police in their investigation.

"More than ever, local authorities need your help in identi-
fying Tara Breckenridge's killer," the *Sentinel* reiterated. "If you

saw Tara on the evening of her death, or were near Madrona Point Park between midnight and two o'clock on that Sunday morning, Mayor Albert Hoch urges you to come forward.

" 'If we are to make Seward Island safe for our children again,' he said, 'we need your support. We cannot let this murderer escape justice.' "

The Breckenridge case was almost three weeks old and going nowhere, and the people were growing restless.

"Why is Tara Breckenridge's killer still at large?" the frightened father of two young girls asked the editor. "Surely, on an island as small as this, the police should already have a suspect in mind, have gathered enough evidence, be close to making an arrest. We pay taxes to have a police force that will keep our community safe. Why aren't they doing their job?"

"Is it possible that he lives just down the street?" inquired an eighty-year-old grandmother. "Is it possible that I've known him since he was a boy, watched him grow up, and never saw the evil that was taking possession of him? Is it possible he played with my grandson or dated my daughter? I've lived here all my life. Do I really want to know?"

"I'm afraid to go out of my house now," a seventh-grader wrote. "I'm afraid the killer might get me."

"I've never seen anything like it," Hoch admitted to Ruben, brandishing the latest issue of the newspaper as evidence. "People are running scared. Parents are locking up their kids at night. They're staying home themselves. Restaurants reported a sixty percent drop in dinner revenues last week; the movie theater says attendance was off by almost half. Nobody ever thought about locking their doors on this island before. Now Jim Petrie down at the hardware store says he can't keep enough dead bolts in stock. Nobody knows who to trust anymore. Folks are suddenly suspicious of neighbors they've known all their lives. Everyone's walking on eggshells."

"That's perfectly understandable," the police chief told him. "Cold-blooded murder is a whole new thing to this community, and people don't know how they're supposed to react to it."

"And, of course, everyone's trying to figure out who the next victim will be."

"Next victim?" Ruben echoed. "Why are they assuming there'll be another murder?"

"Because the maniac lives right here, where he can strike at any time," Hoch declared. "Maniacs don't stop at one killing, do they?"

"Based on the nature of the crime, we believe the killer was enraged," the police chief replied. "But not necessarily that he was deranged. Whether he kills a second time depends on why he killed the first time."

The mayor's eyes popped in his bald head. "Don't you think he'll kill again?"

Ruben leaned against his chair, stretching his back, and contemplated the wall for a long moment while he weighed the pros and cons of telling Albert Hoch what he really thought.

"Mind you, this is nothing more than my own personal opinion, based on past experience," he said at last, knowing that within the hour his words would be reported the length and breadth of the Island as official fact, "but I tend to see this crime as having been a deliberate assault on a single person for a specific reason. There's nothing we've uncovered so far that would lead me to assume that our killer will kill again. Of course, I could be wrong, but all the circumstances of this case seem to indicate that it was an isolated incident."

11

It was just her eyes he saw. In the moonlight, they seemed to burn with a life of their own, as though they had no relation to the rest of her, as though there were no rest of her. Twist and turn though he might, he couldn't get away from them, or from the hideous indictment in them.

He covered his face with his hands so he wouldn't have to see. But even with his face covered, there were the eyes. Always the eyes. He tried to hide himself, whimpering and cowering because he knew what was coming next. He covered his ears, hoping to shut it out. But even with his ears covered, the wretched scream split the night in half as it denounced him to the world.

And then he woke, in a panting, sweat-soaked panic. There was no moon, no scream; the room was dark and silent. He had not been exposed. It was only a nightmare.

For a moment, his throat was so tight he couldn't seem to breathe, the pain in his chest so sharp he wondered if he might be having some kind of heart attack. What an inexcusable blunder it would be, he thought, were he to die right here, right now, over a bad dream, when he had so much of life yet to live.

He forced himself to take several deep breaths, filling his lungs to the bursting point before he let the air out as slowly as he could, knowing this would relax his throat and ease the pain in his chest.

When he was reasonably calm, he pushed his pillows against the headboard, leaned back into them, and began to reconstruct the entire scenario, from start to finish, assuring himself each step of the way that he had taken the only option available to him. What she had demanded would have destroyed him, ruined his entire life. He would probably even have gone to prison. But she never once made an effort to see that from his perspective. As many times as he tried to tell her, she refused to listen. He couldn't believe how stubborn she had been. In the end, she left him no choice.

The stupidity of it was that something could have been worked out. All she had to do was go along. He had more than made that clear enough. So, in reality, she had brought it on herself, out of her own sense of shame or guilt; forced his hand, out of some misjudged sense of power. She had gambled with her very life, and lost. Which meant the consequences were hers.

With a satisfied sigh, he closed his eyes and waited for sleep to return, having persuaded himself that, in the end, at least, she understood what she had done—what she had compelled him to do. It was the reason she hadn't struggled.

12

"For the next several weeks, we're going to be taking a look at World War II, up close and personal, as they say," Jerry Frankel told his sophomore history class on the Monday after Halloween, when Tara Breckenridge had been dead for three weeks.

"As some of you may already know, this was a war that, aside from the loss of life and the defeat of Fascism, had an enormous socioeconomic impact on this country, and we'll examine that impact very closely. But just to get our feet wet a bit, do any of you have family members who were involved?"

Three hands went up.

"My grandfather fought in the war," Lucy Neiland said. "He lost an arm on D-Day."

Many members of the class nodded. They knew Lars Neiland. He owned the sail shop down at South Cove, and could tie a knot faster with his steel claw than anyone with two hands.

"I had a great-uncle who was in the Navy," Jack Tannauer reported. "But I never met him. The Japs sank his boat in the Pacific way before I was even born."

Jerry looked at the teenager for a moment. "You mean the Japanese, don't you?" he suggested.

Jack shrugged. "Yeah, sure, whatever," he said.

"My grandmother's whole family died in the war," Daniel Cohen said. "Her parents, her brothers, and her sisters, all her aunts and uncles and cousins, too. They were gassed at Auschwitz. She was the only one who survived."

There was a loud snicker at the back of the room.

"Hank, did you have a comment?" Jerry asked.

"That stuff about gassing—that's all such garbage," Hank Kriedler said.

"What do you mean by 'garbage'?" the teacher inquired. "Are you saying Daniel just made up that story about his grandmother's family?"

"Well, he might think it's true," Hank said with a careless shrug, "because that's what they told him. That's what they told everybody."

"They? What 'they' are you talking about?"

"The Jews, of course," Hank Kriedler replied. "It's all propaganda that the Jews spread around to give Hitler a bad name because they didn't like the way he was getting Germany back on her feet."

Jerry considered the sixteen-year-old for a long moment before he spoke. "My father has a tattoo on his arm that reads: M4362," he said finally. "He covers it up with long sleeves so no one will see it because he's ashamed. He got it on the day he arrived at Majdanek—which we'll learn was one of Hitler's most notorious death camps—the same day he saw his parents herded into a communal bathhouse and never saw them come out again. He's ashamed because he couldn't do anything to save them. He was twelve years old. Is that what you mean by propaganda, Hank? You think my father made it all up?"

"The Jews were destroying Germany," the teenager maintained. "They controlled all the money. They were strangling the economy. Everybody knows they engineered the Great Depression so they could get even richer and have more power. And they got France and England to start the war with Germany. Hitler was right to get rid of them while he was defending his country. But there were no death camps like everyone thinks—they were just detention camps, like we had for the Japs—uh, Japanese—here. That whole mass murder stuff is crap."

"Then what do you think happened to the six million Jews, and the millions of political dissidents, and others designated as undesirable by the Third Reich, who disappeared during the war?"

"Like I said—propaganda," Hank repeated. "Most of them probably never existed in the first place."

"You seem to be quite well versed in this particular subject," the teacher observed. "May I ask where you got your information?"

Hank shrugged again. "From books," he said. "My dad has real history books that me and my brother have read, books that tell the true story, not the lies they always try to feed us in school."

Jerry Frankel looked around the class of twenty-three, a perfectly ordinary group on the face of it. "Are there any more of you who feel the way Hank does?" he asked. "Who feel that the textbooks we have are feeding you lies?"

Hank glared at his classmates, especially those who were part of his immediate social circle. Jack Tannauer shrugged and raised his hand. After a moment, Kristen Andersen did, too. Several others looked as though they might, but then apparently thought better of it.

"At least three of you," Jerry murmured, feeling the hair at the back of his neck begin to rise. He made a quick decision. "Hank, I'll tell you what," he said. "You bring in those books of your father's. We'll read them together, right here in class, where we can compare them to the texts that have, for almost fifty years now, been accepted by pretty much every educational institution in the country. Then we'll separate the facts from the fiction of the matter, and see if we can come up with the real truth."

The whole room began to buzz. Everyone turned to look at Hank Kriedler. He was big for his age, good-looking, and one of the few sophomores to drive his own car. He was generally acknowledged to be one of the class leaders, and he had been challenged.

"I'll have to ask my dad," the teenager mumbled, his face coloring to the roots of his platinum hair. "They're his books. I don't know if he's gonna let me bring them to school."

"Why not?" Jerry Frankel inquired mildly. "This is a neutral place. Our primary objective here is to learn. You've presented us with a fairly contrary view of history today—one you obviously believe we should all embrace. I'm simply offering you the opportunity to achieve your goal; to back up your beliefs with documentation that can stand the scrutiny of your peers."

In a basement room, lit by a single candle, seven men talked late into the night. It was not a regularly scheduled meeting of any official organization, nor even a social get-together, for few of these men moved in the same circles. Rather, it was a hastily called gathering of certain like-minded citizens who, when the occasion arose, came together for the purpose of discussing a specific issue.

Their voices were too low to overhear, their faces too shadowed to identify. The only thing that was clearly distinguishable in the flickering light was a red banner mounted on the back wall with a distorted Greek cross in its center.

13

Ginger's least favorite part of any investigation was having to go back to people she had already interviewed and press them even harder—perfectly innocent people, who wanted nothing more than to be left alone to live their lives—in an effort to persuade one of them to give up his or her brother, best friend, neighbor.

In the weeks following the funeral, she went back to the group of students who had been closest to Tara Breckenridge. Had anyone seen Tara displaying any kind of special interest in another student, a teacher, an adult man in the community—anyone at all, at any time—that might give the police a lead to follow? The answer was no.

Had anyone seen a student, a teacher, an adult man in the community—anyone at all, at any time—displaying any special interest in Tara? Again, the answer was no.

"Tara was my best friend," Melissa Senn said, "and I happen to know she was very sheltered. She wasn't even allowed to date. I guess her parents felt she was too young and naive about some things. I think they were afraid she might end up getting pregnant or something." The black-haired teenager stopped short, coloring deeply, when she realized what she had said. "I guess they were right, weren't they?"

"There was this sort of 'hands-off' thing about Tara," Bill Graham observed. "I don't think she knew it. I think it was just the way everyone related to her. You know, look but don't touch. She was part of our crowd sometimes, we kidded around, but that's as far as it went."

"And that was okay with you?"

Bill shrugged. "My dad is a mortician, Detective Earley. He dresses dead bodies and digs graves. I'm gonna be lucky if I get to go to college. Hank Kriedler's dad sells cars. Jack Tannauer's dad collects tickets and cleans toilets at the movie theater. We're not exactly the kind of people who'd be welcomed at Southwynd, if you know what I mean. When it came to Tara, I think the Breckenridges had their sights set a little higher than someone from Seward Island."

Ginger moved on to the boys in the senior class. How many of them had known Tara? Had they ever been out with her? Had they ever seen her in any situation that seemed unusual, out of the ordinary? She was met with another blank wall.

Then she interviewed each of them separately. What were you doing on the night Tara died? Is there anyone who can corroborate your alibi? Would you be willing, if asked, to come down to Graham Hall and take a polygraph test?

Next, the detective went to the office and asked to see the victim's academic record. Coming into high school, Tara's grades had been solid As and Bs. By the end of her freshman year, however, they had quietly slipped down to Cs. She had taken three remedial classes in summer school and received Bs in two of them. In the third class, history, she had gotten an A.

Finally, Ginger went back to the teachers. Having had time to consider, did any of them remember anything that might help the investigation? Was there anything about Tara that had changed during the last weeks of her life?

"Her grades certainly weren't what they should have been," her science teacher acknowledged. "I think she was a good deal brighter than the quality of her work indicated."

"Algebra wasn't her best subject," reported her math teacher. "But I do know she was trying. I checked—she got an A on her last exam."

"She was good in grammar and composition, but she really didn't have her mind on school," her English teacher conceded sadly. "I wish I'd been more alert. Certainly, if I'd had any idea what was going on, I would have tried to do something. But I assumed it was just about getting into a new school year, and like a lot of other kids, she would eventually settle down."

"Tara earned that A in summer school," Jerry Frankel, the history teacher, asserted. "It was no gift. She worked hard for it. But she wasn't the same after the fall term started. Her homework assignments were frequently late or missing altogether, and I noticed she had trouble concentrating in class."

Ginger went over to the intermediate school, which was actually an adjunct of the high school, and asked to see Tori Breckenridge. They went to the library and sat at a table at the far end of the room.

"I don't know anything," the twelve-year-old said. "My mother always says that Tara and I were, you know, close, but we weren't. Not really. We got along okay, I mean; she wasn't bad to me or anything. But she never, like, confided in me about stuff going on in her life, or talked to me about her problems or anything."

"Do you know anyone she might have talked to?" Ginger prompted.

Tori shrugged. "Maybe Father Paul. Tara used to be real involved in church stuff."

The massive doors to the Seward Episcopal Church stood open to the autumn wind. Ginger found the aged priest on his knees at the altar, shivering beneath his vestment.

"It's cold, Father Paul," she said gently. "Could we have some tea?"

The priest struggled to his feet and led the way to his office. The man was over eighty and had been in his church for almost fifty years. His assistant, a gaunt man of around forty, brought tea.

"Tara was a true believer," Father Paul said, his tea sitting untouched beside him. "She helped teach the young ones in Sunday School, you know. She never missed a service, never missed communion. It seemed to lift her spirits so, and renew her soul."

"Right up until her death?" Ginger asked.

"No," the priest admitted. "Sometime, I think it was in early September, she didn't come to church for two weeks in a row. I assumed she must have been sick. She came back after that, but she stopped receiving communion, and she wouldn't teach the children anymore."

"Did you ask her why?"

The priest sighed. "I meant to," he said.

"Didn't you wonder?"

"Of course I wondered."

"She didn't come to you?"

"No."

"Was there anyone else here, one of your assistants, perhaps, that she might have confided in?"

"Father Timothy is my only assistant at present," he said. "Unfortunately, Tara didn't come to him, either. She came to no one here. And that's the failure I will take to my grave." Tears filled the old man's eyes. "She was a beautiful child," he said. "As pure and as clean as the angels of heaven, and given to us by God as a gift of love. Whatever befell her here on earth was surely the work of the devil."

◦   ◦   ◦

Ginger's last appointment of the day was with Magnus Coop at the medical center.

"You were her doctor," she pressed the crusty physician. "You really didn't know she was pregnant?"

"No," he sighed, wagging his white head. "I wish to God I had. I gave her a routine school physical at the beginning of August. I noticed nothing amiss, and she didn't complain of anything. Of course, I wasn't looking for a pregnancy. She didn't come to me after that."

"Did she go to anyone else?"

"Not at this clinic," he declared. "Of course, she may have gone to someone in Seattle."

"On her own?" the detective wondered.

"Probably not," Coop conceded.

"But she had to know she was pregnant," Ginger pressed. "Otherwise, none of this would fit. Do you think she might have gotten herself one of those do-it-yourself-at-home tests?"

"That would certainly make sense," Coop agreed.

"She didn't talk to her parents or her sister, she didn't talk to her friends, she didn't talk to her priest, and she didn't talk to you," Ginger reflected sadly. "How horribly alone she must have felt."

Ruben sat at his desk in Graham Hall, eating the lunch Stacey insisted on preparing for him every morning. This was Tuesday, which meant a meatloaf sandwich smothered in salsa, just the way he liked it. But he ate mechanically and hardly tasted a thing.

It was three weeks since the death of Tara Breckenridge, and Ruben was still trying to find something in the few fragments of evidence that Charlie Pricker had retrieved from Madrona Point Park that would put him on the trail of a killer.

The entire department had been working on the case, and all they had to show for it was a piece of bloodstained carpet, a number of hairs and fibers that did not belong to the victim and may or may not have belonged to the person they sought, the partial fingerprint on the cross around Tara Breckenridge's neck that apparently did not match anyone among her close friends and family, a hundred or so other fingerprints that could take months to identify—if indeed they could be identified at all—and the certain and infuriating knowledge that he was out there, somewhere, watching their every move, laughing at them.

Ginger had reported talking to at least two hundred people. In addition to the victim's friends, classmates, and teachers, she had reinterviewed family members, neighbors, and townspeople, asking all of them the same questions: Were they absolutely positive they hadn't seen Tara that evening? Hadn't talked to her? Hadn't known of her dating anyone? Hadn't seen her with anyone? Hadn't heard her speak of anyone?

All of them were positive. They hadn't seen her, they hadn't talked to her, there was no one, there was nothing. Besides, deep down, none of them could really believe that one of their own had committed such a heinous crime. A few of them had voluntarily come down to police headquarters and taken polygraph tests. All of them had been excluded as potential suspects.

And yet there had to be somebody out there, Ruben was convinced, somebody who knew something, even if he or she didn't realize it. There was always something. He sighed and picked up the forensic reports for the twentieth time. Fingerprints, fibers, hair, blood. It was all right here. All they needed was a place to start.

"Knock, knock," said Helen Ballinger. The plump, affable, middle-aged police department clerk stood at Ruben's open office door, wagging her head as she saw the folders in one hand and the sandwich in the other. "You're going to get indigestion doing that," she warned.

"Probably," he agreed.

"Well, take a break. There's a young man out here wants to talk to you."

Ruben dropped the reports onto the desk, set aside his sandwich, and leaned back in his chair. "Okay," he said, "send him on in."

The boy looked to be about seventeen years old, with auburn hair, blue eyes, and acne.

"My name's Owen Petrie," he said, standing awkwardly by the door, his voice cracking slightly.

"No need to be nervous, son," Ruben told him with a reassuring smile. "We're pretty informal around here." He indicated the spare chair. "Why don't you have a seat, get comfortable, and then you can tell me what's on your mind."

The teenager hesitated for a few seconds, as if debating the wisdom of this suggestion, and then slid onto the chair and swallowed hard. "Well, the thing is, I guess I might know something, you know, about the murder," he said, staring down at his Air Jordans.

Ruben's posture didn't change, nor did his expression, but his eyes suddenly began to study the youngster with great care. "If you mean Tara Breckenridge's murder," he said in the same casual tone, "it sure would be helpful if you did."

"Yeah, well, I didn't think it was anything, but then, see, I told my dad about it, and he said, just in case it *was* something, I ought to come and tell you about it."

"Is your dad Jim Petrie, from the hardware store?"

The boy looked up. "Yeah, he is. D'ya know him?"

"Sure do," Ruben said. "He's on the city council, which makes him one of my bosses."

Owen twisted in his seat. "Oh yeah. Well, you see, I was there that night—at Madrona Point Park. The night Tara was killed, I mean. It's a pretty secluded place at night, and sometimes some of the guys go up there to, like, hang out, you know, with girls. Well, you see, I'm not really supposed to go there, which was why I didn't say anything before this, but then I got to thinking, you know, about like what if what I saw was important, and I was the only one who saw it, and so, well, I decided maybe I'd better risk being grounded for a month and tell my dad."

"What did you see, Owen?" Ruben asked carefully.

"Well, I didn't see Tara or anything like that, or I'd have spoke up right away, you understand," the teenager said. "But I did see a car come into the park. It was around eleven o'clock, which was way before, you know, the murder was supposed to have happened, so that's why I didn't really think anything about it. But I'm pretty sure that the car was still there when we left, and that was about eleven-thirty. So, I don't know, maybe it could mean something."

"Did you see anyone inside the car?" Ruben queried.

Owen shook his head. "Not really. Well, I mean, it didn't pull up near us or anything—it went all the way around to the other side of the parking lot from where we were, over near the Dumpster, and there aren't exactly a lot of bright lights around the place." The boy blushed. "That's kinda the reason we go up there, you know, because it's, like, dark and quiet and all."

Ruben nodded. Although his own youth was long past, he could still remember a quiet hill overlooking Los Angeles where he had taken a girl or two. "Could you tell how many people were in the car?"

The youngster shrugged. "Well, there had to be at least one, of course," he said. "There could've been two, I guess. I don't know. To tell you the truth, I wasn't really paying that much attention."

The police chief tried not to smile. "Do you think the young lady who was with you might have seen something?" he asked hopefully.

"No, she didn't see anything," Owen replied, blushing even harder. "She wasn't exactly looking out the window at the time, if you know what I mean."

"Yes, I think I do," Ruben murmured. "Did you know Tara Breckenridge, Owen?"

"Not really," the senior replied, looking straight at the police chief. "I mean, sure, I knew her. Our families know each other; we go to the same church, and to some of the same parties, and we belong to the same country club. But she was just a kid. Jail bait, as my dad says. I never made a move on her, if that's what you're asking, and nobody I hang out with would have, either. Jeez, her father would've killed anyone that tried."

"Getting back to the car," Ruben said, "I don't suppose you got a license number, did you?"

"No, I didn't. How was I supposed to know it would be important? I thought it was just another guy with a girl."

It was too much to hope for. "Well then," Ruben inquired, "could you at least describe the car for me?"

"Oh, sure," the teenager said. "I wouldn't have come talk to you unless I could do that. It was a Ford Taurus wagon, or I guess it could have been a Mercury Sable—they're pretty much the same, you know. My mom drives a Taurus. That's how I recognized it for certain. Except hers is white and this one was dark. Not black, I don't think, but dark green, maybe, or maroon, or brown."

"Three weeks, and finally our first solid lead," Ginger said when she heard.

"First *possible* lead," Ruben cautioned. "It could turn out to be perfectly innocent—just another junior Don Juan out for a hot time."

The detective shrugged. "Well, there can't be that many Taurus or Sable wagons on the Island, so we should be able to find it."

"Start with Kriedler," the police chief suggested, referring to the Ford dealership on Center Island Road. "He ought to be able to give you a list of customers. Then put every uniform we can spare out on the street."

While he might caution Ginger not to get too excited, a lead was still a lead. After weeks of blowing up dust, at least this was something concrete they could investigate. Ruben felt a familiar surge of adrenaline. Old habits, he thought to himself.

14

By the time nine months had passed, Matthew Frankel had decided that living on Seward Island wasn't so bad after all. He had made a best friend, Billy Hildress, who lived several streets over, and that had gone a long way toward making up for the pain of having to leave Scarsdale, his grandparents, his childhood chums, and the only home he'd ever really known.

The boys were in the same fourth-grade class at Madrona Elementary School, and inseparable. Their teacher called them her two peas in a pod. They sat next to each other, teamed up for class projects, and helped each other study. They ate lunch together, spent recess together, walked home together, and played with each other after school. So it was only natural that Matthew would invite Billy to share his ninth birthday celebration.

It was bright and sunny and unusually warm for the second Saturday in November, perfect for a ride on the top deck of the ferry to Seattle. The first stop for the Frankels and their guest was the Museum of Flight down at Boeing Field, where the boys sat in a space capsule, checked out the enormous Blackbird, and climbed aboard a vintage B-52 where they pretended to be pilots and bombardiers. Then there was lunch and games at Chuck E.

Cheese. And now they were back at Matthew's house, playing in the yard with his new golden retriever puppy.

"I named him Chase, because he chases after me all the time," Matthew told his friend.

"Puppies are neat," Billy said. "Our dog is too old to play with me anymore." He flopped down on the grass and the retriever began to lick his face. "Where does he sleep?"

"He'll sleep in my room as soon as he's housebroken," Matthew replied. "And I get to feed him and walk him and take him to obedience school when it's time, too."

"Maybe I'll get a new puppy for my next birthday," Billy said hopefully, "and then the two of them can play together."

From the corner of his eye, Matthew saw a curtain flutter out a second-floor window in the house next door. Justin Keller stood at the window, watching. A serious, solitary boy, Justin was eleven years old and in the sixth grade, and in nine months had not spoken more than a dozen words to his new neighbor.

"It's my birthday," Matthew called up to him. "I got a new puppy. You can come over and play with him if you want."

Almost instantly, Justin disappeared, his round eyeglasses catching a quick glint of late afternoon sunlight as he went. Then a hand reached out to retrieve the errant curtain and shut the window with a wordless response.

"How weird," Billy said.

Matthew shrugged. "I guess so."

"Even weirder," Billy added. "There's a police car coming up your driveway."

Matthew looked. Sure enough, a black Blazer with the Seward Island police seal on its door came to a stop at the top of the drive, and a man and a woman got out.

"That's Chief Martinez," Billy whispered. "And that's Detective Earley with him. She's the one me and my dad talked to the day we found that body in the Dumpster. I wonder what they're doing here."

"I don't know," Matthew said, his dark eyes, which were so like his father's, following the officers up the path to the front door of the house.

The police had identified three Ford Taurus wagons and one Mercury Sable registered on the Island that fit Owen Petrie's description, and Ginger and Ruben were spending Matthew Frankel's birthday interviewing the owners.

The first Taurus on the list, they quickly learned, had been in the repair shop the weekend of the murder.

"That damn car spends more time in Kriedler's garage than it does in mine," the owner grumbled. "I don't know why I let my wife talk me into buying it."

He gave Ruben the receipt for the repairs and the name of the mechanic.

The second Taurus had been in Yakima the weekend of the murder.

"It was my mother-in-law's seventy-fifth birthday," the owner explained. "We left early Friday afternoon and caught the late ferry back on Sunday night. My wife's whole family was there, even the noisy cousins from Albuquerque showed up. Fifty-two people."

He gave Ginger a list of the attendees and his mother-in-law's telephone number.

The Mercury Sable belonged to Dr. Frederick Winthur, a forty-two-year-old divorced father who, it turned out, was the Breckenridge family dentist.

"Where was I the night of Tara's murder?" he asked. "I was right here at home with my two boys. According to my custody agreement, I get them every other weekend."

"How old are your sons, Doctor?" Ruben inquired.

"Eight and ten."

"Do you remember what you did that night?"

"Let's see, we probably went out for pizza—that's what we usually do on Saturday nights. And then I suppose we came home and watched movies on the science fiction channel. That's also what we usually do."

"And, if you recall, approximately what time did your boys go to bed?"

"Probably around eleven," Winthur said. "Although I'd appreciate your not making a big issue of that. My ex-wife has a real fit when I let them stay up past nine."

"And you?"

"Well, I don't really remember, but I guess I'd say I went to bed maybe half an hour after that. I generally hang around for the late news."

"Is there anyone else who would have had access to the Sable that night?" Ginger wanted to know. "Did anyone ask to borrow it? Could a relative or a friend or a neighbor have used it?"

"No," the dentist replied. "I'm not in the habit of lending my car to anyone, and I can't recall anyone ever asking to borrow it."

"Would you mind if Detective Earley and I took a look at your car?" Ruben inquired.

"What for? Do you think I'm lying to you?"

"Not at all," the police chief said smoothly. "It's simply that we have information that a car fitting the description of your car was seen at Madrona Point shortly before we believe the murder took place. We'd like the opportunity to exclude even the possibility that it was your car."

The dentist shrugged. "As long as I can be there to make sure there's no funny business going on, you can look all you want to," he said.

"Thank you," Ruben murmured.

"By the way," Ginger asked, as the dentist led the way to the garage, "when was the last time you saw Tara?"

"Let me see," Winthur said, frowning in thought. "I believe her last checkup was sometime in July. Of course, it could have been June. I think I saw both girls at the same time, but I'd have to review my records to be certain."

It took Ginger less than ten minutes to determine that, on the surface, at least, the car was clean. There were no obvious bloodstains, no suspicious strands of blond hair, no clearly visible "smoking gun."

"One last thing, Doctor," Ruben asked as he and Ginger were about to leave. "Are you right-handed or left-handed?"

"I'm right-handed," came the reply. He pulled back the cuff of his sweater to reveal a contorted left hand. "Good thing, too, because I've had limited use of this one since I was twelve."

"I'm sorry," Ginger murmured.

The dentist shrugged. "I was playing macho man and got careless with a handgun. The damn thing discharged—almost blew away my arm. My boys are never going to come within ten feet of a gun. It's the only thing my ex and I ever agreed on."

The last Taurus on Ginger's list was registered to a Deborah Frankel, the vice president of a major investment firm in Seattle.

As they pulled into the driveway, Ginger saw two boys playing with a puppy in the backyard. As she walked up the path beside Ruben, she could feel three pairs of eyes on her back.

"Good afternoon," Ruben said to the dark-haired woman who answered the door. "I'm Chief Martinez and this is Detective Earley, from the Seward Island police. I wonder if we could talk to you for a moment. It's in connection with the Breckenridge case."

"I beg your pardon?" Deborah Frankel said in surprise. Police officers didn't generally show up at her home on a peaceful Saturday afternoon, wanting to talk about murder.

"The girl who was found in the Dumpster last month," Ginger clarified.

"Yes, I know what case it is," Deborah assured them. "I just don't know anything about it."

"This has to do with a maroon Taurus wagon," Ruben told her. "You do drive one, don't you?"

"No, I don't," Deborah corrected him. "My husband drives it, but you've already talked to him." Ruben glanced at Ginger. "At school," Deborah added. "He was one of the dead girl's teachers."

"Yes, of course," Ginger said. "I talked to a number of Tara's teachers about her grades and general attitude. This is about something else."

The double garage door was open, and Ruben could see the maroon Taurus parked inside. "Perhaps we could talk to your husband, if he's here."

"Yes, of course," Deborah murmured. "Come in."

She led the two police officers to the library where Jerry sat at the rolltop desk, grading a pile of essays.

"Kids," he said with a chuckle. "They think Dunkerque is a city in Iowa, and Churchill used to be President of the United States." He smiled at the intruders. "Hello again, Detective Earley. What has you out working on a weekend?"

"We're following up on a lead we received in connection with the Breckenridge case," Ginger explained. "About a Taurus wagon being seen driving into Madrona Point Park around eleven o'clock on the night of the murder. We're asking everyone on the Island who has such a vehicle whether they were there, and if so, whether they saw anything that might help us, anything at all."

Jerry shrugged. "Well, I do drive a Taurus wagon, but I wasn't out in it that night."

"Is there anyone else who would have had access to the car?" Ginger asked.

"Only me," Deborah replied, "but I didn't drive it that night either."

Ruben looked from one to the other. "Could anybody have borrowed the car? A teenage son or daughter perhaps?"

Both the teacher and his wife shook their heads. "We have only one child," Deborah said. "He's nine—nine today, in fact."

"We're sorry to interrupt such a happy occasion," Ruben said sincerely. "Unfortunately, criminal investigations have a way of intruding at the least appropriate times. To wrap this up then, you're pretty sure that your car was in the garage all evening?"

Jerry's eyes slid past the police chief's shoulder. "As I recall, I was in the shop, working on a kite for my son that evening. My shop area is right in the garage, and I think I would have noticed if the car were missing. I must have been in there from somewhere around ten o'clock until about midnight."

"I was in bed by eleven," Deborah said, although Ruben hadn't asked.

"We were there that afternoon, though," Jerry offered. "At Madrona Point Park, I mean. We took our bicycles and went for a ride around the trails. But we were back home by four o'clock at the latest."

Deborah nodded in confirmation.

"Well, it was a long shot," Ruben said, as he and Ginger prepared to leave.

Jerry gave them a boyish smile. "I thought teaching was tough," he said. "But your job is even tougher. I don't envy you."

"I wonder," Ruben said as though the thought had just occurred to him. "You wouldn't mind letting us take a look at your car, would you?"

"A look?"

"Well, yes. You say you didn't take the car to the park that night, and no one borrowed it, so we'd like to be able to exclude it from our investigation. Occasionally, that's how we have to solve a crime—by excluding everything until we're left with only one possibility."

Jerry looked directly at the police chief. "I thought you came here to find a witness, Chief Martinez—or was it a suspect?"

Ruben shrugged apologetically. "That's just it," he conceded. "Sometimes, we never know."

"Then, by all means, look at the car," the teacher said. "My wife can show you where it is. I have to finish grading these essays."

As with Fred Winthur's Sable, a casual inspection of Frankel's Taurus revealed nothing that either placed the vehicle at the scene or implicated it in the crime.

"Well, what do you think?" Ruben asked as he and Ginger climbed back into the Blazer. "Could he be a reluctant witness?"

"I don't know," Ginger replied cautiously. "From everything I hear, he's one of the good guys. He's got a first-rate reputation at school, and his students say he was all broken up about the murder. I think, if he'd been anywhere near the park that night, he would have told us."

"Unless he had a reason not to get involved," Ruben suggested.

"You mean, he might be stepping out on his wife and had nowhere else to go but Madrona Point, where he witnesses a murder and decides, for the preservation of this illicit relationship, and/or his marriage, to keep quiet about it?" Ginger played out the scenario with a hint of skepticism in her voice.

"Is it possible?"

Ginger shrugged. "I guess anything's possible, but I'd have a hard time swallowing it. To begin with, you saw the wife; she's a knockout. Why would he be looking elsewhere? But let's just say he was. Madrona Point is about teenagers, not adults. Even if he didn't know that, the minute he drove in and saw another car parked there, he would have split."

"He might not have noticed the other car."

"In a town as small as this," Ginger said, "a guy who's doing something he doesn't want anyone to know about would look— very carefully."

"You might be right," Ruben conceded, starting up the Blazer's engine. "Okay, so if he's not a witness—could he be a suspect? He does drive a maroon Taurus—and he *is* left-handed."

"I know," Ginger allowed. She, too, had noticed him grading the essays. "Of course, it could be a coincidence."

"Maybe," the police chief hedged. "But I don't like coincidences. So just to be on the safe side, let's see what we can find out about him."

"Okay," Ginger said. "Drop me off at Graham Hall and I'll get started on it right away."

Ruben looked at his watch. It was after five o'clock. "On Saturday evening?" he protested. "Come on. Don't tell me you don't have something better to do than investigate a murder?"

"Not really," Ginger admitted. "This is just another night in the week as far as I'm concerned." She shrugged. "If you must know, my social life isn't exactly what you'd call active right now. But I don't mind. I love my work."

"If you really don't have any plans," Ruben said without thinking, "maybe we could have dinner together. My daughter is out for the evening, and I guess you could say my social life isn't all that active either."

"You mean a working dinner?" Ginger asked. "To talk about the case?"

Ruben hesitated. What was he doing? Was he crazy? "No," he heard himself say. "I mean a regular dinner, at a nice restaurant, with tablecloths and wine. And we can talk about anything we want to talk about."

15

On the second Saturday in November, Ginger Earley and Ruben Martinez had known each other for exactly twenty-one months and five days, and there had never been anything between them but the job.

As soon as the invitation was out of his mouth, Ruben couldn't believe he had issued it. He couldn't believe he had actually suggested that they go out on what clearly amounted to a date. He had never dated a policewoman before, much less one who worked for him. Come to that, he had hardly dated at all in the past thirteen years. But even as his words took him by surprise, he realized that the idea must have been in his mind for some time.

Ginger had such freshness, and an eagerness about her work that had not yet grown jaded. She reminded him of himself, before the bullet. He liked being around her. And he had to admit she wasn't bad to look at, either. With that red hair and those freckles, it was easy to see the winsome woman she really was peeking through the tomboy facade she had cultivated. He couldn't believe there weren't hordes of suitors tripping all over themselves to get to her, and he felt a strange stab of pleasure in hearing that there weren't.

Of course, he knew he couldn't let himself get carried away with any of this. She was, after all, much too young for the used-up man he knew himself to be. The eighteen years that lay between them was far more than a mere span of months and minutes; it was a lifetime of disappointment and disillusion. But he couldn't help it; he wanted to know what it would be like to sit across a table from her for one evening, away from the turmoil of the office and the pressures of the job. Just once, he told himself—once would be enough. He held his breath and waited for her response.

Ginger was caught completely off guard. In twenty-one months and five days, Ruben had never indicated anything other than a professional interest in her. More than that, he had always been careful not to treat her any differently than he treated the men on the force, or even acknowledge that there *was* a difference. Regardless of the fact that she was the only female officer in the department, she had always felt like one of the guys.

Yet here he was, after all this time, asking her out for dinner on a Saturday night as though it were the most natural thing in the world. What had Ginger so flustered was that she had spent a significant portion of those twenty-one months and five days fantasizing about him doing exactly that.

In the long, quiet evenings alone in the cozy apartment she had leased shortly after returning to Seward Island, as she read a book or listened to music or watched a television program, she would find her mind drifting toward him, find herself wondering what he was doing at that moment, trying to imagine what kind of life he led away from the office, what kind of woman he preferred . . . what he would be like in bed.

Next to her father, she certainly admired him more than any man she knew. His knowledge, his intuitiveness, his patience all spoke of a man who was sensitive, caring, genuinely concerned about people, and dedicated to his work. From the mayor and city council to the members of his staff to the pettiest of vandals, Ruben always treated everyone with respect.

The difference in their ages never entered her mind. There was as yet no gray in his thick black hair, no wrinkles around his intelligent brown eyes, no sag to his square jaw, no telltale thickening in the midsection. Everything about him spoke of vitality and endurance.

He was not overly tall, barely taller than she, in fact. But he kept himself in excellent condition, despite the back brace she knew he wore beneath his shirt, and his body was still lean and hard. Ginger knew about the bullet, of course; everyone in the department knew. The story had become part of office lore, and as far as she was concerned, only added to his appeal.

"Dinner sounds fine," she heard herself say.

Ginger lived on the ground floor of a three-story building on Green Street, two blocks off Seward Way, that had been designed to look more like a mansion than an apartment house. It had a comfortable bedroom and bath, a modest kitchen, a living room with a well-used fireplace and a glass wall that opened into a small backyard, and an alcove that was just big enough for her round oak dining table and four chairs.

She had chosen it in part for the location, being a stone's throw from work, but mostly for the exquisite little garden of rhododendron, rock daphne, andromeda, and ceanothus, surrounded by a high hedge of photinia, that the previous tenants had lovingly planted and left in her care. Ginger wasn't particularly good with plants, but she loved having them, and she made a sincere effort to keep them all well and happy. She did a lot better with animals, and her current cat, an enormous marmalade named Twink, stood guard over the slugs and sow bugs and other parasites that threatened her blooms with bodily harm.

Ruben found the place easily, and then sat in his car for ten minutes until his watch read exactly seven o'clock. Thirty seconds later, he was ringing her doorbell, feeling every bit as nervous and as awkward as a sixteen-year-old on his first date.

One of her mother's homilies that had actually stuck with Ginger down through the years was on the virtue of promptness, and she was ready and waiting in a simple black dress with a scooped neck and a short skirt. Ruben could not remember ever seeing her in a skirt before—she always wore pants to work—and it didn't take him long to notice that she had extremely nice legs. Her fiery hair, normally bound in a neat French braid down her back, had been turned loose to curl softly about her shoulders.

"You look just great," he murmured, wondering what she had done with the tomboy he had invited to dinner.

"You don't look so bad yourself," she replied with a grin. His dark blue suit may have been a little shiny in spots, and his white shirt may have been a bit frayed around the collar, but he was freshly scrubbed and eager, and Ginger couldn't remember him ever looking better.

Because of the murder, quite a number of Island families were still choosing to stay at home these days. Ruben had no trouble getting a last-minute reservation at Gull House, the renowned restaurant crowning the northern arm of the harbor that offered its patrons the finest seafood to be found in the Northwest, and an unparalleled panorama of Puget Sound through a series of leaded glass window walls. The place had much more the atmosphere of an exclusive private club than a public eating establishment. The lighting was soft, the carpets were thick, and the service was as impeccable as the fare.

Ruben had been to Gull House only once before, at a pre-employment luncheon interview with the mayor and members of the city council. The last time for Ginger had been a dinner party to celebrate her twenty-first birthday.

The maître d' showed them directly to a window table in the smallest but most elegant of the three dining rooms.

"My goodness, the best table in the house," Ginger whispered. "I didn't realize I was dining with such a celebrity."

"Neither did I," Ruben whispered back.

They were not unaware of the stunned looks and startled murmurs their entrance garnered from the small contingent of locals who had ventured out, and they let themselves be amused by the sidelong glances that followed their progress across the restaurant.

"What do you think they're thinking?" Ginger asked with a mischievous glint in her eye.

"Why, they're thinking how lucky I am to be out with such an attractive young lady, of course," Ruben replied with a grin.

"I'm delighted you chose this restaurant," she told him carelessly. "Maybe it'll give them something to gossip about besides how little headway we're making on the Breckenridge case."

They ordered Caesar salads, grilled swordfish for him, Dungeness crab for her, and a decent bottle of chardonnay. Over the food, they talked about being on a small island, from his perspective of having more or less recently arrived, and from her perspective of having lived there most of her life.

"How long does it take before you stop feeling like an outsider?" he asked.

"I don't know yet," she replied. "Probably three or four generations."

They talked about what they did when they were away from the office, on weekends and holidays.

"I love to hike," she said. "I've been roaming the Olympics since I was ten."

"I've only gotten as far as Hurricane Ridge," he admitted. "But someday, I'd like to get up to the glacier."

They talked about lifestyles.

"I love the water," Ginger told him. "I'd live on a houseboat if I could figure out how to swing it."

Ruben nodded. "I used to fantasize about living on some

deserted beach one day," he said, "in a little cabin with a dog to keep me company. After I retired, and after Stacey was grown and gone, of course."

They talked about hobbies and favorite activities, and surprised each other when they both put bird-watching near the top of their lists.

"It's not so much the birds," she began.

"As the quiet," he finished.

He applauded her efforts against animal cruelty. She was delighted to learn that he abhorred hunting of any kind. "I know I probably shouldn't say this," he said, "but I think I'd sooner kill another person than a defenseless animal."

They spoke about music and movies and books. It was as easy for them to talk to one another as if they had known each other all their lives, and it didn't take long for them to discover they had a lot in common.

Too soon, much too soon, dinner was over, the last bite of shared satin cheesecake swallowed, the last drop of coffee drunk, and he had driven her back to her apartment house and walked her to her door.

"Thank you," she said, feeling awkward standing there on her front step. "This was really fun."

"Yes, it was," he assured her.

She didn't want the evening to end. She wanted to invite him in, for another cup of coffee, an after-dinner drink, more conversation, anything, because she felt light and carefree and happy, happier than she had in years, and she wanted it to last just a little while longer, like maybe for the rest of her life.

"I guess I'll see you Monday," she said.

"First thing," he promised.

There was just the slightest of pauses, and then he was turning and leaving. The moment was lost. She couldn't go running after him; he'd think her such a fool. She stood on the threshold, watching, until he was out of sight. Then she went inside and shut the door with a resolute click.

He was her boss, after all, and she knew it would be foolish to start anything personal with him. It would only confuse things, or worse, mess up their working relationship, and perhaps even end up costing her a job she loved. Maybe it was the wine that had her feeling so good, she decided, not him. Maybe it was the dinner and the restaurant that made her so giddy, and the fact that this was her first date in over a year.

She kicked off her shoes and padded down the hall into the bedroom to undress. They had chatted on like old friends because, to some extent, they *were* old friends. They had worked within arm's reach of each other for almost two years and that kind of togetherness almost had to create a bond. It wasn't all that surprising; she considered at least half the men on the force to be friends.

As for the things they had in common, well, they weren't such unusual things, really. Hiking and boating—almost everyone in the Pacific Northwest liked them. And as far as bird-watching, classical music, David Lean films, and Tony Hillerman novels were concerned, she supposed she could have those things in common with any number of people.

Ginger scrubbed her face and brushed her teeth and climbed into bed, resolving to make an extra effort to get out more and meet new men. The cat jumped up and stretched out beside her.

"I don't know what I'd do without you, Twink," she said, scratching his ears. "But I'm afraid, when it comes to sharing a bed, you just don't cut it, you know what I mean?"

The cat snuggled against her and began to purr.

Ginger sighed. She loved her job, but the truth of it was, there was a hole in her life that her work just couldn't fill. Surely, there had to be someone out there meant for her—someone who would understand her commitment to her career, who would applaud her work and not flinch from her profession. There had to be someplace where she could meet such a person.

She thought about her girlfriends from high school, most of them married and mothers. She thought about the boys with whom she had grown up. They were either married or gone. The Island was predominantly a family community, not a haven for singles. The chances of meeting Mr. Right here were slim to none, and she dreaded the idea of going into Seattle to hang out at bars.

Maybe she should consider taking an adult education class, or an extension course at the university, or join the Sierra Club. Yes, that was the thing to do—expand her horizons, look somewhere else, somewhere less complicated.

Ruben was a very special person, there was no doubt about that. But what would be the point in getting herself involved in something that had the deck stacked against it right from the start?

Ruben reached home before Stacey. He mixed himself a weak Scotch and water, and sat down in the living room, wondering why he had cut the evening off short of eleven o'clock.

The tables near them at the restaurant had emptied while he and Ginger dallied over each dish, talking and laughing, in no particular hurry to get to the next course. Still, they had run out of food long before they had run out of conversation. Ruben smiled into his Scotch. He had the feeling that, given all the time in the world, they would never run out of conversation.

There had been a fleeting moment, at her door, when he thought she would invite him in, and he wondered how he should respond. But the moment passed, she didn't give him the choice, and he was both disappointed and relieved.

It was easy enough to keep things on a friendly level at the restaurant, with other people around them, but it might not have been so easy once they found themselves alone in her apartment.

He knew it was wiser not to let this go beyond casual, not to get involved. He also knew that neither of them needed complications at work that might hinder their effectiveness or set idle tongues to unnecessary wagging.

It was no big revelation that personal and professional relationships rarely succeeded, and usually ended up hurting one or both of the parties concerned. He had wanted one evening with her and now he'd had it. Dinner was over.

Ruben downed the last of his Scotch with a resolute sigh and pulled himself to his feet. Whatever else, he always tried to be honest with himself. And he knew, despite what he might have believed earlier, that just one evening with her was not going to be enough.

16

The dream woke her—a disturbing dream, not quite a nightmare. Deborah Frankel opened her eyes with a start, expecting to see the girl. But there was only the moonlight slipping through the window, and the shadowy shapes of her solid rosewood bedroom furniture. Who was the girl? Deborah wondered. Where had she come from? And what was she doing in the middle of a dream about Jerry falling off a cliff?

Deborah didn't have a very clear image of her, and even that was fading now with wakefulness, but she had definitely been there, a peculiar spectator who calmly stood and watched and waited—for what?—as Deborah tried frantically to save her husband.

"Help me!" Deborah remembered crying. "Help me!"

But the girl hadn't replied, hadn't moved, hadn't even blinked.

Deborah glanced at the clock on the nightstand. The digital numbers read three-eighteen in ghostly green. She looked over to the other side of the bed. Jerry was fast asleep, safe and sound, all curled up around his pillow like a little boy hugging a teddy bear.

Deborah sighed. It was a major trait of his that she had somehow failed to notice in the beginning: the innocence, the beguiling playfulness . . . the dependency. But that was twelve years ago, and she saw so many things differently now than she had then.

Twelve years ago, she was a junior at Bryn Mawr, trying to decide on a future, and he already had his master's in hand, and was teaching history in an inner-city Philadelphia high school. They met, of all places, at a synagogue on Rosh Hashanah. He was there with his father; she was there with her roommate. Being Jewish wasn't a very big thing in Deborah's life, but it was part of her heritage, and she knew it pleased her parents back home in Scarsdale, New York, when she at least made an effort to observe the holidays.

They spotted each other immediately, across the aisle in the Reform temple, and stole cautious glances whenever they thought the other wasn't looking. After the service, they found a way to meet.

"I haven't seen you here before," he said.

"I haven't been here before," she replied.

He was a taller and much more attractive version of his father, but with the same sensitive, expressive eyes. In retrospect, she decided, it was the eyes she had first fallen in love with. The eyes that had looked so deep into hers that she felt engulfed by them on the night he asked her to marry him. The eyes that danced at the birth of their son, the eyes that cried when their daughter died . . . the eyes that seemed to slide past Ruben Martinez's shoulder when Jerry said he was working in the shop on the night that Tara Breckenridge was killed.

Deborah knew that look. She was sure he meant it to convey concentration, but sometimes she wondered if it hid evasion. She remembered the morning after the murder; the bandaged thumb, the bloody sweatshirt. She hadn't thought anything about it then. For some reason, she found herself thinking about it now, and a cold chill slid down the length of her body as she wondered whether her husband had been telling the truth.

Even after twelve years, she was not quite sure. There had been good communication between them once, or so she thought, when she was young and still impressionable. But as time went on, she came to realize that he had put a barrier between them, like a protective suit of armor which allowed her to know only that part of him that he wanted her to know. In their early years together, she had tried every way she could to penetrate that barrier, but after a while the effort began to seem greater than the reward, and she abandoned it.

Life, she couldn't help reflect, was sometimes like a big black hole—a dark and scary unknown that you plunged into with no clear idea of what awaited you—much like the murky pond behind her childhood home that her mother used to caution her about. You made decisions that seemed to be reasonable and informed at the time, only to learn later that they may have been imprudent. You thought you knew what you wanted, only to discover that perhaps you did not. You saw yourself as wise and worldly and mature enough to make the right choices, only to realize you were not. And then, without quite understanding how you got there, you found yourself in a place you didn't really want to be, with no viable way out.

She remembered how often her elders had waxed eloquently about the particular joys of marriage and motherhood—and wondered why nobody had ever thought to warn her about the mistakes one could make. Not that she was ready to admit that her marriage was a mistake, but there were things she wished she had known beforehand, things she would perhaps have been better prepared for, things she might have been able to handle a little differently.

With a small yawn, Deborah plumped her pillows and snuggled down under the covers. She could go back to sleep now. The analytical side of her brain had taken over—what she always referred to as her working mind. It was already beginning the process of evaluating situations, assessing results, and considering options.

The dream was gone. So was the girl.

17

"Tara Breckenridge has been dead for almost a month now," Gail Brown editorialized in the *Sentinel*, "and yet the police are no closer to apprehending the person responsible than they were on the day it happened. How can this be? With all the modern technology law enforcement has at its fingertips, why does this case remain open?

"Chief Ruben Martinez came to Seward Island three years ago with impeccable credentials, and he has built a first-rate staff. I know most of these people; they are dedicated professionals, and yet they have so far been unequal to the task of solving the single most heinous crime this community has ever known. What's wrong with this picture?

"If we who live here are to blame, if there is someone among us who knows something that will help lead authorities to Tara's killer, and has not come forward, then shame on us, for even the finest police force cannot be expected to work in a vacuum.

"Our idyllic island has been severely rocked and is now being sorely tested. Living here will never be the same. I see fear and distrust everywhere I go. Friends and neighbors who deliberately chose this place to distance themselves and their families from the dangers of big-city life are locking their doors and looking over their shoulders. Tara's death, the way in which she died, touched us all. It's an open wound that will not—and cannot— heal until the person responsible has been brought to justice.

"Whether we knew her well or not at all, we want Tara to rest in peace. We want the Breckenridge family to have some closure. *We* want to be able to get on with our lives. She deserves, they deserve, we deserve to have this matter resolved. If this resolution is being thwarted by someone out there who has pertinent information and has purposely chosen not to share it with the proper authorities, then shame, shame, shame on us all."

"She took aim at the whole island this time," Charlie Pricker remarked, dropping the paper on Ruben's desk.

"It was a mistake," declared Ginger.

"Why?" Ruben asked. The three had once again squeezed themselves into the police chief's tiny office.

"Because she's a native," replied Ginger. "She should know better. All this is going to do is alienate everyone, and make our job even harder."

"I can't see as it matters much," Charlie said, sighing.

Ginger shook her head. "Islanders are basically good people, but they're the kind of people who go to church every Sunday, listen to the sermon, pray piously—and then go home thinking they're square with God. If you rub their noses in it, they'll turn on you. But if you just let them alone, sooner or later, they'll get around to doing the right thing."

"Yeah, but how much later?" Charlie drawled.

Their investigation of the mystery Taurus wagon that had been seen in the Madrona Point parking lot on the night of the murder had come to nothing, and Ginger's look into the life of the history teacher had turned up no indication that her initial assessment of him was in any way inaccurate.

"He's clean," she said. "I haven't found anything to suggest otherwise."

Charlie shrugged. "Back to square one."

"It's infuriating," Ruben said. "The guy we're looking for is out there, right under our noses, and we're just missing him. Here we sit, on an isolated island, with a population of twelve thousand people. That gives us a potential suspect pool of maybe thirty-five hundred males between the ages of eighteen and let's say seventy, only a small fraction of which are going to turn out to be left-handed. Tara obviously had a relationship with one of them, and it didn't happen in a vacuum. So why are we having so much trouble finding him?"

"Maybe because we're coming at it the wrong way," Ginger said slowly.

"What do you mean?"

"Well, instead of investigating Tara, maybe it's the men we should be investigating."

Ruben looked at her. "You want to investigate thirty-five hundred men?"

Ginger shrugged. "Either we can sit around waiting for something to happen, or we can try to make something happen for ourselves."

The police chief frowned. "How exactly would you go about doing this?"

Ginger thought for a moment. "It's the blood that's going to solve this case," she said finally. "So I'd be right up front about it. And I'd start with an easily identifiable group—let's say, high school seniors. That's only around seventy or so. I'd tell them exactly what we're doing. Then I'd ask each of them to voluntarily give us a sample of his blood to be used for a paternity test. If the kid is innocent, it's the best way to clear himself. If he refuses, well, at least we've narrowed the field. Then, of those who refuse, we can strike the ones that are right-handed, and concentrate on the rest. If that doesn't give us what we want, we expand the selection and repeat the process until we get him."

"Those tests cost a fortune," Charlie reminded her, "and they take months to process."

"We can probably eliminate a lot on basic blood typing alone," Ginger replied. "And remember, we're concentrating on left-handers, which will narrow the field dramatically. So we send off only those samples provided by left-handed donors that have a possible chance of matching."

"How do we determine who's left-handed and who isn't?" Charlie inquired.

"Let Magnus do that," Ginger said, "as a casual part of taking the blood sample. You know, you take the blood out of the arm the donor either uses most of the time or doesn't use as much, or something like that. And the technician can mark down which it is."

"Has it occurred to you," Charlie suggested, "that we could be looking for someone who might not be strictly left-handed, but ambidextrous?"

"It's possible," Ginger conceded. "But I think it's safe to assume that the number of ambidextrous men on this island is small enough to ignore at this point. I'd go with the obvious. If we have to increase the sample at a later date, so be it. And if we don't let on that we're only looking for lefties, we won't give anything away."

It was the one piece of information that they had been able to keep from Albert Hoch, and therefore from the Island as a whole.

"Are we clear with the Constitution on this?" Ruben asked. "I don't want to go stepping on anyone's personal freedoms."

"I think we are," Ginger asserted, "as long as we make it strictly voluntary."

Charlie shrugged. "You know, it's so obvious, it might just work."

Ruben had to agree. He looked at the redhead he had known for almost two years, and was just beginning to know. If the department ever got around to solving this case, he felt certain it would be because of her. She combined an instinct for police work that could not be taught, with a thorough understanding of the community in which she performed that work. It was how he had operated in the barrios, blending into the background. It was not like here, where he was so out of place. Here, *she* was the one who blended, and he had come to rely heavily on that.

There had been their dinner together on Saturday night. This was Wednesday afternoon. Hardly a moment had passed between then and now that he wasn't thinking about her, recounting the evening in his mind from beginning to end—every word, every gesture, every smile. It was like returning from a long exile in an Arctic waste to find the world was a warm and wonderful place, and to know, after so many years, that it was okay to be alive.

He was thrown clear of the auto accident that killed his wife—a pickup truck skidding on a slick patch of road, spinning out of control, smashing into the passenger side of the old Chevy. It all happened too fast. There was no time to react, to swerve, to avoid the collision. Everyone said so. But that didn't stop the guilt from engulfing Ruben, or the pain, or the loneliness. He had loved his wife as much as he could. Afterward, he began to wonder whether he had loved her enough. That made it worse.

It was Stacey who saved his life. She was only two years old at the time of the accident, suddenly motherless, and she needed him. He couldn't deny her. He taught himself to shut off all the parts of himself that didn't directly relate to his daughter or his work, and he had been quite successful at it.

Until Saturday night.

Now there were a dozen different doors opening inside of

him, exposing him to the expectations, the uncertainties, the joys, and the fears of connecting with another human being. Because, of course, they *had* connected. As much as he wanted to tell himself—tried to tell himself—they hadn't, he knew better.

It was all wrong, everything about it was wrong—the difference in their ages, their positions, their backgrounds. He was well aware of that. But it didn't matter, because it was clear to him that nothing had ever been or would ever be more right.

He talked it over with Stacey at breakfast on Sunday; they had few secrets between them.

"It sounds like you two really hit it off," she said. She had encountered the no-nonsense redhead at police headquarters on any number of occasions, and pretty much liked what she saw. "So, do you want to see her again?"

"There's really no point in it," her father replied with perhaps more candor than he intended. "This is such a small island. Our working relationship could be jeopardized. Then there's the potential gossip that could cause problems. Not to mention the difference in our ages. She's closer to your age than mine. No, there's no point; it can't go anywhere."

"That's not what I asked you," Stacey observed.

Sometimes, he thought, she was too wise for her years. The obvious answer was yes, but he couldn't seem to say it. He was afraid that he had caught Ginger off guard, giving her no choice but to accept his invitation once she had told him that she was free for the evening. He didn't want her to go out with him just because he was her boss and she didn't know how to refuse, and he wasn't sure he would be able to tell the difference. Ruben had already had enough rejection in his life; he was not particularly anxious to open himself up to more.

"What if I do want to see her again?" he countered. "She may not want to see me. And I certainly don't want her to feel she has to be polite."

Stacey tossed her silky blond hair that was so like her

mother's. "Invite her home to dinner," she suggested. "If she accepts that kind of offer, I think you can assume she's not just being polite. Then I'll get a good up-close, out-of-the-office look at her, and we'll know what's what."

"You really think I should?"

His daughter looked at him quizzically. "What's the worst thing that can happen?" she asked shrewdly. "That she says no—or that she says yes?"

Ever since that conversation, the fearless police chief had been trying to summon the courage.

The Sunday after the dinner at Gull House was brisk and blustery; a steely overcast threatened rain.

Ginger spent the better part of the day holed up inside her apartment, listening to an all-Beethoven concert being rebroadcast from New York's Lincoln Center and cleaning out her closets. Anything to keep herself busy, to keep her mind and her body occupied, to keep from thinking about Ruben.

In the clear light of day, she decided it wasn't fair. To be twenty-eight years old and finally find what could be the right man—only to have him be her highly visible boss in a small town where the gossip alone could destroy them. There were so many things wrong with the two of them being together—and everything right. They thought alike, they shared so many interests, their senses of humor seemed to harmonize. She had no doubt that their bodies would fit together perfectly as well.

Despite her resolution of the night before to get out and meet other men, she began to think about the possibility of finding a job in another police department, in another county, which might then make it permissible for them to see each other. Even though she would hate leaving the Island, if it meant she could have a relationship with Ruben, it might be worth it.

At three-thirty in the afternoon, the Beethoven concert having concluded, Ginger abandoned her closets, changed her clothes, and set off for the rambling farmhouse on the western side of the Island where she had been raised, and where her parents still lived. It was a weekly ritual that she rarely missed because it brought her three brothers and their families back to Seward.

Sunday dinner at the Earley homestead was normally a boisterous affair with her nieces and nephews out of control, and she and her father and her youngest brother squaring off against the rest in a game of touch football. But it was a somber group that greeted Ginger this particular day. The children were strangely silent, her brothers perplexed, her father distracted, and her mother agitated.

"Eleanor Jewel just couldn't wait to tell me," the buxom woman with unnaturally blond hair declared the moment her daughter was past the front door. "Why, she fairly pounced like a cat the moment we walked into church."

"Tell you what?" Ginger asked.

"All about you going to Gull House, of all places, with that Chief Martinez person, of course," Verna Earley replied.

"So what?"

"So how do you think it looks?" her mother complained. "You being seen having dinner with—with your boss?"

"We worked late on a case, and on the spur of the moment, we decided to have dinner," Ginger said. "If I'd thought there was anything wrong with that, I wouldn't have done it."

Verna looked to her husband for support.

"I think your mother is concerned more with how it was perceived than by how it really was," Jack Earley suggested with an unhappy sigh at being put in the middle.

"That's not true," Verna argued. "I'm just as concerned with how it was. It's bad enough you have to work for him, but to be seen with him when you're on your own time, to flaunt your association in the faces of our friends, our neighbors, all the people you grew up with—well, it's not the done thing."

Ginger looked from her mother to her father and back to her mother again. "Did I miss something here?"

"It was a good many years before we became part of this community, young lady," her mother said. "Although you were too young to remember, it didn't just happen. Your father and I had to make it happen. We had to attend a particular church. We had to join the right clubs. We had to cultivate the proper friends. As you well know, Seward Island can be a very cliquish place, and coming from the other side of the state, as we did, your father and I had to work especially hard to be accepted here. It took a long time, but this is our home now, the people are important to us, and their opinion of us matters."

"I guess I must be dense," Ginger said, "because I still don't get it."

Her mother sighed in exasperation. "You were seen giggling and laughing and sharing your food with him, like you were out on a date, for God's sake," Verna said. "Out on a date at the most expensive restaurant in town, in a low-cut dress with—well, I shouldn't even have to mention it, and I'm sorry, but I guess there's only one way to say it—with a Mexican."

The word was aimed like a dart at Ginger, and it landed with the precision of an expert marksman, almost knocking the wind out of her. For a moment, she was so stunned she was unable to speak.

"I never realized there was anything wrong in being friends with a Mexican," she said finally. "You never told me there was anything wrong with that."

"There were never any of them around here," her mother retorted. "So we didn't think there was any reason to tell you."

"And you're saying the whole island feels this way?"

"Well of course I can't speak for the whole island," Verna said, backing off slightly, "but I'm sure I speak for those in our social circle. There are people who belong and there are people who don't, and it doesn't do to mix the two."

"I'm sorry," Ginger said slowly. "I didn't know."

There had always been remarks, passing comments of one sort or another, but never anything as blatant as this, and Ginger had always been able to dismiss them as thoughtless chatter. She looked at her mother as though unsure whether she had ever really seen her before.

"Well then," Verna said, "what's done is done, and now that you understand, we'll say no more about it."

A collective sigh ran through the entire family. Her mother trotted off to the kitchen to tend to her roast. The children began to chase each other around the backyard. The touch football game took over the front lawn. A thorny matter had been dealt with, and now life could return to normal. Nobody seemed to notice that Ginger played with an unusual lack of enthusiasm, or that she hardly said a word to any of them all evening, or that she merely pushed the food around her plate at dinner.

Only when she was back in the safety of her apartment did the anger inside her erupt, and the violence of it made her hurl her handbag at the bookcase crammed into the corner of the entry foyer, knocking several volumes askew and smashing a small porcelain angel that had been a sixteenth-birthday gift from her late grandmother.

For the first time, she realized how apart she had grown from the close-knit family she cherished. More than just the life experiences that had taken her out of the cloistered atmosphere of Seward Island and into the harsh reality of police work, she simply didn't see things the way her parents did. Their values were not her values, their world no longer her world.

She tried to picture herself at ten or twelve, perched on a stool in the big, friendly kitchen as her mother baked cookies, or sitting shoulder to shoulder with her father as they worried over a jigsaw puzzle. Had they really told her that some people were less acceptable than others, and she had missed it? Or had she, like most children, simply allowed them to think and act for her until she was grown up enough to shed their influence and think and act for herself?

Unbidden, a memory pushed its way into Ginger's mind of a Japanese-American girl she had liked in grade school, and how her mother had, for no specific reason, discouraged the friendship. And she recalled a Jewish boy in high school who had been one of the few ever interested enough to ask her out. Verna had clearly not wanted her to date him. So it *was* there, that undercurrent. Never very overt, never too hostile, just there. Never anything specific that you could put your finger on, just something you were apparently expected to understand.

Ginger understood, all right. She knelt down on the floor to retrieve the shattered pieces of the porcelain angel. Gone were all her doubts and fears about an office relationship. Gone was the idea of seeking employment in another district. She was going to stay right here where she belonged, on Seward Island, and live her own life. Because that's exactly what it was—her own life; whatever the pitfalls, whatever the consequences.

There, on her knees, she prayed as hard as she had ever prayed before that Ruben Martinez would ask her out again.

He did. Four days later.

"I guess I should have said something a whole lot earlier," he began cautiously on Thursday morning, when they found themselves alone in his office for a rare moment, "but I really wanted to thank you for having dinner with me the other night. You're a lot of fun to be with, and I had a terrific time."

"So did I," she said. "In fact, I can't recall when I had a better time."

"Really?" he asked, brightening. "Because I thought maybe I didn't exactly give you a choice."

"Of course you did," she told him. "I didn't have to say yes."

"Well then," he said, his courage soaring. "I was—uh—well, wondering if maybe—uh—we might do it again sometime?"

Ginger felt her heart skip a beat. "I'd like that," she replied.

A big grin spread across Ruben's face. "That's great," he said. "That's just great." He turned to the work in front of him and then turned back to her. "I don't suppose you'd be free on Sunday, would you?"

"As it happens, I am," she said without the slightest hesitation.

"Stacey said I should invite you home for dinner so she can look you over, but we can go out someplace, if you'd prefer."

Ginger laughed. "Gosh, I can't remember the last time anyone wanted to look me over," she told him. "I'd be delighted to have dinner at your place."

Ruben shoved his hands into his trouser pockets because he was afraid he might do something stupid, like clap.

"Is six o'clock okay?" he asked.

"Six is just fine, and I think I know the way to your place."

"Oh, no," he said. Despite the desperate life of the barrio, he had been taught his manners. "I'll pick you up at six."

"Okay," Ginger agreed. "I'll be looking forward to it."

Ruben grinned. "So will I."

Ginger grinned, too. Her parents were just going to have to manage without her on Sunday. She began to plan in her mind exactly how she would tell them.

"They're at another dead end," Albert Hoch reported to Kyle Breckenridge. "The car-in-the-park angle didn't pan out. They're back to square one."

The bank president wagged his silver-blond head. "A month and still nothing. This isn't good, Albert. It sends a very dangerous message that our police force is weak at best and incompetent at worst. People are starting to ask how it can be so difficult to catch one murdering bastard on an island with only twelve thousand people."

"I know, Kyle, I know," Hoch said. "But they've got a new plan. They want to use DNA to find him. They want to start with the high school seniors, get them to give a blood sample, and try to match it with Tara's unborn child. If they come up dry, they'll expand the circle to others who knew her. They think they can catch him that way."

"This is terrible," Breckenridge declared. "To have the people in this community subjected to such a thing. What are we coming to—that we must interrogate our lifelong friends and neighbors, invade their privacy, strip them of their dignity?"

"They've got nothing else to go on," Hoch protested. "You want them to find Tara's killer, don't you? Well, they can't just pluck a viable suspect out of thin air, can they?"

"No," Kyle Breckenridge conceded with an unhappy sigh. "They can't just pluck a suspect out of thin air."

Ginger began her telephone calls on Thursday afternoon. By Friday, she had contacted all seventy-two male members of the Seward High School senior class. Of that number, forty-six agreed to be tested, eleven said they would get back to her, and fifteen flat out refused.

"A lot of the parents aren't happy about the idea," she reported to Ruben. "But most of them got the point. If they refuse to let their sons be tested, it could make them look guilty."

She arranged with Magnus Coop to take the blood samples at the clinic on Saturday. Both Coop and Charlie Pricker would be on hand, as well as all three of the clinic's laboratory technicians, who would be instructed to determine whether each subject was right- or left-handed. Once the samples were properly identified and typed, Charlie would hand-deliver those to be tested to the state crime laboratory in Seattle. With a little luck, they could expect to have the results back in two months.

18

Ruben was up, showered, and dressed by seven-forty-five on Sunday morning, but Stacey was way ahead of him. The fifteen-year-old not only was dressed herself, but had his breakfast ready.

"I thought you'd want to go to mass this morning," she said, as she set a plate of scrambled eggs with sausage in front of him, poured his coffee, and then sat down quietly with her hands folded in her lap.

Going to church was something Ruben did as infrequently as possible and mainly on holidays. Even then, it was more for Stacey than himself. Yet there were some things that could not be ignored, that had to be honored.

"Yes," he said, thinking that nobody made coffee like his daughter, thick and black and delicious.

When he invited Ginger to dinner, with Stacey's full approval, he hadn't stopped to think about the date. But this was the thirteenth anniversary of the accident that had taken his wife, and every year since, he and his daughter had observed the occasion by going to mass together.

"We'll have plenty of time to clean up the house when we get back," Stacey assured him. "And do dinner, too."

Ruben nodded sadly, thinking how easy it was for her to slip from past to present, knowing that the ritual they celebrated was his, because she could have no real memory of her mother.

Saint Aloysius Catholic Church was a pristine structure located two blocks west of the Village Green. Built of white clapboard and shingles, with a series of fabulous stained glass windows, it had been destroyed by fire three times in its history and restored, each time just a little bit sturdier, a little bit grander than before. The three percent of the Island population that supported the church did so generously.

A majority of the pews were already filled by the time Ruben and Stacey arrived. As was their custom, they quietly took up seats at the rear. Immediately, Stacey moved forward onto her knees, and began to pray. Ruben stayed where he was. Since the death of his wife, he had been unable to recover his faith. Over the years, he and God had developed a more or less laissez-faire relationship with each other that seemed to work well enough. At least, as far as he was concerned.

The mass was traditional, the sermon a rather bland version of doctrine. The priest was an agreeable enough man, but not much of an orator. Ruben watched with detachment while Stacey took communion, glad if it could bring her a measure of comfort that it no longer brought him. Then he went with her to light a candle for his wife.

It was after the service was over, when the congregation was slowly filing out of the church, that he and Stacey happened to overhear part of a conversation going on ahead of them.

". . . chief favored us with an appearance today," John O'Connor was saying.

"The Breckenridge case must be keeping him busy," Kevin Mahar responded.

"More likely a case of a redheaded detective," O'Connor suggested and laughed.

"Can you believe that?" Lucy Mahar exclaimed. "I don't know what she could be thinking of."

"That she's twenty-eight years old and still unmarried, my dear," Doris O'Connor replied with a shrug.

"For all he's accomplished on the Breckenridge case, we might just as well have hired ourselves a chihuahua," John O'Connor said.

At that, Stacey tucked her arm through her father's. "Come on, Dad," she said in a bright, clear voice. "If we hurry, I can get your kibble on the table before you can say woof."

The O'Connors slunk away without a word. Kevin Mahar had the grace to look embarrassed.

"I'm sorry, Ruben," he mumbled. "We didn't realize you were behind us."

"That shouldn't change your opinion any," Ruben replied with quiet dignity. "One of the great things about this country is the freedom we have to speak our minds without fear of the consequences."

"White American trash," Stacey remarked as they climbed into the Blazer.

"No," Ruben said with a sigh. "They're just ordinary people who aren't used to being afraid of the dark."

The apple pie was cooling, the rib roast was cooking, the little house was scrubbed and sparkling, and the table was set for three by the time Ruben left to pick up Ginger. Stacey selected a red sweater for him to wear over a white shirt, and then liberally dosed his hands with Vaseline Intensive Care lotion.

"Just in case you happen to take her elbow or something, you understand," she said with an impish twinkle in her dark brown eyes. "After all, you don't want her thinking you do housework, do you?"

Ginger was ready when he rang the bell. She was wearing a pair of slacks and a soft sweater in bright blue that looked wonderful with her red hair, which was swept off her face and caught in back with a big blue bow.

"Red, white, and blue," she said in greeting. "We're certainly a patriotic pair."

Ruben Martinez was a straightforward man who believed in tackling a problem head-on. It was simply not in his nature to deceive.

"Look," he said. "Before we go, I think I should tell you that, well—some people are talking. About us, I mean. Normally, I don't pay much attention to that sort of thing, but some remarks were made at my church today, and I just wanted you to know that, well, I'd understand if you thought it best to call dinner off."

"Remarks?" Ginger echoed. "What sort of remarks?"

"Well, I'm afraid they were about you—being seen with me."

"I stopped going to church years ago," Ginger told him with a toss of her head. "Now I know why."

"This is a small town," he said.

"Yes, and some of the people have small minds," she said.

"Still, it's the place where you've lived most of your life," he reminded her. "I don't want to cause you any embarrassment. So the decision is up to you."

"In that case," Ginger declared, "I hope you're a good cook, because I'm starved."

Like an old bathrobe, there was something warm and cozy and familiar about the Martinez home that wrapped itself around Ginger the moment she stepped through the door. Although the place was undeniably small and the furnishings a bit shabby, comfort and caring oozed out of every corner. Had she had the slightest hesitation about going to Ruben's house on just their second date, the feeling vanished the moment Stacey stepped forward with a smile and a hug.

"I hope you like roast beef," the teenager said. "It was the only thing Dad and I could agree on."

The roast was delicious, done just the way Ginger liked it—still red in the middle; the carrots crunched with just a hint of cinnamon; the salad was simple but substantial, and the salsa rice and beans was an unexpected, but perfect, accompaniment.

"Dad wanted to go totally ethnic," Stacey confided, passing a plate of hot buttered tortillas, "but I convinced him that too much too soon might scare you away."

Ginger laughed. "I guess I don't scare that easy," she said with a glance at Ruben.

Dinner lasted well past nine o'clock. No one seemed to be in any hurry. The wine was inexpensive but mellow, the coffee superb. They talked more than they ate, and they ate everything. Several times they laughed so hard they almost cried. Ginger couldn't remember when she had felt so relaxed, so welcome—and so totally content. It was after eleven when Ruben drove her back to her apartment. Five hours had passed in hardly a blink.

"I had a terrific time," she said at her front door, wishing the evening were just beginning and she had five more hours to spend with him.

"So did I," he agreed, hoping this time she would invite him in for a nightcap or another cup of coffee, or even a glass of water, come to that, because he didn't want to leave her just yet.

"I don't know where the time went," she added, wanting to open her door to him but afraid he might refuse. And if he didn't refuse, afraid of the expectations—hers as much as his—and it was much too soon to deal with that. "It's really amazing how we never seem to run out of things to talk about."

"I'm glad you could come," he said. "I guess I'll see you tomorrow."

"Bright and early," she assured him.

They stood there for a moment, neither quite sure what to do next. Then he leaned over and kissed her lightly on the cheek.

"Sleep well," he murmured and was gone, gliding quickly down the pathway, through the shadows, into the dark.

Ginger went inside, alone again, and yet not quite. His kiss was still on her cheek. She touched her fingers to the spot. It felt soft and warm, and the warmth spread down through her body as though he were a part of her.

She wrapped her arms around herself to hold on to him as long as she could. When the feeling began to fade, she went into the bedroom and took off her clothes. Then she ran a hot bath, which was something she rarely did, and soaked in it, trying to recapture the sense of him.

For close to two years, she had talked to him, listened to him, worked beside him, and learned from him, never really believing that he would ever be anything more to her than the chief of police. And now, in just one short week, all that had changed.

The spare cinder block building at the end of Commodore Street was suddenly the most beautiful place in the world to her. Just the thought of going to work made her smile; just the idea of seeing him each day sent her spirits soaring. She no longer thought about how this might end. After all, it was just beginning. And in the beginning, it was always so easy to believe it would last forever.

She tried to recall the young man from Pomeroy, the one in the farm equipment business. But his face had grown fuzzy with time, and it was hard to gauge feelings that no longer existed. How absurd that broken heart seemed to her now; now that her heart was full again, and on the verge of what could well be true happiness.

It was long past midnight by the time she slipped into bed and snapped off the light. She had to be at the office early in the morning, but she didn't bother to set her alarm. There was too much to think about, to dream about while she was still awake enough to steer the outcome. The last thing she wanted to do was sleep.

19

Ginger spent most of Monday going over a list of those high school seniors who had failed to present themselves at the clinic to give a blood sample. There was a total of eighteen names.

"Do you really think he's in there?" Charlie Pricker asked, peering over her shoulder.

"Who knows," Ginger replied with a shrug and a sigh. "But it's a start."

Since Charlie's promotion a year ago, the detectives had shared an office that was barely large enough for two desks pushed against opposite walls, two gray metal file cabinets, and one extra chair. They worked out of each other's back pockets, as they often described it, and had grown accustomed to purloining each other's coffee mug, taking each other's telephone messages, signing for each other's mail, and discussing everything.

"You've been in the department four years longer than she has," Charlie's wife, Jane, complained. "Why don't *you* have seniority?"

"She's been a detective longer than I have," he explained patiently.

"But you've been a policeman for thirteen years," Jane persisted, "and you're six years older than she is. That ought to count for something."

Her husband smiled his easy smile. "It does," he teased, because he loved his wife almost as much as he loved his job. "Sometimes, *she* gets the coffee."

Jane sniffed. "And now that she's playing cozy with the chief, I suppose you'll never get the chance to show how good you are."

"I show how good I am every day of the week," he told her, his smile fading slightly. "By doing my job the best I know how. And I don't particularly appreciate my own wife repeating rumors about the people I work with. It only makes my job harder."

If Charlie harbored any resentment toward Ginger for having seniority, it wasn't apparent. They handled separate parts of an investigation, conferred officially on matters that related to both of them, joked around with each other the rest of the time, and got along well. He thought of her as the kid sister he never had. She looked on him as another brother.

"I like Ruben," he said out of the blue, as he folded his lanky frame into his chair, dropped his glasses over his eyes, and began to peruse a report. "I've known him a while longer than you. He's a good person, but I think he's pretty vulnerable here. I like you, too. You're solid, but I think you're not so vulnerable. That means it's up to you to be careful."

Ginger swung around to face his back. "Is this your own opinion I'm hearing, or is the whole damn island talking?"

"I don't listen to gossip," Charlie replied mildly. "I just call it like I see it."

"We've been out with each other exactly twice," she protested. "Why do people need to make such a federal case out of it?"

"Twice?" he echoed. "Damn, I thought it was only once. Some detective I am."

She couldn't be angry with him. "Thanks," she said with a chuckle. "I know you mean well."

"So then, why don't you give me a copy of those names," he said. "One of the English teachers up at the high school is a pal of mine. Maybe I can get some input on how many of your hold-outs are left-handed."

"It's an outrage," Grant Kriedler wrote to the editor of the *Sentinel*. "We are now being asked to give up one of our most basic constitutional liberties in a blatant attempt to implicate our sons in the Breckenridge case. If the police have just cause to suspect that one of them has committed murder, let them present their evidence and secure a duly executed warrant. If not, let them stay out of our homes and our lives. My eighteen-year-old son has refused to take part in this charade, and I support him."

"It seems to me that we're damned if we do, and damned if we don't," wrote a senior who had kept his appointment at the clinic. "But if giving some of my blood is going to help find Tara's killer, then I say what harm does it do?"

"Three of the kids on your no-show list are left-handed," Charlie told Ginger on Wednesday.

"Thanks," she said, looking at the sheet of paper he laid on her desk and the little red asterisks he had placed beside the three names. "This gives us a starting place."

Stacey Martinez passed a bowl of corn chowder to her father.

"Everyone's talking about it," she said. "It's become the Great Debate. I mean, it's not every day that almost the entire male population of the senior class is asked to give blood to prove themselves innocent of a crime."

"I wish there'd been another way," Ruben replied, taking a generous helping of the soup.

"Do you really think the person you're looking for is sitting in school every day as though nothing had happened?"

"I don't know. Do you?"

"I just don't see it," Stacey declared, buttering a tortilla. "I know you say the killer acted out of anger and circumstance, but I can't believe that any of those kids could have killed Tara that way, and then been able to go on about his life, pretending he didn't know a thing about it. I mean, I see them every day. They're not complicated, they're not alienated, they're not cold and calculating. For the most part, they're normal kids, doing whatever it is normal kids do. This thing about the blood—it's getting to everyone."

"How do you mean?" Ruben asked.

"Well, they're starting to take sides. You're either for or you're against. Everyone's lining up, and they're not just being vocal, either, they're being physical about it, too. The principal had to break up two fistfights today."

Ruben looked at his daughter thoughtfully. "Have you noticed anyone who isn't taking sides?" he asked. "Anyone who isn't being vocal or physical? Anyone who's sort of just standing on the sidelines?"

Stacey started to shake her head, but stopped. A face flashed before her eyes. She frowned because the face was not connected to the question her father had asked; it had just popped into her head.

"Danny Leo," she said, attaching a name to the face.

"Danny Leo?" Ruben repeated. "Is he someone who seems to be playing neutral?"

"No, it's not about that," Stacey said. "Remember, right after the murder, you asked me if I'd ever seen Tara with anyone? Well, there was something I couldn't remember back then, but I remember it now. One day after school, I saw Tara with Danny Leo."

"Come on down to dinner, Danny," Rose Leo called from the bottom of the stairs. "Hurry up now. Your father's waiting."

A good-looking eighteen-year-old clambered down the steps and took his seat at the table. He had curly brown hair that he kept neatly trimmed, and clear green eyes that were known to set a girl's heart to fluttering when they chanced to glance her way.

"You've been locked up in your room for days now, son," Peter Leo said. "What's going on? Is something bothering you?"

"No, Dad," Danny replied. "I'm trying to make a model of the *Bounty*. It's a special project, and Mr. Frankel said he might enter it for the state history award if I got it accurate enough. I'm only locking my door because I don't want the girls to get in there and mess it all up."

The two siblings, seated across the table from their brother, sniffed.

"I just wanted my Fiery Nights nail polish back," the thirteen-year-old said.

"And I want my blue hair ribbon," chimed in the ten-year-old.

"I needed them for my project," Danny told them both. "I told you I'd get you some more."

"See that you do, son," Peter said. "And I don't think you'll have to lock your door anymore. I'm sure, now that the girls understand what it's about, they'll leave your project alone."

The girls looked at each other and then at their father and nodded reluctantly. When Peter Leo spoke, the family listened, and obeyed. The only problem was that he almost always took Danny's side. Not that Danny didn't deserve it much of the time, the girls grudgingly had to admit. The high school senior excelled on both the track and ice hockey teams, served as the sports editor of the school newspaper, was president of the student body, maintained a straight-A average, was in line for a scholarship to Harvard University, and always kept his room spotless. It was just that it would be nice if, once in a while, someone would see things from their perspective; to be more specific—how difficult it was to grow up beside Superboy.

"There's something else," Stacey told her father. "I know I'm not supposed to know about this, but I overheard you say something to Ginger the other night—Danny Leo is left-handed."

"Are you sure?"

She nodded. "I work with him on the school paper. I've seen him writing lots of times."

"It's funny how things happen," Ginger said the next morning. "You start with a forest, and before you know it, there are the trees."

Danny Leo's name was on the short list of left-handed seniors who had not provided a blood sample for the paternity test.

"We can certainly justify having a talk with the boy," Ruben acknowledged. "But I doubt we've got enough for a court order. We can ask him to come in, but we can't force him. How do you want to handle it?"

"I know the family," Ginger said. "Let me go talk to them at home first, informally. Then we'll see."

"I don't know what to do," Rose Leo said, flapping her hands in frustration. "Peter isn't home from work yet."

Ginger stood just inside the front door of the Leo home. It was five-forty-five in the evening. She had waited in her car for almost an hour until she saw Danny jump off the late school bus, trot along Lindstrom Avenue, turn the corner at Dover, and then cut across the lawn that fronted a modest gray-shingled house with brown trim.

Between this morning, when she had first spoken to Ruben, and the time she had gotten into her car to drive to Dover Road, the detective had gathered as much information about the teenager as she could. His school health form indicated that he was five feet ten inches tall and weighed approximately one hundred seventy pounds. Generally speaking, she did not consider that to be an overpowering stature, but as she watched him disappear inside the front door, it was clear that most of his weight was in solid muscle.

Ginger also knew about his grades and his scholarship, that his mother worked part-time as a nurse's aide, and that his father worked the day shift at Boeing's production plant in Everett.

"What time does Peter normally get home, Rose?" she asked.

"He gets off work at four-thirty," came the reply. "If he catches the five o'clock ferry, he's usually here by six."

"I don't mind waiting," the detective said smoothly. "This is rather important."

"Important? Why? Danny didn't have anything to do with that girl who was murdered. He's a good boy. If this is about that blood thing on Saturday, you can't blame Danny for that. It was his father who wouldn't let him go."

"Please, Rose," Ginger said. "I wouldn't be here if I didn't have a good reason. But I'm sure it's nothing for you to get upset about. I just have a few things to discuss with Danny."

"Hey, look," the teenager said from the stairway. "I'll talk to you, Detective Earley. You don't have to wait for my dad to get home. Ask me whatever you like. I have nothing to hide."

"No, Danny," Rose interjected anxiously. "You wait for your father."

"It's okay, Mom," the teenager said. "Really. There's no problem."

"I don't want to go against your mother's wishes, Danny," Ginger said clearly. "I'd prefer to wait for your father."

"Why don't you come on in the living room," the boy suggested. "We can talk there. If you ask me any stuff I don't think I should answer, then we can wait for my dad."

Rose Leo looked from one to the other. "I'll go see to dinner," she said lamely.

The living room was done in Early American style, and didn't look as though it were used very much. Ginger and Danny sat down on two cushioned sofas that faced each other across a maple coffee table.

"I don't know what I can tell you," the boy began. "I'm sorry about not taking the blood test. I would've done it, but my dad said it was a matter of principle."

"Why don't we put that aside for the moment," Ginger said. "Right now, I'm more interested in hearing about your relationship with Tara Breckenridge."

Danny blinked. "I never had a relationship with Tara," he said. "I knew her. We weren't exactly what you'd call friends, but we were—friendly."

"How did you get to be friendly?"

"I knew her from the country club. The last two summers I worked there as a busboy in the restaurant, and she used to come around sometimes."

"And?" Ginger prodded.

"If she sat at one of my tables, she would say hello," he said. "And if she was alone, we would talk about stuff."

"You were several years older than Tara," the detective observed. "What kind of stuff did you talk about?"

"I don't know," the senior replied with an uneasy shrug. "Nothing important."

"Danny, why didn't you say anything about knowing Tara when I first talked to you?"

"Just about everyone knew Tara," he said. "I didn't think *how* I knew her was important."

"Well, it could be very important," Ginger told him. "So why don't you tell me about it now."

The boy hesitated. "I made a promise," he said. "I promised not to tell."

"You promised Tara you wouldn't tell anyone about the two of you being friendly?"

He nodded.

"Well, Tara's dead," the detective said. "I really don't think it would matter if you broke the promise now, do you?"

Danny sighed. "It was her folks, you see. They were real strict with her. They didn't let her date or anything or hang out much. She couldn't even go to parties if her father knew that boys were going to be there. It would've been bad for her if her parents even knew we talked in the restaurant. But we did anyway. It seemed like she really needed to talk to someone. Like I said, we were friendly, but that's all. Maybe we met a couple of times, in private, you know, where we didn't think anyone would see us. She said her folks would've raised hell with her if they knew, so I promised I wouldn't tell. But all we ever did was talk. She was a sweet kid. Real shy, but sweet."

"Are you sure that was all you did, Danny?" Ginger asked softly. "Just talk? Or did you do more than that? Did you meet Tara in places so private that you could do whatever you wanted to do? Is that why you didn't say anything? Is that why you weren't willing to give us a blood sample? Because you knew what the results would be?"

"No," Danny exclaimed. "I swear, we didn't do anything but talk. Okay, if you must know, what was really going on was—I was tutoring her."

"Tutoring her?" the detective asked with a blank look.

"Yeah. She was having trouble in school. The second half of her freshman year, her grades started to slip for some reason.

Her folks didn't like that. They even made her go to summer school. She was real upset about that. So she asked me if I'd help her. I think she was embarrassed. She said she didn't want to have to go back next year. I remember her saying something about wanting her dad to be proud of her, not ashamed of her."

"The times when you and Tara met," Ginger prodded. "Tell me about them."

Danny shrugged. "We met after school," he said. "To keep it secret, we would leave separately and then we would meet up again."

"Where would you meet?"

"There's a place, down by the harbor, that's pretty secluded. We went there a couple of times."

"Anywhere else?"

"Once we went down to the beach."

Ginger looked at the boy intently. "Did you ever meet Tara at Madrona Point?"

"No," he declared. "I never met her there. Most times, we just went right back to school, and hung out behind the bleachers."

"What about at night?" the detective asked suddenly. "Did you ever meet Tara at night?"

The teenager twisted uncomfortably in his seat. "Yeah, once," he replied reluctantly. "That's the time I told you we went to the beach. It was on a Saturday night and she had an algebra test the next Monday. She told me her sister went to bed at nine, and her folks were at some big-deal charity dinner in Seattle and wouldn't be home before midnight. So I picked her up outside her house around ten o'clock. We drove down to the beach and sat at one of the picnic tables and studied the stuff by flashlight." The boy grinned. "She aced the test," he said, and then, apparently remembering himself, sobered. "That was a week before, you know, before she died."

"Was this a business arrangement, Danny?" Ginger asked. "Was Tara paying you for these sessions?"

"No," he said. "She didn't pay me. It wasn't like that. I was just helping her out. You know, like a friend."

"Out of the goodness of your heart?"

The teenager shrugged a bit self-consciously. "Well, maybe I did have what you might call an ulterior motive," he conceded. "I was thinking about asking her father for a recommendation for college. He's a pretty important person around here, you know, and I figured having him in my corner couldn't hurt. I thought that tutoring Tara would be a pretty good trade-off. She said, after her grades got better, she'd be willing to tell him that I was the one who helped her."

"What kind of a car do you drive?" Ginger asked, veering abruptly in another direction.

"I don't have a car of my own," he replied, without hesitation. "I drive my mom's car when she's not using it. But it's not a Taurus, Detective Earley, if that's what you're getting at. It's a Honda."

Ginger gazed at him for a long moment. "Look, Danny, I think you may be telling me the truth," she said finally. "But I've got a real problem here. I've got a corpse who was pregnant, and most likely killed by the person who *got* her that way. Now, you've admitted being friendly with Tara. You've even admitted that you saw her secretly on a number of occasions, including at least one evening. It's only your word that you were just tutoring her."

"But I was," the boy blurted.

"Well then, the best way to prove that would be for you to give us a sample of your blood," Ginger declared. "At this moment, I can't compel you to do that, but considering what you've just told me, I'm pretty sure I could get a court order that would. The thing is, I don't really want to have to do that. What I want is for you to give us what we need voluntarily. Trust me, if you're not involved in Tara's death, there's no blood test that's going to say you are."

"I already told you, it wasn't my idea not to—"

"Danny, don't you say another word." Peter Leo stood in the living room doorway. "Get out of here, Ginger. Get out of here right now."

"No, Dad, it's all right," Danny protested. "Really, I want to—"

"I said be quiet," Leo barked at the boy. Then he turned on the detective. "You have no right to be in my house," he charged. "You have no right to come in here and interrogate my son behind my back, without my permission. Eighteen or not, he still lives under my roof, and I say this is a clear violation of his civil rights. Now get out."

Ginger stood up. "I'm sorry you see it that way, Peter," she said. She looked at the boy and sighed. "I'm sorry, Danny, but an innocent person was brutally murdered, and I'm going to find out who did it."

20

"I guess we've got enough for a court order," Ginger told Ruben on Friday. "Danny Leo knew Tara. From September on, they were meeting as often as three times a week. He even admitted he saw her once on a Saturday night. And his father's acting a lot more like he needs to protect his son than defend a principle."

"You didn't believe the boy?"

"It's not that," she said. "I think he was honest about what he told me, but on the other hand, he may have been telling me only what he wanted me to know."

Ruben stretched his back, taking the moment to think. "The autopsy indicated Tara was ten weeks' pregnant. That puts us in early August, a month before the fall term started. Danny claims he didn't start tutoring her until September, but he admits he knew her through his job at the country club. The question is— is that enough to establish a prior relationship?"

"I don't know," Ginger said. "When she went looking for a tutor, I don't think she would have just picked him out of a crowd because he got top grades. And it wasn't a business arrangement—he said she wasn't paying him, with money anyway, for his services. Besides, if what they were doing was so innocent, why did they go out of their way to keep it secret? Just because her parents didn't allow her to date? I should think Kyle Breckenridge would have been delighted to have his daughter tutored by one of the Island's best students. I think he would have welcomed Danny into his home."

Ruben scratched an ear. "It's possible."

"And there's something else that makes me wonder," Ginger concluded. "Danny is looking at a scholarship to Harvard. While it hasn't been officially confirmed yet, the principal said he looks like a shoo-in. Not exactly the kind of thing a kid like him could afford to forfeit because of a summer peccadillo."

"Okay," Ruben said. "Take it to Judge Jacobs. Let's see if he thinks it's enough."

"What the hell are you doing, Ruben?" Albert Hoch roared the first thing Monday morning. "Going after a court order to test Danny Leo's blood? I thought this whole DNA deal was supposed to be voluntary?"

"His father won't let him come in voluntarily," the police chief replied. "We think we've got probable cause."

"What cause? So he knew the girl from the country club. So he tutored her a few times. So he helped her study for a math test one night. What kind of probable cause is that? That's just crap. Danny Leo is one of our finest young men; an exemplary student, a star athlete, a school leader. Anything else is just crap."

"If that's so, Judge Jacobs will refuse our petition."

"Ruben, I have to tell you, I never really liked that harebrained scheme of yours to test everyone's blood in the first place. But I would have flat out forbid you to do it if I knew it was going to lead you to someone like Danny."

"What did you think?" Ruben countered. "That we were just playing games here?"

"Frankly, you were getting nowhere, so I thought you were trying to make it look like you were actively working on the case," Hoch replied. "You know, so that people would feel better."

Ruben stared at the city official. "You think that's what this investigation is all about?" he charged. "Making people feel better? We've had a murder here, for God's sake. Your own goddaughter's murder. I want to find the person who did it—no matter who he is. Don't you?"

"Well, of course I do," Hoch said irritably. "But you don't really think it's Danny Leo, do you?"

"To tell you the truth, I don't know," Ruben conceded with a heavy sigh. "But at the moment, I'm not about to rule him out."

"This is terrible," Hoch muttered. "This is absolutely terrible. This whole business is tearing the Island apart. I just don't know what to do."

"My son gave his blood in the interests of truth," a mother wrote to the *Sentinel*. "He had nothing to do with Tara Breckenridge's death; he barely even knew her. But he wants her killer caught, and he was willing to do the right thing—help authorities solve a crime that has haunted this community for over a month now. If Danny Leo didn't kill her, what's his father afraid of?"

"Where will it end?" asked a freelance writer. "Should our appointed officials, under the guise of protecting the citizenry, have the right to invade our homes, terrorize our children, and threaten us with prosecution if we object to giving up a single one of our personal freedoms? Has our government finally, and fatally, turned its back on the Constitution?"

"If the chief of police really thinks that a decent young man like Danny Leo could have had anything to do with Tara Breckenridge's murder," suggested the mother of a girl he occasionally dated, "maybe it's time we hired somebody else for the job."

•   •   •

"What's everyone being so solicitous of Danny Leo for?" inquired the father of a senior math scholar heading for Stanford. "Why couldn't he have killed that girl? My son didn't kill her, he didn't even know her, but that didn't stop authorities from taking his blood. Why should Danny Leo be exempt?"

"This witch hunt has gone too far," one of the high school teachers wrote to the editor. "Our classrooms have become battlegrounds, teen against teen. I know how important it is to catch Tara Breckenridge's killer, but must we destroy our island in the process?"

Malcolm Purdy stood well over six feet tall, weighed in at two hundred thirty-eight pounds, wore his head shaved in military fashion, and dressed almost exclusively in camouflage fatigues that he ordered from a surplus store in Seattle. When he drove his Jeep Cherokee down Johansen Street on the Friday after Thanksgiving and pulled into a parking space in front of Curtis House, he stopped foot traffic dead in its tracks. It was more than two years since he had been seen in town.

He swung out of the Jeep, strode into the building, and planted himself at the front counter.

"I want to put a notice in the newspaper," he announced to a wide-eyed Iris Tanaka.

"Certainly, sir," she replied, scrambling for a form.

"I'm offering a hundred thousand dollars to anyone who comes forward with information that leads to the arrest and conviction of the butcher who murdered the Breckenridge girl."

Iris stared at the man. "I beg your pardon?" she sputtered.

"You heard me," he said. "I'm sick of all this shit. Put the notice in the paper, inside a big black box on an important page, so everyone can't help but see it, and keep on running it until I say you can stop. I'll pay you for a month in advance."

"Don't you think you should—uh—maybe go to the police with this first, sir?"

"I have no use for cops," he said shortly. "Just tell me how much I owe you."

Iris figured out the amount and watched as he pulled the bills from his wallet.

"Did you know Tara well?" she ventured.

Purdy shook his head. "Nope. Didn't know her at all."

The editorial assistant was clearly at a loss. "Then—why would you want to do this?"

"I've got my reasons," he told her. "They don't concern you."

Iris hurried into the editor's office the moment Purdy had pocketed his receipt and departed the building. "Can we do this?" she asked.

"The man paid his money," Gail Brown replied with a shrug. "He wants to place an advertisement in our newspaper just like anybody else. We may not like his message, but it's still a free press." She looked out her window after the retreating Cherokee. "My, my, my," she reflected. "This ought to cause a nice little stir."

It caused an uproar.

"Who the hell does this guy think he is?" bellowed Mayor Hoch, secretly annoyed that he hadn't thought of the idea himself—on a somewhat smaller scale, of course.

"I won't have the tragic circumstances surrounding the death of my daughter turned into a three-ring circus," warned Kyle Breckenridge.

"What I want to know is where did he all of a sudden get that kind of money?" asked Jim Petrie of the city council. "And how do we know for certain he's really got it, and that this isn't just some kind of scam he's running?"

"There's funny business going on here, for sure," said someone from the chamber of commerce. "And I think it's high time we found out what it is."

The gossip mill reopened. Locals began to fabricate all sorts of excuses to drive by the Purdy place, some even having enough nerve to get out of their vehicles and walk right up to the gate, being careful not to touch it, of course. But the gate was only twelve feet wide, and the property extended for thirty acres up a narrow dirt road and over a rise; there wasn't much for anyone to see.

"We want an immediate investigation," a contingent of respectable Islanders demanded of the police chief. "We want to know exactly what this fella's been up to all these years. We always thought there was something peculiar going on out there. Now we're sure of it. He's too secretive to be legitimate."

"Do you have any evidence that the man has done anything wrong?" Ruben asked them. "Any *concrete* evidence?"

"Well, no," they admitted.

"When you do, please come back," they were told, politely but firmly. "I assure you we'll look into it."

"Every crackpot in the county is going to come crawling out of the woodwork on this one," predicted Charlie Pricker. "Taking up time we don't have. Using up manpower we can't afford to waste."

"Assign Dirksen to screen the calls," Ruben instructed Ginger with a helpless sigh. "But make sure you apologize to him first."

Officer Glen Dirksen, twenty-two years old and a nine-month veteran of the Seward Island police force, had been the first to reach Madrona Point Park on that second Sunday in October. From the moment he climbed up to peer over the edge of the Dumpster, he had been unable to erase the picture of Tara Breckenridge's mutilated body from his mind. He had two teenage sisters back home in Blaine, and he begged to be involved in the case, gladly accepting the assignment that nobody else wanted.

◦ ◦ ◦

"As if the police department's job wasn't tough enough," an environmental engineer wrote to the editor in disgust. "How will it ever sort through the mountain of garbage that's now bound to come pouring in from every lunatic with a money problem?"

"If someone on Seward has any legitimate information about the murder of Tara Breckenridge that he or she has not already divulged to the proper authorities, it is unlikely that this offer of money will persuade him or her to do so," an Island psychologist felt compelled to say. "Therefore, I predict a mad scramble to see who can invent the most plausible fiction."

"Maybe this offer is exactly what Ruben Martinez needs to jump-start his investigation again," the self-ordained minister of a fundamentalist organization told his flock. "And we badly need funds to pave our parking lot. Perhaps God is showing us the way. If any of you has any information that could help solve this crime, now is the time to come forward."

"I'm getting sick to my stomach," Glen Dirksen reported the following Wednesday. "Over sixty calls have come in already, from under just about every rock on the Island, with theories ranging from the South American Mafia to aliens from the 51 Pegasus system. You know, I'm beginning to think some of these people would turn in their own mothers to get their hands on that money."

"Nobody promised you a picnic," Ginger told him.

"I had one guy on the phone from some church group who told me he had seen his next-door neighbor wielding a knife and dripping with blood the night of the murder. When I asked him why it had taken him so long to contact us, he told me that, until the reward was offered, he had no reason to destroy his neighbor's life."

"It's stuff like this that builds character," Ruben told the young officer. "But go ahead and check out the neighbor anyway."

"More to the point," Charlie wondered, "have we checked out Malcolm Purdy?"

"Yes," Ginger said. She had gone out to the Purdy place herself, pressing the intercom that had been installed beside the electrified gate, waiting for what seemed hours until the man answered.

"What do you want?" the ex-Marine demanded.

"Mr. Purdy, I'd like to talk to you about this reward you're offering," Ginger replied after introducing herself.

"What about it? As far as I can tell, it speaks for itself."

"Well, there are a few questions—"

"Questions?" his voice crackled over the wires. "Last time I looked, this was still a free country. You're not here to tell me the government passed a law saying it isn't anymore, are you?"

"Must we have this conversation over the intercom, sir?" the detective asked.

There was a considerable pause, and then the heavy gate slowly began to swing open.

The service people who had gained admittance to the property during the last decade were right, Ginger decided as she drove up the narrow dirt road; he had done nothing with the place. His great-uncle had been a farmer, but now the fields that once produced much of the Island's corn had gone to weed.

Purdy stood on the front steps, a clear indication that he did not intend to invite her inside. That was all right; the cabin looked like it was about ready to fall down anyway. Ginger could see the bunkhouse he had built out back. It looked solid. The one-eyed dog lay on the porch, too old and complacent to care about visitors.

"So what is it you seem to think you have a right to know?" he inquired.

Ginger sized him up quickly. "For openers," she said, "was your intention to help our investigation or hinder it?"

He chuckled. "To help, of course," he said. "It's obvious that somebody on this rock knows something about that poor girl's murder. So far, appealing to his better nature hasn't gotten you very far, has it? So what's wrong with offering him a little incentive to do the right thing?"

"And what happens if your scheme works?"

"You catch yourselves a murderer, and I guess I'm out a hundred thousand bucks," he said.

"You've lived on this island for ten years, Mr. Purdy," Ginger said bluntly, "and you've never seen fit to involve yourself in local affairs before. Why now?"

He stared at her for a moment, with eyes that were a brilliant blue. "Well, I guess if now it's me and my life you're going to investigate, Detective," he said, in an about-face, "we might as well be comfortable about it." He held the cabin door open for her to enter.

As dilapidated as the little house may have looked from the outside, it was immaculate on the inside, with brightly colored pillows and scatter rugs, highly polished hardwood floors, paintings hung all over the walls, and a pristine open kitchen. It was a little, she thought, like going from Kansas into Oz. There was a coffeepot sitting on one side of the stove, and a kettle of something that smelled wonderful simmering on the other. A warm fire crackled pleasantly in a stone hearth. An easel stood in one corner of the main room, with a cloth draped over it.

"You paint, Mr. Purdy?" Ginger asked, not quite able to keep the surprise out of her voice.

"Sometimes," he answered.

She looked again at the artwork on the walls, and knew that it was all his; at least a dozen renderings of sea and land, from a variety of perspectives around the Island, done in clean, sure strokes, and one haunting portrait of two young girls.

"This is quite lovely," she said.

"I did it from memory," he replied gruffly. "They're a lot older now."

"Your daughters?"

He peered at her. "I don't see as my personal affairs are any of your business," he said. "Your only concern is whether I offered this reward to steer any possible suspicion away from myself."

Ginger couldn't help smiling. "Did you?"

"Nope. Didn't have anything to do with the killing, and no one could ever prove that I did."

"Then why?"

"I have my reasons," he told her. "They don't matter to anyone but me. All you need to know is that I'm good for the money."

"Malcolm Purdy doesn't hunt," Ginger reported back. "He's a vegetarian. He owns guns, not knives, which he claims to use only for target practice, and he was at home on the night of the murder."

"Confirmed?" Charlie asked.

Ginger shrugged. "By the woman who works for him."

"Any clue why he's doing this?" Ruben wondered.

"More from what he didn't say than what he did say," Ginger told him. "I think it may have something to do with a couple of daughters."

"Well then, I guess until we learn different we take him at his word," the police chief said.

"We take the money at his word, too," Ginger said. "He says he has it, but he won't tell me where, and I can't find any record of a bank account in his name in the state. He has one Visa card, which he clears every month with a money order, and he pays all the rest of his bills either with money orders or in cash."

Ruben eyed the detective thoughtfully. "All right, for the

sake of argument, let's assume that he's on the up-and-up," he said. "How do you read the local reaction?"

Ginger shrugged. "Typical," she replied. "When it comes right down to it, people are people. The people on Seward are no different than anyone else. A lot of them believe in live and let live; it's one reason why they moved to a place like this. They won't get involved unless someone gives them a good reason. Malcolm Purdy has just given them a hundred thousand good reasons. For some folks, there's nothing quite like greed to kick the conscience into high gear."

"You mean, there could really be something in some of these calls?" Dirksen asked.

"That's the thing about these people," Ginger told him. "You never know."

The basement meeting ended early. There was only one topic of discussion and it brought little argument. It was barely ten o'clock when the shadow men filed silently back out into the night.

21

Stacey Martinez usually walked the five blocks to her home alone after school. Her close friends took buses to other parts of the Island, and those few classmates who lived in her direction liked to stop off at Pizzazz, the local arcade and pizza parlor, to play a few games, share a snack and a Coke, and generally let off some steam. On Thursday, however, Kristen Andersen caught up with her before she was barely a block away.

"Mind if I walk along with you?" she asked.

"Of course not," Stacey replied, hiding her surprise. Kristen was a nice enough girl. They sat next to each other in history class, they had worked together on a biology project, and occasionally the green-eyed blonde would pass out free cosmetic samples from the pharmacy where her father worked. But she traveled with Hank Kriedler's crowd, and had never gone out of her way to be particularly friendly.

"I—uh—I've been wanting to talk to you," she said hesitantly. "There's something that's like really sort of been bothering me, you see, and I'm not sure what to do about it. I mean, it could be nothing at all, you know, just my imagination, but it's been on my mind, and like well, I thought, you being the police chief's daughter and all, maybe you could tell me what to do."

"I'll be glad to help, if I can," Stacey assured her.

"Well, you see, it's about something I saw a while ago. You know, something to do with Tara."

Stacey looked at her classmate sharply. "If you have information about Tara, you should be talking to my father, not me."

"But that's just the point," Kristen replied. "I don't know if this has anything to do with—you know, her murder or anything. That's why I wanted to talk it over with you first. I can always go to your dad afterward, if you say I should."

The police chief's daughter nodded slowly. "Okay," she said.

"Look, I don't want to get anyone in trouble," Kristen insisted. "What I saw—well, it involves somebody else. Besides Tara, I mean. For all I know, he's already told your dad about it. I mean, he probably has, and the whole thing was all probably totally innocent anyway, so I shouldn't really be worried, right?"

"If you're asking me if there's someone in particular who's come forward to talk to my father about Tara, I don't have any idea," Stacey told her. "But if you know something that might help solve the case, then I don't think I'd worry about getting anyone in trouble."

Kristen let out her breath. "Okay," she said, her words coming in a rush. "Well, as you probably already know, Tara and I were in gymnastics together. And one afternoon, I think it was the Wednesday before—before she died, I stayed on at the end of class because it was my turn to put up the mats and stuff. Well, I thought everyone else would be long gone, but when I came out of the gym, I guess it was like maybe half an hour later, I saw that Tara was still there. She was in the back hall, and she was crying. I was going to go over, you know, to see what was wrong, but then I saw she wasn't alone. There was someone with her. I saw him put his arms around her, and he was holding her, you know, like really close and all, and I didn't want to interrupt, but

I couldn't help it—I had to walk right past them to get out of the building. He let go of her as soon as he saw me. I was pretty embarrassed, and I just dashed out of there as fast as I could."

Stacey thought Kristen was looking pretty embarrassed right now. Her face was all flushed, she was almost tripping over her words in her haste to get them out, and her eyes were fastened on her feet.

"You're saying you saw Tara with someone?" the police chief's daughter prompted.

"Yes, well, Detective Earley asked us about that—if we'd ever seen Tara with anyone, but I didn't really think of it that way then. I thought she meant, you know, like boyfriends. But then, I got to thinking about seeing the two of them there like that." Kristen paused uncertainly for a moment. "I don't know," she added, "maybe there was nothing to it. Do you think I should tell?"

"I don't know if somebody hugging Tara in a hallway at school means anything or not," Stacey said. "It'd probably depend on the circumstances, and on who it was."

Kristen pried her eyes from her feet and looked around as though worried that someone might be listening.

"That's the whole point," she whispered. "That's why I wasn't sure what to do. You see, the police seem to think the killer is one of the seniors, but the person I saw Tara with—well, it might have been at school, but it wasn't a student. It was a teacher. It was Mr. Frankel."

PART TWO

The Suspect

"Nothing is more dangerous than an idea, when it's the only one we have."

—*Emile-Auguste Chartier*

1

Jerry Frankel was the only child of parents who began their marriage knowing very little about each other, and ended it knowing even less. He grew up in a house that never laughed. His mother, Emma, was born in the concentration camp at Buchenwald to a thirteen-year-old Jewish girl who did not survive the birth and a German officer who was later executed by the Allies. She wound up in Philadelphia after the war, adopted by the Kaufman family, who, having barely gotten out of Germany ahead of Hitler, did their best to forget she had been fathered by a Nazi.

But Emma never forgot. She felt the shame of it every day of her life. She was a beautiful girl who had inherited her mother's dark hair and her father's pale eyes in a dramatic blend that, from her earliest days, caused people to stop and stare in admiration. Deep down, however, she felt herself ugly.

She was not much of a student. After graduation from high school at the age of seventeen, she married the first man to show any serious interest in her, because he owned his own business and made a good living, and because he didn't know her father was a Nazi. The Kaufmans did not object. They were decent people, but they were relieved to see her go.

Aaron Frankel was thirteen years older than Emma. He thought she was the most exquisite creature he had ever seen. Further, like himself, she was a survivor of the Holocaust—an event that, in the aftermath of World War II, most Americans seemed to want to forget. He felt that Emma, unlike a girl who had not known the war, would understand his nightmares. He could not believe his good fortune when she promptly agreed to marry him.

After the war, Aaron came from Majdanek to his only surviving relative, a distant cousin who lived in York, Pennsylvania. The cousin was a good man, but he had a wife and five children, and could ill afford to take care of another. So he set the boy up with his wife's uncle, a crusty bachelor who owned a small company near Philadelphia that manufactured surgical instruments.

Aaron had little formal education, but he had a good mind. The uncle, already in his sixties, was delighted with the chance to teach the boy everything he knew before he died. To his surprise, Aaron took to the business. He worked hard and lived cheaply, saving every penny he could toward the day when the uncle would let him buy in. By the time he met Emma, the company was not only his, but one of the fastest growing and most reputable producers of precision surgical instruments in the country. At the age of thirty, having achieved his goal of financial security, Aaron decided it was time he took a wife.

But Emma knew nothing about being a wife, and cared even less. She had never learned to cook, had no interest in making a home, and suffered his attentions in bed with silent distaste.

Aaron forgave her. She was so young and so beautiful, it filled him with joy just to look at her. He determined that he could be patient until she learned. That she flatly refused to discuss anything having to do with the Holocaust was but a momentary disappointment. After all, he reasoned, she had been just a baby, she could hardly be expected to remember. That she showed no interest in his work, and even yawned on those occasions when he tried to explain it to her, was a more lasting disappointment, for it would have thrilled him to have someone with whom he could share his excitement. But then, he decided, her beauty more than made up for any lack of attention she displayed. Over the next ten years, he forgave her everything.

As for Emma, once she realized her marriage was not the fairy tale that the movies and magazines had led her to expect, the discontent returned. Her antidote was to spend money, lots of money, much more than Aaron could afford. It was like a narcotic—the more she spent, the happier she felt. And as soon as the euphoria of one spree wore off, she would set out on another. She bought everything: several sets of fine china and crystal, far more furniture than even their gracious home in Cheltenham could hold, expensive jewelry that she wore once before tossing into a drawer, and clothing that enhanced her lovely figure and overflowed her closets, store tags still attached to them.

When she discovered she was pregnant with Jerry, Emma cried for a week.

"I don't want a baby," she wailed. "It'll make me fat! What would I do with a baby?"

"You'll see," Aaron assured her, elated by the news. "Having a baby will make all the difference. We'll be a real family at last, and you'll love being a mother. Every woman does."

Emma hated being a mother. She was useless at caring for the baby, sometimes forgetting to feed him, frequently forgetting to change him, often leaving him unattended for hours at a time as she resumed her shopping excursions.

Aaron finally hired a nanny to look after the boy. He returned much of the clothing and household items and most of the jewelry to pay for it. He made arrangements with the shops Emma frequented to notify him of her purchases. He hoped that perhaps the buying was enough, and the having was inconsequential. He was right. Emma never missed the items that found their way back onto the racks and into the display cases.

Eventually, though, the antidote began to lose its effectiveness, and then Emma turned to vodka. The clear, almost tasteless liquor made its way into her morning orange juice, her afternoon tea, her dinner coffee, and any time in between.

"This is Mommy's water," she would snap at her son when he reached for her glass. "Go get your own."

When she complained of not sleeping, Aaron found a doctor who would prescribe pills. After that, she slept a great deal, often not awakening until past noon and retiring before eight. Aaron didn't know what to do for her, so he did nothing. Whatever the problem was, he convinced himself it was temporary and would soon go away.

It didn't. Emma sank deeper and deeper into depression. She stopped shopping. She stopped taking care of herself. She ate next to nothing. She began to wander listlessly around the house, vodka in hand, sometimes not even bothering to dress.

The war in Vietnam fascinated her. She would spend hours sitting in front of the television set, waiting for news reports of the carnage.

"It's amazing how a war can come right into your living room and yet not touch you," she would marvel. "You can see everything that's going on without getting hurt."

She was furious with the protesters.

"What do they want?" she would rant. "Do they want to stop the war? Then what would I do all day?"

It was not that Aaron turned a blind eye, exactly. It was more that he couldn't get past his original image of her to see what she had become.

She paid no attention to her son, never noticing how handsome he was, how bright, how sweet-tempered. The only part of him she ever really looked at were his eyes, and she sighed with relief when she saw that he had inherited Aaron's eyes, not pale and cold, but wide and innocent and the color of warm molasses.

Then, on May 4, 1970, the same day that four students protesting the war were shot to death by National Guardsmen at Kent State University, Emma Kaufman Frankel, aged twenty-seven, swallowed half a bottle of sleeping pills with a whole glass of vodka and died.

Jerry found her when he came home from school. She was lying in bed as though asleep, with an expression on her face that the boy had never seen before. She looked happy.

Aaron was shattered. He refused to believe she had done it on purpose. He blamed it on the vodka, claiming she could not have known what she was doing.

It didn't really matter to Jerry. His mother was dead, that was all. He tried to think what that would mean to him. He thought of his friends, and the way their mothers hugged them and fussed over them, and were always there to provide after-noon snacks and chauffeur them to and from Little League games. But his mother had never done any of that. In fact, he could not recall that she had ever done very much of anything for him. He decided her death did not have to make a significant dif-ference in his life.

His nanny, the latest in a long line of women his father had hired to look after him, dressed him in dark clothes and told him he should cry for Emma.

"Why?" asked the pensive eight-year-old. "She's not sad any-more."

Aaron Frankel turned to his son to fill the void. They grew as close as a bewildered man and an abandoned boy could grow. Aaron had tried so hard to re-create a semblance of the family he had lost at Majdanek, and could not understand why he had failed so miserably.

He had no particular interest in other women. To his way of thinking, he had already had the best and would not settle for less. There were many who tried to change his mind—after all, he was a well-to-do widower and considered a fine catch. He was wined and dined by parents from all over the Philadelphia area. He ate their food and drank their liquor, but he did not pursue any of their daughters.

Meanwhile, Jerry grew tall and strong. He excelled at soccer, the debate club, and academics, and discovered that he genuinely liked school, liked learning, liked the *process* of learning. He admired a great many of his teachers, and he thrived on the give-and-take of the classroom. The public library, with its air of quiet authority, its distinct mustiness, and faint smell of sweat, became as familiar and comfortable to him as the teddy bear blanket he had clung to through childhood. Often, he would spend hours after school, wandering through the stacks, pulling out a book here, a volume there, not looking for anything in particular, just to wrap himself inside the walls of the institution. There were many evenings when he would reach home barely minutes before his father.

Outwardly, he was the cheerful, dutiful son he knew Aaron wanted him to be. But it was like looking in a mirror and seeing someone else's reflection, because he knew his real self to be so very different. He preferred shadow to sun, calm to commotion, solitude to society.

As a child, when he was invited to parties, he loved to play hide and seek, but never wanted to be "it." Instead, he wanted to be one of the ones who got to hide. Then he would hunt out a place so secure he could stay hidden for hours. Sometimes, even when there was no party and there was no game, he would hide himself away where he could not be found. He would hear his nanny calling for him and would keep silent. Only when it was his father's voice reaching into the corner of the attic where he crouched under the eaves would he reluctantly crawl out and clatter down the ladder steps.

Jerry was always careful to mask the scary dark moods that

took hold of him for no reason, because he didn't understand what they meant, and he didn't want his father to find out and worry that he would end up like his mother. Or maybe it was he, himself, who was afraid he might end up like Emma.

He had a large circle of acquaintances, but few real friends, unwilling to let anyone get too close. He dated his share of girls, managing to advance past the stage of heavy breathing and feeble protests on more than one occasion, but sooner or later, they all sought a commitment that he found himself unable to make.

The times he treasured most were those when he and his father sat together in the library, reading, listening to music, and talking. It was with Jerry that Aaron finally got to speak about Majdanek. With the boy a willing audience, he would talk for hours at a time, recounting everything he could remember about that piece of the past that had shamed the entire world.

"Those of us who survived," he would say in his still lightly accented English, "survived for a reason. And I think it was not just to bear witness to what happened at that time and in that place, but to make certain it is never allowed to happen again, at any other time or in any other place. Because it is only by studying our past and learning from it that we can prevent ourselves from repeating it."

"How?" the boy would ask.

Aaron would think for a moment. "Each generation must be taught that genocide is not just about Germany thirty years ago," he would say. "It has happened before, and it can happen again, anytime, anyplace—in Europe, in Asia, in Africa. It happened right here, to the American Indians, did it not?"

The boy would nod.

"Well then, it could happen again," his father would predict. "To the Jews, the blacks, the Hispanics, or any other identifiable group that an apathetic public is willing to let be abused. All it takes is the coming together of even a small number of people who require a scapegoat to explain away their own insecurities, lack of abilities, or low self-esteem, and you have the environment for creating another Hitler."

"Do you really think something like that can happen now, Dad?" Jerry would ask. "When the world is so much smaller and people are so much smarter?"

Aaron would wag his head. "It wasn't the intelligentsia who did the bidding of Hitler and his cronies," he would tell the boy. "They were annihilated right along with the Jews and all the others that Hitler determined were political adversaries or of 'inferior breeding.' It was the scum who followed their grand führer; the bigots, the have-nots, the greedy who saw a way to profit by taking what they could never have created on their own. Mark my words, if you let the quality of public education deteriorate far enough, let the economy go sour enough, let unemployment rise high enough, and give people reason enough to lose confidence in their government—it could happen anywhere."

It was those words from his father that cemented Jerry's future. What better way to ensure that the nation's children learned about the perils of the past, he decided, than by being the one to teach them?

He graduated from Cheltenham High School at the top of his class, politely refused an academic scholarship to Princeton because his father could well afford to send him to college, and went on to complete both his undergraduate and graduate work at the University of Pennsylvania.

Jerry loved teaching. Not only was he able to linger in the classrooms and libraries of his youth, where he had always felt safe and protected, but he was fascinated by his subject. The more he learned about history, the more he came to see it as a giant and never-ending tapestry of threads woven together in intricate patterns that kept repeating themselves.

For example, there were so many similar socioeconomic and political threads in the fall of most of the great empires in the world, from Greece to Rome to Russia. And it was a similar set of conditions that had opened the door to Hitler in post–World War I Germany. It began with social unrest, engendered in part by Germany's humiliation over the Versailles treaty, was compounded by severe economic decline resulting from the Great Depression, and ended in a level of moral decay that led directly to the disintegration of respect for the law and the total abdication of personal responsibility. Or, as his father always put it, "thugism."

In many instances, Jerry discovered, life could be as predictable as mathematics; although times and circumstances changed, people basically did not. And he tried to portray this idea of the cycle of history to his classes.

He loved the light of learning he saw go on inside the heads of his students when they finally understood something he had taken great care and patience to explain. It gave him a real rush to stand in front of a class with twenty-odd pairs of eyes trained on him, and know that twenty-odd minds hung on his next revelation. They were like blank computer screens on which he could imprint his lasting images. It was heady stuff, the sense of power that teaching gave him, this daily measure of his own value.

He had just begun his second year of teaching at a public high school in Philadelphia when he met Deborah Stein. She was still at Bryn Mawr, and looked up to him very much the way his students did. Being with her gave him the same kind of rush he experienced in his classroom. She also had dark hair and light eyes like Emma.

"Everyone says you look too much like my mother," he told her, only half joking, when he knew that, this time, he would not be able to get out of the relationship. "If I marry you, they'll say I have an Oedipus complex."

"Perhaps," she returned with a toss of her hair and a mischievous twinkle in her eye. "But if you don't marry me, they'll say you're crazy."

They were married two months later.

• • •

Deborah Frankel graduated from Bryn Mawr, and went on to earn a business degree at the University of Pennsylvania's Wharton School. Each evening over dinner in their cozy little apartment, the young couple would tell one another everything about their day apart, letting even the most inconsequential moments assume major proportions. Then, washing the dishes, they would dream about the wonderful future they would share, the home they would have one day, the family they would raise together, the exciting journeys they would take, the exotic places they would explore, walking in the steps of Jerry's beloved heroes of history. Finally, when the last dish was done, they would whisk the cloth off the table and spread out their homework.

Jerry took enormous pride in Deborah, in her mind, her ambition, her accomplishments. Although, in all honesty, he could not claim much of the credit, he felt like Pygmalion to her Galatea, and it pleased him enormously when she came to him for help with her assignments.

"I don't know why I can't figure this out," she would say.

"Let's see if we can find a way to make it clearer," he would reply.

She asked for his help almost every evening until the middle of her first year at Wharton when she finally passed his level of expertise in her specialty. Two or three nights a week after that, she would come home an hour or so later than usual, having stopped by a friend's place to study.

Then they would throw a quick meal together, provide each other with abbreviated accounts of their respective days as they ate, and hurry to their separate assignments.

"Need any help?" he would ask, poised over his own stack of papers.

"Thanks, but I think I can handle it," she would reply.

Eventually, he stopped asking. He was happy for her achievement, but it was also a loss, and he felt it as a parent would who watched a child grow up and take off on his own—with both pride and pain.

It was during Deborah's second year at Wharton that Matthew was born. She was out of school until after the Christmas break, adjusting to motherhood even as she kept up with the work she was missing. After that, she strapped the baby into a backpack and wore him to class.

Jerry had not believed it possible that he could love another human being as much as he loved his son. The depth of his emotion stunned him. He adored his wife, but there was a distinct difference between what he felt for her and what he felt for Matthew. Here was a brand-new person that was part of him, someone who was totally dependent on him, someone he could nurture and mold and teach from the very beginning.

Standing in the hospital corridor with his nose pressed to the glass wall of the nursery, Jerry could hardly wait to introduce the boy to his grandfather. It meant a great deal to him that he could give Aaron back the family he had lost at Majdanek; this time, a family that would not abandon him.

"I want to go back to New York," Deborah announced when Matthew was seven months old and she had her master's degree in hand. "My parents are there. My whole family is there. I've been recruited by a really good Wall Street firm, and I'd like to take the job. I know you've lived your whole life in Pennsylvania, and you're close to Aaron and all, but I'm close to my family, too, and I've been away from them for six years now, and I want to go home."

The last thing Jerry wanted to do was move to New York, but he couldn't find an objection that she didn't dismiss as selfish. So, reluctantly, he prepared a résumé, and within a month found a teaching position at a private high school in Scarsdale, the town in Westchester County where Deborah's parents lived.

Aaron gave them a down payment for a small house about fifteen minutes from the school. Deborah commuted by train to

New York City. Her mother volunteered to look after Matthew until Jerry could take over, and then Deborah would rush home in the evening to prepare the baby's dinner, give him his bath, and put him to bed.

The following year, after a miserable pregnancy, the Frankels' second child, a daughter, was born with a malformed brain. They named her Emily. She lived twenty-six hours and died. The young couple was devastated, clinging numbly to each other through the ordeal of the funeral and the long week of condolences. Then, surprising everyone, Jerry most of all, Deborah took two weeks of her planned maternity leave and went off to the Caribbean. She returned, tanned and rested, to throw herself back into her work with almost a manic determination, no longer hurrying home at night to her son and husband, and sometimes, if she worked very late, not even bothering to come home at all.

Jerry thought he understood; after all, she had endured an emotionally shattering experience, and as he saw it, her job provided a temporary diversion that could go a long way toward helping her come to terms with that experience.

Eight months later, on the same day her company offered her a major promotion, she told Jerry that she did not want to have any more children.

"The doctors can't guarantee the same thing won't happen again," she said, "and I'm afraid to risk it. I couldn't go through losing another baby like that. But we have Matthew, and he's such a wonderful little boy, I can't help thinking that we're really very lucky. Anyway, I've just been promoted, and I'd like to concentrate on my career for a while."

Concentrating on her career, Jerry soon learned, meant she would now be working late into most evenings and even on weekends. He hid his disappointment. While he was willing to concede that she was bright and talented and had a right to make her mark in the business world, he missed her. He missed the young woman who used to look up to him, who had once believed he had all the answers. Jerry had little in common with the new Deborah. On the increasingly rare occasions when she made it home in time for dinner, she would rattle on about things he barely understood, and then hardly bother to listen when it was his turn to share a few snippets of his daily life.

As more of her energy went into her work, she had less to spend on her husband. They spoke mostly about money now, and about Matthew. Somewhere along the way, they stopped talking about the exciting future they had planned to have, and focused instead on the present.

Jerry never questioned his commitment to his wife. She and Matthew were the center around which his life revolved. Yet, more and more, it seemed to him that he was no longer the center of *her* life; that he had become a satellite to her needs and desires. He tried to talk to her about it, because he wanted desperately to fix what was broken. Only he either couldn't seem to find the right words to use, or she really wasn't listening. After a while, he stopped trying.

They continued on that way, drifting along in different directions, until it became familiar. And with familiarity came a peculiar sense of comfort, and with comfort came no further need for understanding.

Still, there was something that tugged at him, something he was unable to articulate—or probably even acknowledge, given how deeply it was rooted in his past—something he could only sense. Jerry Frankel was lonely.

2

"May I have a word with you, Mr. Frankel?" Ginger asked.

It was Friday, and although well past the last school bell, she found the teacher still in his classroom.

"Sure, come on in," Jerry replied. "I'm just finishing up some paperwork."

He was wearing a navy blazer with a striped shirt and gray slacks, and looked more like a preppy college student than a high school teacher.

Ginger glanced around the room. Some twenty-odd metal desk units were lined up in front of a raised platform on which sat a large wooden desk that clearly showed the scars of time and place. Behind it were suspended two thick rolls of maps. Even without looking, she knew which maps were coiled inside which roll. She knew that blackboards ran the length of three of the room's walls, and that windows lined the fourth.

The detective calculated quickly. If she took one of the student seats, she would in effect be putting herself in a subordinate position. If she remained standing while he sat, she would tend to put him in a defensive position. If she leaned against his desk, her attitude might appear too familiar. If she stayed by the door, it could indicate that she felt somehow intimidated. She chose the first seat in the middle row, directly in front of Frankel.

"This was my seat when I was in school here," she said. "It still feels familiar."

Jerry smiled. "I spend most of my life in classrooms," he told her. "But a couple of years ago, I went to my fifteenth high school reunion, and walked around a building I once knew better than my own home. I couldn't believe how totally lost I got, and how out of place I felt."

In her mind, Ginger flipped through the dossier she had compiled on the history teacher, starting on the Monday morning after she and Ruben went calling about the Taurus wagon, and ending yesterday afternoon after Stacey had brought Kristen Andersen to see her. She knew he was thirty-five years old, and that his fifteenth reunion had been held two years ago. She knew his high school was in Cheltenham, a wealthy suburb of Philadelphia, and that he had graduated first in his class. She also knew he held a *summa cum laude* in liberal arts from the University of Pennsylvania, as well as a master's with honors in education. But of course there was no reason to tell him that she knew all this.

As far as she could determine, his teaching credentials were impeccable. He had taught at a public high school in Philadelphia for five years before taking a position at the Holman Academy, a classy private high school in Scarsdale, New York. The principal at the Philadelphia school had been very sorry to see him go. The headmaster at the Scarsdale school said his resignation had been accepted with great regret.

Frankel had arrived on Seward Island at the end of last January, after his wife's investment firm transferred her to its Seattle office. It was interesting that both of his job moves had apparently been made in deference to his wife's career, but not particularly significant.

In the opinion of Seward High School principal Jordan Huxley, which was based on one spring semester, a summer session and the fall quarter, Frankel was an exemplary teacher, popular with colleagues and students alike, and the Island was lucky to have him. A casual survey of a number of those colleagues and students confirmed Huxley's assessment.

Ginger could find no police record for the teacher, no arrest, no conviction, no trouble of any kind with the law. Not even so much as a parking ticket had shown up in either of the two states where Jerry Frankel had lived and worked. In fact, there was not a shred of information whatsoever that he was anything other than what he appeared to be—a dedicated teacher, a devoted husband, and a proud father.

Still, when Kristen Andersen presented herself at Graham Hall, and repeated the story she had told to Stacey, Ginger could not ignore it.

"It's possible I could be wrong about him," she told Ruben.

"You could," he agreed.

"Of course, at this point, all we've got is a secondhand account of an incident that might have a perfectly reasonable explanation."

"And a bunch of odd little coincidences."

"That's true," she conceded. "So how about if I go talk to him again? One-on-one, you know, friendly like, on his own turf, and see what happens."

The police chief smiled because it was exactly what he would have said under the circumstances, exactly what he would have done.

"As I'm sure you know, we're still investigating the Breckenridge murder," Ginger told Jerry Frankel as he sat behind his desk on the platform, looking down at her.

"I certainly assumed as much," the teacher replied.

"And whenever we receive any information that might be relevant to that investigation, we're of course obligated to look into it."

"I assumed that as well."

"In a case like this, we get all sorts of tips, you know," the detective said, trying to study the teacher without appearing to do so, even as she had the distinct impression that *he* was studying *her*. "People always think they know something they're sure will solve the case for us. Most of what we get doesn't amount to anything, but following up on all of it at least makes us feel like we're doing our job."

Jerry nodded. "And what tip did you get that's led you to my door?" he asked pleasantly enough.

"One of the students here at the high school mentioned having seen you and Tara alone together just three days before her death."

The teacher frowned slightly. "I'm not sure I know what you're talking about, so I can neither confirm nor deny what you've been told," he said. "Perhaps if you gave me some more information, or told me who saw what and where, it might refresh my memory."

"One of your students," Ginger repeated, intentionally omitting Kristen Andersen's name, "claims to have seen you with Tara in the hallway behind the gym at around five-thirty on the Wednesday afternoon before her death."

"It's possible," Jerry said. "I don't seem to remember the specific occasion, but I can't say for sure I didn't see Tara in that particular hall on that particular day."

"I understand she was crying," Ginger prompted. "And that you had your arms around her."

The teacher's eyes widened slightly. "*That* day," he murmured. He stood up from his desk and came down off the platform to take the seat beside the detective. "I do remember now. I was using the inside route past the gym to get to the office, and I did see her there. And she *was* crying. I guess I might have put my arms around her to comfort her."

"Did she tell you why she was crying?"

"No, she didn't," he said, his glance sliding past the police officer's shoulder as though trying to recall. "She just said something about her life being a total mess. I confess I didn't really think that much about it. Kids that age, especially girls, tend to be emotional and often think their lives are a mess."

"After she was murdered," Ginger inquired, "why didn't you tell us about that? Knowing she had been upset to the point of crying shortly before her death might have been important."

"I'm sorry," he said. "I guess it never occurred to me. To be perfectly honest with you, I'd forgotten all about it until just now."

"You'll pardon me for asking this, Mr. Frankel, but was that day in the hall the only time you can recall when you and Tara were alone together?"

"No, it wasn't, Detective Earley," Jerry said, and now he looked her straight in the eye. "On a number of occasions, Tara came to see me after school for extra help. As I think I mentioned before, her grades weren't as good as they should have been. I told her she was welcome anytime."

"Was Tara the only student who needed help?"

Jerry started to smile and then stopped himself. "No, she wasn't. I currently have about a dozen students who come in on a fairly regular basis."

"I wonder if you would be kind enough to give me their names?"

"Of course." He got up and returned to his desk where he scribbled the names on a pad, then ripped off the sheet and held it out to her.

"Thank you," the detective said, rising to retrieve it. "I hope you understand that we're looking for a killer here, and we can't let even the most insignificant of incidents involving the victim go unexplained."

"I understand," the teacher assured her. "It was my fault for not remembering to tell you about it in the first place."

"In police work, you learn to question everything," she added on a sudden impulse. "First, we have someone who claims to have seen a dark-colored Taurus wagon in the park near the time of the murder—and we find that you drive just such a car. And now we have you being observed in a potentially compromising situation with the murdered girl shortly before her death." She was careful to omit any reference to the additional coincidence of his being left-handed.

"And that quite naturally led you to the conclusion that I was a child-molesting monster?" This time he did smile a little.

"Sometimes, it's a lousy world," Ginger said. "But for the record, other than being a concerned teacher, you didn't have any special relationship with Tara Breckenridge, did you?"

It seemed to her that he hesitated an instant before he answered, but she couldn't be sure that it wasn't just her imagination.

"No, I didn't," Jerry Frankel replied.

"And if I were to ask you, on a purely voluntary basis, you understand, to come in for a polygraph test, and maybe to give us a sample of your blood for a DNA analysis, you wouldn't have any objection, would you?"

This time, there was no mistaking the hesitation.

"Probably not," he said. "But I'd want the chance to think about it first."

"Of course," Ginger said.

"I don't know," she declared an hour later, dropping into the spare chair in Ruben's tiny office. "Either this guy doesn't have a thing to do with this case, or he's the smoothest liar I've ever come up against."

"And you can't decide which?" the police chief asked.

"I really leaned on him," Ginger admitted. " 'Forget about the witness thing,' I as good as told him. 'Now we're looking at you for the murder itself.' If he'd been there, if he'd seen anything, knew anything—one way or another, I think he'd have given it up. But I watched him like a hawk. He didn't even blink. Everything he said was exactly what he should have said, every gesture was absolutely correct, every expression had just the right note of sincerity."

"And that's why you think he could be lying?"

"Sounds silly, doesn't it?"

Ruben shrugged. "Do I conclude from this conversation that you're not ready to cut him loose?"

Ginger thought about that for a moment. "Not yet," she said finally.

"Do you consider him a material witness?"

"Probably not," she said.

"Do you consider him a suspect?"

"I'm not sure."

"Do your instincts tell you he could be a killer?" Ruben asked.

"Given the right motivation," Ginger said with a toss of her red hair, "I think anyone could be a killer."

"Does he fit your profile?"

"Sure he does," the detective acknowledged, remembering the characteristics of the killer they had defined. "Right down the line—he's physically strong enough, he has no alibi, he drives the right car, he's left-handed, and he knew the victim. But, except for the car, Danny Leo fits the profile, too. And probably a couple of hundred other people we don't even know about."

"Then what have we got?" Ruben asked.

"An itch I can't scratch," she said. "I've just got this funny feeling he knows something he isn't telling us."

"Okay, supposing you're right, how do you want to handle it?"

"Well, for the moment, the ball is in his court. I invited him in for a polygraph."

"I assume he declined your invitation?"

"He didn't outright decline it," Ginger replied. "He just deferred it."

"Smart."

"What do you think he'll do?"

Ruben shrugged. "I think he'll call a lawyer."

"That's what I figured," Ginger said.

"So suppose he talks to his lawyer and then declines your invitation?"

"I'll take it one step at a time," she replied, leaning back and locking her hands together on top of her head. "I don't really want to harass the guy. But if he's holding something back that has anything to do with this case, I'm going to find out what it is."

She had on navy pants and a blue shirt, and her red hair was bound in a braid down her back. She wore little makeup and her freckles stood out plainly. If it weren't for the gun holster clipped to her belt, she would have looked a good deal more like a troubled teenager than an embattled police officer. Ruben smiled to himself.

It was almost three weeks since she had come to dinner at his place. The longest three weeks he could remember. She was clearly being cautious and he didn't want to move too fast, risk scaring her off by asking her out too often, or give the local gossips any more grist for the mill than was necessary. But he missed her; he missed being able to look at her and talk to her and laugh with her.

They had little time alone together at work, although police headquarters was definitely not the place in which to carry on personal business. There were always people in and out. It was more than a week since they had even had the opportunity to talk in private. He knew he was free to telephone her, in the evening, after hours, but Ruben preferred the direct face-to-face approach, where he could see, not just hear, her reaction and then judge whether she was really interested in going out with him again, or just being polite.

"What about the Leo boy?" he asked.

"I don't know whether that's going to come to anything, but he's still at the top of my list," she told him. The top of a very, very short list, she thought.

Ruben nodded slowly. "People are already yelling witch hunt," he said. "First, we did the blood thing, then we went after one of the Island's top high school seniors, and now we're breathing down the neck of one of the most popular teachers. Whatever you do, make sure you do it by the book, and then make sure you back yourself up, every step of the way."

"I promise."

Ginger smiled to herself, wondering why she had never realized before how cautious he was. It was almost three weeks since she had been to his house for dinner, and the evening had been such fun that she couldn't understand why he hadn't asked her out again. She could read nothing in his behavior at work, but that was to be expected. Without either of them ever saying a word, it was clear that their personal lives had to be kept out of the office. But it was pure hell, waiting for him to speak, and wondering if she had done something to displease him.

Their conversation seemed to be at an end, so Ginger got up and started for the door.

"By the way," she said, turning back, unable to keep the words from coming out of her mouth, "I've acquired two New York steaks, and one of them has your name on it, if you're free tomorrow night."

Ruben's face lit up. "I am," he said. "As a matter of fact, I, uh, was just getting ready to mention something along those lines myself."

"Fine then. How's seven o'clock?"

"Seven is great," he replied. "I'll be there."

As a child, she had often climbed recklessly out onto an untested tree limb. She could remember how fearful she had been to discover that it was much thinner than she expected, and then how exhilarated she was when she realized that it wasn't going to break beneath her. She felt that way now.

Steak, salad, baked potatoes, something for dessert, and a good bottle of wine, she thought quickly. She would stop at the market on her way home tonight. That would give her all day tomorrow to clean her apartment.

"See you then," she said.

"You bet," he said.

Neither of them mentioned that it would be just the two of them, alone together, for the first time.

3

Danny Leo caught the late bus home from school on Friday. It seemed the closer he got to graduation, the more activities he found himself involved in. This particular day, it was a meeting of the holiday dance committee that kept him way past the last bell.

Whenever his mother complained about his hours, or his father chided him for being tardy in doing his chores, Danny would remind them that his school record was not just about good grades, that Harvard University was looking for well-rounded students who displayed a real sense of community commitment. It was enough to get them to back off for a while. Peter Leo had been born and raised in the shadow of Harvard, and had promised himself that, if he ever had a son, the boy would be educated where he himself had been neither bright enough nor rich enough to gain admittance.

"Detective Earley was up at school this afternoon," Danny told his father.

Peter bristled. "Is she harassing you again?"

"No," Danny assured him. "She didn't come to see me. She came to talk to one of Tara's teachers."

"What's so unusual about that?"

"Nothing really," Danny replied, "except that she already talked to all the teachers weeks ago, right after the murder. And today, she made a special trip, after school was out, just to see one of them. I saw her going into his classroom."

"Well, well, well," Peter murmured as a slow smile spread across his face. "Now that's another matter entirely, isn't it? Let's hope it's something that will take the heat off you."

"But I told you, Dad," Danny insisted. "I'm perfectly willing to give blood. I can clear myself if you'd only let me do it."

"You don't understand, son," Peter said, as the boy knew he would. "In this country, you don't have to clear yourself of anything. You are completely innocent until someone can prove otherwise."

"I, uh, won't be home tomorrow night," Ruben told Stacey as they sat down to supper. "I'm going to have dinner with Ginger."

The teenager grinned. "Again, so soon?" she murmured.

"What do you mean so soon?" he protested. "It's been three weeks."

Stacey burst into laughter. "Gosh, Dad, you sound more like a kid than a parent."

"Give me a break," her father retorted. "I'm not used to this father-talking-to-daughter-about-him-dating thing."

"Neither am I," she reminded him.

Ruben frowned suddenly, because the thought had not occurred to him until this moment. "Hey, are you okay with this?" he asked. "I mean, is it a problem, my going out with Ginger?"

Actually, Stacey had not been all that sure how she would feel about her father seriously dating someone. She knew he had seen other women over the years, but rarely more than once or twice, and he had never brought any of them home. She used to wish he would remarry, back when she was little and really needed a mother. But as she grew older, she realized that marriage was not about taking care of children or making a warm, cozy home; it was about a very special relationship between two people that happened when it was supposed to happen and not necessarily when you wanted it to.

"It's no problem," she assured him. "I like Ginger. I like you and Ginger."

He peered at her. "That sounded awfully grown-up," he observed. "When did you get so grown-up?"

Stacey grinned. "Oh, about a minute ago," she said. "So, tell me, are you going to splurge and go into Seattle tomorrow night?"

Much as she might not wish to do anything that would discourage her father's relationship with Ginger, she was all too aware of the gossip that had begun a few weeks ago with the snide remarks at church, and progressed to a fairly steady bombardment of wisecracks from several of her classmates.

Ruben tried to look casual. "As a matter of fact, we're staying on the Island," he said. "Ginger's, uh, invited me over to her place."

The fifteen-year-old digested that bit of information for a moment. "In that case," she said, "be sure and take a condom with you."

Had Ruben's skin been a shade or two lighter, the hot flush that suddenly flooded his face and spread down his neck would have been a lot more visible. His discomfort was in part because this was not exactly the kind of conversation he thought appropriate to be having with his teenage daughter, but mostly because the same thought had already occurred to him.

"Give me a break," he managed to repeat.

"I heard the strangest thing down at the market," Libby Hildress declared over dinner. The wife of the man who had discovered Tara Breckenridge's body was the opposite of her husband in more ways than one. Physically, she was short and plump, with soft blond hair that framed a pretty face, and clear blue eyes.

"What's that?" Tom asked, a spoonful of tomato soup halfway to his mouth.

"Somebody said that the police are investigating Jerry Frankel."

Tom blinked. "For what?"

"I guess maybe they think he might be involved in the Breckenridge case."

"You've got to be kidding," her husband said.

Libby shrugged. "That's what I heard."

"Why would anyone be dumb enough to think that?" Billy scoffed. "I know Mr. Frankel. He's Matthew's dad, a regular person. He can't be the killer."

"Why can't he?" challenged Billy's brother, Bud. "Just because you've been in his house doesn't mean you know anything about him or what he'd do. Besides, the cops have to pin the murder on someone, and it might as well be a teacher." Bud was thirteen years old, in the eighth grade, and not particularly fond of school.

"Dad, the police wouldn't do that, would they?" Billy asked in alarm. "Matthew's my best friend."

"I don't think the police would pin anything on anyone without good cause," Tom assured him.

"We don't even know if it's true," Libby said. "It's just what I heard. Naturally, I called Deborah at her office as soon as I got home." The Frankels and the Hildresses did not really socialize, but because of the friendship between Matthew and Billy, they had exchanged telephone numbers for emergency situations. "She said something about the police wanting to tie up a loose end."

"There, you see?" Tom declared, buttering a biscuit. "Last week, if you remember, the big flap was over Danny Leo. Now it's Jerry's turn. Next week, it'll probably be somebody else."

• • •

"I don't understand," Deborah Frankel declared. "The police already talked to you several times about that murder. Why would they need to talk to you again?"

Jerry shrugged. "Your guess is as good as mine," he replied.

"Oh, come on, they must have had some reason," she persisted. She was furious. She couldn't believe he hadn't called and told her himself about Ginger's visit, that she had to hear about it from the mother of one of her son's friends. "A woman I hardly know interrupts me at work, in the middle of a very important meeting," she stormed. "She wants to know why the police are investigating my husband in connection with the Breckenridge case. I didn't know what to tell her."

"I didn't think it was that important," he said.

"Well, I guess it must be, if the whole town is talking about it."

Jerry could see that she would not be put off, that she was determined to make a big thing out of it.

"One afternoon after school, I guess it was shortly before her death, I came across Tara in tears over something," he said with a sigh. "I don't know, I must have put my arm around her to comfort her. To tell you the truth, I don't really remember doing that, but apparently I did, and somebody saw me, and totally misinterpreted the situation, and reported it to the police."

Deborah felt a cold shiver dart down her back. "You had your arms around the murdered girl?" she asked.

He glared at her. "There was nothing to it," he said coldly.

Scott Cohen was considered by his peers to be among the best criminal defense attorneys in the State of Washington, if not the entire country. He was not bombastic in the manner of an F. Lee Bailey, perhaps, or folksy in the style of a Gerry Spence. But in his own quiet, unassuming way, he could demolish a prosecutor's case with the skill of a precision bomber.

A man of less than medium height and more than medium

weight, Scott had a froth of light brown hair that, by the time he turned forty, had receded almost to the crown of his head, giving him an odd halo effect, and explaining why it amused his colleagues to refer to him as the Cherub. But it was his eyes that drew the attention of most people; they were large, hooded eyes, sea green in color, and filled with a combination of intelligence and compassion that could hearten even the most desperate of defendants.

Scott, his wife, Rachel, and their son, Daniel, had lived on Seward Island for five years, ever since Scott was invited to join the law partnership of Morgan, Kaperstein and Cole, and they had purchased their 1909 farmhouse. Rachel picked the place for the lovely little pond and well-tended orchard that went with it. Scott took to it for all the renovation work he could do in his spare time.

"Are you sure you won't mind having to commute?" Rachel asked, as they packed up the house on Queen Anne Hill that was barely ten minutes from his office.

"Actually, I think I'll like it," he told her. "It'll give me separation time."

Commuters on the seven o'clock ferry from Seward to Seattle got used to seeing the Cherub every morning, sitting in the lounge, looking oddly impish in his three-piece suit, sipping a cup of coffee, and watching the scenery. He never looked at a file nor wrote a note. Only after he reached his office, and settled himself behind his desk with his third cup of coffee, was he prepared to begin his workday.

It was a hard-and-fast rule of Scott's to work Sundays through Fridays, but never on Saturdays; he had been raised to respect the Sabbath. There was no synagogue on Seward Island when the Cohens arrived, barely even a Jewish presence at all. But after two years of trudging back to Seattle for services, Scott became instrumental in urging several local families to form a small congregation. He convinced the rabbi at his old temple to let his assistant take on a part-time flock, and made a deal with the Unitarians for the use of their church on Friday nights, Saturday mornings, and the high holy days in exchange for a reasonable sum. There were fewer than thirty Jewish families on the Island at the time, not nearly enough to support a facility of their own, so Daniel had celebrated his bar mitzvah in the sanctuary of the Cedar Valley Unitarian Church.

"God lives in many houses," the rabbi had asserted. "He rejoices with us no matter which one we are in."

Scott was not an obsessive man, but everyone who knew him knew he took the traditions of his religion seriously. Therefore, when Jerry Frankel came knocking at the Cohens' front door in the middle of a quiet Saturday afternoon, the attorney assumed his friend was making a social call.

"How's it going?" he inquired amiably.

The Cohens and the Frankels had met the previous March, about two months after Jerry and Deborah moved to the Island and chose to attend the Passover service at the church. They discovered that they lived only three blocks from each other, and it was not long before the two couples had become friends.

"Can I talk to you for a minute?" the teacher asked.

"Sure," Scott said. "Come on in."

Jerry shook his head. "Can we take a walk around?" he suggested instead.

The attorney blinked. "If this is business," he said, "can it keep until tomorrow?"

"I'm sorry, I forgot," Jerry said, flustered. "Sure, it's not important, it can keep."

He turned away, but Scott had already seen something in the teacher's eyes that he had seen on far too many other occasions to misread: panic.

"Why don't we take a stroll down by the pond," he offered. "Rachel has been talking about building a little bridge over one end of it, and I've been wanting to ask your opinion."

The two men headed down the slope of lawn behind the farmhouse, Jerry walking with his shoulders bent and his hands shoved into the pockets of his khakis. Scott sighed inwardly.

"I may be getting into something over my head," the teacher said as soon as they were out of earshot of the house. "And I don't know what to do."

"Well, I'm sure it isn't anything that can't be worked out," Scott replied.

Jerry looked at his friend. "I think the police think I'm involved in the Breckenridge case."

"*Are* you?" the attorney asked, caught completely off guard.

Jerry eyes fastened on his friend's halo. "No, of course not."

The Cherub shrugged. "Then I wouldn't worry about it."

"But they want me to take a lie detector test and give them a sample of my blood. If it gets out that they even asked me, pass or fail, I lose all my credibility as a teacher in this community."

Scott took what he liked to call a judicious moment to assess the situation. "You can always refuse," he said finally.

"Won't that look even worse?"

"As I understand it, they've been asking a lot of people to give blood and take polygraphs. How many of them have we heard about?"

"This is different," Jerry muttered. "Most of them were students or regular townspeople. I'm a teacher. I work with kids. My success depends on their trust and respect. Even a hint of scandal will ruin me."

Scott Cohen always prided himself on his instincts about people, and on his ability to evaluate a situation quickly and accurately. "I've been speaking to you so far as a friend," he said now. "Do you want me to represent you as an attorney?"

The teacher sighed. "I guess so," he replied.

"All right then, this is how it works. They can't compel you to take the polygraph. That's strictly voluntary. If you refuse to give them a blood sample, the only way they can force you is to get a court order. For that, they need probable cause. If they *had* probable cause, they wouldn't be asking. So I think we can assume they're on what we call a fishing expedition. Now if, as you say, you're not involved and have nothing to hide, they won't catch any fish, and they'll move on to another part of the pond."

"And it won't look bad that I refused? It won't make me look guilty of anything?"

Scott shrugged. "You have a clear right to refuse; it's called the Fifth Amendment. But you're a history teacher—I shouldn't have to tell you that."

Jerry seemed to perk up at that. "Of course, you're right. I guess I forgot."

The attorney smiled. "In that case, I think your crisis is past."

But the teacher didn't smile back. "If I hear from them again," he said instead, "if they try to pressure me, can I call you?"

"You're my client now," Scott told him. "You can call me anytime, Sundays through Fridays."

4

By five o'clock Saturday afternoon, Ginger's apartment looked like a set for a television commercial to promote cleaning products. The windows were Windexed, the hardwood floors were Johnson Waxed, the carpeting was Hoovered, and the dining room table was Pledged.

Everything that didn't have a proper place had been swept into the back of the bedroom closet. By the time she had Ajaxed the kitchen, it looked as though no one had ever cooked in it. She then Lysoled the bathroom, removed her underwear from the shower bar, and put out a clean guest towel and a fresh cake of soap. At the last moment, she changed the sheets on her queen-sized bed.

With two hours left in which to get dinner, and herself, ready, she headed for the kitchen. She had a salad whipped up in no time. Then she mixed up some sour cream and chives for the potatoes. Finally, she trimmed up a bunch of asparagus to pop into the microwave. She would put the potatoes in the oven at six; they were big and the cookbook said they would take an hour and a half to bake. Since Ruben liked his meat as rare as she did, the steaks would go on the Jenn-Air grill at the last minute.

Dessert was already prepared—chocolate mousse out of a package. Granted, it might not be considered a gourmet meal, but then she was a working woman, not a full-time cook, and she thought Ruben would understand that.

At five-thirty, she jumped in the shower, washed and blow-dried her hair, came out to get the potatoes going, and returned to the bathroom to apply her usual modicum of makeup. At six-fifteen, she headed for her closet. By ten minutes to seven, she had considered and discarded almost its entire contents and was ready to scream.

"We're looking for something simple here," she said to her reflection in the cheval mirror that sat in the corner of the bedroom. "Something attractive, but not too suggestive. Something that says I'm comfortable, but not necessarily available. Something soft; very soft."

From his perch on the bed, Twink, the marmalade cat, let out a low meow.

"Of course," Ginger exclaimed. She raced to her dresser and rummaged around the bottom drawer until she came out with an oversized gray angora turtleneck, a birthday gift from her parents some years back. "Perfect," she said with a wicked smile. "Let's see you try to keep your hands off this, Mr. Chief of Police."

She had just finished buttoning a pair of black wool slacks, slipping her feet into black leather flats, and fastening silver hoops in her ears when the doorbell rang. It was thirty seconds after seven.

"I hope I'm not late," Ruben said.

"Your timing is perfect," she replied.

He, too, was wearing a turtleneck sweater, beige and made of something thick and cuddly, like lambswool, and he wore it with neat brown slacks. He looked so put together, she wondered if he'd had as much trouble choosing his outfit as she had.

He was carrying a bouquet of winter flowers, which he shyly

presented to her. "I'm afraid I'm out of practice," he admitted. "I wasn't sure what to bring."

"You didn't have to bring anything," she told him. "But these are beautiful, so I'm glad you did."

Ginger turned into her little kitchen and busied herself finding a vase. She had been looking forward to this evening all day, but now that he was here, she was suddenly nervous.

"How about a drink?" she asked to cover her jitters.

"Sure," he said.

"Is Scotch okay?" Ginger didn't drink hard liquor. She bought the Scotch because it was what he had been drinking at his house.

"Scotch is fine," he told her.

She fixed the drink the way she remembered he had fixed it, with ice and a little water.

"How did you know?" he asked.

Her hazel eyes twinkled. "I'm a detective, remember?"

She poured a little Scotch over ice for herself, filling the rest of the glass with water, and then they went into the living room. A fire smoldered in the fireplace, threatening to go out.

"May I?" he asked.

"Please do."

He inspected the pile of wood she had stacked next to the hearth, and she watched as he selected a combination of logs and kindling that would best suit his purpose. The beige sweater rippled across his back, and she wondered if he were wearing his brace. He began to rekindle the blaze, alternately rising up to reach for pieces of wood and then squatting to arrange them, while his brown slacks tightened and loosened against his body. Ginger downed her Scotch in two long gulps and went back to the kitchen for more. This time, she doubled the amount of the alcohol and cut the water in half.

At first, tonight had simply been about her wanting to see him again. She would have felt uncomfortable inviting him out to a restaurant, even in the 1990s, and since he had already had her to *his* home, it seemed perfectly appropriate that she ask him to hers. It was only after he accepted the invitation that she began to consider where it might lead. Not that anything was inevitable, of course; not even that it was likely. It was just something to contemplate, maybe even fantasize about while she cleaned the apartment. But now that he was here, she wasn't sure what she wanted.

Ruben reset the fire, taking far more time than the task actually required because it gave him something to do. He had really looked forward to spending the evening alone with Ginger, but now that he was here, he wondered whether he should have suggested they go out to dinner instead.

"There, I think that should do it," he declared as flames began to lick around the fresh wood. He stood up and retrieved his drink from the mantel. Ginger was curled at one end of a dusty blue sofa. He sat down in a green and blue striped chair across from her.

"I'm afraid I'm not very good with fires," Ginger said. "I can start them, but I can't seem to keep them going."

"Well, there's no big trick to it," he told her. "You just have to leave plenty of space around the logs so the air can circulate. It's air that keeps the wood burning."

"I'll have to remember that."

"Of course, you have to use the right combination of wood, too," he said, sipping his Scotch.

"I'll certainly keep that in mind."

"And of course, different kinds of fireplaces react differently," he added. "There are some that don't draw as well as others, and I suppose there are some that might draw too much, but yours seems to work just fine."

"That's good to know," she murmured.

There was silence then, because Ruben had exhausted his

knowledge of fire tending, and didn't quite know where to go next. He took a long drink of Scotch.

"Today certainly was a beautiful day," he said finally, just to say something.

"Yes," she agreed. "Unusually warm for December."

"I walked around my yard in my shirtsleeves."

"I went out without a coat."

"The climate here still surprises me," he said. "You'd think it would get so much colder than it does, being so far north."

"It's one of our best-kept secrets," she told him.

Twink sat by the sliding glass doors, his tail slapping the carpet as though bored with the conversation and impatient for the topic to change.

"I still haven't seen as much of the state as I'd like to," Ruben said, beginning to feel desperate. "I know there are a lot of places we should visit, like the San Juan Islands and Skagit Valley and Leavenworth. Stacey and I keep talking about taking a picnic up to Mount Rainier, and I think a trip to Mount St. Helens would be fascinating. But so far, we haven't been able to make the time."

"Yes, there are some wonderful places around here," Ginger replied.

Sight-seeing? The weather? She couldn't believe they were sitting here, talking like two people who had never met each other before. They hadn't discussed the weather on their first date, or even their second. They had been so comfortable with each other before; he had been so easy to talk to. It made their present conversation seem almost comical. Only Ginger didn't feel like laughing—she felt like crying. The evening wasn't going at all the way she had planned. She downed the rest of her drink.

"I like the way you've done this room," Ruben said, grasping at anything to keep himself from doing something stupid— like fleeing. "The colors you picked work really well together."

"I'm kind of limited," she admitted. "There aren't too many

colors I can live with. Red hair does tend to put a damper on one's options."

"Reds and yellows are my heritage," he told her, "but I like blues and greens. They're softer, and they suit you."

She could feel the warmth of the Scotch wriggling around inside her body.

"I always wanted to wear bright red," she confessed with a sudden giggle. "And swing my hips down Commodore Street. My mother used to tell me that only wicked women wore bright red, but I think I only believed her a little bit."

Ruben was delighted. "So that's where the tomboy came from," he charged. "To cover up your wild side."

A big grin split her freckled face. "Of course. And I did it so well that I talked myself into it."

"Well, be sure and let me know if your true self ever gets the urge to emerge," he told her with a chuckle. "I almost think I'd give up my pension to watch the Honorable Albert Hoch have a coronary right at the corner of Commodore and Seward."

Ginger hooted.

The ice was broken. They sensed it immediately. Both of them sank back into their seats, each with a silent sigh of relief. Even Twink noticed. He came over and stretched out in front of the fire.

"I've never drunk two Scotches before," Ginger said with a giggle.

"I can't tell you how glad I am you did," Ruben said.

While she grilled the steaks, he tossed the salad. While she zapped the asparagus, he rescued the potatoes. While she set the table, he lit the candles. While she turned on the stereo, he poured the wine. Finally, they were seated across from each other, the food between them.

"I was beginning to think I'd made a terrible mistake by asking you over here," she said as she forked up a piece of sour-creamed potato.

"I don't know why, but I can't remember the last time I was so nervous," he admitted, slicing into his steak.

"You'd think we were a couple of teenagers," she said.

"On a blind date," he added.

"Instead of friends . . ." she began.

". . . enjoying an evening together," he finished.

They smiled at each other through the candlelight.

Ruben picked up his wine. "To good food and better company," he said.

Ginger raised her glass to his. "To perseverance," she murmured.

After dinner, Ruben insisted on helping her wash up the dishes.

"You don't have to do that," she protested.

"Of course I do," he replied. "I wouldn't want you to think my Stacey didn't raise me up right."

Ginger chuckled. "She's lucky to have you for a dad."

But Ruben shook his head. "No," he told her with a soft smile. "I'm the lucky one."

When the kitchen was back in order, Ginger took a bottle of Kahlúa from a cabinet and poured two glasses. Then they went back into the living room. A Tchaikovsky symphony had begun to play on the stereo. They sat down on the sofa.

"The *Pathétique*," he murmured. "One of my favorites."

"Mine, too," she said with a nod.

They sat there, sipping the Kahlúa and listening to the music. After a while, he reached over and picked up her hand, entwining his fingers with hers. She didn't pull away. Instead, she let the symphony and the liqueur and the fire and the quiet strength that flowed from his hand to hers lull her into a world of warmth and wonder. A flood of sensations washed over her, from excitement to anxiety to desire to fear.

The last time Ginger had been to bed with a man was almost five years ago, a brief affair with a Seattle reporter assigned to cover one of her small-town cases that left her feeling very used. She concluded that sex, just for the sake of sex, was not a sufficient reason to take off her clothes.

But this time, she hoped it would be different, *wanted* it to be different. In the last few weeks, since she had begun to see Ruben in a new light, she had felt drawn to him in a way that hadn't happened since the young man in the farm equipment business. While she wasn't quite ready to pin a label on what she was feeling, she thought she was at least ready to consider taking the next step.

Of course, she had no idea what was going on in Ruben's head. This was, after all, just their third date, and on both previous occasions he had appeared somewhat reticent. Which meant it was entirely possible that she was no more to him than a momentary diversion, someone to enjoy for a while until the novelty wore off, someone to help push away the loneliness for a time; not someone with whom he would allow himself to get seriously involved. In which case, she would be wise to wait for him to make the next move.

By the same token, it could also mean that he was shy, and awkward at dealing with the unique language of the single set, despite the length of time he had been a widower. In which case, it might very well be up to her to make the next move. For all her intuitive ability on the job, when it came to personal relationships, Ginger had never been much good at reading men's minds.

Ruben, however, had no such problem. He could read his mind quite well. And he knew that, in Ginger, he had found someone quite extraordinary. Not only someone warm and compassionate and singularly compatible, but someone with whom he was beginning to let himself believe he could share the rest of his life. The thought both thrilled and panicked him. In many ways, he had spent a very long and very lonely thirteen years. It was only now that he was beginning to realize what had been missing since the death of his wife; what he had denied himself over grief and guilt. He thought that finding Ginger might be a sign that his penance was over.

All of which was good to know, he acknowledged, but did little to solve his present problem; namely—what to do now? He stole a look at his watch. It read ten minutes past ten. The *Pathétique* was about to conclude. Was he going to thank her for a lovely dinner and depart? Or was he going to seize the moment and let it carry them both as high as they chose to go? Ruben heard the last notes of the symphony. It was time to decide.

He turned to her at the very second that she turned to him, and their words collided in midair.

"Dinner was terrific."

"I'm glad you could come tonight."

There was a sudden pause, during which they both stood up.

She must not be interested, he thought.

He doesn't want to get involved, she thought.

Still, they found themselves searching for something else to say, anything that would keep this evening from ending, until, for the second time, their words, spoken in the same instant, tumbled over each other.

"It's still pretty early."

"Would you like another Kahlúa?"

"Yes," he said.

"Yes," she said.

And then suddenly, without any thought, he was holding her, and her body seemed to melt into his. Ruben couldn't believe how sweet she smelled, how good she felt, how vibrant, how alive. Memories of the handful of women he had clung to out of need over the years vanished in a rush of desire he had not known since his wife.

He had felt guilty on those other occasions, because they meant nothing to him. But he felt no guilt now as he turned Ginger's face to his and began to kiss her, on the forehead, at the corner of her eye, along the line of her cheek, moving down until he reached her mouth. Kissing her softly, because he was still unsure—of her, of himself.

It was only when he realized she was kissing him back that he grew bolder, more insistent, parting her lips with his, drinking from her, deeper and deeper, until he was dizzy and trembling. Then he pulled her close against him and just held her, while the world around him spun wildly.

"I'm a little rusty," he murmured into her hair. "So, if this isn't what you want, tell me now, and I'll go."

"Stay," she breathed.

She was wrapped in his arms and she had never felt so complete, so totally within herself. Not even with Farm Equipment. It was almost as though, at twenty-eight, she was just discovering what being a woman was really about. Every nerve ending in her body tingled, every sense was heightened. She had never been so sure of who she was, and what she wanted. She took him by the hand and led him to the bedroom.

Behind them, Twink curled up on the dusty blue sofa, in the warm spot they had abandoned, and began to lick his huge paws.

The moment they entered the bedroom, they began to reach for each other with their hands, their arms, their lips, their legs. Between kisses, he pulled her sweater over her head, she pulled his sweater over his. With their mouths locked together, he undid the buttons on her slacks, she unfastened his belt. With their tongues exploring each other's depths, he kicked off his loafers, she kicked off her flats. Then they stood there, in their underwear and stockings, and started to giggle.

"This was supposed to be an incredibly romantic moment," he scolded, smiling.

"Well, I guess we'll just have to settle for fun," she replied.

They fell into each other's arms, laughing, losing their balance and tumbling onto the bed.

"That's all right," he murmured. "It's where we were headed anyway."

He pulled off his undershirt.

"You're not wearing your brace," she observed.

Ruben looked embarrassed. "It's not very attractive, and I thought it might, you know, be something of a turnoff," he confessed. "I guess that was pretty presumptuous of me, wasn't it?"

"That's okay," she told him. "I changed the sheets."

He reached for her with a grateful groan. In less than a minute, they had rid themselves of the remainder of their clothing, and then there was no more need for words as their bodies began to communicate with one another.

She smelled of spring flowers, and her skin felt as soft as rose petals. Beneath the tomboy facade, Ruben found a woman's body, expertly molded, eager and welcoming. Ginger was long and lean and nothing like his wife, who had been quite petite, but he felt the same wave of emotion, rising in him like the surf, building toward the moment when it would crest and break and engulf them both.

His body felt strange against hers. The compact shape, the rough skin sliding over taut muscles, the strong hands, the soft warm lips, the dense hair that covered his chest—they were all so unfamiliar. And perhaps because of that, the room, the very bed she had slept in every night for almost two years felt different, as though it were a place she had never been before. But when they finally came together, one and inseparable, she forgot about the strangeness, the self-consciousness. She forgot about everything except the extraordinary sweetness of being with him, the exhilaration of it, and the absolute rightness of it.

Like a hymn from her childhood, she felt as though she were being borne on the wings of an eagle, soaring higher and higher and higher. Sex was not new to Ginger, but this was not just sex. She knew beyond any doubt that what she was feeling was unlike anything she had ever experienced before.

When it was over and they lay apart, their hands clasped together, their energy spent, neither of them could find adequate words to express what had taken place, or what it had meant.

"How awful to think," she said after a while, "that I could have gone to my grave without ever once knowing what it should be like."

"I'd like to think we'll know it more than once," he remarked.

She squeezed his fingers. "Count on it," she told him.

Somewhere along the way, they had remembered the condom, but neither of them could recall exactly when. It had just been handled, at the appropriate time, in the right context, without interruption.

"It's a pity we aren't married," he murmured, thinking of that now. "A night like this should have created life."

5

On Sunday, Ginger drove over to the Earley house shortly after noon, knowing that her brothers would not yet have arrived. Indeed, her parents had barely returned from church.

"What's the matter?" her mother wanted to know, hurrying to answer the doorbell.

"Nothing," Ginger assured her. "I just want to talk to you and Dad before the others get here."

"Talk to us? About what?"

"Do you really want me to tell you right now, on the front porch, in front of God and the neighbors?" Ginger inquired. "Or would you like to let me come in first?"

"Oh, don't be silly," Verna retorted. "Of course, come in."

The three of them sat in the living room, tentatively, her father trying to light his pipe, her mother twisting her hands in her lap.

"I wanted to tell you this myself," Ginger began in a matter-of-fact tone, "before you heard it from Eleanor Jewel, and didn't know how to respond. Ruben Martinez and I are seeing each other . . . socially, I mean. We've had several dates so far, and we've decided that we want to pursue a relationship."

"You mean, you're going to get *married?*" Verna blurted, horrified.

"No," her daughter replied. "I mean we're going to date each other on a regular basis; go to dinner, to the movies, out dancing, anything we like, and see where it leads us."

"You mean, you're *thinking* about getting married?"

"We're not thinking about anything right now," Ginger said, "except spending time with each other."

"But that's exactly where this sort of thing leads, you know."

"If it does, then that's when we'll deal with it."

"You mean, when it's too late to talk any sense into you. Do you have any idea what you're asking for? People like that have no morals. People like that would just as soon get you in trouble and then leave you high and dry."

"People like what, Mother?" Ginger inquired, with a definite edge to her voice. "Decent, hardworking people who earn their paychecks every week, just like Dad? People who dedicate their lives to cleaning up other people's messes? People who stick around to raise children all on their own after their wives die? Are those the people you're talking about?"

Verna looked to her husband for support. "You tell her, Jack. Obviously, she won't listen to me."

Jack Earley sighed. "What do you want me to tell her?" he asked his wife. "I think Sheriff Martinez is a good man, and that's more than I can say for a lot of men I know, wherever they may have come from. If Ginger wants to date him, I don't see as we have any right to tell her she can't."

"Any right?" Verna cried from the very depths of her soul. "After all the years I've spent making a place for us on this is-land—you think she has the right to ruin it?"

Jack puffed on his pipe. "Seems to me," he said after a moment, looking down the last quarter century of life with his wife, "if her dating a Mexican fellow is going to ruin your reputation, maybe it's because you spent all those years circulating in the wrong circles."

"Late Friday afternoon," the weekend edition of the *Sentinel* summarized, "Detective Ginger Earley was back at Seward High School to talk with one of Tara Breckenridge's teachers. This was apparently in relation to the recent report that a classmate of the murdered girl had seen Tara and the teacher alone together several days before her death.

"While details of the conversation between the teacher and Detective Earley were not released, this could mean that the Breckenridge investigation is now headed in a totally new direction."

"Well, they may not have come right out and named him, but you know as well as I do who they're talking about," Libby Hildress told her husband when she read the article. "So I guess I was right about what I heard."

Tom sighed. "That doesn't mean he's involved in the case," he suggested. "It just means they talked to him."

"Of course," Libby agreed. "But where there's smoke, there's usually fire."

They were lingering over coffee, and as was their habit after church and Sunday dinner, they were reading the weekend *Sentinel* to catch up on the Island news. The boys, having been released from the table, were out playing.

"Just the same," Tom said, "do me a favor and don't go making a big thing of it. Matthew is Billy's friend, and I think we owe him and his parents our support."

"I have no intention of saying anything to anyone," Libby promised. "But mark my words, this isn't going to go away next week."

"Every single day, all we ever get is the Breckenridge case, smeared over practically every page of the newspaper," Deborah

Frankel grumbled. "And when they run out of things to report, do they just move on to another issue? No, they invent something, and then spin their wheels speculating about it. You'd think there was nothing more important going on in the world."

"The thing you have to keep in mind is that there's nothing more important going on *here*," Rachel Cohen reminded her gently. The attorney's wife was almost a head shorter than Deborah, with auburn hair, soft brown eyes, and a heart-shaped face.

"That's the difference between us," Deborah said with a heavy sigh. "You like living in the middle of nowhere—I don't."

It was Sunday afternoon, the laundry was done, and the two women were in the kitchen, sharing a cup of coffee while Jerry, Scott, and the two boys were off on a bicycle ride. The newspaper lay on the table between them.

"I hated being here for the first few months," Rachel admitted. "I felt so cut off from everything I thought was important. Now, you couldn't get me to go back to living in the city."

"But don't you get bored out of your skull sometimes?" Deborah cried in exasperation.

The attorney's wife shrugged. "I can get on a ferry and spend a day in Seattle anytime I want to," she said.

While the Frankels had acquired a rather sizable circle of acquaintances on Seward Island since their arrival, Rachel was the only real friend Deborah had made. It wasn't that she was unsociable or snobbish or even shy. It was more that she was a very private person, and did not care to become a topic of small-town gossip.

"I don't think I could stand it if I didn't have my job to go to every day," she confessed. "I don't know how you do it—spend so much of your time here, I mean. It's so claustrophobic."

"You get used to it," Rachel said. "After a while, you start to appreciate things like the peace and quiet, and the clean air, and not having to lock your doors. You find you really enjoy doing things like gardening and baking bread. And pretty soon, you discover the benefits of not having to put on two inches of makeup every day."

"But some of the people here are so small-minded and mean-spirited," Deborah argued. "They smile to your face readily enough, but then they turn around and stab you in the back."

"I don't think the people in our neighborhood are like that," Rachel said.

"Well, no," Deborah conceded. "I guess some of them are okay. But there are others."

In many ways, Rachel was every bit as perceptive as her husband. "You know, I think people are people, wherever they happen to be," she said, casually picking up the *Sentinel* and dropping it on the floor beside her chair. "With all the same dreams, and all the same fears. I don't think it makes much difference whether they live in big cities or small towns."

But Deborah was staring at the spot on the table where the newspaper had been. "Jerry didn't have anything to do with that girl's murder," she blurted suddenly, desperately. "I don't care what they're saying—he just couldn't have."

"Ginger doesn't tell us very much about the case," Verna Earley said over the telephone to Eleanor Jewel, relieved that the topic of the Sunday evening call was going to be murder, not marriage. "After all, the work she does has to be kept confidential."

"But she must have said something," Eleanor insisted. "Now that she and the police chief have become so, shall we say, intimately involved in the case, she surely must know everything that's going on."

On the heels of the conversation with her daughter, Verna bristled. "What my daughter does and what she knows are no concern of yours," she retorted.

"On the contrary, I have two grandchildren up at the high school," Eleanor argued. "If one of the teachers is involved in Tara Breckenridge's death, shouldn't everyone know about it?"

"Well, I wouldn't jump to any conclusions just yet, if I were you," Verna relented, smiling into the receiver because, after looking down her nose at the Earleys for so many years, the gossip queen had finally come begging. "When the time is right, I'm sure you'll be told whatever you need to know."

"You *do* know something," Eleanor pounced.

"I didn't say that," Verna protested.

"You didn't have to say it. I can hear it in your voice, plain as day. That teacher they talked to *is* the one, isn't he? He killed poor Tara, didn't he?"

Ginger had never said a word to her parents about the Breckenridge case, nor did Verna know anything more than the newspaper had reported. But she wasn't about to tell that to Eleanor Jewel.

"I'm sorry," she said sweetly, "but I really can't say any more."

6

"I've spoken to my attorney, Detective Earley," Jerry Frankel said over the telephone on Monday. "He advises me that I am under no obligation to submit to a polygraph test or to give you a sample of my blood."

"Your attorney is absolutely correct," Ginger replied.

"Well then, unless you have some real evidence that I'm involved in this case, I must decline to put myself in a position that would very likely compromise my career."

"If you have nothing to hide, Mr. Frankel," Ginger said smoothly, "your career wouldn't be compromised."

"I'm not that naive, Detective," Jerry responded. "Don't you read the local newspapers? I do. Even the hint that you're seriously investigating me could be enough to get me suspended from my job. And although I'm sure your tests would establish my noninvolvement beyond any doubt, the suspicion would always be there and my credibility at school would be destroyed."

His argument was reasonable; Ginger couldn't fault it. She was, in fact, furious about the article describing her visit to the school, and she resented having to defend any part of it.

"The *Sentinel* didn't refer to you by name," she said.

"It didn't have to," he replied. "This is a very small community. There were still students and teachers and staff at school last Friday when you showed up. How long do you think it will take people to figure it out? I have no information about the murder of Tara Breckenridge. If I did, I would have given it to you a long time ago. Now, please, leave me alone."

There was a definitive click at the other end of the line. Ginger sat there with the dead receiver in her hand. She had assured Ruben that she had no wish to harass the teacher, and she didn't. More than that, he was acting exactly as an innocent man would act in such circumstances, controlling his anger, making his point.

Despite the pressure they were under to come up with a suspect, despite the little itch at the back of her neck that told her he very well might know something that would help the investigation, she wondered if it weren't time to move on.

"First, one of our outstanding seniors was suspected of being involved in Tara Breckenridge's murder, and now it's one of our teachers," the assistant principal of Seward High School complained to the editor of the *Sentinel*. "And not just any teacher, mind you, but one of the finest we've ever been lucky enough to have here on the Island. And for some reason, your newspaper just can't seem to resist reporting every trivial piece of information as though it meant the impending resolution of the case. Perhaps you should display more integrity, and exercise more care before a decent man's career is ruined by innuendo rather than fact."

"I know which teacher it is that the police are now supposedly investigating," wrote the mother of a high school junior. "This is too small a community for anyone not to know. And I can't believe they're serious. My daughter is in one of his classes. She's learned more from him in the short time he's been here than from any other teacher in school, and she has the marks to prove it. A man like that inspires, he doesn't destroy."

"Has anyone noticed what's happening at the high school?" asked one of the English teachers. "It's now a place where learning has become secondary to speculation, and knowledge less important than rumor. If the police really want to find a killer, let them look where killers live, not where young minds are encouraged to grow."

"I don't know who's crazier, the *Sentinel* or its readers," the mother of twin sophomores told the editor. "Does the fact that Detective Earley 'talked' to one of the teachers automatically qualify him for hanging?"

"Where do we draw the line between what is legitimate investigation and what is harassment?" wondered a member of Scott Cohen's modest congregation. "And where do we draw the line between harassment and persecution? The police have now spoken four times to the teacher referred to in your recent article. If there were anything that connected him to the Breckenridge case, wouldn't they be doing a lot more than just talking to him by now?"

"Shouldn't we have a trial first, and see some hard evidence, before we rush out to crucify one of the best teachers we've ever had?" asked a local secretary.

"I have it on very good authority," Eleanor Jewel told a close acquaintance over a double tall latte at The Pelican, a popular coffee shop next to the ferry dock, "the teacher did it. The police know it for a fact, but they just don't have enough evidence yet to arrest him."

"What teacher?" the acquaintance asked.

"Why, my dear," Eleanor cooed, "I thought everybody knew."

"I can't believe the police really think Mr. Frankel could have murdered Tara," Melissa Senn declared during lunch break, between bites of an egg salad sandwich.

As Jerry himself had predicted, Ginger's conversation with the teacher had become common knowledge.

"Well, that's what I heard," Hank Kriedler said.

"How do you hear all these things?" Jeannie Gemmetta demanded.

Hank shrugged. "People talk," he said. "You know how it is."

"More like Kristen Andersen talked," Jeannie scoffed. "She was blabbing that silly story to everyone who would listen to her. All about seeing the two of them together with their arms wrapped around each other."

"What do you think—that she made it up?" Bill Graham asked.

"Maybe not," Jeannie conceded. "But she could have made a lot more out of it than it really was. You know Kristen—she always exaggerates."

"And don't you remember the Monday after Tara died?" Melissa insisted. "I do. Mr. Frankel didn't know a thing about it. We had to tell him what happened. He looked positively sick."

"So maybe the guy's a good actor," Jack Tannauer said.

"If he was that good," Jeannie retorted, "he'd be making movies in Hollywood instead of teaching history on Seward Island."

"I don't believe for a minute there was anything going on between the two of them," Melissa scoffed. "First of all, he's married. Second, Tara might have been pretty, but she wasn't nearly smart enough for someone like him. Third, we see him every day in class, looking perfectly normal, and you know that murderers can't help but give themselves away. And besides, Tara wasn't into going out with guys yet. I was her best friend; she'd have told me if she was."

"Still waters run deep," Hank said.

"What does that mean?" asked Jeannie.

"I don't know about the rest of you," Jim Petrie said, "but I'm getting pretty damned concerned over the lack of progress in the Breckenridge case."

The city council was having lunch, an informal monthly get-together that cleverly preempted the need for public participation, and allowed for what Albert Hoch liked to call "straight talk." As was their habit, they occupied the small dining room at Gull House, with full confidence that the restaurant management would honor their privacy.

"I don't feel any better about it than you do, Jim," Maxine Coopersmith responded. "But as far as I can tell, the police are doing everything humanly possible, and I don't know what more we can expect of them."

"Wasn't that the reason we hired Martinez?" Dale Egaard asked. "Because he was such a hotshot with all that big-city experience?"

"If that was the reason," Petrie countered, "it looks like we made a mistake."

"What are you saying?" Ed Hingham inquired. "You saying you want to fire the guy because he couldn't solve the murder in sixty minutes?"

"How about sixty days?" Petrie shot back.

"Do you think you can do better, Jim?" drawled Henry Lewiston. "Do you want the job?"

"Certainly not," snapped Petrie. "I just want the case solved and the killer caught so we can all get back to living normal lives. But Martinez is going off in all directions, wasting valuable time and resources running down ridiculous leads, and as far as I can tell, getting nowhere."

"Well, I agree the Purdy thing was untimely," Maxine conceded. "Stirring everyone up like it has. And it can't have helped any, to bring out all the crackpots. But no one had any control over that, and we can hardly blame Ruben."

"I'm not blaming anyone," Petrie said. "All I'm saying is that I want results. And if we can't get them from our current chief of police, well then, maybe we should think about bringing in someone else."

"They're looking at some teacher now, aren't they?" Ed Hingham asked. "Maybe something will come of that."

"At this point, I don't think we need to talk about firing anyone." Albert Hoch spoke for the first time. "Let's let the Purdy thing play itself out for a bit, and keep an eye on the teacher situation, and see what happens. The issue is on the table. We know it's there. We can always come back to it later on, if we need to."

"Hey, I've got one for you," Glen Dirksen said, catching Ginger on her way back from lunch. "This twelve-year-old kid says his seventy-year-old grandmother admitted to whacking Tara Breckenridge with an ax. The old lady claimed she needed sweet young bones for her winter soup."

Ginger rolled her eyes. "And I bet you came out of the academy thinking police work was going to be all cops and robbers."

Ruben called to her as she passed his door, heading to her office.

"Fill me in," he requested. "Where are we?"

"It all depends on your point of view," she replied. "We're either in the middle of an intensive investigation, or we're grasping at some pretty skinny straws. Dirksen's got a hot lead on a granny angle."

Ruben shook his head in disbelief. "Anything new on the teacher?"

"No," Ginger told him. "And I'm not so sure there ever will be. But Peter Leo lost his battle in court. Judge Jacobs refused to quash the order on Danny. He's got a week to report to the clinic."

"If his DNA comes up negative, and we cut the teacher loose," he reminded her, "that means we're back at nowhere."

But Ginger didn't need reminding.

"You were right to stand up to them, Albert," declared Kyle Breckenridge. "I'm glad we have one level head at City Hall. Anyone with any brains at all knows you don't change horses in the middle of the river."

"That's exactly what I told them," the mayor agreed, preening a bit from the compliment. "Ruben still has leads to follow. The teacher, for one, although I gather nothing's come of that. And much as it pains me to say it, there's still Danny Leo. Not to mention all the stuff that's been pouring in since the Purdy reward was put up. I told them to wait and see."

Breckenridge nodded. "Something's bound to break," he said. "I don't think it'll be much longer."

Jordan Huxley had been the principal of Seward High School for almost sixteen years. In that time, he had seen a lot of teachers come and go, good ones and bad ones, and he considered himself lucky to have Jerry Frankel on his staff.

The timing had been perfect. First there was Jim Duffy dropping dead of a heart attack the way he had, at the premature age of fifty-two, leaving a rather sizable hole in the history department in the middle of January. And then there was Frankel's wife suddenly being transferred to Seattle, and a letter of inquiry arriving on his desk on the very heels of poor Duffy's funeral. He had just lost a history teacher, and here was a history teacher for the grabbing. After a brief but thorough examination of Frankel's credentials, the principal grabbed. His reward was that Frankel had been able to slip right into Duffy's place, almost without missing a beat.

Huxley was fifty-eight years old, of considerable size, with small brown eyes that tended to get lost in folds of fat when he smiled, and bushy hair that was now more gray than brown. He came from Enumclaw, just east of Tacoma, had gotten his education at Washington State University, and had spent his entire professional life on Seward Island, first as a math teacher for twelve years, and then as assistant principal for seven years before being appointed principal. In all that time, he had never come across a teacher of Jerry Frankel's caliber.

From the start of last year's second semester, through the summer session and right into the fall quarter, the new teacher's performance had been an unqualified success. Somehow, he had managed to arouse a level of enthusiasm for history that the small community had never before enjoyed—an enthusiasm that was now beginning to spill over into other subjects.

"How do you do it?" the principal asked.

The teacher shrugged. "There's no real secret," he replied. "I just try to show the kids that education isn't just some bad-tasting medicine that adults make you swallow in order to matriculate. And that history isn't something old and dry and dead—but something that's living right here with us, influencing everything we do. Once they understand that they're creating history themselves every single day, they begin to realize how important it is to learn from other people's successes and failures."

Truancy in the history teacher's classes dropped to an all-time low. Test scores were on the rise. Frankel had set up an after-school chat room, so to speak, where his students could drop in for help with homework, to participate in informal study groups, or to discuss any of a number of far-reaching topics within the teacher's purview. He was having so much success with this approach that other members of the staff had begun to think about following suit. Despite his brief tenure, Frankel was already being acknowledged by his colleagues as an excellent addition to the school, and an innovator. And Jordan Huxley was getting the credit.

A natural-born leader, the principal thought to himself, dismissing out of hand all those ridiculous rumors about the Breckenridge murder; a leader that might be able to help him with a very sticky problem.

It was no secret that Frankel was Jewish. It didn't matter to Huxley. All he cared about was the quality of a man's work, not the salvation of his soul. But now there was a serious effort afoot to cancel the annual Christmas pageant at the last moment—a pageant that had been held at Seward High School for as long as the principal could remember. In front of him, laid out on a massive polished mahogany desk—his one extravagance after thirty-five years—was a formal petition that contained several hundred names, including the majority of the Island's Jewish residents. To be honest, Huxley hadn't realized there were that many of them.

There had been some grumbling about the pageant, off and on for the last five years or so, but this was the first time any official protest had been lodged. Huxley had two options: he could kick the petition up to the school board and step out of the loop, or he could try to diffuse the situation himself. Not a man to pass the buck, he chose the second option. And he intended to start with the man who was just coming into the front office.

Jerry Frankel knew it was only a matter of time before his effectiveness as a teacher at Seward High School would be compromised. There had been whispers flying around the corridors for the past two days, curious glances, sudden gasps. In class, the students seemed to be studying *him* more than his subject. During the breaks, his colleagues went out of their way to offer support, without really saying what it was they were being supportive about. It was humiliating.

And now this abrupt summons from Huxley: *May I see you after school*, the note delivered during the last period said, and it was not a question.

After everything else, Jerry concluded such a summons could mean only one thing: that his presence at the school had become too disruptive.

"Don't just stand there, my boy, come, come," Huxley beckoned genially, waving Jerry into the private office, and then taking the time to close the door firmly behind him.

At that, Jerry's stomach sank to his feet.

"Sit down," the principal invited, moving back behind his buttress of a desk.

The history teacher sat on the edge of his chair and waited, wondering what form the suspension would take.

"I'm going to come right out and say it," Huxley began. "I need your help."

So his tactic was going to be to ask for a voluntary resignation, Jerry thought. Never mind a suspension and what could be a lengthy and messy investigation—just cut the cancer out, neat and clean. He clenched his teeth.

"You see," Huxley continued, "I've got this petition here, signed by a whole lot of people, and I don't exactly know what to make of it."

Jerry frowned around his clenched teeth, and wondered how a petition about him could possibly have been produced so quickly. Granted this was a small island, and the local newspaper had been eager to jump on his case, but it was hardly more than a weekend since his conversation with Ginger Earley, and only yesterday that he had officially declined to submit to her tests.

"And seeing as it's got your signature on it," Huxley went on. "I was hoping to get your thoughts on the matter."

Jerry looked at the man blankly. What was he talking about? He certainly hadn't had anything to do with signing something that demanded his own dismissal.

"The petition," the principal prompted. "The one I have sitting right here on my desk from all you people who want us to cancel the annual Christmas pageant."

Jerry fell back against his chair in relief. "I thought you were . . . I thought this was . . . well, you know, I thought this meeting was because of the rumors," he stammered.

Now it was Huxley's turn to look blank. "Rumors?" he asked. "What rumors? I'm not talking about rumors, I'm talking about a school tradition here."

Jerry shook his head as though to clear it. "Excuse me," he said. "It's been a rough day. Now, what about the pageant?"

"Well, that's what I was asking you," the principal replied. "You want us to cancel something we've been doing for decades. I want to know why."

"I guess maybe it's because there are enough people now living on the Island who feel that the way it's structured is no longer appropriate," Jerry said.

"But it's just a pageant," Huxley argued. "A nativity reenactment, some recitations, a little dancing, a few songs. Something to get the kids involved. They've been working on it for over a month. What's the harm in it?"

"All the kids, or just some of the kids?" Jerry asked. "Does it include reenactments from all the major religions—or just one?"

"Well, it certainly represents the overwhelming majority of the people on this island, and we do still live in a democracy, don't we?"

"Mr. Huxley, I'm a history teacher," Jerry said slowly, thoughtfully. "A Jewish history teacher. Perhaps that gives me a somewhat different perspective on things, but I don't happen to believe that majority rule should be thought of as synonymous with exclusionary rule."

The little brown eyes blinked between their folds of fat. "So you think the minority should win?"

"If you put it that way, the minority has already won," Jerry replied with a shrug. "It's in the Constitution. But in this case, why can't everyone win?"

"What do you mean?"

"This is a school, isn't it? A place to learn? So why not use the pageant to educate as well as entertain? You can keep your nativity reenactment, but add a skit about Hanukkah and maybe sing a Jewish song or perform a Jewish folk dance. And do the same thing for Ramadan."

"Ramadan, eh?" Huxley mumbled. He hadn't the faintest idea what that was, couldn't remember ever even hearing the word before, but he wasn't about to tell Frankel that.

"Also, I understand we've had a significant Buddhist population here for generations, so why not celebrate some of their traditions?" Jerry added. "And any other religion practiced on the Island. It certainly can't hurt any of our children to learn about the culture and customs of people who are different from themselves. On the contrary, knowledge is always the first line of defense against intolerance."

Jordan Huxley smiled broadly. "Damn if you haven't got a first-rate idea there," he declared. "Don't know why I didn't think of it myself. The pageant's not for a couple of weeks yet. There's still time to make a few little changes. I'll run it past the committee first thing tomorrow, and we'll see how it flies." The principal stood up and came around the desk with an outstretched hand. "I'm pleased you took the time to come in and see me, real pleased. I knew you were the right fellow to talk to."

Jerry took the hand and felt his shoulder almost come out of its socket. "I was happy to help," he murmured as he was ushered out the door.

Martin Keller answered the door himself. "Yes, may I help you?" he asked.

He was a short man, dressed in a dark brown business suit

that befitted his job as senior bookkeeper for a Seattle hospital. It was impeccably shaped to his compact figure, and he wore it with a starched white shirt and a paisley bow tie. A matching handkerchief peeked out of his breast pocket. His brown shoes were polished to a mirror shine. He looked to be somewhere in his early fifties. He had a small mustache and thin hair of a nondescript color, and his eyes, behind gold-rimmed spectacles, were a faded blue.

Ginger pulled out her identification. "I'm Detective Virginia Earley from the Seward Island Police Department," she said, looking down at him from a two-inch advantage. "If I'm not interrupting your dinner, I'd like to ask you a few questions."

"A few questions?" he repeated in a voice that was somewhat high-pitched. "About what?"

Ginger looked around. "About the neighborhood," she replied.

"I don't discuss my neighbors," the man said. He started to close the door.

"It's very important, sir, or I wouldn't be here. It's about the Breckenridge murder."

Martin Keller peered at her through his spectacles. "All right," he said after a moment, and stepped aside to let her enter. He led her across the foyer, a large, high-ceilinged space defeated by dark, gloomy wallpaper, and into the living room.

Like photographs snapping, Ginger absorbed it all in a series of glances. The room was uninspired, decorated in musty browns and rusts and drab earth tones. The furniture was old and ungainly, the scattered rugs well worn and almost colorless. Even the draperies were dull and heavy. Practical was the word that popped into Ginger's head. Little dirt would show in this room; little light would shine in it, as well. The one aesthetic note was a corner curio cabinet that housed an extensive collection of Meissen.

"My wife's," Keller said as if reading her mind. "Left to her by her grandmother."

"Lovely," she murmured.

"Sit down, Detective," he invited, gesturing to two wing chairs drawn up before a neat fire. A well-used book with no jacket lay open on the chair he took for himself. Keller picked it up and closed it as he sat down, and then casually dropped it onto the floor behind him. "I don't believe I know anything about the Breckenridge case," he said. "But I'm curious to know why you think I do."

Ginger sat down opposite him and wondered what it was about him that made her so uncomfortable. He seemed such a harmless little man, and he was being perfectly polite, even gracious. But something about him made her spine twitch. As a matter of course, she was used to taking charge of such conversations, yet she had the distinct impression that he was the one in control; that he was taking her measure even more carefully than she was taking his, analyzing her with those washed-out eyes as intently as a scientist would study a specimen under a microscope.

"We generally get a great many tips from people during an investigation such as this," she began. "And no matter how farfetched they might sound, we're obliged to check them all out."

"That seems prudent," he said.

"We've been given some information that concerns one of your neighbors, and we're trying to determine whether it has any merit."

"Which neighbor?" Martin Keller asked.

"Jerry Frankel," Ginger replied.

The washed-out eyes fixed on her for a full ten seconds before he spoke. "The Frankels live right next door, as I'm sure you already know," he said. "They purchased the house about a year ago. They keep their lawn mowed, they do not have loud parties, and as far as I can determine, they are law-abiding."

At that moment, a boy of eleven or twelve came skidding into the room, perhaps for the purpose of having a word with his father.

"Justin, we do not slide on your mother's floors, and we do not enter a room without permission," Keller said sternly.

The boy, seemingly taken by surprise to see a stranger seated by the fire, blinked several times behind his round eyeglasses, and then darted out without a sound.

"Children," Keller murmured with a sigh. "I apologize for my son's lapse in manners."

"Do you know them well?" Ginger asked, returning to the purpose of her visit.

"Who?"

"The Frankels."

"I don't know them at all," Keller corrected her. "My wife and son and I are very private people, Detective Earley. We don't intrude on others, and by example we expect others not to intrude on us."

"But is it possible," Ginger persisted, "that, without intruding, you may have seen or heard something that might now help us either to include or to exclude Mr. Frankel from our investigation? In particular, on the night of Tara Breckenridge's death?"

Again, there was a contemplative silence.

"I'm sorry to disappoint you," Martin Keller said at last. "But I saw nothing and I heard nothing."

A moment later, Ginger stood in the Keller driveway and looked across at the Frankel house. Lights burned brightly from the windows, spilling out into the chill evening. A boy called out; a dog barked. The family was obviously at home, going about the business of living. It looked just like any of the houses on Seward Island—friendly and inviting.

This had been her last shot. She had interviewed all seven of the teacher's nearest neighbors and learned nothing. The night of the murder, none of them could recall seeing or hearing anything out of the ordinary. As far as anybody knew, Jerry Frankel was a great guy, a fantastic teacher, and a genuine asset to the community.

Ginger sighed. It was almost eight o'clock, she was tired and hungry, and she couldn't think of anything else to do. She got behind the wheel of her car and drove away.

From the slimmest of cracks between the heavy living room draperies, Martin Keller watched her go.

"You don't really think Mr. Frankel murdered Tara, do you?" Stacey asked her father.

"What makes you ask?" Ruben countered.

"Because of what Kristen said," she told him. "It's all over school, you know, that Kristen talked to me, and then I took her to talk to Ginger, and then right away Ginger went back to talk to him. And now, a lot of the kids are going around saying he's the killer."

"Small towns," he said, shaking his head. "To answer your question—I don't know."

"I like Mr. Frankel, Dad," Stacey said earnestly. "He's not just a good teacher. He really cares about the stuff he teaches us, and I think he cares about us, too. He's really into his head a lot, and he knows so much about what makes people tick, from a thousand years ago right up to yesterday. I don't see him as a hothead. I see him as the kind of person like you want *me* to be— one who would think his way out of a problem before he'd act his way out of it. Maybe he was fond of Tara, but I don't believe he could have killed her."

"What do you mean, he was fond of her?"

"Well, I've been thinking about it," the teenager said. "And it's possible that he might have treated her a little differently than he treated the rest of us."

o   o   o

This time there was an angry debate during the basement meeting, snatches of conversation rising well above the usual muted pitch.

". . . never have a better opportunity," declared one.

". . . as subtle as a sledgehammer," scoffed another.

". . . a real chance of exposure here," cautioned a third.

". . . can't risk being identified," warned a fourth.

"Cowards," sneered the first.

"Enough," the acknowledged leader said in a soft but firm voice. "This kind of bickering is getting us nowhere. Let's keep focused."

The men looked at one another. There was a purpose to this meeting, they knew; options to be discussed, a decision to be reached, a plan of action to be devised. All of them had the same objective, personalities notwithstanding. Each took a deep breath and then they began again.

An hour and a half later, the leader rose. "All right, are we agreed?" he asked.

One by one, the men nodded.

7

Gail Brown sat curled on a wicker couch in the living room of her beachfront cottage, which sat at the very edge of North Point, absently tugging at her ponytail. A forgotten cup of tea was balanced on the cushion beside her.

Beyond her window, Mount Baker loomed like a ghost in a clear blue sky. The winter rains were now two months late, and meteorologists, who for weeks had been predicting fronts that never materialized, were beginning to tiptoe around the possibility of a drought.

There was nothing quite like the beauty of the Pacific Northwest on a fine day, but the editor's brown eyes behind the thick glasses stared out at nothing.

Although she was perfectly all right, Gail had called in sick this morning, in the middle of a workweek, a thing she had never done before in her entire professional life. But she had a decision to make, and she needed some distance from the office and her staff in order to make it.

At the heart of it, Gail was a person divided, and being tugged in both directions. The side of her that loved Seward Island and everything it represented was centered in her very marrow and could never be denied. This was not just the place where her family had lived for almost eighty years, or where she had been born and raised. This was her safe haven in an increasingly turbulent world, the one place she knew where she felt unconditionally accepted. There had never been any doubt in her mind, despite electing to go east for her education and experience, that she would come back. It was why she had gone away—to gain the skills she would need to return and succeed.

The little house in which she now lived had been left to her by her grandmother. The old woman had called it her "hut of humble thoughts"; the refuge where she had come whenever she needed to be alone to sort out a problem; the sanctuary where she had insisted on spending her final few months.

Gail felt much as her grandmother had about the rustic cottage perched on Seward's northeasternmost tip, providing as it did a spectacular panorama of Puget Sound from the vantage point of being able to see but not be seen. It was both her window on the world and her preserve of private counsel.

The pull of the Island had cost Gail her marriage. She could not understand why anyone would not want to live on an isolated rock in the middle of nowhere with only a water connection to the rest of civilization; he could not understand why anyone would. He wanted the kind of excitement that only a big-city newspaper could provide, and Seattle apparently wasn't big enough. They left Boston together: he heading for Chicago, she heading for home. She loved him, but she loved the Island more.

That was one side of Gail Brown—the side that would protect this place and these people with her last drop of blood, her final spurt of energy, her one remaining breath.

The other side was the part of her that was smart and determined and totally devoted to her profession. She believed in the Bill of Rights every bit as much as she believed in the Ten Commandments. She was convinced of the people's right to know, and committed to the First Amendment as the only true safeguard of the nation. And for her dedication to that principle, she craved the recognition and respect of her peers.

It never occurred to Gail that the day might come when one side of her would be in serious conflict with the other. But it was two months since the murder of Tara Breckenridge, and notwithstanding the editor's exhaustive efforts to be the conscience of the community, or to put it less charitably, her resolve to milk every ounce of revenue from the story, very little headway had been made in the case. Of course, this was both a plus and a minus. While public confidence was way down, the newspaper's sales were way up—an irony that did not escape her.

The question she now had to answer was—how much further was she willing to go? How thin was she willing to stretch the rules? How narrow was the line she was about to walk?

Although the *Sentinel* had been careful not to identify him by name, Gail knew it was Jerry Frankel who had been the most recent focus of Ginger Earley's attention, and it was likely that, by now, a significant part of Seward knew it, too. The editor could just imagine the conversations taking place in the aisles at the Island Market and under the dryers at Wanda's Hairworks.

She picked up the letter for the hundredth time, and with some measure of cynicism, wondered what people would be saying if they knew about this.

It was typewritten, on plain white paper, and had come with no signature and no return address. Bearing a Seattle postmark, it had been sent, not to the office, but to her home. Under ordinary circumstances, Gail would have dismissed such a letter out of hand. But these were not ordinary circumstances, and she gave in to the little pump of adrenaline that told her this might not be the time to get hung up on ethics.

As a matter of journalistic policy, anonymous letters were never printed in the *Sentinel*. In fact, Gail made a point of personally contacting the author of each letter before it was published to confirm the opinions expressed. Yet there was something about this particular one that could not be dismissed.

Had anyone else received it, he or she would probably have turned it directly over to the police, and let them deal with it. Only Gail Brown was not anyone else. Her hometown ties notwithstanding, she was the ambitious editor of a small daily newspaper that had yet to make its mark, a critical factor that played a part in every decision she made.

On the one hand, she held herself and the *Sentinel* to the highest standards of journalistic integrity. On the other hand, a letter like this, with what it imported, could be the key to breaking the Island's first homicide case wide open, and she was enough of a professional—all right, egoist—to want a piece of the action for herself.

For whatever reason, she had been made part of the equation. In the wake of Malcom Purdy's bizarre offer, the letter had come to her. That gave her an absolute right to use it to her best advantage. The question was—how?

She had never met Jerry Frankel. She had, however, spoken at some length to Jordan Huxley, as well as a couple of dozen assorted teachers, students, and parents. Frankel got top marks from all of them.

"He's a remarkable teacher," said a colleague who taught science.

"He has definitely raised the standards at Seward High School," said another who also taught history.

"He has a true gift," said one of the English teachers.

"He makes learning fun," said a student.

"I like going to his class every day," said another. "All those boring dates of battles and stuff we used to have to memorize— they make sense to me now."

"My son used to be a D student in history," said a parent. "Now he earns As, and he's talking abut majoring in history when he goes to college."

Clearly, Jerry Frankel was a significant asset to the Island. Whatever the subject, Gail knew that a teacher who could inspire his pupils as this one obviously had was a rare commodity in this age of undereducation.

Still, there was the letter. The editor leaned back against the sofa pillows and took a sip of cold tea. With the instincts of a barracuda, she understood its potential value for an obscure newspaper. In fact, she was already envisioning a whole series of articles that would cast the *Sentinel* in the role of mentor to the police. A series that would not only serve to further the investigation, but might aid authorities in the actual capturing of the killer. A series that would give her little newspaper the national recognition she craved. Perhaps, she let herself dream, the kind of recognition that would lead to a Pulitzer.

It was the ultimate dream of every journalist. Just thinking the word sent chills down Gail's back. Despite what she knew her actions might do to the tranquil community she so cherished, it was an opportunity she was not sure she could pass up. The rationalization was easy. What was more important? she debated with herself. To protect a teacher, highly regarded though he may be, educational benefactor though he may be— or to rid Seward Island of a dangerous killer? Besides, there was always the chance that the whole thing was a fool's errand, and would come to nothing.

Put that way, her decision was clear. She picked up the telephone and dialed the number of her travel agent. As it began to ring, she glanced at the letter one more time.

"To the editor:" it read. "Better late than never for the police to get around to a certain history teacher at the high school. If anyone is really interested in solving the Breckenridge case, they should be talking to the people at the Holman Academy in Scarsdale, New York."

8

"I've had over a hundred calls so far," Glen Dirksen reported on Wednesday afternoon. "And more are coming in every day. I've followed up on about two dozen. There's just nothing there."

"Well, we knew it was a slim chance at best," Ruben told him. "But don't give up."

The young officer shook his head. "There was a call from one guy who said he wasn't interested in the money, only in justice. Wouldn't even give his name. All he said was: 'Where there's dirt, there's dirty doings,' and hung up."

"Sounds like one of our Island whackos," Charlie Pricker told him.

"Or an environmentalist," Ginger quipped.

"Hey, Stacey, wait up," Danny Leo called, catching her as she was leaving the high school campus.

The police chief's daughter stopped. "Hi, Danny," she said. "I know I'm a little late with the girls' basketball story. I'll have it in by tomorrow."

"That's okay," he said. "It's not about that." There was an awkward pause. "Look, could I, uh, talk to you about something?"

"Sure."

Danny had gold-flecked brown hair and thickly lashed green eyes that most of the girls at school openly drooled over. Right now, they were fastened on something around the tip of his Reeboks. In the year and a half that Stacey had worked with him on the school paper, she had seen him angry, excited, confused, and even embarrassed, but she had never seen him at a loss for words.

"I guess you know all about me," he said finally. "I mean, your father must have told you about me and Tara."

"Actually, Danny, I was the one who told him," Stacey replied. "I saw the two of you together one time. I'm sorry."

"Yeah, well, that's okay," he said. "I should've been up front about it myself. Anyway, I'm in this kind of jam, and I wondered if maybe you could help me out."

"What kind of jam?"

"Well, you see, Detective Earley got this court order to take a sample of my blood. My dad tried to fight it, but he lost so I have to go to the clinic. But the results of the test won't come back for at least two months, and meanwhile it's screwing up my scholarship to Harvard. Going to Harvard is real important to me, and I swear I didn't have anything to do with Tara's death, and I thought, if I could take the polygraph test, the results of that would be in, like right away, and then everyone would know, and I'd be off the hook."

"Well, if you want to do that, I'm sure all you have to do is go in and see Ginger Earley."

"If my dad found out, he would kill me," Danny said. "He's so hung up on his principles, he doesn't understand it's my life he's messing around with. And I'm afraid he could get himself in a lot of trouble over this. I want to take the polygraph, but I don't want him to know about it until it's done. Do you think you could talk to your dad and see if something could be arranged?"

"I'll talk to him," Stacey promised.

◦ ◦ ◦

"I was happy three years ago when the city council hired Ruben Martinez," a local businessman wrote to the editor. "I knew it was only a matter of time before the rest of the world began to slip across the water, and change our idyllic island for the worse. I read about Ruben's twenty-five years of law enforcement experience, and I felt he was the right man to meet those changes head-on, and deal with them. Now it's been two months since Tara Breckenridge was murdered, and I'm not so sure anymore."

"What do our police do all day?" asked a housewife. "All I see them doing is issuing parking tickets, lying in wait for traffic violators, and assisting elderly people across the street. These are all noble endeavors, to be sure, but Chief Martinez says everyone in his department is working on the Breckenridge case. Do they really think the killer is parking too close to a fire hydrant, or speeding down Center Island Road, or eighty years old and feeble?"

"Ruben, we have a problem," Albert Hoch declared, his voice carrying easily from the police chief's office, despite the closed door. "It's been two months, and you're no closer to solving this murder than you were on the day it happened."

It was Wednesday evening. The police chief, after having a conversation with his daughter, had just arranged for Danny Leo to take a polygraph test. He was getting ready to head for home when the mayor appeared.

"Some things take time," he told Hoch calmly.

"Time? How much time? The more time goes by, the colder the trail gets. You've got Danny Leo giving blood. What about the teacher?"

"We've come up with no evidence that he has any involvement in the case."

"Is there anyone else?"

"Not at the moment."

Hoch sighed heavily. "Three years ago, I went out on a limb for you. A lot of people around here didn't exactly think you were the right man for the job, but I told them you were, that you had the experience we needed. And now look what happens: the first major crime to come along, and you're spinning your wheels like an amateur."

From her office down the hall, Ginger grit her teeth. It wasn't fair. If the mayor wanted to blame someone for the lack of results, he should have come to see her. After all, she was the one running the investigation. If nothing was happening, it was her fault.

"Some cases don't solve easy," she heard Ruben say. "I was hoping this one would, but it hasn't. And unless we're willing to suspend all civil rights, and haul every man on Seward Island down here for mandatory blood and polygraph tests, we're just going to have to rely on something breaking for us."

"How much longer do you think we can wait?"

"As long as we have to, I guess."

"Dammit, Ruben, that's not good enough."

"If you think another man can do a better job," came the response, "that's certainly your decision to make."

Ginger gasped. She couldn't believe that Albert Hoch could really be talking about firing Ruben. Not now. Not when they had finally found each other.

"People are pounding on my door," the mayor said. "They want action. They want to know why our esteemed police force can't seem to solve a simple crime. What am I supposed to tell them?"

"Tell them that Seward Island has a department filled with dedicated professionals whose top priority is the well-being of this community," Ruben replied

Albert Hoch was a glad-hander, not a backhander. He

sighed. "The city council isn't happy," he said. "Frankly, I don't know how much longer I can hold them off."

"My name is Heidi Tannauer," the voice on the telephone said.

"Yes, ma'am," Officer Dirksen replied, stifling a yawn. "How can I help you?"

"I'm a freshman at Northwestern University," she said. "I didn't know anything about the Breckenridge case until I came home for Thanksgiving. But now my parents tell me you think a teacher may be involved?"

Dirksen suddenly sat up in his seat. "I'm sorry, ma'am, but that's not something I'm at liberty to discuss at this time," he said.

"Well, I don't know if this has anything to do with that," Heidi continued, "but I had to take a makeup class in summer school last year, and I distinctly remember seeing Tara several times after school hours with one of the teachers."

"Do you happen to recall which teacher?" the officer asked casually.

"I don't remember his name," Heidi replied, "but I'm pretty sure he was the new history teacher."

9

The telephone was ringing. Jerry Frankel shifted the bag of groceries he was carrying from his left arm to his right and inserted the key into the lock on the back door of his house. He dropped the groceries on the kitchen counter and reached for the receiver.

"Mr. Frankel, this is Detective Earley," the voice at the other end said. "I wonder if you'd be kind enough to come in and see me tomorrow after school."

Jerry sighed. The curious stares and whispers were still following him. And it wasn't confined to the school anymore, but everywhere he went. He had thought, or perhaps hoped, that all the curiosity and speculation would have died down by this time, but it hadn't. Rather, it seemed to be the opposite. Just a few moments ago, two women in line at the Island Market abruptly stopped talking the moment he approached the checkout counter.

"What is it now, Detective?" he asked.

"Well, I really don't want to go into it over the telephone," Ginger replied. "There's something we need to discuss, and it would be better if you'd come in." There was the slightest of pauses. "You're certainly free to bring your attorney, if you like," she added.

"Do you really think that's necessary?"

"It's entirely up to you," she said. "Whatever would make you most comfortable. Shall we say four o'clock?"

"Four o'clock," he repeated dully.

Jerry hung up the receiver and turned automatically to put away the groceries, slipping the jar of peanut butter into the refrigerator and setting the carton of milk on the pantry shelf before he realized what he was doing.

He reached Scott Cohen at his office.

"Are they going to charge you with anything?" the lawyer asked.

"I don't know what they're going to do," Jerry replied. "She said she wanted to talk. She said I could bring you with me."

Scott paused. "Well, it doesn't sound like you're in imminent danger of arrest," he said finally, "but she's putting you on notice that this is more than just a friendly chat. So hold on a minute while I check my schedule."

Jerry waited while the lawyer went off to scan his appointment book and speak to his secretary. His head ached and his brain felt like mush; he couldn't think straight. He wanted Scott to think for him.

"I can meet you there at four o'clock," Scott said, coming back on the line.

"Do you think it will look bad," Jerry asked, "that I'm bringing my lawyer with me?"

"At this point," Scott said bluntly, "that's the last thing you should be worried about."

They gathered in the windowless interview room, the detective on one side of the rectangular metal table, the teacher and his attorney on the other. It was apparently going to be just a conversation; there was no stenographer present, no tape recorder in sight.

"The reason I've asked you to come in, Mr. Frankel," Ginger began, "is because I find myself with so many coincidences here that I feel perhaps you haven't been totally candid with me."

"What sort of coincidences, Detective Earley?" Scott inquired.

"Let's begin with the ones Mr. Frankel and I have already discussed," Ginger said to the attorney. "The fact that a dark-colored Taurus station wagon was seen in Madrona Point Park on the night of the murder, and your client drives such a car; the fact that your client lacks a corroborating alibi for the time of the murder; the fact that your client was one of the victim's teachers, and thereby known by him; and the fact that he was seen with her shortly before her death in what could clearly be construed as compromising circumstances. Now add to that a new report that he was seen alone with Tara several times after school during the summer session. And finally, a piece of information that we have not yet released to the public—the fact that we believe our killer is left-handed, and so is your client. Granted that all this is purely circumstantial, but it does seem to suggest that your client may be more involved in this case than he's told us."

"But I'm not," Jerry interjected.

Scott laid a hand on his client's arm. "Detective Earley, my client has already told you that he was home on the night of the murder. You checked his car and found nothing. I sincerely doubt that he is the only left-handed man who knew Tara Breckenridge. And I could probably find any number of people who were seen alone with the victim prior to her death; such as Danny Leo, such as our esteemed Mayor Albert Hoch, such as Magnus Coop—all of whom, by the way, happen to be left-handed. So since you have nothing that even remotely connects my client to the commission of any crime, I don't see what the purpose of this conversation is, other than harassment."

"Mr. Cohen, I'm not naive," Ginger said. "I'm in no position to charge Mr. Frankel with anything. If I were, I would be standing on his doorstep with a warrant. But I have a brutal murder case to solve, and an intuition that tells me your client is either connected in some way or knows something that could help us. It's not my intention to embarrass him or harass him. I'm just trying to do my job."

"What exactly do you think he knows?"

Ginger looked directly at Jerry. "I think you had something more than just a teacher-student relationship with Tara Breckenridge," she said. "I think, even if you didn't kill her yourself, you know something—whether you realize it or not—that could lead us to the person who did."

Jerry looked at his attorney.

"Would you excuse us for a few moments, Detective?" Scott requested. "I'd like to talk with my client."

"Certainly." Ginger stood up without hesitation and left the room, closing the door behind her.

"How is it going?" Ruben asked.

Ginger shrugged. "They're having a powwow," she said.

Ten minutes later, Scott opened the door. "Would you please come in, Detective Earley. My client would like to make a statement."

"You mean, on the record?" Ginger asked.

Scott glanced at Frankel. "I don't see why not," he replied.

A tape recorder was brought in and set up in a matter of minutes.

"I'd like to have Chief Martinez present, if that's all right with you," Ginger said.

Scott nodded. Ruben entered the room and took a seat beside Ginger. The detective pushed the red button on the recorder and spoke into the microphone.

"This is a voluntary statement being made by Mr. Jeremy Frankel in the presence of his attorney, Mr. Scott Cohen, Chief of Police Ruben Martinez, and Detective Virginia Earley."

She pushed the microphone across the table. The teacher sat up in his chair and cleared his throat.

"Let me say, right from the start, that I had nothing to do with the death of Tara Breckenridge," he said. "I did know her, and we developed a relationship that may have extended, but never ever exceeded, the boundaries of a normal teacher-student relationship." He paused for a moment. "There was something about her that I noticed from the first days of summer school— a kind of melancholy is the best way I can describe it—that clearly went a lot deeper than just the boredom or the embarrassment of having to make up classes. On top of that, she seemed to be far brighter than her grades indicated, which got me curious. I wanted to find out what the problem was and help her work through it, if I could. I might have paid more attention to her than I did some of the other students, because I was trying to get a dialogue going with her, trying to build a rapport. As usually happens when a teacher takes an interest in a student, she responded. Her grades started to improve. I thought that was a good sign, and I acknowledged it. She began to come out of her shell and talk to me—that rapport I mentioned. I've always found that kids who are relaxed absorb more, and sure enough, her grades got better. I saw no harm in that. If she sought me out after school, I didn't turn her off. If I saw her between classes, I was friendly. If she came in for extra help, I gave it to her. I'm in the business of educating, Detective Earley—of opening minds—and different students need different approaches. I was nice to her, I encouraged her, and my efforts paid off. She worked hard and earned an excellent grade, and that was all there was to it."

He stopped. Ginger waited until she was sure he was not going to continue before she leaned toward the microphone.

"You say you and Tara had a rapport, Mr. Frankel," she said. "You say she came out of her shell. What did she talk about?"

Jerry took a moment to think. "Mostly about growing up,"

he said. "She talked about her family. She said she wished she had been a boy instead of a girl."

"Did she say why?"

"I think it had something to do with her father—that she didn't feel she could live up to his expectations. He apparently wanted her to go to a top university and have an important career, but she really wasn't interested in that. She thought he would have been happier with a son."

"Did she say what she wanted out of life?"

"She talked once about becoming a nun," he said.

"I beg your pardon?"

"She said she wanted to be a nun," he repeated. "But she was afraid God wouldn't want her."

Although the Breckenridge family worshiped at Seward Episcopal, Ginger knew that Mary Breckenridge had been raised a Catholic. "Did Tara say why she thought God wouldn't want her?"

"She said it was because she wasn't good enough. That God chose only the best people to serve Him."

"The daughter of the Island's most prestigious family, and she didn't think she was good enough to be a nun?"

Jerry shrugged. "Sometimes, Detective Earley, self-esteem has little to do with wealth or position or even beauty," he said softly. "During the time that I knew her, Tara was a very troubled girl."

"Did she ever talk to you about being involved with someone—a boy, a man?"

The teacher's eyes narrowed as if in thought. "I don't recall that she did," he said.

"Are you sure?" Ginger pressed. "Obviously, you can appreciate how important this is."

"I'm sorry. She never said. Even that day in the back hall that you asked me about. All I can recall is what I told you—she said something very general about how awful her whole life was.

I think her actual words were 'a total disaster.' But kids are always saying things like that and I didn't take it very seriously. I'm sorry now that I didn't. But she never mentioned anyone by name."

"And your own relationship with Tara—are you stating here for the record that it was strictly professional and never sexual?"

Jerry glared at the detective. "What's the matter with you?" he demanded. "She was a child, for God's sake. Just a child."

"Can I borrow the car Saturday night?" Danny Leo asked.

"What for, son?" Peter inquired.

"I'm taking a girl to the movies."

"How nice, dear," Rose said. "Of course you can have the car."

While he was one of the most popular teenagers on Seward Island, Danny dated only occasionally, preferring, in the current local fashion, to socialize with friends in groups.

"What girl?" Peter asked.

Danny took a breath. "Stacey Martinez," he replied.

Peter looked surprised. "The police chief's daughter? Why would you want to date the police chief's daughter?"

"I know her from the school paper, and I like her."

"You know a lot of people. Why this one?"

Danny shrugged. "I'd like to get to know her better."

"Isn't she a little young for you?"

"She's pretty mature for a sophomore."

Peter contemplated the boy. "She's also the police chief's daughter," he said. "I'd be very careful, if I were you."

"It's just a movie, Dad."

"I don't care what you say," Libby Hildress told her husband as they were getting ready for bed. "Something's not right."

"About what?" Tom asked, knowing full well what it would be about.

"I was talking to Judy Parker at choir practice tonight. She told me that Mildred MacDonald told her she saw Jerry Frankel and Scott Cohen going into the police station this afternoon. Now why would he need a lawyer?"

"Scott's also his friend," Tom reminded her.

"Do people normally take their friends with them when they go talk to the police?"

10

If Gail Brown had thought to prioritize all the things she wanted to do in the middle of December, going to Scarsdale, New York, would not even have been on her list. Yet here she was, driving her rental car from Kennedy Airport up the Hutchinson River Parkway, in the dark, through a dense freezing rain.

She had called the Holman Academy before confirming her plane reservations, and was told that, while the school was officially closed on weekends, one or two members of the staff were usually around. Which suited Gail just fine. The fewer people who knew why she had come flying all the way across the country, the better.

From her earliest days as a reporter, Gail had always preferred to slip into a situation, rather than jump into it. That way, she found she offended fewer people and embarrassed herself less often. Such an approach was especially prudent here, where she really wasn't sure what she was looking for.

The anonymous letter may have set off alarm bells and propelled her into this cross-country odyssey, but there were no specifics contained in it, just the cryptic charge. For all she knew, she could be on a wild goose chase.

Gail found the inn her travel agent had booked for her, a quaint little gabled structure adjacent to a friendly-looking restaurant. She checked in, unpacked a few things, and headed for food. The restaurant was doing a brisk business, always a good sign.

"What'll you have," the waitress asked, when she finally made it to Gail's table. The woman looked to be about fifty, with thin brown hair and tired eyes. Her name tag identified her as Sally.

"What's good?" Gail asked.

Sally shrugged. "The stew's always good," she said. "Some of the regulars prefer the chicken. The pasta's fresh. The fish chowder's first-rate."

Gail looked at her. "What do *you* eat?"

The waitress smiled at that, and Gail realized she was a lot younger than she looked, and with a little makeup would have been quite pretty.

"I like the chowder," Sally said.

"The chowder it is, then," Gail ordered.

During all the years that the editor had spent on the East Coast, going to college and graduate school, working on various newspapers, she had never been to Scarsdale. But she knew that it was a fashionable town, with a reputation for having big money. She also knew that most of the people who lived in a town such as this would not be forthcoming with information, preferring instead to protect one another, and by so doing, protect themselves. In a wealthy community, Gail understood, there were always many more closets to hold skeletons.

"Are you here on business or pleasure?" Sally asked conversationally as she set the bowl of chowder, a plate of salad, and a basket of bread down in front of Gail.

"Business," the editor told her.

"Oh? What kind of business are you in?"

"I work for a newspaper," Gail replied.

"Really?" Sally said, because the skinny woman with the bushy ponytail and thick eyeglasses didn't fit the image. "One of those big-city reporters who are always looking to dig up dirt on other people?"

"Not exactly," came the response. "I'm an editor, not a reporter. And I work for a very small newspaper on the other side of the country."

"Oh," Sally murmured, apparently no longer interested.

"You sound disappointed," Gail said with a smile. "Why? Is there a lot of dirt to dig up in Scarsdale?"

The waitress shrugged. "We've got our share, I guess, just like any other town." She walked away before Gail could ask her anything more.

The chowder was as good as advertised, although Gail ate hardly any of it. She left a generous tip.

"For the recommendation as well as the service," she said as she paid her bill.

"Thanks," the woman said, tucking the bills into the pocket of her pink uniform.

Gail went back to her room at the inn and snapped on the television. There was nothing she could do tonight. In the morning, she would locate the Holman Academy.

"What's going on with your dad?" Billy Hildress asked Matthew. The two boys were playing a video game in Matthew's bedroom. Chase, the retriever pup, who was now fully housebroken and allowed the run of the house, sat watching their every move.

"What do you mean?" Matthew asked.

"Well, I don't know," Billy said, "but my mom says that people are saying your dad's got something to do with that body me and my dad found in the Dumpster."

Matthew stared at his friend. "*My* dad?" he replied. "Why would anyone think that?"

Billy shrugged. "I don't know, but it's what my mom heard. Did your dad know the dead girl?"

"Yeah. I think she was in one of his classes," Matthew conceded. "But that doesn't mean anything—he knows lots of kids."

"I gotta tell you," Billy admitted, "it's kinda creepy, having your best friend's dad being talked about like that."

Matthew frowned. Now that he thought of it, his mother had seemed out of sorts the past few days. He wondered if there were some connection.

"Say, Dad, why do people think you're involved in the murder?" he asked at dinner.

"Matthew!" his mother declared. "That's no question to ask your father. He's not responsible for what other people think."

"But Billy said something about it, and I didn't know what to tell him," the nine-year-old replied, not noticing that she hadn't taken exception to his question, only to his asking it.

"Tell Billy that the police have to investigate everyone who could possibly be connected to a crime," his father said. "It's their job. And one of the ways they solve crimes is to eliminate everyone that isn't involved in order to find the one who is. It just happens to be my turn to be eliminated."

That seemed to make sense. "I get it," Matthew said. "They make a list with everybody's name on it, and they keep crossing the names off until they're left with the last one—and that has to be the killer."

"Something like that," his father said.

The Holman Academy was located at the southern edge of Scarsdale, a three-story red-brick building in an upper-class neighborhood that had once been home to a banking magnate. The manager of the inn gave Gail directions, and she found the place easily. A high brick wall surrounded the grounds, just as he said it would. The iron gates stood open. The gravel parking lot that flanked the service wing was empty except for an old Ford pickup and a blue Oldsmobile sedan. It was exactly ten minutes past ten on Saturday morning when Gail pulled her rental up beside them.

It must have been a magnificent estate, she thought as she climbed out of the car and started around toward the front door. The freezing rain of last night had given way to a watery sunlight that set the whole landscape to shimmering. There were acres of lawns, massive elms, graceful maples, and enormous rhododendrons that looked impressive even out of season. Little paths meandered through vast flower beds. And down a little slope, off to one side, she caught a glimpse of a duck pond.

The front door was unlocked and Gail walked right in. The entry corridor was laid in big diamonds of black and white marble; the walls were paneled in rich mahogany. A small brass plaque mounted on the wall made it clear that this was indeed the Holman Academy, an institution of higher education for young women, established in 1943.

The clack of a typewriter came from an open door halfway down the corridor, and Gail followed the sound to a room that might once have been a small parlor but was clearly now an office.

A gray-haired woman was seated behind a vintage Smith-Corona; a plaque on the desk in front of her identified her as Mrs. Quinlan. "May I help you?" she asked, looking up with a bright smile.

"My name is Gail Brown," the editor replied, "and I'm hoping to get some information about a teacher who used to work here."

"Every teacher employed at the Holman Academy has been outstanding," Mrs. Quinlan said, as if by rote. "We're most particular, we have very stringent standards, and we can afford to pay for the highest quality. If you're looking for a reference, I'm sure we'll have no trouble providing you with one." She turned to a file cabinet. "Now which teacher was that?"

"Jeremy Frankel."

Did she imagine it, Gail wondered, or did the woman seem to hesitate for an instant? There was no overt change in her expression or her manner, but Gail was not a journalist for nothing.

Mrs. Quinlan opened the bottom drawer of a metal file cabinet and flipped through a row of folders, finally pulling one out. "Mr. Frankel was on staff here at the academy until January of last year," she said, reading from it. "He taught history. He was with us for six and a half years, and he was a very fine teacher." She replaced the folder and shut the drawer with a sharp click.

"This seems such an ideal place to work," Gail observed. "Can you tell me why he left?"

"Teachers come and teachers go," the woman said. "Now, if that's all, I'm really quite busy."

"I don't mean to bother you, Mrs. Quinlan, but I've come a long way," Gail said. "All the way across the country, as a matter of fact. It's extremely important that I find out why Mr. Frankel left the Holman Academy."

"I don't know what to say that would help you," the woman replied. "All I know is that he resigned in the middle of the school year. I couldn't say why. Why don't you ask *him* why he left?"

"Please understand that, if I could, I would." Gail carefully weighed what to say next. "You see, he currently teaches at the high school in the town where I live, and it's possible that he might be involved in a situation there that could be detrimental to the community. I was told that I could find out what I wanted to know here."

"I'm sorry," Mrs. Quinlan said, and now it seemed that her voice held a note of compassion. "I hope your situation resolves itself appropriately, but there really isn't anything more I can say. Our records are supposed to be confidential, and I've already told you more than I should have."

"Is there anyone else here who might be able to help me?" Gail asked.

Mrs. Quinlan shook her head. "The only other person here at the moment is one of our janitorial staff. He would hardly be in a position to tell you anything."

"Well, thank you for your time," Gail said.

She turned to leave the office and collided with a man wearing blue coveralls with the name "Ezekiel" stitched on the front pocket.

" 'Scuse me, ma'am," he exclaimed, looking embarrassed. "I sure didn't mean to get in your way like that."

"No, please, it was my fault," Gail said quickly. "I'm afraid I have a habit of not always looking where I'm going."

She turned down the corridor in the direction of the front door, but once there, with her hand on the knob, she looked back. Ezekiel was staring after her.

"I think I'll try the pasta tonight," Gail said to the waitress in the restaurant.

"Sure thing," Sally replied.

It was early, not yet six o'clock on a Saturday night, but the place was already more than half full. It was a testament, Gail decided, to modern America's continuing love of home cooking and dislike of cooking at home.

From the Holman Academy, she had gone directly to the local newspaper office, which was housed in the public library building on Olmstead Road, identified herself, and asked for help.

"We have a situation in my community that might involve a teacher who used to be out at the Holman Academy," she said. "I'm trying to determine if there's any connection. Can you give me a hand?"

"What exactly are you looking for?" a pretty redheaded clerk asked.

"Does the name Jerry Frankel ring a bell?"

There was a pause, a blank stare, and then a polite shake of her head. "Aside from graduation and honors stuff, we don't report much on the academy," Gail was told.

"Why not?"

"I guess because it's a private institution, and they go to great lengths to keep it that way."

"Why? What are they hiding?" The question was meant mostly in jest.

"Oh, I don't think they're trying to hide anything," the clerk was quick to reply. "I think it's more that they feel an obligation to protect their students. It's a pretty exclusive school. They've got a lot of rich kids up there, with prominent parents who probably wouldn't appreciate a lot of town gossip. I've been here six months, and we haven't reported a single thing about the academy in all that time."

"Do you think your editor would have any information?" Gail inquired, thinking she might get more from a peer.

The redhead shrugged. "He might, but he's not here. A death in the family. He won't be back until the end of next week."

Gail thanked the clerk, and being right there, stopped in at the library where she spent the afternoon poring over old issues of all of the area newspapers. She went back to the time when she knew Jerry Frankel had first come to the Holman Academy, and worked forward, searching for anything that might give her a clue, suggest someplace else to look, or even, for that matter, give her a hint about what it was she was looking for. There was nothing.

Finally she went to the police station.

"I'm looking into some allegations that were made about a teacher named Jeremy Frankel," she told the officer in charge, a short man with thinning dark hair and a shaggy mustache. "Do you know anything that might help me?"

"No, ma'am," Detective Derek McNally replied without the slightest hesitation. "I can't say as I do."

"Look," Gail said wearily. "I'm not after dirt, and I wouldn't be here if it weren't important. To be honest with you, I'm hoping I'm wrong, that there's absolutely nothing to the allegations. But I have to find out."

"I don't know what I can tell you," he said.

"Did you know Frankel?" she asked.

He shook his head. "No, I didn't. But that's not so unusual. A lot of the teachers around here don't live in Scarsdale, so I'd have no reason to know them."

"My understanding is that Frankel *did* live here."

McNally shrugged. "I still didn't know him."

"Do you know if there was anything that he might have been involved in anytime during his last year? Anything criminal?"

"I believe I spoke to someone in your police department about this guy just a few weeks ago," McNally told her. "A Detective Earley, I think her name was."

"Ginger Earley is a good cop," Gail said. "She's very smart and very thorough. But she doesn't know what I know. And before I tell her what I know, I want to find out if I really know anything at all."

Detective McNally considered the skinny woman with the frustrated expression behind her eyeglasses.

"There have never been any charges brought against your Mr. Frankel," he said. "Not even for jaywalking."

"All right, so there were no charges brought," Gail conceded shrewdly. "But were there any allegations made? Was there any investigation?"

"We have no record of any investigation."

Gail nodded. It had been a long day, and she had spent it running into a series of dead ends. "Well, thanks for talking to me," she told McNally. "I just needed to know, one way or the other. I'm really glad it's turned out this way, because he's an excellent teacher."

"Extraordinary," the detective conceded.

She made her way out of the building and climbed into her rental car. Ginger and Ruben were going to have to solve the Breckenridge case without her help, she decided as she started up the engine. She certainly wasn't going to waste any more time trying to find something that wasn't there. The letter had obviously been a prank. She pulled out into the traffic of Fenimore Road and headed back toward the inn. She had skipped lunch; she would have an early dinner. Then she would see if she could get a seat on tomorrow morning's plane back to Seattle.

Detective Derek McNally stood just inside the doorway of the police station, and watched until she was gone.

Sally brought her salad.

"Did you take care of your business?" she asked.

"I guess so," Gail replied.

"That Holman Academy sure is a pretty place, isn't it?"

"Yes, it is." Gail looked up. "How did you know I was there?"

"I don't know," Sally said with a shrug. "Guess you said something about it at breakfast."

Gail took a bite of her salad and tried to recall the conversation.

"I don't remember mentioning where I was going this morning," she said as Sally returned with her pasta.

The waitress shrugged. "Then maybe I heard it from my husband," she said as she walked away. "He runs the inn."

The pasta was tasty. When she could eat no more, Gail paid the bill and left the restaurant. An icy rain had begun to fall and the walk was slick as she hurried toward the inn. She hoped the weather would clear by tomorrow; she didn't much fancy driving all the way back to Kennedy Airport in the same miserable weather she had driven through to get here.

She did not regret having come. She meant what she had said to Derek McNally; either way, her mission was going to be a success, and truth to tell, she was a lot happier to learn that the anonymous letter was a prank than she would have been to discover that the history teacher was a two-headed monster.

Returning to her room, she called the airline and made a reservation for tomorrow's flight back to Seattle. Then she tuned the television to CNN, and relaxed against the bed pillows to watch the news. Jerry Frankel drifted out of her mind. In ten minutes, she was sound asleep.

It was a little past nine o'clock on the other side of the country. A fire crackled contentedly in the small stone hearth in Ruben's living room. Ruben and Ginger had pulled the cushions off the sofa and now lay propped against them, sipping Kahlúa, as a winter wind whirled and whined around the little house.

"It's all arranged," Ruben said on Thursday. "Danny Leo is going to take Stacey to a movie on Saturday night."

"Where will you do it?" Ginger asked.

"My place," he replied. "We can have everything set up by seven o'clock. He'll be through in about an hour and a half, and that'll still give them plenty of time to catch the nine o'clock show."

"I hope it goes all right," she said. "I'd hate to see Stacey caught in the middle."

Ruben nodded. "So would I," he said uneasily.

Stacey had come to him immediately after she talked to Danny.

"His father doesn't have to know, does he?" she asked. "I mean, before the fact?"

Ruben had to think about that. "The boy is eighteen. If he

comes in voluntarily, it's not our responsibility to determine whether he should have had his father's consent."

"Good," she said, "because I don't think he had anything to do with killing Tara."

"You may be right," Ruben told her, "but I have to warn you: if the test doesn't go his way, we *will* have to notify his parents. And you won't be going to any movie with him."

"But if it does go his way? If he does pass the test?"

Ruben shrugged. "Then it's up to him whether he tells his father or not. And you can tell me all about the movie on Sunday morning."

The polygraph had taken exactly an hour and seventeen minutes. Danny answered every question that was put to him about the death of Tara Breckenridge without a blink.

"Were you having an affair with Tara Breckenridge?"

"No."

"Were you the father of her unborn child?"

"No."

"Did you kill Tara Breckenridge?"

"No."

"What's the verdict?" Ruben asked when it was over.

"There are always ways to beat the test," the examiner qualified his answer. "It's never an absolute. But as far as I can determine, the boy answered truthfully."

Now the teenagers and the machine and the technician were gone, and Ruben and Ginger were alone.

"I guess that knocks Danny off the list," she said.

From the beginning, Ruben had been troubled by the whole idea, especially because the Leo boy had involved Stacey in his plan. As a result, he watched the senior like a hawk, looking for the slightest indication that something was amiss. But the teenager had appeared comfortable throughout the entire procedure, following instructions, taking his time and answering clearly.

"So it would seem," Ruben said cautiously. "But let's run his blood sample anyway."

"Okay," Ginger agreed with a smile. Her boss was a real stickler for detail. They settled down in front of the fire, the unasked question still hanging between them—now what?

"I'd keep after the teacher if I thought there was any more to get," she said. "But I've listened to his statement backward and forward, and I can't find a flaw. I've gone over the notes of my other conversations with him at least a dozen times, and I can't find a single inconsistency. I think he's given us everything he's got, and without a new lead, I'd just be stabbing in the dark." Then she realized what she had said. "Forgive my abominably poor choice of words," she added hastily.

"I think you're right about Frankel," Ruben told her. "We all want to close this case. Me, especially, since it now seems to have put my job on the line. But railroading someone just to stay employed doesn't sit too well with me. The guy looks as clean as snow. So, unless something else surfaces to implicate him, he's off the list, too."

Gail awoke with a sense of urgency, stiff from being cramped in a half-upright position. The lamp beside the bed was still lit; the television was still on. She glanced at her watch. It was after midnight, which meant she had been asleep for more than five hours.

She twisted her neck around to ease the tension, and tried to remember what it was that had jolted her into wakefulness. Was it just a dream, or had something been trying to push its way to the surface? Her mind was blank. She closed her eyes and tried to reconstruct the dream. A montage of the day's events floated into her mind, all out of context: a policeman, a school secretary, a waitress, a newspaper clerk, a custodian in coveralls.

Gail sat up, now positive: there was something about today she had missed. But what was it? She went back over everything—a secretary who was reluctant to talk about a former teacher; an overcourteous policeman who claimed he knew nothing about Jerry Frankel; a chatty waitress who knew she had gone to the Holman Academy; a redheaded clerk who said the newspaper didn't report on the academy; a custodian in coveralls who had stared at her.

Gail jumped off the bed and started to pace around the small room. What was it McNally had said? Not that there had been no investigation of Jerry Frankel—only that there was no *record* of an investigation. And Mrs. Quinlan had said that Frankel resigned, but even when pressed, wouldn't say why, when the record should have listed his wife's transfer as the reason.

The blood began to pound in her temples. It had been right in front of her, and she had missed it. Was she ever rusty! Gail Brown the reporter would have seen it instantly. The newspaper clerk's words echoed in her head: "It's a private institution, and they go to great lengths . . . to protect their students."

She couldn't understand how she could have been so blind. The anonymous letter was no prank. It had sent her in the right direction. The runaround she had gotten was nothing less than the first layer of a major cover-up. And the reason she had missed it was obvious—it wasn't Jerry Frankel these people were shielding.

Her brain was reengaged now, the wheels clicking. It wasn't the teacher and it wasn't the school. Oh, the school would protect itself in any way it could, but she sensed the town as a whole would feel no great obligation to assist in such an effort. Not unless someone was involved whom the town *would* choose to shield, someone prominent or, perhaps, she thought with a shiver, the *daughter* of someone prominent.

Gail called the airline again, this time to cancel her return flight. Then she sat down and began to make a plan.

11

The icy night rain became a fine drizzle by morning. Gail returned to the Holman Academy shortly after eleven o'clock. As before, the iron gates stood open, allowing her to drive right through. And as she had hoped, the Oldsmobile was gone; only the pickup was parked in the gravel lot. Gail pulled up beside it. There was no telling where she would find him; he could be anywhere on the estate.

She climbed out of her car and made her way to the service door that faced the parking lot, relieved to find it unlocked. Pushing it open, she went inside.

It took her twenty minutes to find him, or to be more precise, for him to find her. She was wandering aimlessly down corridors, peering into every room, when a voice behind her said, "You ain't supposed to be here. There ain't no school today."

She whirled around and there he was, in the same blue coveralls, with his name above his pocket.

"Ezekiel, isn't it?" she asked with a smile. "My name is Gail. I was here yesterday, talking with Mrs. Quinlan. Do you remember me?"

Ezekiel squinted at her for a moment and then nodded. "I remember. You talked about the teacher."

Gail's heart bounced. "Yes, I did," she said. "Do you remember the teacher?"

"Sure do," Ezekiel said with a smile. It was a sweet, childlike smile, trusting and toothless. "He was a right fine teacher. Sometimes, he let me come in his classroom after school was done, and he tell me about all sorts of things that happen long before I was even born. I sure did like listenin' to him talk."

"Do you know why he left the school, Ezekiel?"

The man's expression darkened. "It was her fault," he replied. "She said awful things, and the police came."

"The Scarsdale police?" Gail asked.

"Uh-huh. They had nice uniforms."

"What happened then?"

"The headmaster sent them away and told me I shouldn't think about it. But the teacher was all upset and he forgot about lettin' me come in his classroom, so how was I supposed to do what the headmaster told me and not think about it?"

"I don't know, Ezekiel," Gail replied. "But tell me: after the girl said the awful things, and the headmaster sent the police away, what happened next?"

"The teacher went away."

"Right afterward?" Gail pressed. "Did the teacher leave the school right after that?"

"Pretty soon right after," Ezekiel told her. "I know it was after the holidays, 'cause that's when the headmaster told me the teacher was gone and wasn't never comin' back."

Gail held her breath. "Do you know who the girl was?" she asked.

"I miss him," the janitor said wistfully. "Nobody talks to me like the teacher did."

"Ezekiel," Gail repeated, "do you know who the girl was?"

He nodded. "She was a nice girl," he said.

"What happened to her? Do you know what happened to her?"

The janitor shrugged. "Nothin' happen to her, I guess."

Gail stared at him. "What do you mean, nothing? Is she all right? Is she still here?"

"Uh-huh," he said. "I see her all the time. She's a nice girl. All the girls here are nice. Some of them like to tease me." He started to fidget. "But I'm not supposed to talk about her. The headmaster said so."

"That's all right, Ezekiel, you don't have to talk about her," Gail assured him. "You've told me enough. Now just tell me how to get out of this place."

He walked her to the front door and opened it for her. "You don't come from here," he said.

"No, I don't," Gail told him. "I come from all the way across the country."

"Then how do you know about Alice?"

Gail looked at him. "Is that her name?" she asked, holding her breath. "Is that the girl's name—Alice?"

"Alice is a nice name," Ezekiel said as he closed the door.

Gail went back to Fenimore Road and the police station.

"I think you lied to me, Detective McNally," she said. "To begin with, you said you'd never met Jerry Frankel, and didn't know him—yet you referred to him as an extraordinary teacher."

"I thought you were asking me for personal knowledge," the police officer replied smoothly. "I'd heard of his reputation."

"Really? One teacher in a school supposedly filled with out-standing teachers? How did you hear of his reputation? He taught at a school that makes a particular point of staying out of the public eye. How would anything about him have come to your attention?"

"It happens."

"You also led me to believe there was no investigation involving him. That wasn't true, either, was it?"

McNally sighed. "Look, Ms. Brown, I didn't really have to talk to you at all. I was only trying to be polite."

"Then all you had to do was tell me you were not at liberty to discuss the case," Gail retorted.

"And that would have made you go away?"

"Look, McNally, I'm not the enemy. And I didn't come here to take the cure. I came here because two months ago, we had a homicide in my hometown—the first ever. It was the brutal murder of a fifteen-year-old girl, and so far our police department, which is very good indeed, hasn't been able to come up with the killer. Then I get an anonymous tip about a new teacher in the community that directs me right to the Holman Academy. Now, if you were me, what would you have done?"

McNally sighed. "All right, there was an allegation made. We did go up to the school to look into it. The teacher denied it, the headmaster told us it was a private matter, and we went away. No investigation. End of story."

"Can you tell me what the alleged incident involved?"

"It involved a male teacher and a female student."

"Was the teacher Jerry Frankel?"

The detective nodded reluctantly.

"All right, McNally," Gail said carefully. "Jerry Frankel is long gone, which leaves you with no reason to cover for him. So who is it that you've gone to such lengths to protect? By any chance, would her name be Alice?"

The detective looked her straight in the eye. "You got what you came for, Ms. Brown. This conversation is over. It was real nice meeting you, and I hope you have a safe journey home."

An hour later, Gail sat in the restaurant, over an uneaten ham sandwich and a cooling cup of coffee, and put the pieces together.

Obviously, the allegation made against Jerry Frankel by one of his students had been serious enough to cause the police to go out to the academy. And just as obviously, the entire town, while probably willing to give Frankel up without a great deal of concern, was prepared to go to the wall for the student. Which told Gail that she had to be the daughter of someone who had a lot of clout.

The eerie similarity between this Alice and Tara Breckenridge sent a chill through her. Yet Ezekiel had told her that Alice was still a student at the Holman Academy, which meant that whatever had happened between the two in Scarsdale had not resulted in the extreme level of criminal behavior that had occurred on Seward Island.

Gail pondered her options. She now knew that Jerry Frankel had been involved with a female student, but she didn't yet know the nature of that involvement. Had she fulfilled her mission anyway? Could she leave Scarsdale without discovering what that allegation was, and whether there was any merit to it?

While the media in general did not enjoy a reputation for being particularly fair-minded, Gail tried to be. She had always done her best to report both sides of a story, and to give both sides equal weight, distasteful though that often was. Could she now go home and make an accusation without corroboration?

"Coffee need freshening?" Sally asked. "The ham not to your liking?"

Gail looked up. "Thanks," she said. "I guess I could use some hot coffee. But the ham's fine. I just got a little lost in my thoughts."

"Stirring up quite a hornet's nest around here, aren't you?" the waitress observed, exchanging the cold coffee for a freshly brewed cup.

"Am I?" Gail said, her eyes narrowing slightly behind her thick glasses. "I didn't realize."

"The teacher's gone. The rest is best left alone."

"I didn't tell you I was going to the Holman Academy, did I?"

"Does it matter?" Sally replied with a careless shrug.

Gail took a gamble. "I guess Alice is a pretty special girl," she said.

"Which Alice is that?" Sally inquired blandly.

"The one who was involved with the teacher."

The waitress shrugged again. "Well, I wouldn't know about that," she replied.

"Sure," Gail said. "I just assumed. You know, all the trouble they went to, to hush the whole thing up."

Sally let out a short laugh. "You mean, *tried* to hush it up," she said without thinking.

Gail allowed herself a canny grin. "That's what I figured. I was born and raised in a small town myself."

"Yeah, well, then I guess you understand."

"Yes, of course. Someone as special as Alice must be protected at all costs."

"I suppose," Sally said.

"You weren't in favor of the cover-up?" Gail inquired.

The waitress snorted. "I wasn't exactly asked for my opinion," she replied. "But seeing as you managed to find out about it all on your own, let me tell you, those girls up at that academy aren't anything more than a bunch of spoiled rich bitches. None of them will ever have to work a day in their lives—can you imagine that? But does that make them any more special than anyone else? Not in my book. Far as I'm concerned, they deserve whatever trouble they get into."

"Even Alice?"

"Why not? Her daddy's got more money than God, and goes around thinking he's so much better than the rest of us just because he's some hotshot doctor who supports worthwhile causes. I see her, she comes in here sometimes with her friends, acting as if working folk like me are nothing more than dirt on the floor. You can take my word for it, she's no better than any of them."

The gamble had paid off. Gail took a sip of her fresh coffee and a big bite of her ham sandwich, and smiled benignly at Sally. Once again, her stay in Scarsdale was going to be extended.

"I'm not a suspect in the Breckenridge murder anymore," Danny Leo told his parents after church on Sunday.

"What do you mean?" Peter asked. "Have they found the killer? I didn't hear anything about it." He looked at his wife.

Rose shook her head. "I didn't hear anything about it, either."

"I don't know who they've found or not found," Danny said. "I just know they're not interested in me anymore."

"How do you know that?"

"Detective Earley told me so."

Peter frowned. "She made a point of seeking you out to tell you this?"

"Yes sir."

"How come?"

Danny shrugged. "I guess I must have convinced them."

"How did you do that, son?"

"Well, if you must know," Danny said, "I took their polygraph test."

Peter glared at the boy. "I'll sue the uniforms off those bastards," he roared, furious. "They had no right to come after you behind my back!"

"They didn't come after me," Danny corrected him. "I went to them. I wanted to take the test. I wanted to put an end to all this."

"But I told you this was a matter of principle."

"You were making too big a deal out of it. Fighting the court order! Even my friends were starting to look at me funny, like maybe my own father believed I might be guilty or something."

"Your friends must not be worth very much if they can't understand the importance of standing up for a principle."

"The hell with your principles, Dad. Mr. Huxley's the only principal I care about right now, and he told me, flat out, because of what you were doing, I was about to lose my scholarship to Harvard. Is that what you wanted?"

For a moment, Peter looked as though he might strike the boy. Then, in the next moment, he shrugged his shoulders and chuckled.

"Passed the polygraph, huh?"

Danny grinned. "I didn't just pass it," he said. "I aced it."

It took four hours at the library and an hour and a half with the local telephone directory for Gail to come up with Dr. Stuart Easton, his wife, Denise, and their seventeen-year-old daughter, Alice.

The Eastons lived in a six-bedroom Tudor-style home that was rumored to have belonged to a notorious gangster in the 1930s. Dr. Easton was the chief of surgery at a prominent local hospital—an entire wing of which bore his name—and every mention of him included a long list of his medical accomplishments, and a tribute to his many years of community philanthropy.

Gail turned her rental in to the circular drive at ten minutes past eight on Monday morning. A maid answered the door and ushered her down a thickly carpeted corridor to a small parlor where Stuart Easton was waiting. He was about fifty, of little more than average height, slender and dark, with a presence about him that reminded Gail of a stalking panther.

"I have to tell you that I resent your being here, Ms. Brown," he said as soon as the introductions were out of the way. "We're a very private family, and we do not intend to air our dirty linen in public. I've agreed to talk to you as a favor to Derek McNally, but only on the understanding that our entire conversation will be strictly off the record. I warn you—take one step over the line, and this meeting will be over."

"Dr. Easton, I appreciate your seeing me on such short notice, and please understand that I am not here with any intention of embarrassing you or any member of your family," Gail assured him. "As I believe Detective McNally explained, because of a situation in my hometown, I just need to clarify a few things for background only."

He sat down in a leather chair and gestured her to a nearby sofa. "What is it you want to know?" he asked.

She told him about the murder of Tara Breckenridge, and the string of small coincidences that appeared to connect Jerry Frankel to that crime, and then she told him, in general terms, about the contents of the letter.

"Now I don't normally give much credence to anonymous tips," she said. "But under the circumstances, I felt I had to follow up on this one. All I need to know is what the allegation against the teacher was about, and whether there was any real merit to it."

"My daughter was in his junior history class," Easton said. "She was having difficulty with some of the work, and he invited her to come in after school for extra help. He took the opportunity of those private sessions to sexually molest her."

"How did you find out about it?"

"Alice told us. But apparently not until it had been going on for several months."

"What did you do after she told you?"

"What do you mean—what did I do?" he snapped. "I notified the police, of course."

"Did you have Alice examined by a doctor?"

"Ms. Brown," he said irritably, "*I'm* a doctor."

"Please don't misunderstand me, Dr. Easton," Gail said hastily. "I'm simply looking for corroboration."

"Are we still off the record?" he asked warily.

"Of course."

"All right, yes, I had her examined by a doctor."

"And?"

"She was pregnant, of course."

"Were DNA tests done? Was it determined that Jerry Frankel was the father?"

"The teacher was unwilling to submit to any such tests."

"You could have compelled him."

"That would have meant a court battle, and a lot of hurtful publicity," he said with a sigh. "At the very least, my daughter's reputation would have been destroyed. And for what, really? Alice is a very fragile, very vulnerable girl, Ms. Brown. I felt she had been through enough. My first priority was to make sure there would be no baby. After that, I wasn't interested in dragging her name through the mud."

"Detective McNally told me that Frankel denied having had a sexual relationship with your daughter."

"Does that surprise you?"

"No. But without the tests, or a thorough police investigation, it does raise a rather significant he said/she said issue. Frankel has the reputation of being a very dedicated, very caring teacher. Is it possible that Alice could have been, let's say, less than candid with you about her situation?"

"I'm not in the habit of doubting my daughter's word," Easton stated flatly. "If she said he did it, then he did it."

"You mean, she told you Jerry Frankel was responsible, and that was all?"

"In essence, yes."

"Did Alice say she was a willing participant in this alleged affair between the two of them?"

"It doesn't matter whether she was willing or not," he said. "She was sixteen years old at the time—his student. He was in a position of authority—her teacher. She looked up to him. He took advantage of her."

"Can you tell me, Doctor, had your daughter been, well, sexually active prior to the alleged involvement with Jerry Frankel?"

Easton was clearly uncomfortable. "Look, I'm a very busy man. Maybe I'm not at home as much as I should be. Maybe I'm not as close to my daughter as I could be. But I do the best I can. If she was sexually active, I didn't know about it."

"I appreciate how difficult this is for you," Gail said, although, in reality, she found herself feeling very little compassion for the man. "I know, if she were my daughter, I would be every bit as outraged as you are. I hate putting you through this, and believe me, I wouldn't, if it weren't so important."

"I understand," he conceded.

"I only have a few more questions."

"Go ahead."

"What exactly did Alice tell the police?"

The surgeon blinked. "She didn't tell them anything," he replied. "I wouldn't permit it. She told her mother and me what happened, and *we* told the police."

"And based on that, on just what your daughter told you had taken place, Frankel was—what? Forced to resign his position at the Holman Academy?"

"Certainly," Easton declared. "You don't think I would have permitted Alice to stay at the school if he were still teaching there, do you?"

"I see."

"And let me assure you, dedicated teacher or not, a lot of other parents were behind us on this."

"You've told me that there were no DNA tests performed, and Detective McNally told me the police investigation was cut short by the headmaster at Holman. So there was never an objective determination of the facts—just Alice's charge?"

"I'm not sure I appreciate your implication, Ms. Brown."

"Dr. Easton, a man's life is at stake here. If Jerry Frankel molested your daughter and murdered the girl on Seward Island, I want him to pay for it. If he didn't, I don't want to implicate him with innuendo. All we seem to have here is an uncorroborated allegation told to you by your daughter and subsequently related through you to the police." Gail paused. "I don't suppose you'd be willing to let me talk to Alice, would you?"

"Absolutely not."

Gail nodded. You win some, you lose some, she thought as she gathered herself together and stood up. In many ways, she was leaving with more questions than answers.

"Thank you for seeing me."

A moment later, she was back in her car, starting the engine and preparing to swing out of the driveway. She wasn't sure what made her glance toward the house at the last moment; perhaps a sudden movement had caught her eye, perhaps it was just a feeling. A girl with blond hair stood in an upstairs window. It might have been a trick of light, or simply her imagination, but it looked to Gail as though the girl were crying.

He awoke in a panic, his eyes flying open, sockets dry. He was gasping for breath, his heart pounding, sweat pouring from his body. It was the nightmare again, now coming with relentless regularity. Only this time, there was something new—his skull felt as though it were being crushed in a vise. He had never had a headache before, never understood the agony. He wondered if he would have them from now on.

It was the third time this week that his sleep had been interrupted, that he had been jolted out of oblivion. The same faceless eyes stared up at him, indicting him; the same wretched scream split the darkness, denouncing him. Like a snippet of movie newsreel that willfully replayed a piece of history the way it actually happened, rather than the way one might wish to remember it, his nightmare was a moment frozen in eternity that would neither soften, nor blur, nor twist itself around to fit his fancy.

When he was conscious, it was easy to convince himself that *she* was the villain, not he. That, at the very worst, he had acted in self-defense, protecting himself from ruination or worse. It was exasperating that the dream continued to rob him of his rest.

He staggered out of bed and into the bathroom, where he fumbled for the bottle of headache medicine he knew was there, downing three of the tablets with a glass of water. Then he put his head under the faucet and let the cold water run over his hot neck.

When he started to shiver, he dried himself off and crept back between the sheets. The clock on the nightstand told him it was twelve-thirty-five, little more than an hour since he had gone to bed. It was early for the nightmare to have come. He settled down under the covers and began to massage his temples with his fingers. After a while, the pain in his head began to ease, and he went back to sleep.

12

Gail fought a battle with herself all the way back to Seattle. But in the end, she went to Ginger with what she had learned.

"There's not really anything I can ethically use," she conceded, "just a bunch of possibles. But there may be enough for you to move on."

"You couldn't get to the girl?" Ginger asked.

Gail shook her head. "I tried. Her father refused to let me see her. He even admitted that the police had never talked to her. I went back to the school, but the headmaster wouldn't see me. He sent his secretary out to say that under no circumstances would they discuss Alice Easton with me, and that whatever measures they had taken to resolve a specific matter had been taken in the best interests of the school."

"I can't help but say that I wish you'd come to me first," Ginger told her. "I very likely would have gone with you."

Gail shrugged. "Once a journalist, always a journalist, I guess."

"The son of a bitch!" Ginger cried the moment Gail was gone. "He really played me like a violin."

"He's obviously smoother than we gave him credit for," Ruben said.

"Sure, but where were all my finely honed instincts—my professional intuition?"

"Don't be so hard on yourself. He's apparently fooled a lot of people, hasn't he?"

"But I'm a trained police officer," she argued. "I'm supposed to see through all that. He seemed so open, so sincere. Now, of course, I realize he was just prepared. He'd been down the road before."

"Well, not exactly," Ruben suggested. "Alice Easton is still alive."

"A dress rehearsal," Ginger said. She didn't know which was worse—that Frankel was in fact a child-molesting murderer, or that he had manipulated her so easily. She felt so stupid, so betrayed.

"Well, at least now we know," Ruben said.

"Yes." Ginger nodded. "And now that we do, I think it's time to tighten the screws on our dear teacher. I'm going to squeeze him until there's not a lying breath left in his body."

A born cop, Ruben thought.

"Some additional information has come to our attention, Mr. Frankel," Ginger said over the telephone. "I wonder if you'd be kind enough to come in and discuss it with us—perhaps tomorrow afternoon, after school?"

"What is it now, Detective Earley?" he asked with an unmistakable edge to his voice.

"We'd like to talk to you about the Holman Academy."

There was an audible intake of breath at the other end of the line. "How did you find out about that?" he demanded.

"Does it matter?" she responded smoothly.

There was a momentary silence and then a clearly audible sigh. "I'll get back to you," he said and hung up.

• • •

At four-twenty-five the following afternoon, the history teacher walked into Graham Hall, unaccompanied.

"I think you should have your attorney with you," Ginger cautioned.

"He'll be here at five," Jerry told her. "But I came early so I could talk to you first."

She escorted him to the interview room, where he took the same seat that he had occupied on his previous visit. The tape recorder was already in place on top of the table, along with a folder containing a transcript of the teacher's prior statement, and a tray with a pitcher of water and several glasses.

"You are currently being represented by counsel," Ginger said, sitting down across from him. "Which means that you can't waive your rights except in his presence. So we'll wait until he gets here. It's for your own protection." She was not about to play any more games with this man; she wanted every word he said to be admissible in court.

Jerry looked at her with a half smile. "Do I need protecting, Detective Earley?"

"I don't know, Mr. Frankel," she said. "But that's the way it works."

"I didn't kill that poor girl," he said.

"Please don't say anything more."

"I didn't kill her," he insisted. "And you've got it all wrong about the Holman Academy."

"Mr. Frankel," she responded calmly, "as an officer of the court, I can't allow you to continue."

"But I'm trying to tell you," he said. "I didn't—"

"Mr. Frankel, please," she interrupted him. "Unless you agree to say nothing more until you are in the presence of your attorney, I'll have to leave the room."

He shook his head. "This had nothing to do with the Breckenridge case," he said. "It's a totally different matter, and I don't understand why I can't talk about it without my attorney."

Ginger stood up. "I'll wait outside," she told him.

"No, that's all right," he said wearily. "You don't have to go. I won't say anything more. I promise. Please stay."

She retook her seat, and the two of them waited in silence, the teacher fidgeting in obvious discomfort, the detective calmly observing every move he made.

"Can we at least talk about the weather?" he asked after a moment. "I understand it's very mild for December."

"It really would be better if we didn't talk at all," she said.

He sighed heavily and began to look around; blank gray walls stared back at him. After a few moments, he reached for a glass from the tray on the table, poured water into it from the pitcher and drank. When the glass was empty, he returned it to the tray. Ginger sat and watched.

At three minutes past five, Scott Cohen entered the room and sat down next to his client. "All right," he said. "Where are we, and what are we doing here?"

"We are here to discuss some new information regarding an incident at your client's previous place of employment," Ginger said. "Mr. Frankel arrived here half an hour ago, wanting to talk about the matter, but I advised him that he could not do so until he was in your presence."

"As I understand it, you're referring to an alleged incident that is not connected to the Breckenridge case, is that correct?" Scott inquired.

"That's correct."

"Then I see no relevance here."

"Wait a minute," Jerry put in. "I want to talk about it. I want to get this whole thing cleared up once and for all."

"I'd like a moment with my client," Scott said.

Ginger stood up immediately and left the room.

"Jerry," Scott urged. "I don't think this is the time for—"

"I don't care," the teacher said. "This investigation of theirs has turned my whole life upside down, and I want it to stop. Now, I'm going to tell them whatever it is they want to know."

"I'm advising against this."

"They just have the wrong idea about something," Jerry told him. "It has nothing to do with the Breckenridge case."

"Listen to me, and listen very carefully," the lawyer instructed. "Anything you say to them, anything at all, has to do with the Breckenridge case. They're after a killer, and they'll do whatever they have to do to find one. They're looking for a motive, for a pattern of behavior, for whatever they need to make an arrest. The situation at your previous school, as you've described it to me, may just give them all three."

Jerry blinked. "But they already know the other side of the story," he said. "I just want to tell them my side so they have it straight."

Scott sighed. "All right," he said. "But I won't allow you to go on record."

He got up and went to the door. When Ginger returned, Ruben was with her.

"This will be a conversation only," Scott said. "No tape recording, no stenographer. Nothing said here will be on record. Is that understood?"

The two police officers exchanged glances and then Ginger pushed the recorder aside and leaned back in her chair. "Tell us what happened at the Holman Academy."

"As I'm sure you already know, her name was Alice Easton and she was a student there," Jerry Frankel began. "She was the only child of some important doctor and his socialite wife, neither of whom apparently had much time for her. She was a very unhappy girl. She used to tell me she couldn't understand why they'd ever bothered to have a child because she was raised mostly by housekeepers. By the time I met her, she was fourteen years old and so starved for affection, she didn't particularly care where she found it. And I was—there. Alice wasn't the first student to have a crush on me; it goes with the territory. But she was the first who carried her fantasy too far."

"Fantasy?"

"Yes," he said. "That's all it was—a fantasy. She had problems with history right from the beginning of her freshman year, but it wasn't until her junior year that she took to stopping by after school for help. I've always encouraged my students to do that. We don't all learn at the same pace, you know, and sometimes, when we teach at one level, we can lose kids who are at different levels. Alice Easton was an average student, not particularly motivated. She started showing up for help immediately after the fall term began, coming in maybe once or twice a week. By the end of October, she was coming in every day."

"Didn't that strike you as unusual?"

"Of course it did. She had never shown much interest in history before. But I didn't turn her off. I thought of it as at least a safe place for her to hang out, because it was clear very early on that she had nowhere else to go."

"Was she the only student you tutored?"

"No. But if other kids were there ahead of her, she wouldn't join in; she'd sit in the back of the room and wait until they were done. If kids came in after her, she would step aside and insist that I help them first." He sighed. "In the beginning, we talked strictly about history, and her grades even started to improve a little. But after a while, she started to tell me about herself, about her life, and sometimes she would ask me questions about my life and my family—which, by the way, I answered only in the most general of terms. I felt sorry for her. She didn't seem to have many friends, and she apparently wasn't very popular with the boys. She seemed to me to be quite lonely, and I thought it was very sad. She had money and position and advantages that many people would envy, and yet she was depressed and unhappy. So I let her talk. It didn't seem like such a big thing. You know, it's not uncommon for teachers to counsel a student about something peripheral to schoolwork. I thought I was in control of it. A lonely student—a caring teacher; I thought that's all it was."

"But it wasn't?" Ginger prompted.

"One day at the end of November, she came into my classroom quite late," he said. "I was just about to leave. She said she had waited outside on purpose, to make sure no one else would be coming, because we were going to need total privacy. I asked her what she was talking about, and she said she was talking about making love, of course. That she had decided she was ready."

"She came on to you?"

"Came on to me?" Jerry echoed. "She stood there in the middle of my classroom, Detective Earley, and took off all her clothes. Right there, at school, when anybody could have walked in. They prepare you for a lot of things when you're learning to be a teacher, but let me tell you, they don't prepare you to deal with that. I was scared. I tried to be kind, but I guess I wasn't as—diplomatic as I might have been. I'm not proud of myself, but I ended up walking right out of the room and leaving her there, naked. The next thing I knew, I was being accused of child molestation, indecent behavior, statutory rape, consorting with a minor—you name it, her father cried it."

"And none of what she claimed was true?" Ginger asked.

"None of it," Jerry said firmly. "Did I cross the teacher-student line with her? I don't know. Sometimes that line gets a little fuzzy for me when I have an especially needy kid in my class. Did I hug her, did I praise her, did I try to instill in her some measure of self-worth? Yes, I admit to that. But I never did any of the other things they said I did."

"So, you're saying that your attempts to help Alice Easton in your capacity as her history teacher were totally misinterpreted by her?"

"Yes," Jerry declared.

"And it was pure fantasy on her part that the two of you were romantically involved?"

"Yes."

"And that, when you rebuffed her that day in your classroom, she retaliated by accusing you of being the father of her unborn child?"

"Yes," Jerry affirmed. "Now, my attorney tells me I was wrong to tell you all this. He tells me you'll try to use it to build a case against me in the Breckenridge matter. So I want to say that it was my intention to stay at the Holman Academy and fight the accusations, because I know I would have won. But when it became clear that my effectiveness as an educator had been compromised, there was no point. Kids, it turns out, are the harshest judges of all."

Ginger looked him in the eye. "You were not the father of Alice Easton's unborn child?"

Jerry looked right back at her. "No, I was not."

"Did you decline to submit to DNA testing?"

"No. The police never really asked. The officer who interviewed me at school mentioned it in passing as an option if I wanted to exonerate myself. I told him there was absolutely no foundation to the charge, and unless one could be established, I didn't feel I was under any obligation at that point to jeopardize my career."

"Pretty much the same thing you told us, isn't it?"

"And for just about the same reason."

"An interesting coincidence, though, wouldn't you say?"

"They do occur," the teacher replied. "However, the Scarsdale police chose not to pursue an investigation, so DNA testing became a nonissue."

Ruben leaned forward and rested his arms on the table. "I've been a policeman for more than twenty-five years, Mr. Frankel," he said. "Maybe my work has made a cynic out of me, but I don't happen to believe in coincidence. I sit here and I see a man who fits our profile of Tara Breckenridge's killer to a T, who admits to what many would consider an unorthodox pattern of behavior with his students, and who was associated with two pregnant teenage girls—one of whom implicated you in her pregnancy and one of whom ended up dead. Now, that adds up to a whole passel of coincidences. From where I'm sitting, it's starting to look like Alice Easton was responsible for you losing your last job—and maybe you weren't about to let Tara Breckenridge lose you this one."

"Are you prepared to charge my client with anything at this time?" Scott asked abruptly.

"No," Ruben conceded.

"Then this interview is over."

The attorney stood up, took his client by the elbow, and steered him out of the room.

"A pretty cool customer," Ruben observed.

"Which one?" Ginger asked. "The teacher or the lawyer?"

Ruben chuckled. "Take your choice."

"The bastard did it," she said. "It's so obvious to me now, I can't believe I didn't see it before."

"It's happening all over again," Jerry cried as he stumbled toward the parking lot where he had left his car. He had put on a brave show in the interview room, but now he was shaking like jelly.

"It's still a fishing expedition," Scott told him. "They've got nothing more than they had before. So just keep your cool."

"It's all over school, you know. I see it in the way the kids look at me in class. Without their trust and respect, I'm useless to them. Hell, it's not just in school, it's all over the whole damn island. Even Matthew's friends have started asking him about it. Why am I standing on principle? Maybe I should take their damn polygraph and let them test my blood. I don't see how things could be much worse."

Scott shrugged. "That's always an option."

"One you recommend?"

"Right now, I think you're still coming from a position of strength," the lawyer said, weighing his words. "You've denied any involvement in the murder, and while they may have suspicions, they haven't a shred of evidence to the contrary. The Alice Easton matter is most unfortunate, a very awkward parallel indeed, but the argument could be made that it has no real bearing on this case. My advice would be: don't give anything away unless you have to. The winter break starts on Friday. Get some rest. Maybe things will look better after the New Year."

Ginger waited until she was sure the teacher and his attorney were gone and then, very carefully, retrieved the drinking glass that Jerry Frankel had used.

"From what I hear, Scott Cohen is a top-notch lawyer," Ruben said, nodding at the glass. "I'm surprised he let you get away with that."

"He wasn't here," Ginger told him. "I'll get Charlie to take it over to the lab. The teacher thinks we have no proof; he thinks he's going to get away with it. Well, we'll just see about that. If the prints on this glass match the partial on Tara Breckenridge's cross, we've got him!"

"That's twice now that Jerry's been down at the police station," Libby Hildress told her husband that night, her blue eyes troubled. "I saw him myself, this time, around six o'clock. He and Scott were just coming out of Graham Hall, and both of them looked pretty upset."

"Maybe we should call the Frankels, and see if there's anything we can do to help," Tom suggested.

"I don't know," Libby said. "I'm beginning to get bad feelings about this. With everything that's going on, maybe it isn't such a good idea for Billy to be playing over there so much."

* * *

"What did they want *this* time?" Deborah inquired.

"They wanted to know about Alice Easton," Jerry replied.

She gasped. "They found out about that?"

"Apparently."

"I thought the school wasn't supposed to say anything; it was part of the agreement."

"I thought so, too."

She shrugged. "Well, I don't know why either one of us should be surprised. Someone was bound to find out sooner or later."

"I guess so."

"What did you tell them?" she asked.

"I told them the allegation was false, of course," he said with a look of disgust.

"Did they believe you?"

"I don't know, Deborah," he snapped at her. "Why don't you go ask them?"

"Is it the teacher?" Albert Hoch questioned his police chief the following morning, his voice, as usual, resonating throughout the building. "That's twice you've had him down here. Are you on to something? Are you close to an arrest?"

"We're only at the talking stage," Ruben replied. "We have reason to believe he may be involved in the case, but we can't be sure."

"Then why are you pussyfooting around?" the Bald Eagle demanded. "Why don't you go after him, turn his place upside down, find something?"

Ruben sighed. "He's got a very sharp lawyer, and we don't have probable cause for a search warrant," he replied, wishing the mayor would let him alone to do his job. "We have to keep working the situation."

"I gotta tell you, you're running out of time, Ruben," Hoch warned. "The city council is getting pressured. I'm getting pressured. We've got to have a break in the case, something I can take to people and say: 'Here, this is what we're doing; this is what we've accomplished.' You're running out of time."

"I appreciate your efforts in my behalf," the police chief said evenly. "I know you understand that real police work doesn't always happen in an instant; that more often than not it takes great patience and careful strategy to solve a case as complex as this one."

"Do you at least have a strategy for this teacher guy?" Hoch asked.

"At the moment, we're considering several different ones," Ruben told him. "We still have some evaluating to do before we decide which one will be most productive."

"When are we likely to see some results?"

"It's hard to say just now."

Hoch wagged his bald head. "I don't know if that's going to satisfy the city council."

"I'm sorry," said Ruben. "I don't know what else to tell you."

The mayor was clearly frustrated. "What I'm hearing is that you think he probably did it, but you can't nail him for it, is that right?"

Ruben shrugged. "Unfortunately, what we suspect isn't always the same as what we can prove."

Down the hall, Ginger wrapped her legs around her chair to keep from jumping up and running to Ruben's defense. Why couldn't everyone see he was doing his best? With almost no physical evidence, no murder weapon, and no eyewitnesses, what did the damn city council expect?

They had the teacher in their sights, and they weren't about to blink. If they could just get that fingerprint match, they would have their first piece of solid evidence; more than enough to secure a search warrant. And Ginger was positive that a thorough examination of Jerry Frankel's home would turn up all they would need to charge him with murder. It was just a matter of time.

In reality, there was no guarantee that the fingerprint on Tara's cross belonged to the murderer; it was just a possibility. But if it turned out to be Jerry Frankel's fingerprint, then the possibility became a probability. Ginger began to pray for just that. All they needed was a little break; just one thing to show the city council that they were on the right track; something that would get them off Ruben's back. She wondered how much time he had left.

"Stacey?" asked the voice at the other end of the telephone.

"Yes," she replied.

"This is Danny." There was a pause. "Danny Leo."

"Oh, hi," she said. "I didn't recognize your voice. I guess I never talked to you on the telephone before."

"I just wanted to say thank you again for last Saturday night. I really appreciate what you did. I told my folks. My dad was pretty steamed at first, but then I think he was happy about it."

"I'm glad."

"I also wanted to tell you what a terrific time I had—afterward, at the movie, I mean. It was a lot of fun."

"I had fun, too," she admitted.

"You know, working on the paper and all, we've known each other for over a year," he said, "but we really don't know each other very well."

"I guess not."

"Well, I was wondering—do you have any plans for New Year's Eve yet?"

Stacey's heart thumped. Was the school hunk about to ask her for a date? "No, I don't," she told him.

"A classmate of mine is having a party, and I thought maybe you might like to go with me?"

Kids on Seward didn't go in for dating very much, Stacey knew. They went out in groups, usually with other kids in the same grade. She knew very well that Danny Leo showing up at a party with a sophomore would be all over the Island by morning.

"Sounds like fun," she said. "I'd like to go."

It was well after midnight, but a wide-awake Matthew Frankel lay in bed with his arms crossed under his head and thought about school. Outside his window, the world was dark and quiet, the best time for thinking. Chase was curled up on the floor beside him, breathing softly.

Matthew was trying to figure out how he could tell his parents that he didn't want to go to school anymore without having to tell them why. He didn't want to tell them why because he knew it would hurt his father, and there was no one in this world that Matthew loved as much as he loved his father.

He thought of asking them if he could go to private school, but he knew the only one on the Island was a Christian school that Billy had told him about, and that would be, as his mother sometimes said, like jumping from the frying pan into the fire.

But maybe he wouldn't have to go to a real school at all, Matthew thought. Maybe he could just stay home and learn from his father in the evenings. There were parents on the Island who home-schooled their kids; he had heard his father say so. That would be great. He could stay right here, where he was safe, and never have to go back to that place or see those kids again.

"Did you know your daddy's a murderer?" a trio of fifth-graders had taunted him on the playground during recess.

"How does it feel to be the son of a murderer?"

"Son of a Jew bastard murderer!"

"Son of a Jew bastard and a Jew bitch!"

They had grabbed his brand-new jacket and thrown it in a mud puddle and stomped all over it. Then they had pushed him down in the puddle and held his face in the mud until he choked and sputtered.

"Hey, look!" they said, laughing as they walked away. "The kike kid's crying!"

Tears oozed out of Matthew's eyes onto his pillow. No one had ever treated him like that before. He knew he was different from a lot of the kids on the Island, because he was Jewish, but he had always tried his best to be nice to everyone. He didn't understand; he didn't even know those fifth-graders.

"I slipped and fell," he told the playground teacher who pulled him out of the puddle.

"I slipped and fell," he told the school nurse who cleaned him up.

"I slipped and fell," he told his parents.

Matthew didn't like to lie, but something had kept him from telling the truth.

Friday was the last day of school before the winter holiday began. That gave him two weeks to think up a plan that would be persuasive enough to convince his parents not to send him back.

13

On the heels of Jerry Frankel's second visit to Graham Hall came a new spate of letters to the editor that were distinctly different from those previously received, and Gail Brown couldn't resist publishing a cross-section of them.

"It wouldn't come as no surprise to me (sic) that it was a teacher who killed that girl," wrote a high school dropout. "I've seen them get off on power trips where they really think they're like God or somebody."

"I don't care how good a teacher everybody thinks he is," objected the manager of the local liquor store. "Just because he can teach doesn't mean he wasn't involved in that poor girl's murder."

"If the police are seriously considering the possibility that one of the teachers at the high school murdered Tara Breckenridge," inquired a worried mother, "shouldn't he be removed from his classroom until the matter is resolved?"

∘ ∘ ∘

"This is no different than those Wenatchee sex crimes, where that preacher got off," an electrician and the father of six wrote. "Only this time, the victim wasn't just molested, she was murdered. Teachers are supposed to be people we can trust, just like preachers, aren't they?"

Jerry Frankel read the letters and sighed. "Somehow, this whole thing has gotten way out of control," he said. "I don't understand how it happened."

"How did they find out about Holman?" Deborah asked.

"I don't know. They didn't say."

"This place is like a sieve," she complained. "There's no such thing as confidentiality around here. Maybe we should think about moving."

"In the middle of a murder investigation?" he demanded. "Now wouldn't that make me look innocent."

"I was thinking more of Matthew," she said. "This is bound to affect him sooner or later."

"Scott says it'll be okay," Jerry told her. "He says they have no evidence, and without it, they can't charge me with anything. He says he can go to court to get them to stop harassing me."

"It's going to be the same damn thing all over again, isn't it?"

"No, it isn't," he said.

Ginger was not looking forward to the session with her parents, but the feisty redhead intended to stand her ground.

"I absolutely refuse to have that man in my house," Verna Earley declared. "Not on Christmas or any other day. The very idea! What would I tell your brothers? Why, my goodness, I would never be able to hold my head up in polite society again."

"Then I'm afraid you won't have me in your house, either," Ginger shot back. "What will you tell my brothers, then?"

"I suppose I'll have to tell them that you preferred the company of others," her mother replied. "I certainly can't be held responsible for that, now can I?"

"Wait a minute," Jack Earley said. He was a fair-minded man who, when it came to his daughter and his wife, too often found himself in the role of mediator. "Aren't the holidays supposed to be a time for people to come together and forget their differences?"

"The holidays are a time for *family* to come together," Verna retorted.

"How Christian of you, Mother," said Ginger.

"Don't you dare say that to me, young lady. I'm as good a Christian as the next person."

Ginger turned to her father. "Dad, you know Ruben. You work with him. Is he diseased? Does he have horns? Has being around him blackened your reputation in any way?"

"A business association is one thing," Verna interjected before Jack could respond. "Your father can't help who he has to work with, just the same as you can't. But a social association is something quite different. That's a choice."

Ginger shook her head in exasperation. "I don't know how I ever grew up in this house and never saw it," she said.

"Never saw what?" Verna demanded.

"How much of a bigot you are."

"You mind your mouth, young lady," her mother snapped. "I'm nothing of the kind."

"Why don't we all back off a bit here," Jack urged. "I think maybe we're starting to say things we'll regret."

"I don't regret anything," Verna retorted. "I tried my best to instill decent values in her, but she always threw it back in my face. Now she'll have to learn the hard way that like goes with like or there'll be no happiness."

Ginger looked at her mother and sighed. "Ruben and I have a relationship—a committed relationship," she said. "He's part of my life, maybe for a very long time. I'd like you to be glad for me, but I'm twenty-eight years old and I don't need your permission. I'm sorry you feel the way you do, about someone you don't even know, but I'm sorrier for you than I am for me. Now you can deal with this situation in one of two ways. You can cut me loose and tell the world I'm no longer your daughter. That might not say much for your family loyalty, but you'll be able to hold your head way up in the rarefied air of racial snobbery. Or you can take the time to get to know two very special people, and possibly even learn something valuable about what really matters in this world. It's up to you."

Verna looked from her daughter to her husband. It was obvious that she had not anticipated the ultimatum, not seen the trap. She turned on her heel and disappeared into the kitchen.

Jack turned to his daughter and shrugged. "You brought up the heavy artillery for what was probably nothing more than a minor skirmish," he said.

"I know," Ginger replied. "But I'm hoping it won't be a very long war."

"I have a double-edged invitation for you," Ginger told Ruben. "Christmas dinner at my parents' house."

"What's so bad about that?" he asked.

She sighed. "Let me tell you about my mother."

"It could be a little rough," Ruben conceded when he told his daughter. "Her mother isn't exactly ethnically open-minded."

"Oh, great," Stacey said.

"We don't have to go, if you don't want to," he assured her. "We can have our Christmas dinner, just like we always do, and I'll be perfectly happy. The decision is yours."

The very last thing Stacey Martinez wanted to do was spend the most important holiday of the year with a bunch of people who were going to have to force themselves to be nice to her. She already knew enough bigots from school to last her well into the next century. But she didn't have the heart to say no.

"Do you want to go?" she asked.

Ruben thought about that for a moment. "Ginger's pretty important to me," he admitted. "More important than any woman since your mother. I'd be lying to you if I said she wasn't. Which means that, sooner or later, I'm probably going to have to deal with her family. This might be as good a time as any. I know Jack Earley. He's a decent man. As for the mother, I'd like to think that the attitude Ginger describes has more to do with fear of the unknown than any deep-rooted philosophy."

"I guess that means you want to go," Stacey said.

"Never mind me—what about you?" he asked.

"It's okay."

"You sure?"

She shrugged. "Why not? As you say, it has to happen sooner or later."

"I promise you, if it's bad, we'll get up and leave," he told her.

"Dad, I said it's okay. In fact," she added with a malicious smile, "it might be fun to slip a little hot pepper into their stuffing."

"I have attended the high school's Christmas pageant ever since I first moved to Seward Island," a woman wrote to the editor of the *Sentinel*. "It was a source of enormous comfort to me, especially in this age of moral decay, to see our young people carrying on the important traditions of Christianity. But now the pageant has been ruined for me by the intrusion of foreign rituals that have no place in our holiday celebration, and that have undermined its purpose and marred its purity. I will not go again."

"First the Jews objected to prayer in school," wrote Mildred MacDonald. "Then they stopped letting us decorate the won-

derful Douglas fir that was planted on the Village Green a hundred years ago for that very purpose. Now they've ruined our
pageant. It's nothing to do with them, why can't just they go away
and leave us alone?"

"The high school's holiday pageant—for it can no longer be
called just a Christmas pageant," wrote a local pediatrician, "was
a superb example of how a community such as ours can join in
celebrating its diverse heritage. If our young people can come together in such an outstanding effort, is it such an impossible
dream to think that, one day, the rest of us might as well?"

"If the high school wanted to change the Christmas
pageant," Doris O'Connor charged the editor, "why couldn't they
have just sung some different carols? This is our holiday, and we
should have the right to celebrate it the way we want to—which
is the way it always was."

"Since it's the Jewish retail businesses that profit most from
the commercial side of Christmas," wrote an elderly widow, "why
are they always complaining about it?"

"Why do we have to print all this drivel?" Iris Tanaka asked.
"The school board finally had the guts to do a good thing for this
community, and some of these people are being downright big-
oted about it."

"That's why we print it," Gail told her. "To let some light
shine on things that are usually allowed to foment in the dark."

"What is all this garbage?" Deborah Frankel wondered.
"Where is it coming from? Are these people for real?"

"A few, I guess," Rachel Cohen conceded. "They keep it
pretty much under wraps most of the time. I think the stress of
the holidays tends to bring it to the surface."

Deborah snorted. "You mean the universally recognized season of Peace on Earth Good Will Toward Men?"

Although he would never admit it to anyone, not even to himself, Christmas was the most difficult time of the year for Malcolm Purdy. The festive decorations, the holiday spirit, the sound of carols, the eagerness of children—it all reminded him of just how alone he was. Even the woman who worked for him and stayed with him whenever he asked had family obligations at Christmas.

Malcolm had no one. The men who came to his compound meant little to him. They connected for a month or two, but they were not family. He taught them what they wanted to know, they paid handsomely for his services, and then they departed. He never heard from any of them again.

Once a year, Malcolm left the Island and went to a place in Montana where he met with others who were like himself, disillusioned, disenfranchised, lost. The few weeks of camaraderie he shared there came as close to the Corps as anything in his life ever would. The philosophies may have differed, Malcolm agreeing with some of them and disagreeing with others, but the intensity was there, the excitement—the awareness that something was happening in the country, and that things, albeit slowly, might finally be starting to change.

When the holidays came, however, he was alone, with his thoughts, his memories, his shattered dreams. On the day before Christmas, he wrote a long letter to his daughters, sheet after sheet of tightly penned lines that told of his life, and begged their forgiveness. When he was finished, well into the evening, he read the letter through, and then, page by page, threw it into the fire.

Ruben brought a pizza over to Ginger's place. They ate it in front of the fire and washed it down with a bottle of Chianti. Twink was now munching on the last bit of crust left in the box.

"I want to give you this now, while we're alone," Ruben said, pulling a small package from his pocket.

"I hope it isn't too extravagant," Ginger said, eyeing the package.

"Terribly," he told her.

Ginger giggled as she tore off the wrapping. Inside the box, nested in blue velvet, was a thin gold necklace, and hanging from it was a small gold heart.

"I love it," she cried. "It's very extravagant and it's just perfect. Here, put it on for me, will you?"

She lifted her heavy hair away and he fastened the clasp around her neck. Then he leaned over and kissed the little hollow where her neck met her shoulder.

"I love that, too," she murmured. "But first things first."

She reached over and selected a package from the pile she had stacked on the floor.

"For me?" he asked with a smile.

"Well, actually, it was for the mailman," she said, poking him playfully in the ribs. "But you put me on the spot."

He undid the wrapping carefully, preserving the ribbon and the paper, while she wriggled impatiently. She had bought him a pale blue cashmere sweater with an elegant cable knit pattern. It had cost her well over half a week's salary, but she didn't care. She didn't know it was the first cashmere he had ever owned.

"I will treasure this," he said, putting on the sweater and then running his fingers over the fine wool.

She fingered her necklace. "I'll never take this off."

"We've known each other for two years," he said. "We had our first date hardly more than six weeks ago. Why does it seem as though we've been together forever?"

She snuggled against him. "There are some that say we keep meeting up with the people we knew in other lives," she told him.

"Do you believe that?" he asked.

She shrugged. "I don't know," she said. "I don't think I believe in much of anything, except what I feel—I believe in that." She ran her finger slowly down his cheek. "And right now, I feel like taking that sweater off you, and everything else that's on you, and then having you do the same to me. Except for my necklace, of course. That stays on."

Not a moment had gone by since the second Sunday in October that Mary Breckenridge didn't think of Tara. There were many mornings when she would awaken expecting to see her, many evenings when she would sit down at the dinner table and wonder why the girl was late. A number of times, she was almost positive that she heard her daughter's voice echoing down the halls of Southwynd.

On one level, she knew Tara was gone. But on another level, she couldn't seem to let her go.

Christmas was Mary's favorite day of the entire year because it had always meant a time that the family would spend together, laughing, playing, enjoying their presents, having fun. But this year there was no joy, no laughter. The house had not been decorated; there wasn't even a tree.

It snowed on Christmas Day; a rare dusting of white that settled over the Island like a gentle blessing. There was not enough accumulation to clog traffic or cause any major accidents, just enough to lift the spirits and mark the occasion as something special.

Mary never noticed. She spent the day in her room with the curtains drawn, pretending to read. She knew she wasn't being fair to Tori; after all, the girl was only twelve. But she couldn't help it. She felt sick inside, and empty, and her tears were never far from the surface.

What made the pain so much worse was that it wouldn't go away; no one would let it. It was like a worrisome wound that couldn't heal because so many took advantage of every opportunity to pick at the scab. Even when Mary didn't want to think about Tara, the newspaper came to remind her. Every issue carried yet another story, offering a new detail or the rehash of an old theory. And the letters to the editor! Mary wondered whether any of these people, most of whom she didn't even know, realized how hurtful they were being. On top of that, whenever she got up the courage to venture into town, there were all those solicitous souls who looked at her with such pity, or tried not to look at her, or lowered their voices to a whisper when she came near.

"You're making it worse," she wanted to scream at them. But of course she didn't; she hadn't been raised to call attention to herself.

"Don't blame the *Sentinel*," Kyle told her. "They just want to help. They think, if they keep the story going, something they print might lead to the killer. And don't blame the people, either. They're trying to be kind; they just don't know how."

Mary shook her head slowly. Her daughter was gone. What did it really matter?

14

At three o'clock on Christmas afternoon, Ruben and Stacey collected Ginger at her apartment and the three of them drove to the Earley home.

From the outside, it looked like a comfortable house; old and brown with white trim, set back off the road to gain some privacy and an ample front lawn. A giant maple tree stood guard on either side of the driveway, rhododendron beds looked well tended, and window boxes hinted at spring flowers to come. The Earleys had draped colorful lights over the bushes, and a life-sized Santa drove his reindeer across the roof. Through a big front window, Ruben and Stacey caught a glimpse of an enormous blue spruce laden with decorations. It was exactly the kind of place where grandparents would live, Ruben thought; the kind of place he had never known, and had never been able to give his daughter.

"Let's hope looks aren't deceiving," Ginger murmured as though reading his mind. They climbed out of the Blazer, retrieved a pile of gaily wrapped packages from the back, and made their way up the path.

Jack Earley opened the front door. "Merry Christmas," he said, giving Ginger a big hug, offering his hand to Ruben, and smiling at Stacey. "Come in out of the cold. Here, let me take your coats. I've got a good fire going in the living room."

The inside of the house was as welcoming as the outside, with comfortable, well-used furniture, polished hardwood floors, scattered rugs, and a seemingly endless array of family photographs that covered almost every surface. The living room was a spacious rectangle with a great stone fireplace taking up almost one whole wall. On closer inspection, the tree was even more spectacular than the initial glimpse had revealed, with hundreds of lights that sparkled on and off and a magnificent display of ornaments that bespoke a lifetime of collecting.

"What a wonderful tree," Stacey cried, her brown eyes dancing.

"That's my wife's pride and joy," Jack told her. "Takes her three weeks to get the thing up every year."

Stacey took a step closer to look at a miniature wooden sleigh, so exquisitely carved that it looked like lace.

"Don't touch that," a voice barked behind her. "My grandfather made that. It's over a hundred years old."

Stacey turned around to see Verna standing in the doorway. "I wouldn't dream of touching it, Mrs. Earley," she said. "I was just admiring it."

"Humph," Verna said.

"I've never seen a Christmas tree so beautiful."

"You don't decorate a tree of your own?" Verna asked. She could afford to be magnanimous; she knew these people could never have anything that would compare.

"Not with this kind of history," Stacey told her. "My mother was an orphan and my dad's parents are long gone, so it's pretty much just the two of us. I have a few things from my grandmother, but nothing like this."

"That's too bad."

Verna had fully intended to despise the interlopers—these two people who were ruining her holiday. But looking at Stacey, she couldn't stop a pang of sympathy for the motherless child who had no family to fall back on. Why, the girl hardly looked Mexican at all, with her silky blond hair and sweet face and simple velvet dress. All that gave her away really was the color of her skin.

She looked at Ruben. Now there was a different story altogether. Even in his best blue suit and his polished shoes, with his arms full of Christmas packages, there was no mistaking where he had come from. She prayed that none of her neighbors had seen him come in, or would notice his vehicle parked in the driveway, and then go spreading the news all over town. She wondered if Ginger had insisted he drive on purpose. She forced her lips into a brittle smile.

"How do you do, Chief Martinez."

"It's a pleasure to meet you, Mrs. Earley," Ruben replied smoothly. "Thank you for having us to your lovely home."

"Yes, well, you're welcome, of course," Verna replied. So he had some manners and he didn't speak with an accent, she thought. What did that mean? Underneath, he was still what he was.

"This teenage terror with the eyes popping out of her head is my daughter, Stacey," Ruben said.

"Hello," the teenager said politely.

"What a pretty name," Verna murmured. She wondered if these people really believed that their children would be more American if they gave them American names.

Ginger laid her packages under the tree. It gave her something to do so that she wouldn't throttle her mother. She knew exactly what Verna was thinking.

"Ruben, bring that stuff over here," she said, as much to get him out from under the glare as to relieve him of his load.

He did as he was told, giving her an amused wink when he was sure no one could see. He, too, knew what Verna was thinking.

"Don't let it get to you," he said under his breath. "It doesn't matter." But even as the words came out of his mouth, he knew that, this time, it did matter.

"Jack says it takes you three weeks to put up the tree, Mrs. Earley," he said politely. "Do you do it all yourself?"

"I don't actually put it up," she said, preening a little. "Jack does that. But I do the trimming."

"Do you have a set place for each ornament, or do you do it differently each year?"

"Oh, differently, of course," she said, warming to her subject in spite of herself. "The moment it comes down, I forget everything about it, so I won't be tempted to repeat anything the next time. That's the whole fun of it: each year, it's brand-new. I never even—"

She brought herself up sharply. What was she doing, standing here, having a conversation with him when she had intended to ignore him?

"Well, enough chitchat," she said. "I have a dinner to prepare."

Across the hall, Stacey had seen the dining room table; the crisp linen cloth, the candles, the setting for sixteen.

"You're not doing all the work yourself, are you?" she asked. "For so many people?"

"Of course, I am," Verna said. "Who else would be doing it?"

"I'd be happy to help," Stacey offered.

Verna looked at her in surprise. "What do you know about cooking?"

"I think you can trust her, Mom," Ginger said with a chuckle. "She's been cooking for Ruben since she was ten."

"Well, I suppose I could use some help," the woman conceded, wondering if the child had any experience preparing American food. There were a number of simple but necessary chores that needed doing. "Ginger certainly never offers."

"I'm great with stuffing," Stacey said, smiling benignly at her father as she followed Verna out of the room.

"How about a drink?" Jack Earley offered. "We can probably squeeze one in before the rest of them show up."

"Scotch," Ginger and Ruben said together. "On the rocks."

Jack went off toward the bar, and Ginger and Ruben turned to each other with a nervous giggle.

"I've been holding my breath so long, I'm dizzy," she whispered. "I keep waiting for the earthquake to hit."

"My back is so stiff, I can't bend," he whispered in reply.

Jack returned with the drinks. "To a Merry Christmas," he said as they touched glasses all around.

"I'll drink to that," Ruben said.

Somewhere between the afternoon and the evening, Verna had to admit to herself that perhaps she had prejudged Ruben Martinez too harshly. He displayed none of the traits she had always believed were associated with Mexicans. His fingernails weren't dirty, his hair wasn't greasy, he spoke English just like an American, his job apparently didn't permit him to be lazy, his language wasn't crude, his manners were as good as anyone else's around her table, and he wasn't stupid. In fact, he led the conversation on a variety of subjects.

Of course, Verna had never really known any Mexicans personally. Growing up, she had been kept away from the migrant workers who seasonally descended on Pomeroy, and had always relied on second- and thirdhand reports of their behavior for her evaluation of them. She had perhaps been somewhat more willing to make allowances for Stacey, since the girl was obviously half white, but her reevaluation of Ruben came as something of a shock to her. Not that she would ever admit it out loud, of course, but she thought she could see a little of what Ginger saw in him. He sat up straight, he looked a person right in the eye, and he had a very engaging smile.

She was as amazed as anyone that her Christmas dinner was not the disaster she had feared. She noted that the boys made at least an effort to be amiable, engaging the police chief in a game of pool at the antique table that occupied one end of the family room. Even their wives took the presence of the intruders in stride. The grandchildren weren't old enough to know the difference and were delighted to have someone new to bedevil with their antics.

Perhaps most responsible for her altered view of Ruben was the gift he had brought for her. When she first saw the box, she anticipated it contained something cheap or garish or totally inappropriate. But when she opened it, she found a fine lace runner nestled inside a cocoon of tissue paper. It was obviously old, obviously costly, and in exquisite taste.

"Why it's beautiful," she cried.

"Ginger told us a little something about you," Stacey explained. "And when Dad saw this in an antique shop, he thought it might suit you."

"He was absolutely right," Verna said, beaming. Indeed, it would be perfect for her dining room table. Eleanor Jewel had one that she said had been in her family for generations, and it was not nearly so nice as this.

"A thank-you might be in order at this time," Ginger prompted.

"I know my manners, young lady," Verna snapped at her daughter. "I even tried to teach them to you!" She turned to Ruben. "Thank you," she said. "It's quite lovely."

Ruben smiled.

As soon as the holidays were over, Verna decided, she would invite Eleanor over for coffee, and casually escort her through the dining room. Of course, she wouldn't tell the gossip where the runner had come from. Maybe, in time, she found herself thinking, she would be able to forget who gave it to her, and just enjoy it for what it was.

Then, at the very moment of her thought, the most extraordinary thing occurred. She happened to catch Ruben's glance, and knew he had read her mind. But rather than reproach, she saw understanding in his expression. I know how you feel, his eyes seemed to say. I'm sorry you feel that way, but I understand. Verna looked away, feeling both vindicated and ashamed in the same instant.

"I'm going to keep it on the dining room table," she heard herself say. "And I'll think of you fondly every time I look at it."

Ginger did a double take, her father blinked, her brothers stared. But Ruben just smiled.

"You bewitched her," Ginger declared as they drove home. "I wouldn't have believed it if I didn't see it with my own eyes and hear it with my own ears. You absolutely bewitched her."

"Did I?" he replied, a twinkle in his eye.

"Don't sit there looking so smug. You know you did. I don't know how, but you got to her."

"There was no magic involved," he said. "I think it was more a matter of her having the chance to see the enemy up close and personal, and realizing there was nothing to fear."

Verna had even allowed Ruben to hug her when he and Stacey and Ginger were leaving. "I'm glad you could come," she had said, and it wasn't entirely untrue.

"Glad you could come?" Ginger repeated now. "Well, if it wasn't magic, it was certainly a miracle."

The telephone rang in the Earley house at just past nine the next morning.

"Tell me it isn't so," Eleanor Jewel trilled over the line. "Tell me you didn't really do it?"

Verna grit her teeth, wondering how, even on this small an island, word had gotten around so fast.

"Do what?" she asked with a leaden heart.

"Why, have that Martinez person in your home, of course."

"As a matter of fact, I did," Verna replied. "It was Ginger's idea, of course. Apparently the man and his daughter have no family and had nowhere to go. Ginger works with him, you know, and I'm sure she took pity on him. I couldn't very well tell her to uninvite him once the damage was done. That would have been too rude."

"But my dear, it must have been horrible for you."

"Of course it was horrible," Verna replied. "But I'm a Christian woman. What else could I do?"

"You're a martyr, that's what you are," Eleanor declared emphatically. "A real martyr."

"It's all true," Eleanor reported to a friend five minutes later. "He was there for dinner. Verna tried to make it sound like it was nothing more than one of those employer-employee things, but of course we know better, don't we?"

"What can she be thinking?" the friend asked. "That we're stupid? Or blind? Her daughter certainly isn't going out of her way to hide the affair."

"On the contrary, my dear," Eleanor said, "she seems to be flaunting it. Mildred MacDonald saw the two of them together coming out of the movies last week—and they were holding hands."

"Poor Verna," the friend said with a sigh. "She has three fine sons, but that daughter of hers has always been a cross she's had to bear."

15

Stacey Martinez stood in her tiny bedroom putting the finishing touches on an outfit of black velvet pants, a cream silk blouse, and a brocade vest. At fifteen and a half years old, she was about to go out on her first real date.

Ginger had helped her select the clothes. After an hour of frustration with everything in her wardrobe, Stacey had gone looking for advice.

"I want to look soft and maybe a little sophisticated," she said. "I don't mind looking my age, but I want everyone to know I have possibilities."

"Silk," Ginger said at once with a knowing smile. "And velvet. You're perfect in velvet."

They put the ensemble together in five minutes. To finish it all off, Stacey tied a black velvet ribbon around her neck, and then added her mother's pearl earrings, a touch of mascara, and a pale coat of lipstick.

"You look absolutely fabulous," Ginger told her when she came into the living room.

Ruben beamed.

"I don't know how she got to be so terrific," he said after

Danny had come to collect her and they had swept out on a wave of excitement and expectation.

"She had a great role model," Ginger said, sitting down on the sofa beside him and resting her chin on his shoulder.

"You know, I always thought it would be the worst day of my life when I stopped being the center of her universe," he confessed. "Now I'm so proud of her, I could cry."

Ginger smiled. The more she learned about this man, the more she liked him. "I have an idea," she proposed. "Let's not wait for midnight to open the champagne. I think we have something much more important to celebrate right now."

"What?" he asked. "Stacey's emancipation?"

"No," she told him. "Yours."

The New Year's Eve party was at the Petrie home, an imposing two-story gray house on the east side of the Island that sat on a gentle rise well back from the road and was fronted by exquisitely manicured lawns.

"Owen's dad owns the hardware store and garden center in town," Danny told her. "He has a full-time gardener working here, and he writes the expense off on his income taxes as advertising and promotion."

The interior of the house was every bit as splendid as the exterior, featuring large rooms that were filled with an assortment of antiques that, genuine or not, must have cost a fortune. There was an extravagant and apparently endless array of food and drink; two maids in gray uniforms scurried about, serving and clearing; a man in a gray suit stood waiting to take their coats.

Stacey had never been inside such a fine home. It had never occurred to her that there were people right here on Seward Island—other than the Breckenridges, of course—who could afford to live like this, and who would think nothing of putting on this kind of party for a bunch of teenagers.

"Hey, Danny," the acne-faced Owen Petrie called, weaving his way across the foyer with a bottle of beer in his hand. "Glad you could make it. Who's this ravishing thing you got with you?"

"This is Stacey," Danny told him. "Stacey, this is Owen."

"Stacey? Stacey who?" Owen asked. It was clearly not his first bottle of beer.

"Stacey Martinez," she replied for herself.

Owen blinked. "The police chief's daughter?"

"The one and only."

"Well, I'll be damned."

With that, Owen reeled away to greet another guest.

"Is he always this rude?" Stacey asked with a chuckle. "Or is it just on New Year's?"

Danny shrugged. "Maybe we shouldn't have come. Would you like to go someplace else?"

"Oh no," she told him. "I think it'll be fun."

"Happy New Year," Ruben said at midnight, as he and Ginger watched the televised fireworks exploding from the Space Needle in downtown Seattle. "I have a feeling it's going to be a great one."

"So do I," she said.

They had finished the champagne before dinner, so now they toasted each other with glasses of Kahlúa.

"I'm glad we didn't go anywhere tonight," he said. "It's so much better to be here alone with you than out with a lot of strangers looking for an excuse to be happy."

Ginger giggled. "Of course, when you think of it—what's to be happy about?" she pondered. "The world and everyone in it getting another year older?"

"No," he said pulling her close. "What's to be happy about is you and me, finding each other."

The Petries' party was in full swing. Midnight had come and gone; food was still being consumed; punch bowls were being refilled. Many of the kids were walking around with glassy eyes and dumb expressions. The beer was flowing. Danny was drinking ginger ale.

"What's the matter, old man?" Bert Kriedler, a taller, heavier version of his younger brother, Hank, teased. "In training?"

"Nope," Danny replied. "Just the designated driver."

"How about you, Stacey? Did you find the tequila?"

"I found the punch," she told him. "Is there tequila in it?"

Bert didn't reply. He just laughed and turned away.

"I hope he didn't hurt your feelings," Danny said. "He's just a jerk."

"His brother is in a couple of my classes," Stacey told him. "It must run in the family."

Sometime later, as she made her way upstairs in search of a bathroom, she saw Bert and a couple of other senior boys through an open bedroom door. It didn't take an expert, or even a policeman's daughter, to know what they were doing with the lines of white powder in front of them.

"Oh shit!" she heard one of them exclaim as she passed. "Now Miss Tijuana is gonna run and tell her daddy on us!"

"I don't think you had a very good time tonight," Danny said on the way home.

"No, I had fun," Stacey assured him. "It was just—different, that's all. Not what I'm used to."

"I don't hang out a lot with those guys," he told her. "And in case your dad wants to know, I don't do drugs, either."

Stacey smiled. "I didn't think so," she said.

"I've got better things to do with my life."

"I'm glad."

They were silent the rest of the way home.

"Well, uh, d'you think maybe you might want to go out again sometime?" he asked as he pulled up in front of her house.

"Sure," she replied.

"We could go to another movie?"

"That sounds great."

"Well, uh, how about Saturday night?"

"Okay."

Even in the dark, she could see the big grin that spread across his face.

"Terrific," he said. "Do you like pizza? Maybe we could get a pizza before the movie."

"I love pizza."

"Six o'clock then?"

"Okay."

Danny jumped out of the car and came around to open the door for her. On the front porch, he leaned down, and for an instant, his lips brushed her cheek.

"Good night," he whispered.

"Good night," she whispered back.

Stacey watched as he drove off. She was a little high from the punch, but far from drunk. Still, she felt as if the whole world were dancing around her.

Despite the display of opulence, it had truly been a terrible party. Almost everyone there had either made an unpleasant remark or simply ignored her, and she had seen several of the girls staring at her with less than gracious expressions that clearly wondered why she, and not one of them, was out with one of the most sought after boys in school. Stacey had no answer for them; she didn't understand it herself. But she didn't dwell on it. The fact that Danny Leo, the high school hunk, wanted to see her again made the whole evening worthwhile. She opened the front door and floated into the house.

16

"We were willing to give Chief Martinez the benefit of the doubt," a television repairman wrote to the editor of the *Seward Sentinel* on the first Monday of the New Year. "Even though a number of us thought that he was an unusual choice to head up the Island's police department, we were told he had the credentials to handle any law enforcement problem that the 1990s might bring our way. Only it's now more than two months since the Breckenridge murder, and it's clear to me, at least, that we were told wrong. Ruben Martinez is obviously not the man for the job. I say, it's time for a change."

"First it was some unidentified maniac who murdered Tara Breckenridge, then it was an exemplary high school student, then it was an outstanding educator, and now who is it, pray tell?" asked a homemaker. "It seems to me that the police are fishing in some murky pond they can't see into, and just pulling up whatever happens to get snagged on their line. My daughters are now thoroughly frightened of strangers, teenage boys, and teachers. Is that what the city council had in mind when it hired an outsider to be our police chief?"

o o o

"When a project fails," wrote a high-powered business consultant, "management is almost always to blame. Maybe it's time for Seward Island's police department to have some new management."

"All right," a weary Albert Hoch told Jim Petrie over the telephone. "You want to start interviewing, go ahead."

"You mean Kyle has given you his permission?" Petrie asked with just a hint of derision.

"I haven't even talked to Kyle," Hoch snapped. "I'm just sick of all the bickering. I don't happen to think anyone else is going to come in here and do any better than Ruben, but I'm tired of arguing about it."

In fact, he was tired of the constant criticism, the letters that questioned his leadership, the irate phone calls that insulted his judgment. He was hurt by being snubbed on the street by people he'd known for decades, and embarrassed when he realized that he had become the butt of snide jokes. Some less charitable residents had begun to call for his resignation. Even his wife, Phoebe, was feeling the indignity of being ostracized by some of her social circle.

"You can't say I didn't warn you," Petrie said.

"No, I can't," Hoch replied with a sigh.

Before becoming Seward's mayor, Albert Hoch was a successful insurance salesman. Nothing less than a massive coronary at the age of forty-eight could have persuaded him to give up his agency and take on the benign responsibilities of Island leadership.

Being liked, trusted, and accepted were Hoch's stock-in-trade. They were the traits that had made him a millionaire and gotten him elected to office three times. When push came to shove, his principles would always take second seat to his reputation, and his reputation was far too important for him to risk damaging it in a no-win situation.

After his coronary, his doctors had warned him about avoiding stress, and he did not now want to put himself in the unpopular, and therefore stressful, position of going against the city council. Besides, when it came right down to it, he didn't really owe Ruben a thing.

"It's out of my hands now," he told the police chief less than an hour later, having first stopped by Kyle Breckenridge's office at the bank before walking over to Graham Hall. "The city council has decided to look for someone to replace you."

Ruben shrugged. "It's certainly their prerogative," he said with dignity. Not once in his entire career had he ever been fired.

"No one's cutting you off, you understand," Hoch was quick to add, remembering the two years still left on the police chief's contract. "We'll make it right for you. Time to look for another position, references, whatever."

"I wasn't worried," Ruben replied. "And since it's likely that the interview process will take some time on both sides, I want you to know that I'm willing to stay on the job until you've found a suitable replacement."

The mayor nodded. "I was hoping you would say that," he said. "I certainly do appreciate it, and I'm sure the city council will, too."

With that bit of unpleasant business taken care of, the mayor made a hasty withdrawal.

It was after six o'clock. Ruben had gone home, Charlie had gone off to keep a doctor's appointment, the day shift had been replaced by the swing shift. Although she had officially been off duty for more than an hour, Ginger was still in her office, trying to catch up on paperwork. But the anger kept getting in her way.

As far as she was concerned, Albert Hoch was nothing more than a lily-livered coward, and the city council nothing more than a bunch of mealy-mouthed slugs. To hold Ruben responsible for not catching Tara Breckenridge's killer was a little like holding one of those idiot TV meteorologists responsible for failing to predict an earthquake.

Ginger was as frustrated as anyone about the case, even more so now that she knew who had murdered the fifteen-year-old. To have to stand by and watch Ruben get fired because there wasn't enough evidence to arrest Jerry Frankel was almost more than she could bear.

On the heels of the anger came the guilt. It was her fault this was happening. After all, it was she who was actively conducting the investigation, interviewing the teacher, evaluating the information. If the city council had a problem, it was with her, not Ruben.

Hot tears began to sting her eyes. If Ruben left, what was she going to do? Their relationship was progressing, but it was still fragile; she couldn't just pick up and follow him. And if he ended up in some city clear across the country, what would happen to them then? With conflicting work schedules and the cost of travel, long-distance romances were usually doomed; especially ones that hadn't had time to cement. Just when it seemed that life had finally taken the right turn for her, politics stepped in to block the road. She blinked back the tears.

Dammit it, she thought, the teacher was guilty as sin, and being unable to prove it was not only going to cost Ruben his job, but likely going to cost her a future of real happiness. Ginger could no longer keep the tears in check; they began to run freely down her cheeks.

"Knock, knock," Helen Ballinger said, poking her head in the door. She was wearing her coat and obviously on her way out. "This just came in for Charlie."

She held out an envelope.

"I'll take it," Ginger said over her shoulder.

Helen dropped it on Ginger's desk. "See you tomorrow," she said, and hurried off.

Ginger blinked through her tears; the envelope bore the return address of the state crime lab in Seattle. Her heart suddenly skipped a beat. She knew exactly what it was—the report on Jerry Frankel's fingerprints.

The two detectives often accepted mail for the other, but never opened it. Ginger fingered the envelope. Invasion of privacy or not, overstepping the boundaries or not, she felt sure Charlie would understand. With trembling hands, she ripped it open, almost tearing the report in half in her haste to get to it. She read it once, and then she read it a second time, and a third time. Long after the words were imprinted on her brain, she sat there, staring at the piece of paper.

PART THREE

The Victim

"He that is without sin among you, let him first cast a stone. . . ."

—*John 8:7*

1

Malcolm Purdy survived the holidays the way he usually did. He got drunk on Christmas morning, stayed drunk through New Year's Eve, and remembered next to nothing in between.

The woman who worked for him came in now and again to make sure he was all right. Once, she ended up spending the night, trying to get a little solid food into him, cleaning up after he vomited, holding him when he passed out. He rambled on a lot, about people she didn't know and places she'd never been, and about the sorry state of the country, but most of what he said was unintelligible.

When he ran out of liquor, he sobered up, bathed, shaved, and brushed his teeth. He was expecting two men shortly after the first of January, and it would not have been appropriate for them to see him mewling and puking like a baby.

The men arrived late on Tuesday and were shown to the bunkhouse. The woman unpacked for them and then cooked a hot meal. Afterward, the three men sat around drinking beer, talking, laughing. It was understood that they would relax today, and get down to work tomorrow. Sometime around ten o'clock, they went to bed, the visitors staggering out to the bunkhouse, their host collapsing on the sofa in front of the dying fire.

Purdy was a happy man. He knew very little about the two who had come; he would not know much more about them when they left. It didn't matter; he was no longer alone.

"Why, Verna Earley, your table runner is nothing short of magnificent," Eleanor Jewel declared on her way through the dining room. "I don't believe I've seen it before. Was it a Christmas gift?"

"That old thing?" Verna replied. "It belonged to my great-grandmother. I've had it packed away for years."

Eleanor arrived on Wednesday morning in response to the invitation for coffee, bursting with curiosity. It was all she could do to hold her tongue until Verna had propelled her past all her finery and into the breakfast nook, where they sat down with their cups and cake.

"Now tell me just everything," she said at the first possible moment, her triple chins quivering.

"About what?" Verna asked cautiously.

"Well, about the teacher, of course. Are they going to arrest him?" Nothing new had been reported about the Breckenridge case since before Christmas, and the gossip had been itching to get hold of a fresh source.

"Oh, that," Verna said brightly, relieved that the conversation was not going to be about Ruben Martinez. "Well, I expect they'll arrest him when they have enough evidence."

"Then they *are* going to arrest him?" Eleanor gushed. "You mean, he really did it?"

As before, Verna had no more information about the murder investigation than did Eleanor. In fact, when the subject came up at dinner on Christmas Day, both Ruben and Ginger had declined to discuss it. But this was a chance to gain some much-coveted stature, and she wasn't about to let it pass.

"Of course, he did it," she asserted carelessly. "And I'm sure it won't be very long now before Ginger has what she needs to put that horrid man in the hangman's noose."

By the time the holidays were over, Matthew Frankel had reevaluated the incident on the playground, and decided that school probably wasn't such a bad place after all. At least he reasoned that it wasn't fair to judge everyone by the actions of a few.

His grandfather helped him reach that conclusion, during the part of the holiday vacation that the Frankels spent with Aaron in Pennsylvania.

"You're growing into a fine young man," the older version of his father told him. "Tell me, how are you doing in school?"

The two were alone together for an afternoon, and Aaron had taken the boy to the cemetery to visit Emma.

"Okay, I guess, Grandpa," Matthew said. He kicked a stray pebble along the side of the grave.

"Are your grades good?" the old man asked.

"Yes, sir."

"Have you made friends?"

"Sure. Well, one. His name is Billy."

Aaron peered down at the boy and saw an expression that reminded him sharply of Emma.

"What's wrong, son?" he prodded gently.

Matthew squirmed a little. He didn't really know his grandfather very well, but he suspected that Aaron was very much like Jerry.

"Some fifth-graders said some things to me at school one day," he replied hesitantly. "Not very nice things—about me being Jewish." He decided not to mention the other part, the part about his father being a murderer.

Aaron stiffened. He had wondered and even worried when Jerry so abruptly up and relocated his family to the other side of the country. In the past couple of years, he had heard and read some very distressing things about the Northwest; about anti-government militia groups, about small enclaves of neo-Nazis, about skinheads, about the rise in hate crimes.

"Children like that are to be pitied," he told his grandson, a shiver running down his back as he remembered the abusive, goose-stepping youth of the Third Reich. "If you show them you're not afraid, you probably won't have any more trouble with them."

"But why would they do that?" Matthew asked. "I never did anything to them. I don't even know them."

Aaron sighed. "There are people in this world who don't feel very good about themselves," he said. "Some of them aren't very smart, or wealthy, or good-looking; a lot of them have just had bad parenting. Whatever the reason, they're unhappy, and unhappy people somehow get the idea they'll feel better about themselves if they make someone else unhappy. They also have very limited vocabularies."

"*Do* they feel better when they make someone else unhappy?" the boy wanted to know.

"Not for very long," Aaron told him. "You can pretty much hide from the world if you want to, but you can't hide from yourself. Even people who hate others so they won't have to hate themselves sooner or later have to look in the mirror."

"Grandpa," Matthew said, "let's not tell Mom and Dad about this, okay? It's no big deal, and I don't want them to worry."

Aaron nodded. "It'll be just between the two of us," he agreed. "But if it happens again, then you must give me your word that you'll tell your parents. Because they love you and it's their job to protect you."

Matthew considered a moment. "Okay," he promised.

"Again" came four days after school resumed.

The fifth-graders cornered Matthew behind the gymnasium.

"Hey, it's the Jew-boy again!" they exclaimed, closing in.

Matthew stood his ground.

"You're bigger than I am," he said. "And there are three of you. You can push my face in the mud and I probably can't stop you. So if doing it makes you feel better about yourselves, go ahead," he said. "Because after the mud washes off, I'm still gonna like the person I see in the mirror."

The three boys looked at one another for a moment and then back at Matthew.

"The kike kid wants us to push his face in the mud," one said.

"Yeah," said a second. "I heard him ask for it."

"So, what are we waiting for?" asked the last.

The three laughed and started toward him. Matthew didn't fight back. He let them knock him to the ground; he let them push his face into the mud. He shut his eyes and held his breath, and he didn't cry. After a while, they let him up.

"Son of a Jew bitch whore!" they cried.

"Son of a Jew bastard murderer!"

Matthew didn't even let that bother him. He stood as tall as he could. "Did anyone ever tell you that you have a very limited vocabulary?" he told them and then he smiled, his teeth very white in his muddied face.

The three bullies looked at one another, clearly perplexed. None of them stopped Matthew when he turned and walked away.

This time, he told the school nurse who helped clean him up. And he told his parents.

"Are you all right?" Deborah asked in alarm.

"Why didn't you tell us the first time?" Jerry demanded.

Matthew shrugged. "They didn't hurt me the first time; they just scared me. This time, they didn't even scare me, but Grandpa said I had to tell you. They pushed me down in the mud and called me names, that's all. I think doing that makes them feel better about themselves."

Jerry almost smiled because it was exactly the kind of thing Aaron would have said.

"Come on, let's get you into the bathtub, young man," his mother said. She picked him up, hugging him so hard he could barely breathe, and bundled him up the stairs.

Jerry sat down at the kitchen table and clasped his hands until his knuckles turned white. He was a man who was usually slow to anger, but he could feel the burn beginning deep inside him. It was one thing for the police to harass him; it was quite another when a bunch of bullies went after his son. That was hitting way below the belt. Even more, it hinted at something truly malevolent in this serene, pristine community—something that went a good deal deeper than an immature letter to the editor now and then. He had never himself been the target of religious animosity, and despite Aaron's admonitions, he had almost lulled himself into believing he could protect his son from it as well. But now it was here, staring him in the face, and he had to decide what to do about it.

"He's playing naval bombardment as though nothing had happened," Deborah reported ten minutes later.

"But it did happen, didn't it?" Jerry said.

"He's just a kid," she replied. "He doesn't really understand."

"Maybe he doesn't," her husband suggested. "But we do."

"Come on, let's not blow this out of proportion," she responded. "If we make a big deal of it, you know it's likely to make things worse for Matthew."

"We can't ignore it."

"I didn't say we should ignore it. I say we should let the school handle it. That's where it happened; that's where the appropriate action should be taken. You know the principal. You can talk to her and tell her how we feel, and then let her deal with it."

Deborah was a fourth-generation American who had never

been to Germany, hadn't lost any relatives in the Holocaust, and had learned everything she knew about the Gestapo and the Brown Shirts and the Hitler Youth through the filtered light of a classroom.

"You think some kids calling Matthew the 'son of a Jew bastard murderer' is just a school problem?" Jerry asked. "Let them take care of it and that's the end of it?"

"For now, yes," she reasoned. "In case you haven't noticed, there are bigots on this island. And what else is there for people like that to do around here besides giving vent to their fears and ignorance? But if what Rachel says is true, there are just a few of them, and I think we'd be playing right into their hands if we were to sink to their level." That was all she needed, Deborah thought, to have another messy situation in another community.

He looked at her, unconvinced. "Three bullies have targeted your son, and you seem to think it's nothing."

"I didn't say it was nothing," she told him. "But I believe in picking my battles, when I can. A few ten-year-olds calling Matthew names hurts, but it hardly warrants calling in the National Guard. I think he handled it brilliantly, all on his own, and I'd be very surprised if they bothered him again."

"This doesn't end with those kids and you know it," Jerry persisted. "How would they have known what to say if they didn't hear it at home?"

"They probably did," she conceded. "So, what do you want to do—go out and gun down the parents?"

"Of course not," he said. "But it may not be the passing thing you think it is. A couple of months ago, I came up against a student whose parents are apparently teaching revisionist history at home."

"You're kidding," she replied in surprise. "What did you do?"

"I told him to bring in his books and we'd study them along with the traditional texts, and let the class decide the truth about the Holocaust."

"What happened?"

Jerry shrugged. "He never brought the books. He never said another word about them. It became a nonissue, and we went on with the regular curriculum."

"Well, there, you see?" she said. "You didn't have to get down in the dirt and fight him, or make a big fuss about it, did you? A small humiliation in front of his peers was sufficient."

"That approach may have worked in that particular instance, but this is different," he reminded her. "In case you forgot, they called me a murderer, to my own son."

Now it was Deborah's turn to shrug. "The police are desperate to solve the Breckenridge case. In their zeal, they leaned on you a little too hard, and some people got the wrong idea. Maybe some of them were stupid enough to talk about it at the dinner table. You know better than I do that kids are like sponges. They soak stuff up and squeeze it out without any real comprehension. This is probably nothing more than that, and I wouldn't go out looking to find some great community conspiracy lurking in the shadows."

"Are you sure?" he asked.

"Yes, I'm sure," she assured him complacently. "You'll see. It'll all blow over. This'll turn out to be just an isolated incident."

2

So accustomed were the readers of the *Seward Sentinel* to seeing the big black-banded box that had appeared in the classified section with daily repetition for more than a month that they reacted with alarm on the morning it was no longer there.

"What happened?" they wondered on Friday over double lattes at The Pelican.

"Where is it?" they asked as they boarded the ferry.

"Why aren't they printing the Purdy ad anymore?"

"What does it mean?"

"Have the police caught the killer?"

"Who turned him in?"

"Who gets the reward?"

Telephone calls poured into Curtis House at the rate of two dozen an hour.

"First they criticized us for printing the ad in the first place," Iris Tanaka commented, "and now they berate us for canceling it."

"We didn't cancel it," Gail reminded her. "Malcolm Purdy did."

Indeed, the ex-Marine had called late Wednesday, thanked them for their courtesy, and informed them that the notice would no longer be necessary.

"I understand that the police are close to an arrest," he said. "So I don't guess there's anything to be gained by running it any longer."

"An arrest?" Gail echoed, concealing her surprise. "I didn't know that was common knowledge." In fact, she had not even the slightest inkling from her latest conversation with Ginger that an arrest was imminent.

There was a pause at the other end of the telephone.

"Well, that's what I heard," Purdy told her.

"In that case," the editor inquired, "who gets the reward?"

"Too soon to say," he replied.

"My goodness, who are they arresting?" Iris wanted to know.

Gail shrugged. "The teacher, I assume."

"The teacher?" The editor's assistant was clearly bewildered. "They really think the teacher did it? I don't believe it."

"Why not?"

"I don't know. I guess because he seems like such a regular guy. My kid sister's in one of his classes, and she's always saying what a great teacher he is, how nice he is."

"Nice guys sometimes kill," Gail told her.

Iris frowned. "True. But I thought most of that stuff we were printing about him was just hype; you know, just for circulation."

An image of Alice Easton standing in an upstairs window flickered behind the editor's eyes and was gone. Maybe, she thought. "Maybe not," she said.

Ginger hummed the refrain of a current hit song while she ironed. Although this was normally a task she loathed, she had a whole week of work shirts crisply pressed before she realized it.

The secret, she decided, was in not thinking about what you were doing. And Ginger's mind was certainly not on ironing.

It was Sunday night. She had spent the day in Seattle with Ruben and Stacey, wandering through Pike Place Market, sampling the food, admiring the crafts, and laughing at the fishmongers who made a sideshow out of tossing their catch from one to another.

"Dungeness crab, already cooked," one of them encouraged Ruben. "Your missus won't have to cook tonight."

Ruben smiled. "Do you want crab for dinner?" he asked Ginger.

She looked at the price. "No," she said, wrinkling her nose. "I want pizza."

"Me, too," Stacey chimed in.

Ruben shrugged. "Sorry," he said to the fishmonger.

They read the names carved in the floor tiles of those who had contributed to saving the treasured landmark. They bought some fresh vegetables and flowers. And then, coming home on the ferry, they argued over what kind of pizza to have, just like any family.

Ginger had never been happier. She knew that the break they needed in the Breckenridge case was just around the corner, and it would not only save Ruben's job, but also save their developing relationship. Even the city council would find it unreasonable to argue with success.

The teacher was guilty. She knew it for certain. It wouldn't matter that it had taken them three months to zero in on him. There had been few clues, and he had been very clever, very elusive. What mattered was that she had finally seen through his boyish act of innocence and was about to nail him. That's what the people would care about, what the newspaper would report—what the council would have to acknowledge.

It had taken her twenty-eight years to find the man with whom she wanted to spend the rest of her life. While some might think them a strange match, there was no doubt in her mind that Ruben Martinez was totally right for her; so calm when she was wired, so thoughtful when she was impulsive, so wise, so caring, so sexy. She knew she would fight, if she had to, get down in the gutter, if it came to that, and do whatever was necessary to prevent anyone from taking him away from her.

Ginger finished pressing the last pair of work pants and hung them on a hanger on the back of her closet door so they would be handy in the morning. Then she turned off the iron, scrubbed her face, brushed her teeth, and climbed into bed. Twink jumped up and stretched out next to her, purring.

"Well, you're not exactly Ruben," she said, stroking his fur, and remembering with a sigh who had been beside her the night before, "but everything in its time."

She fell asleep with a smile on her face.

Charlie Pricker hated being sick. Even a cold made him irritable because it dulled his senses, and this was no cold.

"It's pneumonia, and there's nothing you can do but take your antibiotics and wait it out," Magnus Coop told him.

"Pneumonia?" echoed Charlie. "How the hell did I get that?"

"You tell me," the doctor retorted. "I told you a month ago to come in about that cough."

"It was nothing," groused Charlie.

"Well, it's not nothing anymore. You've got chills, a fever of a hundred and three, and bloody sputum. Now go home and stay there, or I'll put you in the hospital."

"I can't be out of the office for more than a day or two," Charlie protested. "I've got a stack of work higher than the Space Needle."

"I'll explain it to Ruben," Coop said. "And I'm going to tell Jane to take the phone out of your room," he added. "You're to have complete rest."

"I'll bring you some soup," Jane said when her husband arrived home fifteen minutes later. She had already talked to Coop; the bedroom telephone was in her hand.

"I'll come down for it," Charlie said.

Jane shook her head. "I'll bring it up. I promised Magnus I'd lock the bedroom door from the outside if you went one step further than the bathroom."

He didn't argue. Although he would never have admitted it, Coop's diagnosis scared him. He had one relative who died of pneumonia brought on by a boating accident, and another who had succumbed after traveling in India. Weak lungs ran in his family.

Charlie remained under Jane's house arrest for ten days, until his fever was gone and he had stopped coughing up blood. He returned to work on the third Thursday in January to find a letter from the crime lab in the pile on his desk.

"Hey," he said to Ginger. "This must be the report on Frankel's latents. Sure took them long enough. How long has it been sitting here?"

She glanced over. "It came in late yesterday, I think."

"Why the hell didn't you open it?"

Ginger gave him a blank look. "We don't open each other's mail," she reminded him.

"Weren't you curious?"

"Of course I was," she said. "And I would have called you about it, but Jane said you'd be back to work this morning."

Charlie tore into the envelope and scanned the report. Within seconds, a big grin spread across his face.

"We got him!" he cried. "The son of a bitch—we got him!"

On the basis of the fingerprint match, backed up by an array of circumstantial evidence, Judge Irwin Jacobs was persuaded to sign a search warrant for the person and property of Jeremy Frankel.

Ruben, Ginger, Charlie, and Glen Dirksen arrived at the teacher's Larkspur Lane residence on Friday afternoon at five minutes past three. Frankel and his son were at home; his wife was not.

"I'm sorry, sir, but we have a warrant to search the premises," Ruben said, holding out the official, blue-jacketed document.

Jerry looked at it blankly. "What are you talking about?" he asked. "Search my house? Why? For what?"

"We are looking for evidence related to the Breckenridge case," Ginger said.

"I don't understand," he replied. "There isn't anything here."

"Perhaps not, sir," Charlie said. "But the warrant says we get to look."

"Am I supposed to call my lawyer?"

"That's up to you," Ruben told him. "However, we do have a legal right to be here. I doubt your attorney will tell you anything else. Now, may we come in?"

"You mean, right now?" Jerry asked.

"Yes, sir."

"But my wife's not home from work yet. Shouldn't she be here if strangers are going to go through her house?"

"We have no control over that," Ruben said.

Frankel looked at Ginger. "I don't know what to do," he said. "I have to think. Can you come back in a couple of hours?"

"No, I'm afraid not," she said.

"But my son is here. You can't do this in front of my son. He's only nine years old; he doesn't understand."

Ruben and Ginger exchanged glances.

"Perhaps your son could leave the house for a while," Ginger suggested. "Does he have a friend he can visit?"

Jerry seemed to think about that for a moment and then he nodded.

"Why don't you take a moment to arrange it," Ruben said.

As though in a daze, Jerry turned away from the door, and then immediately turned back. "What do I tell him?" he asked.

"Whatever you need to," Ginger replied.

"These people are going to be here with me for a while," the teacher told his son. "And it would be better if we were alone. I called Mrs. Hildress. She said you can come over and play with Billy until I'm finished."

Matthew took a long look at each of the police officers and then turned his dark eyes on his father. "Okay, I'll go," he agreed reluctantly. "But you call me if you need me."

"Count on it," Jerry said. He helped the boy put on his jacket and guided him to the door. "Stay at Billy's until I come for you," he said. "We'll go get pizza for dinner."

Ginger felt an unexpected catch in her throat. Just like any family, she thought.

The little boy walked down the front path, glancing back toward the house several times. Then he turned onto the street and was gone.

The search was thorough. The police tried to be neat, but within just a few moments, it was clear to Jerry that Deborah was going to know they had been there, and any thought he might have had to keep it from her vanished.

"No, you can't stop them," Scott confirmed from his office in Seattle in response to the urgent call. "What are they going to find?"

"Nothing," Jerry replied.

"So let them search."

The four police officers worked quickly and efficiently, spreading out into all the rooms, leaving nothing unchecked. The teacher followed after them like a lost puppy. An hour later, they met in the kitchen, having found nothing.

"There's still the garage," Ruben said. "And we might as well take a quick look around the outside before it gets too dark."

During the summer months, daylight in the Pacific Northwest stretched until almost ten o'clock at night; during winter, it lasted barely past four-thirty.

It was Glen Dirksen who went inside the part of the backyard that Jerry had fenced off for Chase. The retriever wriggled up to him, and Dirksen stooped down to pet him. Taking that as a sign that the stranger would play, Chase bounded off and returned a moment later with one of his favorite toys—a dirty gray sweatshirt, rolled up and knotted at two ends, that he and Matthew used for tug-of-war.

In the gathering dusk, Dirksen took up one of the ends. It was a full minute before he realized that the rag wasn't just dirty, but had dark stains on it. He untied one of the knots and unrolled the material. The stains were splattered all across the front of the sweatshirt.

His heart pounding, Dirksen hurried toward the garage. "Take a look at this," he cried. Ruben and Charlie stopped what they were doing and came over to see.

"It's just an old shirt the dog chews on," Jerry said.

Charlie examined the material. "These look like they could be bloodstains," he said.

"They are," Jerry confirmed. "I cut my thumb a while back and bled all over myself. The stains didn't come out when my wife washed the shirt, so we gave it to Chase."

"We'll have to check this out," Charlie said. He knew that, in addition to the blood, a number of unidentified light gray fibers had been found on Tara Breckenridge's body. He folded the sweatshirt and placed it in a paper bag. Then he stapled the bag shut and scribbled something across the outside with a black felt marker.

A matter of seconds later, Ginger came toward them with an expression on her face that was half disbelief and half exultation.

"Take a look at this," she said. In her hands was a piece of newspaper; inside lay a knife with a thick black handle and a six-inch curved blade.

"Where did you get that?" the teacher asked.

"From the hidden compartment in the back of your car," Ginger replied.

"My car? What was it doing there?"

"That's a good question, Mr. Frankel," Ruben said. "One I was just about to ask you."

"I have no idea," Jerry said, as he peered down at the object. "It's not mine. I've never owned a knife like that."

"We'll have to check this out, too," Charlie repeated, and everyone watched as he duplicated the procedure he had followed with the sweatshirt.

"Mr. Frankel," Ruben said. "I now have to ask you to accompany us down to the medical clinic, where a sample of your blood and hair can be taken for testing."

"The search warrant says you can do that?" Jerry asked.

"Yes, sir, it does."

"Will it take long?"

"Not very," the police chief told him. "You should be able to pick up your son by six at the latest."

The teacher sighed. "I'll get my coat."

Gail Brown knew about the search before it began. It was just the way things happened in small towns. She didn't have all the details, but she had enough to draw some reliable conclusions and get her ace reporter on the story.

"I'm holding a full column," she told him. "It's tomorrow's lead. You have an hour. Don't disappoint me."

He didn't. Fifty-nine minutes later, he handed her a cogent account of the conditions under which the search warrant had been granted, and an accurate description of who had participated in the search and how long it had taken. All it lacked was a specific accounting of what the police had found at the Frankel home, because Ruben was apparently not yet willing to release that information.

She scanned the paragraphs quickly, noting that no mention of the Holman Academy or Alice Easton appeared in the warrant particulars. Without knowing exactly why, Gail felt a strong sense of relief. Admittedly, she had gone to Scarsdale looking for information that would break the Seward Island case wide open, images of Pulitzers dancing before her eyes, but she was uncomfortable with what she had found—or more precisely, what she had not found. When she took the information to Ginger, it was with the hope that it would be used only to keep the police focused on the teacher long enough to uncover some concrete evidence of his complicity in the Breckenridge murder, should there be any.

Apparently, from what her reporter had learned, there was.

Unlike Eleanor Jewel, Mildred MacDonald, and a few others of similar ilk, Libby Hildress was not considered an Island gossip. She belonged to several community organizations and had a wide circle of acquaintances, which placed her in a position to gather numerous snippets of information, but the only person with whom she ever discussed any of the things she overheard was her husband.

"In the middle of the afternoon, he calls," she said as soon as Bud and Billy had been excused from the dinner table and sent off to do their homework. "Can Matthew come over to play for a while?"

"So?" Tom responded.

"So, Matthew tells Billy the police are over at his house, talking to his father."

"That again?"

"Tom, don't dismiss me. I tell you, it means something. Why would Matthew have to leave his house just because the police were there? Does that make any sense?"

"What are you getting at?" he asked.

"I don't think the police were there to talk. I've got a pretty good hunch they were there to search the house. I think they were looking for incriminating evidence. That's why Jerry sent the boy away."

"They have to have a search warrant for that," Tom told her. "And they need a lot more than a hunch to get it."

"My point exactly."

Tom looked at his wife. "You think he killed her, don't you?"

"I don't want to think that, but I don't know what else to think," Libby said. "This interest in him has been going on much too long. When he came to pick Matthew up, he was trying real hard to act normal, you know, but I could tell he was frazzled."

"Frazzled?"

"Well, you know what I mean," she said. "He looked wild-eyed and like he was sort of coming unglued. Well, I don't know how else to say it except to come right out and say it: he looked guilty."

3

Ruben and Ginger couldn't resist indulging in a little private celebration. They had uncovered the direct evidence they believed was going to solve the Breckenridge case, and they were relishing the moment over fish and chips and a pitcher of beer at the Waterside Cafe.

"I knew once we got a search warrant, we'd find what we needed," Ginger exulted, being careful to keep her voice down because they were not yet ready for public disclosure.

"What's scary is to think we'd already cut him loose," Ruben said.

"It was Gail who saved the day," Ginger acknowledged, giving the editor her due. "If she hadn't dug up that stuff at the Holman Academy, we wouldn't have had any other choice—we wouldn't have anything at all."

"Maybe so," Ruben allowed, "but it was your brilliant water glass maneuver that locked it up. Without that latent match, we were dead in the water."

Ginger shrugged carelessly. "It doesn't matter how it happened," she said. "What's important is that we got the son of a bitch, and now the city council is going to have to dance barefoot on broken glass to keep you."

Ruben chuckled. "Well, maybe nothing quite so drastic."

"Oh come on," she teased him. "You've got to make them crawl just a little."

"You know, I always credit good police work," he said thoughtfully. "But it's amazing how many times a case is cracked just because the suspect was careless."

"What do you mean?"

"Well, we searched Frankel's Taurus that first day we were out there, and we didn't find the knife."

"Yes, but we didn't have a search warrant then," she reminded him. "So I never opened that compartment in the back."

"But that's my point," Ruben said. "He's not a stupid man. He knew we suspected him. Why would he keep a murder weapon in his car?"

Ginger considered the question. "Because he didn't think we'd search there again?"

"No, I mean why would he keep it at all? There are plenty of places on this island where he could have gotten rid of a knife, places where we never would have found it, and he had three months to do it."

"Who knows," Ginger suggested. "Killers do stupid things. Maybe he thought he'd outsmarted us and was going to get away with it, so he figured he didn't need to throw away a good knife. Maybe he wanted a souvenir."

In twenty-five years, Ruben had dealt with his share of killers: smart ones, stupid ones, and smart ones who did stupid things. It had been his experience that, while some had been inclined to keep guns, they invariably got rid of knives.

"That's what I mean by being careless," he said. "It never makes sense."

"Does it matter?" she asked. "He did it—isn't that what counts?"

"You have a point," he conceded.

"I have to tell you," Ginger confided, "for a while there I was really afraid that he was going to get away with it, and that you were going to get fired, and Seward Island's first homicide was going to go unsolved. It's scary to think how close we came."

"Then let's not think about it," he suggested.

"Tell me, if you were in his place, would you try to run?" she asked.

"I don't know," Ruben replied. "Maybe, if I didn't have a family to consider. But he does, and besides, he's got one of the best criminal lawyers in the country."

"Well, just in case the idea occurs to him," she said, "I assigned Dirksen to watch him."

Ruben laughed appreciatively. "You're a damn good cop, you know that?" he told her. "You're thorough, you're professional, you cover all the bases, and you have a healthy distrust of all mankind."

"I'm so excited," Ginger said with a giggle. "I think I could jump off the top of Eagle Rock and fly. Frankly, I was devastated at the thought of having to break in a new police chief."

"I was rather concerned about having to leave here myself," Ruben conceded with a shy smile. "Although, I must admit, my concern wasn't entirely about the job."

Ginger grinned. "I should hope not," she said. Under the table, where no one could see, they clasped hands. "The *Sentinel* will probably run a story tomorrow about the search. When are you going to tell Albert what we found?"

"Charlie should have preliminary results on the knife and the sweatshirt by Monday," he said. "On the assumption that they'll go the way we think they will, we'll get the paperwork over to Van Pelt. Then I'll tell the mayor."

Harvey Van Pelt was the Puget County prosecutor. He

would determine if the case against Jerry Frankel was solid enough for an arrest. Ginger sighed contentedly. It would be the first step in nailing the bastard who had so mutilated Tara Breckenridge.

Deborah Frankel spent Friday night putting her house back in order: folding, arranging, replacing, rearranging. She felt totally violated at having had strangers paw through her possessions without her presence, her permission, or even her prior knowledge. She was outraged that this kind of thing could happen. And much as it appalled her to admit it, she was frightened—more frightened than she had ever been in her life—that the police might know something she hadn't yet allowed herself to consider.

"But how could they have gotten a search warrant?" she demanded when there was nothing left to rearrange, and Jerry was finally able to persuade her to come to bed. "On what grounds?"

"They said they matched my fingerprint to one they found on the cross the Breckenridge girl was wearing," he replied.

Deborah stared at her husband. "Is that possible?" she breathed.

His eyes slid past her shoulder. "I don't know how," he said, "but I suppose so."

It was then that the fear gripped her, like a cold fist in her stomach, and the unthinkable thought she had tried so hard to keep out of her mind crawled in. And with the thought came all the protective, maternal instincts she had been developing, without fulling realizing it, since the day so long ago when she first came to acknowledge that her husband needed a mother more than a wife.

"Let's take the weekend off," she suggested suddenly, recklessly, forgetting the packed briefcase that had accompanied her home. "Let's just get in the car and go someplace."

"Where?" he asked.

"I don't know—out to the coast, maybe. Or up to the mountains. Or we could even take the ferry over to Victoria. I don't care where. We just need to get away from here for a couple of days. I feel like the walls are closing in on me."

"I'm not sure we should do that," he said slowly.

"Why not?"

"All things considered, this may not be such a good time to leave the Island. It might look—funny."

"You mean, because somebody might get the wrong idea and think you're trying to run away?"

He shrugged. "Something like that."

She stared at him, the question she couldn't bring herself to ask filling the space between them. After a while, she turned off the light and pulled up the covers.

It was barely an hour later when the telephone rang, but the shrill sound jerked Jerry out of a deep, dreamless sleep. He groped for the receiver in the dark, wondering where he was and what time it was.

"Murderer!" a nameless, faceless voice cried. "We know you killed that poor defenseless girl, and you won't get away with it. Filthy Jew bastard murderer!"

Beside him, Deborah was fumbling for the switch on the bedside lamp. "Who would be calling us at this hour?" she demanded irritably. "For heaven's sake, it's one o'clock in the morning." Then she saw his face—drained of all color. "What is it?" she gasped. "Has something happened to Aaron?"

Jerry did not respond. He simply lay there with the receiver clutched in his hand. Deborah snatched it from him and put it to her ear, but heard only a dial tone.

"Tell me," she insisted.

"It wasn't about Aaron," he told her in a dead voice. "It wasn't about anything. It was just a crank call."

"A crank call?" she muttered in disgust. "You look like you've seen a ghost from the past."

A ghost from the past, he thought, that was not a ghost at all, nor from the past, but alive and well and living on Seward Island.

"It woke me up, that's all," he replied.

Deborah yawned. "With a little luck, maybe we can get back to sleep." She reached over and snapped off the light.

"Remember what you said about wanting to go someplace over the weekend?" he said into the dark. "Well, the hell with the timing; the hell with what anyone thinks. Let's go."

"Okay," she mumbled into her pillow. "It won't take more than a few minutes to throw some things into a suitcase. We can take the early ferry."

"Have you seen the morning *Sentinel*?" Rachel Cohen asked her husband at breakfast. News of the search was splashed across the newspaper's front page.

Scott nodded.

"I'm sorry, but I just can't believe that Jerry could have had anything to do with that girl's death."

The Cherub shrugged.

"I know you can't talk about a client," she said. "But these people are our friends . . . They're going to arrest him, aren't they?"

"It's possible," he conceded.

"This is terrible. That poor family."

"Have you spoken to Deborah?"

Rachel shook her head. "I called first thing, but the machine picked up. I can only imagine what she's going through. She puts up a good front, you know, but I think inside she's scared to death. She might have made light of that incident at school with Matthew, but I know it had to have upset her."

"What incident with Matthew?"

Rachel blinked. "Those bullies who beat up on him and called him anti-Semitic names. I'm sure I told you about it."

Scott frowned. "If you did, I don't remember. Tell me again."

As best she could, Rachel reconstructed what Deborah had told her. "I know there are certain elements here on Seward who feel that way, but as I told Deborah, they usually stay pretty much underground," she concluded. "I don't remember anything as blatant as that ever happening before."

"Anti-Semitism, eh?" he murmured.

Scott's hooded green eyes narrowed and his wife smiled. It was Saturday, the day of the week on which he officially did not work, but that had never kept him from thinking. Almost as though there had been an audible shifting of gears, she knew his mind was now fully engaged in its own kind of processing. She got up and began to clear away the breakfast dishes. There was no point in her saying another word; she knew her husband would not hear her.

The telephone in Ginger's apartment rang shortly before one o'clock on Saturday afternoon.

"I'm out at Ocean Shores," Glen Dirksen reported.

"What the hell are you doing there?"

"Following Frankel," the young officer replied. "You told me to watch him, didn't you? Well, they were up at dawn this morning, and on line for the early ferry—teacher, wife, kid, and dog. I didn't know what they had in mind, so I thought I'd better follow them."

He had sat a discreet half block from the Frankel house all night, dozing off only when the upstairs lights had gone out for good, and awakening every half hour or so until the lights went back on.

"What are they doing?" Ginger asked, suddenly alert.

"They checked into the Lighthouse Suites Inn, then they

went into town and ate lunch at the Dairy Queen, and now they're walking on the beach."

"What kind of luggage do they have?" Ginger asked.

"One small suitcase, weekend size."

"Do they know you're there?"

"I don't think so. I'm not in uniform and I'm driving my pickup. There aren't a heck of a lot of people out here this time of year, but I'm being careful."

"Get as close to them as you can," she instructed. "I don't care if they spot you. I want you to stick to them like glue."

"I can do that," he assured her.

"Do you have enough money for a room and food?"

"Yeah," he replied. "But it's my rent money, so I hope I can get reimbursed."

"Don't worry about that," she said. "Now listen, if they so much as glance in the direction of Canada, stop them. Arrest him, if you have to, on any pretext you can concoct. Otherwise, just keep me posted."

"You see, I was right," Libby Hildress declared, waving the *Sentinel* under her husband's nose. "That's why Matthew was sent over here—so he wouldn't be home when the police found the incriminating evidence."

"The newspaper didn't say anything about anyone finding any incriminating evidence," Tom reminded her. "It could all be much ado about nothing."

"If the police were able to get a search warrant, it isn't about nothing," Libby insisted. "We haven't heard about anyone else's home being searched, have we?"

Tom had to concede they hadn't. "Still, let's not be in such a hurry to tie a noose around his neck until we know something more specific," he suggested.

"I'm sorry," she said. "Matthew may be a nice enough boy, but I don't think we should let Billy have any more to do with that family. He's spent hours and hours over there when neither one of us really knew what was going on. I know I haven't said anything about it before, but I was never very comfortable about that friendship from the beginning."

"Why not?" Tom asked.

"Because we don't know how those kind of people think," she told him. "Or how they might have tried to influence an impressionable boy like Billy."

"Influence him about what?"

Libby shrugged. "I don't know," she said. "All sorts of things. Against Jesus, maybe."

"You're not serious?"

"Of course I am. Jews don't believe in Jesus. They might have tried to convert him."

"Libby, I think you're stretching. Billy's never said anything that would lead us to believe the Frankels ever talked to him about religion."

"Well, who knows what they might have said, or even what they practice?" she persisted. "For all we know, they could be members of one of those weird mind-control cults out there that parents have had to deprogram their kids from."

"Oh come on," Tom declared. "What would make you think they were into anything like that?"

"I don't know that they are. I'm just saying we should be careful," she replied. "After all, what do we really know about them?"

"They're people, just like us," he said.

"Oh no, they're not," Libby shot back. "They're not like us at all. They don't look like us. They don't think like us. They certainly don't believe in the same things we believe in. And with people like that—well, how do we know what they'd do?"

4

Including the night of the polygraph test, Stacey Martinez had been out with Danny Leo four times: on New Year's Eve, a second time to the movies, and once to a concert in Seattle. Tonight would be their fifth date, and they were going ice skating.

Because of the moderate winter climate, there was no natural ice on Seward Island. About fifteen years ago, the city fathers had been persuaded, by a majority vote of the population on a special bond issue, to build a covered outdoor rink. For a remote area, with little to occupy its youth, the project was promoted as a potential antidote to skyrocketing drug use.

The Ice Pavilion was located on a bluff that jutted out into Puget Sound, just north of town. It was maintained by the city parks department. A well-stocked snack bar helped to defray costs, as did the school district, which leased the facility during the winter for its hockey team. With its glass roof and three open sides, the rink afforded skaters a wonderful mural of the mainland at any time of the day. At night, they could watch Seattle's lights dance across the water as they glided and twirled to the music.

Three times a week, from November to March, Danny Leo trained at this rink. He knew every inch of it.

∘ ∘ ∘

"You're seeing quite a lot of this young man, aren't you?" Ruben observed as Stacey waited for her date. "Three weekends in a row."

"I like him," she said. "He's a whole lot more mature than most of the boys at school. He's really got his act together. Do you know he's got his whole life planned out already? He knows exactly what he wants to do."

Ruben looked at her. "It's my fault," he said sadly. "You had to grow up way before your time. Now you're too old in your head to think about parties and pretty clothes, like other girls, and boys your own age are too young for you."

Stacey came over and gave her father a hug. "I don't know why I am the way I am," she told him, "but right now I wouldn't want to be anyone else."

He couldn't remember ever loving her more than he did at that moment. Tears crowded his eyes. He blinked them aside and cleared his throat.

"You're—uh—not doing anything foolish with this boy, are you?" he asked.

Stacey giggled. "Nothing as foolish as you and Ginger, if that's what you're asking."

"It is, and I don't appreciate the comparison," he said, but he couldn't quite keep from smiling.

"Danny's a perfect gentleman," she assured him. "And since you taught me to be a perfect lady, you can put all those worries right out of your head." She gave him a mischievous look. "At least for a while anyway."

"How long a while?"

She screwed up her face in thought. "I guess until I get with someone who makes me feel the way Ginger makes you feel," she said.

"And Danny Leo doesn't?"

Stacey considered that. "Maybe he could," she replied with a toss of her silky blond hair. "If I gave him the chance."

"You're seeing an awful lot of this girl," Peter Leo remarked, standing in the bathroom doorway, watching his son shave, and wondering where the years had gone. "Is it such a good idea?"

Danny blinked at him through the mirror. "I can't see as it's hurting anyone," he said.

"She's young," Peter reminded him. "If anything should happen—if she should get herself in trouble—she's underage, you know. It would ruin you."

"Then I'll just have to make sure nothing happens," Danny replied with a trace of a smile.

"Don't be cocky," Peter retorted. "Sometimes, things can get out of control despite our best intentions."

"Stacey and I are friends, Dad," Danny assured him. "There's nothing more going on."

The evening was clear and unusually cold, even for January. A thousand stars smiled down through the glass roof, and the lights of Seattle glittered across Puget Sound. The ice was crowded, mostly with teenagers. The snack bar was doing a banner business in hot chocolate.

Danny was an excellent skater. There was no question that he would be playing hockey for Harvard next year. Stacey was graceful, but not nearly as comfortable on the ice.

"That's okay," he said easily. "Just hold on to me and you'll be fine."

He put his arm around her waist and guided her smoothly over the ice, in perfect time with the music. She felt as though she were floating.

"I've never skated almost outside before," she told him, used to the sterile, air-conditioned rinks of California. "I can't believe how different it is."

He looked up at the stars and out across the water. "This is the way it's supposed to be," he said, and whirled her around until she was dizzy and laughing.

"Are you two an item?" Bert Kriedler asked them when they stopped to catch their breath. "I mean, like officially together?"

Danny looked at Stacey and smiled. "We're officially friends," he said.

"What's your secret?" Melissa Senn wanted to know when she cornered Stacey in the rest room. "I could never get the high school hunk to look twice at me."

"I don't think I have any big secret," Stacey told her honestly. "We're just friends."

"Do you think she's putting out?" Melissa asked Jeannie Gemmetta. "Is that why he's interested?"

Jeannie shook her head. "Not Stacey. She's Catholic and cautious, and she knows her daddy would kill anyone who touched her. When she spreads her legs, it'll be for nothing less than a ring and a ceremony."

"Yeah, but remember," Melissa cautioned, "that's what we thought about Tara, too."

Two shots of Scotch, half a bottle of wine with dinner, several sips of his Kahlúa, and a warm fire had made Ruben uncharacteristically loquacious.

"I'm a simple man, with simple needs," he told Ginger as they lay curled up on her living room floor, Twink at their feet. "I never wanted a lot of money. I never wanted to be famous. I just wanted to do something worthwhile with my life, and have a crack at being happy."

"Well, it's for sure you don't have a lot of money," Ginger said with a chuckle, "and you aren't famous, and you do very worthwhile work. So all that's left is—are you happy?"

"I think so," he replied. "But you can ask me that again after we collar the teacher."

She reached over and poked him in the ribs. "You're such a romantic," she chided.

"It depends on your definition of romance," he told her, teasing. "I think miracles are romantic, and solving the Breckenridge case was nothing short of a miracle. Getting Frankel to drink out of that glass before his attorney showed up was more than just luck."

"Sometimes miracles happen," she said with a shrug.

Twink blinked.

"True," Ruben conceded. "But this one probably saved my job. And while I wouldn't admit it to anyone but you, I'm just a little bit happier about saving my job than I am about solving the case."

Ginger sighed a very self-satisfied sigh. "Me, too," she said.

Twink yawned.

"You know, I never cared that much about where I worked," Ruben went on. "As long as the schools were good and safe and the environment was healthy, a job was a job, and I was always ready to move on to the next one. But things are different now, and I admit I'm struck by the irony."

"Of what?"

"Let's face it, I don't fit in here. I'll never fit in. I'm about as outside as an outsider can get on Seward Island, and it's not likely that I'll ever be welcomed into the bosom of this community. And yet, this is where I want to be; these are the people I want to serve; this is the department I want to run; this is the staff I want to go on working with. This is where I want Stacey to finish high school and where I want her to come home to from college. This is where I'd like to grow old. I didn't realize how important the place had become to me until I thought I was going to have to leave it."

In response, Ginger put her arms around him and hugged him. She didn't want to tell him how frightened she had been at the thought of losing him.

Twink purred.

"And as long as I'm running on at the mouth here," Ruben added, "I guess I should tell you that I'm getting a little tired of spending all these wonderful evenings with you and then having to get up and go home. I think it's time for a change."

"Exactly what sort of change did you have in mind?" Ginger asked, pulling back to look at him.

"Well, that's just it, I'm not sure," he replied. "You see, I'm selfish enough to know that I want to marry you, but I'm also smart enough to know that a young girl shouldn't marry an old man."

"Last time I looked," she responded breathlessly, "I wasn't so young and you weren't so old."

"You know what I mean," he said. "When a woman like you marries for the first time, it should be about starting a brand-new life—not picking up in the middle of someone else's. And what about children? Every woman dreams of having children. I wouldn't want to rob you of that joy. But I'm old enough to be your father. If we had children, I'd be more like a grandfather to them."

"I don't think anything in life is ever perfect," she said slowly. "Even the best parts require some kind of accommodation. I'd be lying if I said I hadn't thought about having children someday. I guess it's natural for a woman to think about that. But I'd also be lying if I said having children was more important to me than you are."

"You may think that now," he cautioned. "But what about a year from now, or ten years from now, or twenty, when it would be too late?"

"I don't have any idea how I'll feel then," she told him honestly. "I only know how I feel now. And how I feel now is that I would be silly to give up what I *know* I want for some future perfection that might not even exist."

Ruben peered at her in the firelight. "You sound like you've already thought this all through."

"I have," she admitted, smiling softly. "The night of our second date. I've just been waiting for you to catch up."

He wondered if she would always be a step ahead of him, and decided he really wouldn't mind if she were. "Well then," he said, taking a deep breath, "will you marry me?"

Ginger took a moment to stare into the fire and let his words sink in. She wanted to be sure that she understood all the ramifications of what this would mean. She looked down the twenty-eight years of her past, at the path that had led her here. Then she looked at Ruben, her future, waiting for an answer.

"Yes," she said.

"I guess you can't do anything in this town without everyone trying to second-guess you," Danny said as he walked Stacey to her front door. "Everyone's sure we're getting it on."

"I don't care what they think," she replied. "We know we're just friends."

"Well, that's just it," he said, scuffing the tip of his shoe against the porch steps. "I'm beginning to think maybe we could be more than just friends."

She giggled. "Peer pressure getting to you, is it?"

"Not a chance," he replied with a grin. In fact, his friends were telling him he was crazy to spend so much time with a sophomore when he could just about have his choice of the senior class.

Stacey looked up at him through the moonlight. "I like you," she conceded. "Does that make us more than friends?"

"Well, I don't know," he said. "Why don't we find out?"

He leaned over and pressed his lips lightly against hers. They felt soft and warm and tingly. The world slipped a notch off center.

"How was that?" he asked.

"I don't know," she murmured breathlessly. Not for anything in the world would she tell him that this was her first real kiss and therefore she had nothing to compare it to.

"Well then, how about this?"

He brought his lips down to hers again, only this time they were slightly open and moist, and he seemed to want to suck the air right out of her. The world turned upside down.

"That was nice," she admitted skittishly, not sure where this was going and not sure she was ready to find out, "but I think maybe I'd better go inside now."

Danny chuckled. "That's okay," he whispered, touching her cheek with his hand. "There's no hurry."

5

"Three months ago, a terrible crime was committed in our midst," intoned the minister of the Eagle Rock Methodist Church at the Sunday morning service, "and it now appears as though a reckoning may finally be at hand. We are decent and law-abiding people with no animosity in our hearts. We were horrified by the thought that one of us might be guilty of this heinous act, and so we prayed to the Almighty to be merciful. It is with enormous relief that I am standing here today to tell you that our prayers have been answered. The monster who murdered Tara Breckenridge was not one of us."

Here the good reverend paused and several members of the congregation looked at one another and began to smile.

"But let this be a warning to you that we cannot relax our vigil," the minister continued. "Satan walks among us and he takes many forms. He may try to look like us and he may try to act like us, but he is not one of us, and we must always be on our guard, ready to ward off his evil whenever and wherever we encounter it, and protect ourselves and our loved ones from him. In the name of our lord, Jesus Christ, amen."

"Amen," said the congregation.

"You see?" Libby Hildress whispered to her husband sitting beside her in the second pew. "Isn't that just what I told you?"

"Ruben and I are going to be married," Ginger announced in the middle of Sunday dinner.

Verna Earley dropped her salad fork. "Married?" she gasped, although she had been steeling herself against this moment for over a month now. In fact, this was the first Sunday dinner since Christmas that the police chief and his daughter had not been in attendance.

"Married," Ginger confirmed.

"Hey, congratulations, Sis," her eldest brother said. Despite his mother, he didn't see anything so terribly wrong with Ruben. In fact, the police chief played a pretty decent game of pool.

"Yeah," echoed the others. "Congratulations."

"Have you set a date yet?" one sister-in-law asked.

Ginger shook her head. "Not yet. But sometime in the spring would be nice. I don't think either one of us is interested in a long engagement."

Jack Earley got up from the table and came around to give his daughter a hug.

"If this is what you want for yourself," he whispered, "then this is what I want for you."

"Thanks, Dad." She beamed. "Thanks, everyone." She looked pointedly at her mother.

"Well, I suppose this means a wedding," Verna said as brightly as she could, under the circumstances. "You're my only daughter, so this is going to be my only chance."

"A small affair, Mom," Ginger requested. "It's Ruben's second trip to the altar, you know. We don't want to make a big fuss; just the family, and maybe a few friends."

"That sounds fine," Verna assured her, relieved to have a legitimate reason to exclude certain members of her social set. "No one ever said that small weddings can't be every bit as elegant as big ones."

Ginger regarded her mother with surprise. "Thank you," she said. "I was afraid this was going to be a battle."

"It's your life," Verna told her. "Besides, now that you and Ruben are about to wrap up the Breckenridge case, I expect he's going to be a very popular man around town."

"It isn't wrapped up yet," Ginger said, cautious as always about what she revealed, but unable to keep a note of satisfaction from her voice. "But I wouldn't be surprised if it didn't take much longer."

"It'll be a small wedding," Ruben told Stacey. "Just something quiet and official."

"Gee, Dad, you're not committing a felony, you know," Stacey responded. "You're getting married. Make the most of it."

"You don't think it's a mistake?" he asked. "I mean, there are so many things against it."

"Do you love her?"

"Very much," came the immediate response.

"Do you think she loves you?"

"Yes, I do."

Stacey shrugged. "Then what are you worrying about?"

"For one thing, I'm concerned about the big difference in our ages," he said. "And for another thing, I'm concerned about what *you* think."

The teenager cocked her head as if in thought. "Yeah, I guess the age thing could be pretty sticky for you," she agreed. "But if you can handle having another daughter, I can handle having a big sister." And she quickly ducked out of his reach.

The maroon Taurus rolled off the late ferry and headed north with Jerry behind the wheel. In the back of the wagon, Matthew and Chase slept, one curled around the other. In the front passenger seat, Deborah was thinking that the two days they had spent at the shore had done wonders for all of them.

They had run and played and sucked in the ocean air as though they didn't have a worry in the world. And now, as they turned into their neighborhood, the Taurus's headlights flashing across a familiar house here, singling out a well-known tree there, she was ready to believe it was true.

"I'm glad we went," she said with a yawn. "This is the first time in I don't know how long that I've felt truly relaxed."

"Then we'll have to do it more often," Jerry suggested, making a right onto Larkspur Lane.

"But let's not plan it," Deborah replied. "I think it was the spontaneity that made it work. I never thought I'd hear myself say it, but I'm even glad to see our street."

"Then we're definitely going to be more spontaneous," he said with a chuckle.

"You know, maybe this isn't such a bad place, after all," she conceded. "Maybe we shouldn't let the attitudes of a few contaminate the whole."

Jerry swung left into the driveway. "I think you're right," he agreed.

And then they saw it, caught in the headlights as they pulled up in front of the garage—big and black and spray-painted across the double-wide door.

They sat there, disbelieving and believing.

"How could anyone . . . ?" Deborah sputtered. "Why would they . . . ? What did we ever . . . ?"

All of her questions had answers of a sort, but Jerry knew there was little point in providing them. He had heard about it from the time he was ten, learned about it in the classroom, and read about it in a dozen different books. But for the first time in his life, Jerry now knew what Aaron had known as a boy: the humiliation, the betrayal, the fear, and the overwhelming sense of helplessness.

First it was Matthew and the bullies on the playground, and he had let that pass. Then it was the telephone call, and he had allowed himself to dismiss it. Now it was this Nazi obscenity on his garage door. He knew it was the Breckenridge investigation that had triggered it all, but he wondered who was behind it, and how much further it would go, and whether he could keep his family safe.

He looked at his wife with a heavy heart. "Do you still think this is just an isolated incident?" he asked.

Officer Glen Dirksen was tired and hungry and glad to be home. He had seen the Frankels off the ferry, followed them until they turned onto Larkspur Lane, and then made a beeline for his own apartment, a roomy ground-floor unit in a recently renovated Victorian on Johansen Street, just three blocks south of the Village Green.

It was a far bigger place than he could ordinarily have afforded, but the landlord had given him a nice break on the rent because the other tenants liked the idea of having a policeman in residence. So far, his furniture consisted of two futons, one in the bedroom on which he slept and one in the living room on which he watched television, a big oak cabinet from a secondhand store that housed the television as well as a stereo system and an eclectic collection of CDs, and an old wooden dining table with two chairs that he had painted dark green enamel.

There wasn't much of anything in his refrigerator, so he contented himself with two peanut butter sandwiches and a bag of chocolate chip cookies, washing it all down with a glass of milk. He had eaten little during the past two days and slept in his truck, because he didn't want to let the Frankels out of his sight any more than he absolutely had to. He would never have been able to explain having them slip away in the dead of night while he was sound asleep in some comfortable motel bed.

His big adventure to the coast had turned out to be pretty routine. The family seemed content to eat fast food, take leisurely walks along the beach, and poke around the few local shops that were open at this time of year. They had made no move toward Canada, nor in any other direction, nor did they show any particular interest in the out-of-uniform policeman who followed them.

"The place was almost deserted," Dirksen reported to Ginger. "He couldn't help but see me, but I don't think he remembered who I was, because he smiled at me a few times; you know, like strangers do when they're away from home."

"Good work," Ginger told him. "Now get some sleep."

But sleep didn't come right away. Instead, Dirksen lay on his futon and thought about Jerry Frankel, and what he thought about most was that the history teacher had acted completely normal, and not like someone who had committed a brutal crime.

The young police officer had been trained to look for signs of guilt in a suspect's body language, in the way he made eye contact, in his basic demeanor and in his general attitude toward his surroundings, even when the suspect was unaware that he was being watched. But in two days of undetected observation, Dirksen had seen no clues at all, and he marveled at the man's ability to control himself. Which only goes to show, he decided, how cool some murderers could be. He would remember to tell Ginger that the teacher would not be likely to crack under pressure.

Jerry and Deborah lay open-eyed for the better part of the night, separated by their thoughts, neither dozing off until almost dawn. They forgot to set Deborah's alarm, and would likely have slept well into the morning had they not been awakened at seven-thirty by what sounded like a power washer.

"What the hell?" Jerry mumbled. He struggled into his

bathrobe and made his way to the front door. Sure enough, half a dozen of his neighbors stood in his drive, scrubbing down the garage door.

"This must have happened after dark yesterday," one of them said. "I came home at four o'clock and I'd have seen it if it was there then."

"We don't have that kind of neighborhood," said another. "We want you to know that this is an embarrassment to all of us."

"We know you, Jerry, and we like you and Deborah and Matthew," said a third. "You've been a fine addition to the block, and we're proud to call you friends."

"Thank you," Jerry said, but he was unable to tell them what it really was that he was thanking them for.

"We couldn't type the bloodstains on the sweatshirt," Charlie reported to Ruben and Ginger. "Too much bleach. The lab boys may have some luck with DNA, but I wouldn't hold my breath. However, the fibers are consistent with the ones we found on Tara Breckenridge's body. Of course, that might not be very helpful; the shirt is local—you can buy it in half a dozen stores around town."

"What about the knife?" Ginger asked.

"We had better luck there. Magnus says it's definitely the same kind and size of knife used in the killing, and we found a speck of blood right where the blade joins the hilt. It matches Tara's blood type. As it happens, it also matches half the rest of the population on the Island. So we'll need DNA to tell us for sure."

"That it's the victim's type is enough for now," Ruben said.

"And there's something else," Charlie added. "The newspaper we found the knife in—it was the wrap-up edition of the *Sentinel* for the second weekend in October."

"I'll be damned," murmured Ginger.

"Of course, it's still all circumstantial. Fingerprints on the knife would have been the clincher. But we couldn't get any clean ones."

"Well, it figures they'd have gotten smudged," Ginger said.

"What about the newspaper?" Ruben asked.

"Nothing clean there, either," Charlie told him. "But the important thing is," he added, "we've got what is in all likelihood the murder weapon."

"Okay," Ruben said. "Let's take it to Van Pelt."

Harvey Van Pelt was nearing the end of his professional life without ever having had that one headline-making, career-defining case that most attorneys dream of having.

Large and lanky, with a bushy head of salt-and-pepper hair, a bristly mustache, and a pleasant, smile-creased face that seemed reassuring to most people, Harvey had some years ago toyed with the idea of entering politics.

"If you want to get elected to something other than the prosecutor's office," he was told by a member of his party who was in the know, "get yourself a reputation."

"What kind of reputation?" he asked.

"On second thought," came the response, "you're probably better off staying where you are."

Van Pelt had stayed. He was now sixty-two and in his twenty-ninth year as Puget County prosecutor, having been re-elected every four years virtually unopposed. Although nobody except his wife yet knew it, this was his last term in office. The cancer that was slowly destroying his liver was not going to grant him another four years.

He wasn't bitter. All things considered, he'd had a good run for his money. The view of Gull Harbor from his office window was prime, his chair was comfortable, and his home was a mere ten minutes from the courthouse in one direction, and five minutes from the golf course in the other. He had a time-share on Maui, he drove a Lincoln, and he had put all four of his children through college and two through graduate school.

More than that, Van Pelt genuinely liked his job. It was interesting work, not overly demanding, and occasionally rewarding, and it gave him a degree of stature and respect in the community—a significant accomplishment on Seward Island for the son of a seamstress whose husband had abandoned her when the boy was only six months old. But the prosecutor was only human, and he would periodically reflect on the fact that, while his career in Puget County had been gratifying, it had provided him limited opportunity to shine.

At shortly past ten o'clock on the third Monday in January, however, all that changed. The case of a lifetime reached the desk of Harvey Van Pelt.

What could be more perfect, he thought, than to close out his career with the conviction of the bastard who had butchered poor little Tara Breckenridge? Here in front of him seemed to be motive, opportunity, intent, circumstantial evidence galore—and even the probable murder weapon. All that was missing were the DNA results, which would likely be icing on the cake for a jury who could accept them or not as it wished. In sophisticated legal terms—it was a slam dunk.

Well, almost a slam dunk. There was the small matter of Frankel's attorney. Van Pelt had never gone up against Scott Cohen in court, but he knew the attorney's reputation. He knew that, in more than twenty years of practice, the Cherub had never lost a murder case. And therein lay the challenge. What a victory it would be, he exulted, to convict a murderer and hand Cohen his first defeat in the same instance.

"It looks to me like you've done a good, thorough job of this," he told Ruben. "I can't see a reason to waste any more time. Go get him."

o   o   o

The second lunch period had just begun at Seward High School. As usual, Melissa Senn and Jeannie Gemmetta were seated at a table with Hank Kriedler and Bill Graham. What was not so usual was that Stacey Martinez had been invited to join them.

"You and Danny Leo are the talk of the school," Jeannie informed her.

"We are?" Stacey replied. "Why?"

"Well, I guess because you've been seeing so much of each other."

"We're just friends," Stacey said automatically. She had no intention of sharing anything about her relationship with Danny with these people.

"Hey," Melissa said. "You've landed the neatest guy in school—enjoy it."

"Yeah, us sophomores aren't good enough for you anymore, are we?" Hank teased.

Stacey smiled benignly. Neither he nor his friends had ever shown any interest in her. In fact, they had pretty much ignored her. She was exactly the same person she had been before, but now, because of her relationship with Danny Leo, she had apparently gained some measure of value in their eyes.

"How would I know?" she told him. "None of you ever asked me out."

Hank and Bill exchanged leers. "I guess we'll have to do something about that," they joked.

"Guess what?" Jack Tannauer said, plunking down beside them. "I just saw your father, Stacey. He and Detective Earley were going into Huxley's office."

"Really?" breathed Melissa. "What do you think that means?"

"Do you think it means they're going to arrest Mr. Frankel?" Jeannie gasped. "The newspaper said they searched his house on Friday, remember? They must have found something."

Jack shrugged. "Maybe Stacey knows."

But Stacey shook her head. "Sorry to disappoint you," she told them, "but my dad doesn't tell me about his cases. I don't know any more about this than you do."

"Wouldn't that be a kick," Hank mused. "If the teacher did it, after all."

"Hey," said Bill, jumping up. "Why don't we go find out?"

Ruben and Ginger entered Jerry Frankel's fifth-period history class ten minutes before the bell sounded, leaving Jordan Huxley to hover in the corridor outside. The teacher was writing on the blackboard with his back to the door.

"Jeremy Frankel?" Ruben said, moving toward him.

Jerry whirled around, startled. "Yes?"

Ginger stood in front of the door, her gun drawn. Ruben stood less than two yards from him, one hand poised on his holster. "Jeremy Frankel, you are under arrest for the murder of Tara Breckenridge."

The teacher blinked. "What are you talking about?"

"May I ask you please to turn around and put your hands on the blackboard."

"Wait a minute, I don't understand. There must be some mistake."

"Turn around, please," Ruben repeated, "and put your hands on the blackboard."

"You have the right to remain silent," Ginger began to recite. "If you waive that right, anything you do say can and will be taken down and used against you in a court of law. You have the right to an attorney . . ."

In the hallway, Jordan Huxley was holding Jerry's fifth-period students at bay. "You can't go in there right now," he told them. "Just stand over here, against the wall, please."

It took less than a minute for Ruben to determine that the teacher was not carrying a weapon and only a few seconds to secure his hands behind his back.

"Is this really necessary?" Jerry asked. "I'm perfectly willing to go with you. Must you drag me out in handcuffs in front of the kids?"

"I'm sorry," Ruben replied. "Regulations."

Ginger opened the door, and positioning the teacher at her side, walked with Ruben down the hall, past a crowd of curious eyes, and out of the building.

6

"Rachel, I need you to go pick Matthew up from school," Scott Cohen instructed his wife less than an hour later. "Right now. Take him home with you and keep him inside, if you can. I've called Deborah. She'll be on the next ferry, and she'll come by to get him. I'll be on the next ferry, too, but I'm going over to the courthouse first."

"This is awful," Rachel said.

"It doesn't look good," her husband agreed.

The Puget County Courthouse was a three-story, gold-domed rectangle built of limestone that had survived half a century of ridicule for its pomposity. It sat on Seward Way, at the north end of town, in the middle of three landscaped acres that were meticulously maintained by the ladies of the Garden Club.

In addition to two fully appointed courtrooms, the larger one of which was almost never used, the building housed the spacious offices of Judge Irwin Jacobs and his associates, the more modest office of prosecutor Harvey Van Pelt, plus a score of others on a lesser level.

The third floor of the west wing contained the county jail, recognizable from the outside only by a row of iron-barred windows. It was here that Jerry Frankel was taken to be booked, fingerprinted, and photographed. His allotted telephone call had been to his attorney, and on the Cherub's advice, he had afterward declined to make any statement, or answer any questions.

Scott found him sitting on the edge of a bunk in a small cell, looking dazed.

"I don't understand what's happening," he said after they had been escorted to a room, just big enough to hold a table and two chairs, and left alone. "They can't have uncovered any evidence that links me to the Breckenridge murder."

Scott was flipping through the file he had demanded upon entering the courthouse. "They say otherwise," he reported. "They say they found your fingerprint on the cross the victim was wearing. They also say that a bloody sweatshirt having fibers similar to those found on the body was discovered in your backyard, and that a knife which the medical examiner has declared to be consistent with the murder weapon was found hidden in your car."

Jerry shook his head as though to clear it. "It was *my* blood on the sweatshirt. I cut myself on something in the shop. And I have no idea where that knife came from. I've never owned anything like it. I'm not a hunter—why would I have a hunting knife? Besides, even if I did kill that poor girl, do you really think I'd be stupid enough to keep the murder weapon lying around for anyone to walk right in and find?"

Scott looked intently at his client, the hooded green eyes missing nothing. "If you did hunt, we might be able to argue that the knife was a weapon of opportunity, not intent. That would be murder two, which would mean prison, but maybe not life," he said slowly, carefully. "However, if you don't hunt, then a good case could be made for premeditation with special circumstances, and Van Pelt would almost certainly seek the death penalty."

Jerry blinked. "If you're trying to scare me, you're doing a first-rate job of it."

"I'm trying to tell it like it is."

There was no mistaking the message, and Jerry took a long moment to stare back at his attorney. "I don't hunt," he said finally.

"All right, then," Scott said with a brief nod, "let's go to work."

"Ruben, let me be the first to congratulate you," boomed Albert Hoch, stalking into Graham Hall shortly after two o'clock, much as Ginger had predicted. "I knew you were the right man for the job, first time I met you. There was no doubt in my mind you were going to get that bastard."

"I'm glad we were successful," the police chief said, neither his face nor his voice revealing his thoughts.

"Now don't you worry about the city council and all that firing nonsense," Hoch went on. "Mark my words, when I get through with them, they're going to be begging you to stay on."

"I appreciate that, Mr. Mayor," Ruben said, making a supreme effort not to smile.

In her office down the hall, Ginger could barely keep from laughing out loud.

The parade began about four o'clock when, one by one, members of the city council, who somehow just happened to be in the neighborhood, dropped by to express their gratitude for the excellent work Ruben and his department had done, and to offer the hope that he would understand the tremendous pressure they had been under to see results.

"Of course I understand," Ruben told each of them in turn. "I was under the same pressure myself."

"I'm so glad everything worked out," Maxine Coopersmith confided. "I wasn't really in favor of replacing you."

"Well done, old man," declared Dale Egaard. "Among other things, you've saved us a lot of unnecessary headhunting."

"We behaved like a bunch of old farts," Ed Hingham admitted. "We hired you for the job; we should have had more faith in you doing it."

The only member of the city council who did not present himself was Jim Petrie.

"He's probably too busy down at the hardware store," joked Charlie, "returning all those dead bolts he won't be able to sell anymore."

Deborah couldn't seem to concentrate on anything. She went through the motions of getting on and off the ferry, of collecting Matthew from Rachel's house, of bringing him home and feeding him, but she couldn't have said what she fixed or whether he ate any of it. She brushed aside his worried questions because she didn't have any answers for him. She didn't have any for herself.

Scott came by about six and told her that Jerry was all right and had sent his love.

"When will they let him come home?" she asked.

The attorney shook his head. "We won't get bail," he said. "It's a capital offense."

"You mean he has to stay there?" she cried, horrified, picturing the kind of place and people she had seen only in movies.

"He isn't in prison," Scott assured her, as though reading her mind. "It's a county jail. He's in a cell all by himself. It's small, but it's clean and safe and the Waterside Cafe provides his food. He's only been accused of a crime; he hasn't been convicted of anything. No one is going to bother him."

As soon as Scott left, Deborah called Scarsdale and talked to her parents.

"No, don't come out now," she said, feeling so horribly ashamed when she told them what had happened. "Matthew and I are okay. There's no point. Maybe later."

Then she made herself call Cheltenham.

"I was afraid of something like this," Aaron said at once. "I've had a worry ever since you were here, ever since Matthew and I talked. My son's being used as a scapegoat."

"We have a really terrific attorney," Deborah told him. "He's also a good friend. Believe me, if Jerry is being set up, he'll find out, and then he'll make the whole thing go away."

"I want to come out," Aaron said.

"I know, but not yet. When the trial starts—if it comes to a trial, of course—that's when he'll need you, when we'll all need you." The last thing she wanted was to have to deal with his pain when she didn't know how she was going to deal with her own.

Around eight o'clock, the neighbors started to arrive, bringing with them cakes and pies and solemn faces as though it were the aftermath of a funeral. Deborah knew they were trying to be kind, but they only made things worse.

"I don't understand how this could be happening," she cried. "Jerry couldn't have done what they say he did."

"Sometimes the police make mistakes," they told her, although they weren't really certain anymore. But they didn't want to hold the woman and the boy responsible for something the husband might have done.

Somehow, she got through the condolences, got the dog fed, got the dishes done, got Matthew to bed. Much later, as though she actually thought she was going to sleep, she went into her bedroom and put on her nightclothes. Then, as she stood in the bathroom and began to wash off her makeup, she caught sight of her pale face and hollow eyes in the mirror.

"He didn't do it," she said to her reflection. *Are you so sure?* a little voice answered back.

And then the tears began to flow.

• • •

"Teacher Charged in Breckenridge Case," screamed the headline in the morning *Sentinel.*

"Authorities arrested a popular Seward High School teacher yesterday in connection with the death of Tara Breckenridge.

"Jeremy Frankel, 35, was arrested in his classroom, concluding a three-month murder investigation. Breckenridge, 15, was stabbed to death at Madrona Point Park in October.

"Frankel, who has been a history teacher at Seward since last January, left his former teaching job in New York State under a 'possible cloud,' according to police detective Ginger Earley."

"Maybe it did take three months, Kyle, but we got him, didn't we?" Albert Hoch declared. "I know a lot of us were looking for an overnight solution, but like Ruben says, some things just don't happen before their time. In the end, it was patience and determination and damn good police work that did it. I know for a fact that the whole bunch of them down at Graham Hall never gave up, not for a minute."

"The case they've got against the teacher—is it really solid?" Breckenridge asked. "The bastard isn't going to slip through any legal cracks, is he?"

"Oh, I wouldn't worry about that," the mayor assured him. "Ruben is a very cautious man. He isn't sloppy, and he's not the kind who would spring a trap until he was sure he was going to snare the right prey."

"Martinez is a good man, after all," Breckenridge conceded. "I admit I had my doubts, but obviously I was wrong."

"Well, you were in good company," Hoch told him with a slight smile. "I've got a city council over at Graham Hall eating a lot of crow right now."

Breckenridge shrugged. "A little humility won't hurt them," he said.

Hoch inspected his fresh manicure. "You know," he commented, "it wouldn't be such a bad idea if you were to maybe drop by and say something to Ruben yourself."

"Coaching me, are you, Albert?"

The mayor flushed. "Just making a suggestion, Kyle, that's all."

"Don't worry," the bank president said. "I fully intend to make my own appearance at Graham Hall before the day is out."

Hoch smiled. "It'll mean a lot," he said.

"The important thing is that we can finally begin to put our lives back together," Breckenridge said with a long sigh. "It's been a dreadful three months; not only for me and my family, but for the entire island, I think. What we need now is a proper trial, a swift conviction, and justice. It'll be difficult for all of us, especially Mary, having to relive it again, but it's the only way for the healing to happen. I just hope there won't be any delays."

Mary Breckenridge spent the day in bed, with the lights out and the curtains drawn and her headache medicine on the nightstand.

She had come down to breakfast with her husband and daughter, as she did every morning, as she had when Tara was still there. In fact, she still insisted that the place to her left at the magnificent oval rosewood table be set for every meal, as though her elder daughter would claim it at any moment, a rather macabre ritual that Kyle and Tori did their best to ignore.

"Humor her, Mrs. Poole," Kyle instructed. "We all grieve in different ways."

On this morning, as always, the housekeeper brought Kyle his juice, his cereal, and the morning editions of the *Seattle Post-Intelligencer* and the *Wall Street Journal*. Then she brought Mary her coffee, her buttered toast, and the morning edition of the *Sentinel*.

One glance at the headline was all it took. The coffee spilled all over the table, a piece of toast got stuck in her throat, and without explanation, she fled upstairs.

The last thing Mary wanted to know was that someone had been arrested for killing her daughter, especially after all the effort it had taken to convince herself that Tara was not really dead, but simply not here. That was how she was dealing with the loss, the only way she could deal with it, as a temporary condition that would one day correct itself and make her world right again. Let everyone else think what they liked.

While the story had never really died down, the daily reports in the newspaper had been mostly speculative; perhaps this, maybe that—all vague enough to discount. An arrest was not vague, it was vivid, and it threatened to bring Mary face-to-face with the truth she had worked so very hard to ignore.

She waited for what seemed like hours, until she was sure that Kyle had left for the bank and Tori had gone off to school and Mrs. Poole was occupied somewhere else in the big house. Then, summoning a courage she hadn't realized she possessed, she picked up the telephone from the table that separated her bed from her husband's, and dialed the number at Graham Hall.

"Hello, I want to talk to Chief Martinez," she told the clerk who answered.

"I'm sorry, but he's not here at the moment," Helen Ballinger replied to the unidentified caller. "Can I connect you to someone else?"

"No," was the answer. "No one else. I want to talk directly to him."

"Then perhaps I can give him a message?"

Mary considered that for almost a minute. "Yes," she said finally. "Please give him a message. This is Mrs. Breckenridge calling. Will you tell Chief Martinez that the teacher he arrested didn't kill my daughter."

"I beg your pardon?" Helen replied, stunned.

"I said the teacher didn't kill her."

"How do you know that, Mrs. Breckenridge?" the clerk asked gently.

"I know because—because he's a fine teacher. Tara says he's the best teacher she's ever had. He's been helping her with her work, you know. He would never hurt her. You must tell Chief Martinez."

With that, Mary hung up, knowing she had done as much as she could do, and hoping it was enough to keep reality at bay, at least for a little while longer.

"That poor woman," Helen said later when she related the conversation to Ginger.

"She's in denial," Ginger said. "If we arrest someone for her daughter's murder, it forces her to admit that her daughter is really dead."

7

Word got out about the swastika having been painted on the Frankels' garage door, as it was bound to. It happened not so much out of maliciousness as out of disbelief. Most people simply couldn't accept it. It was inconceivable to them that a symbol of so much brutality and bigotry would ever be openly exhibited in their community, and in such a cowardly fashion— an anonymous somebody with a spray can under cover of darkness.

While the power washer had removed most of the paint, a recognizable impression still remained. Soon, those who could not help themselves were cruising slowly along Larkspur Lane, intent on getting a glimpse of the stigmata.

"I didn't believe it until I was standing right there in front of it," Paul Delaney, the *Sentinel* photographer, told Gail Brown. "This is my hometown, for God's sake. People here don't do things like that."

"Don't they?"

"Come on, I was born here, same as you," he replied. "And I've never seen anything like that before."

"Did you get a good shot of it?" the editor asked.

Delaney grinned. "You bet I did," he said.

"Under no circumstances do we support or condone the piece of graffiti recently put on public exhibit," half a dozen different religious leaders quickly stepped forward to avow. "Regardless of what may have instigated this open display of depravity, we are dismayed that such a thing could happen on our harmonious island."

"It's probably the first time those roosters have agreed on anything," Charlie Pricker observed.

"While freedom of expression is the bedrock of our nation," the city council said in a carefully worded release, "we condemn the crude example of ideology that has defaced a structure in our community. This sort of thing hurts us all, in our own eyes, as well as in the eyes of the world."

"Well, if those people hadn't come here in the first place," a devout Presbyterian wrote to the editor, "Tara Breckenridge would still be alive and no one would have had any reason to paint that garage door."

"What people is she talking about?" Rachel Cohen asked rhetorically. "Nathaniel Seward and his crew?"

"Anti-Semitism has reared its ugly head on a remote island in the Puget Sound," Peter Jennings began his report on the ABC evening news. "Someone has painted a swastika on the garage door of a Jewish teacher who has been charged with the murder of a local fifteen-year-old girl."

"Oh, terrific," Albert Hoch said in disgust. "Now the whole country is going to think this place is nothing but a hotbed of Nazis."

"Don't worry about it," Jim Petrie told him. "We'll have our fifteen minutes of fame and then it'll all be over, and we'll be forgotten again."

"Maybe," the mayor groused. "But if we had to be famous, I'd just as soon it was for something else."

It was a very somber group of residents who gathered in the apse of the Cedar Valley Unitarian Church. Called together at the last moment, they represented fifty-nine of the Island's seventy-three Jewish families.

"What are we going to do?" they asked one another.

"What does it mean?"

"We didn't know there were people who openly thought that way here."

"How are we supposed to react?"

"I can't believe this is happening."

"We've only been on the Island for a short time, but we've always felt so comfortable, so . . . unnoticed."

"Just because they think one of us murdered that girl, does that mean they have to condemn all of us? When one of them does something wrong, do we condemn all of them?"

"When it comes to us, one bad apple in the barrel, and we're all rotten. That's the way it works."

"All right everybody, let's sit down," said the leader, a well-respected cardiologist, "and see if we can make some sense of this."

"We've lived on the Island for close to ten years now," a local real estate broker began. "Aside from a letter to the editor every now and again, there's been no real problem that I know about."

"You mean the sort of drivel that came out at Christmas about Jewish retailers making all the money?" asked a tax accountant.

"Yeah, that sort of thing."

"And you don't think that means anything?"

The broker shrugged. "The people writing those letters are malcontents. They're anti-Semitic, anti-black, anti-gay, anti-everything but their own personal interpretation of the New Testament. They're fringe elements, they don't represent the mainstream. Look at me—I'm selling houses, my wife's boutique is selling *chachkas*, and my kids are friends with everyone."

"Well, my brother's nursery went under when the hardware store put in its fancy new gardening department," a computer consultant complained. "They undercut his prices so drastically he couldn't compete. And then the minute they closed him down, their prices shot up higher than his had ever been."

"That's not discrimination," someone said with a dry chuckle. "That's free enterprise."

"The truth is, we're a minority here," said the local chiropractor. "And like most minorities, if we offer a service that the majority wants, we're tolerated. Otherwise, we're ignored."

"Until now," the cardiologist said with a sigh. "Now we have a Jewish teacher accused of murdering a gentile teenager and somebody seems to want to make a statement about that. The question is, what are we going to do?"

"You mean, are we going to protest it?" a successful insurance agent asked. "How? Make a march down Commodore Street? Take out an ad in the *Sentinel*? Assure people that we're really good folk and don't deserve to be gassed?"

"Well, what do *you* suggest?" someone asked.

"I say, don't rock the boat. I think it's fair to assume that most of us live here because we like it. It's relatively safe, and it's a low-key kind of place where the overwhelming majority of the people are content to live and let live. If we start making waves, mark my words, it'll backfire on us."

Everyone looked at everyone else. "You mean, we should just pretend it never happened?"

"Why not? Let's be practical. We're talking about a teacher who's been arrested for murder. So somebody paints a swastika on his garage door. So that's his problem. It's not on any of our doors, is it?"

"Not yet," someone murmured.

"Wait a minute," someone else interjected. "The last time I looked, wasn't Jerry Frankel one of us?"

There was some foot scraping and seat shifting at that, and a number of eyes looked down at the floor.

"Of course he's one of us," the cardiologist took the opportunity to emphasize. "And putting that thing on his garage door is the same as putting it on all our garage doors."

"Oh no, it's not," said the real estate broker. "I didn't murder anyone."

"Is that what this is all about?" the tax accountant wondered. "Let us be the first to cast Jerry out so we won't be painted with his spray can?"

"Why not?" asked the insurance agent. "If he's guilty, he deserves to pay for his crime."

"You don't get it, do you?" the tax accountant said. "This isn't just about Jerry Frankel. This is about all of us. Someone is simply taking advantage of Jerry's misfortune to send us a very clear message."

"Rubbish," scoffed the real estate broker. "This is no time for hysteria. There's no ominous message here. There's no master plan behind that stupid swastika. It's ridiculous to think that sort of nonsense could ever happen on Seward Island, in practically the twenty-first century. It was just a prank, probably done by kids, and put up to it by one of our famous Northwest nut groups. I admit it wasn't in very good taste, but those people *have* no taste, so what do you expect?"

"You're absolutely right," agreed the insurance agent. "We're making a *tsimmes* out of nothing. And as long as it doesn't cost me any clients, I intend to stay well clear of it."

A murmur of assent rippled through the majority of the

group. Almost everyone looked relieved. The cardiologist and the tax accountant exchanged glances.

"So those of us who see something sinister in this are just being alarmists?" the cardiologist asked.

"Yes," said the insurance agent. "Come on, this is our home. We know these people. We live next door to them. We do business with them. I've even been invited to their country club. They haven't turned on us. Whatever happened, you'll see, it was nothing more than an isolated incident."

8

In the days that followed Jerry Frankel's arrest, the residents of Seward Island began to come out of their three-month, self-imposed seclusion. People stopped bolting their doors, locking up their children, and looking over their shoulders, and started to trust one another again.

"I invited my next-door neighbor in for coffee today," a home-maker wrote to the editor of the *Sentinel*. "It's the first time in months I've done that. It's the first time in months that I didn't have the thought in the back of my mind that her husband or her son might be a murderer."

"Our streets are once again safe, our daughters are safe," penned the local barber. "And we owe it all to Chief Ruben Martinez and his outstanding police department. On behalf of my wife and our three girls, I would like to take this opportunity to express my thanks for a job well done."

"Three cheers to Chief Ruben Martinez and Detective Ginger Earley," agreed the owner of Seward Island Stationers. "And to all the members of the police force who contributed to the investigation and apprehension of Tara Breckenridge's killer."

"When we make a decision, we don't always know for sure whether it will turn out to be the right one," wrote city councilwoman Maxine Coopersmith. "But it is clear now that our decision to hire Ruben Martinez as our chief of police was the right one."

Both Ruben and Ginger were overwhelmed by the Island's show of appreciation. Boxes of candy, baskets of fruit, and bouquets of flowers began arriving at Graham Hall, running the gamut from simple to downright extravagant. Cards were delivered by the dozens. Commendations were being proposed, ceremonies were being suggested.

"A week ago, they were clamoring for our heads," Ginger observed with a smile. "Now we're heroes."

"We were just doing our job," Ruben said with genuine modesty. "I don't know what all the fuss is about."

"For all these months, I've been so afraid that the murderer was one of us," the secretary of the Puget Sound Lutheran Church wrote to the editor. "I thank God that it wasn't."

"What does she mean by that?" Deborah asked Rachel. "Who is this 'us'?"

"Jerry Frankel's employment has been terminated," Jordan Huxley informed the *Sentinel* in the midst of all the furor. "On paper, I must say, he seemed ideal. There certainly was no indication of any aberrant behavior. I feel as though in part I'm to blame for Tara's death. But how could I have known?"

"I home-teach my three children," wrote the wife of an environmental engineer. "I always thought I was doing it because my husband and I wanted our kids to have a better education than we felt they could get in the public school system. But now I see it was really to protect them."

"There has to be a better screening process for hiring teachers in our community," wrote a parent whose daughter was a freshman at the high school. "We must find a way to safeguard our children from anything like this ever happening again."

"Why does everyone all of a sudden think we're so safe?" a forty-nine-year-old spinster who lived a life of caring for her invalid mother demanded to know. "Just because one of them is behind bars doesn't mean we're safe. What about the rest of them who've moved in on us and walk around as if they owned the place?"

"I say a jury trial's too good for someone who preys on little girls," wrote a man who was the product of an abusive family. "Especially someone in such a position of authority over children. Anyone care to join me at the old maple tree?"

This last was a reference to the giant first-growth maple that sat in the middle of the Village Green, and according to Island lore had, in bygone days, been used as a hanging tree.

"Freedom of the press is one thing," Scott Cohen sternly cautioned the editor of the *Sentinel*. "But publishing a letter that flat out calls for a public lynching is going too far."

"It's one man's opinion," Gail replied with a shrug. "But you might as well know, that opinion happens to be representative of more than half of the letters we've been receiving."

"My client is innocent until proven guilty," Scott told her. "And that's not an opinion—it's the law of our land. Be sure you tell your readers that."

Gail smiled brightly. "May I quote you?"

* * *

"They've already got me convicted, and now they can't wait to hang me," Jerry protested to his attorney.

"Sentiment doesn't seem to be running in our favor right now," Scott agreed.

"So what do we do?"

"We stay calm, we proceed with caution, and we don't rush into anything for which we are not fully prepared."

"Easy for you to say."

"Look, I know this isn't the nicest position you've ever been in, but bear with it. The preliminary hearing is coming up, and then we'll see what kind of a case Van Pelt thinks he has. I'm also going to move for a change of venue."

"Will we get it?"

Scott nodded. "I think so," he said. "The *Sentinel* seems to be doing everything it can to hand it to us on a silver platter."

Harvey Van Pelt was thrilled with the Frankel case. The deeper he got into it, the more convinced he became that this was indeed the big one—the one for which he had waited his entire career.

Ruben had seen to it that every bit of documentation had been laid out for the prosecutor as precisely as a road map to his own front door. There had been no mistakes made, either with the warrants or with the collection and handling of the evidence. Everything had been done by the book. All that was wanting were the scientific analyses and the DNA results. Van Pelt wondered how long it would take Scott Cohen to come looking for a plea bargain.

And go away empty-handed, he thought with an inner smile. Taxpayers' dollars notwithstanding, this was one case that was going to go all the way to the gallows. For the first time in his twenty-nine years in office, Van Pelt was glad that hanging was the state's primary method of execution. Barbaric though it was, it certainly suited the perpetrator of this crime.

The legal gamesmanship that generally marked the first stages of a trial had already begun. Motions had been filed, disclosure issues were being argued, schedules were being discussed. It was like a chess match, each side attempting to size up the other, second-guess the other, get one step ahead of the other. It was the part of a case that Van Pelt liked best. He was an excellent chess player.

Not that he didn't appreciate the actual trial itself. He did. In particular, he enjoyed the sound of his own voice resonating throughout the courtroom as he loomed over a jury and hammered home his points. He was a charter member of the local chapter of Toastmasters, and had always prided himself on being a good public speaker.

More than that, though, Harvey Van Pelt was a good public servant. In over a quarter of a century, no hint of corruption had ever attached itself to him or to his office. He was known as fair, honest, and totally dedicated to the principles of justice and the law.

Although his was an elected position, Van Pelt did not play politics, and never allowed himself to be swayed by outside influences of any kind. With an impartial eye, he evaluated every case that came across his desk on its own merits, and he never undertook a prosecution in which he didn't thoroughly believe. After a careful review of the Breckenridge file, he thoroughly believed in the guilt of Jerry Frankel.

"I rarely speculate about a pending matter, especially in the early stages," he told the *Sentinel* reporter who came for an interview. "There's always a real danger of poisoning the jury pool, you know. I believe in trying my cases in the courtroom, not in the media. All I'm prepared to say at this time is that I'm confident that justice will be done."

◊　◊　◊

"Van Pelt's a good man," Scott told Jerry. "And I think a much better lawyer than his record might indicate. So, at this time, I'm obliged to ask you if you would entertain any kind of plea?"

"What do you mean?"

"I mean I don't know what Van Pelt's thinking is at this point, or how confident he is about a conviction, but it's possible we could plead down to murder two."

Jerry blinked. "What does *that* mean?"

"It's saying that you killed her, but you didn't really intend to," Scott replied, his expression revealing nothing. "It was more or less a heat-of-the-moment kind of thing. You were arguing. Maybe the knife was only supposed to scare her. The argument got out of hand, you went a little crazy, and you didn't realize what you were doing. It would mean a long prison sentence, but it's better than the alternative."

"It's not better than an acquittal," the teacher said.

"No, it's not," the attorney agreed.

"I'm not pleading to anything," Jerry declared. "If Van Pelt thinks he has enough evidence to get a conviction, let him try."

"Perhaps I'd better tell you a little something about our court system," Scott said. "A conviction sometimes has a lot less to do with the evidence than with how the jury perceives the defendant, which in this case is you. If they see you as guilty, they'll tend to believe the evidence. If they see you as innocent, they'll make every effort to ignore the evidence."

"Wait a minute—I thought I was innocent until proven guilty."

"That's always the ideal," Scott said. "Unfortunately, it's not always the reality."

Jerry frowned thoughtfully. "It's obvious that folks around here want to lynch me, regardless of the evidence. Will a change of venue make a difference?"

"It might. But the murder of a pregnant fifteen-year-old girl might not sit too well with a lot of people, no matter where the case is heard."

"Are you recommending that I plead?"

"No," Scott told him. "The decision is yours. My job is to make sure that your decision is an informed one. Clearly, there was enough evidence to warrant an arrest. Van Pelt must feel he has enough to prosecute. But that doesn't automatically mean there's enough for a conviction."

There was a moment of silence then, while the teacher considered his options and the attorney waited.

"I think I can beat this," Jerry said. "They can't prove that was my knife, and even if they find Tara's blood on it, mine isn't, and neither are my fingerprints. So what's to say that the real murderer, who knew I was under suspicion, didn't plant it in my car? It wouldn't have been all that hard to do. My garage was never locked."

"That's certainly a point we would try to make," Scott confirmed.

"Also, I've been doing some reading about DNA while I've been stuck in here, and I say that it was *my* blood on the sweatshirt, and I don't think anyone's going to come up with any convincing evidence that it wasn't."

"You may be right."

"As for that partial fingerprint they say they found on her cross, who knows how it got there? It could have happened anytime. That day in the back hall, for example. There's certainly no proof it was left there on the night of the murder."

"That's true," Scott conceded.

"And you assured me that the Alice Easton incident is not going to be admissible in court."

"It isn't," the attorney confirmed.

"Then I think that adds up to reasonable doubt. I say we go to trial."

"Okay," declared Scott, "we go to trial."

Matthew Frankel had become a commuter. Two days after his father's arrest, the three bullies dragged him into the bathroom and stuck his head in a dirty toilet bowl, holding him there, thrashing and gagging, until the boy almost passed out. They might well have finished the job—they were having such a good time of it—but a sixth-grader walked in on them.

"What're you doing?" he asked.

"Nothing," they said.

The intruder took in the entire scene, studying the three fifth-graders through round eyeglasses, memorizing their faces.

"Get out," he told them.

The bullies fled, leaving the eleven-year-old to pull Matthew out of the toilet. He laid the boy on his stomach, turned his head to one side, and pumped until the fourth-grader threw up, and it was clear that he would be all right. Billy Hildress found his best friend on the bathroom floor five minutes later.

"Somebody pulled me out," Matthew related afterward, "but I couldn't see who it was."

"What's the matter with you people?" Deborah stormed at the principal. "He's only nine years old, for God's sake. He hasn't done anything to deserve this."

"I quite agree with you, and I'm most dreadfully sorry," the principal said solicitously, fearful that the outraged mother seated across the desk from her might be tempted to bring legal action. "And just as soon as we identify the boys who did this terrible thing to Matthew, they will be dealt with, I assure you."

"Why wasn't anyone paying attention?"

"I realize now, of course, that we should have been," the principal was forced to concede, "but the truth is, we don't have the personnel to watch every child every minute of the day."

"After two previous incidents involving *this* child, I think you should have found the personnel," Deborah retorted.

The principal swallowed her anger. What did you expect? she wanted to shout. Your husband murders someone else's child, and you think it isn't going to rub off on yours?

"We've never had this kind of situation before," she said instead. "If you'll just be a little patient, I'm sure we can come up with an appropriate solution."

But Deborah didn't wait. She contacted a private school on the mainland to arrange a transfer, and within a matter of days, mother and son could be seen riding the ferry to and from Seattle together five times a week.

Matthew didn't miss his old school very much. He liked his new teacher and got along well with his new classmates. Best of all, nobody seemed to know who he was, and he didn't have to be afraid to walk down the hallways or across the playground.

The worst of it, though, was that he and Billy didn't get to see each other every day anymore, only on Saturdays, when they would try to catch up for the whole week. Sometimes, Deborah would take them on excursions off the Island, or they would take Chase for a romp at Madrona Point Park, or go skating at the Ice Pavilion, or just hang around the house, playing video games. And if something came up that just couldn't wait until Saturday, they would call each other in between.

It was to Billy that Matthew confided his deepest fears about his father, in the dark days and weeks that followed the arrest.

"My dad couldn't hurt anyone," he told his best friend. "He's not like that. Why, he never even gets mad at anyone. My mom, she gets mad, but not my dad. He's always nice to everyone, and he's always willing to talk things over. He's really a lot like *your* dad."

Billy nodded. "That's exactly what I think," he replied. "Probably this whole thing is just a big mistake."

"But I'm so scared that nobody else besides us knows that."

"Don't you think Mr. Cohen knows?"

"I guess," Matthew conceded. "But if he can't convince the police, they might lock my dad away for the rest of his life for something he didn't do."

"I don't think that's the way it works," Billy said. "I think it's something called a jury that decides."

"What's a jury?"

"I don't know," Billy confessed. "But my dad says Mr. Cohen has to convince a jury not to lock up your dad if he didn't do anything wrong."

"Oh," Matthew said, feeling a little better, although not exactly sure why.

It was his lifeline, his friendship with Billy; someone he could talk to, someone he could trust to tell him the truth, someone he could count on to be there for him when things got really rough.

"I'm sorry, Matthew, but Billy's not here right now," Libby Hildress said into the telephone one Wednesday evening, while her younger son scowled at her from less than ten feet away.

"Oh?" came the puzzled reply. "He left a message for me to call him as soon as I got home. It sounded important."

"Well, I guess it wasn't so important, after all."

"I guess not."

"Or maybe he was calling to tell you that he won't be able to spend Saturdays with you anymore," she said.

There was a pause.

"He won't?" Matthew asked.

"No, I'm afraid he won't," she said firmly. "We've decided that Saturdays are going to be family days from now on. The four of us realize we haven't been spending nearly enough time together."

"Oh."

"I hope you understand that we have nothing against you personally, Matthew," Libby took the opportunity to add. "But under the circumstances, we feel it would probably be better all around if you didn't call again."

9

The preliminary hearing took place at the Puget County Courthouse on the second Monday in February, in the larger of the two courtrooms—the one that was almost never used.

It was an impressive space of high windows, gleaming wood paneling, ornately carved moldings, and oak flooring. By nine o'clock in the morning, the room was packed with as many spectators as could be crammed into the six rows of benches that rather closely resembled church pews.

The proceedings were separated from the gallery by a low wooden railing that extended the entire width of the room. Just inside, and accessible by a swinging gate at the center, were two long tables. Harvey Van Pelt and three members of his staff were seated at the table to the left of the aisle, while Jerry Frankel and Scott Cohen occupied the table to the right. The jury box, a raised platform set off by its own polished wood railing, ran beneath the row of windows on the left. It held fourteen armchairs that, for this particular event, would remain empty. On the right side of the room, at a small desk with a telephone on it, sat Jack Earley, dressed in his bailiff's uniform, his gun strapped to his hip.

Above everything loomed Judge Irwin Jacobs, a small, bald

man of sixty-six, with a prominent nose and thick dark eyebrows that appeared to run together in an unbroken line. Other than his head, his hands were all that could be seen of him; the rest seemed to be lost inside his black robe.

It took little more than three hours for a handful of people to be sworn in, take the witness chair, and offer their testimony.

Kristen Andersen was first, looking extremely nervous, her voice barely above a whisper.

"So three days before her death, you saw Mr. Frankel put his arms around Tara Breckenridge in what you considered to be an inappropriate embrace, is that correct?" summarized Harvey Van Pelt.

"Yes."

"Your witness," he said to the Cherub.

"Can you recall any time in your life when you were upset to the point of crying about something, and someone, let's say your father or some other adult male, put his arms around you?" asked Scott Cohen.

Kristen darted a look at her parents, who were seated in the second row of the gallery.

"I guess so," she mumbled.

"Can you give us any reason why he would do something like that?"

"Because he wanted to make me feel better."

"Precisely," Scott agreed. "So, can you now state, with absolute confidence, that what you saw take place in the back hall at the high school was inappropriate?"

"Well . . ."

"Is it even possible, Miss Andersen, that Mr. Frankel could have been trying to comfort Tara Breckenridge, much the same way your father would try to comfort you?"

Kristen thought about that for a long moment. "I guess it's possible," she said.

"Thank you."

• • •

"Can you tell us what time you saw the maroon Taurus wagon drive into Madrona Point Park?" the prosecutor asked Owen Petrie.

"About eleven," the teenager replied.

"What time did you leave?"

"About eleven-thirty."

"Was the Taurus still there when you left?"

"Yes."

"Your witness."

"Mr. Van Pelt just described the Taurus you say you saw drive into the park as maroon," the Cherub said. "Is that the way you described it to Chief Martinez?"

"Well, not exactly," Owen allowed. "I said it was a dark color, not black but maybe green or maroon or brown. I wasn't sure. I also said it could have been a Sable."

"Have you ever seen Mr. Frankel's car parked at the high school?"

"Sure. Every day."

"And when you saw the Taurus you've described in the park that night, did you automatically think to yourself—'There's Mr. Frankel's car'?"

Owen blinked at the Cherub several times before he answered. "No."

"Did you happen to see the license plate?"

"No."

"Well then, can you positively identify the car you saw at Madrona Point Park as my client's car?"

"No," he replied. "And I never said I could."

"Can you tell us exactly what you personally witnessed between the victim and the defendant during summer school?" Van Pelt asked Heidi Tannauer, who had made a special trip back from Northwestern for the hearing.

"I saw Tara and Mr. Frankel alone together several times after class."

"What were they doing?"

"Walking, talking, laughing together. Once I saw him sitting on one of the benches, and Tara came over and sat down beside him. Another time when I saw them, they were sharing an apple."

"Did you ever see Mr. Frankel walk and talk and laugh with any of his other students after class?"

"No."

"Your witness."

"The apple that you say you saw Mr. Frankel and Tara Breckenridge sharing," Scott inquired, "were they both eating from the same piece of fruit?"

"What do you mean?"

"Were they passing a whole piece of fruit back and forth to each other? Or did one hold the apple out to the other to take a bite?"

"No," Heidi replied. "They each had a half."

"In all the times you say you saw the two of them together during summer school—uh, I'm sorry, how many times was that?"

"Two or three."

"Yes, well, in all those two or three times, did you ever see Mr. Frankel touch Tara Breckenridge? Put his arms around her? Hold her hand? Caress her in any way?"

There was a pause. "No. Not that I remember."

"As a result of your autopsy, Dr. Coop, what did you determine was the cause of Tara Breckenridge's death?" the prosecutor inquired of the medical examiner.

"She died as a result of multiple stab wounds," the physician replied.

"Can you please describe the murder weapon to the court?"

"It was a hunting knife, with a curved blade about six inches in length and approximately one and one eighth inches at its widest point."

"Were all of the injuries that the victim sustained consistent with having been made by that weapon?"

"They were."

"And were you able to determine whether they were inflicted by a single perpetrator?"

"I believe they were."

"And from your thorough examination, have you determined anything else about the perpetrator?"

"From the nature and angle of the wounds, I estimated that he was between five feet ten inches and six feet two inches tall, and reasonably strong," Coop said.

"Do you happen to know how tall the defendant is?"

Coop squinted at Frankel. "As I recall, I measured him last August at five feet eleven and one half inches."

"Anything else?"

"It is my opinion, based on my analyses, that the killer is most probably left-handed."

"Do you happen to know, Doctor, whether the defendant is left-handed?"

"I happen to know that he is," said Coop.

"Your witness."

"Doctor, how many of your regular adult male patients would you say are between five feet ten and six feet two inches tall?" asked Scott.

Coop pursed his lips. "At least two hundred."

"And how many of them are left-handed?"

"Perhaps twenty."

"And without naming names, how many of those twenty would you say knew Tara Breckenridge?"

Coop eyed the attorney for a brief moment. "In all likelihood," he replied, "I'd say at least seventy percent of them."

"Now, Doctor," Scott went on. "The knife you described as the probable murder weapon—is it an uncommon kind of knife?"

"No."

"Well, if you were to rank it in popularity, say between one and ten, with one being the least, how common would you say it was?"

"Nine or ten," the medical examiner replied.

"And if you were to estimate how many such knives would be found, as a matter of course, in homes around the Island, what would your guess be?"

"Objection," Van Pelt cried. "Calls for speculation, Your Honor. How would the witness know how many knives there are on the Island?"

"There's no jury here, Mr. Van Pelt," Judge Jacobs said mildly. "And I believe I'm an experienced enough jurist to evaluate the testimony. I'll allow it."

Coop shrugged. "I'd say at least five hundred."

"One last question," Scott concluded smoothly. "Based on whatever personal knowledge you might have, how many of your twenty left-handed patients who are between five feet ten inches and six feet two inches tall currently own such a knife?"

"I personally know of eleven that do," the doctor replied.

After Magnus Coop left the stand, Ginger testified about the defendant's statement, and about the discovery of the knife in Jerry Frankel's car.

"Will you please describe that knife," prompted the prosecutor.

"It's a hunting knife," Ginger replied. "It has a black handle and a six-inch curved blade that measures an inch and an eighth at its widest point."

Next, Glen Dirksen took the stand to explain how he had happened to find the stained sweatshirt in Jerry Frankel's backyard.

"Was it buried?" asked Scott on cross-examination. "Did you have to dig it up?"

"No, sir."

"You mean, it was in plain sight, for God and everyone to see?"

"Yes, sir. The dog was playing with it."

At that, a nervous giggle rippled through the courtroom.

Charlie Pricker was the final witness, testifying to the match of Jerry Frankel's fingerprint with the partial print on Tara's cross, and the identification of the fibers on the victim's body as being consistent with the bloodstained shirt in the teacher's possession.

"We were unable to type the blood on the sweatshirt, but we are hoping for something from the DNA analysis," Charlie said.

"Did you find any blood on the knife?" Van Pelt asked.

"Yes," Charlie replied. "We were able to get a small sample of blood from the knife, and we determined that it's the same type as the victim's."

"Your witness."

"Tell me, Detective Pricker," Scott asked, "did you find any bloodstained pants in your search of the Frankel home?"

"No, sir."

"Did you find any bloodstained shoes, or socks?"

"No, sir."

"What do you think happened to them?"

"I'm sorry, sir?"

"Well, if my client was foolish enough to keep an incriminating sweatshirt around where you could so easily find it, what do you think he did with the rest of the clothing he was wearing that night?"

"I don't really know, sir," Charlie replied. "Maybe he disposed of it. Or maybe none of the rest of it had blood on it."

"Given the brutality of the crime," Scott prodded, "does that seem reasonable to you?"

"I just do my job, sir," the detective said. "I don't spend much time thinking about what should or shouldn't be."

At twelve minutes past noon, Jerry Frankel learned that he would be required to stand trial for the murder of Tara Breckenridge. There was no fanfare, no drumroll, just a crack of a gavel and an eleven-word ruling.

"I find sufficient cause to bind this defendant over for trial," Judge Jacobs declared in a throaty voice devoid of any inflection.

"Is that all there is to it?" the teacher asked his attorney as Jacobs stood up and left the room, and Jack Earley came over to escort him back to his cell.

"That's all there is to it," Scott told him. "What did you expect?"

"I don't know," Jerry said with a shrug. "This is my life that's being decided. I guess I expected more."

A magnum of champagne greeted Ginger, Charlie, and Glen Dirksen when they returned to Graham Hall.

"Good heavens, where did this come from?" Ginger asked.

Ruben grinned. "The city council," he replied.

"News sure does travel fast," Dirksen said. "It's only a ten-minute walk from the courthouse."

Ginger laughed. "Welcome to a small town."

"It may have taken only a couple of weeks to get to the preliminary hearing," an irate taxpayer wrote the editor of the *Sentinel*. "But I hear it could be at least a year before there's a trial. I can't afford to sit around reading books and watching television and eating three meals a day from the Waterside Cafe. Why should I have to pay through the nose so some bloody murderer can?"

"The wheels of justice turn too slowly in this country," wrote the manager of the Island Market. "Even if we get a conviction in the next year or so, it will take decades to wade through all the appeals that are sure to be mounted. Tara Breckenridge never saw her sixteenth birthday, but her killer might live another twenty years before he has to pay for his crime."

"We got the change of venue," Scott said two days later. "The case will be heard in Whatcom County."

"But that's only three hours away," Jerry said.

Scott shrugged. "It's the best Judge Jacobs would do. Van Pelt was chewing nails as it was."

"Too bad," Jerry said with a sigh. "I sort of had my heart set on Bucks County."

"We don't have a Bucks County in Washington," Scott told him.

"No," Jerry conceded. "It's in Pennsylvania."

The hooded green eyes blinked. "Well, at least you still have your sense of humor," the attorney said. "That's good."

"What difference does it make?" the teacher declared. "I sat at that hearing and listened to what those people were saying about me. And the truth is, if I didn't know I was innocent, I would have believed them. *I* would have thought I was guilty."

"That was only one side of the story," Scott reminded him.

"I know that," Jerry conceded. "But tell it to me straight— do we really have a chance? In any county? With any jury?"

"We always have a chance," Scott replied, looking his client in the eye. "There are a lot of loose ends in this case—ends Van Pelt is going to have to find a way to tie up if he wants a conviction."

"Four months ago, I had a life," Jerry said. "I had a family. I had a job doing something I thought was important. I was full of lofty ideals about making this a better world. Now all I want is to kiss my son good night again, hug my wife, and look out a window that isn't covered with steel bars."

"This case isn't over yet," Scott assured him. "Trust me, it hasn't even begun."

"What's wrong with this picture?" an outraged mother asked the editor. "Jerry Frankel butchers Tara Breckenridge right here on Seward Island, but he has his trial moved to Bellingham? Is this what happens when we let killers hire shyster lawyers to get them off?"

"I say it's *our* murder and it's *our* trial," wrote the owner of the auto parts store. "And the jury should be made up of people who knew and cared about Tara Breckenridge. That's all the impartiality this murderer deserves."

"I argued against a change of venue as vociferously as I could," Harvey Van Pelt defended himself on the steps of the courthouse. "But Judge Jacobs ordered it." There was the slightest of pauses. "I'm sure he had his reasons."

"Sure he did," someone muttered in disgust. "One Jew looking out for another."

Van Pelt, who was a good enough lawyer to know that the judge had made a legally appropriate ruling in this case—in fact, the only appropriate ruling, given the nature of the pretrial publicity—pretended not to hear.

10

It didn't make a bit of difference to Ginger where the trial was held. That was somebody else's responsibility. She had already done the job she was required to do. She had helped build the case that eventually caught a vicious murderer, and for her efforts, she had become something of a local heroine. She had also become engaged to be married. It was the happiest time of her life.

At two months before her twenty-ninth birthday, she felt as though the pieces of her life had finally come together in the right pattern—very much like those jigsaw puzzles she and her father had worried over during so many of her childhood evenings.

While Ruben might never be welcomed into the upper echelons of Seward society, he had at least been accepted as someone of stature in the community. It was some of her mother's friends who, surprisingly, were among the first to acknowledge him.

Verna had taken it upon herself to insert a small announcement of the engagement in the *Sentinel* soon after Jerry Frankel's arrest. In a matter of days, little handwritten notes on flowery, perfumed paper found their way to Graham Hall, congratulating Ruben and Ginger on a job well done, and taking the opportunity to remark rather favorably on the upcoming nuptials.

"What a pity the two of you have decided against a big wedding"—Verna pouted, riding the tide of her daughter's success, "when the whole island wants to help you celebrate. Why, it could be the social event of the decade."

"They tried so hard to hide it, didn't they?" Helen Ballinger cooed.

"Yep," Charlie Pricker agreed with a grin. "And they failed so miserably."

"Er, well, I guess you're going to be outgrowing that little house of yours," Albert Hoch boomed, shaking Ruben's hand so hard the arm almost came out of its socket. "I'm going to have a chat with Ed Hingham. He owns half the Island, and I happen to know he's got a real pretty place over on Somerset that Ginger might like. It has three bedrooms and two baths and a great view of the harbor. And we're going to want to renegotiate your contract, too. You know, to make sure we can keep you happy for the next five years or so. I'm going to get with the council on this as soon as possible, and I don't want you to worry about a thing."

"He may have a point," Ruben said to Ginger. "My house is awfully small."

"They're worried that you're going to jump ship because they treated you so badly," she told him. "I know the house on Somerset. It's a beauty. I say, let's take advantage of their generosity for the brief time it's being offered."

"I wouldn't really have thought of it, but they're so perfectly suited to each other, aren't they?" Maxine Coopersmith suggested to Dale Egaard.

"Of course they are," said Egaard. "I just wonder what took them so long to figure that out."

"Congratulations, Ruben," Keven Mahar said one Sunday when the police chief came to pick Stacey up after church. "You not only caught yourself a murderer, you seem to have caught yourself a wife in the bargain."

"Ginger is a very lucky girl," Doris O'Connor added with a genuine smile.

"Have the two of you set a date yet?" Lucy Mahar asked. "June is such a beautiful month on the Island, you know."

"In the aftermath of tragedy, comes healing and even love," Gail Brown began an editorial.

Ruben was embarrassed. "I wish they'd stop," he said. "I guess I don't mind the hullaballo over the Breckenridge case so much, but I'd really like our private lives to be just that."

Ginger was much too happy to care. In a few short weeks, Ruben had gone from scapegoat to savior, and she had helped to make it happen. Soon they were going to be married and live in a wonderful home. Forever linked with that was a history teacher who would be tried for murder and no doubt convicted of his crime, and she had helped make that happen, too. While it was all too true that one might well never have occurred if not for the other, she refused to let herself dwell on it.

If the Island wanted in on the celebration, Ginger had no objection. After all, occasions such as these were the public measuring sticks of a person's life; events that would be remembered, times that would be cherished, singular moments that would secure a past and define a future. If she lived to be a hundred, she knew it would not get any better than it was right now.

So why was it, she wondered, that she had lain in bed, tossing and turning, unable to sleep through a single night for the past six weeks?

Deborah Frankel also lay awake nights. A few short months ago, she had been in control of her life; her son thriving, her career moving forward, her marriage surviving. Now everything had been turned upside down. The boy barely smiled, she was falling woefully behind in her work while her colleagues at the office were whispering behind her back, and her relationship with her husband was being conducted in a visiting room, through a slit in a Plexiglas wall.

"How's Matthew?" Jerry asked at the beginning of every visit.

"He's doing as well as can be expected," Deborah lied. There was no point in telling him the truth—that she could hear his son crying himself to sleep every night. "He's adjusted very well to his new school, he's now an avid Sonics fan, and he and Chase have become inseparable."

"I miss him."

"He misses you, too. Maybe I could ask Scott to arrange a visit."

"No," Jerry said quickly. "I don't want him to see me in here. I don't want him to have to talk to me through a damn hole in a wall."

"Okay."

"Does he understand any of what's going on?"

"A little," she told him. Probably more than either of us realizes, she thought.

"And how are you?"

"I'm putting one foot in front of the other," she said truthfully. "It's the best I can do right now."

Deborah hated these visits. She didn't want to sit and make small talk with him, she wanted to scream. She wanted to pound her fists against the Plexiglas wall. She wanted to reach through that damned little hole and grab him by the throat and demand to know why he had done this to them. Then she would lie in bed at night and count the hours as they passed, and wonder if perhaps she couldn't blame it all on him; if perhaps she had played a part in the terrible tragedy unfolding around them.

"It takes one to make a bad marriage," her mother had always told her. "It takes two to make a good one."

Had she been too wrapped up in herself and her career? Had there been too little of her left for him? Had she not cared enough to recognize his needs? Was a nine-year-old boy the only thing that was keeping them together?

There had been any number of times that Deborah had thought about divorce. But it was a thought in the abstract only, as a convict might think about executing an impossible escape from a maximum security prison; it was more a mental exercise than a realistic possibility. And as quickly as the idea came, it was gone. Whatever had happened to their marriage, she would never leave her husband. Not because she didn't sometimes yearn for a different kind of relationship, but because she knew he would not survive it.

Aaron had raised his son to believe that there was nothing more important than family, nothing else you could count on, nothing else you could trust in. Then Emma had abandoned him in the cruelest possible way. Deborah could not even guess at the scars that her suicide must have left, because Jerry never spoke of her death. In fact, he rarely mentioned his mother at all, and then only in passing.

To the world, he was the outgoing, optimistic, dedicated visionary that had first captivated her as a junior at Byrn Mawr. But she had learned that he also had a dark side. She saw occasional glimpses of it when she would come upon him unexpectedly. Sometimes it was an expression, sometimes a gesture. Sometimes it was a mood that overtook him and drove him away from her and Matthew.

Everyone had a dark side, she knew, but Deborah could never really get a firm fix on the extent of Jerry's. All she understood was that it was mixed up in his fragility, his dependence, and his reluctance to deal openly with pain.

For ten years they had shared the same bed, and it had been a safe haven; a gentle place where they could put down the burdens of responsibility for a while; a neutral place where they could turn out the lights and confide in one another; a tender place of truce and comfort that, even if it didn't involve the kind of intimacy that it once had, was nonetheless satisfying.

Until Alice Easton. Then everything had changed.

Deborah had stood by his side through that whole sordid business; protecting him, defending him, holding her head high despite the invective, the censure, the mud. But it wasn't the same after that; they weren't the same. Even though he had repeatedly protested his innocence, nothing had been the same.

"I never touched that girl," he had proclaimed. "You do believe me, don't you?"

"It makes no difference what I believe," she replied wearily. "It's what everyone else believes that's going to count."

It was Deborah who had thwarted his attempt to stay and fight the charges. What was the point of staying in a place where his reputation was already ruined? she reasoned.

"Tucking my tail between my legs and running away is like saying I'm guilty," he argued. "I can't do that to my students. What will that teach them?"

"I don't care about them," she declared. "I care about us, and about Matthew. Even if you win, your job is lost anyway. Alice Easton's father will see to it that you never teach at Holman again. Or at any other school within a thousand-mile radius, for that matter. So what's the point? It'll be much better if we just go away and start over someplace else, someplace where nobody knows us, and we can put this all behind us. So take the deal they're offering you and let it go."

He had given in to her, of course; he always did. And the place she chose was as far away from Scarsdale, New York, as her company could send her. It just hadn't been far enough.

Now, lying alone in their bed, Deborah stared dry-eyed into the darkness, looking for an answer that wasn't there—the answer to a question that had dogged her like a shadow from one coast to the other. Had her maturity, her refusal to have more children, her commitment to her career, their slow alienation from one another helped to send him off some precarious edge?

The Jerry Frankel she knew, and had lived with all these years, could never have molested Alice Easton or murdered Tara Breckenridge. But what about the Jerry she didn't know?

Mary Breckenridge was another who waited for the hours of the night to pass.

She didn't want to think about Jerry Frankel, she didn't want to have to see his face or hear his name, but she couldn't help herself. Even in the sanctity of her bedroom, in the darkness, she could picture him—the straight brown hair, the intelligent eyes, the boyish looks, the set jaw. And in the silence, she could hear his name ringing in her ears, over and over and over again.

Her desperate attempt to convince Ruben Martinez had accomplished exactly nothing. The history teacher was still in jail, and every detail of his life was being endlessly dissected on the television, in the newspapers, across the front pages of the tabloids.

Every gruesome detail of the crime that had consumed the Island for so many months was now being played and replayed for a national audience. It seemed to be all anyone could talk about—or write about.

"CNN has finally discovered Seward Island," a nursery school teacher informed the editor of the *Sentinel*. "What a pity it had to be because of the one thing that makes us ashamed rather than the many things that make us proud."

◦ ◦ ◦

"The next thing you know," wrote a conservative, "the liberal media will stick its noses and its cameras into our courtroom and try to direct the trial."

"Why do we need a trial at all?" asked a fisherman. "We know he did it. Why don't we just save the taxpayers a lot of time and money, and feed the bastard to the sharks. Now, that would be justice."

Mary couldn't stand it. Every word about him was an assault, every picture of him a defilement, and she felt them each as a thrust of a knife plunging deep into her very soul. Like Tara must have felt.

She knew she couldn't risk another call to Graham Hall for fear Kyle would find out and be furious with her. Or worse, send her away to some hospital for the mentally sick. But she had to do something. Something that would make it all go away. So she shut herself off from the television and the newspapers and the people she had known all her life, and retired to her room, to lie awake at night, to doze fitfully during the day. But each time she fell asleep for more than a few moments, it was Tara she saw, with tears overflowing her eyes, reaching out, silently begging for comfort and help. And the harder Mary tried to get to her daughter, the further away the girl slipped. Then the pain was so sharp it would jolt her awake in an agony that was becoming too much to bear. By the end of February, Mary Seward Breckenridge knew what hell was.

Gail Brown spent most of February closeted away in her office, creating five articles that she believed constituted the finest work of her career to date. She called the series *The Anatomy of a Tragedy*, and it chronicled the murder investigation in a fascinating and detailed step-by-step account that had her readers, a great many of whom thought they already knew everything there was to know about the Breckenridge case, riveted to their seats.

As soon as the fifth article, articulating all the legal maneuverings that surrounded the trial, had been published, Gail decided to add two more to the series: the sixth to be written when the case actually went to trial, and the seventh when the verdict was rendered. She had already scoped them out, with the intention of making the long round-trip to Bellingham herself each day to bear witness to every moment of the court proceedings.

"I decided to follow one case from beginning to end," she said about the series. "I wanted people to know what an honest-to-goodness, everyday criminal investigation is all about. And then I want them to know what really goes on during a trial—both inside and outside the courtroom. This seemed like the best way to do it."

Accolades were coming in from all over the country, calling her work powerful, insightful, masterful. The *Seattle Post-Intelligencer* asked for permission to rerun the entire series. Other major publications wanted excerpts. Television newsmagazines were requesting interviews.

"You're famous," Iris Tanaka declared when she took a telephone call from a producer of *Nightline*. "Even Ted Koppel wants you."

Gail grinned. "If that's what it takes to put Seward Island on the map, I guess I can suffer through it."

The skinny brunette thought about her current wardrobe, and wondered whether her bank account could withstand a trip to Seattle and a major spending spree at Nordstrom's.

Libby Hildress read Gail Brown's series in the *Sentinel* and felt vindicated. It seemed ordained that her husband would be the one to find Tara Breckenridge's body, and then that she would be among the first to consider the involvement of Jerry Frankel. She secretly wondered if, perhaps without realizing it, she had received a message from God. Just the thought was enough to buoy her spirits and strengthen her conviction.

"If you suspected him all along, why didn't you say something?" her friend Judy Parker whispered during choir practice.

"Because I'm a good Christian," Libby whispered back, "and I don't like to think ill of another person, even if he isn't one of us. But I guess, after a while, with everything that was going on, I knew that two and two just had to add up to four."

"And to think you let your Billy spend so much time with those people."

Libby sighed. "I have only the good Lord to thank for keeping him safe."

But Billy Hildress didn't realize how safe he was. All he realized was how lonely he was.

"Matthew's my best friend," he complained. "I don't understand why I can't play with him anymore."

"Because his father's done a very bad thing," Libby patiently explained to him.

"But Matthew didn't do anything bad. What does what his father did have to do with him?"

The apple doesn't fall far from the tree was the thought that came immediately to mind, but Libby knew she couldn't tell that to the boy because, for some unfathomable reason, he remained very loyal to his friend.

"You're just too young to understand," she took refuge in saying. "Someday, when you're older, I'll be able to explain it to you better."

Not satisfied with her evasion, the nine-year-old tried his father.

"I think maybe you'd better discuss it with your mother," Tom Hildress suggested. "She has it all worked out in her mind."

"She says I'm too young to understand," Billy said. "But I'm not. She thinks Mr. Frankel is guilty, and that somehow that makes Matthew guilty, too. But it doesn't, does it?"

Tom sighed. "No, it doesn't," he replied. "But I don't think that's exactly what she meant."

"If Matthew hasn't done anything wrong, why can't we be friends anymore?"

"Until the situation with his father is resolved, I think Mom feels you might not be safe at Matthew's house," Tom told him.

"But his dad isn't even *at* his house," Billy protested. "He's locked up in jail. And anyway, Matthew could come here."

Tom tried never to lie to his children. "Billy, we don't always know what other people will do, especially under stress. I think Mom feels it would be better to let things with the Frankels settle down a bit. In a few months, it all might be resolved happily, and then you and Matthew can start seeing each other again, the same as before."

"Dad, tell me honestly," the boy asked, "do you think Mr. Frankel murdered that girl?"

"Honestly?" Tom replied. "I don't know. It kind of looks that way right now, but I keep remembering that we're only hearing one side of the story so far."

"Mom seems pretty sure he did it," Billy said. "But is it okay if I wait with you to hear the other side?"

"I think that would be all right," Tom replied.

11

The case against Jerry Frankel began to unravel in the middle of March.

"We didn't get a match on the hair," Charlie Pricker said on the second Wednesday of the month. "Not one of the samples we took from Frankel is consistent with any of the hairs we found on the victim."

"That's odd," Ruben said with a frown. "You'd have thought there'd be at least one."

"Could he have worn a cap of some kind?" Ginger asked hopefully.

"There's no indication of that," Charlie said. "And we certainly didn't find any caps in the search. Of course, there's always the possibility that he *was* wearing a cap and he got rid of it with the rest of his clothes."

"Could whatever hairs he might have left on the body been dislodged when he rolled her in the rug?" Ruben inquired.

Charlie shrugged. "I suppose," he said. "But we didn't find any of his hairs on the rug, either."

* * *

"What does that mean, no match on the hair?" Albert Hoch asked.

"It means that the lab didn't find any hairs, consistent with Frankel's hair, on Tara's body or on the rug," Ruben replied.

"No, I mean what does this do to our case against him?"

"Well, a match certainly would have helped," the police chief conceded. "Another forensic nail in the coffin, so to speak. But it doesn't necessarily hurt us that much. There are ways of explaining the absence of hair. He might have been wearing a cap. Or whatever hair he may have deposited on her body simply came off when he rolled her in the rug."

"You found other hairs on her, didn't you?"

Ruben nodded. "But they might have come from the rug itself."

The mayor rolled his eyes. "I can hear Scott Cohen gloating all the way from Seattle."

"We've got to go with what we've got," Ruben reminded him. "We can't manufacture what isn't there."

"But are you sure what you've got is enough?"

"I think we gave Van Pelt a very strong case," the police chief responded. "Granted most of it is based on circumstantial evidence, but I'd have no problem leaving it up to a jury."

"The sweatshirt came back from the lab," a dejected Charlie reported on Thursday. "No go on the DNA. We can't prove the blood was Tara's."

"What about the fibers?" Ginger asked.

"They're consistent, positively," he confirmed. "But we did a little checking, and we found three stores on the Island that have been selling the identical sweatshirt—same dye lot and everything—for at least the last six months."

"We didn't get much from the car," Charlie related the following Monday.

They had impounded Jerry Frankel's maroon Taurus on the day he was arrested. The crime lab in Seattle had then spent the better part of two months putting it through every test known to man.

"Let's have it," Ruben said.

"No fingerprints," Charlie told him.

"None at all?"

"None belonging to Tara."

"He wiped them off," Ginger said flatly.

"That's possible," Charlie conceded, "but there was also no hair—again. At least, none consistent with the victim. No skin traces, either."

"He vacuumed," Ginger declared. "Don't forget, we didn't get the car until three months after the fact. He had plenty of time to be very thorough."

"Is there any *good* news?" asked Ruben. "I find it very hard to believe, even after three months, that Tara could have ridden all the way from Southwynd up to Madrona Point without leaving some microscopic clue behind."

"Well, we may be in luck here, but then again," Charlie replied with a shrug. "The lab boys found some blue denim fibers lodged in the front passenger seat cushion, which are consistent with the skirt she was wearing that night."

"Does that do it?" Ginger asked anxiously.

"Not exactly," Charlie cautioned. "You see, they can't positively identify them as coming from that particular skirt. Just like the sweatshirt, turns out the skirt was one of the hot items on the racks last fall. In fact, there's a store here in town that purchased two dozen of them, again the same dye lot and everything, and sold them all."

"Okay, we've got no prints, no hair, and questionable fibers," Ruben said. "What about blood?"

"That's the biggest problem," Charlie said. "The car is clean."

Ginger looked stunned. "There must be some mistake," she cried, and now there was a definite note of desperation in her voice. "That's just not possible."

"That's what I told the boys at the lab," Charlie said. "But they told me the only substance they could identify in that car was a common household cleaning product."

"In other words," Ruben said with a heavy sigh, "the lab hasn't come up with one piece of conclusive evidence that Tara Breckenridge was ever in Jerry Frankel's car."

"That's about it," Charlie agreed. "We have a possible, maybe even a probable, but not a positive."

"Could it be that she was never in the car?" Ginger wondered aloud. "That she got to the park some other way and met him there?"

"That doesn't fit with everything else we have," Ruben reminded her.

"No," Charlie concurred. "The timing, the sequence of events—everything we have hinges on him picking her up near Southwynd sometime after ten o'clock and driving her up to Madrona Point at about eleven, when the Petrie kid said he saw the Taurus. And we did get some pieces of gravel from the tires that are totally consistent with the type they use in the parking lot. But of course, we can't prove that they got there on that night."

Ruben began to rub his temples with the tips of his fingers. "No conclusive evidence of the victim ever being in the car I can maybe live with," he mused. "But no blood? The job he did on her—he had to have been covered in it. Is it possible he could have gotten every single trace of it out of the car?"

"With enough time and enough cleaner?" Charlie replied. "The answer is . . . yes."

The police chief sighed. "First there's none of Frankel's hair on the victim, then we strike out with the sweatshirt, and now we've got next to nothing from the car—I'm not sure I like where this is going," he told them.

"What's happening, Ruben?" Albert Hoch bellowed over the telephone.

"I don't know," the police chief replied uncomfortably.

"Is this case about to blow up in our faces?"

There was a long pause. "Not yet," Ruben said finally. "There's still the DNA to come in, and we're pretty confident about that. In the meantime, we still have the knife, and we still have the fingerprint."

Ginger scrubbed her face and brushed her teeth and slipped into her pajamas. But she didn't even bother to look at her warm, inviting bed; she knew she would not be sleeping in it tonight. Instead, she pulled on her bathrobe and a pair of heavy socks, and padded out into the living room.

A fire crackled smartly; she had laid it the way Ruben had taught her. Twink was curled up on the dusty blue sofa, basking in its warmth. Ginger sat down beside him, and idly began to scratch him behind the ears.

Things were not going at all the way she had thought they would. Like a row of clay pigeons, every piece of evidence she had been so sure would point an irrefutable finger at Jerry Frankel was being shot down by their very own investigators.

The case she had helped to build, one excruciatingly small piece at a time, was now threatening to come crashing down around her. What had, just days ago, seemed to be unequivocal was now beginning to appear insufficient.

Ginger sighed. Two months earlier, she had made an agonizing decision—her little deal with the devil, as she thought of it. Although it had sent the investigation rolling in what she firmly believed was the right direction, she was now faced with having to undo that deal—and it was likely to destroy more than just the rest of the case against Jerry Frankel.

She stared into the fire most of the night, as though searching for an answer among the embers. Occasionally, she would get up and set another log to burn. Then she would sit back down again and pick up her thoughts. Every once in a while, almost as if he were reading her mind, Twink would slap his tail and whine.

While it might have been very much on Harvey Van Pelt's mind, Scott Cohen rarely thought about the fact that he had never lost a murder case. He preferred to concentrate on each case as it came before him, as though it were the only one that had ever come before him. Each situation was unique, with a series of defining circumstances that set it totally apart from any other. For that reason, no two cases could be prepared alike, or tried alike.

He had represented clients in whose innocence he had believed one hundred percent, and he had searched through the prosecution's case to find the one inevitable flaw that would result in an acquittal.

Similarly, he had defended clients in whose guilt he had believed one hundred percent, and he had searched through the prosecution's case to find the one obscure mistake that would create reasonable doubt.

Whichever way it went, Scott had no trouble sleeping at night, because he believed absolutely in the law. Imperfect though justice could sometimes be, his entire professional life was predicated on the single principle that, before a man could properly be found guilty of murder, the case against him must be solid enough to withstand a major assault from any direction.

In the hundred or more cases he had tried over the past quarter of a century, the Cherub had never lied to a jury, or misrepresented the facts of any matter, or put forth a theory he could not evidentially support. The secret behind his success lay in the fact that he was a superb strategist. He knew exactly where to look for the weak points in an argument, and then how to keep digging at them until they came apart, one by one, and the whole case collapsed in the prosecution's lap.

"I have nothing against the state," he said once in a *Seattle Times* interview. "But I wouldn't be willing to put my life into the hands of unchallenged civil servants. The same goes for my clients. We are fortunate to have an adversarial system in this country; many countries in the world do not. And it is this system, which holds the state accountable for the capability of its employees and the integrity of their work, that protects us all."

The case against Jerry Frankel perplexed him. While the individual pieces fit together in a nice neat little pattern, they did not appear to have been cut from the same cloth, but rather from various pieces of fabric that were then hastily sewn together, and were now beginning to fray.

The fingerprint on the cross; the sighting of the Taurus in the park; the bloody sweatshirt; the knife; the eyewitness accounts that placed the teacher and the student together—much of it was apparently being mitigated, if not out-and-out contradicted, by the scientific evidence. There were holes in that fabric through which the attorney knew he could drive a herd of buffalo.

Despite the fact that Jerry was a friend as well as a client, Scott had no clear certainty one way or the other about the teacher's guilt or innocence. On the surface, the man was a gentle philosopher, incapable of violence. But underneath, Scott had always sensed an unsettled soul. It didn't matter, really; it was not an issue with which he had to concern himself. All that mattered was that the state's case was falling apart.

"You've got nothing," he told Harvey Van Pelt on Tuesday. "Nothing that puts my client at the scene of the crime; nothing that puts my client in contact with the victim; nothing that conclusively puts the victim in my client's car. You don't even have positive identification that it *was* my client's car at Madrona Point. Your case is nothing but smoke and mirrors and wishful thinking."

"What are you talking about?" Van Pelt scoffed. "I still have motive and opportunity, I have the murder weapon found in his car, and I have the fingerprint on the cross. And any day now I'll have the DNA to corroborate."

"Are you so sure?" Scott asked softly.

"Of course I am," came the irate response.

"I'm sorry," said the Cherub. "I know how important it is to everyone on the Island to prosecute Tara Breckenridge's killer, but I'm afraid your people haven't done their job." He handed the prosecutor a blue-jacketed document. "I'm moving for a dismissal."

"Ruben," Van Pelt entreated, "I need your help on this. Cohen's going before Judge Jacobs in the morning. Do we have anything we can use to fight this?"

"I'll get back to you," the police chief replied.

They sat in the interview room, with Ruben and Charlie at either end of the metal table and Ginger in the middle. She was strangely quiet, her face pale, her eyes little more than dark holes.

"Are you okay?" Ruben asked, because she looked bad enough to worry him.

But she simply shrugged him off. "I didn't sleep very well," was all she said.

"I checked with the lab," Charlie reported. "The DNA analysis isn't complete yet, and they can't tell us anything concrete until it is. Without those results, and given what's happened to some of our other evidence, I don't know what you can say to Van Pelt."

"Maybe what all this means is that we weren't really meant to get him," Ginger said in an emotionless voice.

Ruben stared at her. "That's strange talk coming from you," he observed. "The Seward Island holdout for truth and justice."

"If we don't have the evidence," she said with a shrug, "Van Pelt isn't going to get a conviction."

Now both men stared at her.

"Wait a minute, what's going on here?" Charlie asked. "It was you who convinced the rest of us that Frankel did it. It's not like you to give up."

"I'm not giving up," Ginger replied with a sigh. "I'm just being realistic."

"But we have solid evidence," Charlie said. "Maybe the shirt and skirt fibers are a little iffy, but the knife was in his car."

"Yes," she said dully, clasping her hands until the knuckles turned white because she knew what was coming next.

"And his fingerprint was on her cross."

It was here, the moment she had been dreading, the moment that had kept her awake so many nights. And she realized, as though looking down a long tunnel, that it had been inevitable, right from the beginning.

"No," she whispered, so softly that neither of the men was sure he heard her right.

"I beg your pardon?" Ruben asked.

Ginger took a deep breath that came out as more of a shudder. "It wasn't his print," she said.

"Yes, it was," Charlie corrected her. "I saw the report."

"No," she said again. "You saw the *second* report."

The two men were clearly confused.

"I don't follow," Ruben said.

"The print we took off the glass Frankel used didn't match the latent we had from Tara's cross," she explained in the same flat voice. "I made up a new one and sent it to the lab."

"You did what?" Charlie asked in disbelief.

"I switched the latent to get a match," she said.

"Whatever possessed you to do a thing like that?" Ruben demanded.

"I knew he was guilty," Ginger replied. "And I knew the only way we were going to prove it was to get inside his house. All we needed was one piece of solid evidence for the warrant. I figured, if the search came up empty, no harm was done. But if we found what we were looking for, well then, the killer was caught. And I was right—we found the murder weapon."

A heavy silence descended on the windowless room.

Charlie twisted uncomfortably in his chair. "I've got to go do something," he mumbled finally and escaped.

Ruben just sat there. He didn't move, not even a muscle twitched, but Ginger could feel him pulling away, distancing himself from her. She had come so close to having it all, she thought, everything she had ever wanted. The brass ring had actually been in her grasp, and she had unceremoniously dropped it.

"They were going to fire you," she whispered, tears filling her eyes. "I'd just found you. I didn't want to lose you. I knew he was guilty."

He didn't know what to say to her, what to feel, what to do. The woman he had waited so long to find; the lovely, warm, witty, exciting woman he was planning to marry in three short months and spend the rest of his life with, had turned out to be someone he was suddenly afraid he didn't even know.

He had worked with cops before who had considered it acceptable to help evidence along in order to nail down a particularly elusive case, and it had always been done with the best of intentions—to put the guilty son of a bitch behind bars where he belonged. It didn't matter; Ruben had fired them all. The law was the law, and he had taken an oath to uphold it. More than that, he believed without exception that police officers who bent the law were no better than those who broke it.

"I have to call Van Pelt," he said at length.

Ginger nodded numbly.

Ruben got slowly to his feet and went to the door. "We'll have to sort all this out, of course, but not now," he said. "Why don't you take a couple of days off . . . Call in sick or something." And then he left the room without looking at her.

"Please, Your Honor," Van Pelt protested on Wednesday morning when Judge Jacobs did indeed dismiss the charges against Jerry Frankel. "We still have what is almost certainly the murder weapon, and we have the right defendant. The DNA results will nail him."

"If they do, you can always refile," the judge told him in a world-weary voice. "But this man has no priors, he appears to be an upstanding member of the community, and I'm not going to keep him in jail based on the current state of your case."

Van Pelt looked as though smoke and fire would burst from several of his orifices at any moment. He was embarrassed beyond words; not because Jacobs had summarily dismissed his case of a lifetime, but because he knew in his heart that the judge was right to do it.

"I should have dropped the charges myself, the moment Cohen showed up," he told his assistant. "I knew it was the right thing to do. Now I look like such a fool. I should have waited for the DNA before I filed. I was in too much of a hurry."

"What do you mean, I'm out of here?" Jerry asked.

"I mean, the judge has dismissed the charges against you for lack of evidence," Scott told him.

Jerry wasn't sure he had heard correctly. "I thought you said they had such a strong case."

The Cherub shrugged. "It seems to have fallen apart on them," he said.

"Fallen apart?" the teacher asked, dumbfounded. "You mean the DNA came back negative?"

"No, that's not in yet. But there isn't enough other evidence to hold you. Of course, they can always refile if the DNA goes their way."

The teacher began to giggle, a borderline hysterical sound. "You ever had the feeling you were tied to a train track?" he asked his attorney. "You see the train coming right at you, closer and closer, and you know it's going to hit you, pulverize you, but you can't get away? And then at the last moment, the train stops, just inches away from you, and you don't know why? That's how I feel right now."

"Give it a couple of hours to sink in," Scott told him. "Give me one more night to get all the formalities taken care of, and by tomorrow morning you'll be on your way home where you can kiss your son and hug your wife anytime you like."

"Okay, so Jacobs turns the teacher loose," Glen Dirksen said on Wednesday afternoon. "Then what happens when the DNA comes in?"

"If it nails him, Van Pelt will refile," Ruben replied. "If it doesn't, we reopen the investigation."

"Van Pelt won't get the chance to refile," the officer predicted, clearly upset. "I watched Frankel during the preliminary hearing; he knows what the DNA results will be, and he's not going to hang around for them. I wouldn't, if it was me. And once he's released, I could follow him to Timbuktu and it wouldn't matter. There's not a damn thing we can do to stop him."

"We did our best with what we had," Ruben responded. "We just didn't have enough."

"Well, look at the upside," Charlie Pricker said. "No one will blame us for not making the case. Everyone knows he did it. They'll blame his hotshot lawyer for getting him off."

"Jacobs is letting Frankel go?" Gail Brown exclaimed.
"That's what I heard," Iris Tanaka said.

"Unbelievable," the editor breathed, already beginning to figure how she could rework the sixth and seventh articles in her exemplary series to show how a diligent investigation could sometimes go awry. "Get someone on it right away and scratch tomorrow's editorial. I'll do a new one."

"After all that," Iris remarked. "To end up with the wrong man."

Gail sighed as an image of Alice Easton came into focus. She had never revealed the contents of the anonymous letter to anyone but Ginger, nor the results of her trip to Scarsdale.

"That's the trouble," she said now. "What if he's not the wrong man?"

It surprised Malcolm Purdy that he should have taken the death of Tara Breckenridge so personally. But he had, and as a result he had followed the official investigation every inch of the way, and had even gone to the trouble of running a private little investigation of his own, calling on a few well-placed sources around the country. He had, of course, reached the same conclusion as the authorities, only way ahead of them. It never ceased to amaze him how slow the police were to react, how laborious the process was, how far backward they had to bend not to trample the precious rights of a murdering piece of filth.

There was no doubt in the ex-Marine's mind that Jerry Frankel was guilty. The psychological abnormality of the man was obvious to Purdy: the classic symptoms of inadequacy, stemming from the background of a Holocaust-surviving father and an unbalanced mother, steering him into a profession where he could manipulate the minds of children, leading to the abuse of that position. Anyone with even limited intelligence could see it, anyone who had studied human behavior as he had . . . anyone with daughters.

After the preliminary hearing, Purdy had celebrated. Until then, he'd had little faith in the bleeding-heart liberal legal process. But the system had prevailed. The good guys had come out on top. Tara Breckenridge had won.

There was a young man with him at the time, and the two of them split a case of beer and a bottle of bourbon as they sat around a crackling fire well into the night, the woman trying to get them to eat something, and cleaning up after them.

"The motherfucker's gonna hang," Purdy predicted as he whirled the woman around the room in an off-balance version of a jig.

The night he learned that Frankel was going to be cut loose, he paced the floor until dawn. He felt betrayed. His reborn faith had been short-lived—the system had failed after all, and Tara Breckenridge was not going to have her day in court.

It didn't take a genius to figure out that the bastard wouldn't wait around for the DNA results to come in, but would take off at the first opportunity. Purdy spent the dark hours wondering if the police, crippled by their rules and red tape, would be able to stop him.

The nightmare was about to end, Deborah Frankel thought, having spoken briefly with Jerry and then at length with Scott. Or was it just beginning? When she faced herself in the mirror, she wasn't sure. At the very least, the case against her husband had been discredited; enough so that the judge had agreed to let him go. Well, for the time being anyway, until the fancy blood analysis was complete.

She found herself wondering what the DNA would show. Had Jerry had an affair with Tara Breckenridge . . . was he the father of her unborn baby . . . did she really want to know? He had denied both vehemently and repeatedly, and she had taken some measure of comfort from that, but in the uncompromising glare of the bathroom light, she wasn't sure she really believed him. In many ways, it would have been easier to let a jury tell her what was true.

For Matthew's sake, she was glad that Jerry was coming home. The boy adored his father, hung on his every word, and trusted him implicitly. How uncomplicated childhood was, she thought. For her, however, there were decisions that needed to be made. Whether the DNA would eventually prove Jerry guilty or innocent, she had to protect her son and herself, and if it came to that, her husband. For Matthew's sake.

Putting the house on the market was an obvious option. It was what she would have done had Jerry gone to trial and been convicted. It was what she should do now. Living on Seward Island had become pure hell for both her and her son, and Jerry would certainly never teach here again, so what was the point of staying on one moment longer than necessary? Deborah put a note on her calendar to call the real estate agency first thing in the morning.

She would quit her job, of course. That is, if the firm didn't fire her first. Given the renewed media coverage the Breckenridge case was getting, going into the office each day had become as difficult for her as it had been for Matthew to go to his former school. Deborah knew that, as good as she was at her job, she had become a public relations liability, and the company would be only too glad to be rid of her. But that was all right. They had some savings to tide them over, and she knew she would have little trouble hooking up with a different firm in another state. Her track record spoke for itself. All she had to do was contact one of the big head-hunting outfits, and then wait for the offers to come in.

Jerry, however, was another story. Even were he to be exonerated of Tara Breckenridge's murder, Deborah doubted that he would ever teach again. There would be no bargain this time, as there had been in Scarsdale, no deal with the school, no protection.

A charge had been filed, an arrest had been made, an indictment had been handed down. True or false, upheld or not, it was part of the record, and it would follow him wherever he went. Besides, she was certain he could not possibly have the stomach for teaching anymore.

But an idea had been turning around in her mind for a while now. There were so many different aspects of history that fascinated Jerry; he was always jotting little notes to himself, and promising that one day he would organize the notes into a book. That was something he could do—spend his life writing. Why not? It was a perfect way for him to stay in his field, and out of the classroom. And it wouldn't matter if he were published or not; they wouldn't really need the second income.

Deborah made a mental note to broach the idea when she and Matthew went down to the courthouse to collect him after his release.

12

For the first time since the day he had been arrested, Jerry Frankel slept the night through. No nightmares haunted him, no sense of panic jarred him into consciousness. The deputy who brought him his breakfast at seven-thirty Thursday morning had to wake him.

"I'd have thought you'd be up and ready to go by now," the officer said without a smile.

"Me, too," Jerry agreed with a sheepish grin.

He couldn't remember when coffee had tasted so good, or orange juice so fresh. He marveled at how crisp the bacon was, how perfectly the eggs had been scrambled, how the toast had just the right amount of butter melting into it. He knew that never again would he take the small pleasures of life for granted. He decided there was no narcotic as powerful as freedom.

Scott had brought him a fresh set of clothes: gray slacks, white shirt, blue sweater, underwear, socks. He changed into them as soon as he was finished eating, leaving the onerous orange uniform he had been forced to wear in a heap on the floor.

Sunlight filtered through the barred window of his cell. A new day, he thought, a new beginning. Deborah had said she would bring Matthew with her when she came to pick him up. Jerry hadn't seen his son for two months, and he couldn't wait to wrap his arms around the boy and promise never to leave him again.

A crowd began to gather on the courthouse plaza, made up of silent, somber people who had been drawn to this place to witness something, but were unsure of exactly what or why. They stood in little clusters that grew larger as the minutes ticked by, until there was just one large mass of bodies overrunning the sidewalk, the circular drive, and even the grassy slope that flanked the imposing building. Only some measure of timidity seemed to have kept them off the broad flight of steps that led up to the front entrance.

"This is unbelievable," Gail Brown murmured to Paul Delaney. "There must be a thousand people here."

They maneuvered themselves to the edge of the steps for a preferential view, only to find a dozen other reporters and photographers with the same idea. Ever since the swastika had been painted on Jerry Frankel's garage door, the case had been attracting a lot of attention.

"What are they all doing here?" Glen Dirksen wondered aloud from inside the lobby of the courthouse as he peered through the massive leaded glass entry doors.

"They've come to observe a travesty of justice, young man," Harvey Van Pelt, overhearing, replied. "That's what they're doing here."

"Why did the time of my client's release have to be publicized?" Scott Cohen asked.

"The people have a right to know, and a right to be here, if they so choose," the prosecutor reminded him. "Besides, the newspaper didn't ask our permission before printing the information. Maybe you'd feel more comfortable going out the back door."

"My client is guilty of no crime," the Cherub responded.

"He doesn't have to sneak out of here. He has every right to walk out the front door, a free man."

"I don't think there'll be a problem, Mr. Cohen," Jack Earley said. "They don't look like a lynching mob. I think they're just curiosity-seekers."

"Can you at least clear the drive so we can get the car in?" Scott asked.

It was ten minutes past one. The paperwork was done, the formalities and technicalities had been taken care of. All that remained was for Deborah Frankel to drive up to the courthouse and take her husband home.

"We can do that," Glen Dirksen said. He gestured to two other uniformed officers standing in the lobby and the three of them left the building, jogged down the steps, and began to make their way through the crowd, directing people to back off.

At twelve minutes past one, Deborah maneuvered the maroon Taurus wagon up the plaza drive and brought it to a stop at the bottom of the steps. A murmur rippled through the crowd at the sight of the car.

"Okay, let's go," Scott said.

Jack Earley escorted Jerry out of a small waiting room off the lobby, and with the Cherub on one side and the Puget County bailiff on the other, the three men walked through the front doors of the courthouse into the sunlight.

"Here he comes," Gail cried, directing her photographer. "Get everything."

Jerry never really saw the crowd. His eyes were fixed on the car, searching until he located his son in the rear seat. Then a broad smile spread across his face, and he started to run down the steps.

"Wait a minute, Mr. Frankel," Jack Earley called, but the history teacher paid no attention.

At exactly the same moment that Jerry broke from his escort, Matthew scrambled out the back door of the Taurus and started up to meet him. The boy could not remember ever having been so excited. It was such a special day that his mother had taken off from work and allowed him to skip school.

When the two were twenty steps apart, a cold chill, like a gust of Arctic air, swept over Scott Cohen. When they were fifteen steps apart, the attorney, acting on an instinct he would not later be able to explain, suddenly bolted after his client. When father and son were ten steps apart, Scott began to shout at Glen Dirksen and the uniformed policemen who were still among the crowd. When the man and the boy were but five steps apart, the Cherub heard the sound he had feared he would hear, like the distant backfire of a car, and saw Jerry Frankel collapse into his son's arms.

Few among the onlookers paid much attention to the sound, so intent were they on getting a view of the scene unfolding before them. At first, most thought they were witnessing a heart-wrenching reunion. Then those at the front of the crowd began to realize that something very different was taking place. They could see that the attorney was bending over his client, gesturing frantically, the bailiff was thundering down the steps, and the three policemen were closing in on the scene with their handguns drawn.

Jerry lay with his head in Matthew's lap, his eyes open, staring sightlessly at his son.

"Dad? What's the matter, Dad?" the boy cried, even as his jeans were being soaked by blood and brain matter.

He got no answer. A single bullet in the forehead, leaving a hole no bigger in diameter than a pencil, had blown off the back of his father's skull.

Inside the Taurus, Deborah couldn't seem to move. She had watched Jerry's descent, had seen his progress halted by a force that snapped his head backward and buckled his knees, and had grasped the reality of it immediately. She knew she had to get to Matthew, to shield him, to get him out of there. But she found herself unable to move, her hands frozen to the steering wheel, caught somewhere between a gasp of horror and a guilt-ridden cry of relief.

Outside the Taurus, the crowd pressed forward, finally comprehending what they had just witnessed, and erupted in a resounding cheer.

The entire event had taken twenty-six seconds.

They took the body over to Magnus Coop at the clinic. The coroner put it in the morgue, on the same table that had held Tara Breckenridge's remains, and covered it with a sheet.

"This is terrible," he muttered over and over again. "This is absolutely terrible."

"Get that stuff developed and on my desk as soon as you can," Gail instructed Paul Delaney as the two of them rushed back to Curtis House. "Clear the entire front page," she barked at her assistant. "We're going to have one hell of an issue tomorrow!"

"What happened?" Iris Tanaka demanded.

"Somebody assassinated Jerry Frankel as he was leaving the courthouse," Gail told her.

"Oh my God, who?"

"Don't know. Chances are, we'll never know. But get someone on it anyway."

"Did you actually see it?" Iris asked.

"Sure did," Gail said. "Peter and I were right up front. There must have been, oh, at least a thousand people there. And as soon as they realized what had happened, they went wild—cheering, dancing, singing in the streets. I've never seen anything like it."

"That's awful," Iris murmured.

"It wasn't pretty," Gail agreed. "And we got it all on film. Call the printer. Tell him to double tomorrow's run."

• • •

Charlie Pricker was back in the office by three o'clock. It didn't take him very long to reconstruct the event. An evaluation of the angle of the entry wound and a survey of the buildings along the perimeter of the courthouse plaza brought him to the widow's walk of a three-story Victorian about four hundred yards away that was undergoing extensive remodeling to suit an assortment of trendy boutiques. The construction would have afforded a sniper unlimited roof access.

"Judging from the distance, I'd say the shooter used a hunting rifle with a scope," he said afterward. "Judging from the entry wound and the bone and shell fragments I found on the courthouse steps, he used some kind of varmint slug, not more than thirty-caliber. That thing exploded inside Frankel's head like a miniature hand grenade. The chances are slim to none we'll ever be able to trace it. Whoever this guy was, he knew what he was doing."

"Not exactly the way we wanted to close the case," Ruben observed with a sigh.

"But when you think about it," Glen Dirksen remarked, "it *is* justice, even if it's only poetic justice."

"I see your point," the police chief said tonelessly. "But that doesn't make it right."

"Maybe not," the officer agreed. "But he was this close to getting away with it." Dirksen held up his thumb and index finger, separated by a bare eighth of an inch. "And you know as well as I do that someday, somewhere, he was going to do it again. We might not like the method, but there's at least one teenage girl out there who'll appreciate the result."

"It's not our job to protect society from a crime that hasn't yet been committed," Ruben instructed him.

"Well, it's done," Dirksen replied, "and I can't say I'm very sorry about it."

Ruben sighed again. "I don't imagine there'll be any great

push for us to find the shooter," he said. "But we at least have to open a case file."

"Are you kidding?" Charlie declared. "This guy'll be the new town hero. Legends will grow up around him. 'The man who set Seward Island free,' they'll call him."

"He's still a murderer," the police chief declared, "and it's our job to get him if we can."

"Don't get me wrong," Charlie said. "I really feel for Frankel's wife and son. Especially the boy, to have something like that happen right in front of him. I can't imagine anything more horrifying than what they've just gone through. But I doubt anyone else will be grieving tonight. A murderer has been murdered—that's all anyone will think about."

"You may be right," Ruben conceded. "But just for the sake of argument, what if he didn't do it?"

Dirksen stared at him. "Are you saying you have any doubt?" he asked.

"I always have doubt," Ruben replied. "Our work is never perfect. That's why I rely on the system. It's what keeps us honest."

"But the system failed," the officer said. "The lawyer got him released."

Ruben shook his head sadly. "No," he said. "The system worked. It was lack of evidence that got him released."

"But he was guilty," Dirksen argued. "I don't care what happened with the evidence, I know he was guilty. So maybe the victim wasn't in his car, so what? Maybe he wasn't even driving his car that night."

"What about the Petrie kid?" Charlie asked.

"He could have been mistaken," the officer declared. "Maybe we got it all wrong, and they met at Madrona Point. Frankel lived less than a mile away, maybe he walked there. Either way, we found the bloody sweatshirt, didn't we? Even if we couldn't get it to test out. And we found the knife. And he had a

motive, and he had the opportunity, and we know he'd done almost the same thing at least once before. As far as I'm concerned, he got what he deserved. And if that means I care more
about justice being done than I do about the system working,
well then—maybe I do."

At three-thirty-eight, Ginger walked resolutely through the
doors of Graham Hall, down the corridor, and into Ruben's office, and dropped an envelope on his desk.

"My resignation," she said simply, and turned to go.

"Wait," he said. He had spent the better part of two nights
thinking it through, staring at his bedroom ceiling, trying to find
a way to hold on to what he believed in, and still make room for
her in his life. In the end, he decided that, right or wrong, emotions could sometimes distort one's judgment. He rationalized
that what she had done had been as much for him as for herself
or the Breckenridge case, and that meant he had to accept some
of the responsibility. "We need to talk."

She shook her head. "There's nothing to talk about," she
told him. "I did what I did for what I thought were all the right
reasons. But when I looked at it through your eyes, I realized
how terribly wrong it was. I can't work here anymore. We both
know that."

"You're a good cop," he said.

"I was," she conceded.

"We all make mistakes."

"Ruben, I falsified evidence in a homicide case."

"Yes," he agreed. "But only up to a certain point. You were
willing to let a search warrant hang on that fingerprint—but you
weren't willing to let the whole case hang on it. That's the difference."

"It seems a small point to me now," she said. "A man is
dead."

"That isn't your fault."

"Of course it is," she cried. "He wouldn't have been in jail in the first place if it hadn't been for me."

"You don't know that," Ruben told her. "You don't know how the investigation might have gone. We might have come to him from a totally different direction."

She looked at him wearily. "We were at a dead end."

Ruben shrugged. "You believed he was guilty. You didn't want anyone else to get hurt."

"What I did violates every principle you live by," she said thoughtfully. "And here you are, trying to justify it. How can you do that?"

He considered his words very carefully before he spoke. "I'm not justifying it," he said. "But I can't ignore the fact that you're only human, and you were under a great deal of pressure. Yes, what you did was wrong. But when it came right down to it, even though you knew it would cost you your career, you came clean about it. If I can't cut you a little slack for that, well then, I'm not much of a police chief—or a man."

"I'm sorry I let you down," she said. "I'll have my desk cleaned out in half an hour."

Ruben had to accept her resignation—he had no choice, really. He was only grateful that she hadn't left it up to him, because he didn't know how he would have been able to fire her.

"I think it would be better all around if you give a month's notice," he said. "You can cite exhaustion, or a career reevaluation, or something along those lines as the reason. That way, we don't disrupt the department, and we keep speculation to a minimum."

She stared at him. He was offering her a graceful exit instead of the public humiliation she deserved. It was a straw and she desperately wanted to grab it.

"But what about Van Pelt?" she asked.

Ruben shifted a bit uneasily in his chair. "All I told him was that there was a mistake," he replied, "a mix-up with the lab, and that we only found out about it when we went back over everything."

Ginger stared at him. "You lied to him?"

He shrugged. "It wasn't exactly a lie. There was some truth to it."

She seemed to hesitate for a moment, and then she shook her head. "There's also Charlie," she said.

"I've already squared it with Charlie," he told her. "So what happened will stay right here between the three of us."

Ginger blinked. "You owe me nothing," she said. "I betrayed my oath, I betrayed your trust. I deserve to be kicked out of here in a city garbage truck. Why would you compromise yourself because of me? Why would you want me to stay on the job one more minute, much less a month?"

He smiled, a wistful little smile. Perhaps her image was a little tarnished in his eyes. Perhaps there might be an occasional moment during the next few weeks when he would find himself wondering whether he could ever trust her again. But perfection, he knew, was something that, while frequently sought, was rarely attained.

"Because I love you," he said. You don't stop loving someone, he thought, just because they disappoint you.

The Cohens took Deborah and Matthew home with them. Rachel gave Deborah a Valium and put her to bed in the guest room. She stripped the boy of his bloody clothes and put him into the bathtub, running the water as hot as she could to counter the shivers that had wracked his small body since the moment he realized what had actually taken place on the courthouse steps. She sent Daniel to fetch Chase. By the time the puppy arrived, Matthew was sitting in the kitchen, wrapped inside a terrycloth bathrobe, trying to eat a bowl of chicken noodle soup.

"We'll keep them here with us tonight, of course," Rachel told her husband. "This is no time for them to be alone. Deborah's parents are catching the red-eye; they'll be here first thing in the morning. Jerry's father is due in at noon."

Scott nodded. "This is a terrible day," he said. "A terrible day for the Frankels, and a terrible day for Seward Island."

After Matthew had swallowed all he could of his soup, Rachel gave him a Valium and tucked him into bed beside his mother. Chase curled up on the floor. Then she went into the living room and sat with Scott, saying little—for what was there to say?—until it grew dark and the friends and neighbors began to arrive.

"We never dreamed it would come to anything like this," they said.

"This is a civilized island. We can't believe that such a thing could happen here."

"Why?" someone asked. "We thought, when they dismissed the charges, it meant he was innocent."

"I guess somebody saw it differently," Scott replied.

"We're in total shock," a neighbor exclaimed. "People actually cheered?"

"Yes, a lot of them did," Scott confirmed.

"Do you think this was related, you know, to the other thing?" the cardiologist and the tax accountant wondered in private.

"It's hard to tell," Scott acknowledged.

"A couple of months ago, we brought you the story of a Jewish teacher who had been accused of murdering a teenage girl on a remote island in Washington State, and an incident of anti-Semitism connected with it," Peter Jennings reported on the evening news. "Now the story has taken a bizarre twist."

"Well, I certainly didn't want him to get murdered," Libby Hildress told her husband. "I just went down there to see what was going on."

"What did you think would happen?" Tom asked wearily. "The way this island was all riled up, it's a wonder they didn't fall on him and tear him to pieces right in front of the boy."

"You can't blame the Island," Libby declared. "If you want to blame someone, blame that lawyer of his."

"Why? Did the lawyer shoot him?"

"Oh, you know what I mean."

"And now I suppose you're going to tell me that you were one of those who celebrated?"

"Well, maybe a little bit," she confessed. "I couldn't help myself. None of us could. There was such a sense of—I don't know—relief. And well—everyone was doing it. Of course, now I wish I hadn't."

"Really?" Tom inquired. "Why?"

She bit her lower lip and looked up at him. "Because I realize it's going to get all distorted in the media, to a lot of people who don't even know us. It's going to make us look like we're a bunch of . . . of heathens."

The doorbell at the Martinez house rang at seven-thirty, and Stacey went to answer it. Danny Leo stood on the front porch.

"Hi," he said.

"Hi," she echoed.

"I heard about what happened today," he began. "I felt just awful, and I wanted to come talk to your dad about it. Is this a bad time?"

Stacey shook her head. "He's pretty upset," she told him. "But I don't think he'll mind."

They went into the living room where Ruben sat on the sofa, an untouched glass of Scotch in his hand, staring at empty space. Ginger had agreed to giving a month's notice, and they had put off the wedding.

"We both have things we need to work through," she told

him. "Maybe we can find a way back to each other with this between us, maybe not. Only time will tell."

She was right, of course. And he knew, probably better than
she, that their future together was uncertain at best. Rebuilding
their relationship would be a painstaking process, with no guarantee of success. At any moment, the most insignificant issue
could come along and topple it for good. The one thing they had
going for them was that they both still wanted it; they had established that much, at least. He looked down the months, if not
years, that now lay ahead, and the loneliness was almost overwhelming. It was the second lowest point of his life.

Danny cleared his throat to catch Ruben's attention.

"I wanted to say how sorry I am, sir," the boy began.

Ruben glanced over. "What is it you're sorry about, Danny?"
he asked softly.

"I'm sorry because this isn't the way it's supposed to happen," he replied. "For a while there, I know you thought maybe
I was the one who murdered Tara, but I had the chance to clear
myself. Mr. Frankel never got that chance, and now there'll always be a question. I think those people who celebrated out
there today were wrong. And those who think that whoever murdered Mr. Frankel is a hero are wrong, too." He stopped, a little
embarrassed by his monologue. "I just wanted you to know how
I felt," he said.

Ruben took a moment to study the boy. "I admit I wasn't exactly thrilled when you started dating my daughter," he said. "But
I've always trusted her judgment, and tonight, I think I can see a
little of what she sees in you."

Danny grinned. "That's good, sir," he said, "because I really
like Stacey a lot, and with your permission, I sure would like to
go on dating her."

How uncomplicated childhood was, Ruben reflected sadly.
Why did it all have to change when you grew up?

• • •

As hard as she tried to shield herself from the world around her, Mary Breckenridge heard about the death of Jerry Frankel.

Irma Poole told her when she brought a tray of tea to Mary's bedroom. "It's over," the woman said firmly. "For better or worse, it's done with. God willing, we can put it behind us now, and go on."

Mary looked up at the housekeeper who had cared for her and her family for almost a quarter of a century.

"Is it?" she asked pathetically. "Can we?"

13

Curtis House was quickly flooded with letters about the killing of Jerry Frankel, and true to Charlie Pricker's prediction, they ran five to one in support of the assassin.

"If our mighty legal system couldn't take care of one murdering teacher," a garage mechanic told the editor, "it's lucky for us that someone else could."

"I don't ever want to know who pulled the trigger," a romance novelist wrote. "I'd much prefer to imagine him as a handsome crusader on a prancing white steed."

"Whoever he is, he did us all a favor," opined a local plumber. "We should applaud him, not prosecute him."

"Well, Ruben, you dodged a real bullet," Albert Hoch confided. "If that bastard had gotten away with it, there would've been hell to pay. This way, we can mark the case closed, and get on with other business."

"There's still the matter of the shooter."

The mayor shrugged. "Oh, I wouldn't spin too many wheels over that, if I were you," he said.

"It's my job," Ruben reminded him.

"Well, if it'll make you feel better," Hoch conceded with a broad wink, "you can spend a few hours rounding up the usual suspects."

"As long as I have your approval," Ruben said smoothly, "I may as well tell you that Kyle Breckenridge is at the top of that list. He had more motivation than anyone else I can think of to kill his daughter's killer."

The mayor's eyes bulged. "Well, you can take him right back off that list," he snapped. "It just so happens that Kyle and I were in a meeting together at exactly the moment Frankel was being shot."

"You'd testify to that?" Ruben asked. "Under oath, if necessary?"

Hoch didn't even blink. "Yes, I would," he replied. "And since you seem to be having some difficulty reading the climate of this community, let me strongly urge you to move along to something else."

"I wonder if it's occurred to anyone on this island that the only thing that makes our country work is that we live by a system of laws," Ruben said irritably.

"I think everyone is so relieved that it's finally over, they haven't gotten to that point yet," Ginger told him with a touch of irony. "Give them time."

"Time is something we don't control," he said, "and our esteemed mayor notwithstanding, we have an investigation to conduct."

"All right, then," she said affably because she was, after all, still on the job, "aside from Kyle Breckenridge, who else is on your list?"

◦ ◦ ◦

Malcolm Purdy opened the electrified gate, and watched calmly as Ginger pulled her black-and-white to a stop in front of his ramshackle cabin.

"What took you so long?" he asked with a cynical grin.

"You were expecting me?" she parried.

"Yesterday."

"Good," she said. "Then you know why I'm here, and we don't have to waste any time with preliminaries."

"Hell, you can waste your time any way you like," he offered. "But it seems to me that someone has just saved the taxpayers a whole lot of money. If you find the guy, you ought to give him a medal."

"I'll certainly keep your suggestion in mind," Ginger replied.

Purdy chuckled. "I was here the entire day," he told her. "I have two witnesses, if I need them: a man who is staying with me for a few weeks, and the woman who works for me. Both of them were here with me the whole time."

"Do you mind if I take a look at your guns?"

"Do you have a search warrant?" he asked.

"Do I need one?" she countered.

He shrugged and led the way around to the back of the cabin where he unlocked the door to a converted wood shed, revealing a small arsenal that ran the gamut from assault weapons to target rifles to hunting rifles to shotguns, all of them freshly cleaned and oiled and standing in felt-lined racks. On a shelf above sat every kind and size of scope imaginable.

"You could wage quite a little war here, if the occasion ever arose," Ginger observed.

"My war days are over," he told her. "Now I just amuse myself."

The detective took her time scrutinizing the collection before reaching out to lift a Winchester rifle from its rack. It was a beauty. She ran her hand over the smooth wood stock and down the length of the blue steel barrel, observing the 270-caliber designation stamped into it. She noted that the Winchester was fitted for a scope. Next, she pulled back the bolt, noting the fluid action, and smelled fresh oil in the firing chamber. Finally, she returned the rifle to its rack, and allowed Purdy to accompany her back around to the front of the cabin.

"I guess you're off the hook," she said as she was about to climb into her car.

"Am I?" he asked with a smile.

"For the reward," she clarified. "The hundred thousand dollars. That ad of yours was worded 'for the arrest and conviction,' wasn't it?"

He cocked his head. "Far as I'm concerned, the terms were met. And the way it looks right now, Detective, you're in line to collect."

"Me?"

"You're the one who came up with the first piece of real evidence, aren't you—the fingerprint match?"

"Sorry," she said abruptly, closing the car door and starting up the engine. "I'm not eligible. If you're determined to give your money away, you'll have to look somewhere else."

Purdy waited until he was certain there had been enough time for her to pass through the gate before he pressed the button to close it. Then he went back behind the cabin to lock up the shed.

The woman was standing at the rear door. "You took a big chance," she said.

"No, I didn't," the ex-Marine assured her with a small smile. "She could have been holding it right in her hands, and would never have been able to prove it. She knew that."

"He has two witnesses who'll swear he was with them the entire time," Ginger reported to Ruben, "and a beauty of a Winchester he knows we'll never be able to identify."

"Do you think he's our shooter?"

"I'm sure of it. We can investigate every other guy on the Island who owns a rifle capable of shooting a thirty-caliber or less varmint slug, but it would be a waste of time."

The police chief sighed. "All right, then," he said. "Let's not spin our wheels on it; put the investigation on an indefinite hold."

"And the Breckenridge case?"

Ruben shrugged. "As soon as the DNA results come in, close it."

Charlie Pricker stood in the doorway to Ruben's office. "Well, you're halfway there, then," he said.

"What do you mean?" Ginger asked.

He held up an envelope. "The DNA on the knife just came in," he replied. "It was Tara's blood, all right."

A big grin split Ginger's freckled face, and it was much more about relief than about joy. "I knew it," she cried. "I knew he did it. I knew the DNA would prove it!"

"It sure looks that way," Ruben said.

"The paternity report should show up sometime next week," Charlie said. "But that's just a technicality now."

"What a weight off my mind," Ginger exclaimed. "Oh my God, I was so afraid I might have been wrong—that I might have gotten an innocent man killed."

"Well, apparently, you didn't," the police chief was quick to concede.

"I feel like climbing to the top of Eagle Rock," she said exultantly, "and shouting at the top of my lungs—'Yes!'"

"Yes," Charlie echoed, "but will you settle for a normal voice and a plain old press conference? As soon as this gets out, we're going to be swamped. We didn't just make the local stations on prime time last night, you know, we made the networks."

"You do the interviews, Charlie," Ginger told him, sobering instantly. "You're much better at it than I am, and you can talk all that technical stuff that I don't know a thing about."

Glen Dirksen popped his head in the door. "I just got a call from one of the real estate agents here on the Island. He says he talked to Deborah Frankel at nine o'clock yesterday morning, and she told him to put her house on the market."

"What do you know about that," Charlie murmured.

"So I was right," Dirksen said. "She would have picked him up at the courthouse and never looked back. They'd probably still be going."

"Charlie," Ginger suggested. "I think you should let Officer Dirksen here do the press conference with you. Give him some experience."

"Really? Me on TV? Wow, wait'll I tell my folks!" Dirksen exclaimed and dashed out.

"He's got the makings of a good cop, that boy," Charlie said with a chuckle.

Ginger looked at him. They had been so close and shared so much. Next to Ruben, she knew she would miss him most. "The fact that Frankel turned out to be guilty doesn't erase what I did, and I know that," she told him. "I appreciate your willingness to keep it between us, and to let me leave on my own legs. But if the day comes, anytime in the next month, when you decide you can't live with it, I'm out of here—no explanations necessary. Are we absolutely clear on that?"

Charlie shrugged and then nodded. "Who knows," he said gently. "If I'd been wearing your shoes, I might have been tempted to do the same thing."

This time, the basement meeting was not really a meeting at all, but a boisterous celebration. There were cheers and laughter, and an ample quantity of champagne as the seven men sat around in the ambient candlelight, and congratulated themselves and each other. Everyone had at least one toast to make.

"To the fools who never knew what hit them," said Axel Tannauer, who managed the local movie theater.

"To us," said Tavis Andersen, the pharmacist.

"To the beginning," said Grant Kriedler, of the local Ford dealership. "Now that we know we can do it, no one can stop us."

"When you think about it," Andersen marveled, "it was all so ridiculously easy."

"Most of it," Tannauer agreed. "The stroke of genius was sending that letter to Gail Brown."

"It was pure luck that I happen to have a cousin living in Scarsdale," Jim Petrie, hardware store owner and city council member, confessed. "The genius was in knowing that Brown wouldn't quit until she found a way to dig the story out."

"What I can't get over was that swastika business," Barney Graham, the mortician, said, shaking his head.

"Why?" Anderson asked. "We didn't do it. That was somebody else."

"That's my point," Graham declared. "We started the ball rolling, and someone else got up and ran with it."

"It was perfect," Tannauer concurred. "It proves our effectiveness even more."

"It was a stupid thing to do, and it could have ruined everything for us," Kriedler said with a sharp edge to his voice. "I could tell right away that it made the Jew lawyer suspicious."

"You worry too much," Andersen said. "You're starting to sound like a Jew yourself."

The other men laughed and stamped their feet.

The noise ricocheted through the house and awakened the eleven-year-old boy who slept in the second-floor bedroom. Or perhaps he had not really been asleep at all, just waiting for an opportunity. He crept down the stairs in his pajamas, his feet bare so he would make no sound.

No one heard him as he opened the basement door a few inches. No one saw him as he crouched down beside it. His eyes squinted through his round spectacles to identify the men in the flickering light, to memorize their faces. His ears strained to hear their boasts and their claims, to catch a name, to attach it to a face, to store it away in his mind for another time, when he knew it would be important that he had been witness to this night.

He didn't understand a good deal of what he observed, but it was more than he needed to conclude that something was very wrong. He knew better than anyone that those fifth-grade bullies might have killed Matthew Frankel in the school bathroom that day, and now somebody had indeed killed Matthew's father . . . and for some inexplicable reason, these men were celebrating.

"Any of you have any idea who the shooter was?" the boy heard Petrie ask.

The men shrugged.

"I could make a pretty educated guess," Kriedler said, "about a certain ex-Marine who was so all fired anxious to give away his money."

"If that's the case, I say, we should elect him mayor," said Andersen.

The others chuckled.

"I expect now he'll probably figure he earned the reward himself," Tannauer said.

When they ran out of toasts and champagne, they declared the evening at an end and made their unsteady way out of the basement. The boy slipped off, unnoticed. He had seen and heard enough. Someday, when he was older, when he could find people who would listen, maybe he would tell.

The night was bright with stars, the air was crisp and buoyant and smelled of early spring. For no apparent reason, the men found themselves stopping on their way to their cars to look across the drive. The house next door was dark and still; no boy's voice broke the silence, no dog barked. The garage door had a fresh coat of paint. A "For Sale" sign had been impaled beside the front walk.

"One last toast," Tavis Andersen said as he waved an imaginary glass. "To improving the neighborhood."

Their host, Martin Keller, chuckled.

"Now that it's all over," Axel Tannauer wondered, "do you think he really did it?"

"Who knows?" replied Jim Petrie.

"Who cares?" asked Grant Kriedler.

"Does it matter?" questioned Keller.

"He must have done it," Graham said. "They found the knife in his car, didn't they? Although God knows why he kept it, the idiot."

The six of them looked at the seventh man, the quiet one, the leader.

"Of course he did it," Kyle Breckenridge said. "No doubt about it. All we did was make it a little easier for everyone else to figure it out."

14

It was just her eyes he saw. It was always that way. In the moonlight, they seemed to burn with a life of their own, as though they had no relation to the rest of her, as though there were no rest of her. Twist and turn though he might, he couldn't get away from them, or from the hideous indictment in them.

He covered his face with his hands so he wouldn't have to see. But even with his face covered, there were the eyes. Always the eyes. He tried to hide himself, as he invariably did, whimpering and cowering because he knew what was coming next. It always came next. He covered his ears, hoping to shut it out. But even with his ears covered, the wretched scream split the night in half as it denounced him to the world.

He awoke, soaked in sweat, his chest heaving, his head ready to burst. The nightmare had come again, to ruin his sleep, to jeopardize his health, to threaten his very sanity. To expose him for what he was.

Child molester! Murderer!

There was no escape.

Why now? he wondered, as he gasped for air. Now that it

was over, now that the teacher was dead and the case as good as closed, now that he was finally free?

It wasn't fair. Not when he had orchestrated everything so brilliantly: devising the clues, planting the knife, manipulating the public, making sure that someone else, someone expendable, would pay the price—and no one had been the wiser.

Except for her.

But he had only done what anyone in his position would have done—he had protected himself. It was clearly self-defense. She had given him no other choice. Why couldn't she understand that? Why wouldn't she let him alone?

He pressed his hands against his head, willing the pain to pass, willing her to let go. But she remained. *How much more of this do you think I can take?* he screamed at her soundlessly.

It didn't matter now whether he was asleep or awake, she was always there to taunt him, to test him, to make his life a living hell. He was no longer able to think her away, no longer able to put reason between them, no longer able to fend her off with rationalization.

He couldn't bear the thought of living the rest of his life like this, in emotional isolation. He craved the comfort of another person; someone who would not judge him; someone who, without having to understand, would absolve him. But it couldn't be just anyone. He needed someone who trusted him implicitly and loved him unconditionally to put her arms around him and hold him and make the pain go away.

He got out of bed and stumbled blindly to the door, yanking it open, in too much agony to care about being quiet. He stood for a moment, blinking in the soft light that lit the hallway. Then he staggered forward, toward a room at the far end, a room directly across from the pink and yellow room where he used to find solace.

In total horror, Mary Breckenridge watched him go.